of love & life

ISBN 978-0-276-44449-4

www.readersdigest.co.uk

Published in the United Kingdom by Vivat Direct Limited (t/a Reader's Digest),
157 Edgware Road, London W2 2HR

and in Canada
www.rd.ca

The Reader's Digest Association (Canada) ULC, 1100 René-Lévesque Blvd. West, Montréal,
Québec, H3B 5H5 Canada

# of love & life

Three novels selected and condensed
by Reader's Digest

The Reader's Digest Association Inc., London, Montreal

CONTENTS

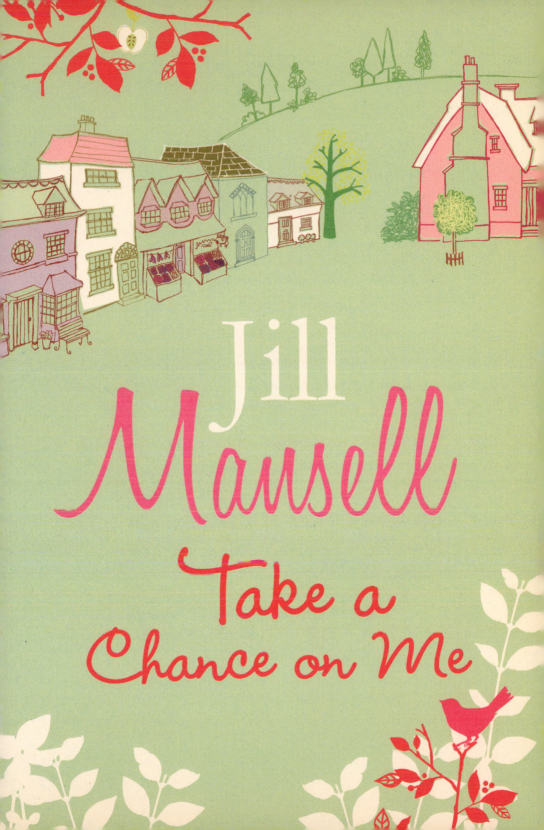

Jill
Mansell
Take a
Chance on Me

Hello—

I do hope you'll enjoy 'Take a Chance on Me'. As a writer you never know when and where inspiration will strike, but with this book it came from two distinct events.

The first happened when I was spending the day at the Badminton International Horse Trials and saw some amazing, larger-than-life wire sculptures of horses. The second idea came when I was lucky enough to be driven in a limo to a literary event—I know, get me! The chauffeur told me so many brilliant stories about his job that I knew I couldn't let them go to waste.

So that was it! My heroine was a chauffeuse for a limo company, my hero was a wire sculptor, and the story is set in the Cotswolds . . .

Jill

Chapter 1

'COME ON, COME ON, late as usual.' Waiting in the porch, Ash Parry-Jones tapped his watch as Cleo Quinn and Will Newman hurried up the gravelled path. 'Better get in there and grab a seat. Place is filling up fast.'

Like it was an Elton John concert or something. Cleo paused to straighten Ash's wonky yellow-and-grey striped tie. 'Don't nag. And I can't believe you're wearing this shirt.'

He looked offended. 'Who are you insulting?'

'You.' She gave his collar an affectionate tweak. 'Stripes and swirls don't go.'

They found somewhere to sit in a pew on the left-hand side of the church. As the organ music played, Cleo composed herself. Of course it was a sad occasion—it was the end of a life, after all—but as funerals went, it had to be one of the cheerier ones she'd attended.

Then again, as deaths went, Lawrence LaVenture's had been better than most. As Lawrence himself had been fond of remarking, the family name was descended from the French word for lucky or fortunate, and he'd taken enormous pleasure in living up to it. And what rakish 73-year-old widower, given the choice, wouldn't want to go as he had gone, following a sublime meal and a bottle of delicious St-Emilion, in bed with an attractive brunette *many* years younger than himself?

Peering round, Cleo whispered, 'Do you think she'll turn up?'

'Who?'

'The woman who was with him when he died! I want to know what she looks like.'

'She'll be the one in the black leather basque,' Will murmured. 'Stockings, suspenders, spike-heeled stilettos . . .'

Cleo dug him in the ribs then slipped her arm through his, grateful to him for having come along. Will had never met Lawrence LaVenture but she'd wanted him with her today and he'd obligingly taken the afternoon off work. Meeting Will in a nightclub three months ago had definitely been one of the happier accidents in her life. She'd been nudged from behind in a crowded bar in Bath, her drink had splashed over his sleeve, they'd got chatting as a result . . . and what a result it had turned out to be. Will was handsome, hard-working and intelligent . . . basically, he was perfect in every way.

'Could be her.' Pointing helpfully to a roly-poly woman in her sixties, squeezing into an already-full pew across the aisle, Will said, 'There's a high-class hooker if ever I saw one.'

'That's Effie Farnham from Corner Cottage.'

'There's a studded leather whip hanging out of her handbag.'

'She breeds Cairn terriers. It's a dog's lead.'

'Are you sure?'

'Trust me, Effie's not the whippy kind.'

'You never know. Under that coat she could be wearing something completely outrageous.'

Thankfully, before Cleo could start picturing Effie in a tasselled thong, distraction was provided by the arrival of Lawrence's family. Well, such as it was. She watched as the three of them made their way up the aisle, two ancient, creaking older sisters swathed in politically incorrect fur and supported by silver-topped ebony canes. And between them, matching his pace to theirs, Johnny LaVenture.

He was looking smarter than usual in a dark suit and with his habitually wayward black hair combed back from his forehead. For a split second he glanced to the left and their eyes met, prompting a Pavlovian jolt of resentment in her chest. She couldn't help it; old habits died hard. Then Johnny looked away, carried on past and took his place between his ancient aunts in the front pew.

Cleo bent her head. OK, don't think about him. Just concentrate on the funeral. Lawrence might have been an off-the-wall character, fond of a drink and, well, various other lusty pastimes, but he'd been entertaining to have around. They were here to celebrate a life well lived.

After the service, everyone made their way across the village green to the Hollybush Inn, where food and drinks had been laid on.

Ash, catching up with Cleo and Will, rubbed his hands together as he said cheerfully, 'I really enjoyed that, didn't you?'

And *still* he was managing to make it sound like an Elton John concert. Cleo said, 'You're not supposed to enjoy funerals. Next you'll be giving it five stars on Amazon.'

'Actually, that's not a bad idea. We could do it on the show, get the listeners to call in with reviews of their favourite—'

'No you couldn't. That's just wrong. Oh God, look at my *heels*.' As they reached the pub, Cleo leaned against one of the outdoor tables and used a tissue to clean away the clumps of mud and grass. 'Did you see me sinking into the ground while we were standing around the grave?'

'That's why I didn't wear mine.' Ash nodded sympathetically. 'You know, you're looking good today. Scrubbed up well. Even if you don't deserve a compliment because of all the grief you give me.'

'It's not grief. It's constructive criticism. Which you badly need, by the way.' Having more or less cleaned her heels, Cleo lobbed the muddy tissue into the bin and adjusted her narrow cream skirt. Of course she was looking good; hadn't she put in a whole heap of extra effort making sure of it? But that was pride for you. It was also the reason she'd dragged Will along for the occasion. When you'd spent your teenage years being mercilessly teased and humiliated, you didn't want to turn up to meet your tormentor looking like a . . . a *donkey*. You felt compelled to prove to him that you weren't still a complete loser, not to mention capable these days of bagging yourself the kind of boyfriend any girl would be thrilled to, well, bag.

And here he was, standing just inside the entrance to the pub, greeting everyone as they came in and gravely receiving condolences in return. Oh well, on an occasion like this at least he wouldn't call her—

'Hello, Misa.' Dark eyes glinting with amusement, Johnny gave her hand a cross between a shake and a squeeze.

I can't believe he just called me that.

'Hello, Johnny. I'm sorry about your dad. We'll all miss him.'

'Thanks. I guess this village is going to be a quieter place from now on.' His gaze flickered over her and the smile broadened. 'You're looking very well.'

Damn right I am. Turning to indicate Will, Cleo said, 'This is my boyfriend, Will Newman.'

'I'm so sorry for your loss,' Will said politely as they shook hands.

'Thank you. So, Misa, gone and got yourself a new man. Excellent. From what I hear, the old ones haven't been much cop.'

See what a nightmare he was? Cleo quelled the urge to retaliate with something cutting; it would hardly be seemly, after all. Plus, dammit, she couldn't think of anything fast enough. Instead she turned away.

When they were safely out of earshot, Will said, 'Why does he call you Misa?'

'Oh, it's a hilarious nickname. I used to work hard at school, pay attention in class, ask loads of questions, answer them too. One day I was so excited about knowing the answer to a really difficult question that I stuck my hand up and yelled, "Me, sir!" Well, everyone practically wet themselves laughing. And that was it, I was stuck with it for the next three years of school.'

It went without saying that she had never once put her hand up in class for the rest of her time at school, had stopped asking questions and paying attention to the answers. OK, she couldn't blame everything on Johnny LaVenture, but he certainly hadn't helped. When her GCSEs had been a complete car crash, she'd felt an almost perverse sense of pride at their awfulness. *See, look at me, look at these abysmal grades! Here's the proof that I'm not a teacher's pet any more!*

'Poor baby. Want me to beat him up for you?'

'Yes please. Except you'd better not. It's his dad's funeral, after all.'

An hour and a couple of drinks later, the party had begun to warm up; everyone had started to relax and Cleo's skin had stopped prickling every time she glanced over at her nemesis. Was it stupid still to feel like this? Maybe, but she couldn't help herself. It was thirteen years since they'd been at school together. She had left at sixteen and plunged into the first of many jobs. Johnny had stayed on to take his A levels—ha! *Now* who was the swotty teacher's pet?—before heading off to art school. After that he'd moved to New York, returning only occasionally to Channings Hill to visit his father, although Lawrence had evidently kept him updated on the subject of her less-than-dazzling successes on the boyfriend front. Meanwhile, he had begun to make a real name for himself with his wire-constructed sculptures. When it came to the luck of the LaVentures, he'd inherited his share too. As time went by, the sculptures grew and so did Johnny's reputation, culminating in an exhibition during which every last one of the larger-than-life-size pieces had been snapped up by the billionaire owner of a chain of casinos. Overnight, Johnny became a recognised name, a celebrity in his own right with a stunning supermodel girlfriend to match.

Will checked his watch and said apologetically, 'I have to go.'

'Of course you do. Thanks for coming.' He had a work meeting in Bristol to get back to. Cleo hugged him, kissed him quickly on the mouth and said, 'I'll see you on Friday.'

'Can't wait. Will you be all right here?'

'I'll be fine. I've got my big sister to look after me.' Abbie, fifteen years older and light years more sensible, was over by the bar chatting to some neighbours.

'Well, make sure she does. I'll be over after work on Friday. Bye.'

'Or I could come to you,' Cleo offered, 'if it's easier.'

'Hmm, you know what? I think I'd rather stay at your place.' He smiled and pulled a you-know-why face; the two friends with whom he shared an untidy flat in Redland were the boisterous, heavy-drinking types. Will, reluctant to subject her to their ribald remarks, had explained that it wouldn't matter so much if she were just a casual one-off fling, but she wasn't, she was way more important than that.

Hearing this had caused Cleo's heart to expand with hope. She watched him leave and exhaled happily. Will Newman. Cleo Newman. He really could be The One.

Then her skin started prickling again and a voice behind her said, 'So that's the boyfriend, is it, Misa?'

Was her blood actually *physically* heating up or did it just feel that way? Cleo kept herself under control and nodded.

'And now he's run off and left you?'

'He had to get back to work for an important meeting. He has a very responsible job.'

'He does? Good for him.' Johnny sounded amused.

How did he manage to make even those few words sound as if he was taking the mickey? Cleo marvelled at his talent. Logically she might know her own lack of further education wasn't his fault, but deep down inside, it still felt that way. She loved her job at Henleaze Limos, but who knew, if her schooldays hadn't been blighted, she might have gone on to do anything.

'So is this Will New-Man the love of your life?'

See? Even now he was making fun of Will's surname.

'Maybe. It's all going very well at the moment. How about you?'

Johnny grinned and pulled a face. 'Not so great. Temperamental creatures, women. They can be pretty hard work.'

They. Just to let her know how popular he was, subject to the attentions of hordes of besotted females. Cleo smiled politely, registering lack of interest, and said, 'What's going to happen to Ravenswood?'

'Sell it, I suppose. If I can.' Johnny shook his head. 'Not the ideal time, of course, but you never know. It'd be great if we could find a buyer before Christmas. There's an opportunity to bag the apartment below mine if we can get a quick sale. I could turn it into a fantastic gallery.' He stopped and looked at her. 'Why are you asking? Might you and your chap be interested in putting in an offer?'

Oh, that was *so* on the cards, what with Ravenswood being a seven-bedroomed detached house with a garden bigger than a football pitch.

'I could mention it to Will.' *And start buying extra Lotto tickets.* 'How much will you be asking?'

He shrugged. 'I've got a couple of estate agents coming over tomorrow to look the place over and come up with a valuation. I'm pretty out of touch, but somewhere around two and a half, at a guess.'

Two and a half million pounds. Ah well, maybe she and Will would give it a miss after all. 'Well, good luck. I'll leave you to get on.'

As she made to move away, he said, 'This chap of yours. Does he work in private health insurance?'

'What? No! Why?'

'Just curious.' A smile lifted the corners of Johnny's mouth. 'He just looks as if he might, that's all.'

Ooooooh . . .

'**O**h dear, look at you.' Abbie greeted her sympathetically. 'Johnny been getting under your skin, has he? Here, have a sip of my Malibu.'

Cleo could always rely on her sister to make her feel better. Abbie was looking lovely today, her fine honey-blonde hair falling in waves to her shoulders and her gentle face glowing.

Then again, sisterly sympathy only went so far. 'I've got a better idea. Why don't I have my own drink? Seeing as Lawrence is paying. Which means Johnny is. Dry white, please.' Cleo signalled to Deborah behind the bar. 'Lovely, thanks. Honestly, he doesn't change, does he?' She knocked back some much-needed wine. 'Two and a half million pounds he's going to be asking for his dad's house. He wondered if Will and I might like to make him an offer. And he's keen to get it sorted before Christmas because he wants to buy another apartment in New York and turn it into a gallery. I mean, does he even *care* that Lawrence has just died? As far as he's concerned, it's a nice little windfall coming along at just the right time . . . God, it's enough to make you *spit*.'

'Is this a diatribe?' Tom, Abbie's husband, looked pleased with himself. 'Ha, there's a word I've never used before. But it is, isn't it?'

Cleo smiled, because Tom was looking so smart in his dark funeral suit and a bright blue shirt that matched his sparkling eyes. It always seemed strange to see him out of his work clothes of dusty polo shirt and jeans. 'Oh yes, it's a diatribe. Some people just deserve one.'

'But you liked him once,' said Tom.

'What?' Cleo froze. 'No I didn't!'

'You must have done. If you didn't fancy him, why would you have said yes when he asked you out?'

Her heart beginning to thud in double time, Cleo said, 'I don't know what you're talking about.'

Tom was actually laughing now, wagging a finger at her. 'Come on, I know Johnny LaVenture asked you out at the school disco and you agreed, then—*hey*, mind my drink!'

'Tom.' Abbie, who had given him a nudge, shot him a warning look.

Staring at them open-mouthed, Cleo said slowly, 'Oh my God, you *know* about that? *Both* of you know?'

It was her deepest, darkest, most shameful adolescent secret. All these years she'd kept it buried, telling herself that, OK, she'd made an almighty fool of herself but at least her family didn't know.

Except . . . she looked from Abbie to Tom, then back again . . . it rather looked as if they did.

'Honestly, you're such a blabbermouth,' Abbie scolded.

'Hey, it was years ago.' Tom's grin spread across his face as Ash approached them. 'What does it matter now?'

'What are we talking about?' Ash, whose nosiness knew no bounds, looked interested.

Cleo blurted out, 'Don't tell him!'

'The time Johnny LaVenture told Cleo he was crazy about her and she agreed to go out with him.'

'Oh right, at the school's end-of-term disco.' Ash nodded solemnly.

Right, that was it. Ash had moved into the village only three years ago. Facing him, Cleo's voice rose. 'Does *everyone* know about this?'

'Well, yes. Although I thought it was supposed to be a secret. You weren't meant to *know* that we know.'

Cleo swallowed. What had taken place had been enough to scar a girl mentally for life. In fact, she was fairly sure it *had* scarred her mentally for life. She'd gone along to the end-of-year disco with no expectations other than drinking a few alcohol-free shandies, dancing with her friends and having a fun time. When Johnny LaVenture had come up to her and asked to speak to her outside, she had initially refused, but he'd practically begged her until curiosity had got the better of her and she'd eventually given in. Then, once they were outside, Johnny had haltingly confessed his true feelings for her. He'd teased her so much, it transpired, only to cover up the fact that he really liked her, but now he could no longer hide how he really felt. And as he'd been telling her this, his beautiful dark eyes had gazed beseechingly into hers.

Cleo, hypnotised by the declaration, had leaned back against the girls' changing rooms and been unbelievably moved by the admission; he must have been plucking up the courage to say this for months.

Then Johnny had falteringly asked her out on a date the following week and, although she didn't want to go out with him, she'd known she couldn't refuse. It would shatter his confidence. Sixteen-year-old boys had easily bruised egos; it would be cruel to turn him down . . .

So she'd smiled up at Johnny and said yes, of course she'd go out with him. It had been a heady moment, the kind of turnaround any downtrodden sixteen-year-old could only dream about, but it had actually happened and it felt . . . God, it felt fantastic! And now he looked as if he was about to kiss her. Tilting her face up to his, Cleo closed her eyes, encouragingly puckered her lips and waited for—

Snorts of laughter directly above her head *wasn't* what she'd been waiting for. Someone was eavesdropping. Several someones, from the sound of it. Still, did it really matter if they'd overheard? Putting out a hand to reassure Johnny, Cleo said, 'It's all right, don't worry about them,' and wondered why he wasn't looking at her any more.

The giggles turned to shrieks of hysterical laughter and the head of Mandy Ellison poked through the open window. Crowing with delight, she yelled, 'Ha ha, I can't believe she fell for it; you were brilliant!'

Bewildered, Cleo turned to Johnny. 'What does that mean?'

Half smiling and backing away, Johnny said, 'Sorry, she bet me a fiver I couldn't do it.'

Everyone was laughing harder and harder. As the realisation sank in that she'd been well and truly set up, colour flooded Cleo's cheeks.

Johnny shrugged and raised his hands, absolving himself from blame. 'I never thought you'd say yes.'

She was torn between wanting the ground to swallow her up and an overwhelming longing to burst into tears. 'I only said it because I felt sorry for you!'

'Ha ha ha ha ha! Yeah, of course you did,' jeered Mandy Ellison.

'It's *true*. I don't fancy him!'

'But you seriously thought he fancied you,' Mandy sniggered. 'Like that's ever going to happen, *Misa*. Ha, you've just given us the best laugh we've had in months. And all for a fiver.' As she said it, she grinned at Johnny. '*Bargain*.'

Now, here in the front bar of the Hollybush, the humiliation was every bit as acute as it had been all those years ago.

Cleo looked at Ash, Tom and Abbie. She said, 'Who told you?'

Ash shrugged and pointed at Abbie. 'You told me, didn't you?'

'Tom told me,' said Abbie, 'straight after it happened.'

'Honestly, why do I have to get the blame for everything? Everyone was having a laugh about it in the pub the day after the disco,' Tom protested. 'Stuart Ellison told us about it. His sister Mandy was there when Johnny did it. It was just a bit of fun.'

So all this time she'd been the laughing stock of the entire village. And like one of those well-kept secrets you never imagine could actually be kept secret, she'd had no idea.

What's more—talk about adding insult to injury—the chances were that if you were to ask him about it now, Johnny himself probably wouldn't even remember that evening at the school disco when he'd earned himself the easiest fiver of his life.

Chapter 2

THE FOR SALE SIGNS had been up for over a week now. Having instructed his solicitors to take care of everything, Johnny had flown back to the States the day after the funeral. Busy cleaning the windscreen of the Bentley she was due to take out again this afternoon, Cleo paused as, across the green, two cars slowed to a halt outside Ravenswood.

It wasn't nosy to watch them, was it? It was being neighbourly, making sure the place wasn't about to be burgled. Although it had to be said, the couple emerging from the maroon Volvo didn't look like your archetypal burglars. And the other chap was visibly an estate agent. Of course, where Johnny was concerned, it would be just typical that the first people to view his old family home would buy it on the spot.

Cleo was kneeling across the Bentley's back seat, vigorously vacuuming under the driver's seat, when someone pinched her bottom.

'Oof!' She collapsed, rolled over onto her side and pointed the vacuum nozzle like a pistol at Ash. 'Don't *do* that.'

His eyes danced. 'Can't help myself. If I see a cute little backside sticking up like that in front of me, I just have to pinch it.'

He was home from work. The downside of hosting a breakfast radio show might be the inhumanly early starts, but the upside was that it was all done and dusted by ten o'clock and he was back at Channings

Hill by eleven. Switching off the vacuum cleaner and picking up her polishing cloth, Cleo said, 'Pass me the beeswax. How'd it go today?'

'Bloody brilliant. If you'd bothered to listen to it, you wouldn't have to ask.' Since taking over the breakfast slot three years ago, having been poached from a smaller commercial station in London, Ash had conjured up a seventy-per-cent increase in listening figures. He was the star of BWR, much loved by his ever-growing audience. As well as local listeners, fans from all over the world were now tuning in to hear him online. On his show he exuded confidence, wit and irresistible charm. Women and girls of all ages adored him.

In reality, out of the studios, his confidence melted away. Actually that wasn't true; in the company of friends, people he knew, he was fine. But plant a new and attractive woman in front of him and Ash completely lost it every time. Along with the vanishing confidence went the easy wit and charm, their places usurped by clunky awkwardness as Ash Parry-Jones reverted to being a cripplingly shy, overweight and unattractive teenager.

He may have lost some of the excess weight that had haunted his adolescence but his solid frame was always going to be chunky. His hair was fairish, messy, unremarkable. And lookswise, he had the kind of face that gave the impression of having been put together using leftovers—a wonky nose, double chin, wayward eyebrows and slightly asymmetric ears. Cliché it might be, but his was a face perfect for radio.

'I couldn't listen to your show. I was on a job,' said Cleo.

Ash raised his wayward eyebrows. 'On the job?'

'A job.' She flicked the polishing cloth at him. 'It was really sweet, actually. A couple celebrating their golden wedding anniversary. Their children clubbed together to send them on a fantastic holiday as a surprise present. And this morning they thought they were being picked up by an ordinary taxi.' Clients like these, thrilled and excited to be taking the first ride of their lives in a limo, were the kind Cleo loved the most. They made up for the silent high-flying businessmen who took the service for granted, the ear-splitting racket generated by overexcited children leaving junior school for the last time, and having to control groups of wildly inebriated women on hen nights. This morning's lady, bless her, had burst into tears in the back of the Bentley. Through the sobs she'd hiccupped, 'Oh my days, whatever did I do to deserve a family like mine? I'm the luckiest woman in the world!'

'And just think how much more they'd have enjoyed the journey if they'd been allowed to listen to my show.'

'You never give up, do you? You're nothing but a ratings tart. If you want to be useful,' said Cleo, 'you could make me a cup of tea.'

Ash ambled inside, returning five minutes later with two mugs of tea. As Cleo settled herself on the wall separating their adjoining front gardens from the road, the three visitors emerged from Ravenswood. They stood chatting together for a minute before the estate agent jumped into his car and with a cheery wave drove off. The remaining couple surveyed the village before climbing into their Volvo.

'Do you think they'll buy it?' said Cleo.

'Might do.'

The immaculate maroon Volvo pulled away in stately fashion, made its way past the pub then, instead of turning left out of the village, carried on around the green towards them at a menacing ten miles per hour. Watching it, Ash hummed the theme tune to *Jaws*.

'Morning. We've just been to view Ravenswood,' the woman said. 'Seems like a quiet-enough village. Are people happy to live here?'

'Happy?' Ash said good-naturedly, 'They're ecstatic. So you're interested in the house, then?'

The woman pursed her lips like a VAT inspector. 'Possibly. But we need to know more about Channings Hill before we make any decisions. My husband and I like peace and tranquillity. Is this a quiet village?'

'I wouldn't say quiet, exactly,' said Ash. 'It's just . . . normal.'

'What does *that* mean?' The woman's husband surveyed them intently.

'Not too many people have parties,' Cleo explained. 'It's more kind of . . . unstructured noise. Like the teenagers on their motorbikes . . . they're good kids really, they just don't think about the noise when they're racing round the green.'

The dual intake of breath was audible. The woman shuddered and said, '*Motorbikes?*'

'Not all of them,' Cleo rushed to reassure her. 'Some just have mopeds. But it all stops at midnight.'

The man's eyes bulged. 'The estate agent didn't mention this.'

'I'm not surprised! But the rest of the village is great.' Cleo nodded with enthusiasm. 'Fantastic pub, loads going on there. You'll make lots of new friends in no time, especially if you're into karaoke!'

The Volvo left the village a lot more speedily than it had arrived.

Ash reached for Cleo's hand, gave it a smack and said, 'You're a bad girl.'

'So. I didn't like them. They wouldn't have fitted into the village.'

'And it's nothing at all to do with wanting to muck things up for Johnny LaVenture.'

Putting on her most wounded face, Cleo said, 'That's a terrible thing to suggest.'

'But a great opportunity to get your own back. He's desperate for a quick sale. You've probably stopped that happening. Just how fond of your kneecaps are you?'

'Oh, come on, somebody else'll come along and buy it. Anyway,' said Cleo, jumping down from the wall and handing back her mug, 'Johnny's in New York, so how's he ever going to find out?'

Something had happened; Abbie's stomach was in knots and she didn't know what to do. Maybe if she'd more experience with relationships, like her younger sister Cleo, it would be easier to cope.

But when you'd been married for twenty-three years to a cheerful, uncomplicated man who had become withdrawn practically overnight, it turned your whole world upside-down. There was no getting away from it—Tom had the air of someone with a terrible secret.

Abbie had spent the past three days eaten up with fear. Top of her list of suspicions was the possibility that, healthwise, there was something seriously amiss. Had he visited the doctor and been given terrible news? Number two, and a suggestion that until this week she would have dismissed as unthinkable, was that he was having an affair. But Tom's behaviour had veered *so* wildly out of character, maybe it wasn't unthinkable after all. Oh God, what if he *was* seeing another woman?

Snap went the stem of the pink and gold glass apple in her hand. Bugger, and these were the expensive ones, three pounds fifty each.

'I don't believe it. *Another* one.' Des Kilgour, who owned the garden centre, spotted the broken Christmas ornament as he loped past. 'I bet it was that little kid in the red coat, he was over here just now—'

'It wasn't, it was me. I broke it.' Tempting though it was, Abbie knew she couldn't let an innocent four-year-old take the blame. 'It just snapped in half, I'm really sorry.'

Seeing that she was upset, Des backed down at once. 'No problem, accidents happen.' He paused, raking pale fingers through his reddish fair hair and surveying her with concern. 'You OK?'

Abbie nodded, determined to keep it together. Des was a good boss, and he'd always had a bit of a soft spot for her, which was why he wasn't yelling blue murder now.

'Sorry, I'm fine. It's just been one of those days.'

'Well, don't break any more, will you?' He gave her a jovial pat on the shoulder. 'Those apples don't grow on trees!'

Good boss, terrible stand-up comedian. Summoning a halfhearted smile, Abbie said, 'I won't.'

'I'd better get on. Cheer up, Abbie. It might never happen, eh?'

All her life she'd hated that expression. What if Tom had fallen in love with another woman? What if she was young and fertile and he wanted to have babies with her? Abbie busied herself sorting the jumbled-up Christmas decorations into their respective colour-coordinated compartments. What if everything she most dreaded was happening now?

You knew you'd got it bad when you tried to cook for someone and pretended it was the kind of thing you did all the time. Uncorking the wine and pouring herself a glassful—just to check it was all right—Cleo wondered why she was doing it. Except she knew the answer to that; it was all Nigella's fault. She'd watched the programmes. Nigella had made preparing a three-course meal look *soooo* easy. Tricking her, Cleo, into believing it was and, in turn, encouraging her to invite Will to come on over after work so she could cook dinner for him.

And yes, she truly *had* believed it was actually within her powers to dazzle Will with her culinary capabilities to the extent that he'd realise she was indisputably The Perfect One for him. Well, that had been the plan. Instead of which, she was surrounded by lumpy cheese sauce, worryingly odd-tasting chicken and incinerated parsnips.

'Everything OK?' Will wandered into the tiny blue and white kitchen, clearly wondering if they were going to be eating before midnight.

'Fine, fine, I'm just . . . getting everything together . . .' Frantically stirring the sauce, Cleo wondered how on earth you were meant to get the lumps out. 'Won't be long now!'

'What are those?'

'Parsnips.' She knew she sounded defensive. How were you meant to get the fat ends cooked without burning the pointy ends anyway? How did Nigella deal with triangular vegetables?

Eyeing the cheese sauce, Will said valiantly, 'The chicken looks nice.'

Oh God, the chicken. It had tasted too salty so she'd counteracted it with sugar, then that had been frankly weird so she'd added a coating of satay paste but the sweetness had still been there and now it was all hideously reminiscent of peanut toffee. With garlic. It was no good, she couldn't let him taste it; the look of horror on his face would be too much to bear. She was going to have to confess. Taking another glug of wine, Cleo shook her head and said, 'You know what? I've made a—'

The crash of the door knocker stopped her in her tracks.

'Who's that?' said Will. 'Have you invited someone else for dinner?' There was a note of hope in his voice, as if having another person here to help eat the food might not be a bad thing.

'No. It might be carol singers.' Equally glad of the reprieve, Cleo went to the front door and opened it.

Yeek, not carol singers. Standing on the doorstep, wearing a Barbour with the collar turned up against the cold, was Johnny LaVenture.

'Cleo, I'd like a word.'

Cleo wavered; whenever people said this, she experienced a wild urge to shout, 'Kittens!' or 'Brassiere!' or 'Nincompoop!' But he didn't look as if he'd find that amusing. In fact his expression was grim.

'Fine.' She stood her ground, wondering what had brought him here. 'I thought you'd gone back to the States.'

'I did. And now I'm here again. What's that diabolical smell?'

Cheek. Then again, he had a point. The broccoli she'd cooked earlier was still sitting in a pan on the hob, waiting to be covered with the cheese sauce just as soon as she worked out how to de-lump it. Offended, she said, 'It's dinner.'

'It's burning.' Stepping into the house *without even being asked*, he headed past her through to the kitchen.

'Excuse me!' Cleo bridled with indignation as she followed him.

'Bloody hell, can't you smell it?' Johnny went straight to the stove, picked up the blue enamel pan of drained broccoli and dumped it in the washing-up bowl in the sink. A mushroom-cloud of steam instantly enveloped the kitchen, along with an ear-splitting hiss.

'That gas ring wasn't supposed to be on.' Defensively Cleo blurted out, 'I thought it just smelled horrible because it was broccoli!'

He tilted the still-steaming pan towards her. The broccoli florets were blackened and stuck to the bottom. Oh well, at least it meant she didn't have to wonder how to get the lumps out of the cheese sauce. Raising an eyebrow at the half-charred parsnips, the sauce and the chicken quarters, Johnny said to Will, 'Are you seriously going to eat that?'

Wonderful though it would be if Will were to punch Johnny in the face, there was the danger that he might agree with him instead. Cleo said heatedly, 'Hang on, I don't remember inviting you into this house.' It might not compare with Ravenswood but it was her home, and she loved every cosy, crooked, cottagey inch of it.

'No?' Johnny looked at her. 'Well, do you remember talking to the couple who were interested in buying *my* house?'

Oh. Bugger.

'What?'

'Don't pretend you don't know. I spoke to the estate agents. Then I called the couple who'd been put off after talking to someone in the village. Before that, they'd been really interested.' His eyes glittered.

'Until they heard about the gangs of Hell's Angels we have marauding around this village every night.'

'And you're saying Cleo told them that?' Will was defending her at last. 'I don't think she did, you know.'

'Well, I'm sure you're right,' Johnny drawled. 'It's just that when I asked them to describe who they'd spoken to, they said it was a girl in her late twenties with magenta streaks in her hair and a big freckle under her right eye.' He paused. 'So you can see why I'd jump to conclusions.'

'OK, so it was me.' Cleo defiantly straightened her back. 'But you should have seen them. They wouldn't have fitted into the village *at all*.'

'And I expect you thought it would be fun to piss me off,' said Johnny. 'Well, congratulations, you managed it. If I don't find another buyer before Christmas I'm going to lose that apartment I've been trying to buy. So the reason I came over is to ask you not to do it again. Because, trust me, I don't find it funny.'

And that was it. He turned, he left.

When the front door had closed behind him, Will gazed across the kitchen at Cleo.

'I can't believe you didn't tell me.'

Oh God, a man with morals. 'I just hate it that he always gets everything he wants.' She heaved a sigh. 'Are you shocked and disappointed?'

A slow smile began to spread across his face. 'I'll forgive you.'

Phew, thank goodness for that! And while they were on the subject of confessing their faults . . . 'There's something else,' said Cleo. 'I'm really bad at cooking.'

'You don't say. I'd never have noticed.' Grinning now, Will moved towards her. 'Who wants to eat vegetables anyway?'

'Or chicken. That's awful too.' Between kisses, Cleo said, 'We can get something to eat at the pub. What are you doing?'

His hands had slid under her top . . . whoops, and now he was unfastening her lilac satin bra.

'Bed first,' Will murmured in her ear. 'Pub later.'

The smell of scorched broccoli had pretty much spoiled her appetite too. Wrapping her arms around his neck, Cleo said happily, 'That sounds like an excellent idea to me.'

Abbie, lying beneath a layer of bubbles in the bath on Saturday evening, was listening to a problems phone-in on the radio. Hearing about other people's difficult lives and dilemmas was meant to be taking her mind off Tom but it wasn't having the desired effect.

He'd gone away for the weekend on a fishing trip with a couple of friends from work. *Allegedly*. Then again, the trip had been arranged months ago, so maybe it was true.

Someone on the radio was talking about her adulterous husband and searching for clues. It hadn't occurred to Abbie to do that. Which just went to show how completely . . . well, *clueless* she was. If she hunted through the house, who knew what might turn up?

And what was she waiting for? Anything would be better than this awful not knowing. With a swoooosh Abbie hauled herself out of the bath, dried herself, threw on her dressing gown. Then, hair dripping, she ran into their bedroom and pushed up her sleeves. OK, if she was Tom with something incriminating to hide, where would she hide it?

Forty minutes later, she found it. In Tom's sock drawer, of all the unimaginative places. The moment she heard a crackle of paper and her fingers closed around the folded-up envelope, she knew this was what she'd been searching for.

Trembling, Abbie sank down onto the edge of the bed. Oh yes, this was it, no doubt about it. A blue envelope, first-class stamp, postmarked eleven days ago. Tom's name and this address on the front. If this was from his mistress, she'd taken a risk sending it.

Abbie closed her eyes. Once you knew something, you couldn't unknow it. Her life was about to change for ever. Right, here goes. She slid the sheet of writing paper out of the envelope. As she unfolded it, a photograph dropped to the floor.

Her bare toes scrunched with fear, Abbie left it there and began to read.

> *Dear Tom,*
>
> *OK, you haven't been back in touch and you promised you would, so I'm writing again. Were you hoping that if you ignored me, I'd go away? Because I promise you, that's not going to happen!*
>
> *All my life I've wondered who my dad was, and now I've tracked you down, I'm not giving up—no way. I'm glad you aren't questioning it, by the way, or trying to say you might not be my father, but Mum says I do look a lot like you. Anyway, here's a photo of me taken last year (during my mad hat phase!), so you can judge for yourself. I'm not too ugly, am I?!*
>
> *And I'm really sorry if it's awkward for you with your wife but that's not my fault, is it? Please ring me soon so we can fix a date to meet. You have no idea how desperate I am to see you! (Mum says hi and she's sorry too, but you already know what she's like!)*
>
> *Love,*
> *Your very-keen-to-meet-you daughter,*
> *Georgia xxxxx*

Abbie bent down, picked up the photograph and turned it over. As if any further proof were needed, Tom's laughing, light-blue eyes gazed up at her out of a teenager's heart-shaped face. A girl, beaming away, with Tom's cheekbones and the unmistakeable outline of his mouth. Tendrils of fair hair were escaping from her purple butcher-boy cap. She was wearing big hooped earrings and a white denim jacket.

She wasn't too ugly. She was beautiful. And she looked so like Tom it was ridiculous.

So that was it; now she knew the truth. Tom wasn't ill. He wasn't having an affair either. But he'd had one years ago. Her loving, straightforward, utterly trustworthy husband had been unfaithful to her and his mistress had given birth to a girl who was now—understandably—desperate to meet her father.

After everything they had been through together, it was like being stabbed in the stomach, over and over. Clutching her chest, Abbie let out a low-pitched broken wail of grief as her world crumbled.

The phone rang an hour later. Caller ID told her it was Des from work. Feeling utterly wretched, Abbie answered and mumbled, ''Lo.' Oh God, her throat was so swollen from crying she didn't even sound like herself. Too late, she wished she hadn't picked up.

'Abbie? Is that you?' Des sounded surprised.

'Yes.' She cleared her throat, tried again. 'Hello.'

'Listen, I'm here doing the rota and Magda's got her uncle's funeral on Wednesday, so we're short-staffed. Any chance you could swap your day off to Thursday?'

'Um . . . er . . .' Her brain was like cotton wool; he was talking about four whole days away.

'Are you all right?'

'Yes, yes . . . yes, I'm fine . . .'

'No you're not. What's wrong?'

'Nothing . . .' The fact that he was being kind, sounding as if he really cared was what finished her off. A huge uncontrollable gulpy sob burst out like a cannonball.

'Right, that's it. Is it Tom?' His voice rising, Des said urgently, 'Is he beating you up?' Like Superman, ready to swoop to the rescue.

'N-no, Tom's not here. He's gone f-fishing.' Another involuntary sob escaped. Her face was tight and salty from all the tears.

'And you're on your own? OK, don't move. I'll be five minutes.'

'No . . . you don't have to . . .' But it was too late, Des had already hung up. He was on his way.

Abbie just had time to wash her face and gaze miserably at her piggy-eyed reflection in the mirror before the doorbell rang downstairs. Now that Des was here she was grateful for the company; the urge to talk things through was welling up unstoppably like water in a garden hose and Des, a genuinely kind soul, would be a good listener.

When she opened the front door he took one look at her face and exclaimed, 'Oh Abbie, tell me what's wrong.'

'It's Tom. He's had an affair.' As she led the way into the living room, Abbie saw it with fresh eyes. Everything was immaculate, because they had both always taken great pride in their house. From the pale yellow Colefax-and-Fowler wallpaper and matching curtains to the polished wooden floor and cream rugs, it was all perfect. She looked at the happy smiley framed photographs of her and Tom together, and tipped the nearest one over. 'And a baby.' Saying the word aloud caused her to shudder. 'A daughter.' *Crack* went the glass in the silver frame containing a picture of them taken on their wedding day. 'Called Georgia.'

Des looked appalled. 'And she's just been born?'

Abbie shook her head, pulled the envelope from her dressing-gown pocket and gave it to him. She watched him look at the photograph first, then read the letter.

When he'd finished, Des said, 'This is pretty major. But she doesn't say how old she is. Maybe it happened before you two got together.'

'Nice try.' Abbie's jaw ached with the effort of keeping the muscles rigid. 'But it didn't. We've been together since we were fourteen. Childhood sweethearts.' The words curdled on her tongue; everything was spoiled now. 'All we ever w-wanted was each other, for ever and ever, for the rest of our lives. Ha, and to think I actually believed that!' *Craaaacccckkkk*, glass from the next frame shattered on the floor and she flinched as a shard ricocheted off her bare foot.

'Right, stop it. Come here.' Grabbing hold of her by the hand, Des yanked her away from the glass. 'You're going to hurt yourself.'

'And you think I'm not hurt already?' Hyperventilating with rage and grief, Abbie howled, 'You can't *begin* to understand how I'm feeling! Des, did you ever wonder why me and Tom didn't have children?'

There was bemusement in his grey eyes. It had clearly never occurred to him to question it. 'No.'

'Well, it's because I *couldn't* have children. At all. Ever.' Was she completely losing it now? Abbie didn't care. Dimly aware that Des was herding her away from the broken glass, she burst into tears and sobbed, 'Which makes all this quite h-hard to bear, really, seeing as it was all I ever w-wanted in my life.'

Superman took charge, guiding her firmly out of the living room and in the direction of the stairs. 'Tell me where you keep your vacuum cleaner. Then go and get dressed. You're not staying here on your own.'

When you were at the end of your tether, being given clear, simple instructions was such a relief. Getting dressed; she could manage that. While the Dyson crackled and roared downstairs, slurping up splinters and shards of glass, Abbie pulled on jeans and an old oversized blue V-neck sweater. Everyone had always said she and Tom had the happiest marriage they knew, and she'd been gullible enough to believe them. Whereas behind her back, while she'd been feeling ridiculously happy and loved, Tom had kept the secret of his own infidelity. And once you'd had one affair . . . well, why stop there? For all she knew, he could have had dozens.

It didn't bear thinking about. So she didn't.

Were you meant to vacuum up broken glass with a Dyson or would it irretrievably shred the innards and render it useless?

Oh well, she knew how *that* felt.

Des's flat, above the garden centre, was plainly furnished, decorated in shades of magnolia and tidier than she'd imagined. He was being so kind. When he offered her a drink, Abbie said, 'Wine please, white if you've got it,' and Des said apologetically, 'Sorry, I don't have any wine. There's some brandy left over from last Christmas.'

He evidently wasn't a great drinker, which was no bad thing. In the narrow beige kitchen, discovering lemonade in the fridge, Abbie said, 'Well . . . brandy and lemonade then, that'll be fine,' and didn't have the heart to complain when Des, knowing no better, poured equal quantities of each into a half-pint beer mug.

Actually, it kind of grew on you after the first few shudder-making sips. And the spreading warmth in her stomach was definitely helping her to relax. You could see why people in times of trouble turned to drink. Next to her on the faded leather sofa, in front of a real fire, Des was being a brilliant listener, nodding sympathetically and being completely on her side.

'. . . We found out when I was seventeen. I had to go to the hospital and have all these tests done, then they told me I didn't have a viable womb. And that was it.' Abbie sank her head back against the sofa cushions. 'I just wanted to die. I thought Tom would leave me. Why would he want to stay stuck with someone who could never have children? But he was fantastic.' Tears slid down her face and dripped off her chin. 'He said it didn't matter and he loved me too much to let me go.

Of course, he forgot to mention that he'd be taking his mind off things by screwing other women behind my back.'

'It might have happened only the once,' said Des.

Abbie wiped her eyes. 'And that's meant to make me feel better, is it? You're sticking up for him now?'

'No, no, I'm really not.' Covering her hand, Des gave it a squeeze. 'I don't know how he could do it to you.' He shook his head. 'What about adoption? Did you never want to try that?'

'Oh, we did want to. But we were too young to adopt.' Abbie closed her eyes as the painful memories of that time came flooding back. 'So we tried surrogacy but that was traumatic and it didn't work . . . then we couldn't face any more tries after that, so we saved up for a couple more years and investigated adopting from abroad instead. But it was all so complicated and hard and I ended up getting into such a state that my doctor had to put me on tranquillisers. She told me I was obsessed, that it was taking over my life and if I wasn't careful I'd have a complete nervous breakdown. And that was when Tom said it had to stop. He put his foot down and told me he wanted a wife, not a gibbering wreck. And you know what? It was almost a relief. We'd tried everything and nothing had worked. So we gave up and told ourselves we'd leave it for another four years. But then every time we started thinking about adoption after that, Tom saw me getting wound up all over again and said he wasn't going to put me through it. And when I went along to my doctor in a state, she told me I wasn't doing myself any favours, and that with my mental history I might not be considered suitable to adopt anyway.' She paused, turned to look at Des. 'So that was it. We drew a line, gave up for good, told ourselves that at least we still had each other.'

He gave her hand another sympathetic squeeze. 'I'm so sorry.'

'It's not your fault.' Frowning at the empty glass in her other hand, Abbie said, 'Did I spill this?'

Des smiled. 'You drank it. Stay there, I'll get you another one.'

By the time he returned from the kitchen, Abbie was in tears again.

'Sorry, I don't know where it's all coming from.' She fumbled for another tissue. 'This must be the most boring night of your life.'

'Don't be silly. We're friends, aren't we?' He sat back down. 'You've had a rotten thing happen and you don't deserve it.'

A rotten thing happen. Well, that was one way of putting it. But he was trying so hard to help.

'I don't know what to do.' Abbie's voice broke. 'I still can't believe he did it. I just want to hurt him like he's hurt me . . .'

Oh no. Oh God. The moment Abbie opened her eyes, the events of the night before came flooding back in technicolour detail.

Every single detail.

Her stomach clenched with horror, she gazed at the unfamiliar curtains and felt the unfamiliar arm draped over her side, the warm breath on the back of her neck. How had she got herself into this situation? Except she already knew the answer to that. Fuelled by the second half-pint mug of mostly brandy with a dash of lemonade, she had carried on ranting and raving while Des had been . . . well, lovely, really. Kind, patient and endlessly understanding. Until finally she'd cried, 'I mean, how would Tom like it if I did it to him?' and Des had gazed wordlessly into her eyes until the penny finally dropped.

A combination of alcohol and the desire for revenge was what had propelled her to do it. She had leaned over and kissed him. That was all, just a kiss, but Des had responded with alacrity. They'd kissed some more and it had felt strange, but it was a way of getting back at Tom, so she'd carried on. Then after a while, Des had helped her to her feet and led her through to the bedroom. By that stage the alcohol had well and truly kicked in. Recklessly, she'd almost made up her mind to have sex with him. *There you go, Tom, see how you like that.* But when it came down to it, she hadn't been able to see it through. And to his eternal credit, Des hadn't pressed her to change her mind. He had stopped at once, comforted her when she started sobbing all over again, and told her that it didn't matter, just being here with her was enough. Not long after that, overwrought and exhausted and unaccustomed to the alcohol she'd drunk, she'd fallen asleep in his arms.

Still fully clothed, thank God.

Abbie blinked and shifted to the edge of the bed. Her mouth tasted sour and last night's torrent of tears had left her eyes sore and gritty. The clock on the bedside table showed that it was ten to six. Outside, the sky was still pitch black; it wouldn't start to get light for another hour.

'Where are you off to?'

Guiltily, she turned and saw that Des had been watching her. If last night had been embarrassing, this morning already felt worse. 'Sorry, did I wake you? I need to get home.'

'You don't have to. You're welcome to stay.'

He was her boss. She had nearly-but-not-quite slept with him. And he was still being kind. Feeling sick and dreading Tom's return from his fishing trip this evening, Abbie said, 'Thanks, but I want to go.'

'OK, I know you've got stuff to sort out with Tom.' He pushed back his tousled reddish fair hair with the flat of his hand. 'But . . . I meant it when I said you didn't deserve to be treated like that. You're lovely . . . amazing . . .' He saw her flinch and went on hastily, 'Look, you can call me or come over whenever you want. Anything I can do to help, please, just say the word.'

'Right.' Abbie nodded. 'Thanks.' If it wasn't so tragic it would almost be funny; they sounded so clipped and British, like something out of a 1940s black-and-white film.

He blinked. 'Will you tell him about spending the night here?'

'Don't worry.' As she shook her head, she saw the relief in Des's eyes. 'I won't. It's just between us. No one else is going to know.' Awkwardly she added, 'And you won't tell anyone either?'

Des's expression softened. 'Whatever you want.'

'Thanks. Well, bye then.'

He cleared his throat. 'I hate to ask, but will you be able to work Magda's shift on Wednesday?'

God, this was what he'd phoned up to ask her last night. If he hadn't, none of this would have happened.

'Yes. Fine.' Abbie nodded helplessly. She'd spent the night in Des Kilgour's bed and nearly ended up having sex with him, and it was all Magda's dead uncle's fault.

Chapter 3

'CLEO!' SASKIA CAME hurtling towards her, mittens on strings flapping as she flung out her arms.

'Sass!' Picking her up and swinging her into the air, Cleo pretended to stagger. 'Oof, you're heavier than a house.'

'I'm not. You are.' Saskia had inherited her mother's slender frame, dancing green eyes and infectious giggle. 'When are we going? Soon?'

'Sorry, sorry.' Shelley, her mother, ran her hands over her neatly tied-back dark hair and grimaced by way of apology. 'She hasn't stopped going on about it all weekend. Are you sure you don't mind?'

Of course she didn't mind. Cleo knew how much she owed to Shelley. Following a series of less-than-thrilling jobs—waitressing, office work, tour guide—she had been more than ready for a change three years ago when she'd heard about a vacancy for a chauffeur at Henleaze Limos. Grumpy Graham, who owned the company and ran the tiny office from his home just off Henleaze Road in North Bristol, had wanted another male driver. Shelley, in her late thirties and divorced, had persuaded Graham to take Cleo on instead. She had then been the one who'd shown her the ropes and taught her how to stand up to Graham, who took his grumpiness seriously. She and Shelley had hit it off from the word go, and Saskia—three and a bit then, six years old now—was the light of her mum's life. She also had the memory of an elephant; many months ago, Cleo had mentioned in passing that next Christmas Saskia might enjoy a trip to Marcombe Arboretum, where an illuminated path through the woods led to a hut in a snowy clearing where good children got the chance to meet Santa. When she'd said, 'You should ask your mum to take you there,' Saskia had replied brightly, 'Or you could take me.'

And the moment Shelley had mentioned that she had a pick-up at Heathrow on Sunday afternoon, Saskia had announced without hesitation, 'That's fine, Cleo can take me to that tree place to see Santa.'

'You're a star,' said Shelley, heading for the door. 'I'll come and pick her up at seven, is that OK?'

'Perfect.'

'Bye, Mummy!' Tugging hard at Cleo's hand, Saskia said eagerly, 'Come on, hurry up, let's go.'

Once they'd reached Marcombe, parked in the arboretum car park and trudged along the winding, lit-up path through the woods, it was magical. Strategically positioned uplighters shone differently coloured lights into the trees, others were strung with garlands of twinkling white stars and a snow machine had been brought in to dust the entire clearing with a festive layer of biodegradable snow.

'Is he really in there?' breathed Saskia, gazing in wonder at the gingerbread-style wooden hut with Santa's helpers at the entrance and a pair of real reindeer being fussed over by families at the head of the queue.

'He really is.' Squeezing Saskia's mittened hand, Cleo felt her eyes prickle with sentimental tears. This was what Christmas was all about, wasn't it? Creating wonderful memories for children while they were still young and innocent enough to believe in Father Christmas. All around them, happy families were laughing and chattering, clouds of condensation puffing out of their mouths as they stamped their feet and rubbed their hands together.

'Are you cold, sweetie?'

'No.' Saskia, who had been picking bits of white papier-mâché fluff off the front of her pink flowered Wellingtons, said, 'It's not real snow.'

'It's better than real snow. It doesn't melt.'

'But it's the real Santa?'

'Oh yes, definitely the real Santa.'

Saskia did an excited skip. 'Can we see him now?'

'Soon, sweetie. We have to get in the queue.'

It was while Saskia was busy twirling around and gazing skywards that Cleo glimpsed something that gave her a jolt. Several feet ahead of them in the queue, someone was wearing a tan leather jacket just like Will's, and for a split second as the man gestured with one hand he even looked like Will. Wait until she told him she'd thought she'd seen him in the queue for Santa's grotto with two small children in tow.

Except . . .

Oh God, no, *surely not.*

But of course it was him. It was Will, her boyfriend, not in Manchester preparing for a conference. Instead, unbelievably, he was here, just a few paces away, waiting to see Father Christmas.

Cleo's heart was banging so hard against her ribs she could barely hear all the different voices around her. Will wasn't married and he didn't have children but somehow, inexplicably, a small girl in a pink coat was hanging on to his hand and behind her a boy aged six or seven was stealthily filling the pockets of her coat with fake snow.

Cleo became aware of a tugging on her own arm. Saskia was saying urgently, 'How many presents am I allowed to ask for? Can I ask for six?'

'Um . . .' It was so hard to concentrate. 'No, just one.'

OK, let's be logical about this. She was here with Saskia, but did that automatically make Saskia her daughter? No, of course it didn't. So it stood to reason that the same went for Will. He was simply doing a friend a favour, bringing the friend's two children along to the arboretum out of the sheer goodness of his heart and . . .

'Mummy? Mummy!' A child in a Postman Pat anorak was pointing an outraged finger at Cleo. 'That lady just said you're allowed to ask Santa for only *one* present! But you said we could ask for *three.*'

Oh God, get me out of here. Hurriedly, apologetically, Cleo stammered, 'S-sorry, I made a mistake . . . it's three.'

'*Ha.*' The child shot a look of triumph at Saskia.

'Three?' Saskia gazed up at Cleo for confirmation. 'Three *big* presents?'

Distracted, Cleo nodded. OK, it would be useful if Will could turn round now, catch sight of her and break into a huge delighted smile.

He'd exclaim, 'I don't believe it, have you been roped into this too?' before going on to explain that the Manchester conference had been cancelled at the last minute and his boss had asked him for this huge favour and, hey, now they could all queue up together . . .

'Does an Xbox count as a big present or quite a small one?'

'What? Um . . . big.' Reaching for her mobile, Cleo dragged her gaze away from the back view of Will and scrolled through to his number. She pressed Call. Watched, dry-mouthed, as his phone began to ring. Saw Will take it out of his jacket pocket, glance at the screen and calmly switch it off.

Straining her ears, Cleo heard the girl holding his hand say, 'Who was that, Daddy?'

Will smiled down at her. 'No one, darling. Just work.'

Just work.

Of the extracurricular variety.

Cleo didn't often find herself at a loss, but watching the three of them, she couldn't for the life of her figure out what to do now. If it had just been Will and herself here, she would have confronted him, *obviously*. But how could she do that with his children present?

So confrontation was out.

Ditto, murder. Sadly.

And she couldn't leave, because that would break Saskia's heart.

So basically she was stuck here, while Christmas music piped out from speakers hidden in the trees and fake snow drifted down, watching the cheating, lying bastard who had, up until this afternoon, been her lovely boyfriend . . . then again, hang on, might it be possible that he was a liar but not a cheat? Thinking fast, it occurred to Cleo that he could still be single; he just hadn't plucked up the courage to tell her about the children by a previous girlfriend in case it put her off him. Because if *that* was the case, discovering the truth like this could actually turn out to be quite romantic, like the heart-warming ending of one of those schmaltzy films you only ever see on TV at Christmas.

It was a fabulous idea, scuppered in moments when a thirtyish woman squeezed past, the sleeve of her navy coat brushing against Cleo's arm as she murmured, 'Sorry . . . excuse me . . .' before reaching Will and the children.

'Yay, you're back from having a wee,' sang the girl, beaming up at her.

'Yes, well, thanks for sharing that information.' The woman exchanged an amused look with the couple ahead of them in the queue.

'You're always going to the loo,' the son chimed in. 'Every time we go out. Doesn't she, Dad?'

'She does.' Will nodded solemnly.

The woman mimed outrage and pretended to hit him. Will ducked away and used his son as a human shield. Everyone around them was laughing now. The perfect family sharing a perfect moment, with pretend snow tumbling down, fairy lights twinkling in the trees and Christmas carols being piped out, creating the perfect festive mood.

Cleo wondered how Will had managed to spend the past three months conducting an affair while he was married. The woman was wearing a wedding ring and now she was affectionately brushing fake snow out of Will's hair, which wasn't something you'd do to an ex-husband.

There was no getting away from it, she was his wife.

The nerve, the colossal *nerve* of the man . . .

'Aaaaaalllll is calm, aaaaaallll is bright,' Saskia sang. People in the queue turned to smile at her and that was when it happened. The woman nudged Will and he turned to look at Saskia. Then, like a join-the-dots picture, his gaze travelled from Saskia's face to her arm to the mittened hand holding Cleo's before travelling upwards and finally reaching Cleo's stony face.

Ha, now whose heart was hammering in his chest with shock and fear? She saw it in his eyes, raised an eyebrow fractionally in return but otherwise didn't react at all. Will looked away first, turning back to his children. Even from this distance she could see the tension in his shoulders.

'Cleo?' Now that the music had stopped, Saskia tugged her hand again. 'Is an iPod a big present or a small one?'

'It's a big present, sweetie.'

'But it's only *tiny*.'

'They cost a lot.'

'Oh.' Saskia's eyes were huge. 'So . . . would a dog be cheaper?'

'Your Mum's already told you that you can't have a dog.' Cleo had wondered how long it would be before the D-word was raised; getting a dog was Saskia's latest mission in life. 'Dogs need too much looking after.'

'And they wee a lot.' Breaking into a grin, Saskia pointed ahead of them. 'Like that lady over there.'

This was unbearable.

Forty hellish minutes later, it was Will and his family's turn to be led inside the grotto to meet Father Christmas. He hadn't looked round once since discovering who was in the queue behind him. Cleo wondered if Will was having a go on Santa's knee: 'Dear Santa, I haven't been a very good boy this year; in fact, I've been very *naughty*. But could I still get a Christmas present? All I want is for my wife not to find out about my mistress.'

Oh God. She shuddered at the word, up until that moment it hadn't occurred to her that this was what he'd turned her into.

'Cleo? Is it our turn soon?' Saskia's nose was pink with cold but she was still zinging with pent-up anticipation.

'Not long to go now.' Cleo lifted her into her arms for a cuddle to warm them both up and take her own mind off the fact that she may as well have Evil Harlot scrawled in red felt-tip across her forehead.

Then the door of the wooden hut opened and Will and his family emerged. The children were excitedly clutching wrapped presents and their mother was exchanging cheerful words with the next people to go in. Passing Cleo and Saskia, she said, 'Don't worry, he's worth the wait!'

Meaning Santa, presumably. Not Will.

'Can we open them now, Daddy?' The boy rattled his parcel.

'No, come on, let's get back to the car.' As he hurried both children past Cleo, Will's glance met her unwavering gaze. There was pleading apology in his eyes and with his wife safely out of sight, his left hand came up to shoulder level, thumb and little finger extended to indicate that he would call her.

Pointedly Cleo looked away. Three whole months of her life, wasted. And to think that she'd actually had high hopes for Will. Apart from the disappointment and the fury at having been strung along, she just felt so used and gullible and *stupid.*

'You look funny.' Saskia, with not a care in the world, beamed and said, 'You've got all pretend snow in your hair.'

Ha, not to mention murder and retribution in her heart.

Abbie had been going relentlessly over and over the moment of Tom's return, working out what she was going to say, but when it actually came to it, she didn't need to say anything at all.

His key turned in the front door, the overnight case, cool box and fishing rods were dumped in the hallway and he yelled out, as he always did, 'Hi, honey, I'm home!'

It was their little joke, the way he always greeted her, and every time he did it, Tom varied the accent. Today, in honour of the fishing trip, it was Irish, and just to prove it—because some of his accents weren't instantly recognisable—he added, 'Bejaysus, it's frayzin' out dare tonight!'

Ironically, he sounded more cheerful than he had done for the past fortnight. Was that because he'd spent the weekend with his daughter?

Then Tom appeared in the kitchen doorway and his expression changed. The moment he saw her sitting there, he knew.

Abbie knew she looked a fright but she didn't care. *He* had done this to her. It was his fault she'd spent the day a trembling wreck, red-eyed, dry-mouthed and with a whole world of pain in her chest.

'Oh God.' The colour drained from his face. His hand rasped over his unshaven jaw and he shook his head. 'How'd you find out?'

'About Georgia, you mean?' Abbie barely recognised her own voice. 'Your . . . *daughter*?'

Tom exhaled noisily. 'Oh God. Did she turn up on the doorstep? I *told* her not to do that. Abbie, I'm so sorry, I was going to tell you—'

'*Were you really?* How considerate of you!' As her voice rose, Abbie realised he was moving towards her, arms outstretched. CRASH went the kitchen chair as she leaped up, sending it flying. Backing away, she shouted, 'Keep away from me! Do you think I want you *near* me?'

Tom stopped dead in the middle of the kitchen. 'Look, I've said I'm sorry. And I knew you'd be upset. That's why I didn't tell you before. I was trying to work out a way of breaking it to you gently . . .'

'Wow, what a hero!'

'Abbie, it's been as much of a shock to me as it has been for you. I still can't believe it's happened.' Will shook his head. 'But we'll get over this, I promise. We just have to work through it together.'

'Are you *serious*?' Had he *no* idea how she felt? 'Tom, how can I ever trust you again? Our whole marriage has been a sham! Maybe some women could put up with what you've done, but I'm not one of them. I feel sick just looking at you . . . I never want you to *touch* me again!'

Tom was staring at her. 'Abbie, that's not fair.'

Not fair? *Not fair?* Rage surged up through her. 'So as far as you're concerned, the fact that you had an affair with another woman is something I should just . . . *forgive*.' Abbie's fingernails dug into the palms of her hands as she spat the words out. 'Does that mean you wouldn't mind if I did it? Would you just say oh dear, never mind, I'm sure we can *work through it together*? Because if that's what you think, let me—'

'Hang on. Whoa.' Tom frowned and raised a hand to stop her. '*What* did you say? What are you talking about? There was no . . . *affair*.'

'Fine,' Abbie bellowed, 'like it makes any difference! So she was just a casual fling, a one-night stand, some tart you had sex with . . . '

'No, no, *no*.' Shaking his head in disbelief, Tom said, 'Is that what she told you? Georgia . . . did she say it was an affair?'

'I haven't seen her! I never *want* to see her!' Abbie wrenched the letter from her jeans pocket and slammed it down on the scrubbed oak kitchen table. 'It's all in there.'

Something altered in Tom's face. He looked at the letter. Then he looked up again at her.

'Not quite all.' Even his voice sounded different now.

'You've got a daughter.' As she said it, Abbie felt her mouth twist with misery. 'What else is there to know?'

'Oh Abbie . . . sweetheart . . . I love you so much.'

'Don't say that.'

'But it's true. And there's one question you haven't asked yet.' Closing his eyes briefly, Tom said, 'The name of Georgia's mother.'

Feeling sicker by the second, she said, 'Go on then.'

Tom rubbed his hands on the sides of his worn corduroy trousers and said, 'It's Patty Summers.'

Patty.

Patty Summers.

Patty Summers from nearly twenty years ago, with her silver-blonde hair and her long floaty skirts? Abbie was confused, struggling to take this information in; it was *the* most unlikely name he could have come out with. Had Tom carried on secretly seeing Patty afterwards?

'I've never cheated on you, Abbie. Never wanted to, never have.' Sensing her bewilderment, Tom moved towards her. His voice infinitely gentle, he said, 'Sweetheart, she lied to us. *She lied.*'

Nineteen years ago. Abbie remembered it as clearly as if it were yesterday. She had been twenty-five and frantic, a seething hormonal maelstrom of desperation and impatience. The more everyone had told her just to relax and stop worrying, the more desperate she had become. Surrogate mothers had been in the news and being told by her disapproving doctor that this wasn't something she should even consider had been the final straw. Who needed an official organisation to make the arrangements anyway? Thanks to all the reading up she'd done, Abbie knew it was a straightforward-enough process, and taking matters into their own hands seemed to be the only way to go. Using a box number, she had placed an advert in the local Bristol papers: 'Could *you* be a surrogate mother for a couple unable to have children of their own? Please help! Generous expenses paid.'

Tom was wary but supportive, Abbie's overwhelming need overcoming his own natural reticence. And four days later, the letter had arrived from Patty Summers offering to be their surrogate.

It was as if a miracle had been granted. They made arrangements to meet up at a café in Clifton, the upmarket area of Bristol where Patty lived. Not knowing what to expect, meeting Patty for the first time was a revelation. She swished into the café, greeted Abbie and Tom like long-lost family and dazzled them with her warmth and *joie de vivre*.

She was beautiful, like Claudia Schiffer, with dancing eyes and a wide smile. Spotting their ad in the paper, she told them emotionally, had captured her heart. It had reached out and touched her. What better way could there be to help others than by carrying a baby for a couple who weren't able to procreate themselves . . . she would be *honoured* if they would allow her to do this for them.

Abbie was mesmerised, completely entranced by Patty Summers. It was left to Tom to ask the sensible questions. And no, Patty didn't have children of her own—she'd never been the maternal type, never *wanted* any—but she just knew this was something she was capable of doing. She was twenty-six years old, completely healthy, didn't take drugs or even smoke cigarettes. Her last job, working in a bar, had come to a bit of a sticky end when she'd broken up with her boyfriend, who happened to own the bar in question. This was why she'd been flicking through the local paper in search of work. And that was why it all made such perfect sense. Either she could start some boring new job, or she could relax, chill out for a year and grow a baby instead!

After an hour, Abbie's mind was made up. In order to pay the rent on her flat in Clifton and cover the rest of her bills, they agreed to pay Patty a thousand pounds a month. More than they'd been expecting, but not unreasonable when you thought about what she would be doing for them. And the beauty of going with Patty was her willingness to start straight away.

'A thousand pounds a *month*,' hissed Tom when Patty left them to visit the loo. 'For nine *months*.'

But Abbie wasn't to be swayed. Nothing was going to stop them now. They had their savings, Tom could work overtime and she would take an extra evening job. 'We're not going to haggle.' She clutched his hand beneath the table and gave it an iron squeeze. 'Tom, think of the beautiful baby we'll have! We're going to do it and it'll be worth every penny. This is the answer to our dreams!'

'But we don't even know her. We met her only an hour ago.'

'Don't you dare spoil this.' Abbie's chest was tight with anxiety.

'She could be anyone.'

'He's right.' Patty, back from the loo and overhearing their exchange, said, 'I *could* be anyone, but I'm not. I'm me.' She looked at the pair of them. 'OK, how about if I show you my flat? Would that help?'

So they'd done that, gone along with Patty to her attic flat on the fourth floor of a Georgian house in Cornwallis Crescent. Photos of Patty with friends and family chronicled her life to date, she'd painted the walls a sunny shade of yellow, and there were books and CDs everywhere. 'Sorry, I'm a messy pup.' Busy checking her calendar, Patty said, 'So, looking at dates, I reckon next weekend's when we want to make a start. And I'm free on Saturday afternoon.' She looked at them brightly. 'That OK with you?'

'Next Saturday.' In a daze, Abbie nodded. It was February . . . if everything worked first time, they could have a baby by Christmas.

'Brilliant!' Patty's silver bracelets jangled as she clapped her hands together in delight. 'We'll do it here!'

'Hang on.' Reddening, Tom said, 'There won't be any . . . you know, *contact*. I mean, you and me won't be . . . um, doing anything together.'

'Oh bless, is that what you were worried about? All this time?' Patty burst out laughing. 'Of course we won't be having sex! We use one of those baster thingies, don't we? You do your business into a teacup or whatever, then I'll take care of the girly side of things . . . ' Shaking her head at Tom, she went on, 'No offence, but you're really not my type.'

The following Saturday they had gone back to the Clifton flat. They handed over the first cheque for a thousand pounds, and thirty minutes later the deed was done and Patty hugged them both goodbye, taking Abbie's hand, placing it over her flat stomach and exclaiming, 'Just think, it could be happening in there right now, at this very minute! Can you picture that? Isn't it the most amazing idea *ever*?'

The next two weeks crawled by with agonising slowness. Abbie barely slept, convinced it had worked and that their longed-for baby was already on its way. Was it a boy? Was it a girl? What names would they choose? Would it be wrong to start buying clothes for it?

Sixteen days after insemination day, Abbie phoned Patty's number.

'Hi, it's me. Um, any . . . news?'

'Oh, hello Abbie! No, nothing yet . . . '

'So that's *good* news.' Abbie sent up a heartfelt prayer of thanks.

'Well, it's too soon to tell, really. I might just be, you know, a bit late.'

'But you could do a test. I can buy one and bring it over, if you like!'

'Oh, you're so sweet, but I really think it's too early to do an accurate test. Look, I'm popping over to France to see my mum for a week. I'll be back next Wednesday. So if my period still hasn't started, I'll do the test then and we'll really know for sure!'

Somehow Abbie made it through the next week and then, on Wednesday evening, the phone rang and there was Patty's voice on the other end of the line.

'Oh Abbie. I'm so sorry, it didn't work. My period started today.'

Abbie slid down the wall until she was sitting on the living room floor. No baby. So sorry.

'Abbie? Are you all right? Look, we tried. We did our best. Sorry.'

OK, it's not the end of the world. *Although it felt as if it was.* Forcing herself to keep it together, Abbie said, 'Well, we'll just have to try again.'

'Yes.' Pause. 'Except, um, could you use someone else next time? Because I don't think I want to do it any more.'

'But you *promised* . . .'

'I didn't promise. We *agreed* that I'd keep going if it didn't work straight away. But, you know, I didn't enjoy it as much as I thought,' said Patty. 'So I've changed my mind about doing it again.'

'But we're paying you!'

'Abbie, don't get upset. I'm not trying to con you out of your money. Of course I won't take any more . . .'

'*Don't get upset?*' bellowed Abbie. 'How do you expect me to feel?'

'OK, now you're shouting at me. And I'm not going to change my mind.' There was an edge to Patty's voice. 'Anyway, it wouldn't be practical,' she went on, 'because I'm leaving Bristol. My mum's asked me to go down to France, move in with her.'

'Please. Just . . . give it one more try . . . please, I'm begging you . . .'

It wasn't dignified and it didn't work. Patty hastily ended the call and Abbie collapsed in a heap on the floor.

Now, nineteen years on, Abbie realised Tom was holding her hands in his own. What he'd told her simply wasn't believable, it couldn't be real. But, deep down inside, she knew it was.

'Patty lied to us,' Tom said again. 'She did get pregnant but she realised she wasn't going to be able to hand the baby over. As soon as the hormones kicked in, she knew she wanted to keep it herself. So she told her mother, who promised to help her . . . and that was it.'

'She took our baby. She stole her.'

'Legally, it wasn't *our* baby.' Tom's voice was gentle but she could feel the pain he was suffering too. This eighteen-year-old girl was half Patty's, half his. She was his biological daughter and he'd been cheated out of knowing her, loving her, seeing her grow up.

And speaking of cheating . . . oh God, Abbie felt sick all over again, at the thought of last night. She might not have slept with Des but it could so easily have happened. And she'd spent the night with him in his bed. It would kill Tom if he ever found out.

Well, he just mustn't, that was all. Anyway, she couldn't even think about that now.

'Sweetheart, I'm so sorry.' Tom stroked her hair. 'I didn't know how to tell you before.'

None of this was his fault. She had the best husband in the world and she didn't deserve him.

'Never mind.' Would he and Georgia form a father-daughter relationship? Would she be excluded and left out? Abbie's heart felt as if it was breaking, but the least she could do now was support Tom. Summoning a weak smile, she said, 'Well, I think you should give the girl a ring. I bet you can't wait to meet her.'

Bursting to talk about Will, Cleo was hoping to pounce on Shelley the moment she arrived to pick up Saskia at seven o'clock.

'Hi! Sorry I'm late—the client's flight was delayed!'

Shelley sped past her into the house at seven thirty, grabbing Saskia's coat from the banister and calling, 'Sass? Come on, darling, we've got to rush home and get you to bed, it's school tomorrow.' Over her shoulder she said to Cleo, 'How was Father Christmas? Did you have a good time?'

'Great. Um, but you won't believe what happ—'

'Here you go, put your arms in there . . . good girl, now your boots . . . sorry, can't stop, got your present from Santa, sweetie? Ooh, isn't that lovely! Right, we're out of here! Bye!'

No one could out-whirlwind Shelley when she was in a rush. Within milliseconds they were out of the door, into the car and whizzing back to Bristol, leaving Cleo open-mouthed like a cod on the doorstep.

Still bursting to share what had happened and tragically minus a sympathetic ear. She'd just have to tell Ash instead. And threaten to punch him if he laughed his head off.

Nimbly she vaulted the wall separating their cottages and rattled the knocker on his front door. What wasn't a promising sign, though, was the fact that the house was in darkness.

She went back to her own cottage and rang Ash's mobile, only to find it switched off. Frustratedly, Cleo tried her sister's number and got Tom.

'Oh hi. Abbie's upstairs in the bath. I'll tell her you rang, but she's not feeling that great just now.' Sounding pretty subdued himself, he said, 'So she'll probably call you back tomorrow, if that's all right.'

OK, was this some kind of conspiracy?

Well, she couldn't stay here. She'd explode. Maybe Ash was at the pub.

Except he wasn't. The pub wasn't that busy at all. Still, now that she was here she may as well make the walk worthwhile. Perching on one of the stools at the bar, Cleo ordered a gin and tonic and debated whether to tell Deborah behind the bar about the evils of married men.

Then the door leading to the loos opened and Johnny emerged, and she realised the half-full pint of Guinness on the bar three feet away from her belonged to him.

'It's OK, no need to move.' He looked amused as he swung himself back onto the stool next to hers. 'I'm not in a biting mood tonight.'

Cleo, who was most definitely in a biting mood, said tightly, 'I didn't know you were still here. Shouldn't you be back in New York?'

'Well yes, strictly speaking I should. But it seemed safer to stay and keep an eye on the house. Guard it from anyone who might be wanting to put off potential buyers.'

Trust him not to forget that. 'I already told you, I won't do it again.'

'I know you won't. I'm making sure of it. Well,' Johnny amended, 'I would be, if only we could *find* another buyer.'

Was he trying to make her feel guilty? Cleo crossed her legs, coolly examined her drink then took an elegant sip in the style of Audrey Hepburn. The effect was slightly spoiled by her phone bursting into life, her glass slipping and a sloosh of icy gin and tonic dribbling down her chin into her cleavage.

OK, maybe it didn't quite *count* as a cleavage, but that was where it would have dripped if she'd had one.

Johnny passed her a bar towel. Glancing at the phone lying on the bar, he said, 'It's your boyfriend. Aren't you going to answer that?'

She'd already seen Will's name flash up on the screen. How he had the nerve to call her, she didn't know.

Leave it? Answer it? What the hell. She picked up the phone on the fifth ring and said, 'Not interested,' before hanging up.

'Oh dear.' Johnny raised his eyebrows. 'Problems?'

'Don't be nosy.' Cleo finished dabbing at the wet patch on the front of her white T-shirt.

'I'm not nosy. Just concerned. You seemed so happy together.'

Now he was definitely taking the mick.

Bee-eep, chirruped her phone, signalling the arrival of a text: I can explain everything.

Cleo texted back: You're hilarious.

Bee-eep. This time his message read: I'm coming over.

'You know, this is what I love about the good old-fashioned village pub,' said Johnny. 'The sparkling conversation.'

Ignoring him, Cleo texted back: No No No.

Bee-eep: Please. I need to see you.

'The badinage,' Johnny continued, 'the dazzling repartee.'

Oh, for crying out loud. Cleo quickly sent a final text: NO WAY, then switched off her mobile and said, 'Debs? I'll have another drink.'

She may as well, seeing as staying here was preferable to going home.

'I'll get that.' Johnny was reaching for his wallet.

'No thanks. I'll buy my own.'

'That's the other thing I love, the friendliness of the locals.'

'Look, I'm not in a friendly mood.'

He shrugged. 'Maybe I could cheer you up.'

'You know something?' said Cleo. 'You really couldn't.'

The pub began to fill up, Johnny played a couple of games of pool with three members of the local football team, and Cleo took her mind off Will by chatting to Deborah about salad dressings, Renée Zellweger's love life and all-time favourite shoes. She was just describing her beloved red boots, bought in a sale and gorgeous beyond belief to look at but sadly a size too small, when the door swung open behind her and she caught a faint waft of Armani aftershave.

It didn't take a genius to know who'd just turned up. Cleo swivelled round on her stool and looked at the man who until a few hours ago had been her boyfriend.

'Go away, Will.'

'Cleo, we need to talk.'

'You might need to. I don't.'

'Please.' Aware of interested eyes upon him, he said, 'Can we just go to your place?'

'Um . . . how can I put this? *No.*'

'I'm *sorry.*' Moving towards her, he said pleadingly, 'I love you.'

Cleo's breath caught in her throat. All her life she'd dreamed of someone saying those three little words to her. In the romantic sense, anyway; of course her parents had said it while she'd been growing up. But somehow she'd managed to reach the age of twenty-nine without ever once hearing it from a boyfriend. And now, finally, someone was telling her he loved her. In public, too. He was announcing it in front of everyone in the pub, not caring who heard him, which would have been *so* romantic, if only the circumstances could have been different.

As it was, Cleo was filled with fury and disappointment that he had ruined it for her; her first I-love-you would always be this one, about as unromantic as it was possible to get.

'You lied to me.'

Will spread his arms wide in desperation. 'Because I love you.'

'That flat in Redland. You said you lived there.'

'I know.' There was a faint sheen of perspiration across his forehead. 'It's Rob and Damon's place. I had to do it; I didn't want to lose you.'

Cleo gripped her drink tightly. 'Go away, Will. Go home.'

'Not until we've had a proper talk. Come outside,' he begged.

'I think she wants you to leave.' When had Johnny abandoned his game of pool and resumed his old position at the bar?

Will eyed him evenly and said, 'This is between me and Cleo.'

'Cleo doesn't want to speak to you.'

'She needs to hear what I have to say. In private.'

Johnny turned his gaze on Cleo. 'Did he hit you?'

'For God's sake,' Will exploded. 'Of course I didn't hit her!'

'Well, you've done something to upset her.'

'He's married,' Cleo said flatly. 'And he has children.'

Will's eyes darted around the pub.

'He's been lying to me for three months. I just found out today.'

'Just come outside,' Will begged. 'For two minutes.'

With a hiss of exasperation, she slid down from the stool. Next to her, Johnny said, 'Sure about this?'

Cleo nodded. Will's wife was the innocent party here; she didn't deserve to be publicly humiliated, even if Will did.

Outside, the temperature had plummeted, a thick frost was spreading across the parked cars, and the grass was crisp beneath their feet.

'Nothing you can say is going to make me change my mind.' Cleo wrapped her arms tightly around her shivering torso.

'I love you,' said Will.

Don't say that.

'You're a liar and a cheat.'

'You don't know what it's like. My marriage is over. But it's different with you . . . when we're together, I feel alive again!'

Oh yes, the clichés were really piling up now. 'You're disgusting,' Cleo shot back. 'And how do you suppose I feel? I believed everything you told me! I *trusted* you.'

'That's because we're perfect for each other.' Will took a step towards her. 'We're *meant* to be together. Look, I made a mistake before; I thought Fia was the one for me, but she isn't. My life at home is a nightmare—'

'Apart from when you're out at clubs, picking up girls and pretending to be single.'

'Once. *Once* I did that. And it was the best night of my life,' Will said fiercely. 'Meeting you changed everything . . . it was fate!'

'Don't touch me.' Cleo backed away as he reached out to her.

'But you have to believe me, it's the *truth*. Cleo, when I—'

'OK, time's up.' Johnny had emerged from the pub. 'You can leave now. Head on home to the wife and kids. I'll take care of Misa.'

Will looked at him with loathing. 'She hates you.'

'Maybe so.' Johnny's mouth began to twitch. 'But right now, I reckon I'm the lesser of two evils. So, bye!'

'Don't tell me what to do,' countered Will.

The air was thick with testosterone. Oh God, don't let them fight.

'Wouldn't dream of it. Just making a suggestion. Take care driving home now,' Johnny drawled. 'The roads are slippery.' He paused for a moment, then added, 'A bit like you, really.'

There was no fight; it all happened in a split second. Will took a furious swing at Johnny, who simply put out an arm and blocked the punch. The next moment Will was flying backwards through the air as if twanged by a giant elastic band. Then he hit the ground, his feet shot out from under him, and he was sprawled flat on his back on the frosty grass.

'Oh dear,' said Johnny. 'Slipperier than I thought.'

Leaving the pub by unspoken mutual agreement, Johnny beckoned to Cleo and together they started off across the village green. Behind them, Will got to his feet, brushed himself down and made his way to his car.

As the grass crunched underfoot, Cleo shoved her hands into her jacket pockets and sighed. 'I suppose I've got to thank you now.'

He laughed at her tone of voice. 'Not if you really can't bear to.'

'How did you do that thing, anyway?'

'What thing?'

'Stick your arm out and send him flying.'

Johnny sounded amused. 'Ah, that's the joy of self-defence. You use your attacker's strength against him. I did Shoto Ryu for a few years. You should give it a go. Never know when it might come in handy.'

It was a nice idea, but Cleo knew what she was like. She'd join the self-defence class bursting with good intentions, then lose interest a week later. As her teachers had so often written in her school reports during her unbothered phase, she lacked application.

Actually, speaking of her traumatic schooldays . . . 'Could you stop calling me Misa, by the way?'

'Sorry, didn't realise I still was.'

'You said it in the pub.'

'Did I? Force of habit. I'll try,' said Johnny. 'Scout's honour.'

'You never were a scout.' Cleo glanced over her shoulder as they approached the cottage, double-checking that Will had gone. 'Thanks for walking me back.' It seemed strange to be on relatively cordial terms with someone you'd disliked for years. Taking out her keys, she said, 'Next time I bump into you in the pub, I may even buy you a drink.'

This was her way of signalling goodbye, seeing as a handshake would be weird and she definitely didn't want to give him a kiss on the cheek. Johnny, however, ignored the hint and headed on up the path.

'He might decide to come back. I'll keep you company for a bit.'

'Honestly, there's no need.'

'You don't know that. Anyway, it's not a problem.'

Cleo fitted the key into the lock. 'For you, maybe.'

'Hey, I'll just stay for a coffee. You can manage that, can't you?' Deadpan, he said, 'It's not as if I'm asking you to cook me a meal.'

At least there was no evil smell of burning this time. In the kitchen, she added an inch of cold water to Johnny's mug of coffee before handing it to him.

'You know, it's almost as if you don't enjoy my company.'

'It's been one of those days.'

'Pretty miserable, I suppose. Finding out your boyfriend isn't the catch you thought he was.'

Cleo reached for the biscuit tin and pulled it across the table towards her. Unlike men, chocolate digestives never let you down.

'You had high hopes for him, didn't you?'

'Not really,' Cleo lied.

'Oh, come on, you did. It was pretty obvious. Can I have a biscuit?'

There were only four left. Reluctantly she offered him the tin.

He took two.

'Anyway, he's a dick,' said Johnny. 'You're well rid of him.'

'Thanks. I do know that.'

'You'll find someone else. Eventually.'

'OK, one, I know I could find someone else if I wanted. Two, Will was *a* boyfriend, he wasn't the great love of my life. And three, I don't need another man anyway.'

Johnny leaned back against the fridge. 'Ah, the old don't-need-a-man thing. I love that line.'

She sighed. 'What's *that* supposed to mean?'

'I mean it sounds great, and girls love to say that stuff because it makes them sound all strong and independent. But it's not actually true, is it? Deep down they're panicking, getting more and more desperate, and the next thing, they're hurling themselves into a new relationship.'

'I don't do that. I *wouldn't* do it.' Cleo was indignant.

'Trust me, give it a few weeks and you'll change your mind. I'm guessing you'll go for whatsisname . . .' he indicated the wall on the right, '. . . radio guy . . . the boy next door.'

'*Ash?* No way! He's a friend, that's all. And don't tell me I'm desperate,' said Cleo, 'because I'm not. I'm just fine on my own.'

'Don't get ratty. I'm sure you're right.' His eyes glittering with amusement, Johnny said, 'I'll ask you again in six months, shall I?'

'Fine, do that.' Seeing as it had taken her twenty-nine years to find a man she'd liked as much as Will, the chances of bagging another by then were practically non-existent.

'Look, thanks very much for seeing me home, but you can go now. Will isn't coming back and I'm going to have a bath.'

Johnny took a card out of his jacket pocket. 'That's my mobile. If he turns up and you need a hand, give me a call.'

That was *so* not going to happen.

'Bye.' Briskly she ushered him to the door.

Pausing in the doorway, Johnny said, 'I'm flying back to New York tomorrow. So have a good Christmas.'

'You too.' Cleo wondered if she would.

He raised an eyebrow. 'And we'll see if you're still single next summer.'

'I will be.' Did he think he was setting her an impossible task? It was the easiest challenge she'd ever been set.

Chapter 4

HOW HAD SHE MANAGED to get herself into such a mess? Abbie could barely breathe as she arrived at Kilgour's to start her shift on Monday morning. Oh God, and there was Des now, carrying Christmas trees from the shed and stacking them outside.

Des was wearing an unfamiliar red sweater and cleaner jeans than usual. When he saw her and whipped off his knitted grey beanie hat she saw that he'd had a haircut. His just-washed, reddish fair hair stood up in a whoosh of static.

Oh God, he'd only gone and given himself a makeover.

'All right, Abbie?'

'Not really, no.' Now that she was within six feet of him, she could smell the lavishly applied aftershave. Double-checking that there was no one else within earshot, she took a deep breath and said, 'Look, I need to talk to you, it's really important—'

'Des, are we bringing out the rest of the ten-footers?' Huw poked his head out of the shed and Abbie came out in an icy sweat. OK, *this* was why she would be such a useless adulterer, should she ever seriously contemplate it. Huw was married to Glynis, who worked in the shop and *lived* for gossip. It didn't bear thinking about . . .

'No, that's enough for now.' Addressing Huw, Des said, 'Half a dozen of each size is plenty. Give the customers too much choice and they can't make up their minds.' He turned to Abbie and added calmly, 'Is this about your shifts? Better come up to the office.'

Abbie couldn't believe it; there was no trace of a quaver in his voice, not a nanosecond of hesitation. He'd said it like an absolute pro.

Des said to Huw, 'When you've finished here, can you unload the poinsettias? I'll be back in five minutes.'

Upstairs, he firmly closed the door of the office behind him.

'OK, tell me what happened. Did you confront him?'

Dry-mouthed, Abbie said, 'I did. And it wasn't what I thought. Oh God, this is so complicated . . .'

'Worse than you thought? Or better?' Des searched her face for clues.

Faltering at first, then speeding up as the words spilled out, Abbie explained everything. Finally, her eyes filling with tears, she said, 'Georgia's coming to stay next weekend.'

'So . . . you're not going to leave Tom?'

'Of course I'm not going to leave him! He's my husband and I love him. But now it's more important than ever that he mustn't find out about, you know . . . what nearly happened the, um, other evening.'

'You mean on Saturday?' Des looked taken aback. 'When we spent the night together?'

'Oh, don't say it like that!' It came out as a panicky squawk. 'We just have to forget about it. *Completely.*'

Des's shoulders slumped. 'OK, don't panic. If that's what you want, it's what we'll do.' She saw it sinking in that the raised hopes and self-administered makeover had been for nothing. Summoning up a regretful smile, he made a clearing gesture with his outstretched hand and said, 'There, forgotten. Gone.'

Pink coat—turquoise scarf, pink coat—turquoise scarf, pink coat—turquoise scarf. The words were drumming through Abbie's head in time with her racing heart as the train drew into Temple Meads station and slowed to a halt. The doors opened and passengers spilled out onto the platform, streaming towards the exit.

This was it, this was the one with Georgia on it. Any moment now, a teenager in a pink coat and a turquoise scarf would step down from the train and she would see the girl who should have been her daughter.

And then it happened. Next to her, Tom took an audible breath before saying in a carefully controlled voice, 'There she is.'

Abbie squeezed his hand before releasing it. As the girl scanned the area beyond the gates, Abbie moved away from Tom. He had insisted she came along this evening but the first meeting had to be between father and daughter. Melting into the background, bracing herself, she watched as Tom raised his hand and stepped up to the barrier.

Georgia was gazing at Tom now, a huge smile spreading across her face. The next moment she let out a squeal of excitement, shoving her ticket at the startled ticket collector and barrelling through the gate, before abruptly screeching to a halt six feet away from him and pulling out her phone. She pressed a couple of buttons, held the phone up to record Tom's face, and yelled joyfully, 'Hi, Dad!' Then she threw down her rucksack and launched herself like an Exocet missile into Tom's arms.

It was hard to watch but impossible to look away.

Then father and daughter pulled apart and gazed wordlessly into each other's eyes. Abbie's stomach twisted with envy and emptiness. With her heart-shaped face, slender figure and long, rippling, silvery-blonde hair, Georgia resembled her mother but she was also, without question, a part of Tom. As in the photograph, there were those shared cheekbones, that exact same mouth shape. Even from this distance you could see that their eyes were an identical shade of sky-blue.

Abbie watched as Tom said something to the girl then led her over to where she was standing. He was trying so hard not to show it, but the pride he was feeling was inescapable.

'Abbie, this is Georgia.'

'Hiya, nice to meet you.' Politely Georgia held out a hand for her to shake. 'Isn't this amazing? Look, I recorded it all on my mobile! Hang on, let me play it again . . .'

Her throat so tight she could barely swallow, Abbie was forced to watch as the video clip was replayed on the mobile's tiny screen.

Twice.

'I'm going to keep that *for ever*.' Georgia clutched the phone to her chest. Then, putting her face next to Tom's, she said, 'Can you take another one of us? Do we look alike? We do, don't we!'

Eventually they made their way out of the station to the car park. Having chucked her rucksack in the boot of the car, Georgia automatically jumped into the passenger seat, so she could sit next to Tom. Abbie, relegated to the back seat, listened to her chattering excitedly in the front and felt more left out than ever.

Back at Channings Hill, Georgia climbed out of the car and surveyed the house, currently in darkness but with the trees in the front garden decorated with twinkling white Christmas lights.

'And this is where you've been living since before I was born.'

'It is.' Tom nodded in agreement. 'We like it here.'

'Pretty.' She followed him up the front path. 'So if Mum had given me to you like she was supposed to, this is where I'd have grown up.'

'You would.' He unlocked the front door, then showed her into the living room and began switching on the lights.

Georgia clapped her hands at the sight of the tree. 'You've got a real Christmas tree! All my life I've wanted a real one. Mum always said they were too messy.'

Eighteen Christmases they'd missed out on. Abbie said, 'I'll put the kettle on, shall I? Make us all a nice cup of tea?'

'No thanks, I don't drink tea. I'll have a coffee.' Grabbing Tom's left hand, Georgia held out her own and exclaimed, 'Hey, our fingers are the same shape! Spooky!'

In the kitchen, Abbie fumbled to undo the packets of biscuits she'd bought specially. As she waited for the kettle to boil, the lump in her throat grew and grew, and the girl who should have been her daughter carried on laughing and exclaiming and comparing various body parts in the living room with the man who actually was her dad.

Abbie opened the back door and slipped out into the garden. It was a relief to be able to let the tears out. She must be a truly horrible person to resent all this so much, but she just couldn't help herself. It was only now that she truly appreciated how happy and uncomplicated and easy her marriage *had* been.

Georgia's arrival had ruined everything. Hopefully, once this weekend visit was over and her curiosity had been satisfied, she would disappear again and leave them to carry on with their lives.

Well, you could always dream.

The kitchen door creaked open and Abbie hurriedly wiped her face before Tom could see that she was upset. But when she turned, she saw that the figure silhouetted in the doorway wasn't Tom's.

'Hello?' Gazing through the darkness, Georgia said, 'Are you OK?'

'Fine, fine! Just . . . fancied some fresh air. Where's Tom?'

'He went up to the bathroom.' There was a pause. 'Are you crying?'

'Of course I'm not crying!' This was now technically true; the embarrassment of being caught had stopped the tears dead in their tracks.

But Georgia was coming across the garden towards her. When she reached Abbie, she peered closely at her face and said, 'Liar.'

'Really, I'm OK. You go back inside. I'll be in in a minute.'

Georgia didn't move. 'Do you hate me?'

'No. No.' Shaking her head, Abbie said, 'I definitely don't hate you.'

'Mum, then. I bet you hate my mum.'

Oh God, this was difficult. 'I don't think *hate* is the right word. But yes, she made me . . . very unhappy.' Which was about as inadequate an explanation as you could get, but how else could she put it?

'She didn't mean to,' said Georgia. 'She told me all about it. The reason she did it in the first place was because she really wanted to help you. But when she knew she was pregnant, it all kind of began to sink in that she was having an actual baby. And her feelings began to change and she started to panic . . . basically, she was falling in love with me, and she realised she couldn't bear to give me away after all.'

Abbie nodded; how could she dispute that?

'So she told her mother, my grandmother, and they decided they'd raise me between them,' Georgia continued. 'But if they'd told you and Tom, you'd have gone mental and nagged her to change her mind, and you might have got the police involved, and it would have been upsetting for everyone. So it was easier just to lie and say she wasn't pregnant.' She shrugged. 'Under the circumstances, it was the best thing to do.'

'Did you miss having a father when you were growing up?' Abbie had to ask.

'I don't really know. A bit, maybe, sometimes. It's hard to know if you really miss something you've never had.' Georgia's teeth gleamed in the darkness. 'Then again, it's pretty cool meeting him now.'

That was the point of all this, Abbie reminded herself. It was happening for Georgia's benefit, not theirs.

'And I'm sorry if I made you cry,' Georgia went on.

'That's OK. It wasn't your fault.'

'If my mum hadn't decided to keep me, you'd have been my mother.' Her blonde hair swung as she shook her head. 'That's definitely weird.'

'I know.'

'The thing is, all my life I've been wondering who my dad is and wishing I could meet him.'

Abbie nodded. 'I know.' God, she sounded like a stuck record.

'So, no offence, but I haven't spent years and years wondering who my mum is,' said Georgia, 'because she's always been there.'

This was stupid; she couldn't say 'I know' again. Searching for an alternative, Abbie said, 'Of course she has.'

'What's going on?' From the kitchen doorway, Tom called across, 'Are you two planning on staying out there all night?'

Georgia was shivering, her arms wrapped tightly around her midriff.

'I could light a bonfire,' said Tom.

Georgia looked uncertainly at Abbie. 'Is he joking?'

'That's something you'll just have to get used to, your dad's sense of humour.' Smiling, Abbie said, 'Let's go inside, before we get frostbite.'

'I just saw them leaving.' Cleo gave her sister a hug. 'How did it go?'

Abbie heaved a sigh. It was late on Sunday afternoon and Tom was driving Georgia to the coach station; she was heading back to London, to the Paddington flat she shared with her mother.

'Well, I suppose it could have been worse.' At least she could be honest with Cleo. 'She's a sweet girl. But I'm glad it's over.'

'Over?' Cleo looked doubtful. 'You think she'll leave you alone now?'

'Fingers crossed.' Pushing up her sleeves, Abbie began running hot water and Fairy Liquid into the sink; having spent hours cooking an elaborate roast dinner, it would have been nice if Tom and Georgia could have told her to put her feet up and let *them* do the washing-up, but of course it hadn't occurred to them to offer.

'I wondered if she'd want to stay for Christmas.'

'Me too, but it's OK. She's off to Portugal with her mother. Patty's got this semi-boyfriend who lives out there. He's invited them to stay for a few weeks.' Drily Abbie said, 'He has a massive pool.'

'Well, good. Maybe now she's met Tom, the novelty'll wear off.'

This was what she was hoping too. Something told Abbie, though, that it wasn't likely to happen. Scrubbing hard at a plate, she said, 'How about you?' Even in the midst of her own misery, Abbie could still feel sorry for her sister, who had never had much luck with men. 'Tell you what, how about if we get you a lie detector for Christmas? Then the next time you meet someone, you can give them a good old interrogation first.'

'Oh wow, wouldn't that be brilliant? I'd love one of those! Think of the stuff you could find out, the havoc you could cause! Speaking of lies, you know what this place is like.' She pulled a face. 'They were gossiping about Georgia in the pub last night. The O'Brien brothers were joking about Tom playing away. I think some people just don't want to believe the whole surrogate story.'

'Great.' Abbie had expected as much, but it still hurt; the downside of living in a village was the gossip. As soon as Georgia's startling resemblance to Tom had been spotted, they'd been forced to explain her existence and knowing nods had ensued.

'Don't worry, I had a real go at them in front of everyone. I said it was sick of them even to think that, because Tom had never done anything behind your back and he never would. I said the two of you had the perfect marriage.'

Oh God. 'Well, thanks anyway.' Here came the guilt again; she concentrated all her attention on vigorously scrubbing an already-clean gravy jug. She could be honest with Cleo about a lot of things but there was no way she could tell her about Des Kilgour. Cleo would be shocked. Some secrets you just had to keep to yourself.

Bristol Airport was busy, packed with people arriving, leaving and waiting. Cleo, her greetings board tucked under her arm, watched as the doors slid open to disgorge the latest stream of arrivals.

She was here to pick up a client flying in from Amsterdam, a Mrs Cornelia Van Dijk, and take her to the Hotel du Vin, where she would be having lunch, then chauffeuring her wherever she wanted to go after that, until six o'clock. And, as always when all she had was a name to go on, she had formed a picture in her mind of Mrs Van Dijk: she would be tall and grey-haired, in her sixties and thin. Her nose would be long and she might even have a pointy beard and moustache . . .

OK, probably not. But her art teacher had been a fan of Van Dyck the painter, and once you had an idea lodged in your head it was hard to—

Oh my God, look who was coming through the glass doors!

Cleo experienced that jolt of shock you always got when you saw someone out of context. Johnny LaVenture was wearing a sand-coloured suede jacket, white shirt and black jeans. He was also pushing a trolley piled high with dark-blue cases. Glancing up at the arrivals board, she saw that he'd just flown in from New York.

Breaking into a smile, Johnny came towards her. 'Misa! Sorry . . . Cleo.' He shook his head, correcting himself. 'Look at you in your uniform. Have you come to pick me up and take me home?'

He was wearing a new aftershave, lemony and intriguing. Different smell, same old deliberately provocative manner.

'Not unless you're in the middle of having a sex change.' She showed him the name on her greetings board.

'No, that's not me. Shame. How do you pronounce it?'

'Van Dyke,' said Cleo breezily.

He frowned slightly. 'Really? Sure it's not Van Deek?'

Damn, he'd been testing her. Trust him to know. Changing the subject, Cleo nodded at his mountain of cases and said, 'That lot must have cost a fortune in excess baggage.'

'All my worldly goods.' He gave the uppermost case a pat.

'Why?'

'Why d'you think?' Johnny raised an eyebrow. 'Ravenswood still hasn't sold. *Somebody* managed to scare off the only serious buyers. So I'm getting out of New York and moving back to Channings Hill.' He paused, noting with amusement the dismay on her face. 'I know, and it's all your fault. So you don't have anyone to blame but yourself.'

Ouch. Well, that served her right. She'd done a bad thing and now she was being punished for it.

'What's happened with your married guy?'

Because that was the thing about Johnny, he never had been able to resist taking the mickey out of other people, reminding them of their own imperfections and failures.

'I haven't seen him since that night.' Glancing up at the arrivals board, Cleo saw that the Amsterdam flight had landed.

'Found yourself another chap yet?'

'No. I don't need another man.'

'That's the spirit.' He half smiled.

As patronising as ever. But . . . what *was* that aftershave he was wearing? Breathing in surreptitiously, Cleo inhaled the herby lemoniness and attempted to commit it to memory. Mrs Van Dijk would be emerging soon. She looked at Johnny and said, 'Are you waiting to be picked up?'

'Always.' His dark eyes glittered. 'Sorry. Yes, I am. So, do you like it?'

Deliberately cryptic. It was slightly puzzling, though, that he should seem so cheerful about coming back to live in Channings Hill when he'd been so keen to sell the house. Patiently she said, 'Do I like what? Being single? Waiting to be picked up? Snails in garlic?'

'My aftershave. Actually,' Johnny amended, 'it's not mine. I tried it in Duty Free and I think it might be OK.' He leaned towards her, inviting her to smell his neck. 'Here, what do you reckon?'

Had she been snuffling the air like a truffle-hunting pig? No, she definitely hadn't been doing that. Cautiously Cleo moved forward an inch and breathed in again. 'It's . . . fine.'

'Fine?' He looked disappointed.

Oh, this was ridiculous. 'Actually, it's really nice,' said Cleo. 'What is it?' At least now she could find out.

Johnny frowned. 'Damn. I can't remember. I picked up loads of different ones and smelled them . . . then this one seemed good so I gave it a go . . and now I have *no* idea which one it was.'

'That's just stupid, then, isn't it?' More people were beginning to emerge through arrivals; Cleo kept an eye out for Mrs Van Dijk. There was a tall, beaky-looking woman in her sixties coming through now;

stepping away from Johnny, she held up her greetings board and assumed a smiley, welcoming expression.

'Ah good, you are hjere!' The client approached her and, not for the first time, Cleo's preconceptions flew out of the window. As the beaky woman strode towards the exit, a curvaceous, sultry brunette in her late thirties, with cushiony crimson lips and smoky eyes, offered her the handle of her expensive-looking case-on wheels. 'I am hjere too!'

Which just went to show, you never could tell. Cleo said cheerfully, 'Welcome to Bristol, Mrs Van . . ?' This was how she handled tricky names; if in doubt, let the client tell you themselves.

'Van Dijk.' It was Johnny's voice, pronouncing it Van Dyke. He broke into a broad smile. 'Or as I call her, the wonderful Cornelia.'

'Johnny! You beautiful man, Ij didn't know you were there behijnd the sign!' Exclaiming with delight, Cornelia threw her arms around him and kissed him extravagantly on both cheeks.

'Looking rather spectacular yourself. And is this a new bracelet?' Diamonds glittered as he held up her arm.

'Just a little Christmas gift,' Cornelia confided. 'From me to myself.'

'When you live in Amsterdam, it'd be a crime not to.' Johnny regarded her with affection. 'It's so good to see you again.'

'Oh, dear Johnny, it ijs wonderful to see you too! Well, Ij am hungry! Shall we go?'

Cleo nodded. 'Absolutely. I'm taking both of you, then? Hotel du Vin?'

'That'd be great.' Steering his trolley towards the exit, Johnny said, 'I booked the car just for Cornelia, originally. I was planning to fly in yesterday. Then I had a last-minute meeting, switched my flight to today . . . and we've managed to arrive at the same time, which is a miracle.' He beamed at Cleo. 'Good of me to use your limo company, wasn't it?'

Hmm. As far as she was concerned, it had less to do with generosity and more to do with his eternal bid for one-upmanship. But Cleo smiled and nodded and said obediently, 'Very good. Thank you.'

With the luggage stowed in the boot of the car—today she was driving the midnight-blue S-class Mercedes—Cleo pulled out of the short-stay car park and headed towards Bristol, still with no clue as to who Cornelia Van Dijk actually was.

Apart from absolutely loaded, if the diamonds were anything to go by, and in possession of a stupendous pair of gravity-defying breasts.

'We'll be a couple of hours. Will you be OK out here?' asked Johnny. They were parked outside the Hotel du Vin.

Cleo nodded. 'No problem. It's my job to be OK out here.'

He hesitated. 'You will wait here, won't you?'

The cheek of it! 'Don't worry,' said Cleo, 'I'm not planning to dump the car in some NCP with all your worldly goods in the boot.'

'Darling, Ij am sure she'll keep everything safe.' Shaking back her glossy hair, Cornelia said, 'Shall we go inside? Ij am gasping for a drink!'

Johnny reappeared shortly after three.

'See?' Cleo climbed out of the driver's seat, indicated the car. 'Still here. I didn't even sell your stuff on eBay.'

He inclined his head. 'Excellent. Cornelia's just freshening up. She'll be out in a moment.'

'Good lunch?'

'Great, thanks. So, are you curious about Cornelia?'

What a question—of course she was curious.

Aloud, Cleo said, 'No, why would I be?'

'Oh, OK.' He shrugged, shoved his hands in his pockets.

Pause.

Longer pause.

Oh, for heaven's sake. 'Go on then,' said Cleo. 'Who is she?'

'A client.' Johnny smiled briefly at her capitulation. 'A very wealthy one. Her husband died last year.'

'Really?' She was shocked. 'How awful.'

'Not really. He was eighty-six.'

Euw. Careful not to pull a face, Cleo gulped and said, 'And she's . . ?'

'Think of a number, then double it.' Amused, he explained, 'She has a great plastic surgeon. But that's beside the point. She isn't my girlfriend, if that's what you were thinking. Cornelia bought two of my pieces last year and now she's interested in commissioning a third.'

Cleo nodded, because this was how the other half lived. If normal people wanted to treat themselves, they ordered something off the Internet or popped down to the local shop to see what caught their eye. Whereas when Mrs Van Dijk fancied a new sculpture for her drawing room, she hopped onto a plane to meet up with the artist.

And here she came now. Crikey, was she really in her sixties? Smiling fondly at Johnny as Cleo held the car door open, she trailed the back of her hand along his cheek and said, 'Darling, you do smell delicious. Acqua di Parma, am Ij right?'

A flicker of recognition crossed Johnny's face as the name rang a bell. 'In a bright-yellow box? I think that's the one. Clever you.'

'Colonia Intensa.' Inhaling appreciatively, Cornelia purred, 'I'm always right. Cary Grant used to wear it, you know. And David Niven.'

Crikey, Cornelia was older than they thought.

It was five o'clock. Having dropped Johnny and Cornelia at Ravenswood an hour ago, Cleo was now back to take Cornelia on to Cheltenham, where she was due to spend a couple of days with an old friend before flying back to Amsterdam.

Johnny answered the door and said, 'We'll be a few more minutes, is that OK?'

'Absolutely.'

She took a couple of steps back but he opened the door wider. 'No need to wait in the car. Come in and see my studio.'

Curiosity got the better of Cleo. Having never seen inside a proper artist's studio before, she followed Johnny across the oak-panelled hall.

'Well,' he amended, 'it'll be my studio when I've finished with it.'

They were in the drawing room, a vast, high-ceilinged space with tall sash windows and French doors that opened on to the garden at the back of the house. Given that Lawrence LaVenture's priority in life had been socialising in the pub and not interior design, the decor was on the tired side. The wallpaper was peeling at the edges, the carpet was a riot of swirls and none of the sofas matched. There were book-cases crammed with books, and the TV, Cleo saw with a start, was balanced on the back of a three-foot-tall, bright-red clay statue of an elephant.

'I know.' Watching her reaction, Johnny said drily, 'but this was how Dad liked it. The estate agents were marketing the house as an excellent opportunity for the buyers to stamp their own personality on the place. Meaning basically that it needed a total refurb.'

'I love the elephant!' Cleo moved towards it, unexpectedly entranced. There was a quirky, cheeky glint in the creature's eye.

'So did Dad. It's the first piece I did that he ever really liked.'

She looked at the elephant again. 'You made this?'

He nodded. 'When I was sixteen.'

Back when they'd been enemies. But he'd had real talent, even then.

'Anyway,' said Johnny, 'now that I'm going to be living here, there are going to be some changes. And this room will be perfect to work in.'

Cleo could see that it would be. She headed over to an octagonal dining table, across which were strewn oversized sheets of paper covered in sketches. As she studied the charcoal drawings of horses grazing in a field, Cornelia burst into the room and said, 'Hjere Ij am, all ready to leave now! Ah, you are admiring my beautiful horses? Johnny is going to make them for me. He's brilliant, isn't he? I'm such a lucky girl! Thank you,' she exclaimed as Johnny helped her into her coat. 'Shall we go?'

Chapter 5

A week after Christmas, Cleo was on her way home from a job when the first snow of the year began to fall. Tiny dissolving snowflakes at first, followed by faster, fatter ones that stuck to the windscreen and whitened the fields on either side of the motorway. Just enough snow to settle and look picturesque would be nice. But not enough to bring Gloucestershire to a grinding halt, especially when she had another pick-up this afternoon.

Her stomach rumbled loudly as she neared the village. A mug of tea and a plate of hot buttered currant buns, that was what she wanted right now. Which was frustrating, seeing as she didn't have any at home, but unless there'd been a mad rush on buns this morning, she'd be able to grab some from the village shop.

Oh yes, toasted currant buns dripping with butter. The more Cleo thought of them, the more badly she needed to have them. Finally reaching Channings Hill, she pulled up on the forecourt outside the shop and jumped out of the car.

Waving at Glynis behind the counter, Cleo hurried towards the bread section and screeched to a halt when she saw Johnny ahead of her. With his dark hair tousled and sweatshirt spattered with paint. And two cellophane packets of currant buns in the crook of his left arm.

Stiffening in disbelief, she stared at them, then at the empty shelf where *no more packets of buns sat.*

Was he doing this on purpose? Had he been reading her mind?

'Morning! Sorry,' Johnny checked his watch and corrected himself. 'Afternoon!'

Never mind about that. Cleo pointed to the buns. 'Are you having both packets?'

He looked surprised. 'Well, yes. That's why I'm holding them.'

'So you're buying . . . *all* the buns?'

'Not for my own personal use,' said Johnny. 'I've got a crew of painters and decorators waiting back at the house. If you're working undercover for WeightWatchers,' he added, 'and worried I might be guzzling the lot myself, I can promise you I'm not.'

It was no joking matter. The thought of not being able to have currant buns was sending Cleo's blood pressure sky-high. She blurted out,
'How many in the crew?'

'Five. Plus me. That's two each.' Johnny frowned. 'Is that a problem?'

Could she say it? Yes, she could. 'OK, here's the thing. I came into the
shop because I really, really want toasted currant buns with butter.'

'Oh.' He nodded in amused recognition. 'I've just realised why.'

'Why?'

'Mrs Clifford.'

Heavens, he was right. Mrs Clifford, the lovely cuddly cook at
Channings Hill village school all those years ago. Whenever the snow
had fallen, she had made currant buns and brought them into the class-
room, halved and toasted and laden with butter. It had been a tradition
that everyone would eat two halves before piling outside to pelt each
other with snowballs. How funny that she'd forgotten that.

So, the fact that Johnny was here buying them too wasn't such a
coincidence after all. More of a Pavlovian reaction to snow. 'We could
have one packet each,' Cleo offered reasonably.

He raised an eyebrow. 'Have you *seen* my team of decorators?'

'Look, there's Scotch pancakes! I bet they'd prefer those.'

Johnny gave her a look. 'Nobody in their right mind would rather
have a boring Scotch pancake than a toasted currant bun.'

'There are crumpets.' She picked a packet off the shelf and waggled it
persuasively. 'Crumpets are the *best*.'

'Are they?' said Johnny. 'Why don't you have them, then?'

Ooh. 'Because I want a bun!'

'You could buy plain bread rolls and poke currants into them.'

'Or,' said Cleo, 'I could poke currants into you.'

Johnny laughed, thinking she was joking. He didn't know her at all.
'OK,' he said finally. 'I'll give you two.'

If he'd been Ash, she'd have made some bawdy quip about it being
better than him giving her one. But he wasn't Ash. Instead, Cleo went
along with Johnny to the counter and watched him pay for both packets of buns. Then he tore open the cellophane on one of them, asked
Glynis for a paper bag and handed it over with two of the buns inside.

'Here.' In return, she tried to give him a fifty-pence piece.

'Have them on me,' said Johnny.

'Thanks.' Much as she'd have preferred not to be beholden to him,
Cleo wasn't going to get into an undignified grapple over fifty pence.

As they left the shop, Johnny paused next to the ancient Land Rover
he'd driven down in. 'You could come up to the house if you want. See

what's being done to it. We can have a communal tea break, all toast our buns together.'

A flurry of snowflakes swirled around them. Cleo shivered in her thin uniform. 'No thanks. I've only got an hour before my next job.' And *nothing* was going to spoil her enjoyment of the hard-won buns.

Johnny reversed the Land Rover across the shop forecourt and roared off up the hill. Hungrier than ever and practically salivating by now at the prospect of toasting the buns, spreading them with Lurpak and biting into their curranty, butter-soaked heaviness, Cleo followed suit.

At the top of the hill, Johnny gave her a wave and turned right at the village green. She took the left-hand fork and made her way between the avenue of chestnut trees, passing a metallic-blue Fiesta parked up by the play area before pulling up outside the cottage.

There was someone sitting at the wheel of the Fiesta. Just sitting there, not speaking on a phone or anything. Which was slightly unusual, given the weather. Mildly curious, Cleo glanced over as she climbed out of her own car. Was it a man or a woman? She couldn't even tell. And what were they *doing*, sitting there? Reaching the front gate, she stopped and turned again. Were they lost, or ill, or—

Rurr-rurr-rurr-rurr went the engine of the Fiesta as the driver turned the key in the ignition. Rurr-rurr-rurr.

The engine wasn't firing. So that was why the car was there. It had broken down. What a rotten time for it to happen, in weather like this.

Rurr-rurr-rurr-rurr-*rurr*. As the driver banged the steering wheel in frustration, Cleo saw that it was a woman.

Oh God. Her stomach was rumbling like a cement mixer, her feet were cold and in less than an hour she had to be out again. The last thing she wanted to do now was see if she could help a stranger in trouble.

Oh *God*. With a sinking heart, Cleo took her hand off the wooden gatepost. As she approached the car, the woman behind the wheel stopped turning the key in the ignition. She was looking at Cleo.

Cleo's heart lurched up into her throat as her eyes met those of the woman and recognition hit her. This was Will's wife—*his wife!*—and she was here in Channings Hill, parked fifty yards from her house.

OK, had Will told his wife about her? Was she here for a confrontation? Or was this . . . please God . . . simply a coincidence? And did she know who she was about to speak to? Cleo had recognised her because she'd spent forty minutes queuing behind her to see Santa, but Will's wife wouldn't remember her from then. That was impossible.

Which meant there was still the faintest of possibilities that she didn't know who was standing in the snow beside her car.

The woman opened the driver's window. She had a clear complexion, huge amber eyes and glossy gold-brown hair pulled back from an oval face to reveal exceptionally pretty ears. *The stupid things you notice when you're in shock.*

'Hi. Um, problem with the car?' Cleo had never felt more ridiculously British. Plus, it was a completely idiotic question.

'Er, yes. I don't know what's wrong. It just . . . died on me.'

Dry-mouthed, Cleo said, 'I could give you a push, if you like. See if we can bump-start it on the slope.'

Will's wife was still gazing at her intently, as if she wasn't sure whether Cleo was the one or not. She was also shivering.

'OK, we'll give it a go. Thanks.'

'No problem.' Slinging her bag satchel-style over one shoulder, Cleo braced herself against the back of the Fiesta and gave it an almighty shove. She was strong, she could do this . . . *heeeavvve* . . .

Nothing. The car didn't move an inch. Stopping and making her way round, she said to Will's wife, 'You have to take off the handbrake.'

'*Oh.* Sorry!'

They tried again. This time the car began to roll slowly forward. Pushing hard, then harder still, Cleo yelled, 'Try now!' but the engine didn't catch and they ran out of downward momentum. Brilliant; now the car was stuck right outside her cottage, which was *worse*.

'Hang on, I've got some WD-40.' Fetching the can from the Mercedes, she flipped up the Fiesta's bonnet and sprayed every available lead.

Still no joy. Her hands were numb by now, her nose pink and stinging with the cold.

'Oh well. Thanks for trying, anyway.' The woman's teeth were chattering. 'I'd better call the RAC.'

She took out her mobile. Cleo stood next to the car like a lemon and listened to the brief exchange on the phone. Finally Will's wife hung up. 'It's going to be at least an hour before they can come out.' She shivered. 'Typical.'

If anyone else were to have been stranded in a freezing cold, broken-down car, Cleo wouldn't think twice about inviting them into her house. Which meant she was going to have to invite Will's wife or it would look suspicious and it would become blazingly obvious to Will's wife that she *was* the one who'd been having an affair with her husband . . .

OK, this was too confusing. Blowing on her icy hands, Cleo said, 'Well, you can't wait out here. You'd better come in.'

'Are you sure?' Will's wife looked startled, then relieved. Recovering herself, she reached for her bag and jumped out of the car. 'Thanks.'

If the situation had been surreal before, it became even more so once they were inside the cottage. Cleo put the kettle on, sliced the currant buns and popped them into the toaster.

While she buttered the buns, Will's wife was making the tea, spooning sugar into mugs.

'It's kind of you to invite me in. What's your name?'

Did Will's wife know her name? Had Will told her? 'Uh, Cleo.'

'Hi. And I'm Fia. Short for Sofia.'

'Right. Um . . . bun?'

'Thanks.' Fia paused, taking the plate and gazing at her. Then she looked directly at Cleo and said, 'You're having an affair with my husband, aren't you?'

Shit. Cleo's hand flew to her mouth. Collapsing onto a stool, she said, '*Did* have. Past tense. I didn't know he was married, I swear.'

'How did you find out?'

'I saw him with you and the children. Queuing at the arboretum to see Father Christmas.' Feeling awful, Cleo said, 'As soon as I found out, that was it. I finished with him that same night.'

Fia thought back for a moment, then nodded and shrugged. 'Will's a good liar. It's always been one of his special talents.'

Cleo was still finding it hard to believe they were having this conversation. 'I felt terrible. You all looked so happy together.'

'We probably thought we were.'

Of the two of them, Cleo realised she was the one finding this more of an ordeal. Her buttered toasted bun was growing cold in front of her and she could no longer even face eating it, which was something that had *never* happened before.

'Oh, I wouldn't call it the surprise of the century.' Making short work of her own bun, Fia shook her head and said, 'He did it last year too.'

'He *did*?'

'With a girl from his office. When I got to hear about it, he begged me to forgive him. On his knees.' Her lip curled at the memory. 'And he swore he'd never do it again. Silly me, I believed him. Decided to give him one more chance.'

She didn't want to ask, but she had to. 'And now?'

'Well, he's blown it, hasn't he? I'm not a complete doormat,' said Fia. 'And he's never going to change. So it's all over.'

'Oh God. I'm sorry.'

'I'm sure I'll get over it.' She eyed the untouched bun on Cleo's plate. 'Are you going to eat that, or can I have it?'

Cleo pushed the plate across the table. Those poor kids, how would they cope with their parents' divorce? 'Why did you come here today?'

'I just wanted to see what you looked like. I wasn't going to speak to you.' Wryly Fia said, 'The car breaking down wasn't part of the plan.'

'And how did you know where I lived?'

'Ah well, that was a teeny bit illegal.' Fia pulled a face. 'I happen to have a friend whose brother works for the phone company. He got me a copy of Will's mobile bill. Your number cropped up all the time so I persuaded my friend's brother to look up your address. But it's OK, he made me promise not to set fire to your house.'

Cleo looked out of the living room window and saw that the snow was still falling in flurries. 'Look, I can't be late for my next job. I'm going to have to leave early.'

Fia flipped open her phone and rang the RAC again. She frowned, listening to them. 'Another two hours.' Hanging up, Fia said with heavy irony, 'Apparently they're snowed under.'

'Um . . .'

'It's OK, I know. I'll wait in the car.'

Damn. Cleo was torn; turfing her out was going to be even more embarrassing now. But how *could* she go off, leaving a complete stranger in her house? Except Fia was *worse* than a complete stranger; she was Will's emotionally tortured, cheated-on wife. Who was to say she wouldn't go completely ballistic, cut up all her clothes and smash everything she could get her hands on?

On the other hand, I did have an affair with her husband.

'Hang on.' Picking up her own phone, she speed-dialled Ash. 'Hi, it's me, what are you doing?'

'Nothing much. Googling myself, seeing how popular I am. You know, I can't believe how much everyone loves me, they—'

'Come round,' Cleo interrupted. 'I need a favour.'

She opened the door to him twenty seconds later. Ash, wearing a torn checked shirt over a faded Superman T-shirt, struck a pose and said, 'Damsel in distress? I'm here to help. What is it, something electri-cal? Or another jam-jar lid you can't get undone?'

'I have to get back to work. Can you look after someone for me? Her car broke down.' Cleo pointed to the Fiesta, wonkily parked by the gate. 'Just keep her company until the RAC turns up.'

'OK, no problem. Do I smell toasted buns?' Breezing past her, Ash headed into the living room and stopped dead in his tracks. 'Oh. Hi.' He stared at Fia and promptly flushed an unbecoming shade of red.

She gave him a curious look in return, taking in the uncombed hair, blotchy complexion and scruffy outfit. 'Hello.'

'Fia, this is my friend Ash.' Cleo didn't have time to play nursemaid; if he was going to be shy, that was his problem. 'Ash, this is Fia.' Having rapidly introduced them, she grabbed her bag and keys. 'And I need to go.' She waved goodbye to Fia. 'Hope your car gets fixed soon. And good luck with, you know . . . the other stuff.'

'Thanks.' Fia nodded and smiled. 'Bye.'

The front door slammed behind Cleo and Ash felt his hands go clammy. This was it, the story of his life. On the outside everyone thought he was so confident and cheerful. And a lot of the time they'd have been right, he *was* confident and cheerful. Until the moment he found himself in the company of a girl he fancied, and his entire personality shrivelled and dried up like a grape.

He was used to it. It had been happening for years.

Fia was covertly watching him. She was wearing a plain black V-necked sweater and grey jeans tucked into boots. Her hair, a kind of shiny, golden brown, was pulled back in a ponytail and she had really nice ears. And he couldn't think of a single solitary thing to say to her. God, she was gorgeous.

Say something, you plank.

Ash cleared his throat. 'What other stuff?'

She looked taken aback. 'Sorry?'

This was what it was like, every time. He gazed out of the window, praying to see an RAC van pulling up outside. 'Cleo said good luck with the other stuff.'

'Oh, right.' Fia nodded. 'Well, she was seeing this guy, Will Newman? Did you ever meet him?'

Blinking fast, Ash said, 'No.' What was going on here?

She gave him a look. 'It's OK. You're allowed to say yes.'

See? He'd even lost the ability to lie. Usually he was world-class at it. He shrugged. 'Yes.'

'Well, I'm his wife,' said Fia.

'Shit.'

'Yes, he is.' Her half-smile only made her more irresistible.

An awkward silence fell. Ash checked again that there was no sign of the RAC van. 'Tea?' It came out like a frog's croak.

'No thanks, we just had one.'

'OK.' It was his biggest fear that one day this would happen while he was live on air; some girl with whom he was secretly besotted would walk into the studio and his listening audience would hear him grind to a halt and turn into a monosyllabic moron.

'Are you all right?' said Fia hesitantly.

Humiliation made him defensive. 'I'm fine. Just, uh . . . never mind.' The TV remote control was balanced on the arm of the sofa. Seizing it with relief, Ash said, 'Shall we watch TV?'

Cleo pulled up outside the cottage and stared in disbelief at the snow-covered blue Fiesta still parked in front of her gate. This was ridiculous; it was eight o'clock at night. How could Will's wife still be here? She should have been gone hours ago.

More to the point, where was she now? Because both Ash's cottage and her own were in darkness.

Oh well, ask a silly question.

'We're in the pub.' Ash had to raise his voice to be heard above the racket. 'Coming over?'

'Did the RAC not turn up?' Cleo was outraged.

'Oh yeah, they did. They fixed the car,' said Ash.

'Oh, for God's sake! So why's Fia still here?'

There was an edge to his voice that she couldn't identify. 'I don't think she wants to go home.'

Cleo changed out of her uniform into combats and a hoodie, then set off across the green. A rush of warmth and noise greeted her as she pushed open the door. Frank, the landlord of the Hollybush and a life-long Elvis fan, was clutching the microphone and swivelling his hips. His audience was applauding and yelling encouragement. There was Ash, observing the proceedings from the safety of the bar. A little way away, Fia was clapping wildly. And next to her, holding a pint of Guinness and grinning at Frank's more extravagant pelvic thrusts, was Johnny LaVenture.

'What's going on?' Joining Ash, Cleo gave him an accusing nudge.

'I didn't know what to do with her, did I?' Ash wasn't looking too thrilled either. 'We sat and watched TV for ages. Then it got to five o'clock and she saw the lights coming on outside here and there was still no sign of the RAC, so I thought why not, it'd be something to pass the time. Then just after we arrived, Johnny and his crew came piling in.' Drily he said, 'That's when she perked right up.'

'But eventually the RAC did turn up.'

Ash nodded. 'They did. And they got the car going in five minutes flat. But then Johnny persuaded her to stay for one more drink . . . then another . . . and she's been here ever since.'

'Oh God.' Cleo groaned and looked over at their unwanted guest. 'Is she completely wellied?'

'Not yet. But give her time.'

Frank's moment in the spotlight had come to an end and he was now shamelessly milking the applause. Leaning across to whisper something in Johnny's ear, Fia confidingly clutched his arm.

'So what did she tell you about Will?'

'Not a lot.' Ash shrugged. 'He's a dickhead, it's over, she's leaving him. That's pretty much it.'

Yet again, Cleo felt the weight of a responsibility she didn't deserve. 'Those poor kids.' Flinching, she said, 'Oh help, she's going to sing . . .'

A roar went up as Fia took Frank's place on the tiny raised stage. Seizing the microphone and blasting everyone's ears with high-pitched feedback, Fia announced, 'My husband cheated on me and as from today my marriage is *over*. But guess what? Life goes on and he's the one who's going to be missing out. Because I can promise you one thing. I-I-I . . . wiiiiillll . . . surviiiiiiiiive!'

More cheers as the opening bars of the great Gloria Gaynor classic filled the pub. Fia's singing voice was way worse than Frank's, but what she lacked in vocal skills she made up for with reckless alcohol-fuelled enthusiasm. Johnny's painters and decorators all joined in the chorus, everyone was clapping and Fia carried on singing her heart out.

At last the song was over. Having soaked up the applause, she jumped down and returned to Johnny who was looking after her drink. Cleo watched as he put a reassuring arm around Fia's shoulders and gave her a congratulatory you-did-it hug.

Finishing his own drink, Ash said, 'I'll leave you to it. Good luck.'

Moments later, spotting Cleo, Fia came over.

'Did you see me up there? I've never sung karaoke before in my life!'

And if she knew what she sounded like, she'd never do it again. But that was mean, and it was beside the point—it had been the very *act* of singing that had been cathartic—so Cleo said, 'You were . . . incredible.' Because she'd certainly been that.

Joining them, Johnny said easily, 'Didn't she do well?'

'Yes. Really brave. So!' Cleo turned brightly to Fia. 'Your car's fixed!'

'Yeah, the chap was really nice. He couldn't stop apologising because of the wait, but I told him it didn't matter. If he'd turned up two hours earlier, I'd have just driven straight home. We wouldn't have come over here to the pub.' Fia was still flushed from her exertions. 'And I'd never have met all these fantastic people!'

No prizes for guessing which fantastic person in particular she was so delighted to have met. Honestly, weren't people whose marriages had just broken down meant to be miserable for the first six months at least? Fia appeared to be having trouble stringing it out for six *hours*.

And as for those two innocent children . . . shouldn't she be at home comforting them, gently preparing them for the imminent upheaval in their young lives?

'Another drink?' said Johnny. He reached for Fia's empty glass. 'Cleo, what'll you have?'

'Actually, it's half past eight already.' Cleo looked at her watch; surely it was time for Will's wife to leave now. 'Shouldn't you be going home?'

Fia looked appalled. 'Home? You mean, where Will is? I don't think so.' Pulling out her phone, she glanced at the screen and said with satisfaction, 'Seven messages from him so far. Ha, good. Let him wonder where I am for a change.'

Was she for real? 'But what about the children?'

Puzzled, Fia said, 'What about them?'

OK, she was now officially heartless.

'Oh lovely, thanks so much!' Fia smiled up at Johnny and took the brimming glass from him before turning her attention back to Cleo.

'Who's looking after them?' Cleo couldn't help herself, she had to know.

Fia gave her an odd look. 'Well, their mother of course. Will sees them only every other weekend.'

Clannnggg, the penny finally dropped.

'You mean . . . they're not yours?'

'God, no! Did you seriously think they were?' Shaking her head vigorously, Fia burst out laughing. 'No, no, no, the kids are from his first marriage. I mean, they're really sweet and I've always got on well with them, but they're definitely not mine. They live with their mum and her second husband in Birmingham. I only met Will three years ago and he was already divorced by then.'

Good grief, this country was littered with Will's wives. Up on the stage, one of the painters was belting out 'Do Ya Think I'm Sexy?' Every time he sang the question, his work colleagues yelled back, 'Nooooo!'

'Sorry. I thought they were yours,' said Cleo.

'I wondered why I was getting interrogated. So anyway, that's that sorted out.' Waving her hand in a forgiving manner, Fia said, 'Look, seeing as it's kind of your fault I'm here, I couldn't crash at yours tonight, could I?'

Honestly, hadn't she already done enough? Cleo hesitated. While she was prevaricating, Johnny passed Cleo a glass of white wine.

'Please? I wouldn't be any trouble,' Fia wheedled. 'I promise.'

'Um, the thing is, the spare bed isn't made up . . . and I have to be at work *really* early tomorrow morning . . .'

'Tell you what,' said Johnny. 'You can stay at my place.'

Cleo saw the way Fia's eyes lit up and something in the pit of her stomach tightened. No, no, this wasn't the answer.

'Really? Gosh, *thanks!*'

Hastily backtracking, Cleo said, 'Look, it's fine, we can make up the bed. Of course you can stay with me.'

'But you have to be up *really early*.' Evidently overjoyed by Johnny's Far Better Offer, Fia did a poor job of pretending to be grateful to Cleo. 'And you've helped me so much already.'

'But you can't stay at Johnny's house . . .' It wasn't Fia's fault; she didn't know what he was like. Cleo did her best to signal discreetly with her eyes that she could well be risking life and limb.

'Hey, it's OK, I'm not a serial killer.' Intercepting the look, Johnny said with amusement, 'She'll be safe, I promise.'

'That's really kind. And you won't even know I'm there,' Fia promised him. 'Just leave me with a blanket and I'll sleep on the sofa.'

'No need for that. There are plenty of spare bedrooms.'

'Plenty?' Fia giggled. 'What do you live in, some kind of *mansion*?'

Frank the landlord, handing Johnny his change, said, 'Biggest house in the village, love. Gives Buckingham Palace a run for its money.'

Fia did an astonished double take. She turned to Johnny, still wearing his paint-splashed sweatshirt and torn jeans. 'Is he serious? But . . . you're a painter and decorator?'

Cleo raised her eyebrows and took a big glug of wine.

'It was my father's home. He died before Christmas and now I've moved back in. We did try to sell it,' Johnny said innocently. 'But no luck.' He indicated the team clustered around the stage, still heckling their unsexy coworker. 'So that's why we've been working on the house. But I'm not a decorator by profession.'

'But I asked Ash. He *said* you were a painter,' Fia said.

'I do paint.' Johnny nodded in agreement. 'But canvases, not walls.'

'You mean you're an artist? That's amazing!' She was now gazing at him as if he'd sprouted celestial wings. 'What kind of work do you do?'

'Well, all sorts.' Looking suitably modest, Johnny said, 'But my main thing these days is wire sculpture.'

'Oh my God,' breathed Fia, recognition dawning. 'Don't tell me you're the one who does those huge great ones . . . Johnny LaVenture . . . ?'

Cleo couldn't believe Fia even knew his work, let alone his name. It wasn't as if he was as famous as Damien Hirst or Banksy.

'I'm impressed.' Johnny smiled slightly. 'And flattered.'

'Are you kidding? I love your sculptures!' exclaimed Fia.

Cleo's jaw ached from smiling. This was Will's *wife*. She didn't want her staying here in Channings Hill any longer than necessary.

'Well, this is a treat. Compliments are usually pretty thin on the ground around here.' Evidently enjoying himself, Johnny said, 'I'm glad you turned up.'

'Me too.' Her eyes shining, Fia visibly came to a decision and scrabbled in her bag for her phone. 'Right, well, if you're sure I can stay. . . .'

Rod Stewart had been replaced by Amy Winehouse; Deborah had come out from behind the bar and was performing 'Rehab', with three of the decorators singing and dancing in unison behind her.

'Hi, yes, I'm fine. Sorry? Oh, because I didn't want to. Anyway, this is just to let you know I won't be home tonight.' Moving the phone away from her ear, Fia said, 'No need to shout. I've met an extremely good-looking man and he's invited me to spend the night with him.' She smiled up at Johnny, enjoying being in control for possibly the first time. 'Well, I can do whatever I like. Same as you always have.'

Cleo watched her. Fia's eyes were bright, her mind made up. She was tipsy but not that drunk, galvanised by adrenaline rather than alcohol. Would she wake up tomorrow morning and regret it?

Having listened to Will at the other end of the line, Fia replied, 'Because you've been shagging another girl behind my back, and that means our marriage is over, that's why. Yes, you have. No, she didn't tell me.' Catching Cleo's eye, she winked. 'If you must know, you've had a private detective following you for the past three months. Anyway, I have to go now. I'll be home some time tomorrow; we can talk about solicitors and stuff then. Byeeee!'

She switched off the phone with a flourish, dropped it into her bag and exhaled.

Johnny surveyed her. 'Are you OK?'

'I think so.' Fia pulled a shaky-scared face. 'Phew, who knew so much could happen in one day?'

Cleo glanced over at Johnny. *Not to mention one night.*

'I haven't had anything to eat.' Fia sounded surprised. 'Not since those currant buns ages ago. Do they serve food in this place?'

'No.' Cleo shook her head.

'Oh. Damn, I'm starving.' Pleased, Fia said, 'And my marriage just broke up. That has to be a good sign, doesn't it?'

'They sell crisps,' said Cleo. 'And nuts.' She was hungry too. At home in the fridge was a sausage casserole ready-meal for one, not easily split between two famished people, but if she didn't offer—

'OK,' Johnny said, as Cleo opened her mouth to speak. 'How about we finish our drinks and then head to my place? I can do you steak and chips or a mushroom risotto, or there are pizzas in the freezer.' As an afterthought he added, 'And there's blackberry crumble too.'

Honestly, who did he think he was? Jean-Christophe Novelli?

'Wow!' Clearly thinking the same thing and wildly impressed, Fia exclaimed, 'Not only a world-famous artist, but you can cook as well.'

'Well, not quite.' Johnny shrugged. 'Chips and risotto out of the freezer. But I can chargrill a mean fillet steak.'

Ten minutes later, up on the stage, a couple of new arrivals were being Elton and Kiki, making a surprisingly good job of 'Don't Go Breaking My Heart'. Taking advantage of Johnny's visit to the loo, Cleo managed to take Fia to one side.

'Listen, you don't know Johnny. I really don't think you should go home with him. You can stay at my house, it's no trouble.

She could see the thought processes going on in Fia's head. Hmm, tiny cottage versus stonking great mansion. Husband's somewhat grumpy ex-girlfriend versus flirtatious, seriously attractive sculptor . . .

Fia searched for the right words. Finally she came out with, 'Thanks, but I've already said I'd stay at his place. It'd be rude to back out now.'

Surprise, surprise.

Cleo nodded. 'OK, but can I just say? Johnny has a bit of a reputation, so don't do anything you might regret.'

Fia considered this for a bit. Then she replied, 'You know, I never thought I'd be getting moral advice from my husband's mistress.'

'I wasn't a mistress! I didn't even know he was married!'

'Well, exactly. So you're hardly an expert, are you? This could be fate, couldn't it? I've come here today for the first time in my life. I came to see you, and I've ended up meeting Johnny. And he's been incredibly kind and he seems *really* nice . . .'

Cleo wondered how to respond. Should she explain that the whole point of men like Johnny LaVenture was to make you *think* they were really nice?

'In fact what I'm starting to wonder,' Fia waggled a mischievous index finger at her, 'is if you might not be a little bit envious because you're secretly quite keen on him yourself.'

Ew, what a thought.

'Johnny and I grew up in this village. We went to school together. I'm kind of the opposite of keen,' said Cleo.

Chapter 6

'WOW!' HURRYING INTO the pub on Saturday at lunch time, Cleo screeched to a halt when she saw Ash. 'You're eating!'

'I don't know how you do it,' Ash marvelled. 'It's some kind of sixth sense. You should be a psychic detective. Oi, give me that back.'

Cleo dug his fork into the lasagne and sampled a mouthful to see if it tasted as good as it smelled. Her eyes widened. 'Mmm . . . mmmmm!'

'Oh no you don't.' He snatched the fork back before she could steal any more. 'Get your own. Actually, have the fish pie, then I can see what that's like.'

'Fish pie? I *love* fish pie!' Whirling round, Cleo saw that a menu had been chalked up on the blackboard that had remained menu-less ever since Tony-the-temperamental-chef had broken up with his boyfriend and stropped off to work in Malaga.

Then Cleo's mouth dropped open as the new chef emerged from the kitchen carrying a tray of food.

Fia Newman, wearing a blue-and-white striped apron and with her hair tied back in a high plait, made her way over to one of the other tables. As Cleo stared in disbelief, she greeted the customers and deftly unloaded the plates. Finally, spotting Cleo, she waved and came over.

'Hi!' Fia's amber eyes danced. 'Surprised to see me?'

Cleo had spent the past four days and nights chauffeuring a visiting American businessman around the country. She felt as if she'd been away for four months. 'Are you the new chef?'

'Morse,' murmured Ash. 'Marple. Holmes. You're up there with all the greats.'

'Well, I really wanted to be the resident karaoke queen, but Frank said no to that. So I thought I'd give this a go instead!'

'But . . . how . . . ?'

'I know! It's like fate, isn't it? That night I stayed at Johnny's house, I was saying how crazy it was that this place didn't serve food and he told me what had happened with the chap who used to work here, Mad Tony. I didn't think any more of it, but then I went home the next day and had my big showdown with Will. That was when I realised I'd have to find somewhere else to live, because there was no way he'd move out of his precious house.' Fia pulled a face. 'And I was definitely going to have to find a new job, because I was working for Will's mother, and as far as Vivien's concerned, her boy can do no wrong. If he had an affair, I must have driven him to it.'

'God . . .'

'Oh, I never liked her anyway. Walking out of that china shop of hers was a joy. So then I thought about this place,' Fia said cheerfully. 'And I knew everyone was friendly, so I gave Frank a call. Well, he seemed keen on the idea, so long as I could cook. So I came over with some of my food. He liked it, I liked the flat upstairs and bingo, here I am!'

'Well, gosh, that's . . . great.' Mixed emotions didn't begin to describe how Cleo was feeling.

'How's that lasagne?' Fia looked over at Ash.

Ash chewed, swallowed. At last he said scintillatingly, 'Um . . . nice.'

'Good-good.' She turned to Cleo. 'Can I get you anything?'

'I'll have the fish pie.'

Fia gave a nod of satisfaction. 'You'll love it.'

Twenty minutes later, Cleo called her back over. She said, 'You know what? You're right, I do love it.'

Not being entirely thrilled about having Will's wife living here was one thing, but she cooked like an angel.

'I don't do fancy food.' Fia looked pleased. 'Just the basics.'

'Which is just what we need. Mad Tony was forever trying out new stuff that didn't work. Chicken with marmalade sauce, curried peas and mango. And last summer he was serving everything with rose petals and tarragon.' Cleo looked over at Ash. 'Remember that?'

'Uh . . . yes.'

Oh, for heaven's sake. As soon as Fia had disappeared back into the kitchen, Cleo grinned and said, 'You fancy her, don't you?'

'No.'

She gave him a gleeful prod. 'You do! You've gone all stupid again!'

Ash put down his drink and heaved a sigh. 'OK, now listen to me. If you were fourteen years old, you might think it'd be funny to blurt it out in front of everyone. But you're *not* fourteen, so I'm sure you can understand that it wouldn't be funny for me. It would be embarrassing all round. What's more, I'd never forgive you.'

'You're no fun.' Cleo pulled a face.

'But I mean it.' She could tell he did by the look in his eyes. 'She's living here, which means I'm going to be seeing her practically every day.' Ash leaned farther across the table. 'And if you tell her, it'll make it unbearable. So you need to keep that . . .' he made a zipping gesture in front of Cleo's mouth '. . . shut. Or we won't be friends any more. I'll get over it, I promise.'

Crikey, he did mean it. 'OK, I won't say anything. Cross my heart. How long, d'you think, before you get over it?'

'Oh, a couple of hours.' Exasperated, Ash said,' How the bloody hell do I know? She's only just left her husband.' He shook his head. 'So it's going to be months before she's even ready to look at another man.'

Which just went to show how naive Ash could be. The very next moment, as if to prove it, Johnny came into the pub and Fia was out of the kitchen in a flash.

'Hi, I was wondering when you'd be in!' Her whole face was lit up, her body language unambiguous. 'It's all going *really* well!'

Fia clearly subscribed to the theory that the best way to get over one man was to meet another. Preferably in less time than some people took to Hoover their carpets. Eagerly she said, 'What are you going to have?'

'Sorry, busy, can't stop.' Holding up a carrier bag, Johnny offered it to one of the lads standing at the bar. 'Dave, you left your brushes behind—I found them in the sink in the utility room. Thanks for finishing up last night. Great job.' Turning, he grinned and said, 'Cleo, hi! I tell you, it's going to be weird not having that lot around any more. I came downstairs this morning and made six mugs of tea before remembering I was on my own.'

He hadn't called her Misa. It was a miracle. To show that she could be civil too, Cleo said, 'So the house is all done, is it? How's it looking?'

'You wouldn't believe the difference. Come on over if you want. See for yourself.'

'Oh, um . . .' Now she didn't know what to say. She hadn't been expecting an invitation. Next to him, Fia was also looking taken aback.

'I'll show you what I'm working on too,' Johnny added. 'For Cornelia.'

OK, now that was something she'd definitely like to see. Not that Johnny would ever know this, but she'd been Googling him on the quiet and had—even more secretly—fallen in love with his work. Some of the larger-than-life sculptures were breathtaking.

'One of her horses? I'd love to.'

His grin broadened. 'Come round when you've finished your lunch. I'll be the one wrestling with a mile of wire.'

All of a sudden the mental picture this conjured up seemed quite exciting. Oo-er, what was *that* about? Was this how it felt to fall under Johnny LaVenture's spell? Johnny was an inveterate charmer who loved to flirt for his own amusement. Only a fool would believe he meant it.

Or a Fia.

'Fine, yeah, maybe later.' Cleo waved her fork and went back to her meal. Johnny said his goodbyes to Dave and the boys at the bar and moved towards the door.

Fia, her face falling, called after him, 'Will you be in this evening?'

'Who knows? Never say never.'

When he'd gone and Fia had once again vanished into the kitchen, Ash echoed, 'Fine, yeah, maybe later,' mimicking Cleo's casual tone.

'Behave yourself.' Having jabbed the back of his hand, Cleo wiped her fork on a napkin. 'Would you rather Fia went over there instead?'

'So that's what you're doing, is it? Selflessly offering yourself in her place, like some kind of noble sacrifice? Don't take her, take me.' Ash shook his head. 'I had no idea you were so brave, so heroic.'

'And I had no idea you were such a philistine. He's an artist. I'd love to watch him at work.'

'Why? You've never wanted to watch *me* work.'

'He's creative!'

'Bloody hell, so am I! I create a radio show,' Ash retorted. 'Which is *also* art, and is a damn sight more difficult than bending bits of wire in this direction and that direction. Any idiot could do that.'

Cleo smiled. 'Are you jealous?'

'Maybe. A bit. OK, of course I'm bloody jealous.' He jerked his head in the direction of the kitchen. 'She's crazy about him. It's so obvious.'

Bless. Cleo's heart went out to Ash. 'I know, but I'm going to talk to him about that, tell him not to get involved.'

Ash nodded slowly, acknowledging that this made sense. 'Well, be careful. He probably works with his shirt off.'

OK, delete that thought before it could take hold. Chasing the last fat prawn around her plate, Cleo shrugged and said, 'Don't we all?'

'**H**ey, you came.' Answering the front door and thankfully not topless, Johnny looked pleased to see her. He was wearing faded jeans and desert boots, and a white T-shirt with a diagonal reddish-brown smear across the front.

'Is that paint?' Cleo pointed to it, hardly a cheerful colour for a room.

'What?' He glanced down at the smear. 'Oh, right. No, it's blood.'

'Did somebody stab you?'

'Ever the optimist. No, I've just been having a fight with a horse.' Lifting his T-shirt, he showed her the cause of the bleeding, a long, freshly inflicted scratch. 'Occupational hazard. You wouldn't believe how many T-shirts I get through in a year. So,' he led her into the house and gestured around the hall. 'Is it looking better in here?'

It was. Better, fresher, cleaner. The smell of paint still hung in the air but all the clutter had gone. There were new rugs on the polished wooden floorboards, the light fittings had been replaced and the windows glittered.

'Much,' said Cleo.

'Just as well. It's cost a fortune.'

She kept a straight face. 'You poor thing. I'm welling up.'

'OK, sorry.' Johnny smiled briefly. Then they reached the drawing room and he threw open the double doors.

'Oh *wow* . . .'

No more worn, threadbare carpet. No more peeling outdated wallpaper. The entire room, including the floorboards, had been painted white. Sunshine streamed in through the full-length windows. Lined up against the far wall were huge bales of wire and in the centre of the room stood the current work-in-progress, a half-completed, twelve-foot-tall sculpture of a horse. It was an arresting, magnificent sight. No wonder Cornelia was such a fan of Johnny's work. Looking at photographs of the creations on his web site gave no inkling of the emotional impact to be gained by viewing them in the flesh. So to speak.

Watching her with a faint smile on his face, Johnny said, 'You like it?'

Cleo nodded, barely able to tear her gaze away from the horse. Stepping over the coils of wire strewn across the white dust sheet upon which it stood, she moved towards it. 'Am I allowed to touch?'

'Go ahead. It's not as fragile as it looks. Watch out for sharp edges—I haven't turned them in with pliers yet.'

She ran the flat of her hand wonderingly over the horse's flank. How could something made of lengths of galvanised steel seem so alive? It was extraordinary. Finding herself smiling in disbelief, Cleo moved round to the front and stroked the proud curve of its neck. Imagine being able to create something as—*yeesh*, that windswept mane was *sharp*.

A bead of blood grew on the end of her finger. Stepping up and taking hold of her wrist, Johnny examined the wound.

'Oh dear. We're going to have to amputate.'

Cleo retrieved her hand and sucked the blood from her finger. She moved back. 'Show me how you do it.'

'How I amputate? Well, I generally get a big old electric saw . . .' He picked up a pair of safety glasses, then nodded at the only piece of furniture in the room. 'Go and sit down. You'll be safe over there.'

The sofa was long and sleek, upholstered in deep purple velvet. Sitting on it, the view was of Johnny and the sculpture, then the French windows behind him, then the terrace and the grounds beyond that. As he worked, illuminated by the afternoon sunlight flooding into the room, Cleo was able to see the play of tendons and muscles in his body. No wonder he had broad shoulders and a washboard stomach; the galvanised steel wire needed to be strong enough to bear the weight of the piece when it was completed. Johnny flexed and stretched as he bent and sculpted each section into place. Perspiration gleamed at his throat and on his forearms. Behind the safety glasses his eyes were narrowed, constantly judging and gauging and checking that every new addition was exactly right. You could see the intensity of his concentration as he moved around the figure, making endless additions and improvements.

Watching Johnny at work was a magical, mesmerising experience. When he finally stopped, Cleo would have guessed she'd been sitting there for fifteen, maybe twenty minutes. But when she looked at her watch she saw that it had been an hour and a half.

'I can't believe it's four o'clock.' She shook her head in amazement. 'This is definitely how time travel should be. Just think, if airlines supplied wire-sculpture demonstrations on long-haul flights, you'd find yourself on the other side of the world in a flash!'

'It's like that for me too.' Pushing his fingers through his hair, Johnny stepped back to survey his work from a distance. 'Once I start, I lose all track of time. I can go through the night.'

Now there was an image to conjure with.

He flexed his shoulders. 'Come on, let's get a coffee.'

'OK, *oof*.' Her left leg, which had been tucked under her on the sofa, had gone dead. Gingerly uncurling it and levering herself upright, Cleo shook her head when he offered a hand. 'It's fine, I can manage.'

'Stubborn as ever,' Johnny remarked. 'Either that, or you're scared of my irresistible animal magnetism.'

'Or your incredible modesty.' Cleo limped into the kitchen after him and leaned against the polished granite worktop as her foot began to fizz and prickle back to life. 'Listen, what's going on with Fia Newman? Was it your idea for her to move here?'

He began making the coffee. 'No. She was trying to figure out what she could do. I happened to mention that a live-in job would kill two birds with one stone, but I didn't suggest the Hollybush. I just dropped in yesterday evening and there she was, carrying her stuff into the flat upstairs.'

'And the other night?'

'The other night what?'

'When she stayed here with you.'

He turned to look at Cleo. 'What are you asking?'

'Nothing.' They were two consenting adults and it was none of her business what they might have got up to, but she felt it only fair to warn him. 'It's just . . . she spent the night in your house. You were kind to her. And now, bam, she's moved into the village! I don't know if you realise this, but you're probably the reason she's done it.'

Ha, she caught the flash of genuine surprise in his eyes. So he hadn't cottoned on. 'Me?'

'Oh yes.' Cleo rotated her recovering ankle.

'Riiight.' Johnny nodded slowly. 'OK, I see what you're saying.'

Cleo reached for the mug of coffee he was holding out to her. 'She's vulnerable.'

'Because you had an affair with her husband.'

She gave him a look, but he was right, she did feel responsible. 'You don't want to mess her around. That wouldn't be kind.'

'OK, spare me the lecture. And you should have a bit more faith in me,' said Johnny. 'I'll have you know I can be a gentleman when I want to be. When Fia stayed here the other night she slept in the spare room.' He paused. 'And I slept in mine.'

'Well, good.' Cleo smiled, relieved to hear it.

'Do I get a reward for that?'

'Yes you do. You get a nice warm glow from knowing you did the right thing.'

'Fantastic.' He nodded. 'A nice warm glow. Who could ask for more?'

Cleo drank her coffee. 'Getting involved with her would just be asking for trouble.'

'Fine, I get the message. Sounds like you're not too thrilled about having her here.'

'She seems nice. Normal enough. Apart from having a crush on you.'

'Touché.' He acknowledged the dig with a brief smile.

Cleo sighed; did he think she was a complete bitch? 'But it's just . . . difficult, you know? Every time I see her, I'm going to be reminded of Will. And I'll keep on feeling guilty.'

'It wasn't your fault, though.'

'I know that logically. But I'm still the reason she left him.'

Johnny said, 'Sooner or later it would have happened anyway. You've done her a favour. And at least the children weren't hers.'

Cleo nodded. 'That's true.'

'If she'd stayed with Will for a few more years, chances are they'd have had kids of their own. And she'd have ended up a single parent. So you've saved her from all that.'

'You're right.' It was Cleo's turn to look modest. 'I'm a heroine.'

'A heroine with terrible judgment when it comes to picking a man. I mean, there's me,' he tapped his chest, 'pretty much perfect in every way and you're not remotely interested.'

She dipped her head in agreement. 'So true.'

'But a complete arse like Will Newman comes along and you think he's the answer to your prayers.'

'OK, you might find this hard to believe, but he did actually do a pretty good job of hiding his complete arsiness. He's like a lot of people.' Cleo's tone was meaningful. 'They can give the impression on the surface of being nice. But deep down, they're capable of all sorts.'

Johnny raised an eyebrow. 'Let me show you upstairs.'

Hmm, there was an offer.

'Not like that.' He tut-tutted, demonstrating his unerring ability to read her mind. 'Well, not unless you really want me to.'

'Very generous of you, but no thanks. I have to go. But it's been fun.' Cleo made to leave. 'And remember what I said about Fia, OK? Don't do anything . . . you know.'

'Fine. For now.' Johnny's eyes glinted with mischief as he showed her out. 'Although it still feels like you're the one who wrecked her marriage and I'm the one getting punished for it. Seems a bit harsh.'

She smiled up at him. 'Just concentrate on that nice warm glow.'

Abbie was in the bath waiting for her face pack to set when the doorbell rang downstairs.

And Tom was still at work.

She waited for whoever it was to go away. No way was she answering the door with a pale-blue clay mask slathered over her face.

But the person on the doorstep kept on ringing the bell. Again.

And again.

And agaaaaaain—

'OK, I'm coming, just *stop* it.' Sloshing water, Abbie climbed out of the bath and pulled on her towelling robe. She padded downstairs and paused in the hallway before calling, 'Who is it?' through the front door.

Then she heard, 'It's meee!' and felt her stomach turn to concrete.

Oh God. Without even any warning. Completely forgetting the face pack, Abbie opened the front door and gazed at Georgia, very tanned and blonder than ever. And with a huge battered suitcase at her feet.

'Hi, Abbie! *Euw*, look at you! Dad's not home from work yet, then?'

She didn't mean for her breezily worded question to hurt, but the effect was like fingernails scraping down a blackboard. Actually, the setting face pack came in handy, keeping Abbie's features immobile and her true feelings hidden. While inwardly her brain screamed, *Go away, leave us alone and don't even think of bringing that case into this house.*

Aloud, Abbie said, 'Not yet. Does he know you're here?'

'No, it's a surprise! I called him this afternoon and told him I was sunbathing on the beach in Praia da Rocha, and he said lucky old me. But I'm not there, and when he comes home I'm going to go whoo-hoo, I'm back!' Georgia beamed at her. 'Won't he just love it?'

'Well, it'll definitely be a surprise.' The drying clay meant she sounded as if she were speaking through clenched teeth. And of course she couldn't stop Georgia bringing the case into the house. Abbie stepped to one side as the girl lugged it past her over the front step and into the narrow hallway. 'Have you come straight from the airport?'

'No, we've been in London for the past couple of days. I've left Mum packing everything up before she flies back to Portugal.'

Abbie followed her through to the living room. 'Why?'

'Because she's doing another of her flits, surprise surprise.'

Georgia peeled off her coat to reveal a stripy top and lime-green shorts. 'We've had a bit of an argument about it. She's dumped Christian, right, and now she's met this new guy, Ted. I mean, this is a middle-aged woman we're talking about, d'you know what I mean? She can't keep chasing men for the rest of her life. It's not dignified.'

'So Ted lives in Portugal too?'

'Lives and *drinks* in Portugal.' Pulling a face, Georgia said, 'And he's made it perfectly clear he doesn't like me. Which is fine, because it's absolutely mutual. I was in the way there and he wanted me out of the picture. So I said that was cool, I'd live in the Paddington flat by myself . . . so then, well, we ended up having a falling-out.'

'Oh dear.'

Georgia looked at her. 'Can I make a cup of tea, is that all right?'

'Yes, yes . . . sorry, I should have offered.'

'It's OK. Why don't I make the tea while you go upstairs and wash all that blue stuff off?'

Abbie didn't ask the question that was uppermost in her mind and Georgia didn't answer it. Instead, like the elephant in the room, it remained unmentioned for the next seventy minutes while they talked instead about Portugal, their respective Christmases, and how weird it was that people would gag at the sight of mouldy yoghurt but would happily tuck into blue cheese, the mouldier the better.

Basically, she didn't need to ask the question because she already knew the answer. Even a chimp could guess.

Then Tom arrived home and Abbie saw his face light up at the sight of his daughter. Georgia yelled, 'Surprise!' and almost sent him flying, wrapping him in an exuberant hug. The little knives were out in force in Abbie's stomach, twisting with envy and dread.

'So is that all right then?' said Georgia when she'd finished explaining the story of how she happened to be here. 'It's OK if I stay with you?'

This was it, this was the question. Abbie carefully kept her expression neutral, while inside her head she shouted, No no no no no.

'Well . . .' Startled but hopeful, Tom had turned to look at her. 'That sounds . . . um, what do you think, Abbie?'

Cruel. Cruel and unfair. He had to know what she was thinking.

Georgia was looking taken aback too, as if it hadn't occurred to her that she might have to beg. 'Oh God, is this really awkward? I'm sorry,' she blurted out to Tom. 'I thought you'd be pleased!'

'Sweetheart, don't get upset.' Tom was mortified. 'Of course we're pleased . . . it's just a bit sudden. How long were you thinking of—'

'Don't worry, Dad, it's fine, I'll go back to London.' Georgia's blue eyes swam. 'Sorry to bother you . . . I'll find someone to put me up . . .'

'Wait, you can't go, of course you can stay!' Tom turned to Abbie and blurted the words out in a panic. 'That's all right with you, love, isn't it?'

Cleo was painting her toenails when the phone rang.

'Hello?' Whoops, she managed to blob pink polish onto the side of her foot as she clasped the phone between shoulder and chin.

'Hi, it's me.' Abbie's voice. 'Come over to the pub.'

'Hm? Oh, no thanks, I'm having a lazy night in. Actually, I'm just doing my toes and you've made me—'

'It wasn't a question,' Abbie cut in. 'I'm telling you to come over because I need you.'

'What? Why?' Putting the lid back on the bottle of Rimmel polish, Cleo straightened. 'And why are you sounding all weird and echoey?'

'I'm in the loo. Hiding. How soon can you be here?'

Whatever was happening? 'Well, it says this stuff dries in sixty seconds. So all I've got to do is put some clothes on. Oh, except I've just plucked my eyebrows. As soon as the redness goes down, I'll—'

'Never mind your eyebrows,' Abbie blurted out. 'Get yourself over here *now*.'

Which was easy for her sister to say, but Cleo knew from experience that after a vigorous plucking session, the skin around her eyebrows stayed red for ages. Then again, Abbie had sounded desperate. Heroically, Cleo got herself dressed, roughly dried her hair and spent a couple of minutes applying minimum-level make-up plus white highlighter under the eyebrows to disguise the worst of the damage.

Cleo surveyed the end result in the mirror. She still looked ridiculous but never mind. In a way, it was nice to be wanted. And since Abbie didn't make a habit of needing her company in such dramatic fashion, she could even hazard a guess as to what this might be about.

The guess was confirmed when she arrived at the pub and saw the blonde girl with Tom's eyes standing with Tom and Abbie. She hadn't met Georgia last time, but the girl had evidently turned up again. Poor Abbie; hopefully it was only a flying visit.

'Oh look, it's Cleo.' Feigning surprise, Abbie beckoned her over. 'Georgia, meet my younger sister. Cleo, this is Georgia. And you'll never guess what? Georgia's come to stay with us! Isn't that lovely?'

Bloody hell. No wonder Abbie was looking a bit wild-eyed.

'Hi. Great. So how long are you staying?'

'Who knows? I'm moving in!' Leaning towards Tom—oh God, it was so weird to think he was her father—Georgia said cheerfully, 'I could still be here when I'm seventy!'

So that was why Abbie had sounded frantic on the phone.

'Drink, Cleo?' Tom already had his wallet out.

'Yes please.'

'Actually, I hope you don't mind me saying.' Georgia peered more closely at her. 'But are you allergic to your eye shadow? Only your eyes are, like, really *red*.'

'**W**hat could I do?' Abbie murmured thirty minutes later when they visited the loo. 'How could I say no? She doesn't have anywhere to go.'

'Oh God, it's not fair on you.' Cleo gave her a hug.

'And Tom's thrilled; it's like a dream come true for him. He's trying to hide it, but he can't. And every time I think about it I just feel sick.' Abbie shook her head. 'But then I tell myself it's not her fault and I hate myself for being so horrible. I must be some kind of monster . . .'

'Look, you're in shock. And you're definitely not a monster. It'll get easier. Everything'll settle down and you'll all get used to each other.' Cleo knew she was probably spouting rubbish, but what else could she say? 'And this is Channings Hill we're talking about. She's used to living in London. A couple of weeks here and she could be going out of her mind with boredom. She'll be begging to leave.'

'That'd be too much to hope for,' Abbie sighed.

The door was pushed open. Georgia said brightly, 'Talking about me?'

She hadn't heard them. 'No,' Abbie managed a smile.

'We were a bit,' said Cleo.

'Of course you were. I'm not stupid. It's OK, I don't mind.'

'Actually, Abbie's got a headache, but she was worried you might think she was just using it as an excuse to leave. She's feeling rotten,' Cleo went on, 'so really she should go home and take some painkillers.'

'Oh poor you. Of course you must go,' Georgia exclaimed, over-sympathising in that way people do when the least popular member of the party says they might leave. 'Me and Dad'll be fine.'

'And I'll be here too.' Cleo nodded at Abbie, who was so obviously not enjoying herself. 'Go on, off you go.'

Grateful for the excuse, Abbie left and Georgia and Cleo rejoined Tom at the bar. Georgia said interestedly, 'Who's that, over there?'

While they'd been in the loo, Johnny and Ash had both arrived and were setting up a game of pool. Johnny was looking handsomer then ever tonight in a white cotton shirt and jeans, with his hair falling into his dark eyes. Ash, never the most sartorial of dressers, was wearing a baggy red sweatshirt that made him look like an off-duty Father Christmas.

'Just a couple of locals.' Changing the subject, Cleo said, 'So, what are you going to be doing jobwise? Any ideas?' This was the girl who had just spent several weeks lazing by a pool in Portugal; she hoped Georgia didn't think she could just move in with Tom and Abbie, and sponge off them like . . . well, OK, like millions of bone-idle teenagers the world over, but that was beside the point.

Leaning forward, Georgia said eagerly, 'How funny, I was just about to ask you about that. Now, my plan is to start up a business. Minimum outlay, maximum profit, flexible working hours, how does that sound?'

'What kind of business?' said Cleo.

'Ironing.'

'Seriously?'

'Why not? I love ironing. I've always done all our stuff since I was eleven.' Dreamily Georgia said, 'It's brilliant, taking something crumpled and messy and making it all smooth and perfect. And you can charge one pound twenty a shirt! How long does it take to iron a shirt? Five minutes. Easy peasy. And you can watch telly while you're doing it.' She looked pleased with herself. 'All I need is an iron!'

'And an ironing board,' said Cleo.

'That too.'

'And hangers. Lots and lots of hangers.' Oh dear, was she raining on the girl's parade?

'Fine. They're cheap.'

'And leaflets to advertise the business.'

'Okaaay.'

'And transport.'

'Not if I tell people just to drop the stuff off at the house and pick it up again once it's done.'

Tom shook his head. 'That won't work. Ironing services collect and deliver. You'd definitely need a van.'

'Fine then, forget the ironing.' Georgia puffed out her cheeks, exhaled noisily and shook back her hair. 'I thought it was a good idea, but it wasn't. *And* I was going to subcontract work out to pensioners. But never mind, I'll just become a pole dancer. That pays well, doesn't it? Then I can save up for a van. Look, they've finished playing now. Shall we challenge them to a game of doubles?'

'No.' Cleo glanced briefly across at Johnny, who was laughing, and at Ash, who was juggling pool balls and being generally boisterous. 'Anyway, he's too old for you.'

'Why? How old is he?'

'Thirty.'

Georgia's eyes widened. '*Is* he?'

Sensing that they were being watched, Ash turned round to look at Cleo and demanded, 'Are you ogling my irresistible backside?'

Cleo opened her mouth to retort that she could think of prettier sights but was beaten to it by Georgia who said, 'Cleo was just telling me about you. I can't believe how old you are.'

What? Cleo did a double take.

'Bloody cheek. So how old do you think I am?' Ash demanded. 'Sixty-five?'

Beaming, Georgia said, 'I'd have said mid-twenties.'

'But I *am* in my mid-twenties.' Ash raised his eyebrows. 'What has that witch been telling you?'

'She said you were thirty!'

Cleo was stunned—so much for jumping to conclusions. 'I didn't. I meant *Johnny* was thirty.'

'Who's Johnny? Oh, I suppose that must be you.' She briefly acknowledged Johnny before turning back to Ash.' So what's your name?'

And within moments she was over at the pool table, chatting away to Ash, the two of them getting along together famously. Cleo heard him tell Georgia that she, Cleo, was in fact fifty-seven years old.

'She's too young for Johnny, surely.' At her side Tom was panicking, having made the same assumption. 'Oh God, how am I supposed to deal with all this? I've missed out on eighteen years of practice.'

'I'll have a word with her.' Cleo took a gulp of her drink; if things had been different, she would have been Georgia's aunt. Fabulous, trendy, Auntie Cleo who was always fun and never nagged.

'I'll buy her a van,' said Tom.

'What?'

'Just a cheap one, so she can set up the business.' He'd obviously been mulling it over in his mind. 'Can't have her pole dancing.'

'Well, no.' Georgia had pretty obviously only said that to terrify him into buying her a van, but he couldn't take the risk that she might do it.

'So, you've met her now.' Tom tried and failed to keep the pride out of his voice as he watched his new-found daughter from a distance. 'What's the verdict?'

Cleo touched his arm and said gently, 'I think she's a character, and she's going to change your life. But this isn't as easy for Abbie as it is for you. Don't let her feel left out of all this, will you?'

He looked surprised. 'She isn't left out. We're all in it together.'

Cleo nodded slowly. She'd always loved Tom but he wasn't necessarily brilliant at understanding how women might feel. 'OK. I'm just saying it might not feel that way to her.'

Tom had already headed off for work. Abbie, busy buttering toast and drinking tea, was due to leave in ten minutes. Having crept around upstairs in order not to disturb their new house guest, she got a shock when the door was pushed open and Georgia came padding into the kitchen in a green-and-purple striped nightie and with her hair askew.

'Hi!' Abbie knew she sounded overbright but she couldn't help herself; it just kept happening. 'Did you sleep well?'

'Yeah, thanks.' She raked her fingers sleepily through her tangled hair. 'Is it OK for me to have a cup of tea?'

What did she expect the answer to be? *No you can't?*

'Of course! Help yourself to anything you like!' Abbie cringed; here she was, off again and drowning in a forest of exclamation marks

'Thanks. Is your head better?'

'Oh!' She'd forgotten about last night's fictitious headache. 'Yes, thanks, all gone! So, what are your plans then for today?'

Georgia shrugged and dropped a tea bag into a mug. 'Don't know. Just watch a bit of TV, I suppose.' She wrinkled her nose at the radio, currently playing a Neil Diamond track. 'Is that Radio Two?'

She made it sound like Radio Born-in-the-Ice-Age. Was this Georgia's way of telling her that from now on they would be listening to a station that was hip and happening? Feeling about a hundred years old, Abbie said defensively, 'No, it's—'

'Actually, d'you know what time milkmen finish work?'

'Sorry?' Was this a trick question?

'You know, people who do a milk round. They start work dead early so they must finish early. I just wondered if you knew when.'

'No idea. Midday, possibly.' Surely Georgia wasn't considering that as a job? In a hurry now, Abbie took a big mouthful of toast and checked her hair in the mirror. She liked Neil Diamond. Having a hypercritical teenager *in situ* was going to change her life in more ways than she'd imagined. The chances were that Georgia wouldn't share her taste in TV programmes either, would flinch at the prospect of having to watch a wildlife documentary or chatter distractingly all the way through a vital episode of a series Abbie was addicted to.

Oh God, listen to me, I'm just a horrible human being who—

'Hang on!' Georgia held up a hand. She was listening intently to something. Had she heard an intruder trying to break in through the back door? A bird singing in the garden? Maybe she was interested in wildlife after all.

'What is it?' Having listened for several seconds, Abbie said, 'I can't hear anything.'

'Him.' Georgia pointed in disbelief to the radio on the windowsill. 'That voice! It sounds just like the person I was talking to yesterday in the pub . . . wow, that is so *spooky* . . .'

Realisation dawned. 'Oh, did you meet Ash?'

'Ash! Yes, yes!' Georgia gestured wildly at the radio. 'Can you believe it? This guy sounds *exactly* like him!'

'That could be because it's the Ash Parry-Jones show.'

Georgia's teaspoon clattered onto the worktop. 'Get out of here.' Her head swivelled between Abbie and the radio, where Ash was now exchanging banter with his newsreader. Her eyes widened. 'But . . . but he told me he was a milkman!'

'It's kind of a running joke. He lives next door to Cleo. Look, I'm going to have to go—'

'He's an actual DJ! That's amazing! I thought he was brilliant before, but now he's even *better.*'

Abbie moved towards the door. 'Will you be OK? I'll see you later.'

'I'll be fine,' Georgia said absently. 'This is so cool! It's like I'm going to have my very own Chris Moyles!'

Fia marvelled at the difference a month could make. Just a few weeks ago, her morning routine had involved getting up at eight, starting work in her mother-in-law's shop at nine and, in between being polite to customers, listening patiently to her mother-in-law's nonstop stream of gossip, criticism and social commentary. Regularly interspersed, needless to say, with paeons of praise for Will.

Fia would have found another job months ago but each time she'd mentioned it, Will had been upset. She'd be letting both him and his mother down. And like a complete pushover she'd believed him. Whereas in reality he'd been controlling her, keeping her mentally tethered to him and Vivien while he conducted his own life as he pleased.

Looking back on it, she couldn't believe she'd been so gullible. Well, she'd put all that behind her. Who dares wins, and all that. She had been daring and she was definitely winning so far.

Best of all, she was loving her unexpected new job. Even if it did mean getting up at six in order to go and buy the food she'd be cooking that day, then spending the next three hours doing all the prep.

'La la la, laaa laaaaa.' Humming along to her CD, Fia finished peeling and quartering the King Edwards for the shepherd's pie and slid them into the pan of water on the hob. From the kitchen window she was able to look out over the pub garden, where wild rabbits hopped about and birds swung like acrobats from the trees, feeding on berries and seeds. She loved the utter peacefulness of the mornings, then the contrast of the buzzy conviviality of the pub when it was open. Of course it was hard work, but everyone was so appreciative of her cooking, it more than compensated.

Frank, the landlord, came into the kitchen as she was frying the sliced onions in butter and oil.

'Morning, pet. Smells good. Coffee?'

'Hi, Frank. Yes please.' She sprinkled caster sugar onto the onions. 'I'm doing shepherd's pie, mushroom stroganoff, beef curry and chicken and leek casserole.'

'Great. We've already got twelve booked for lunch. Bunch of women who usually eat at The Bear are coming over because they've heard good things. Word's spreading, pet.'

Frank sloshed boiling water into two mugs and nodded at the CD player on the shelf above the fridge. 'What's that you're listening to?'

'*Carmina Burana*. By Carl Orff. Like it?'

He grinned. 'Never really bothered with all that classical stuff. It's Elvis for me, every time.'

'It's relaxing. I just like to have it playing in the background.'

Frank listened for a few seconds, clearly underwhelmed. Finally he said, 'Wouldn't the radio be more cheerful? You want to give BWR a go. Have a listen to Ash's show. He's a right laugh, that lad.'

Fia's hackles rose instantly. A right laugh. Except, hard though it was to believe, it actually appeared to be true. Last night while she'd been working away here in the kitchen, she'd heard Ash laughing in the bar. Ash had been playing pool with Johnny, joking around and generally being the life and soul of the party. Yet when she'd squeezed past and smiled at him he'd practically cut her dead, turning away as if she didn't exist. And this wasn't the first time it had happened either. Everyone else in Channings Hill had been welcoming and friendly, but Ash Parry-Jones invariably treated her like some unwanted intruder. At first she'd assumed he was simply the quiet, keep-himself-to-himself type. Discovering over the course of the past fortnight that he was actually completely confident and outgoing with everyone else had come as a shock, not to mention a slap in the face. Because that meant he was being cold for a reason. He just didn't like her.

And if he was going to be such an unfriendly miserable sod, she was buggered if she was going to listen to his precious radio show, no matter how hilarious it might be.

Frank left the kitchen. Fia powdered the frying onions with flour, then added a glug of red wine. Ten minutes later, curiosity got the better of her and she switched off the CD. If BWR hadn't been one of the preset radio stations she wouldn't have found it. As it was, she jumped at the sound of Ash's voice. God, it was weird to hear him being himself, playful and good-humoured and utterly relaxed.

'. . . and that was Katie Melua, for those of you who like that kind of thing. Although if I had to be buried in my coffin with an iPod and only one artist playing on it, I'd kill myself if it was her. Or George Formby.'

'Who?' He had a young-sounding female in the studio with him. 'The boxer guy who sells Lean Mean Grilling Machines?'

'Do you know what? You're thinking of George Foreman, who I'd love to have on my iPod in my coffin because he's a legend, even if he doesn't sing. But *I'm* talking about George Formby, who played the ukulele and sang in a *really* annoying way. And I wouldn't want Lonnie Donegan either. The King of Skiffle. Because I don't like skiffle music,' said Ash. 'Although I have to say, the actual word *skiffle* is one of my all-time favourite words. It's right up there with *knickerbocker* and *lollygagging*.'

'You just made that last one up!'

'I didn't. It's a real word,' Ash protested. 'It means hanging around. Which is a lot nicer than you might think, because you'd *think* it meant gagging on a lolly.'

The girl said, 'I like pernickety.'

'That's our producer's favourite word,' said Ash. 'Can't imagine why. Probably because he wears knitted pullovers and—'

Footsteps sounded outside the kitchen, signalling Frank's return. Before she knew it, Fia's arm had shot out and switched from radio back to CD. OK, maybe it was childish, but she wasn't going to give Ash the satisfaction of hearing that she'd listened to his show.

If he could be cold and unfriendly for no apparent reason . . . well, that was fine. So could she.

'I bet you couldn't believe your luck, could you?'

Cleo glanced in the rearview mirror at her passenger and nearly got dazzled by his teeth. 'Sorry?'

'When you found out who you were picking up. Not just your lucky day either. Your lucky three weeks.'

'Right. Absolutely.' She nodded and flashed a professional smile of assent. Oh joy. Five minutes into the first of many journeys and already the client was proving himself to be a dickhead.

And to think Grumpy Graham had thought, in his own grumpy way, that he was doing her a favour when he'd allocated her the job.

'You can take this one.' Graham had actually winked—winked!—as he'd handed her the booking sheet last week. 'Nice and regular, and a bit of a looker by all accounts. Don't say I never do anything for you.'

'Ooh, Casey Kruger!' Coming into the tiny cluttered office to drop off some keys, Shelley had peered over Cleo's shoulder. 'I used to have a poster of him on my bedroom wall when he was in *On the Beach*.'

Cleo hadn't watched *On the Beach*, one of Australia's most successfully exported soaps, but she knew who Casey Kruger was. Like Kylie and Jason and so many other soap stars, he had gone on to have a career in music.

And now here he was, lounging in the back of the car in an unbuttoned black shirt and supertight black jeans, drinking Diet Coke and autographing a pile of publicity photos of himself. For the next three weeks he was starring at the Bristol Hippodrome in a new musical called *Beach Party!* It was her job to pick him up every afternoon from his hotel and deliver him to the theatre, then collect him again after each performance and return him safely to the hotel.

'Here.' Casey leaned forward and tapped her on the shoulder as they waited at a junction.

Turning, Cleo saw that he was presenting her with one of the photos he'd just signed.

'Oh thanks. That's really kind.'

Well, what else could she say—no thanks, that's really nauseating?

'See what I've put on it?' Casey looked pleased with himself. Glancing at the words, Cleo read: 'To Cleo, You're a babe and you're driving me crazy! All love, Casey Kruger xxx.'

Which was less flattering than it sounded, because 'You're a babe!' was Casey's catchphrase and he said it to everyone he met.

'You know what? We're going to have fun, you and me.' Chuckling, Casey lowered his darkened window so the people waiting at the bus stop could recognise him. He nodded and waved graciously before buzzing the window up again. 'So, Cleo, tell me all about yourself. Were you a big fan of *On the Beach*, back when I was in it?'

Oh dear. Maybe she could persuade Shelley to swap jobs.

Lunch with his producer meant it was four o'clock by the time Ash arrived home. As he got out of the car, he heard footsteps behind him. For a split second his heart leaped at the thought that it could be Fia. Turning, he came face to face with . . .

OK, not Fia. It was Georgie—no, *Georgia*, Tom Wells's eighteen-year-old, sperm-donated daughter. What a weird situation *that* was.

'Hey, how are you doing?' She was looking and sounding exceedingly perky. 'I've been waiting for you. Guess what?'

He shrugged. 'No idea. You're my long-lost sister?'

'Shut up! No, listen, I am your biggest fan! I can't believe you didn't tell me last night that you're a DJ!'

'I'm very modest,' lied Ash.

'Seriously, I heard your show this morning . . . and you were *brilliant*. You're *way* funnier than Chris Moyles.'

'I happen to agree with you there.'

'You're fantastic.' She fixed him with her unblinking vivid-blue gaze. 'I absolutely completely fancy you rotten.'

'OK, who put you up to this?' If it was Cleo, he'd wring her neck.

'No one!' Raising her hand, Georgia reached out and gently brushed the backs of her fingers against his face. When he leaned away, she said, 'I felt it last night. I kind of hoped you did too. And that was *before* I knew you were on the radio. Which proves I'm not a screaming groupie.'

Ash shook his head. 'This is a trick.'

'It's not. OK, you're not pretty. But that's not what I go for. Never have done. It's character every time for me.' She moved a couple of inches closer. 'And you must want me.'

This was surreal. 'Why must I want you?'

'Because I'm pretty *and* I have a great personality. What's not to like?'

Reaching up on tiptoe, she planted a quick kiss on Ash's unsuspecting mouth. 'And you're going to be glad too.'

Ash wiped his mouth, now sticky with melon-flavoured lip gloss. 'OK, stop right there. I don't know what you think you're playing at . . .'

'Come here, then, and let me show you.'

'No. Get *off*.' It was like trying to wrestle an octopus. Unpeeling her hands, he said firmly, 'This isn't going to happen. No way.'

'Why not? You can't tell me I'm not pretty enough.'

He could understand her confusion. On the scale of physical attraction, she was stratospherically out of his league. Ash said, 'Look, you're stunning. But you're eighteen.'

'So?' Her voice rose.

'That's too young for me.'

'So you're not interested in me. You'd prefer someone older and uglier. And probably way fatter too.' Her hands on her narrow hips, Georgia said, 'Do you have any idea how . . . *wrong* that is?'

Ash broke into a smile. 'Yeah, I suppose it is.'

'Oh well, I'll leave it for now. But don't think I'm going to give up. I can still try to win you over with my dazzling personality.'

'Of course you can try, but it's not going to happen. Now, I have calls to make, business to take care of.' Inching towards his front door, Ash said, 'So I'm afraid I'm going to have to—'

'OK, I'm off. But I know what I want and I don't give up until I get it.'

As he went into his cottage, Ash wondered why, *why* he couldn't be shamelessly lusted after and chased by Fia?

'**I** had a call from Ash this morning.' Cleo had dropped in on Abbie after work. 'He's being sexually harassed by Georgia.'

'Lucky old Ash.' Abbie carried on basting a chicken.

Cleo switched on the kettle. 'Except he's not the least bit interested. She's not his type. He says—'

'Not that one,' Abbie blurted, stopping her in her tracks as she took a carton of milk from the fridge. 'That's the full-fat.'

'It's OK, I like full-fat.'

'But it's Georgia's. Use the other one, the semi-skimmed, otherwise there won't be enough for her cereal and it'll be my fault.'

Abbie was clearly stressed. Her hair was escaping from its scrunchie, her cheeks were flushed and she was spooning melted butter over the chicken at warp speed. Cleo said carefully, 'Where is she?'

'Out with Tom. Looking at vans. She needs a van for her ironing business so he's buying her one.' Baste, baste, baste.

'Abbie, sit down.'

'I can't, I'm making the dinner.' Prodding the chicken with the basting spoon, Abbie said, 'Except we can't have the stuffing *in* the chicken because that makes it *claggy,* apparently. So we have to cook it in a separate tin and make sure it's all crunchy on the outside, because doing it the other way is just *gross.*'

'Poor you.' She gave Abbie a hug. 'Things'll settle down, though. You'll get used to each other.'

Abbie shook her head. 'I'm trying my best, but I feel like such a spare part. And we were planning to go on a cruise this summer, remember? It's always been my dream. But when I asked Tom about it yesterday, he said it might be a bit awkward now. He doesn't think we can just swan off, the two of us, and leave Georgia here on her own. But if she came along too, we'd have to book another cabin just for her, and that would almost double the price of the holiday, which would mean we couldn't afford it anyway, so basically that's that. We're not going anywhere. But hey, it's probably for the best, because who needs a lovely cruise around the Mediterranean anyway when they can stay here and spend all their hard-earned savings on some crappy old van instead?'

Her voice had spiralled up to bat-squeak level; it was almost painful to hear. Cleo's ears were saved by a car pulling up outside. She glanced out of the window. 'They're back.'

'Right. OK, calm, *calm.*' Taking deep breaths and vigorously fanning herself with the tea towel, Abbie said, 'Sorry, just having a bit of a moment. I'll be fine.'

The front door slammed and there was a squeal of laughter out in the hallway. Then, two voices chorused, 'Hi, honey, I'm ho-me!'

Which was what Tom always said in his jokey way, but before Cleo could smile at Abbie to signal that everything would be OK, they heard Georgia exclaim, 'Oh, wow, you live here too? That's amazing, so do I! Oh, honey, look at us, we're both *home!*'

'Home!' echoed Tom. 'And honey, do you smell cooking?'

'Honey, I do! In fact I think I smell . . . chicken!'

The next moment they burst into the kitchen together, but not before Cleo had seen the look in her sister's eyes. Once, she had been the person Tom called honey. Now, Georgia had managed to hijack that shared endearment and she and Tom were calling each other by that name. And if they hadn't meant to make Abbie feel even more left out, they'd managed it anyway. She minded a lot.

So much for telling Tom last night to be a bit more sensitive. He was clearly besotted with Georgia and unable to help himself.

'Hiya! Is it crunchy stuffing?'

'Yes, I've—'

'But you won't undercook the carrots, will you? I hate crunchy veg.'

Abbie summoned a cheery smile. 'No, don't worry, I won't—'

'Ha! Guess where we've been?' Georgia blurted out, 'To look at vans! And guess what we've done?'

Abbie opened her mouth to guess. 'Did you—'

'WE'VE BOUGHT A VAN!' Launching herself at Tom, Georgia hugged him and kangaroo-jumped around the kitchen. 'Well, my dad bought me a van! Isn't that just the coolest thing ever? Tomorrow morning, as soon as we've got the insurance sorted out, I'm picking up my very own van! And it's blue!'

Abbie was like a nervous bride posing for the photographer, forced to hold her smile for too long. 'Blue! How *lovely* . . .'

OK, enough. 'It wasn't just your dad, though, was it?' Cleo had to say something. 'It was Abbie too. That money came from both of them.'

'Did it? Oh right, I didn't realise.' Shaking her head, Georgia said gaily, 'Thanks, Abbie,' and let go of Tom just long enough to give Abbie a quick embrace and an air-kiss close to her cheek.

'No problem, sweetheart. It's our pleasure.' Abbie gave her an affectionate hug in return, but within seconds Georgia was back at Tom's side, clutching his arm and chattering excitedly about how early tomorrow morning they'd be able to collect the van.

Cleo glanced at Abbie, longing to say something, but Abbie was shaking her head. Never before had she had to work so hard to bite her tongue.

Chapter 7

'GREAT SHOW THIS MORNING,' said Frank, taking Ash's order for chicken curry. 'Loved all that stuff about the nun.'

'Thanks,' Ash replied cheerfully.

'I was laughing so hard I snorted coffee out of my nose.'

'You could go on *Britain's Got Talent* with that,' said Ash.

'Chicken curry for Ash, love.' Frank waylaid Fia as she emerged from the kitchen and Ash felt the muscles in his face begin their familiar contortion. OK, just ignore it, distract her with your trademark lightning wit and dazzling charisma . . .

'How about you? Did I make stuff come out of your nose too?'

Fia stared at him. So did Frank. There was a stunned silence that probably lasted a second or two but felt more like twenty.

'Sorry, sorry.' Ash felt a great woosh of heat shoot up his neck. 'I didn't mean that. We were talking about something on my show this morning . . . the stripping nun . . . don't know if you heard it . . ?'

'No,' said Fia evenly. 'I didn't.'

'Oh. Well, it was funny.' He didn't mean to sound so defensive; it just came out that way, probably as a result of his clenched muscles.

Frank said, 'Fia doesn't listen to your show. She's into Carmen Miranda and all that malarkey.'

A mental image flashed into Ash's mind, of Fia scantily clad and dancing saucily towards him with an explosion of fruit on her head.

'*Carmina Burana*,' Fia corrected him. 'I like classical music.'

God, bloody classical. Ash nodded. 'Yeah? Me too.'

Her look of surprise said it all. 'Really?'

What, did she think he was too thick to appreciate it? Too much of a heathen? 'I do,' said Ash.

'How about opera?'

'*Love* opera.'

'What's your favourite?' There was a note of challenge in her voice.

'*Madame Butterfly*.' Ha, take *that*.

'By?'

'Puccini.' *And that.*

'What else did he compose?'

'*La Bohème. Tosca. Manon Lescaut.*' *With knobs on.*

Grudgingly impressed, Fia said, 'Didn't have you down as an opera lover. I'll bring your chicken curry in a few minutes. Rice or chips?'

Ash loved chips. Only heathens ate their curry with chips. *Telegraph*-reading, opera-loving, sophisticated men of the world—and the women who found them attractive—turned their noses up at people who ordered chips with their curry.

'Rice please,' said Ash.

'Bloody hell,' Frank barked with laughter, 'there's a first. What's up with you, lad? Trying to shift some of that flab?'

By the time Fia arrived with his food, Ash had formulated a plan.

'There you go. Chicken curry with basmati rice.'

'Thanks.' There was an awkward pause while he watched her place a bowl of poppadoms and a ramekin of mango chutney on the table. 'So the thing is, sometimes we get given tickets to . . . er, things. At the radio station. So if I got some for . . . you know, something classical, would you be interested, d'you think?'

Fia paused, as if struggling to work out what he was actually saying. Finally she said, 'Well, that sounds . . . brilliant. Yes, I would. Thanks.'

'Great!' Ash did his best to keep the adrenaline surge under control. 'Thanks . . I mean, right, I'll see what comes in! Probably we'll have some in the next few days . . . because we get sent these things a *lot* . . .' Uh oh, he'd gone from tongue-tied to full-on burble in under ten seconds. 'Better than us giving the tickets away in some stupid phone-in like we usually do. They always end up going to complete idiots anyway, like the drunk guy last week who won seats for *Don Giovanni* and thought he was going to see Jon Bon Jovi . . .'

'Right, well, food to cook, people to serve.' Backing away with a look of bemusement, Fia said, 'Enjoy your curry!'

Parked in the side street, Cleo watched from a distance as Casey Kruger worked his way through the crowd of fans gathered on the pavement by the Hippodrome's stage door.

Although to call them a crowd was pushing it. At ten thirty on a cold and rainy evening in March, there were barely enough to form a gaggle. Cleo counted eleven and most were fans she'd seen before, the diehards who congregated there night after night and revelled in the knowledge that Casey recognised them, sometimes even greeting them by name and making them feel loved in return.

'I'm a celebrity,' Casey announced, falling into the back seat eight minutes later. 'Get me out of here.'

He made the same 'joke' every night. Weaving past the fans as they dispersed, Cleo said, 'Good night?'

'Pretty good.' He heaved a sigh. 'We sang, we danced, they applauded, they cheered, we sang some more.' Pause. 'I tried calling my ex and she hung up on me.'

'Oh dear.' *Good move, ex.*

'Then I tried to call my parents back home, but no reply.'

'Oh.'

'My dad's bald. I mean, completely.' Casey shook his head.

'Is he?' Where was this heading?

'Yup.' He nodded morosely, rubbed his hand through his hair. 'And guess what I saw when I looked in the mirror tonight?'

Cleo negotiated the car through the city-centre traffic. 'Well, if you were looking in the mirror, I'm guessing you saw . . . you?'

'Funny.' Clearly, her attempt at a joke was on a par with his. Sinking back against the leather upholstery, Casey said, 'I saw a bald spot. At the back of my head. Not totally bald.' His hand explored his scalp, searching it out. 'But it's thinning. Definitely starting to go.'

'Well, I can't see anything.' Poor guy; she had to say something to try and cheer him up.

'It's there.' Casey sounded resigned. 'Nature's way of telling you your time's up, you've had your fun, your heart-throb days are over.'

'Oh, come on, it doesn't have to be that bad.'

'No? Eight years ago I was mobbed in the streets. I had a double platinum album and sold out Wembley. And now I'm thirty-four.' Catching Cleo's eye in the rearview mirror, he said, 'OK, thirty-six. And it's all downhill from here.'

The journey from Bristol back to Casey's hotel took twenty minutes. Cleo pulled into the courtyard and he said, 'Sorry, sweetheart. I've been a miserable sod tonight, haven't I?'

'It's allowed.' Who would have thought she could feel sorry for Casey Kruger? He was usually so full of himself.

'It's my parents' wedding anniversary today. That's why I wanted to get hold of them.' He held up his mobile. 'Oh well.'

'You're just feeling a bit homesick. That's normal.'

'Just because it's normal doesn't make it any easier. I don't suppose you'd like to come in for a drink?'

Cleo hesitated. Which would be the best way to say no?

'Go on. If you leave now, I'm going to sit on my own in a corner of the bar, feeling homesick and crying into my beer. But if you stay for one drink,' said Casey, 'just to keep me company for twenty minutes, I'll feel better.'

The windscreen wipers swished back and forth. Rain fell out of the blackness and drummed on the roof of the car.

'Please,' said Casey.

There was a lucky parking space right next to the hotel entrance, with an overhang of honeysuckle that would shield them from the rain on their way in.

'OK.' Cleo executed a swift three-point turn and reversed into the space. 'Just the one drink.'

Except it never worked out that way, did it? One drink was never enough. Certainly not for Casey, who was now on to his fifth bottle of beer and third whisky chaser. Keeping him company, Cleo had drunk orange juice, sparkling water, still water and an Appletiser. It was thirsty work having to sit and listen to a former superstar, now relegated to being your average bog-standard star, complain to you about how crap life was.

'. . . see, I should be settled down by now, married with kids, the whole shebang. I'm thirty-four . . .'

'Thirty-six,' Cleo reminded him.

'That's even worse. And I want to be married, I *do*.' He shook his head sorrowfully. 'But I just can't find the right girl. Everyone I get involved with ends up selling stories about me to the papers.'

This was true. Then again, Casey didn't do himself any favours when it came to selecting girlfriends. The ones he went for were invariably blonde, perma-tanned, micro-skirted and pouty-lipped.

'You need to find yourself a nice girl.' Cleo swirled the ice cubes around her tumbler.

'I know.'

'Who does tapestry, and flower arranging, and knows how to cook.'

'And has a hot body.'

'You see? This could be where you're going wrong.'

Casey looked offended. 'Hey, I have my standards. I don't want some ropey old dog with fat ankles and saggy tits.'

'Is that what the women in your world are divided into? WAGs with boob jobs and ropey old dogs?'

He frowned. 'That's a bit harsh. It's just a case of women I fancy and the ones I don't.' He half smiled. 'Does that sound terrible?'

'So, just out of curiosity, am I a WAG or a dog?'

He looked confused. 'Um . . .'

'OK, would you go out with someone like me? In theory?'

'God . . . well, no. S'pose not. No offence.'

'That's fine, none taken. So that makes me a dog,' said Cleo.

'No, no!'

'It's late.' Cleo rose to leave.

Following her out to the wood-panelled reception hall, Casey said, 'You know what, babe? I've enjoyed this, being with you tonight.'

Babe. Cleo let it slide. 'You mean I'm not bad company for a dog.'

'I told you before. You're not a dog.' Catching hold of her elbow, he swung her round to face him. 'There's something about you, babe. You've got . . . character.'

'Shall I let you into a secret? *I* don't mind being told that, but most girls would be really insulted.'

'I wouldn't say it to most girls. Because their characters don't tend to be that important. But you're different.'

'Yup. I don't wear PVC and have gravity-defying E-cups.'

Casey laughed. 'See? You're good company. Entertaining.' Abruptly leaning back against the wall, he pulled her with him. 'Maybe I've been getting it wrong all these years . . . come here, babe . . .'

His right arm grasped her waist. For a split second his mouth clamped down on hers and alcohol fumes stung the inside of her nose. Damn, she should have seen this coming. Cursing herself for letting it happen, Cleo jerked her face away, slid sideways and ducked under the left arm propped against the wall.

And saw Johnny LaVenture watching her from the other end of the reception hall with a faint, unreadable smile on his face.

'Whoa, hey, where'd you go?' Casey took a steadying step forward and did a bewildered double take.

'Cleo.' Acknowledging her with a nod, Johnny said, 'Fancy bumping into you here.'

Mortified at the thought of what he'd just witnessed, she straightened her jacket. 'I'm just leaving.'

'Someone you know?' Glancing over his shoulder at Johnny, Casey said, 'She's a great girl, this one. A real character.' He gave Cleo a nudge. 'Even if you do have to pay her to keep you company.'

Johnny's eyes glittered. 'How much does she charge?'

Hilarious.

Ignoring him, Cleo turned back to Casey. 'Bye. I'll pick you up at four tomorrow.'

'I'd have paid more,' said Casey. 'You only had to ask.'

Cleo left the hotel, ran down the stone steps and splashed through the puddles to the car.

The tap on the passenger window came as she was pulling out of the parking space under the dripping honeysuckle. Through the rain-dappled glass, his face looked as if it were melting.

She buzzed the window down and Johnny said, 'Hey.'

'Hey.' In the glimmering darkness he had cheekbones like Johnny Depp.

'Off home?'

'Amazingly, yes.'

He didn't say anything, just steadily held her gaze.

'Go on then, get in,' said Cleo.

'Thanks.' He jumped into the seat next to her.

'I'm not a taxi service, you know.'

He grinned. 'You're a friend. That's even better.'

'Hm.' Cleo's stomach curled like a prodded oyster. A friend. Was she really?

'I tried four cab companies but they were all booked up for the next couple of hours. It's my own fault; should have called earlier.' Johnny raked his fingers through his damp hair. 'Never mind. You came along at the perfect time.'

'I have my uses. And just so you know, I don't charge Australian soap actors for my company.' As they drove out through the hotel's impressive iron gates, Cleo said, 'He was drunk.'

'I guessed that, when I saw him kissing you. Sorry,' Johnny raised his hands in self-defence. 'That came out the wrong way. Of course he'd want to kiss you. Who wouldn't?'

OK, what was *that* supposed to mean? 'If you're going to start taking the mickey now, you can jolly well get out and walk.'

'I'm not.' The corners of his mouth twitched. 'Anyhow, you can do better than him. What was all that about PVC and E-cups?'

'Nothing that would interest you. Well,' Cleo amended, 'it probably would, but never mind. What were you doing at the hotel anyway?'

'Having dinner with the Hart-Berkeleys. They want to commission a piece for their stud farm.' He paused. 'Do you have a thing for Casey Kruger?'

'No!'

'Sure?'

'Weren't you watching? I *escaped* when he kissed me.'

Johnny shrugged. 'Could have been playing hard to get.'

'Trust me, I wasn't.'

'Shame. I'd have won my bet.'

So he hadn't forgotten.

'Well, you haven't won.' Cleo's insides were back doing the squirly oyster dance and she had a horrible feeling she knew why. She didn't want Johnny to think she had any designs on Casey Kruger. If she was completely honest, and this was something she wouldn't tell another living soul, there was only one person she'd be interested in having designs on and he was currently sitting beside her in this car.

Oh God, there, she'd admitted it to herself at last. Cleo swallowed with difficulty. Her confused feelings about Johnny LaVenture had settled into something recognisable. He'd always been seriously attractive and charismatic but it had recently begun to dawn on her that personality-wise, he was also actually a lot nicer than she'd always thought. She took shallow breaths, genuinely scared by the turn events had taken. She liked him. A lot. But that still didn't mean it was a sensible idea; he might have good qualities but he was also a—

'Fox,' Johnny observed as a blur of reddish-brown fur darted across the road before diving into the undergrowth.

Which was apt, because he and the fox shared so many traits. They were both clever and confident, rapacious and sly. They knew what they wanted and they didn't stop until it was theirs.

And they usually left a trail of headless chickens in their wake.

Johnny said, 'You've gone quiet.'

'Just thinking.'

'What about?'

'Foxes.'

They'd reached Channings Hill. Seeing as it was still bucketing down, Cleo pulled in through the gates of Ravenswood and drove up to the house.

'Door-to-door service,' Johnny observed.

'Only because it's raining.'

'You're a star. I owe you one.'

The security lights had come on; he was giving her that indecipherable look again. Wiping her cheek, Cleo said self-consciously, 'What's wrong? Do I have something on my face?'

'Yes, you do.'

As she'd climbed into the car a great swathe of wet honeysuckle had brushed against her hair. *Oh God, please don't let it be a slug . . .*

'This.' He raised his hand and with the back of his index finger touched the big freckle beneath her right eye. 'Your beauty spot.'

Phew, not a slug then. 'It's a freckle.'

'D'you know something? I've always liked it.' Johnny nodded slowly. 'That's a great freckle you have there. Makes you look like Pierrot.'

Oh God, he had *no* idea what he was doing to her insides when he touched her face like that.

Either that or he knew exactly what he was doing. Which, let's face it, was infinitely more likely. She concentrated on keeping her breathing even, not betraying her emotions. Letting Johnny know how she felt about him would definitely be a terrible idea.

'OK. Well, bye.'

'Thanks for the lift.'

She managed an easy smile. 'No problem.'

Johnny climbed out of the car, then leaned back in through the open door and said, 'I'd have given you a goodnight kiss, but you didn't seem to enjoy the one you got earlier.'

'Not much, no.'

He grinned. 'I couldn't cope with the rejection.'

Cleo's mouth was dry; her lips were actually tingling at the thought of what she'd just missed. Aloud she said, 'Good job then that you didn't try.'

The doorbell rang while Abbie was in the kitchen. Answering it, she found Fia Newman on the doorstep.

'Hi.' Fia held up a black bin bag. 'Frank's rushed off his feet so he asked me to bring his stuff over for Georgia. Is she in?'

'Yes, I'm here! Come on through!'

Abbie bit her lip; she knew she should be glad Georgia was working, but she was beginning to feel like an intruder in her own home. Showing Fia into the living room, she breathed in the steamy smells of Lenor and spray starch. Freshly ironed shirts, trousers and dresses were festooned around the place, arranged on hangers and dangling from picture rails and pieces of furniture. The radio, tuned to BWR, was blasting out. Piled up on the sofa were bags of clothes still waiting to be dealt with. In the centre of the room, wearing a Snoopy vest top and a pair of stripy pink and white shorts, was Georgia, working away like a thing possessed. True to her word, she had indeed turned out to have a talent for ironing; her work was speedy and meticulous.

'Wow, look at you.' Fia was visibly impressed. 'How much stuff have you got there?'

'Loads.' Beaming, Georgia expertly flipped over the shirt on the ironing board and smoothed out one of the sleeves. 'I'm undercutting all the other ironing services in the area, so it's all flying in. Isn't it great?'

It was great, thought Abbie, so long as you didn't want to sit down with a cup of coffee and watch the TV in peace. The living room was pretty much off limits these days.

'Isn't she amazing?' Fia was in a chatty mood. 'To be honest, I never thought she'd do it. Most teenagers wouldn't be bothered.'

'Oh, she's a hard worker.' Abbie wondered how Fia would feel if Georgia were to set up her ironing board in the middle of the pub.

'Right, where shall I put Frank's stuff?'

'Over there by the fireplace. I'll have it all done by tomorrow night. Abbie, can you do a label?'

Abbie reached for the roll of sticky labels, scribbled Frank's name on one and slapped it onto his bag.

'You're going to be working all day and night at this rate.' Fia watched as Georgia finished a shirt, lovingly hung it up and pulled the next one from the basket at her feet. 'Oh, I know who that belongs to!'

Georgia gave the crumpled shirt an ecstatic hug. 'It's Ash's. His body has been inside it. This material has had physical contact with his *chest*.'

Abbie said by way of apology, 'She has a bit of a thing about Ash.'

'I know.' Fia looked baffled. 'Everyone in Channings Hill knows.'

'It's not a "bit of a thing".' Georgia lovingly wrapped the arms of the shirt around her neck and dreamily began to dance along to the radio. 'It's true love.'

'One-sided love,' Abbie pointed out. 'Ash isn't interested.'

'*Yet*. But I'm going to win him over. With my wit and my charm and my dazzling skill with an iron.'

Fia was clearly amused. 'It's not as if he's even good-looking. He can't afford to be too picky.'

'Exactly.' Georgia nodded in agreement. 'I've already told him that.'

The trouble with having a bit of a clear-out downstairs and hauling three bin bags of assorted clutter up into the loft was that you never actually dumped them and came straight back down again. While you were there, you always somehow managed to spot something you hadn't seen for years and get sidetracked.

Cleo, sitting cross-legged with her back to a bundle of blankets, had been up in the loft for the past two hours. She'd looked through a suitcase of her dad's favourite clothes. Losing her mum at eleven had been devastating, but she knew how lucky she'd been to have her loving, gentle father, who had become two parents rolled into one and done such a good job, along with Abbie, of bringing her up. One day she'd feel able to donate his old woolly jumpers and faded checked shirts to the charity shop, but not quite yet.

She had then examined a cardboard box containing all the books she had adored as a child; OK, the charity shop definitely couldn't have these because one day she planned on reading them to her own children, whether they wanted to hear them or not.

Ouch, her foot had gone numb. Cleo shifted position, bent forward and reached for the next packet of photos in the trunk in front of her.

This was what had kept her up here for the past hour. Her father had never gone anywhere without a camera. He'd taken endless photographs throughout her childhood and at the time she'd wished he wouldn't. Back then, it had been a source of embarrassment and shame.

But almost two decades later, the embarrassment factor had faded and she was glad he'd done it. Village life had been captured to a T and it was brilliant to see everyone as they'd looked all those years ago. Sorting through the snaps, she came to one of herself with an ill-advised high fringe, showing off her new lemon-yellow dungarees in the back garden. Flipping on, she came to one featuring Abbie and Tom looking young and in love, and—ha!—there was Johnny, in jeans and a dodgy striped T-shirt, fooling around with a couple of friends. Next was one of herself—oh, good grief—wearing a homemade hula skirt and crepe flowers in her hair for the fancy dress competition. Then another of Johnny stretched out on the grass, feeding crisps to the vicar's yappy Jack Russell terrier.

Her mobile burst into life and she answered it.

'Hi, it's me.' Her pulse quickened; there was no mistaking Johnny's playful drawl.

'This is a coincidence. I've just been looking at old photos of you!' Hastily Cleo added, 'Not in a stalkery way.'

'How did I look?'

'You've had better hairstyles.'

'And how did you look?'

'Stunning, of course.'

He laughed. 'Listen, remember you liked my new dining room?'

'Um . . . yes.' When he'd shown her over his house the other week, she'd fallen in love with the shade of paint he'd chosen for the walls, a rich, velvety topaz yellow.

'Well, I've just been sorting through junk in the garage and I've found another ten-litre tin of the stuff. I knew we'd ordered too much, I just didn't realise how much. And you said you were thinking of redoing your living room, so I wondered if you wanted it.'

'Great, thanks!'

Ten litres of good-quality paint, for free? Brilliant.

'If you're at home, I can bring it on over.'

'I'm in the attic. It's easier to get into than it is to climb out of,' said Cleo, 'so give me five minutes. But the door's on the latch.'

Johnny didn't hesitate. 'In that case, just stay where you are. I'm on my way.'

Three minutes later Cleo heard the front door open and close, then footsteps on the stairs. Peering over the edge of the hatch, she said, 'Where's the paint?'

'I left it in the hall. What are you doing up there?'

'Looking at old stuff.' Cleo let go of the photo in her hand and watched it twirl down towards him like a leaf. Catching it, Johnny studied the snap of himself and shook his head.

'I was fourteen. God, look at the state of me.' He grinned and climbed onto the chair beneath the hatch, then expertly—impressively—hauled himself up into the loft and gazed around. 'You've got a lot of stuff to look at.'

'I've been here for ages.'

'I can see why. It's nice up here. Cosy.'

'I think I have abandonment issues. I can't bring myself to throw anything away.' Bending her head to avoid the slanted beams and the forty-watt light bulb, Cleo made her way back to where she'd been sitting before. She patted the rolled-up blanket next to her. 'Come and have a look at the photos. I daren't take this lot downstairs; they'll never get back up here again.'

The next thirty minutes flew by. She and Johnny may not have been friends during their teenage years but they'd known all the same people. He exclaimed with delight as he recognised places and events from their shared-but-separate pasts. There were assorted Christmases, bonfire-night parties, school sports days, Badminton Horse Trials . . .

'Now that's what I call style,' said Johnny.

Cleo looked at the photograph of herself on her thirteenth birthday, proudly cutting a star-shaped, Smartie-studded cake and evidently delighted by her choice of puff-sleeved purple blouse and green-and-purple checked waistcoat.

'I dread to think what I had on on the bottom half.' In the photo she was standing behind a table but Cleo had a distinct memory of orangey-brown trousers from C&A. Oh well, he didn't need to know that.

'Ha!' Johnny spluttered with laughter as the damn things were revealed in the next photo.

'Fine, you weren't always so sartorial yourself.' Retaliating, she flipped through an earlier batch until she found the one of him leading the fancy dress parade at the summer fete. Aged ten or eleven, he was wearing dark-brown tights, a brown turtleneck jumper and a hat decorated with huge branches and swathes of greenery.

Pointing to them, Cleo said, 'Tights.'

'I was a *tree*.'

'With transvestite tendencies.'

'I try to keep those under control these days.'

'You looked ridiculous.'

'But I came third. I won a book token.' Pause. 'I got to keep the tights.'

She groaned aloud at the next photo of herself eating candy floss, with pink gunk around her mouth and bits of it attractively stuck in her hair. 'Look at the state of me there.'

'Ah, but you've improved with age.' Johnny was half smiling. 'In fact you've scrubbed up pretty well.'

'Shut up.' Cleo squirmed.

'You don't take compliments very easily, do you? But it's true.'

And she'd been doing so well up until now. Hopefully he couldn't tell how fast her heart was beating. Casually she said, 'Maybe it depends on who's giving them.'

'You're a beautiful girl. That's a fact. Trust me.' His green eyes glittered with amusement. 'I'm an artist.'

Ha, a smarty-pants con artist, more like. But even as she was thinking this, her body was reacting to his voice.

Johnny's voice softened. 'I mean it. I don't think you have any idea how attractive you are.'

For the life of her she couldn't speak. If he were to reach out and kiss her at this moment in time, Cleo knew she would kiss him back. Last time, in the car, it hadn't happened. But now they were teetering on the brink of the next stage. Every inch of her skin was prickling with adrenaline; she wanted it to happen and there was only so much anticipation a girl could take. Up here in this shadowy, dusty, cobwebby attic, it seemed as if he was about to make his move at last. And she wasn't going to stop him. OK, maybe it wasn't the most romantic of locations but—

Dee-de-deee, da da da deeee dah!

Cleo froze. Sometimes, just sometimes, didn't you just wish mobile phones had never been invented?

In her ear, Johnny murmured, 'You could always not answer it.'

'I have to. One of the other drivers wasn't well this morning, so I'm on standby.' Cleo winced when she saw Grumpy Graham's name pop up on the screen. She pressed reply, crossed her fingers and said, 'Hi, what's happening?'

'Don's gone down with food poisoning, big time. He can't do the Edinburgh trip. And they need picking up in forty minutes so you'll have to get your skates on.' Graham's tone was brusque.

Her heart sank. There was no point arguing or trying to wriggle out of it. She had a job to do and that was that. 'Fine, no problem.'

Next to her, Johnny mouthed, 'Job?'

Cleo nodded.

'Shame,' he said under his breath.

Which was just about the understatement of the year. Cleo said, 'Where are the clients now?'

'The Marriott Hotel.'

The Marriott was the five-star hotel in the city centre, which at this time of day meant she had roughly five minutes in which to shower off the dust and change into her uniform. Scrambling to her feet, not even daring to signal regret with her eyes, Cleo glanced at Johnny and said into the phone, 'I'm on my way.'

'I've been given a couple of tickets,' said Ash, 'for *Madame Butterfly* next Tuesday at the Pargeter Theatre in Clifton.'

'Are you serious?' Fia's face lit up. 'That's my favourite opera!'

He'd had an inkling it might be.

'It's a touring production. They're supposed to be pretty good.'

'That's *fantastic*. Ash, thanks so much, this is really kind of you!'

'The thing is, I have to review the show for the radio station, that's why they've given us the tickets.'

'Oh.' Fia's change of expression was like a knife between his ribs. 'I see.'

'But it's still *Madame Butterfly*.' His mouth was dry; he couldn't fall to his knees and beg her to go. But it was obviously not what she wanted to do.

She hesitated and he could see her wrestling with her conscience. Thankfully good manners won out and, mustering a brave smile, she said, 'Well, that'll be great. Thanks for inviting me.'

'Yes.' Ash mentally kicked himself; once he got tongue-tied, he couldn't get even the simplest response right. Belatedly he said, 'No problem.' Jesus, what was *wrong* with him? This was his big chance; he'd actually managed to trick Fia into going out on a date with him.

Despite everything, Ash couldn't help feeling a squiggle of excitement and hope. It might not be much. OK, it *wasn't* much. *But it was a start.*

Chapter 8

THERE WAS A JOLLY feature on dance aerobics on the TV and Abbie joined in as she vacuumed the carpet. Turning up the volume so she could hear the music above the roar of the Hoover, she danced and sang along with the instructor and knocked the Hoover against the metal legs of the ironing board that was a permanent feature in the living room.

And if she was being noisy, well, so what? It was almost lunch time. Georgia should be up by now.

'And stretch and *bend* and stretch and *bend*,' yelled the fitness instructor on TV. 'And *reach* and twist and *reach* and twist those hips, that's it! Now *stretch* and *reach* and *bend* and—'

'WAAAH!' Abbie let out a shriek as a hand touched her shoulder.

'Sorry, sorry, I didn't mean to frighten you.' Georgia pulled an apologetic face as Abbie pressed the mute button on the TV.

'I thought you were still in bed.' Abbie flushed; had she looked completely ridiculous? Had Georgia been laughing at her?

'I've got loads to do. I was up ironing till three o'clock this morning.'

Hadn't they all known it; the irregular clunk-clunk of the iron and the burble of the TV had driven Abbie demented when she'd been trying to get to sleep.

'Anyway, just to let you know I'm off now. I've got deliveries, pick-ups and a trip to the printers for more business cards, so I won't be back before tea time.'

'OK, fine.' Was it wrong to feel this delighted at the prospect of having the house to herself on her day off?

'Oh, and we're out of milk, so you might want to get some more. Bye, then. See you later!'

Abbie bit her tongue until Georgia had packed the completed ironing into the van and driven off. *This* was what drove her insane, the utter thoughtlessness. In the kitchen, she found the empty milk carton and a drained glass sitting in the sink. This was teenagers for you.

Oh well, she'd finish the cleaning first, then change out of her track-suit bottoms before heading on over to the shop. Reaching for the remote control, Abbie de-muted the TV and switched the Hoover back on. Seeing as it now promised to be an extra-nice, home-alone day, she might treat herself and see if Glynis had any toffee doughnuts.

Straightening up after Hoovering under the sofa, she glimpsed a flash of dark red through the front window as a car pulled up outside.

Her stomach did a little flip because it was Des's car and the faint awkwardness between them was still there, even if no one else was aware of it. She switched off the vacuum cleaner and watched him climb out of the driver's seat. OK, there was absolutely no need to be nervous. He'd dropped by to ask her to swap shifts with someone, that was all. They saw each other at work every day and it had been months since . . . the *thing* that had happened.

Forcing herself to sound and behave in a completely normal fashion—and God knows, she should be used to doing it by now—Abbie opened the door and said cheerfully, 'Hi, Des! Let me guess, Magda wants me to do Sunday for her so she can have loads to drink at her neighbour's party on Saturday night.'

'No.' Following her into the house, Des ran his fingers through his hair and shook his head. 'I just needed to see you. We have to talk.'

The fading anxiety did an abrupt about-turn. 'What about?'

A muscle was twitching in his forehead. 'I love you.'

The vacuum cleaner nozzle dropped from her hand. 'What?'

'I'm sorry, I can't help it. I can't stop thinking about our night together.' He moved towards her. 'I've tried, but I just can't. I've never felt like this before, about *anyone* . . .'

'Des, I'm married!'

'I know, but he doesn't love you as much as I do. He *can't*. Abbie, I want us to be together. Just give me a chance.'

'No, no, I've told you before, that was just one night.' The fear had her by the throat now, but it was mixed with annoyance. 'You know why it happened, and it's never going to happen again, *ever*.'

'Look, you're not even giving me a chance.' Desperation made him reckless. 'I can make you happy, we could live—'

'*Shhh!*' Abbie froze and held out a hand, her skin prickling with terror. Something had just creaked upstairs. But how could there be anyone up there? Until Des had arrived she'd been alone in the house.

Oh shit, shit, there it was again. And this time Des had heard it too. Nausea rose in her chest and perspiration broke out as she turned and went out into the hall. There was no one on the stairs. Nor on as much of the landing as she could see from this angle.

But the shadow on the landing wall was human-shaped.

Never before had Abbie prayed so hard for a burglar. Oh God, please let the figure on the landing be a complete stranger who'd climbed up the drainpipe and broken into the house . . . he could take her jewellery, as many electrical items as he could carry. If he needed a hand she'd even help him. Her voice tight with fear, she said, 'Who's that up there?'

The shadow moved and a voice said, 'Me.'

Abbie gazed up the stairs at Georgia. Georgia in turn looked first at her, then at Des standing in the living room doorway. Abbie said, 'Des, you can go.'

He shook his head. 'I'm sorry.'

'I bet you are.' Georgia's expression was stony.

'Look, this isn't what it sounds like.' So many explanations and excuses were tumbling around inside Abbie's head, she couldn't coherently voice any of them.

'Isn't it? Well, that's a relief, because from where I'm standing it sounds like you're having an affair with your boss who's in love with you.'

'Des. Tell her it's not true.'

Des looked like a rabbit caught in headlights. 'But she heard me say it. I *do* love you.'

'*Out.*' Trembling all over, Abbie yanked open the front door. When he'd gone, she closed it behind her and eyed Georgia again. 'And what are you doing here anyway? You left the house twenty minutes ago.'

'I wasn't spying on you, OK?' Georgia's arms were tightly folded, her tone defiant. 'I was a couple of miles down the road when I realised I'd left the drop-off list on my bed. And on the way back I thought I'd stop in at the shop and pick up a carton of milk, to save you the bother. So that's what I did. I actually thought I was doing a nice thing.' As she carried on, she stomped down the staircase. '*Then* I thought how about if I parked behind the house, sneaked in through the back door and left the milk out by the kettle so you'd get a huge surprise when you went into the kitchen? Because you wouldn't have a clue how it had got there and it'd be like the fairies had left it for you! So I did that too, and you were still busy hoovering away, you didn't hear me come in, and then I went upstairs to pick up my list.' Pausing for breath at last, she concluded evenly, 'Which is when your boyfriend turned up.'

Abbie had never felt more sick. 'He's not my boyfriend, you don't—'

'Oh please, are you seriously going to tell me I don't understand? I've spent my whole life watching it happen! My mother was either cheating on men or having them cheat on her. That's why I loved it that you and my dad were a proper married couple who trusted each other and I thought that was fantastic. Well, more fool me.' Georgia's blue eyes, so unnervingly like Tom's, registered disdain. 'Because you're exactly the same as my mother, cheating on my dad behind his back. And that is just . . . *disgusting*.'

'OK, stop.' Abbie's voice rose in panic. 'Stop right there. I *haven't* cheated on Tom and I'm *not* disgusting!'

'Hello? I heard it with my own ears . . . you and your boss spent the night together!'

'Nothing happened!'

Georgia looked repulsed. 'Dad's going to be devastated.'

Oh God. 'I'm going to explain everything and you're going to listen. Because I never meant any of this to happen and it's not my fault.'

'You're sounding more and more like my mum.'

'If this is anyone's fault,' Abbie retaliated, 'it's your mother's.'

Ten minutes later, Georgia knew everything. And while she was less angry than before, she was nowhere near ecstatic. Frankly, Abbie couldn't blame her. She'd been forced to share information neither of them was comfortable with. There had been kissing, yes. In a double bed, yes. But no sex, absolutely not. So no actual physical betrayal.

'OK, so if you came home from work and went upstairs and found Dad in bed with some other woman, you'd be fine with that, would you?'

'No, no, of course I wouldn't. But it happened only because I thought Tom had been unfaithful to me. I was distraught. And I wouldn't *ever* have contacted Des.' Abbie was vehement; how could she persuade Georgia to believe her? 'He just happened to phone . . . and I was in such a state, he came over. But I didn't cheat on Tom. And he doesn't need to know what happened that night. I love him. More than anything. And he loves me. It would break his heart.' Her fingers digging into her palms, she pleaded, 'It's best if you don't tell him.'

Georgia twirled a strand of hair round and round her thumb. She studied Abbie in silence for several seconds before finally speaking.

'You'd better be telling me the truth.'

'I am.' Scarcely able to breathe, Abbie nodded then shook her head. 'I never wanted any of this to happen.'

'What are you going to do about your boss?'

'Nothing. You heard what I was telling him. Des knows I'm not interested in him. He'll get over it.' She prayed Des would be discreet.

Georgia gazed down at the floor. Finally she looked up. 'OK, I won't say anything to Dad.'

A lump expanded in Abbie's throat. 'Good.' *Good* was the understatement of the year. 'Thanks,' she added, even though she knew Georgia was doing it for Tom's sake, not hers.

Georgia's don't-thank-me shrug was a nerve-wracking echo of her father's. 'Anyway, I'd better get going. Lots to do.' Still clutching her van keys, she moved towards the door.

'See you later.' Spotting the condensation-dotted carton next to the kettle, Abbie said hurriedly, 'Oh, and thanks for the milk, that was really thoughtful of you. Um, so what would you like for dinner tonight? Tell me what you're in the mood for and I'll cook it.'

Georgia gave her a pitying look. 'I think you have to learn that the first rule of lying is to act normally. Because if you suddenly start being extra-nice to me, Dad's going to be suspicious.'

'Sorry.' It was both a salutary lesson and a slap in the face. Abbie glanced down at her hands, which were still shaking.

Pausing in the doorway, Georgia turned and said, 'Can you make the spicy prawn thing?'

'Come in. Oh, hello.' Des coloured when he saw who had knocked on the door to his office. 'Come on in.'

He waited until she'd closed the door behind her then said, 'Look, I'm sorry about yesterday.'

He looked as if he hadn't slept all night. Well, welcome to the club. Abbie said, 'So you keep telling me. But you have to promise you won't come to the house again *ever*.'

'I promise.' He nodded unhappily. 'What happened?'

'Georgia's not going to say anything to Tom. For now. But last night was just . . . horrible.' A sob escaped Abbie's chest without any warning; the strain of pretending everything was normal had been agonising. She'd spent the evening cooking dinner, washing up afterwards, then cleaning the kitchen. When Tom had innocently asked, during the meal, if she knew if Des was signing up for the cricket team this year, Georgia's stony gaze across the table had caused her stomach to clench with fear.

How on earth was she going to keep this up for the next week . . . month . . . year?

'Don't cry.' Hurriedly patting his pockets and failing to come up with a handkerchief, Des yanked open the desk drawer and pulled out a Burger King serviette instead. 'Here, use this.'

'I can't b-believe she found out like that. It's just a nightmare.' Abbie wiped her eyes with the thin, scratchy paper. 'She said she thought me and Tom were happy together, she couldn't believe I'd done something like that to him. She's on his side all the way.'

'Do you want me to talk to her?'

'God, are you mad? No way! She heard what you said, all that stuff about . . . you know . . .'

'Loving you? I said it and I meant it.' Des stayed calm. 'But I won't tell Tom. And I won't tell him about our night together either. Whatever happens from now on, it's up to you. If he hears it from anyone, you'll know it won't have been me.'

Was she stupid to trust him? Abbie decided she knew Des well enough to believe what he said. He was an honourable man who wouldn't betray her.

'We're just going to carry on as if nothing's happened.' She wondered if this was actually possible, but what other choice did they have? 'I was going to hand in my notice here, but then everyone would want to know why, and I can't think of a reason.'

'Good.' Des shook his head. 'I don't want you to leave. We'll get through this, you'll see.'

OK, this wasn't funny. As if he didn't have enough to contend with already.

Ow, ow, fucking *ow*.

Right, just breathe slowly. That's it, in and out, you can do it—

OWWWW!

Ash caught sight of his reflection in the mirror and clutched the shower door for support. He looked like Quasimodo. A fat, pale, pathetic, naked Quasimodo.

Carefully, inch by inch, Ash eased himself out of the shower cubicle in a stooped, Neanderthal way. You saw the government health warnings on packets of cigarettes and on all those drinks ads on TV, but it never occurred to the bloody government, did it, to slap stickers on bottles of shampoo?

Warning: dropping this in the shower and bending down to pick it up could seriously damage your health.

Not to mention your bendability.

And it had to happen today of all days, less than four hours before embarking on the date of a lifetime. At seven thirty he was due to pick Fia up from the Hollybush, drive her into Bristol and sit next to her through a two-hour performance of *Madame Butterfly*. He'd been counting down the minutes, so excited he hadn't even been able to eat anything today.

And now he'd gone and put his bloody back out. Typical. Gingerly wrapping himself in his dressing gown, he made his way ultra-slowly downstairs. Every step was agony. Right, just keep moving and maybe things would improve, the muscle spasm would somehow loosen up.

After twenty minutes the pain was, if anything, worse. Already aware of the outcome of the conversation he was about to have, out of desperation Ash gave it a shot anyway.

'I'm sorry,' drawled the receptionist who answered the phone, 'if you want to see the doctor, you have to phone this number between eight thirty and eight fifty in the morning.'

She didn't sound remotely sorry.

'But something just went in my back.' Shit, it even hurt to *speak*. 'At eight thirty this morning I was fine.'

'In that case, try calling us tomorrow morning and we'll see if we can fit you in then.'

Try being the operative word, because the line was usually jammed with desperate sick people dialling over and over again.

'But I need to see someone today. It's urgent.' Ash spoke through gritted teeth.

'Can you move at all? Or are you completely immobile?'

'I can move a bit. But it's very painful.' *And I have a date tonight, you hideous old bag. When did you last have one of those, eh?*

'If you can move, you can wait till tomorrow. Or if you really want to be a nuisance, get yourself off to Casualty. We can't help you.'

Which kind of made you wonder why she'd bothered picking up the phone in the first place. And now she'd ended the call, not even allowing him the satisfaction of hanging up on her.

Hissing air out between his teeth, Ash inched his way over to the kitchen drawer that doubled as a medicine cabinet. He searched through the jumble of antacids, Elastoplasts, cans of Deep Heat and antiseptic spray, Night Nurse, sun cream . . . hang on, Night Nurse? That had pain stuff in it, right? He scanned the side of the bottle. Contains paracetamol.

Negotiating the childproof top took some doing and increased the spasm in his back but he breathed through the pain—God, this had to be worse than childbirth—and glugged down a couple of mouthfuls.

By five thirty he'd ordered a cab to take them to the theatre, taken another *small* sip of Night Nurse and spent fifteen minutes getting his boxer shorts on. One final desperate trawl through the medicine drawer came up with a lone orange tablet left over from his mother's last visit when she'd been over here recuperating from her neck-lift, eyebag-reduction and whole-body lipo. She was a mass consumer of painkillers. Ash peered at the tablet, badly in need of help.

But since he wasn't stupid, he phoned his mother first.

'Mum? Those orange tablets you were taking when you were here last year. What were they for?'

'Hello, darling! Goodness, let me see, orange, orange . . . were they oval or circular?'

'Oval.'

'Glossy or matt?'

'Um, glossy.'

'Oh, I know, something beginning with B . . . God, listen to me, memory like a thing with holes in! Darling, why do you want to know?'

'There's a leftover one here. And I've done my back in,' said Ash. 'I'm desperate.'

'Oh, go on, darling, take it. Those things got me through post op. So how are you otherwise? Lost any weight yet?'

'No.' He swallowed the tablet.

'Thought any more about liposuction?'

'Funnily enough, I haven't.'

'Now, now, darling, don't get huffy, you should give it a go! They sucked *gallons* of fat out of me!'

'Bye, Mum.' Ash hung up the phone before she could start interrogating him about girlfriends.

'**P**oor you.' Fia said. 'Are you sure you don't want to cancel?'

'No, no, I'll be fine. Can't let the radio station down.' Ash shook his head. 'They need the review. Anyway, nearly there now.' In truth, the pain was less than it had been earlier. The various pills had done a good job of numbing it. They appeared to have numbed his brain too, relaxing him. Which helped. He was actually thinking of witty things to say to Fia, which was a first. He couldn't always be bothered to *say* them, mind you, but at least they were there in his head.

Oh well. Never mind, at least they were having a conversation of sorts, which had to be better than sitting in awkward silence. A bump in the road made him flinch. 'I really hope this isn't the early stages of labour. I don't want to give birth in the middle of the theatre.' Damn, that wasn't funny. Why had he said that?

Humouring him, Fia said, 'Could be messy.'

'And I'd have to call it Butterfly. Which would be awful,' said Ash. 'Especially if it was a boy.'

When they reached the theatre he eased himself out of the back of the cab with Fia's help.

'Here, hold on to my arm,' she offered, which was an excellent idea.

'God, I should have thought of this ages ago!'

Fia looked perplexed. 'Thought of what?'

'Nothing.' Together they made their way verrrrry slooooowly up the steps. 'We're like a couple of geriatrics. Which probably means I'm not about to have a baby. Don't worry,' said Ash to the couple ahead of them who had turned round to look at him, 'I used to be a woman, had a sex change, but now I'm thinking of going back again. That's the trouble with us females, eh? Can't make up our minds.'

'Look, we don't have to do this.' Fia stopped in her tracks. 'You seem a bit . . .'

'Thingy. I seem a bit thingy. I know, and I apologise, but I promise you I'm OK to do this.' He turned and winked at the elderly woman behind him. 'And I'm not drunk, if that's what you're wondering, madam. It's probably just the drugs.'

Now it was the elderly woman's turn to look shocked. Fia said firmly, 'He's not on drugs.'

'Hey, I like it when you defend me. Very masterful. Ha, or mistressful!'

Quite sexy, in fact.' Dimly aware that he'd meant only to think this but appeared to have said it out loud, Ash made amends by nodding at the woman and patting Fia's sleeve. 'She's a very good cook, you know. Oscar-winning roast potatoes.'

When they finally reached their seats, Fia whispered, '*Are* you on drugs?'

She was looking beautiful tonight. 'No. Just, you know, painkillers.'

'Strong ones?'

'I think so. But I'm fine.'

The man in the seat beside him said, '*Sshhhh.*'

'What? Excuse me?' Gesturing to the crimson velvet curtains, Ash said, 'The show hasn't even started yet.'

'You're being a bit loud,' Fia murmured in his ear.

God, that felt fantastic. She could murmur in his ear for ever and it wouldn't be long enough. Turning to the man on his right, Ash said loftily, 'I'm allowed to be loud. I'm the arts critic for *The Sunday Times*. So basically,' he added, 'I can make as much noise as I like.'

Distant music soaring in the distance . . . high voices warbling . . . and emotion, lots and lots of emotion . . . *ow* . . . more music . . . different voices . . . heart-rending . . . *ouch* . . . and now the faraway music was reaching a crescendo . . . the sound of clapping . . . cheering . . . getting louder . . . oh for God's sake, *shut up* . . .

'What? What's going on?' His eyes snapping open, Ash attempted to jerk upright in his seat. A spasm of pain gripped his spine, hurling him back. Bewildered by the applause, he said, 'Is it starting now?'

'It's finished.'

'*What?*'

Fia was busy clapping. 'Wasn't it fantastic?'

Oh no, don't say he'd missed the whole thing, *please* don't say that. But then why was Fia asking him if he thought it had been fantastic?

Then he saw that she'd been addressing the woman on her left, not him at all. Giving her a nudge, Ash said, 'Did I . . . um, fall asleep?'

'Yes.'

'Oh *God.*'

'And you snored.'

'No!' He went hot and cold with shame.

The man to his right said drily, 'Oh yes.'

Ash's heart shrivelled further still when he saw the small wet patch on the shoulder of Fia's cream jacket. 'Don't tell me I did that to you?'

Fia looked down at the damp mark. 'Oh yes, you dribbled a bit. Doesn't matter.'

He'd leaned against her and rested his head on her shoulder. It was practically his lifetime's ambition. And he hadn't even been aware of it.

'I'm so sorry.' To add insult to injury, the pain that had been effectively numbed earlier was now back with a vengeance. He needed Fia's help to stand upright as the audience began to make their way out of the theatre.

Fia said she wasn't bothered about her jacket; it was machine washable and the production of *Madame Butterfly* had been excellent. It might not have been Ash's finest hour, but it wasn't his fault he'd fallen asleep. And he'd been so funny before the performance, completely different from the way he usually was with her.

'Now she tells me.' They'd reached the foyer and Ash had switched his phone back on. Having briefly scrutinised it, he showed Fia the text on the screen: 'Remembered at last—the orange one is a tranquilliser. VV strong!!! Love, Mum xx.'

'Is that what you took?' Fia laughed at the expression on his face. 'Serves you right for pinching other people's tablets.'

'She told me it would help with the pain.'

'Well, it certainly did that. You slept right through it.'

'Fia? Is that *you*?'

Fia stopped dead, the little hairs at the back of her neck prickling at the sound of a voice she instantly recognised.

She turned to face her mother-in-law. 'Hello, Vivien. How are you?'

'Pretty good, pretty good. Busy training up the new assistant in the shop.' This was one of Vivien's Pointed Remarks, emphasising the inconvenience Fia's departure had caused. 'And Will's doing *very* well. Got himself a lovely girlfriend, she's an absolute joy!' This meant that she, Fia, had always been hard work and probably unworthy of her beloved son. Vivien's miss-nothing, lilac-shaded eyes flickered over Ash and widened in recognition. 'Are you the person who fell asleep during the performance? The one who was snoring?'

'I may have dozed off during the boring bits,' said Ash.

Vivien gazed at him askance. 'Gracious me, and you two are together? Fia, is this your new . . . boyfriend?' As she said it, she took in every detail, from Ash's slightly glazed expression to his crumpled jacket, from his in-need-of-a-comb hair to the straining buttons on his shirt. Her mouth began to twitch, as if she couldn't wait to contact Will and tell him what a physically inferior character his wife had hooked up with. The clear inference was: *After my son, is this the best you can do?*

And Ash, who had never even met her before, knew exactly what was going through her mind.

'Actually, Fia just came along as a favour to me.' Having assumed a very upper-class drawl, he now stuck out his hand for Vivien to shake. 'How d'you do? My name's Humphrey Twistleton-Jakes. Pretty dull production this evening, didn't you think?'

'We should go,' said Fia. 'Our car's waiting outside.' Smiling at Vivien as they moved past her, she indicated Ash and said proudly, 'He's the arts critic of *The Sunday Times*.'

Passing the village shop on her way to work, Cleo saw Johnny's car parked outside it. Oh God, the feelings hadn't gone away; if anything, they were stronger than ever. Jamming her foot on the brake, she pulled up and gave her pounding heart a moment to calm down.

Well, calm down a *bit*. OK, just be casual. Walk into the shop, pick up a newspaper or a packet of mints or something, then glance over and spot Johnny and look surprised. Easy.

Pushing through the door just as it was pulled open from the other side, she catapulted into Johnny's chest and let out a squeak like a mouse caught in a trap.

'Whoops.' Steadying her, he said, 'Cleo, hi. How are you?'

'Fine! You? Been busy? Haven't seen you for a while? Oh look, milk!' *God, had she ever sounded more like a complete cretin?*

'I've been away in—'

'Away? Oh, fantastic!'

'Not really. One of my aunts has had a stroke.'

'Oh no!' She'd last seen the aunts teetering around on walking sticks at Lawrence's funeral. They were both in their late seventies and had looked incredibly fragile back then. And they both lived at the same nursing home. Remembering that their names were Clarice and Barbara, Cleo said, 'Which one?'

'Barbara. She's the older sister.' There were dark shadows under Johnny's eyes, as though he hadn't slept for a week. 'She's still unconscious in the ITU at the Norfolk and Norwich University Hospital. It's touch and go at the moment.' He looked exhausted but seemed pleased to see her. 'Look, you couldn't spare ten minutes, could you? Come over for a quick coffee and a chat?'

'Of course I can!' Cleo checked her watch, did some rapid calculations in her head. 'I've just got to pick up Casey Kruger and get him to Bristol. I can be back in an hour and a half.'

But Johnny was already shaking his head. 'I'll be gone by then. This is just a flying visit to pick up some things. I need to get back to Norfolk as soon as I can.'

Bugger. Cleo briefly considered persuading Casey to get off his lazy celebrity backside and make his own way to the Hippodrome, but she couldn't let him down. 'Sorry, I can't come over now. I have to work.'

Again.

Johnny's smile was rueful. 'Shame. Oh well, never mind. I'll see you when I see you.'

A quick pat on the arm and he was gone. Cleo watched his car disappear from view. Poor Johnny. Poor Aunt Barbara.

But on the bright side, at least it meant he hadn't been busy conducting a torrid affair with someone infinitely more gorgeous than the freckly female chauffeur from across the green, whose idea of a seductive location was a dusty, cobwebby attic.

'I'm going to make you an offer you can't refuse,' said Georgia.

Her eyes were bright and she was wearing a tight purple T-shirt with 'Dyslexics of the world, UNTIE!' emblazoned across the chest. She was also holding something behind her back.

'Or I'll end up swimming with the fishes?' Switching off the ignition, Ash slowly slid his legs out of the car. He was on the mend but it still hurt. A lot.

'Fishes?' Georgia wrinkled her nose as she jumped down from his garden wall. 'You don't say fishes. It's *fish*. Anyway, I was listening to your show this morning. And I've got something for you.'

'Oh yes?'

'Something you're going to *love*.'

'This doesn't bear thinking about.'

'Don't be so grumpy! OK if I come in?'

'Can I stop you?' Ash clutched the fence for support as she followed him up the path.

'Shouldn't think so, not in your state.' When he'd unlocked the front door she danced past him into the house and said triumphantly, 'Ta-daaa!'

She was holding up her surprise, a small bottle of liquid.

'If that's white wine, it's not nearly enough.'

'It isn't wine. Take off your jacket.'

'Excuse me?'

'And your T-shirt.'

'Why?'

'Because I heard you going on about your bad back. And I am brilliant at giving massages. Not the mucky kind, strictly above-board. But I promise you, you won't regret it. I'm fabulous.'

Ash dropped his car keys on to the table. It sounded like the worst idea he'd ever heard.

Then again, his back was still killing him and there was no denying a massage would be nice.

'Go on then.' He took off his jacket. 'Where do you want me?'

'Upstairs on the bed.'

He caught the glint in her eye. 'Not a chance.'

'Spoilsport.' Grinning, Georgia said, 'Fine then, we'll do it on the living room floor instead.'

She brought a bath towel downstairs, laid it on the carpet and fastened her hair back in a loose plait. In too much pain even to contemplate sucking his stomach in, Ash cautiously lowered himself onto the towel and lay face down, still fully clothed.

'You have to take your T-shirt off,' said Georgia.

'No way. I'm not getting semi-naked in front of you.'

She rolled her eyes. 'I won't be able to use the oil now.'

'It's this way or nothing at all.'

Grinning, she said, 'Prude.'

To give Georgia her due, it turned out she did know what she was doing. Kneeling beside him, she rubbed her hands together to warm them. Then she began moving her fingers over his back in gentle rhythmical circles.

'Let me know if I hurt you.'

'You're all right,' Ash mumbled.

'I'm better than all right. I'm genius at this.' Her hands pressed each vertebra in turn, then fanned out on either side of his spine.

'So how long does this last?' mumbled Ash. He could actually feel it doing some good. The tension was seeping out of his knotted muscles.

'Fifteen minutes, twenty. For as long as you like.' Playfully, Georgia said, 'So will I get a mention on tomorrow's show after this?'

He smiled. 'You might.'

'Cool! Could you also slip in a bit about me doing ironing at really reasonable rates?'

'Is that all I am to you? A source of free advertising?'

'No, but I wouldn't mind if you just happened to mention it.'

'Well, I can't, because—'

TAT-TAT.

'Ooh, who's that?' Springing to her feet, Georgia bounded to the door. Stuck there on the floor, all Ash could do was listen to the sound of the front door being opened and her exclaiming, 'Hi! Oh, isn't that good of you? You must have been listening to the show this morning too!'

Was it too much to hope that his GP, overcome with remorse at not having been able to fit him in yesterday, had decided to grant him a home visit instead?

And had *apparently* brought along some kind of takeaway?

Then the wafts of herbs and garlic grew stronger and Ash heard Fia say, 'Um, yes, that's right. How's his back?'

Oh God . . .

'About to get *much* better.' Cheerfully Georgia led their visitor into the living room. 'Just as soon as I've finished working my magic!'

Having finally managed to turn his head, Ash saw Fia giving him a startled look from the doorway. Hardly surprising, considering she was seeing him lying on his front like a beached walrus.

Thank God he hadn't let Georgia bully him into taking off his T-shirt.

'Oh, sorry, I just thought you might not feel up to coming over to the pub for lunch.' Indicating the basket she was holding, Fia said uncertainly, 'I brought you a dish of cannelloni.'

'Th-th-thanks.' The word juddered out of his mouth as, without warning, Georgia dug her knuckles into his ribs.

'Just leave it in the kitchen,' she told Fia between kneadings. 'I'll heat it up for him later when we're finished. Now, just relax and stop trying to hold your stomach in.'

Ash felt her fingers pressing into his sides, only too clearly able to imagine the unattractive view with which Fia was being presented.

'Ooh, you're so *lovely*,' Georgia burst out, clutching handfuls of flesh through his T-shirt and waggling them like dough. 'Like a great big cuddly seal!'

Abbie was helping a dithery woman choose from the various types of solar-powered garden lighting on display when she heard Magda say playfully, 'Oh my, who's that handsome hunk coming in now?'

It was Tom. Even after all these years, the unexpected sight of him made Abbie's heart soar. Breaking into a smile, she lifted her arm to wave before realising he wasn't looking in her direction. Instead his attention appeared to be focused elsewhere.

Oh, good grief . . .

Approaching Des in the middle of the shop, not slowing for a second, Tom drew back his arm and unleashed a mighty punch that would have done Ricky Hatton proud. Des went down like a sack of gravel. Screams rang out from women in the vicinity; nothing like this had ever happened before in Kilgour's Garden Centre.

Tom didn't utter a word. Without so much as a glance around the shop, he turned and left. Everyone was in a state of shock, their eyes like saucers and their mouths agape. People gasped as Des hauled himself into a sitting position and blood dripped from his nose onto the tiled floor.

Then slowly, one by one, faces began to turn in Abbie's direction. Fear squeezed her stomach and bile rose in her throat as she saw their expressions alter, slide from astonishment and confusion to suspicion and then realisation that, logically, the chances were that this had to be something to do with her.

The stunned silence gave way to a kerfuffle, a rising babble of voices. Assorted bystanders helped Des to his feet and tissues were produced to staunch the bleeding and mop the mess from the floor.

'Has anyone called the police yet?' This came from dithery solar-powered woman in a high-pitched, panicky voice.

Fresh blood spattered over Des's grey checked shirt as he shook his head. 'No, no, don't do that.'

Magda said, 'Abbie? What's this about? What's been going on?'

'I . . . I don't know.' Her cheeks were so hot they felt as if they might burst into flames.

Huw's overgrown eyebrows were bristling as he helped Des to his feet. 'Come on, lad, let's get you cleaned up.'

Abbie tried to swallow but her mouth was too dry. Her hands were shaking. She needed to talk to Tom, needed to explain.

'Um . . . I'll go and see Tom.' Was that her own voice, calling across the shop after them? It didn't sound like her at all.

Des turned and nodded. Like an automaton, Abbie headed for the door. Somehow she had to sort this out, explain that she hadn't—

'I'm coming with you.' Magda's hand grasped her arm.

'It's OK, you don't have to.'

'What are you going to do, walk home? Come on, I'll give you a lift.'

Back in Channings Hill, Tom's dusty silver-grey van was parked outside the house.

'I'll come in too.' Magda was firm.

'No, please don't.' The last thing they needed was an audience.

Taking a deep breath, Abbie opened the front door.

Ironing, ironing everywhere. The living room was awash with it. No Georgia, thank God. Just Tom standing with his back to her, his arms tightly folded and his whole body radiating fury.

This was what she'd been dreading for months. Now it had happened. And it was fairly obvious how he'd found out.

'How could you?' Tom's voice vibrated with emotion. Slowly he turned to face her. 'How *could* you?'

Abbie saw red. Without warning, fear turned to defiance. 'How could I? Look what you've just done!' The words came spilling out, a desperate form of retaliation. 'If you wanted to talk about it, you could have just asked me and I'd have told you everything. It would have been just between us. But oh no, you had to come into work and cause a scene, and now everybody knows!'

'I DON'T CARE.' Tom, who never raised his voice, roared, 'I WANT EVERYONE TO KNOW! YOU AND DES KILGOUR . . . YOU AND HIM TOGETHER . . .'

'I haven't had sex with him.' Abbie blurted the words out, terrified by his fury. 'It was just one night, I thought you'd had an affair and I was upset—'

The front door swung open and Georgia called out, 'Why's there a woman trying to hide in the bushes under our front window?' Then she appeared in the living room doorway and her expression altered as she took in the scene. Her gaze flickered between them and Abbie knew then who had told Tom.

'Thanks.' Abbie shook her head at Georgia.

Georgia said indignantly, 'What? It wasn't me. I didn't tell him.'

Tom looked at his daughter in disbelief. 'Hang on. You mean you knew about it? You *knew* about Des Kilgour?'

'He turned up here once, and they didn't know I was in the house. Abbie made me promise not to tell you. Oh Dad, I'm sorry . . .'

Could Georgia make it sound any worse? And she was lying; she had to be behind this. Abbie demanded, 'So who told you?'

Tom took a folded sheet of paper out of his jeans pocket. 'This was left on my windscreen.'

Her legs still trembling, she crossed the room and took it from him. In capital letters, the anonymous note said: 'FROM A FRIEND WHO THINKS YOU SHOULD KNOW THAT YOUR WIFE IS HAVING AN AFFAIR WITH DES KILGOUR.'

'It isn't true.' Abbie swallowed hard; how many more times did she have to say it? 'Nothing happened, I *swear*.'

'You spent the night with him,' Georgia butted in. 'In his bed. You can't say *nothing* happened.'

Had she written the note? So that Tom would find out, but she could insist she hadn't been the one to tell him?

'There was no sex.'

'But you kissed him.'

'Look, I'd like to talk to Tom about this. Could we have some privacy, d'you think?'

Any normal person would instantly leave. But Georgia, who wasn't any normal person, shook her head. 'No, I'm staying. Look what you've done to my dad.'

Tom was barely recognisable, his face gaunt and his eyes dead. Of course Georgia was siding with him, protecting him.

'Let me explain.' Abbie pleaded, but he held up his hands.

'You've lied to me. You've been keeping secrets, doing God knows what, so why would I believe anything you say now?'

This wasn't an argument, this was her whole world slipping away. Abbie blurted out, 'It was when you were off on that fishing trip and I found the letter from . . . her.' She indicated Georgia, who reacted as if she'd been slapped.

'So it's all my fault, is it? Oh no, you're not going to pin the blame on me, just because you've been caught out!'

'Look, I'm just trying to tell you what happened.' Abbie's voice rose. Georgia's interference was the last thing she needed.

'Well, don't.' Tom surveyed her with disgust before turning away. 'Don't bother. Because I don't want to hear.'

You're sure you don't mind?'

'Of course I don't!'

'You're really sure?'

'Really.' How could she mind her sister moving in? Cleo carried a cup of tea over to Abbie, who was in a terrible state. Apart from anything else, it had been a fait accompli; by the time she'd arrived home from work this evening, Abbie had already let herself into the cottage and taken over the spare bedroom. Staying in her own house was no longer an option.

When she'd heard the reason why, Cleo had been stunned. It was surreal, on a par with Abbie announcing that she was becoming an astronaut and going off to train with NASA.

But it was true. Beyond belief though it seemed, her sister had managed to get herself entangled, however briefly, with Des Kilgour. Who was now, somewhat inconveniently, in love with her.

And possibly also suffering from a broken nose.

It just went to show.

'I couldn't stay there. I *couldn't*.' Distraught and repeating herself, Abbie rattled on. 'Not with the two of them ganging up on me. Oh yes, this is Georgia's dream come true. From now it'll just be her and her dad together. She definitely put that note on Tom's windscreen. I tried so hard to be nice to her and this is the thanks I get. And to think I *trusted* her . . .'

It was eleven thirty. Cleo was shattered after a long day. 'But what if it wasn't her?'

'Who else could it be? Des hasn't told another living soul. And neither did I. Because I knew it was the only way to be safe.'

'Maybe somebody saw you.'

'But that's just it. They couldn't have. There hasn't been anything to see!'

There was no answer to that. Cleo said, 'I can't guess how it happened, then, but I'm sure Tom'll come round. You know how much he loves you.'

'I didn't tell him about Des because I didn't want to hurt him. Now I've made things much worse.' Tears were leaking from Abbie's eyes. 'He doesn't believe me any more. The trust has gone. You know how proud Tom is. God, *sorry* . . .' Abbie was shaking so much she knocked over her cup.

'Doesn't matter. Let me do it.' Bending to retrieve the smashed sections of her favourite teacup, Cleo managed to kneel in a puddle of tea and simultaneously slice her finger on a shard of china.

'Sorry, I'll help you clear up . . .'

'No, really, it's fine.'

'I just can't believe it's happened.'

'Abbie, it's only a cup.'

'I didn't mean that. I'm talking about my life. My hopeless l-life . . .'

Eleven thirty-five. Cleo grabbed a handful of tissues from the box Abbie was working her way through and began to mop up the mess. It was going to be a long, long night.

Chapter 9

IT WAS THE FINAL performance of *Beach Party!* at the Hippodrome and the Casey Kruger fan club had turned out this evening in force. They had a nice night for it. Which was just as well really, seeing as the show had ended fifty minutes ago and they were still waiting with their cameras and autograph books for their hero to emerge from the theatre. But no one seemed to mind. Apparently Casey had been fantastic tonight.

Cleo was having to wait too, but at least she was getting paid for it.

Settling back in the driver's seat, she picked up her phone. She'd already called Abbie to let her know she wouldn't be back before midnight. Earlier, too, she'd spoken to Tom and discovered him in no mood to forgive his wife for almost-but-not-quite sleeping with another man. Nor had he taken kindly to being lectured (his choice of words) on the subject of love and trust by someone who'd never even *had* a proper relationship in her life.

Which had hurt.

Well, she'd leave Tom alone for the moment. But still she fidgeted restlessly with her phone; yesterday's bombshell regarding Abbie and Tom had affected her in more ways than one. Because theirs had always been the ultimate perfect relationship, the one against which all others were held up, measured and invariably found wanting.

Call it warped female logic, but if things could fall apart for Abbie and Tom, what hope was there for the rest of them?

Which in turn meant that if you were going to end up getting your heart broken anyway, why not have a bit of fun with the most gorgeous man you could think of.

Ooh now, hmm, let's see, and who might that be? Cleo smiled inwardly, mocking the fact that she was a girl with a guilty secret. Because like it or not, Johnny LaVenture appeared to have taken up more or less permanent residence inside her head.

But it wouldn't be out of order, would it, to give Johnny a quick call, just to find out how things were going with his aunt? If he was going through a difficult time, wouldn't he be glad to hear a friendly voice?

The stage door burst open at last and Casey emerged to a rousing cheer from his fans. They clustered around him as if he were a conquering hero. And he was waving a bottle of champagne in each hand, which was only increasing their excitement. By the look of him, it wasn't the first champagne he'd encountered tonight.

Cleo scrolled through the numbers stored in her phone and felt her breath catch in her throat as Johnny's name came up. Which was kind of a giveaway. OK, all she was doing was calling *as a friend* to see how things were going in Norfolk.

Or maybe not. His phone was switched off, which probably meant he was at the hospital.

Cleo ended the call; she'd try again tomorrow.

Casey reeled over to the car. Shaking his head to stop Cleo opening the rear door, he threw himself into the front passenger seat instead.

'I can't talk to you properly from back there. C'mon, let's go, my work here is done.' He glugged back more champagne as she put the car into gear and pulled away from the kerb. 'You know what? I'm gonna miss this place. Gonna miss you too.'

'Thank you. That's nice.' Cleo turned her attention to navigating the busy multi-laned city centre. Moments later she saw that Casey's eyes had closed and his mouth had fallen open. Hooray, just pray he didn't snore like a warthog all the way back to the hotel.

Before long they'd left Bristol behind them. Cleo drove while Casey slept, his head lolling onto his shoulder, the half-empty bottle cradled like a baby in his arms. She was three miles from the hotel when he woke up with a whole-body jolt and said, 'How 'bout you, then?'

'How about me what?'

'Gonna miss me, babe?'

Oh please. Aloud she said politely, 'Of course I will.'

'Ha, knew it!' He slapped his leg. 'Changed your mind about me now, haven't you? Don't want to miss your chance with Casey Kruger. Stop the car, babe.'

'Listen, we'll be at the hotel in five minutes—'

'No no no no *no*! C'mon, babe, pull over, just do it for me, eh?'

He was absolutely plastered. Cleo had no intention of slowing down. 'Let's just keep going, shall we, then—'

'Babe, for crying out loud, stop the car NOW!' As he said it, Casey launched himself without warning across the car and grabbed the steering wheel, wrenching it from her hands. The car swerved wildly to the left as the narrow country lane bent to the right. In slow motion, with Casey's belated yell of, 'Oh fuck a duck!' ringing in her ears, Cleo jammed on the brakes too late to prevent the car crashing through a fence and assuming a sideways momentum of its own as it hurtled down a steep slope on the other side.

It was like being trapped against your better judgment on the world's scariest roller coaster. Flung left then right then upside-down, Cleo gave herself up to the rolling. Was this it, was this how she was going to die? Would everyone blame her for the accident? Would Casey Kruger fans disrupt her funeral and call her names? Oh no, poor Abbie, as if she didn't already have enough on her plate. Damn, and did this mean she'd never find out what Johnny was like in bed? That was so unfair, why hadn't she just . . . oh, hang on, stopping now . . .

Stopping . . .

Stopped now.

Slowly Cleo opened her eyes. Was she still alive or did she just think she was, like Patrick Swayze's character in *Ghost*?

'Oooooh fuuuuck,' groaned a voice next to her.

OK, if they were both dead, this could mean she was shackled to Casey Kruger for all eternity. That would definitely be too much to bear, stuck with the world's most irritating ghostly sidekick.

No, they were still alive. Cleo croaked, 'Are you all right?'

'Fucking stupid question. What did you do?'

Hello? What had *she* done? 'You grabbed the steering wheel,' Cleo reminded him.

'What? No I didn't!' Casey was outraged. 'It was you.'

OK, now wasn't the time to get into a fight. They were trapped in complete darkness, hanging upside-down in a smashed-up car on a steeply sloping wooded escarpment. Cleo felt blood trickling down her face. There was shattered windscreen glass all over her. Her neck hurt. So did her legs. Oh God, this was serious. The driver's side of the car was buckled in. Who was to say the petrol tank wouldn't ignite? Fumbling for the door handle with her right hand, she attempted without success to open the door.

'Look,' Casey complained, 'not being funny, but can we stop mucking about now? Just get me back to the hotel, yeah?'

'We need an ambulance.' Cleo tried to work out where her phone was.

'Fine then, tell 'em to hurry up. I need to get back before they close the bar . . . wha's happened to this bottle anyway? S'empty.'

Fingers trembling with the effort, Cleo managed to reach her mobile. It almost slipped from her grasp and the back of her neck prickled with panic because if she'd dropped it, they'd really be stuck. Right, got it; all she had to do now was press nine nine nine and—

'Cleo? Hey, how are you!'

What?

Confused and in a state of shock, Cleo wondered how she could possibly be hearing Johnny's voice. Was he working on the switchboard for the emergency services? Hang on, no, she hadn't called them yet. Belatedly she realised she must have pressed last number redial when she was making a grab for the phone.

'Cleo? Are you there?'

Tears welled up in her eyes because he sounded so close, when in reality he was two hundred miles away. 'Yes, I'm here . . . Johnny, we've had an accident . . . we're trapped in the car and my neck hurts . . . I need to call an ambulance but the battery's almost gone on my phone . . .'

He didn't hesitate or waste a moment. 'I'll call them. Where are you?'

'Pennywell Lane, we came off at the bend opposite Parson's Barn . . . Casey's with me . . . I'm frightened to move and we're stuck here . . .'

'Tell 'em to bloody hurry up,' Casey bellowed. 'I don't want to miss last orders.'

'Right, I'm calling nine nine nine. Hang up now,' Johnny ordered. 'And don't panic, OK? Everything's going to be fine.'

He'd gone. Cleo closed her eyes. All they could do now was wait. A fresh trickle of blood slid across Cleo's forehead into her ear. It felt horrible but she couldn't turn her neck to stop it happening. There was glass in her hair too. She started to shiver as shock set in. How long would it be before the ambulance turned up?

Not long at all, thank God. Within minutes they heard a vehicle racing along the lane, coming closer and closer. No sirens though. Maybe when there was no other traffic on the road they didn't bother with them. Cleo listened to the ambulance pull up, followed by the sound of a door slamming and footsteps racing towards the car.

Then she opened her eyes again, and there was Johnny, which was so clearly impossible that she had to be hallucinating.

'About time too,' slurred Casey. 'Get us out of here, mate. Got any whisky on you?'

'Johnny?' His name came out as a croak. 'Is it you?'

'You're OK. Don't try to move.'

Johnny managed, finally, to wrench open the buckled driver's door. Crouching beside Cleo, he stroked her hair out of her eyes. 'Can you feel your legs?'

She managed with some difficulty to wiggle each foot in turn. 'Yes. How can you be here?'

'I got back to Channings Hill earlier this evening.'

'Your aunt?'

'Barbara died last night,' said Johnny.

'I'm sorry.' Cleo tried to shake her head and winced with pain.

'Keep still. The ambulance'll be here any minute. I can't believe I beat them to it.' Johnny was stroking her hand. 'Then again, I was only three miles away. And I drove like a maniac.'

His presence was such a comfort. 'I'm glad you came.' A tear leaked from Cleo's right eye and she felt him wipe it away.

In the distance they heard the wail of a siren—so it was being used after all. He stayed with her, gently picking bits of shattered windscreen glass out of her hair, until help arrived in the form of two police officers and two ambulance crew.

While they checked her over, one of the paramedics asked, 'Had anything to drink this evening?'

'No.'

'Ha, don't you believe it,' said Casey. 'She's been knocking back the vodka shots all night, saucy minx.'

The second paramedic raised an eyebrow and said drily, 'And how about you, sir?'

Casey waved an airy hand. 'Nothing at all, officer. Completely teetotal, me. Never touch a drop.'

'**H**ow can I put this?' said Ash. 'You've looked better.'

'Thanks.'

'So what's happening with Kruger? Going to sue the pants off him?'

Hmm, that was a tricky question. She'd already been visited by Casey Kruger's manager, his agent and his lawyers. Casey, miraculously unhurt himself, was emphatically denying having caused the accident. According to his statement, a muntjac deer had leaped out in front of them and Cleo, panicking, had swerved off the road. If she didn't agree with this version of events, he would be forced to accuse her of dangerous driving. The publicity for Henleaze Limos would be dreadful, the repercussions potentially horrendous.

Or they could keep the matter out of court and he would pay for the considerable damage to the car.

Just as well it hadn't been the Bentley Continental.

'It's complicated.' Grumpy Graham was currently seeking legal advice on the matter. Easing herself off the bed, Cleo said, 'Ow, *ouch.*'

Ash shook his head. 'You have to go one better, don't you? Just because I hurt my back, you have to crash a limo and end up in hospital. Has anyone ever told you you're a copycat and an attention-seeker?'

Cleo took his arm. 'Yes, but you're better now. So you can help me out to the car.'

'So long as people don't see us like this and think we're a couple.' Grinning, Ash said, 'I do have my standards, you know.'

The discharge forms had been filled in and she was free to leave. Cleo knew she was lucky. The X-rays had been clear. She had cuts to her face and whiplash but it could have been so much worse. And the doctors had told her she only had to wear the surgical collar for a week.

A pretty nurse, pink-cheeked and sparkly-eyed, came hurrying up to them. 'Oh, you're just off? You've got another visitor!'

Grumpy Graham? Casey Kruger? More legal people? Turning stiffly to survey the double doors at the entrance to the ward, Cleo's heart did the rabbity, skippety thing it quite often did, nowadays, when she saw Johnny LaVenture.

'Hey.' Johnny smiled slightly when they reached him. 'So they're kicking you out.'

Nodding hurt. And, thanks to the high soft collar, probably gave her an unattractive double chin. Thinking that if Ash hadn't had a proprietary arm around her, Johnny might have greeted her with a kiss, Cleo said, 'I'm fine. Thanks for, you know, last night.'

'No problem. Glad I was able to help.' He glanced at Ash. 'I can give her a lift home if you like. If you're busy . . . ?'

Yes please, yes please!

'It's OK, I came here to pick her up.' Ash's arm around her tightened. 'I'll take her back.'

Johnny nodded slowly. 'OK. I'll see you soon then. I'm heading back to Norfolk to organise Barbara's funeral.'

'Well, thanks again. For everything.' This time Cleo disentangled herself from Ash's grasp and leaned forward to plant a kiss on Johnny's cheek. Kissing was even more painful than nodding, but the smell of his aftershave and the warmth of his cheek made it worth it. Also, out of the corner of her eye she could see the envious expression on the face of the pretty nurse.

'**Y**ou can thank me as well if you like,' said Ash on the way home.

'Thank you for what?'

'You wanted to go back with him, didn't you? And what would have been the point of that? You've got a thing for Johnny LaVenture. He might even have a bit of a thing for you, seeing as he hasn't had a chance yet to tick you off his To Do list.' Ash could be very blunt when he wanted. 'But let's face it, you're in no condition to do anything right now. Plus, you look dead rough. So, if you really want to make a fool of yourself, at least wait until you're better.'

As he drove through Winterbourne, Cleo pulled down the sun visor and studied her reflection in the tiny mirror. Hair a mess, cuts all over her face and a giant plastic-and-foam neck brace.

Ash had a point.

'Cheers.' You could always rely on your friends to give you a boost. To pay him back she said, 'How's it going with you and Fia?'

'I tell you what.' Ash kept his attention on the road ahead. 'You don't ask me cruel questions. And I won't stop the car and make you walk.'

Fia couldn't believe she was having such a fantastic time. Who'd have thought a trip to the zoo could be so much fun? But it was, and it had all been her idea! When she'd invited Ash to come along with her, he'd looked stunned. But then he'd said yes and that had been the start of a truly brilliant day.

'Where next? Gorilla Island!' Taking his hand, she raced across the grass separating the lion enclosure from the monkey house. 'I want to see the baby gorillas . . .'

'No, no, penguins first.' Ash pulled her in another direction. 'They're being fed in ten minutes. Have you ever fed a penguin?'

'It's not allowed.' Fia had seen the signs. 'The keepers have to do it.'

'Ah, but I used to work here. Didn't you know that?' He shook his fair hair out of his eyes and gave her a wink. 'Which means we can.'

And unbelievably, they had. The crowds of zoo-goers, watching enviously from behind the barriers, laughed and applauded Ash's comic antics as he interacted with the penguins. Finally she exclaimed, 'You're so different today! I love it when you're like this!'

And Ash replied, 'But I've always been like this. You've just never noticed before.' Then he reached for her hand and pulled her towards the ledge where the deep water glittered in the sunlight. 'Come on, let's go for a swim!'

The crowd gasped as, together, they raised their arms and launched themselves like dolphins into the air. A split second before hitting the surface of the water, Fia woke up.

Wow, that had been bizarre. That was dreams for you. They were weird. God, though, this one had felt so real. And it wasn't fading away either, as dreams usually did. Every last detail was still vivid and intact.

Even thinking about Ash made her feel a bit funny. He'd been so brilliant in the dream, and there'd been this amazing connection between them, as if they'd been best friends for years. In fact, *more* than best friends . . .

Rolling over in bed, Fia turned off her alarm, switched on the radio and scrolled through the channels until she came to BWR. Did Ash's show start at seven?

'. . . on your marks then for the great Spacehoppathon. On the orange spacehopper we have Gay Pete and on the manly dark-green spacehopper we have Big Bad Bruce in his motorbike boots. OK, twice round the studio, no pushing and shoving, three two one . . . go!'

Gosh, it felt strange to hear his voice again so soon after they'd been feeding penguins together. But Ash sounded just as jolly and relaxed on the radio as he had at the zoo. Anyway, time to get up. Hauling herself out of bed, Fia stumbled through to the bathroom and switched on the shower. At least this would be warmer than the icy blue waters of the penguin pool.

By seven thirty she was out of the shower and brushing her wet hair. On the radio, Ash was consoling Gay Pete, who hadn't covered himself in glory during the race.

'Poor you, came last *and* broke the heel on your pink stiletto.'

'Bruce cheated! I would've won if he hadn't stabbed my space-hopper with his penknife.'

'Oh now, come on, a bad hopper always blames his punctures. Just face up to it, Pete, you lost your race. Big Bad Bruce is the champion. And now I'm afraid you have to pay the price . . .'

By the time Fia had finished drying her hair, Rihanna was singing her latest single. When the music came to an end, Ash began chatting to Megan the traffic girl about the date she'd been out on last night with the drummer in a local band.

'It went really well.' Poor Megan, she was trying to be discreet; it couldn't be easy, being interrogated when her date could be listening in.

'I love it. This is so romantic,' Ash exclaimed gleefully. 'How did the date come about, then? You can tell us that. How does a long-haired thrash-metal drummer with tattoos and multiple piercings go about romantically asking out a pretty little Doris Day type who loves puppies and hairbands and cupcakes with pink glittery icing?'

Fia pulled open her underwear drawer and selected her favourite peacock-blue bra and knicker set.

'Fine then.' Megan was laughing but her tone was defiant. 'If you must know, he didn't ask me out. I asked him.'

'*What?*' Ash affected shock. 'You mean he might not even *like* you?'

'Shush, I knew he liked me. I'd seen the way he looked at me. But I'd waited and waited and he *still* didn't say anything. In the end I knew I'd have to be the one to make the first move.'

'So why didn't he do it?'

'Because he was scared I'd turn him down.'

'Oh, right. You're telling me the long-haired tattooed thrash-metal drummer is shy.'

Megan sounded proud. 'He is. And I like that in a man. It's an attractive quality. Not that you'd know anything about that.'

'Ha, now that's where you're wrong,' Ash countered. 'I have no confidence. Deep down, I'm very shy.'

Everyone in the studio was laughing now. Megan said, 'Yeah, yeah, you're about as shy as Russell Brand.'

'I can be shy. Sometimes.' He paused, and for a moment Fia almost believed him. Then he continued smoothly, 'So d'you fancy going out on a date with a real man now? What are you doing tomorrow night?'

They kept up the banter while Fia buttoned herself into her kitchen whites. Megan protested that her new drummer boyfriend probably wouldn't appreciate her going out with someone else and Ash told her she was a fool to throw away her big chance, that she didn't know what she was missing. Then female listeners started texting in, eagerly offering themselves as replacements and begging for a date with Ash.

'Right, all you girls out there have to calm down,' he ordered. 'There's only one of me to go around and, you know, I do still have my bad back. Oh God, and now we've had another text from Keira Knightley. Keira, love, how many times do I have to say it? You're just not my type. Leave it now, give it a rest. Move on.'

Megan said, 'So who *do* you like?'

'Ah, a gentleman never tells. Plus, he definitely wouldn't tell *you*. There might be someone capable of making my heart beat faster,' Ash's tone was playful, 'but that's my business, not yours.'

'Ooh!' Gay Pete chimed in. 'Is it me?'

By seven thirty, thanks to three glasses of wine, Cleo was feeling pleasantly fuzzy around the edges. A few people might still be giving her funny looks but she no longer minded. Here at the Hollybush she was among friends.

She heaved a sigh. 'What's going to happen? When's it going to end?'

Ash said, 'Are we talking about the world?'

Cleo gave him a prod. 'I'm talking about Abbie. My sitting tenant. Except she never does sit, she just keeps on cleaning.'

'When she's finished your place, send her round to do mine.'

'She can move in with you if you like.' Cleo sank her head back against her chair. 'Oh God, I'm horrible. She's my sister and I love her to bits, but I really don't want her living with me until I'm forty.'

'What makes you think she'd want to live with you?'

'Who wouldn't? I'm irresistible and gorgeous.' As she said it, her stomach rumbled.

Ash reached for a menu. 'And hungry?'

'Now you come to mention it,' said Cleo, 'that too.'

Fia put the finishing touches to Ash's hotpot and Cleo's chilli baked potato, ready to carry them out of the kitchen. Unbelievably, last night's dream was still vivid in her mind. Having felt compelled to listen to the rest of Ash's show this morning, she now understood why it was so popular. In the studio he'd created a little world to which his listeners yearned to belong. Everyone joined in and the banter was a two-way process. Ash was razor-sharp, brilliantly funny and capable of going off on the most surreal of tangents when the mood took him. He was clearly adored by his many fans.

Yet when she'd taken their food order twenty minutes ago, he'd barely glanced at her. She still felt, in his presence, as if she'd inadvertently committed some hideous faux pas. Having intended to tell him about her dream, her nerve had failed her.

But this was ridiculous. Fia snipped flat-leaf parsley and sprinkled it over the hotpot. She loaded the plates onto a tray. If she'd done something to upset Ash, it was up to him to tell her what it was. He couldn't expect her to guess.

'There you go,' she said cheerfully as she put the plates down in front of them. 'One hotpot, one baked potato.'

Ash's jaw tightened. 'Thanks.'

'Yum!' Unwrapping her napkin, Cleo said, 'This is *just* what I need!'

OK, ignore the fact that Ash hadn't even looked up. Fia said, 'I had the weirdest dream last night. And guess what? You were in it!'

'Me? Oh no, was I naked again?' Cleo pulled a face. 'I'm always dreaming that I'm out and I've forgotten to put any clothes on.'

'Not you. Ash.'

'You dreamed about Ash? Ha, was he naked?'

'No. We were at the zoo, feeding the penguins.'

'Oh now, that sounds *romantic*.'

When she'd mentioned his presence in her dream, Ash's shoulders had visibly stiffened. Now he shot Cleo a look of horror mingled with revulsion. Hurriedly Fia said, 'Oh God no, it wasn't romantic at all! That's the last thing it was. He was trying to make me dive into the freezing water with him . . . and there was this awful smell of raw fish and all these seals lolloping around . . . *yeurgh*, it was *gross*.'

'Sounds it.' Ash dug his fork through the layer of crispy potato slices on his hotpot; featuring in other people's dreams clearly wasn't something he enjoyed.

Embarrassed by the snub, Fia said, 'Yes, well, I didn't dream about you on purpose. If I had a choice I'd have preferred David Tennant.'

Ash looked as if he wished she'd leave them in peace. Evenly he said, 'Me too.'

'We'd all prefer David Tennant!' Cleo chipped in to cover the awkward silence.

See? She'd done it again. What *was* Ash's problem with her? It was on the tip of Fia's tongue to demand an answer, but the pub was busy and causing a scene would be awful. Instead she flushed and said evenly,

'Enjoy your meal,' before turning and heading back into the kitchen.

When she'd gone, Cleo said, 'You're such a div.'

'Shut up.'

'You went all weird again.'

'Look, I *know*, OK?'

'Why don't you just let me have a quiet word with—'

'Don't even think it. No way.' Vehemently Ash shook his head. 'If you do, you'll die a horrible death.'

'But—'

'You said her dream sounded romantic and she was appalled. I saw the look on her face. She couldn't have been more disgusted. Last week she saw me being massaged by Georgia and this week she dreamed about me swimming with a load of fat blubbery seals. So just leave it, OK?'

'OK. Could I just—?'

His voice rose. 'Cleo, *NO*.'

'Just try a bit of your hotpot,' Cleo blurted out, 'to see what it's like.'

Ash sighed. 'Go on then. You're a nightmare.'

'Ooh, can I try some too?' Georgia had just come in. Bounding up to them, she snatched the fork from his hand and helped herself to a mouthful. 'Mmm, that's good. How are you, anyway?'

'Looking forward to the rest of my hotpot,' said Ash.

'How's your back?'

'Better.'

'See? That's all thanks to me! Didn't I tell you I was brilliant?' She waggled her hands at him. 'There's magic in these fingers. If you want me to give you another go with them, just say the word.'

Cleo looked hopefully at Tom, who had come in with Georgia. Maybe they could have a chat. In response he shook his head and said, 'I don't want to talk about Abbie. We've just come out for a quiet drink.'

'Not too quiet,' Georgia retorted. 'I'm not going to sit in a corner and be boring.'

Ash said, 'That would be too much to hope for.'

'You love me really.' Georgia's eyes danced. 'Look, we'll leave you to eat your food. Join us afterwards if you fancy a game of doubles.' Indicating the pool table, Georgia said playfully, 'But only if you're brave enough to take us on.'

'Maybe later,' said Ash.

Georgia and Tom headed over to the pool table. Too busy watching them to pay attention to the food on her fork, Cleo dripped sauce down her front. 'Oh God, why does it always happen to me?'

Ash raised his eyebrows. 'And you were so flawless up until that moment.'

Cleo knew she wasn't looking great, what with the cuts all over her face, her super-attractive neck brace and her hair in need of a wash because Abbie's frenzy of cleaning had used up all the hot water in the tank. Oh well, never mind. As she rubbed at the stain on her top, she stuck her tongue out at Ash. 'Lucky I'm only here with you.'

Twenty minutes later the door swung open and Welsh Mac came in. Hoisting himself onto a stool at the bar, he said to Deborah, 'Pint of bitter, love. Johnny's back, just seen him. He's on his way over.'

Johnny was back? On his way over? Cleo sat up straight, simultaneously thrilled and mortified. This was something else that always seemed to happen to her. 'I'm just going to the loo for a second.'

'To try and tart yourself up?' Pretending to feel in his jacket pockets, Ash said innocently, 'Want to borrow my lipstick?'

'You're hilarious.'

'Damn, haven't got it with me. How about a brown paper bag to put over your head?'

Cleo aimed a kick at his legs beneath the table. 'How about I tell Fia you *luuurve* her, you want to *kiss* her, you want to *marry* her?'

Sorrowfully Ash shook his head. 'See, you had the chance to rush off and try to make yourself a bit less scary. But now it's too late, he's here.'

Cleo swung round as the door opened. Oh well, it wasn't as if Johnny hadn't seen the cuts to her face before. Hastily she scrubbed with her serviette at the stain on her top. Then Johnny appeared and the sight of him prompted her strongest-yet adrenaline rush. Oh God, she'd really got it bad. He was wearing a white cotton shirt over a navy T-shirt and age-softened Levis. His dark hair was flopping over his forehead, his profile was chiselled and gorgeous, and he was laughing at a comment someone to the left of him had just made.

Then his previously obscured companion moved into view and the fizzing excitement deflated like a popped balloon. Not only was the girl tall, blonde and ridiculously attractive, but Cleo knew who she was. Thanks to the wonders of the Internet, she knew far more than she wanted to know. Because this was Honor Donaldson, one of Australia's most famous exports. She was a plus-size supermodel, just short of six-foot tall and not remotely plus-size in terms of the real world. But with her lusciously voluptuous size-fourteen curves and flawless gilded skin, she had taken the modelling industry by storm. Then, when interviews followed and her vivacious character had become known, the rest of the world had fallen in love with her too.

One other small detail about her had come to Cleo's attention while she'd been—oh, the shame of it—Googling Johnny. This was that prior to his return to Channings Hill, for several months he and Honor had been a couple.

And now here she was, making Johnny laugh and holding his hand. Not to mention looking out-of-this-world stunning.

No, no, no, this isn't meant to happen.

Next to Cleo, Ash frowned and said, 'Isn't that thingy?'

'Yes.' If only she looked like a thingy.

'Oh my God!' Abandoning her game of pool, Georgia exclaimed, 'Are you Honor Donaldson? I love you!'

'Sweetie, thanks so much! And look at you, you're so gorgeous!' Honor, whose ability to charm was legendary, smiled at Georgia as if it was the nicest compliment she'd ever received. 'Hey, I like it here already! Johnny, you have to introduce me to *everyone.*'

'Don't worry, I will. Just let me get some drinks in first.' For a brief moment Johnny's gaze met Cleo's and she saw him attempt to signal something . . . God knows what . . . with his eyes, before turning back to the bar.

'Wow,' murmured Ash.

Cleo realised that Fia was standing right beside her, a tray of dirty plates in her hands and a look of dismay on her face as she took in the sight of Johnny and Honor together. Evidently she wasn't the only one who'd just had her hopes dashed.

Under her breath Fia muttered, 'This is so unfair.'

Then Cleo saw the utter devastation in Ash's eyes, because more than anything he wanted Fia to feel that way about *him.* And it was clear that she never would. He was about as desirable, as far as she was concerned, as a mouldy old fridge. It was a tossup who she felt more sorry for, Ash or herself.

Within minutes, much like the dreaming-you-were-naked scenario where you prayed no one would notice, Johnny brought Honor Donaldson over to meet them. Up close she was even more jaw-droppingly beautiful. She was wearing a casual outfit of loose sand-coloured linen trousers, a paler sandy-gold top, cream waistcoat and espadrilles. Her hair was every shade of gold, her eyes chestnut brown.

'Oh my Lord, look at your face! You poor *thing.*' Honor shook her head in sympathy. 'Are you the one who had the accident?'

What else could she say? Cleo nodded. 'That was me.'

'Johnny *told* me about it. Casey Kruger, right? I met him a couple of years back. Jeez, what an annoying little tit.'

Cleo's heart sank. She'd wanted to dislike her, but how could you not love someone who said that? 'Well, yes.' It certainly summed Casey up.

'Anyway, great to meet you. It's so cool to be here finally, after hearing Johnny talk about this place for so long.' As she spoke, Honor leaned back against Johnny's chest, tilting her head affectionately towards his. 'And it's fantastic to be back with Johnny. I bet he's kept some of the girls around here on their toes, am I right?'

Cleo was numb. She said faintly, 'Oh, I'm sure he has.' Next to her, Ash was having trouble keeping his eyes off Honor's goddess-like cleavage. OK, now she definitely knew who she felt more sorry for. And it wasn't Ash.

In the harshly lit toilets, Cleo surveyed her reflection in the mirror. Flat chest, beige plastic neck brace, attractive sauce stain on T-shirt, face full of healing cuts. Nice. It was pointless but she took the mini powder compact out of her bag and attempted to cover the unsightly marks.

If anything, that looked even worse, bumpy and seriously amateurish. Hopeless, hopeless. And what did it matter now, anyway?

Outside the toilets, she bumped into Johnny. *Of course.*

'I just wanted to say sorry.' He forced her to look at him. 'None of this was planned. Honor turned up out of the blue . . . but, you know, she's here now . . .'

Oh God, did this come under the category of Being Let Down Gently? Nausea crawled up Cleo's throat. It did, didn't it? His conscience had been pricking him, forcing him to acknowledge that up until recently he might have considered having a bit of a fling with her, but things were different now. His old girlfriend was back in his life and she just happened to be one of the most desired females in the world. So basically she, Cleo, had to understand that in comparison . . . well, sorry, there *was* no comparison. At all. End of.

Luckily these thoughts ricocheted through her mind in a nanosecond. Without missing a beat she was able to say breezily, 'Hey, no need to apologise. Honor's great, and it's about time you got yourself a nice girl and settled down. You're not as young as you used to be, after all!'

It actually sounded pretty convincing, even if she did say so herself.

'Thanks.' Johnny's gaze dropped to her front; was he looking at the sauce stain or at her sadly inferior breasts? 'Well, that's it, I just needed to explain.' Eager to change the subject he went on hurriedly, 'Anyway, how are you? How's the neck?'

Cleo's hand went up to the plastic contraption that was currently holding her head on her shoulders and forcing her to walk around looking as if she had a poker up her bottom. Cheerily she said, 'Not so bad.'

Unlike her heart.

'It could have been worse.' He looked as if he wanted to say more, but Cleo couldn't bear it. Her control was in danger of slipping so she headed back to the bar before she said or did something she'd regret.

As the door swung shut behind them, she saw that Honor was getting a round in. She called out, 'Cleo, there you are! Another white wine?'

'Um, no thanks.'

'Oh go on, we're all having a drink! Please let me get you one.'

OK, slightly surreal. Honor Donaldson was begging to buy her a drink. Under other circumstances it would have been the highlight of her year. But not when Honor had just triumphantly reclaimed the man she, Cleo, had been on the brink of plunging into a relationship with. No matter how unsuitable and doomed to disaster that relationship would undoubtedly have turned out to be. He had captured her heart, and maybe it wasn't completely shattered but it definitely had a crack in it.

'I'd love to,' Cleo lied, 'but I'm shattered. I really need to get home.'

'She's a lightweight,' Ash explained to Honor. See? The presence of Fia rendered him practically mute but with Honor, whom he evidently didn't fancy, he was completely relaxed.

'And I'm taking strong painkillers that don't mix with alcohol.' Waving goodbye to everyone, Cleo said to Honor, 'Why don't you ask Ash to tell you what happened when he tried it?'

Outside the pub she stopped and gulped down lungfuls of cold air. At least she'd left with some shreds of dignity intact. A few more drinks and those shreds could so easily have deserted her. And then where were you?

Chapter 10

IT WAS A GUILTY relief to be escaping from Abbie at home but Cleo's spirits had risen as she'd made her way over to the Hollybush on Sunday at lunch time. Her face had pretty much healed up, it was her first time out without her neck brace and she was actually looking normal again.

But Cleo's spirits were currently taking a bit of a tumble, because while Honor Donaldson was undoubtedly cheerful, chatty company and a genuinely nice person, having to listen to her chattering on about just how ecstatically happy she and Johnny were together wasn't exactly top of Cleo's want-to-hear list.

'I mean, it was all my fault in the first place. When I look back now, I can't believe I was so stupid. This other guy came into my life and I was just, like, wow, this is *amazing*, because I had all his attention and he was so full-on. And he was a movie producer, which helped. He knew everyone, all the A-listers. That makes me a horrible person, right? I'm not proud of myself, but at the time I really thought I was in love with him. So I left Johnny, just like that. Broke his heart. And he was *devastated*.' Honor shook her head sorrowfully at the memory. 'I felt bad about it, of course I did, but I was so wrapped up in this fantastic new relationship I told myself I was doing the right thing.'

She stopped, waiting for the reaction. Forced to oblige, Cleo said, 'But you weren't?'

'Of course I wasn't! The guy was a complete nightmare, super-possessive, paranoid, the works. I realised I'd made the biggest mistake of my life. I mean, he bought me stuff, diamond bracelets, a Picasso . . . but he wasn't making me happy. And I was really missing Johnny by then, but I told myself I shouldn't contact him. I'd made him so unhappy, he deserved the chance to rebuild his life. Then I bumped into his New York agent at a gallery opening and he told me about Johnny's aunt. Well, that was it.' Honor pressed her clenched fist to her chest and said, 'I couldn't help myself, I knew what I had to do. He was all on his own in Norfolk and I just couldn't bear it. I caught the first flight to London. Do you know how I knew I really loved him?'

'Um . . . no.'

'They didn't have any seats left in first class *or* in business.' Honor said proudly, 'So I flew economy.'

Cleo shook her head. The unimaginable horror.

'But it was worth it. I caught a cab to Norfolk and turned up at Johnny's hotel. Then I got the manager to call him down to reception . . . oh wow, it was like something out of a movie.' Her eyes shining, Honor said, 'All these people were watching as Johnny came down the stairs. I just held out my arms and said, "Oh baby, I love you so much! I'm here for you now." And the tourists were all going "Aaaahhh," and it was the most amazing romantic moment . . . oh Jeez, look at me, I'm welling up just thinking about it!'

She was, too. In the prettiest way imaginable. Even the whites of her eyes stayed Persil-white.

'If I tried something like that, it'd all go pear-shaped. I'd turn up and the guy'd say, "Sorry, love, bit late, I've met someone else now."'

Honor said confidently, 'Oh, I knew that hadn't happened.'

'Did you?' Cleo felt sick. 'How?'

'I Googled him. Typed in his name plus new girlfriend.' Honor shrugged as if it were obvious. 'Not a bean.'

'What if he was seeing someone secretly?' God, was she some kind of masochist?

'It's OK, I did double-check.' Smiling, Honor said, 'I asked him myself. There hasn't been anyone else. And now we're back together there isn't going to be, I can promise you that!'

So, officially a masochist.

Rescue arrived minutes later in the form of Johnny himself, come to take Honor away. They were driving back to Norfolk ahead of tomorrow's funeral. Sliding gracefully off her bar stool, Honor planted a lingering kiss on his mouth. 'We've just been talking about you.'

Cleo's own mouth was dry; how did it feel to be kissed by Johnny? She'd never find out now. And look at the two of them together; they made such a perfect couple. Honor was stunning in an amethyst wraparound dress and silver jewellery. Johnny was wearing a pale-grey shirt and black trousers. They were visiting Aunt Clarice in the nursing home and making the final arrangements for the service. For a second he met Cleo's gaze and her heart turned over.

'You're on the mend. Looking better. How's the neck?'

'Good, thanks.' She nodded to prove it.

'Great. Well, we need to get off.' He jangled his keys at Honor.

'Hope the funeral's OK tomorrow.' Was that a ridiculous thing to say?

'Thanks. Bye.' Johnny's hand rested in the small of Honor's back as he ushered her out. *She imagined what that felt like . . .*

'See you when we get back, guys!' Honor waved over her shoulder.

Fia, finished in the kitchen, said resignedly, 'She's so nice, isn't she? I suppose he was always going to end up with someone like that.'

'I suppose so,' murmured Cleo.

Peering out of the bedroom window, Abbie shivered at the sight of the rain hammering down and the branches of the trees behind the house being battered and swept sideways by the howling gale. Poor Cleo, on her first day back at work after the accident, was having to drive a car full of executives up to Gatwick.

Guilt kicked in then, because at least she was warm and dry and comfortable, and shouldn't that be enough to make her happy? But it wasn't. Unrelenting misery was now an inescapable part of her life and she knew she was no fun to live with. How Cleo was managing to put up with her, she had no idea. It was time to sort herself out and start thinking about the future. She couldn't impose indefinitely. She also needed to get another job.

Abbie headed downstairs in her dressing gown. She would make herself a cup of tea, curl up on the sofa and find something easy to watch on TV.

The doorbell rang halfway through *Britain's Got Talent*. A manic magician had just—apparently—sliced off his arm with a circular saw. The audience let out a collective gasp of horror as blood spurted across the stage. Abbie gasped too when she opened the front door and saw Des Kilgour standing wet and windswept on her doorstep.

'Abbie? Can I come in?'

She hesitated. 'Why?'

'I need to talk to you.'

'Des, I don't think so.' God, had he come here to tell her he still loved her? Her pulse quickened with anxiety. 'Really, there's nothing to say.'

'Look, this isn't like last time. It's nothing to do with that.' He paused, clearly embarrassed. 'It's about . . . something I've found out.'

Abbie wavered. Des was a good-hearted soul; it wasn't as if she was afraid of him.

'Please,' he said again.

She took off the chain and opened the door properly. 'OK.'

Rain dripped from Des's Barbour and formed puddles on the parquet floor. Sitting back down on the sofa and wrapping her dressing gown tightly around herself, Abbie said,' What's this about, then?'

'You know you thought it was Georgia who told Tom about us?'

Us. She wished he wouldn't use that word. 'It had to be Georgia. No one else knew anything.'

'It wasn't her.' He shook his head, causing Abbie to feel sick.

'So what are you telling me? It was you?'

'God no!' Stricken, Des said, 'Of course it wasn't me!'

'Who, then? Who stuck that letter on Tom's windscreen?'

'Glynis.'

'*What?* Glynis from the shop?' This made no sense. How could Glynis have found out? It wasn't physically possible.

'She wasn't snooping. She just . . . heard us.'

Abbie still couldn't believe it. 'And she actually told you this?'

'Huw did,' said Des. 'She only told him last night. He came to see me this evening, thought I should know.'

'I don't see how it happened.'

'It was my fault.' He shifted awkwardly from foot to foot. 'Glynis was working in the shop when the phone rang. She picked it up and heard our voices. I know, I know how it happened,' Des hurried on. 'I worked it out. Before you came into my office that morning, I'd been trying to contact Huw. Then when you turned up and we were talking I must have accidentally knocked my phone and hit redial. Glynis answered the phone and heard us. I suppose it sounded as if we were having a full-on affair. And she's pretty straight, you know. It shocked her. She didn't want to be seen to be the one spreading gossip, but she thought Tom deserved to know what was going on.'

'Oh God.' Abbie rubbed her face as the information sank in.

'Sorry. But I had to tell you.' Des raked his fingers through his reddish fair hair. 'Huw feels bad about it too.'

'Right. Well, thanks. At least now we know.'

As she showed him out, Des said, 'Everyone misses you at work, you know. Not just me. If you wanted to, we'd have you back tomorrow.'

'Thanks, but it'd be too difficult. I couldn't.' Abbie knew that Tom wasn't going to take her back, but the superstitious part of her wouldn't let her even consider returning to Kilgour's in case he found out just as he might be on the verge of changing his mind.

The trees creaked and swayed and leaves swirled up like ghosts as the storm raged around her. Everyone else was inside tonight. Abbie's umbrella had been blown inside out; giving up on it, she let the rain hit her in the face. Within minutes she'd reached her old home. It was eleven o'clock but there were still plenty of lights on. And it didn't matter how horrendous the weather was, she wasn't going inside.

Not that she was likely to be invited.

Abbie braced herself. She didn't even know yet if Georgia was there. She could be out. And Georgia was the only person she wanted to speak to. Oh well, only one way to find out.

But it was Georgia who answered the door and was visibly shocked to see her. 'Oh. Dad's not here.'

Good. 'That's OK, it's you I wanted to see.' Abbie noted the bandage on Georgia's right hand.

Opening the door wider, Georgia stepped aside and said, 'You'd better come in.'

'No, um, I'd rather not . . .' As she spoke, a blast of wind hit Abbie from behind, almost knocking her off her feet.

'It's all right, you can come in, it's OK.'

Relieved, Abbie stepped over the doorstep.'

The living room was festooned with more clothes than ever. Georgia winced with pain as she picked up the steaming iron.

Right, let's get this done before Tom comes back. Abbie plunged straight in. 'Look, I've come to apologise. I accused you of telling Tom about . . . you know. And you told me you hadn't, but I didn't believe you. Well, now I know it wasn't you. I was wrong and I'm so, so sorry.'

Georgia stopped ironing. She carefully upended the iron on its rest and said, 'So who was it, then?'

Abbie explained who had composed the anonymous letter and how it had come to be written. 'I think Glynis's conscience was pricking her, because she knew I thought it was you.' She shook her head and clutched at her battered umbrella. 'Anyway, that's how it happened. And I'm sorry.'

'Thanks. But you should have believed me.' Georgia looked relieved and sad at the same time. 'I'm a very honest person.'

'I know. And there's nothing worse than being accused of something you didn't do. That's why I had to come over and tell you, because I felt so terrible . . .' Abbie's voice trailed off as Georgia bent her head and a tear plopped onto the ironing board. First one, then—*plop*—another. 'Oh please, don't cry. You didn't do anything wrong!'

'That's not quite true though, is it?' Raising her chin, Georgia said unsteadily, 'I've messed up everything. I should never have come here. No wonder you hate me; look what's happened since I turned up. I've ruined your life.'

Oh God. Abbie was horrified. 'You haven't . . . you didn't . . .'

'I have.' Georgia's mouth wobbled with the effort of not bursting into tears. 'I'm not stupid, I know what it's been like for you. I've wrecked everything and I'm s-sorry . . . if I hadn't come along, you and Tom would still be t-together.'

Unable to bear it a moment longer, Abbie rushed over. Georgia let out a howl of misery and crumpled into her arms.

'Oh sweetheart, don't cry, ssshhh.' A lump sprang into Abbie's throat as she folded her into a hug.

'*Ow* . . .' Flinching, Georgia pulled her bandaged hand free.

'I'm sorry, I'm sorry.' Attempting to let her go, Abbie discovered she couldn't; Georgia was clinging to her like a baby koala.

'And you mustn't blame yourself. I'm the one who messed up. It's not your fault . . . oh God, now you've set me off . . . listen to me, you haven't done *anything* wrong.' Her own tears were now falling into the hair of the daughter she'd never had. She stroked Georgia's silky head and patted her like a baby. 'Don't cry. Goodness, what do we look like? If your Dad comes in now . . .'

'He's got a job on in Bournemouth so he's staying down there for a couple of days. It's just me here tonight.'

'And your hand? What happened to that?'

'Burned it with the iron.'

'Let me see.'

Georgia reluctantly peeled off the bandage.

'*Ouch.*' Abbie winced at the sight of the triangular burn on her palm.

'I know. I sent the iron flying and tried to catch it.' Georgia said wryly, 'That's how smart I am.'

'How can you even *hold* an iron now?' It had to be agonisingly painful.

Georgia indicated the bags of clothes. 'That's how. It all has to be done and I can't let people down. I took Sunday off to go out with Dad, so yesterday I was ironing for eighteen hours straight. And I still haven't caught up.'

She was in pain, emotionally wrung out and physically exhausted. Abbie said, 'Oh sweetheart, just look at you,' and took off her coat.

'It's OK, you don't have to help me.' Georgia's eyes filled with fresh tears as she watched Abbie roll up her sleeves.

'I know I don't. But I want to.' Abbie smiled at the girl she would have been unbelievably proud to call her daughter. 'And I'll keep going for as long as it takes. If you want to do something useful you could put the kettle on. I'd love a cup of tea.'

'**H**i, can you pop over? I've got something for you to say thanks for the other night.'

'Oh sweetheart, you didn't need to do that.' Abbie melted at the sound of Georgia's voice; it was so lovely to hear her sounding cheerful again. 'You don't have to buy me presents.'

'Ha, bit late now, it's here. I'd bring it over in the van,' said Georgia, 'but it's too heavy for me to lift on my own.'

Was it a bay tree in a pot, a garden table, a gigantic vase, a life-size pottery crocodile? With Georgia, who knew?

As Abbie reached the house and raised her hand to ring the bell, the front door was pulled open and Georgia threw her arms around her.

'Hello, I've got to go! Your present's in the living room. Hope you like it!'

And she was gone. The van sped off down the lane and Abbie's knees turned to spaghetti. Because her present was no longer in the living room. It had moved into the hallway.

'I've been given a big talking-to by my daughter,' said Tom. 'And she's explained some things I should have been adult enough to work out for myself.'

Abbie's heart was in her mouth. Tom's voice wasn't completely steady. Instead of his dusty work clothes he was wearing clean jeans and the blue-and-green striped shirt she had bought him for Christmas. She could tell by the set of his shoulders that he wasn't comfortable; talking about his feelings had never come naturally to him. Aloud she said faintly, 'What kind of things?'

'Oh, I don't know . . .' Tom licked his lips and gazed up at the ceiling. 'Things like I've missed you so much and I love you and the last couple of weeks have been the most miserable of my life . . .' Now that he'd started, the words came tumbling out. 'And I can either carry on being proud and miserable or I can get over what happened and put it behind me and tell you I don't want to live without you. Because that other stuff doesn't matter, it was a mistake and I just want us to be like we were before.' He shook his head. 'I knew I had to sort things out, but it took Georgia to bring me to my senses and realise that I need to do it now. It was just my stupid pride stopping me.' This time Tom's voice cracked with emotion. 'I was an idiot and I'm sorry, and I might have left it too late because you could be loving every minute of your new single life. But I love you so much, I really do. And if you do want to come back, you'd make me the happiest man in the world.'

Abbie managed a wobbly smile. This was why she'd spent her entire adult life loving him. Tom was honest, principled, loyal and strong. He might find it hard to express his feelings but that only made it all the more special when he did. Her throat tightening, she said, 'Are you sure?'

'I'm sure.' He nodded, keeping his gaze fixed on her. 'And you'd make Georgia pretty happy too.'

Was this really happening? She threw herself into his arms and this time Tom was the one whose eyes were damp with tears. Tom, who never, ever cried.

'I'm sorry too. I wish it hadn't happened but it did. I was out of my mind with misery and I made a hideous mistake. But I didn't have sex with Des Kilgour, I swear I didn't—'

'Sshh. It's OK, I believe you. I just want you back.'

Dizzy with joy, Abbie kissed him. 'I've missed you so much. I want to come back more than anything.'

He squeezed her, overcome with emotion. 'Good. And there are going to be some changes around here.'

Was he laying down the law? Were there going to be *rules*? Taken aback, Abbie said, 'Like what?'

Tom took a half-step back and drew her into the living room doorway. 'Take a look. Notice anything different?'

What was different? And then she saw. *Oh, good grief!* There were no clothes hung up, no crammed-full bags, no ironing board set up in front of the TV. The room was back to its pristine, uncluttered, pre-Georgia state. It looked so *empty* . . .

Abbie's heart thudded with fear. 'Is Georgia moving out?'

Tom looked carefully at her. 'Would it help if she did?'

'No! I don't want her to go!'

He broke into a smile. 'That's OK then. She's not going anywhere.'

Abbie gestured around the room. 'So where's . . . everything?'

'You know Georgia, she doesn't hang about. One of her clients runs an ad agency in Cheltenham. He offered her a job as his receptionist. She's taken on Ethel and Myrtle Mason to do the ironing at their house from now on. She'll take care of the pick-ups and deliveries before and after work. So that's it, all sorted. We've got our house back.'

'I've got my husband back.' Abbie stroked his dear familiar face.

'And I've got my beautiful wife back.' Kissing her, then kissing her again, Tom said, 'Now that's what I call a result.'

An hour later, Abbie's phone went. Smiling when she saw who was calling, she answered and said, 'Hi.'

'I've waited and waited, and now I can't wait a single second more. *Well?*' demanded Georgia.

Patience had never been one of her strong points.

Abbie said, 'What time are you coming home and what would you like for dinner?'

'Yay! Is everything really OK now?'

'It's more than OK. Thanks to you. How about roast chicken?'

'Yes please! With loads of roast potatoes. And can you do the stuffing separately? Because—'

'It's OK, I know.' Abbie realised that what she was feeling was unconditional love. Her happiness knew no bounds. Squeezing Tom's hand, she said into the phone, 'Because stuffing's always better when it's crunchy.'

Having switched on the radio expecting to hear Ash, Fia couldn't believe it when she found herself listening to the voice of a complete stranger.

For heaven's sake, who was this man burbling on about supermarket queues? He wasn't even funny! What was he doing on Ash's show?

Was it weird to be this indignant and put out? Oh well, too bad. Fia carried on listening until the usurper said chummily, 'And for those just joining us, a big hello from me, Max Margason, filling in for Ash this morning. Poor old Ash, he's only gone and lost his voice! Has he tried looking under the sofa cushions, that's what I want to know, ha ha ha!'

God, he was so *annoying*. But at least now she knew what had happened to Ash. Laryngitis, hardly ideal for a radio presenter. Poor thing; hopefully he wasn't feeling too rotten. Maybe she'd call round after lunch and see if there was anything he needed.

'Unless he's pulling a sickie,' Max burbled on. 'Eh, Megan? That could be it, couldn't it? Maybe he met a pretty young thing and . . . well, wa-heyyyy, just didn't feel like getting out of bed this morning, ha ha ha!'

How dare he say that? What an idiot, what an annoying, unfunny *prat*. Fia had never wanted to slap someone so badly in her life.

Emerging from the kitchen at lunch time, Fia was startled to see Ash sitting up at the bar. So he wasn't ill after all. Did that mean he'd lied to his bosses at the radio station? *Had* he pulled a sickie because he'd had a riotous night last night?

'Hi.' She felt . . . not jealous exactly. Just kind of needing to know.

Ash looked up and waggled his fingers by way of greeting. His fair hair was tousled and still damp from the shower. He was wearing a blue-and-white striped cotton shirt over a white T-shirt and faded jeans. Beckoning her over, he scribbled something on a fluorescent pink Post-it pad: Laryngitis. Hi!

Oh, the relief. Fia knew she was beaming like an idiot but she couldn't help herself. She was glad he hadn't got lucky last night.

'I know. I heard the other guy on the radio this morning.'

Ash raised an eyebrow and wrote: He's a dickhead.

'You can say that again.'

He tore off the Post-it and wrote on the next sheet: He's a dickhead.

Fia laughed. 'How are you feeling?'

Ash scrawled: Fine! It's just my voice that's gone. Saw Dr and he said rest it completely.

'Poor you.'

Ash wasn't looking at her. Instead he concentrated on writing the next message: When did you start listening to my show???

The fact that his eyes were fixed on the Post-it pad meant she didn't have to blush. 'Oh, a while back. I like it. I can listen to classical music during the rest of the day. You and Megan make me laugh.'

As he scribbled the next words, she noticed that Ash's neck was reddening. Maybe he was running a temperature and didn't realise it.

Fia watched him write: Excellent! But I'm funnier than Megan.

'That goes without saying.'

Smiling slightly, Ash scrawled: That's why I didn't say it.

'Are you hungry? Does it hurt to eat?'

He nodded then shook his head.

'So you'd like . . . ?' Fia indicated the blackboard with today's offerings chalked up.

Ash made horns of his index fingers.

'Chicken.'

He gave her a look.

'Sorry. Beef. OK, salad or curry?'

Ash fanned his mouth vigorously.

She smiled as his phone started to ring. 'Coming right up. Want me to answer that for you?'

He glanced at caller ID, shook his head and scribbled: Only my agent.

Ten minutes later, returning with the curry, she found Ash gazing into space and looking preoccupied.

'Everything OK?'

He paused, then grimly passed his mobile over to her, indicating that she should listen to the message.

Never mind preoccupied, he was in a state of shock. Had someone died? Had he been sacked? Fia put down the plate of beef Madras and took the phone.

'Ash? Listen, kid, we've had an approach from KCL. I've just taken a call from the big boss—he's a major fan of yours. He wants you to fly over there, meet the team, see what you make of the place.' Ash's agent had a gravelly, agenty type of voice. His words sent an icy tremor down Fia's spine. 'But they really want you, so it's pretty much a done deal. And they're talking big bucks. So how about that then? Bit of a result, eh? Told you it was worth a shot. Call me back, kid. See ya!'

Fia switched the phone off and swallowed hard. 'Wow. Where's KCL?'

She peered at the pad as he wrote: Sydney.

'Australia?' Idiotic question. And she already knew how many enthusiastic Australian fans he had; they were endlessly emailing the show. Ash called them his Possum Posse.

He nodded.

'I didn't know you were thinking of moving abroad.'

He shrugged helplessly.

'Well, good for you. Sydney. Wow.' OK, this was getting stupid, she had to stop saying wow. Fia dredged up a smile. 'Bondi Beach.

Barbecues. Beer . . . all that *sun* . . .' Oh God, listen to her, and now she was practically pushing him onto the plane.

Deborah joined them. 'Fia, table three are ready to order. D'you want me to do it?'

Did she? Fia couldn't even tell. All she knew was that she was seized with a strange panicky fear teetering on the edge of tearfulness.

OK, get a grip. She shook her head at Deborah. 'No . . . no, it's fine, I'll take care of them now.'

Probably just as well, before she made a massive fool of herself in the middle of the pub without even quite understanding why.

Sometimes dreams trick you into believing they're real. And then there are other times when, completely out of the blue, life suddenly becomes so surreal that you wonder if perhaps you're dreaming after all.

Cleo stared at Fia, who had come hurtling across the green to see her. It was nine o'clock in the morning, bright and sunny, and she'd been washing the red Bentley prior to picking up a married couple later who were celebrating their ruby wedding anniversary. She switched off the power hose.

'Sorry, say that again?'

'I don't want Ash to move to Australia. I don't want him to go.' Out of breath and with an air of desperation about her, Fia blurted out, 'The thing is, I really like him but he's always been really weird with me . . . I didn't know what I'd done wrong but he obviously couldn't stand me, then something changed and he seemed different and then I started to feel differently, but it's all so weird and confusing, and now there's this Australia thing happening and I'm just so *scared* . . .'

Blimey. Cleo was stunned; she'd never seen Fia in a state like this. 'So what do you want me to do?'

'Oh God.' Fia raked her fingers through her hair. 'I suppose I'm asking if he's said anything to you.'

'About Australia?'

'About me! I'm asking if he's said he really doesn't like me.' She paused, shaking her head. 'Or if you think, deep down, maybe he likes me a bit . . . you know, just enough to give me something to work with.'

Cleo surveyed her seriously, taking in the ruffled blonde hair, the absence of make-up, the air of agitation. 'It's neither of those.'

'Oh. Oh.'

'He doesn't dislike you.'

'Oh?' Hope flared in Fia's eyes.

'He doesn't like you a little bit.'

'Oh.' Fia's shoulders slumped. 'Right.'

'He likes you a lot.'

Confusion reigned. 'What?'

Honestly, how could some people be so blind? Cleo said, 'I thought you knew! It was so obvious, I thought you'd figured it out and were just being polite and pretending you hadn't noticed.'

Fia did a double take. 'He ignored me! He hardly ever *spoke*. Most of the time he wouldn't even look at me!'

'Hello?' Cleo gave her a *duh* look. 'That's kind of what shy people do.'

'*Shy?*' Fia clapped a hand over her mouth in disbelief. 'He said he was shy once, on the radio. I thought it was a joke.'

Cleo shook her head. 'Ash has had a massive crush on you from day one. I did offer to tell you but he threatened to chop me into small pieces. And to be honest, I never thought for one minute you'd go for him. The only person you were interested in was Johnny.'

'Maybe I was, at first. But some things are never going to happen, are they?' Fia shrugged, casually eradicating that idea. 'Anyway, forget about that. Let's talk about Ash. What am I going to *do*?'

Cleo wished she could fall in love with someone else and dismiss Johnny from her life as easily as Fia. Sadly he appeared to be stuck in her brain for good. But never mind that now; if there was anyone with a more disastrous love life than her, it was Ash. This was stunning news for him.

'Easy. Just tell him.'

'Oh God, my *heart*. I don't know if I can.' Fia was trembling and clutching her chest at the mere thought of it. 'He hasn't been over to the pub for the past two days. And I'm working tonight . . .' Fia fiddled with her watch strap. 'Perhaps I'll leave it until the weekend . . .'

Honestly, how could people *do* that? Never one of life's procrastinators—at least where good news was concerned—Cleo exclaimed, 'This is something *nice*! We're not talking about filling in a tax return here. You want to tell him straight away!'

'I know, but this is all a bit sudden.' Fia was hyperventilating and edging backwards. 'I kind of need to think about how to say it.'

Right, enough faffing about. A kick up the backside was definitely called for. Thinking on her feet, Cleo said, 'Except you can't afford to hang about, can you? Because it'll be too late. You have to do it now!'

Fia's eyes widened. 'Why?'

'Because he's jacking in his job, didn't you know?' Cleo shook her head and crossed her fingers behind her back. 'He told me yesterday, said there was nothing to keep him here so he may as well go to Australia. He's going to resign live on air this morning.'

'He's doing it *today*?' Fia's throat went blotchy with shock.

'At the end of the show.' God, she was brilliant.

Fia checked her watch. 'It's ten past nine. Oh my God, you have to stop him!'

'*You* have to stop him,' said Cleo.

'How can I do that?'

'Phone him. Now.'

'Oh God, no, I couldn't. On the phone?' Vehemently Fia shook her head. 'No way.'

Cleo put down the power hose and gave her a measured look. Then she eased her mobile out of her jeans pocket. Finally she said in a firm but kind voice, 'If you don't want to lose him, you don't have a choice.'

Panicking and caving in, Fia whispered fearfully, 'OK then.'

Hee!

Inside the cottage, Cleo made her sit on the sofa. She pressed out the number of the radio station and asked to speak to Megan. The call was transferred in a matter of moments.

'Megan? Hi, it's Cleo Quinn. Now listen, have you ever wanted to be a fairy godmother?'

Megan, Ash's traffic and weather girl and all-round sidekick, was always up for some fun. 'Hi, Cleo! You mean with a wand and a tiara? Always!'

'Well, listen, don't let Ash know who's calling, but I've got a friend here who has something very important she'd like to say to him. And let me tell you, it'll be good.'

'Yeah?' Megan was immediately interested. 'Ooh, give me a clue!'

'I can't, it's better if it's a surprise, but you'll love it, I promise. So, can you put her on after the next record?'

Fia let out a squeak of alarm. 'I'm not saying it on the radio! Can't I just talk to him off-air?'

'No, because the hands-free thingy's broken on my phone so I wouldn't be able to hear what's going on at the other end. This way,' Cleo explained cheerfully, 'I can!'

'Is that her in the background?' Megan said, 'What's her name?'

'It's Fia.'

'Oh, *Fia*.' Megan sounded even more intrigued. 'The one who does the food in the pub? Ash is always talking about her.'

'That's because he's secretly in luuuuurve with her.' Beaming across at Fia, Cleo said, 'But nobody else knows it yet.'

'Hallelujah, I am loving the sound of this.' Megan, who spent her life being mercilessly teased by Ash, let out a whoop of delight. 'Let's do it, baby. Put her on!'

Fia's palms were slick with perspiration. Gripped with terror, she almost dropped the phone when Cleo passed it across. How was this happening to her?

'Listen,' said Cleo encouragingly, 'it's got to be easier than doing it face to face.'

But Fia could barely hear what Cleo was telling her, because Megan was saying in her other ear, 'Fia? Hi there, I'm going to bring you in at the end of this track that's playing now. You just say what you have to say to Ash, but do keep it clean, OK? And don't try to listen to yourself on the radio there, because we operate with a two-second delay and you'd get in a muddle.'

Fia croaked, 'Right.' How much more of a muddle could she get into than the one she was already in? Glancing across at Cleo, who was busy fiddling with the tuner on her old transistor, she shook her head and said, 'You can't have it on in here. Take it into the kitchen.' She couldn't cope with Cleo watching while she possibly turned herself into an international laughing stock.

Then the track that had been playing on the radio came to an end and in her ear Fia heard Megan announcing, 'That was Leona Lewis with her new single, and now we have a mystery caller on the line for our Ash. And I want all of you out there to pay attention to this, because I have it on good authority that it's going to be worth listening to.'

'What's this?' protested Ash. 'Some kind of set-up? It had better not be that barking psychotherapist again, calling to tell me—'

'It's not the psychotherapist,' Megan interrupted. 'It's a lady by the name of Fia, who I believe you already know. Hello, Fia! Ooh, and can I just tell everyone that Ash has now gone a very fetching shade of pink!'

'Hi. It's me.' Fia discovered that her mouth was managing to produce the words despite the fact that her brain felt as if it had just been whizzed up in a blender.

'Fia?' Ash sounded stunned.

OK. Fia closed her eyes; she had to do this, she just had to. Don't think about who else might be listening. This was just the two of them now. She cleared her throat and said, 'The thing is . . . someone's just told me that, um, you might quite, um, like me. And I wondered if it was true. Because if it is, I just want you to know that I feel the same way about you, and the reason I'm telling you this now is in case it might make you change your mind about Australia.'

'Australia . . .' Ash repeated the word as if in a trance.

She couldn't give up now. She'd started, so she'd finish. 'So basically, I don't want you to go.'

Ash said dazedly, 'Why not?'

Fia unstuck her tongue from the roof of her mouth. 'Because I'd miss you. I can't believe I'm saying this on the radio. And if you're taking up the job in Sydney because it's what you want more than anything in the world, that's fine. Just forget any of this happened. But if it makes any difference at all, I need you to know that if you *did* decide to stay here . . . well, I'd be glad about that, because I really, really like you. A lot.'

'This *liking* thing,' said Ash. 'Excuse me for asking, but can I just double-check that this isn't liking in a platonic kind of way?'

Fia took a deep breath. 'No, definitely not platonic.'

Oh heavens, she'd actually said it now.

Ash cleared his throat and said huskily, 'Fia? Is this true?'

As if she'd be doing this if it wasn't. 'Yes, it's true.'

'God, I can't believe it.'

A laugh bubbled up without any warning at all. 'Neither can I!'

'This is . . . amazing.'

'I know. Do you really like me?'

'Yes. Oh yes. You have no idea.'

'Are you going to Australia?'

'No. I called them days ago and told them I wasn't taking the job.'

Jolted, Fia wailed, '*Days ago?* But I thought you were handing in your notice today . . . I mean, er . . .'

The kitchen door swung open, bursting the bubble and bringing her crashing back to reality. Cleo poked her head round and said gaily, 'Whoops, sorry, I made that bit up!'

What? 'Why?'

'Duh. Otherwise you wouldn't have done this!'

On the other end of the line, Fia realised, Megan and other people in the studio were now whistling and cheering. Megan was saying gleefully, 'Oh my word, you should see how many texts and emails we've got coming in—this console's lit up like the Starship *Enterprise*!'

'Look, I've just got to finish the show,' said Ash, 'then I'm coming home. I can be there in an hour. Where will you be?'

Unable to wipe the ridiculous smile off her face, Fia said joyfully, 'I'll be right here, waiting for you.'

In Channings Hill, Abbie and Georgia listened to the rest of the show in silence, then Abbie switched off the radio. 'Oh sweetie, are you upset? I know how much you liked him.'

Georgia dabbed a finger across her plate, carefully collecting up crumbs and wondering how she felt. So that was it, Fia from the pub was in love with Ash. And Ash, it turned out, had been secretly in love with her for months. And now they were a couple, so besotted with each other that you could almost *feel* it over the airwaves.

Whereas Ash might have been her type but, for whatever reason, she hadn't been his. Anyone would be disappointed, wouldn't they? But the thing was, it wasn't her fault. The reason he hadn't wanted her wasn't because she was unattractive and a complete turnoff, but simply because she hadn't been Fia Newman.

Which was actually quite a comforting thing to know.

'I liked him. But it's no big deal.'

Abbie gave her shoulder an affectionate squeeze on her way to the sink. 'Don't let it get you down. You're a gorgeous girl and you'll find someone else. It's his loss.'

Georgia smiled and relaxed. So far this year she'd acquired a new home, a new family and two new jobs, which was probably enough for anyone to be going along with for now. Aloud she said happily, 'Yeah.'

When Ash arrived home fifty minutes later, Fia was waiting for him outside his cottage. His heart began to thud at the sight of her, in her grey top and skirt, her gold-brown hair lifting in the morning breeze.

Somewhat less romantically, Cleo was there too, looking incredibly pleased with herself.

Ash climbed out of the car, pointed to her open front door and said, 'Off you go.'

'Spoilsport.' Triumphantly she said, 'This is all thanks to me, you know.'

'All the same. Bye.'

Amazingly, she disappeared inside her cottage. He turned his attention back to Fia. Her amber eyes were glowing. His voice cracking with emotion, Ash said, 'You're beautiful.'

Fia visibly relaxed. She broke into a huge, uncontrollable smile. Without even hesitating, she moved towards him and kissed him on the mouth. Oh God, this was fantastic . . . her lips were warm and soft . . . she was pressing her body against his . . . Like magic, he discovered that all the excruciating shyness had melted away. It was no longer there, paralysing his mind and rendering him practically unable to think, let alone speak. Still holding her, Ash broke away and said, 'Not that I'm complaining, but what brought this on?'

'You didn't come to the pub,' said Fia. 'It's been three days since you got that message from your agent. Last night I couldn't sleep for thinking about you. Then I came over here this morning to see Cleo and she said you were off to Australia. And she told me all about you resigning live on air at the end of today's show.' Fia shook her head. 'So I realised I had to stop you before you did that. Except what I didn't know was that she'd made the whole story up.'

Ash stroked her face. Her skin was like silk. 'You're amazing.'

Fia wrapped her arms tightly around him. 'And as it seems to have worked, I suppose I can't be too cross with her. Tell me why you decided against Australia.'

He regarded her with amusement. 'OK, can you seriously picture me on Bondi Beach? A million fit, tanned bodies and one beached whale?'

'Stop it. You're not fat. OK,' Fia amended, 'you're a *bit* fat. But I like it. You're *you*.' She ran her hand down his front. 'And you're definitely not a whale.'

'I'll never have a six-pack,' said Ash.

'My husband had one of those. Six-packs are nothing to write home about. They're not even comfortable, just rock-hard and bumpy.'

Ash smiled. 'That's it then, I definitely don't want one now.'

Then he took her by the hand and led her up the path and into the house. The real reason he hadn't seriously considered taking the job in Sydney was because Fia was here. But he'd tell her that later.

Right now they had more important things to do.

Chapter 11

'HI, IT'S ME.' The moment she heard his voice on the other end of the line, Cleo's stomach did its habitual swoop-and-dive. 'Look, I have a big favour to ask you.'

Cleo hesitated. Did she even want to do Johnny any more favours? Since returning from Norfolk last week following the funeral, he and Honor had been seen coming and going. In yesterday's *Daily Mail* there had been a photo of them arriving at a high-profile fashion event in Knightsbridge. Honor had looked stunning in a scarlet taffeta mermaid-style dress that showed off her signature curves. Johnny had been wearing a designer suit. Honor was quoted as saying, 'Sacrifice?

What sacrifice? Love's all that matters and I've never been happier in my life!'

Which was how Cleo, upon reading the accompanying piece, had learned that Honor Donaldson had turned down a multimillion-dollar deal to front a major cosmetics campaign because it would have meant working in Venezuela and being apart from Johnny for three months. Explaining her decision, Honor had said, 'It was pressure of work that broke us up last time. We're not going to let that happen again. Being together is more important than any amount of money in the bank.'

Which was undoubtedly true, but didn't make it any easier to read. There was something about other people's happiness—well, Johnny and Honor's happiness—that was hard to bear. Anyway, back to the present. Cleo braced herself. 'What kind of favour?'

Unless . . . wouldn't it be great if he was calling to say that it was all over between him and Honor and could she possibly come over and give them a hand packing up her stuff?

God, that would be fantastic.

Johnny said, 'Are you doing anything this evening?'

Hmm, one of *those* questions, the kind where you had to commit yourself before discovering what you were letting yourself in for. Well, she wasn't going to fall for *that* old trick.

Cleo said cautiously, 'What's the favour?'

'The thing is, we've got Clarice here at the house. She's come to stay for a few days. Now mentally she's fine, but physically she's pretty frail and I don't want to leave her on her own. But we've been invited to a gallery opening tonight and they're raising money for charity . . . I promised to help out and I don't want to let them down.'

That was it, then. Basically, she would be Cinderella left at home while he and Honor swanned off to the prince's ball.

'So you're wanting me to baby-sit?'

'Just for a few hours. We'd be home by midnight. But only if you want to. If you're busy, that's fine,' said Johnny. 'I'll ask someone else.'

Cleo hesitated; the way her brain was programmed meant she found it hard to refuse anyone requesting a favour. It was one of those genetic things; you could either do it without a qualm or you couldn't.

Plus, it wasn't as if she had anything else planned for this evening.

'OK, I'll do it. What time do you want me?'

For a moment there was no reply and she wondered if her phone had gone dead. Then Johnny said, 'You will? That's great, you're a star. Eight o'clock all right with you?'

He'd come to her rescue when she'd crashed into a ditch. Of course she had to help him in return. And anyway, it might turn out to be fun. Forcing herself to sound cheerful, Cleo said, 'No problem. Eight's fine.'

'**O**h hooray, you're here, come on in, thanks so much for doing this!' Honor greeted her warmly at the door and ushered her through to the living room. 'Come and meet Clarice. Poor old darling, she's a bit crotchety but we've only got her for a few days. Here we are, then!' She pushed open the door and raised her voice. 'Aunt Clarice, this is Cleo, she's going to be keeping you company this evening, isn't that nice?'

'How would I know if it's nice? She might be the most boring creature on the planet.'

Okaaaaaay.

'Well, she isn't,' said Honor. 'She's lovely, so there.'

'And I'm crotchety.' Johnny's aged aunt eyed her over the top of her reading glasses. 'Mainly because you keep calling me a poor old darling and acting as if I'm stone deaf.'

'Hey, how's it going? Thanks for doing this.' Johnny hurried into the room, pulling on his jacket. He nodded at Cleo, then at his aunt. 'You'll be fine with Cleo. There's whisky in the cupboard and food in the fridge. We won't be late home.'

'Baby, can you do this for me?' Honor approached Johnny holding out a narrow gold chain. Sweeping up her hair and turning her flawless back to him, she waited while he fastened it around her neck.

'There, done.' He stepped back.

'And that's us all ready to go!' Flashing them the kind of smile that made Cleo feel about as alluring as a squashed frog, Honor waggled her French-manicured fingers and said, 'See you later! Have fun!'

They let themselves out of the house and Clarice echoed drily, '*Have fun. If only I'd remembered to bring my time machine with me.*'

She was in her late seventies, as thin as a whippet and with practically translucent skin. Her hair was grey and fastened back in a ballerina's bun. She was wearing a plain white shirt, pale-green wool skirt and darker green cardigan. No make-up. Miss-nothing grey eyes.

Cleo sat down opposite her. 'I'm so sorry about your sister.'

'Thank you. Yes.' Clarice nodded briefly and closed the book on her lap. She removed her rimless reading glasses and said, 'First Lawrence, then Barbara. Only one of us left now.'

'Are you down here for long?'

'Just a few days. Then it's back to the nursing home.'

'What's that like?'

'Full of old people. Who keep *dying*. Oh, it's a laugh a minute. The conversation just sparkles.' Clarice heaved a sigh.

'If you don't like it,' said Cleo, 'why are you there?'

'Oh, God knows. It was Barbara's idea, when the house got too much for us. And she seemed to like it. She was happy there.' Clarice paused. 'I wouldn't call it my idea of heaven.'

'So couldn't you leave?'

'What, run away and join the circus?' With a brief smile, Clarice said, 'Unfortunately I'm a decrepit old bat, just in case you hadn't noticed. I have heart problems, joint problems, eye problems, you name it. Oh yes, it's a bundle of laughs being old and in possession of a body that's falling to bits.' She dismissed the topic with a shrug. 'Anyway, enough about me and my disintegrating bones. Why don't we talk about something more interesting? Johnny tells me you're a chauffeuse . . .'

The next couple of hours passed effortlessly. Contrary to expectations, Cleo really enjoyed herself. Clarice might be a decrepit old bat, but she was hugely entertaining, as sharp and scurrilous as Paul O'Grady and with a wicked sense of humour to boot. She also spoke about her family and told brilliant tales of Johnny's childhood.

'He came to stay with me once when he was . . . ooh, six or seven. I was driving us along when all of a sudden a mouse ran across my foot. Damn near crashed the car! And Johnny said, "Oh no, I forgot I had Harry in my pocket. Poor Harry, if we'd had an accident he could have been *killed*."'

Hopeless case that she was, just the mention of Johnny was enough to cause a flutter of excitement in her chest. Quelling it, Cleo said, 'That almost happened to me once. I had a client in the back of the car and we were heading along the M5 when he said, "Now don't panic, Miss Quinn, but I have to warn you that my snake is heading for your gearstick."'

'Ha!' Clarice almost spilled her tumbler of whisky and water. 'I once had a work colleague like that.'

'Except this was a real snake.' Shuddering at the memory, Cleo said, 'And I was doing eighty in the outside lane.'

Johnny and Honor arrived back just before midnight.

'We're home!' said Honor, and Cleo's heart sank, because she said it as if she meant it. Ravenswood was her home now, and she and Johnny were a proper couple. A golden couple with everything going for them.

Johnny surveyed them from the doorway. 'Everything OK?'

'Perfect. We've had a wonderful evening.' Patting Cleo's hand, Clarice said, 'Couldn't have asked for a nicer baby sitter.'

He smiled briefly. 'Good.'

'How about you two?'

'Great.' Johnny shrugged. 'The evening was a success. The art was . . . interesting.'

'It was modern,' Honor cut in. 'Basically, it looked like it had been done by a bunch of drunken monkeys. Paint spattered everywhere. But we raised a ton of money, so that's the main thing. Right, I'm off to bed. Night, everyone! See you, Clarice!' She blew kisses and retired upstairs.

Clarice said drily, 'See you.'

'Clarice isn't happy in that nursing home. She was only putting up with it to keep her sister company. And now she doesn't have to stay there any more.'

Johnny had offered to walk her home and Cleo had taken him up on it. This was something he needed to hear and she suspected that for all her straight talking, Clarice wouldn't dream of telling him herself.

He nodded thoughtfully. 'I did wonder.'

'She hates it.'

'That bad?'

'Yes.' She was firm.

Johnny shoved his hands into his jacket pockets as they made their way across the wet grass. 'Well then, we need to get something else organised.'

'Can I say something?'

In the darkness she detected a glimmer of a smile. 'Can I stop you?'

Only with a kiss. But that's not going to happen, so don't even think about it.

Aloud she said, 'Your aunt is brilliant. I really like her.'

'So do I.'

'But when she told me about how much she hated the nursing home, I said hadn't she thought about moving to this part of the country? And she said she couldn't do that because then you'd feel obliged to visit her all the time. She doesn't want to put you under pressure.'

Johnny stopped walking. 'She's my only living relative. Why would she think I'd feel pressurised?'

'Because she says you have your own life to live and you don't need some ancient relative taking up your time. Which is why I'm telling you now.' Cleo looked at him. 'Even though she made me promise I wouldn't. But I do happen to know a good nursing home in Bristol. One of my regular customers lives there and she loves it.'

'And when I'm at home she could come and stay here . . . it'd be easy if she was that close.' Johnny said, 'Whereabouts is this nursing home?

What's it called? God, she used to be a consultant obstetrician and spent forty years terrifying the life out of young doctors. She's such a professional battleaxe I can't believe Clarice didn't want to ask me herself.'

'She's doesn't want to be a burden.' Brimming with fresh emotion, Cleo said, 'Look, if you ever needed a hand with her, I'd be more than happy to help out.' Oh God, did that make her sound like a creep, desperate for contact with him no matter how tenuous it might be?

They'd reached the cottage. Johnny lightly touched her on the arm and the unexpected contact made her shiver with suppressed longing.

He looked down at her and said, 'What is it?'

Cleo shook her head helplessly; it wasn't as if she could blurt out how she felt about him and how utterly bereft Honor's reappearance in his life had made her feel.

'Nothing. I'm OK, just . . . you know, tired . . .'

Johnny's dark eyes glittered. 'I meant what's the name of the nursing home?'

'Oh God, sorry . . .' Just as well it was dark; she felt her cheeks heat up. 'It's Naish House in Clifton, up on the Downs.'

'I'll have a look at the web site when I get home.' He paused. 'Thanks for tonight. I owe you one.'

Owed her one what? A favour? A moment of rampant passion? For a long moment they looked at each other and Cleo wondered if he was thinking what she was thinking. What would happen if she were to grab him now, just go for it and, God, *launch* herself at him? And was she imagining it or did he—

'Yee-ha!' The whoop came out of the darkness, closely followed by the sound of running footsteps and panting and muffled laughter. Together they turned and saw Ash racing across the grass towards them with his striped shirt untucked and Fia in his arms giggling and shrieking to be put down. On their way back from the pub, it wasn't hard to guess why they were in such a hurry to get home. Watching them, Cleo was glad they were so ecstatically happy, but Ash's timing definitely left something to be desired.

Then again, maybe it was just as well.

'Evening!' Grinning broadly at the sight of them, Ash lowered Fia to the ground but kept his arm around her; practically inseparable for the past few days, it was as if they couldn't bear to let each other go.

'Evening.' Johnny smiled briefly and said, 'Right, I'd better get back then.' He looked at Cleo, his expression unreadable. 'Thanks again.'

She dragged her gaze away from his mouth and heard herself say as chirpily as a Girl Guide, 'No problem, I really enjoyed it. Good night!'

From her darkened bedroom window Cleo watched as Johnny made his way back across the green to Ravenswood. And to Honor Donaldson, curvy and irresistible and more than likely currently lying naked in his huge king-sized bed.

Not that she'd ever seen it, but she'd bet any money it was king-sized.

From next door came whoops and squeals of helpless laughter. Cleo rubbed her hands over her face and turned away from the window. It wasn't much fun feeling unwanted, unloved and like a gooseberry in your own house.

The past eight days had been a whirlwind of work. The upside to this, Cleo had discovered, was that it kept your mind occupied and stopped you daydreaming hopelessly about your last unsatisfactory encounter with Johnny LaVenture before he and Honor had disappeared from the village. Well, it almost stopped you daydreaming about him. The downside was that she was exhausted and today had been another long day. A long, loooonnnngggg day. Nor, sadly, was it over yet. When she called Grumpy Graham and tried to wriggle out of the third booking, he informed her in no uncertain terms that she was out of luck.

'But I did the Heathrow run this morning.' She wondered if he had a heart at all. 'And I've done the wedding anniversary thing in Devon. Couldn't someone else do this one?'

'Bloody hell, no, they flaming well can't.' Graham heaved a sigh of annoyance. 'I've already told you, everyone else is *busy*.'

With resignation Cleo gave up and ended the call. It looked as if she had a couple more hours to go yet. And another hundred miles at least, in order to collect someone called Lady Rosemary from her home outside Stratford upon Avon and take her to Shepton Mallet.

Cleo could guess what Lady Rosemary would be like. Loud for a start, with an offhand manner. She would complain about bumps in the road, be wearing nostril-shrivelling perfume and she would exhale with irritation every time they were forced to stop at a zebra crossing, because how *dare* people in ghastly track suits want to cross the road.

Cleo gave herself a mental shake; she was tired, her back was aching and her life was shit. But hey, the job was booked and she had to do it. Served her right for being indispensable.

An hour later she was almost there. Compton Court was in the depths of the Warwickshire countryside, and it was proving to be extremely well hidden. The battery on the satnav had died and she was due to pick up Lady Rosemary at eight o'clock. Finally arriving at a junction, Cleo saw that the rustic wooden road sign had had its arms wrenched off—evidently what passed for teenage entertainment in these parts. Pulling into one side of the narrow lane, she reached across to retrieve her map from the glove compartment. Maps didn't have annoying robotic voices, they didn't run out of batteries, they were reliable and trustworthy and they—

Oh *fuck*.

And they were held together with a spiral of wire that had sharp ends capable of snagging a hole in your tights just when you *really* didn't need it to happen.

A hole *and* a ladder now, on the one day she didn't have an emergency pair stashed in her bag. If this wasn't a shining example of how crappy her life was at the moment, she didn't know what was.

Two miles down the road, possible salvation presented itself in the form of a tiny petrol station of the postwar kind. Two old-fashioned pumps stood on a minuscule forecourt amid piles of used tyres and several rusty cars. But by some miracle it appeared to be open. A fat man in dusty overalls was tinkering with the engine of an old van. Cleo jumped out of the car and said, 'Hi, I'm looking for Compton Court.'

He straightened up and wiped sausagey fingers on a cloth. 'Lady Rosemary's place? Straight along this road, take the second right, then half a mile along and you'll see the entrance on your left.'

'Thanks. Um, is your shop open?'

The man nodded and said, 'Feel free.'

Calling it a shop was possibly overstating the case. The tiny room was part of the garage and the air tasted of dust and oil. There were crisps on sale, cartons of UHT milk, bottles of limeade and crates of fresh-from-the-garden vegetables. In addition, on a series of shelves, were piled assorted motoring magazines, petrol cans, bottles of engine oil, stretchy steering-wheel covers and a box of wheel nuts.

And then, the second miracle: Cleo spotted a selection of rain hats, plastic macs and packets of tights.

This was the good news. The bad news was that the tights were all forty denier, extra large and American Tan in colour.

Cleo turned to the man who had followed her into the shop. 'Um, do you have any other tights?'

'No, sorry.'

'Oh. It's just that these are a bit grannyish.'

He lit a cigarette. 'They're my wife's tights.'

'Oh. Sorry.'

'She died last year.' He breathed out a lungful of smoke. 'So I thought I might as well sell them.'

Oh, good grief. At least they were still in their packets; his wife hadn't actually worn them. 'I'm sorry. I'll have this pair.' Cleo hurriedly paid for them; bare legs would look so much better, but her uniform demanded that she wear tights and Lady Rosemary would be bound to complain if she didn't.

A mile down the road she pulled into a gateway and changed into the Nora Batty tights. They were the colour of really strong tea and absolutely huge, wrinkling around her legs like a snake halfway through shedding its skin. Oh well, never mind.

Cleo followed the garage owner's instructions and finally reached the entrance to Compton Court. The sun had just set, a misty dusk was falling and the driveway leading up to the house was lined with chestnut trees.

Very nice too. Quite Jane Austen-esque, in fact. Cleo's mood began to improve as she reached the top of the driveway. You could imagine the lady of the house holding a Regency ball here, greeting her guests on the steps and graciously—

'Oh hi, you the driver?' The front door had swung open to reveal a teenage girl with multiple facial piercings, fluorescent pink eye shadow and leopard-print jeans. Clutching her mobile phone to one ear and gesturing with her free hand, she said, 'They're round the back, just follow the path down past the rose garden and go through the arch in the yew hedge . . . yah, I know, I *told* Zan she was a slapper but he didn't believe me!'

Probably not Lady Rosemary. Engrossed once more in her phone conversation, the girl wandered back into the house and kicked the door shut with her bare foot. The good news was that she hadn't even noticed Cleo's legs.

The tights were loose around the waist too. She was forced to hold them up as she made her way through the misty gloom. Her shoes crunched on the gravel and the smell of freshly mown grass hung in the air. Rooks were cawing in the trees, disturbed by the drone of a single-engined plane as it crossed overhead. As Cleo passed the carefully tended rose garden, she began to hear voices in the distance. Ahead of her stood the yew hedge, twelve-foot tall and with an eight-foot arch carved into it. Something was happening beyond the arch; as she moved towards it, the voices grew louder and she glimpsed flashes of colour and movement through the gap.

Some kind of garden party, by the look of things. Cleo bent and attempted to smooth out the accordion pleats in her tights then grabbed the waistband and yanked them up, Benny-Hill style, as high as they'd go.

As she reached the archway a switch was flicked, and the area beyond it was suddenly flooded with light and the assembled audience burst into applause.

Behind them, Cleo's heart did a dolphin leap of disbelief. A surge of adrenaline shot through her body and her skin prickled with recognition, because there in the centre of the clearing, illuminated by the expertly angled uplighters, stood a family of deer. The proud stag, antlers stretched and like wings, directly faced them. To his right stood the graceful female, her neck bent as she grazed. And between them, playful and inquisitive, was their faun.

Not a real family of deer, but constructed from stainless steel and larger than life-size. The stag was over twelve-foot tall. Bathed in silvery-white light and surrounded by trees, the effect was ethereal and otherworldly. And the woman leading the applause was now drawing their creator forward.

Johnny was smiling, wearing a dark-blue shirt and jeans, looking modest and unbelievably gorgeous. Cleo couldn't help herself; just seeing him unexpectedly like this was enough to set off a whole cascade of emotions. Ravenswood had been standing empty for the past week. No one had known where he was.

'Thanks so much to Johnny for making my dream come true. He's absolutely exceeded my expectations, I couldn't be happier with my beautiful sculptures and I know I'm going to love them until the day I die!' The woman—could this be Lady Rosemary?—was in her early fifties, plump and smiley in a padded gilet and corduroy trousers. So much for preconceptions. She hugged Johnny before announcing, 'Well, it's getting a bit chilly so shall we all head back inside? Ooh, hello!' Spotting Cleo hovering at the back of the crowd by the giant yew hedge, she added, 'Have you come to whisk my favourite artist away?'

As they passed her on their way back up to the house, Cleo felt herself being scrutinised by the assembled guests. Were they laughing at her Nora Batty corrugated tights? When it was just the three of them left, the woman clasped Cleo's hand in both of hers and said warmly, 'I've heard all about you, my dear. I'm Rose, by the way.'

What was going on? Cleo said, 'Hello, I'm Cleo. Um . . . am I driving you to Shepton Mallet?'

'No, dear, you're taking Johnny home. Now, I'll just go and start pouring drinks for my thirsty friends. And you're both more than welcome to join us if you'd like to.' Beaming at Johnny over her shoulder as she disappeared through the archway, Rose said cheerfully, 'Pretty girl. Gorgeous freckles. Funny tights!'

And then it was just the two of them left in the clearing, with the surrounding trees and the family of silver deer artfully spotlit, dusk falling around them and the grass wreathed in white mist.

Cleo met Johnny's gaze for the first time. Something was definitely going on and nobody was explaining it to her. It was like one of those dreams where you find yourself on stage but nobody's told you the name of the play you're meant to be appearing in.

OK, first things first. Her mouth dry, she said, 'What happened to Shepton Mallet?'

Johnny took a deep breath. 'Sorry, that was down to Rose.' He sounded less sure of himself than usual, which was weird for a start.

'Why has she heard all about me?'

'I've been working here for the past eight days. We got talking.' He paused. 'I had to talk to someone or I'd have gone mad. And getting you here like this was all her idea. If you'd known you were coming over to see me, it wouldn't have been a surprise.' Drily Johnny added, 'Surprises are very much Rose's thing.'

Cleo's heart had never beaten so fast. To give herself time to think, she said, 'How's Clarice?'

'Very well. She's going to be moving into Naish House next month.'

'That's . . . great.'

'I know.'

She braced herself. 'And how's things with Honor?'

'Honor's fine. She's very well too.' Another pause. 'We're not together any more. I finished with Honor last week.'

Oh good grief, was he serious? Unable to contain herself, Cleo blurted out, 'You did? Why? Why would you *do* that?'

He held up his hand to stop her. 'OK, let me explain something. When I was living in the States, Honor and I were seeing each other and things weren't really working out. The relationship had pretty much run its course, but Honor panicked when I tried to end it. Then she met this other guy and told me our relationship was over. That way, she wasn't the one being dumped. Which was absolutely fine by me. I was relieved. But then last month that all went pear-shaped when she realised what a prat he was. And that was when she turned up while I was in Norfolk and Barbara was about to die. And she'd turned down this multimillion-dollar deal to be with me, so what could I say? Tell her thanks but no thanks?' He shook his head. 'I couldn't do that.

She's a sweet girl with a good heart. So I felt I had to give it another try.'

'Until a week ago.' Cleo's teeth were chattering. 'What happened?'

'You really want to know?' He gazed steadily at her. 'OK, I'll say it. You happened.'

'What?'

'Remember when I asked you to come over to the house and keep Clarice company for the evening?'

'Yes.' *Oh God, what was she supposed to do with all this adrenaline?*

'You said you'd do it. Then you said, what time do you want me?' Johnny waited, then dipped his head. 'And I wanted to say, *all the time*.'

Silence. In the distance an owl screeched. Cleo shivered; was this really happening? It *felt* as if it was happening, but how could she be absolutely sure?

'And that was the moment I knew what I had to do,' said Johnny. 'Even if I end up looking like a complete idiot. Because maybe you don't feel the same way about me, but ever since I came back to Channings Hill, I haven't been able to stop thinking about you.'

Could he hear how fast her heart was beating? It was like a kangaroo trying to batter its way out of her chest. Risking a brief smile, Cleo said, 'Thinking what about me?'

'Only good things. I'm serious now. Since the day of Dad's funeral, you've been . . . in here.' He tapped the side of his head.

Oh God, how brilliant. 'Why me, though? Why me and not Honor?'

'OK, off the top of my head.' Johnny counted off on his fingers. 'If you broke one of your nails, would you call up your manicurist and tell her to get on a plane and come and sort it out?'

'I might,' said Cleo.

'If I frowned and my forehead moved, would you go on and on and on at me, telling me I really should get myself Botoxed?'

'It's a possibility.'

'If I told you I was making arrangements for my aunt to move down to a nursing home in Bristol, would you say, "Ah Jeez, does she have to? That means she'll keep wanting to come and stay!"'

He'd captured Honor's accent to perfection. Shocked but at the same time delighted, Cleo said, 'God, did she really say that?'

Johnny shrugged. 'It's not why I finished with her. I did that because she wasn't you. OK, shall I make a confession now?'

'Yes please.'

'You're funny and stroppy and have no idea how gorgeous you are.' He paused. 'You're the reason I came back to live in Channings Hill.'

She blinked. 'I don't believe you.'

'It's true. Would you like another confession?'

'Definitely,' said Cleo.

'This is a shameful one.'

'My favourite kind.'

'When I bet you couldn't last six months without a boyfriend, it was because I didn't want you getting involved with anyone else.'

Cleo's stomach squirmed with joy. 'Remind me again how much money was involved? I can't wait to win this bet.'

'I haven't finished yet with the confessions.'

'Sorry. Carry on.'

'All these months I've wanted to kiss you.' Johnny shook his head. 'So badly. God, all this time and I haven't even *kissed* you . . .'

Cleo swallowed. 'You're making me nervous now.'

'Why?'

'Because what if I'm rubbish at it? I might kiss like a washing machine.'

Johnny said, 'Has it occurred to you that I might be nervous too?'

She shook her head. 'Now you're the one talking rubbish. You're never nervous.'

'I never have been before.' He moved closer. 'But I am now. Apart from anything else, I've told you how I feel about you and you haven't said anything back. You could be about to tell me to take a running jump.'

Cleo gazed up at him. He sounded as if he meant it, but this was the most confident man she'd ever encountered in her life. Without warning she reached out and pressed the flat of her hand against the warm triangle of chest exposed by his open-necked shirt . . .

Thudthudthudthudthudthud . . .

Johnny exhaled, mortified. 'Could you *hear* my heart beating?'

How funny that in all these years it had never once occurred to her that men might worry about this too. A smile spread across Cleo's face as she reached for his hand and placed it at the base of her own throat.

Dahdahdahdahdahdah . . .

Johnny felt it, then visibly relaxed. 'Nearly as fast as mine.'

Did he kiss her or did she kiss him? Cleo had no idea how it happened; all she knew was that they met in the middle, their mouths touching and magically appearing already to know each other. Johnny wrapped his arms around her; she ran her fingers through his hair and it felt so perfect she never wanted it to end.

Which, for quite a long time, it didn't. Until finally they had to come up for air.

Johnny was smiling and stroking her face. 'Not a bit like a washing machine.'

'Nor you.'

He touched the freckle below her right eye. 'Final confession?'

'Go ahead.' How were her legs still managing to hold her up?

'I love you. I really do. And I feel like such a novice, because I've never felt this way about anyone else before.'

I love you. There it was. The last time someone had said those words to her, it had been Will, in the pub that day when she'd told him she wanted nothing more to do with him. Her very first *I love you*, and it had been horrible, so completely wrong.

But this time it felt wonderful. Johnny was saying it and it felt blissfully, perfectly *right*. Faintly she said, 'This had better not be a joke . . .'

'Oh God, don't even think that! I've felt guilty about that for *years* . . .'

'Guilty about what?'

'That stupid bet. The night of the school disco. I've wanted to apologise so many times, but I just didn't have the nerve. Then I thought—hoped— that maybe you'd forgotten all about it, so what would be the point of bringing it up again? But you hadn't forgotten, had you? I'm so sorry.'

He truly meant it. Magically, the burden of embarrassment rose up and floated away. Cleo said happily, 'I've forgotten about it now. Anyway, carry on with what you were saying.'

'OK, maybe this is jumping the gun,' Johnny went on, 'but all these years, you're the one I've been waiting for. Because I know I could spend the rest of my life with you. I *want* to spend the rest of my life with you . . .' Another kiss, then he said in a voice that wasn't completely steady, 'Will you give me a chance to prove it?'

Cleo said, 'Don't make promises you might not be able to keep. Let's just take it one day at a time, shall we?'

'Fine, but I know how I feel and I know this is a promise I can keep. I'm not going to change my mind about you.' The look in his eyes told her how much he meant it. 'You're everything I've ever wanted.'

Cleo felt her heart expand with joy. Until he'd said them, she hadn't dared to admit even to herself that hearing those words from Johnny LaVenture was all she'd ever wanted too. If it had happened years ago, it would never have worked. But now . . . now it was right, it was *perfect*. She tilted her head. *Hang on . . .*

'What's that noise?'

Johnny straightened up and listened. It was only faint but there was some kind of whooping.

'Oh, don't worry about that.' Having turned to look behind him, he said with amusement, 'It's just Rose, celebrating because she's been proved right.'

Earlier, Cleo had briefly wondered why anyone would commission a truly spectacular sculpture and situate it in a wooded clearing, obscured from general view by a twelve-foot-tall yew hedge.

Now she discovered that, like Stonehenge, the sculpture had been carefully positioned so that from the orangery at the side of the house you had a perfect view of it through the archway cut in the hedge.

It was also apparent that, along with the family of steel deer behind them, she and Johnny were illuminated in the glow of the spotlights.

And Rose wasn't the only one cheering. All her guests were gathered at the full-length windows; they were quite the centre of attention.

'We'll have to stay for a quick drink,' said Johnny. 'Let her have her moment of glory.'

'This is going to be so embarrassing,' said Cleo.

'It won't, it'll be fine, I promise. Hey, where are you going? Are you taking all your clothes off?' Alarmed, Johnny said, 'Hey, I don't want to wait either but we can't do anything here, not with everyone watching.'

Behind the hedge, just about hidden from view of the orangery, Cleo did what she had to do and said, 'Don't panic, I'm not getting naked. Just taking these godawful tights off. Here, hide them in your pocket.'

Johnny held them up and fondly contemplated them, wrinkled and ugly and the colour of builder's tea. 'Fine, but we're never going to throw these away. They'll be a memento of an unforgettable day.' Sliding his arm around Cleo's waist as they made their way beneath the yew arch, he murmured, 'You can wear them under your wedding dress when we get married.'

Did he think she was completely stupid? 'I've got a better idea,' said Cleo. 'Why don't you?'

Jill Mansell

Take a Chance on Me—was the title of your novel influenced by the Abba song?
Some authors start their books by coming up with a title. Others—me—finish writing their book then have to think of titles, ninety-five per cent of which are promptly rejected by their publisher. I'd already had quite a few ideas turned down when I found myself watching the film, *Mamma Mia,* again, and realised that *Take a Chance on Me* would be perfect for my book. I suggested it to my editor and she loved it too. And now people keep telling me that they hear the song in their head every time they see my book, which I think is great. I love the film. It's funny, upbeat and romantic—perfect. Pierce Brosnan's inability to sing just makes it seem more real and I love him for being brave enough to do it.

I believe that LaVenture is your mother-in-law's family name. Did it make it harder to create Johnny LaVenture's character with real-life family members in mind?
LaVenture is such a great surname, isn't it? Some people have criticised my use of it because it sounds so over the top and made up, but my lovely mother-in-law was thrilled when she saw I'd used it. She said it made her feel a little bit famous! It didn't seem strange to be using it in the book, but at the time I didn't realise there is a distant cousin called Johnnie LaVenture. If I'd known that, it might have felt a bit funny . . .

I read that you are going to be a writer in residence. Do you enjoy doing this?

Yes, I'm spending a week visiting 5-star hotels on the Costa del Sol—it's a hard life but someone has to do it! Standing up and giving a talk is scary, although lovely when the audience laughs and applauds. More popular nowadays is the chat show format, which is so much more relaxed and informal, and that's what I'm going to be doing there.

Would you like to own a Johnny LaVenture wire sculpture?

As I said in my introduction to the novel, I saw these amazing larger-than-life wire sculptures of horses at the Badminton International Horse Trials. I wanted to buy one, obviously, but my other half reminded me that our garden backs onto a rugby training ground and we might end up getting rugby players vaulting over the fence and jumping onto our wire horse. So I wasn't allowed to have one. But I'm nothing if not a consumer and had to have something, so I chose a lamb and she's gorgeous. Real ones grow up and become fat old sheep but mine will be an adorable little lamb for ever!

Did you model Johnny LaVenture on anyone?

No, but I think we all knew boys like that at school, super-attractive and confident, who we secretly fancied but only ever got teased by . . . Anyone? No? Oh God, really? Just me then.

Would you enjoy being a chauffeuse like your heroine Cleo Quinn?

I would love to be a limo driver for the opportunities to meet all sorts of fascinating characters, but the drawback is that I hate driving for longer than about twenty minutes at a time, which could be a bit of a problem! I find it boring and it makes my back ache, and if I'm driving a nice car I fret non-stop about accidentally bumping or scraping it. Also, I hate getting lost but don't trust satnavs. All in all, I don't think limo driving is the ideal job for me!

Who was your favourite character in the novel?

I love all my characters but Georgia is a particular favourite. She's eighteen, untidy, hardworking in some ways and spectacularly lazy in others; she's also thoughtless and careless, impulsive and loving, upfront and charming . . . hmm, much like my own eighteen-year-old daughter . . .

On your website, www.jillmansell.co.uk, there is a link to Twitter. Are you a fan?

Oh, I love Twitter, it's such fun! It was originally my publisher's idea and I told them I'd hate it, but it's been a total joy. Writers and people who work from home are especially keen because it's like a magic coffee shop, always open, that you can pop into whenever you like and make contact with friends. Being a novelist means sitting at home on your own, which can become a bit tedious. Twitter has changed that, and it's also brilliant for research. Ask any question and someone will instantly have the answer. So it's not only great company, it's a vital research tool. And it's free!

WINTER
GARDEN

KRISTIN HANNAH

I know we writers aren't supposed to say that we have favourites; our books are supposed to be like our children, each one unique and beloved in its own way. But I'll let you into a little secret: 'Winter Garden' is my favourite book so far.

It started with an ordinary sentence: 'Sometimes when you open the door to your mother's past, you find your own future.' I thought of this sentence and I was on my way.

'Winter Garden' is really my favourite kind of book —part epic love story, part family drama, part historical novel —and I hope that you love it as much as I do.

Kristin

PROLOGUE

1972

ON THE BANKS of the mighty Columbia River, in the icy season when every breath became visible, the orchard called Belye Nochi was quiet. Dormant apple trees stretched as far as the eye could see, their sturdy roots coiled deep in the cold soil. As temperatures plummeted and colour drained from land and sky, each day became indistinguishable from the next. Everything froze, turned fragile.

Nowhere was the cold and quiet more noticeable than in Meredith Whitson's own house. At twelve, she had already discovered the empty spaces that gathered between people. She longed for her family to be like those she saw on television, where everything looked perfect and everyone got along. No one, not even her beloved father, understood how alone she felt within these four walls.

But tomorrow night all of that would change.

She had come up with a brilliant plan. She had written a play based on one of her mother's fairy tales, and she would present it at the annual company Christmas party.

'How come I can't be the star?' Nina whined. It was at least the tenth time she'd asked this since Meredith had finished the script.

Meredith turned in her chair and looked down at her nine-year-old sister, who was on their bedroom floor painting a mint-green castle on an old bedsheet. Meredith bit her lip. The castle was all wrong. Too bright, too messy. It would have to be fixed. Script in hand, she knelt beside her sister. 'We've talked about this, Nina.'

'But *why* can't I be the peasant girl who marries the prince?'

'Jeff is playing the prince, and he's thirteen. You'd look silly next to him. Besides, your part is important, Neens. Without the younger sister, the prince and the peasant girl would never meet.'

'I guess.' Nina sat back on her heels. With her short, tangled, black hair, bright green eyes and pale skin, she looked like a perfect little pixie. 'Can I be the peasant girl next year?'

Meredith put an arm across Nina's narrow back. 'Of course.' She loved the idea that she might be creating a family tradition. All her friends had traditions, but not the Whitsons. There was no stream of relatives who came to their house on holidays, no turkey on Thanksgiving or ham on Easter, no prayers that were always said. Heck, they didn't even know how old their mom was.

It was because Mom was Russian and alone in this country, Dad said. Mom didn't say much of anything about herself.

A knock at the door surprised Meredith. She looked up just as Jeff Cooper and her father came into the room.

'Jeff,' she said, her voice catching only the smallest amount. Her cheeks grew hot at the obviousness of his effect on her. They'd been best friends since fourth grade, but lately it felt different to be around him. 'You're right on time for rehearsal.'

He gave her one of his heart-stopping smiles. 'Just don't tell Joey and the guys. They'd give me a ton of crap for this.'

'About rehearsal,' her dad said, holding out the script. He'd just come home from work. His curly black hair reached the collar of his brown leisure suit, and his bushy moustache made it hard to tell if he was smiling. 'This is the play you're doing?'

Meredith got slowly to her feet. 'Do you think she'll like it?'

Nina stood up. Her heart-shaped face was solemn. 'Will she?' The three of them looked at each other over the expanse of mint-green castle. The truth they passed between themselves, in looks alone, was that Anya Whitson was a cold woman; any warmth she had was directed at her husband. Precious little of it reached her daughters. When they were younger, Dad had tried to pretend it was otherwise, to redirect their attention like a magician, mesmerising them with the brightness of his affection. But like all illusions, the truth ultimately appeared behind it.

'I don't know, Meredoodle,' Dad said, reaching into his pocket for his cigarettes. 'Your mother's stories—'

'I love it when she tells them to us,' Meredith said.

'It's the only time she really talks to us,' Nina added.

Dad lit a cigarette. His brown eyes narrowed through a swirl of grey smoke. 'Yeah,' he said, exhaling. 'It's just . . .'

Meredith understood; none of them ever really knew what would set Mom off. But if there was one thing her mother loved, it was this fairy tale. 'It takes ten minutes, Dad. Everyone will love it.'

He hesitated, almost as if he wanted to tell her it was a mistake, but she knew he loved her too much to say no. 'OK,' he said.

She felt a swell of pride. It would work. For once, she'd be the centre of her mother's attention. This play would prove that Meredith had listened to every precious word Mom had said to her, even those few that were spoken softly in the dark, at story time.

For the next hour, Meredith directed her actors through rehearsal, although only Jeff needed help. She and Nina had heard this fairy tale for years. And what a story it was! Meredith had added some bits and pieces, like a magical wishing well and an enchanted mirror. But even without extras, it was as good as any movie.

When the rehearsal was over, Meredith made a sign: ONE NIGHT ONLY: A GRAND PLAY FOR THE HOLIDAY. She touched up the painted backdrop. When the set was ready, she added sequins to the ballet skirt-turned-princess gown she would wear at the end. By the time she went to bed, she was so excited it took a long time to fall asleep.

The next day seemed to pass slowly, but finally, at six o'clock, the guests began to arrive. It was not a big crowd, just the men and women who worked for the orchard and their families, a few neighbours, and Dad's only living relative, his sister, Dora.

Meredith sat at the top of the stairs wondering when to make her move. Just as she was about to stand up, she heard Nina in the kitchen banging a pot with a spoon and yelling, 'Show time!'

No one knew how to steal the limelight like Nina.

There was a smattering of laughter as the guests made their way to the living room, where the painting of the green castle hung from an aluminium movie screen set up beside the massive fireplace. To the right of it stood a large Christmas tree. In front of the painting was their 'stage': a small wooden bridge that rested on the hardwood floor and a cardboard street lamp made with a flashlight.

Nina and Jeff were already there in their costumes. Meredith dimmed the lights and turned on the fake street lamp, then slipped behind the backdrop and began the narration: 'Her name is Vera, and she is a poor peasant girl, a nobody. She lives in a magical realm called the Snow Kingdom, but her beloved world is dying.'

She heard a sound, like a sharp intake of breath. Leaning sideways, she peered round the screen. Everyone was smiling, nodding. Meredith went on: 'An evil has come to this land; it rolls across the cobblestone streets in black carriages sent by a dark, evil knight who wants to destroy it all.'

The audience clapped enthusiastically. Someone whistled.

Meredith walked onstage, taking care not to trip over her long, layered skirts. She looked out over the gathering and saw her mother at the back of the room, her beautiful face blurred by cigarette smoke. For once she was looking directly at Meredith. *Finally.*

'It is so cold this winter,' Meredith said loudly, pacing in front of the faux castle. She clapped her mittened hands together.

At the sound, Nina made her entrance. Dressed in a ratty nightgown with a kerchief covering her hair, she wrung her hands together. 'Is it the Black Knight?' she practically yelled, drawing a laugh from the crowd. 'Is his bad magic making it so cold?'

'No. I am chilled at the loss of our father. I am so worried. When will he return?' Meredith pressed the back of her hand to her forehead. 'The carriages are everywhere. The Black Knight gains more and more power. People turn to smoke before our eyes . . .'

'Look,' Nina said, pointing towards a picture taped to the fireplace. 'It is a white carriage with gold. The prince . . .'

Jeff came out from behind the tree. In his sports coat and jeans, with a cheap gold crown on his blond hair, he looked so handsome that for a moment, Meredith could hardly breathe. And he was smiling as if she really were a princess.

He held out a pair of silk roses. 'I have two roses for you.'

Meredith touched his hand, but before she could say her line, there was a crash and a sound like a cry.

Her mother stood in the crowd, her face pale, her blue eyes blazing. Blood dripped from her hand. She'd broken her cocktail glass.

'Enough,' she said sharply. 'This is hardly entertainment.'

The guests seemed to freeze; the room went quiet. Dad made his way to Mom and tried to pull her close.

'I'm sorry.' Meredith didn't know what she'd done wrong.

'I never should have told you those ridiculous fairy tales,' Mom said, her Russian accent sharp with anger. 'I forgot how romantic and emptyheaded girls can be.'

Meredith was so humiliated she couldn't move.

She saw her father guide her mother into the kitchen, where he probably began cleaning up her hand. The guests left as if this were the *Titanic,* rushing for lifeboats stationed beyond the front door.

Only Jeff looked at her. The pity in his eyes made her feel sick. He started towards her, still holding the two roses. 'Meredith—'

She pushed past him and ran out. At the end of the hall, she skidded to a stop, her eyes burning with tears. As if from far away, she could hear her dad's voice as he tried to soothe his angry wife.

'What did you do?' Nina asked quietly, coming up beside her.

'Who knows?' Meredith wiped her eyes. 'She's such a bitch.'

'That's a bad word. Should we say we're sorry?'

Meredith reached down for her hand. 'She won't care, trust me.'

'So what do we do?'

Meredith knew what would happen: Dad would calm Mom down, and then he'd come up to their room and make them laugh and tell them Mom really loved them. By the time he was done, Meredith would want to believe it. Again. 'I know what I'm going to do.' Staring through to the kitchen, she could see Mom's side—just her slim, black velvet dress and her pale arm, and her white, white hair. 'I'm never going to listen to one of her stupid fairy tales again.'

CHAPTER ONE

2000

WAS THIS WHAT FORTY looked like? Really? In the past year, Meredith had gone from miss to ma'am. Just like that, with no transition. Even worse, her skin had begun to lose its elasticity. Her neck was fuller. She hadn't gone grey yet; her chestnut-coloured hair, cut in a shoulder-length bob, was still full and shiny. But her eyes gave her away. She looked tired. And not only at six in the morning.

She turned away from the bathroom mirror and stripped out of her old T-shirt and into a pair of sweats and a running shirt. Pulling her hair into a ponytail, she walked into her dark bedroom, where her husband's soft snoring made her want to crawl back into bed. In the old days, she would have done just that—snuggled up against him.

Leaving the room, she headed down the hall, passing the doors of her children's bedrooms. Not that they were children any more. Jillian was nineteen, a sophomore at UCLA who dreamed of being a doctor, and Maddy was eighteen and a freshman at Vanderbilt. Without them, this house felt emptier than she'd expected.

She kept moving. Lately that seemed to be the best way to handle things. Downstairs, in the mudroom, the dogs leaped up at her, yapping and wagging their tails.

'Luke, Leia, no jumping,' she scolded the huskies, scratching their ears as she led them to the door. When she opened it, cold air hit her face like a slap. Snow had fallen again, and though it was still dark on this mid-December morning, she could make out the pale pearlescence of road and field. By the time they were on their way, it was six ten and the sky was a purplish grey. Right on time.

Meredith ran slowly at first, acclimatising herself to the cold. As she did every weekday morning, she ran along the gravel road down past her parents' house, out to the lane that ended a mile up the hill. From there, she followed the loop out to the golf course and back. Four miles exactly.

It was a routine she rarely missed; she had no choice, really. Everything about her was big by nature. Only exercise and diet could keep her looking good. She was tall, with broad shoulders, curvy hips. Even her Julia Roberts-type mouth and her huge brown eyes seemed just a little too much for her oval face.

As she turned back onto her road, the rising sun turned the mountains pink. On either side of her, thousands of bare, spindly apple trees showed through the snow. She came to a stop at her front porch just as the valley filled with bright golden light.

She fed the dogs and hurried upstairs. She was just going into the bathroom as Jeff was coming out. Wearing only a towel, with his greying blond hair still dripping wet, he turned sideways to let her pass, and she did the same. Neither of them spoke.

By seven thirty she was dressed for work in a pair of black jeans and a green blouse. A little eye-liner, mascara and a coat of lipstick and she was ready to go.

Downstairs, she found Jeff at the kitchen table reading the *New York Times*. The dogs were asleep at his feet. She went to the coffeepot, pouring herself a cup. 'You need a refill?'

'I'm good,' he said, without looking up.

She stirred milk into her coffee. It occurred to her that they only talked about work or the kids lately. She tried to remember the last time they'd made love, but she couldn't. When you'd been married as long as they had, there were bound to be quiet times. Still, it saddened her to remember how passionate they used to be.

They'd married early, and she'd followed him to college in Seattle. She'd been happy in their cramped, tiny U District apartment. Then, when they were seniors, she'd become pregnant. It had terrified her at first. She'd worried that she was like her mother, and that parenthood wouldn't be a good thing. But nothing could have been further from the truth. She had discovered, to her profound relief, that she was the complete opposite of her mother. Perhaps her youth had helped in that. God knew Mom had not been young when she first gave birth.

Jeff shook his head. It was a minute gesture, but she saw it. 'What's the matter?' she said.

'I just asked you something.'

'I didn't hear you. Ask me again.'

'It doesn't matter.'

'Fine. Will you be home for dinner at seven?'

'By all means,' he said, turning the page.

Meredith was at her desk by eight o'clock. As usual, she was the first to arrive and went round the cubicle-divided space on the warehouse's second floor flipping on lights. She passed by her dad's office, pausing only long enough to glimpse the plaques on his door. Thirteen times he'd been voted 'Grower of the Year'. It didn't matter that he'd been semi-retired for a decade; he was still the face of the Belye Nochi orchard.

She had had a part to play in the company's growth, to be sure. Under her leadership, the cold storage warehouse had been expanded and a big part of their business was now storing fruit for other growers. She'd also turned the old roadside apple stand into a gift shop that sold hundreds of craft items and speciality foods.

For the next three hours, Meredith threw herself into work. She was rereading the latest crop report when her intercom buzzed.

'Meredith? Your dad is on line one.'

'Thanks, Daisy.' She picked up the call. 'Hi, Dad.'

'Mom and I were wondering if you could come for lunch today.'

'OK. But I have to be back by one.'

'Excellent,' he said. Meredith could hear the smile in his voice.

She hung up and went back to work. Lately, with demand down and transportation costs skyrocketing, she often spent her days putting out one fire after another, and today was no exception. By noon, a low-grade stress headache had crawled into the base of her neck. Still, she smiled at her employees as she left her office. In less than ten minutes, she pulled up in front of her parents' garage.

Surrounded by poplars on a gentle rise, the house was something out of a Russian fairy tale, with its turret-like, two-storey verandah and elaborate fretwork trim. The hammered copper roof was dull today in the grey weather, but on a bright day it shone like gold. The house was so famous that tourists often stopped to photograph it.

Leave it to her mother to build something so absurdly out of place. A Russian dacha, or summer house, in western Washington State. Even the orchard's name was absurd. *Belye Nochi*. White nights indeed. Nights here were dark as new asphalt. But whatever Anya Whitson wanted, her husband gave her.

Meredith knocked and went inside. The kitchen was empty; a big pot of soup simmered on the stove. In the living room, light spilled through the windows of the rounded north wall. Wood floors gleamed with beeswax. Richly upholstered antique sofas and chairs clustered round a huge stone fireplace. Above it hung an oil painting of a Russian troika— a romantic-looking carriage drawn by matching horses sailing through a field of snow. Pure *Doctor Zhivago*. To her left were dozens of pictures of Russian churches, and below them her mother's 'holy corner', where a table held antique icons and a single candle burned year-round.

She found her father in the back of the room alongside the Christmas tree, stretched out on the ottoman, reading. His hair—what he had left of it at eighty-five—stuck out in white tufts. Too many decades in the sun had pleated his skin, and he had a basset-hound look even when he was smiling, but the sad countenance fooled no one. Everyone loved Evan Whitson. It was impossible not to.

At her entrance, his face lit up. He reached out and squeezed her hand tightly. 'Your mom will be so glad to see you.'

Meredith smiled. It was the game they'd played for years. Dad pretended that Mom loved Meredith and Meredith pretended to believe him. 'Great. Is she upstairs?'

'I couldn't keep her out of the garden this morning.'

Meredith wasn't surprised. 'I'll get her.'

She left her father and walked through the kitchen to the formal dining room. Through the French doors, she saw an expanse of snow-covered ground, with acres of dormant apple trees in the distance. Closer, beneath the icicle-draped branches of a fifty-year-old magnolia tree, was a small rectangular garden defined by antique wrought-iron fencing. Its ornate gate glittered with frost.

And there she was: her eighty-something-year-old mother, bundled up in blankets, sitting on the black bench in her so-called winter garden. She sat motionless, her hands clasped in her lap.

As a child, it had scared Meredith—all that solitude in her mother— but later it irritated her. A woman of her mother's age had no business sitting alone in the cold. She claimed it was because of her vision—she saw only white and black and grey—but that never struck Meredith as a reason for staring at nothing.

She opened the door and went out into the ankle-deep snow. 'You shouldn't be out here, Mom. You'll catch pneumonia.'

'It takes more cold than this to give me pneumonia.'

It was the sort of ridiculous comment she always made. 'I've only got an hour, so you'd better come in.' Meredith's voice sounded sharp, and she winced. What was it about her mother that brought out the worst in her? 'Did you know Dad invited me for lunch?'

'Of course,' her mother said, but Meredith heard the lie in her voice.

Her mother rose from the bench. Her face was remarkably smooth, her skin flawless and almost translucent. She had the kind of bone structure that made other women envious. But it was her eyes that defined her beauty. Deep-set and fringed by thick lashes, they were a remarkable shade of aqua flecked with bits of gold.

Meredith took her elbow. 'You should have gloves on in cold—'

'I do not want to be warm, thank you. It is December the fourteenth.' Mom eased her arm away gently, as if perhaps the quietness of the move could mask its purpose, but Meredith knew better. A lifetime spent watching her mother pull away left her sensitive to every movement, big or small. They went up the steps into the house.

Meredith watched her mother go to the stove to stir the soup; she set the table, and for a few precious moments there was noise in the room, an approximation of a relationship, at least.

Dad came into the kitchen. 'My girls.' He looked pale, his once-wide shoulders whittled down to nothing. He put a hand on each of their shoulders. 'I love it when we're together for lunch.'

'As do I,' Mom said in her clipped, accented voice.

'And me,' Meredith said.

'Good. Good.' Dad nodded and led them to the table.

Mom brought a tray of warm, feta-cheese cornbread slices, put a piece on each plate, then brought over bowls of soup.

'I walked the orchard this morning,' Dad said.

Meredith sipped at her soup; homemade lamb meatballs in a savoury saffron broth with silken egg noodles. 'Oh, yeah?'

'I want to change field A to grapes.'

Meredith lowered her spoon. 'Grapes?'

'The Golden Delicious are not our best apple any more.' He held up his hand. 'I know. I know. We built this place on Golden Delicious, but we need to diversify. We could make ice wine.'

'In these times? The Asian markets are tightening. Our profits were down twelve per cent last year. We're barely hanging on.'

'In business, you don't hang on. You either innovate or die.'

'We can't just pull up those trees and plant something else. It would cost too much, and the return would be a decade away.'

'You should listen to your father,' Mom said.

'Oh, please, Mom. When was the last time you looked at year-end statements?' Meredith stood up. 'I need to get back to work.'

She carried her bowl over to the sink, where she washed it. Then she put the leftover soup in a Tupperware container, stored it in the impossibly full refrigerator and washed the pot.

'That was delicious, Mom. Thanks.' She said a quick goodbye and put her coat on. She was out on the porch, breathing in the sharp, frigid air, when her dad came up behind her.

She couldn't help smiling. She loved that he couldn't stand to see her leave angry. 'I'm OK, Dad.'

'You know how she gets in December. Winters are hard for her.' He pulled her into his arms and held her tightly. The pattern had played out through the decades: Meredith fought with Mom, and Dad made it all better. 'You two need to try harder.'

'I will,' she said, completing their little fairy tale as she always did. 'I love you, Dad.' She kissed his cheek.

'I love you, too, Meredoodle.' He grinned. 'And think about grapes. Maybe I can be a vintner before I die.'

She hated jokes like that. 'Very funny.'

As she started her SUV, she saw her parents through the living-room window. Dad pulled her mother into his arms and kissed her. They began haltingly to dance, although there was probably no music. Her dad always said he carried love songs in his heart.

Meredith drove away from the intimate scene, but for the rest of the day she found herself remembering how in love her parents had looked.

At six thirty, she glanced at the clock. She was late. Again. After organising her paperwork into neat piles, she headed out.

Snow was falling. It blurred the view through her windshield. Meredith slowed and hugged the shoulder of the road.

At home, she slammed the door shut behind her and hurried into the kitchen. She put her bag on the counter. 'Jeff?'

'I'm in here.'

Meredith followed Jeff's voice into the living room. He was at the bar, making himself a drink. 'Sorry, I'm late. The snow—'

'Yeah,' he said. They both knew she'd left late. 'Want a drink?'

'Sure. White wine.' She looked at him, not knowing what she even felt. He was as handsome as ever, with dark blond hair only beginning to grey, a strong jaw and steel-grey eyes that always seemed to smile. He didn't work out, but his body never seemed to age. He was dressed in Levi's and an old Pearl Jam T-shirt.

He handed her the drink. 'How was your day?'

'Dad wants to plant grapes, and Mom was in the winter garden. She's going to catch pneumonia.'

'Your mom is colder than any snowfield.'

'Amen to that.' She leaned back against the wall. All at once, her hectic day caught up with her and she closed her eyes.

'I got a chapter written today. It's short. Only about seven pages, but I think it's good. I made you a copy. Mere?'

She opened her eyes and found him looking at her. A small frown creased the skin between his eyes, made her wonder if he'd said something important. She tried to recall. 'Sorry. Long day.'

'You're having a lot of those lately.'

She couldn't tell if there was a hint of accusation in his voice or just a simple honesty. 'You know what winter is like.'

'And spring. And summer.'

There was her answer: definitely accusation. Even last year she would have asked him what was wrong with them. She would have told him how lost she felt in the grey minutiae of her life, how much she missed the girls. But now that kind of intimacy felt impossible. Distance seemed to be spreading between them, like spilled ink. 'Yeah, I guess.'

'I'm going to the office,' he said suddenly.

'Now?'

'Why not?'

She wasn't sure if it was really a question. 'No reason.'

'Yeah,' he said, kissing her cheek. 'That's what I thought.'

CHAPTER TWO

IT HAD TAKEN two weeks' hiking through the jungle to find the kill. Insects had alerted them to it, along with the smell of death.

Nina stood back. For an instant, she experienced it all: the buzzing flies; the maggots that turned the carcass almost white; the stillness of the African jungle that meant predators and scavengers were nearby.

Then she began to compartmentalise the scene, to see it as a photographer instead of as a human being. She chose a camera and focused on the bloodied body of the mountain gorilla. *Click.*

She stepped round, focusing and snapping shots. Changing cameras, adjusting lenses, checking the light. She paused to put a little more Vicks under her nose, then squatted down closer. *Click.*

There were places in the world where a gorilla's hand was an ashtray in some rich jerk's library. *Click. Click.*

For the next hour, Nina framed and shot. When dusk finally fell, they began the long, hot, trek back down through the jungle. The descent was quiet, solemn. The immediate aftermath was always worst for Nina. It was difficult to forget what she'd seen. Often the images would return as nightmares and wake her from sleep.

At the bottom of the mountain, the group came to the small outpost that served as a town in this remote part of Rwanda. Climbing into the jeep, they drove several hours to the conservation centre, where they asked more questions and Nina took more photos.

'Mrs Nina?'

She was standing by the door, cleaning her lens, when she heard the centre's head guide say her name. 'Hello, Mr Dimonsu.'

'I am sorry to bother you, but we forgot to give you important phone message from Mrs Sylvie. She say to tell you to call her.'

'Thank you.'

Nina took the bulky satellite phone out of her bag and carried all the gear to a clearing in the camp. When the signal strength looked good, she made the call.

'Hey, Sylvie,' she said when her editor answered. 'I got the poachers. Sick bastards. Give me ten days to get you the photos.'

'You've got six days. We're thinking of the cover.'

The cover. Her two favourite words. Some women liked diamonds; she liked the cover of *Time* magazine. Or *National Geographic*. 'You'll have it. Then I'm meeting Danny in Namibia.'

'Lucky girl. But be ready to be back to work next Friday,' Sylvie said. 'I won't call unless a new war breaks out, I promise.'

A few days later Nina was in Namibia in a rented Land Rover, with Danny at the wheel.

It was seven in the morning, and already the December sun was bright and warm. By one o'clock, the temperature would be around 115 degrees. The road—if you could call it that—was a river of sand that sent them careening one way, then the other.

Nina stared out at the desolate, blistering landscape. As the hours took them deeper into one of the last true wildernesses of southern Africa, she noticed more herds of starving animals by dry riverbeds, dying where they stood as they waited for the rains to come.

'You sure you want to find the Himba?' Danny asked, flashing her a grin as they slammed sideways and almost stuck in the sand. The dirt on his face made his white teeth and blue eyes look startlingly bright. Dust powdered his shirt and collar-length black hair. 'We haven't had a week to ourselves in months.'

She brought up her camera. Studying him through the viewfinder, she saw him as clearly as if he'd been a stranger: a handsome forty-year-old Irishman with pronounced cheekbones and a nose broken more than once. Pub fights as a lad, he always said. She could see tiny frown lines between his eyes. He was worried he'd followed bad advice on the road, though he'd never say so. A war correspondent, he was used to following a story to hell and back. Even if it wasn't his story.

She took the shot. 'I owe you one.'

'Indeed you do, love, and I'll be collecting, you can be sure.'

Nina leaned back into the seat and tried not to close her eyes, but she was exhausted. After two weeks tracking poachers, and four weeks before that watching people kill each other in Angola, she was tired to the bone. And still there was nothing in the world she'd rather be doing.

She'd known that sixteen years ago, at twenty-one, when, with a journalism degree and a camera, she'd gone in search of her destiny. At first, she'd taken any job that required a photographer, but in 1985, she'd met *Time* editor Sylvie Porter. Next thing Nina knew, she was on her way to Ethiopia. What she saw changed everything.

Almost immediately her pictures began to tell stories. In 1987, when the Ganges River flooded, leaving 25 million people homeless, it was Nina's photograph of a woman up to her neck in dirty water, carrying her baby above her head, that graced the *Time* cover. Two years ago she'd won the Pulitzer for her photographs of the ethnic cleansing in Kosovo.

'Look. There,' Danny said, pointing.

At first, all she saw was an orange-and-red sky full of dust. Gradually the silhouettes on the ridge materialised into people, gazing down at the dirty Land Rover and its even dirtier occupants.

'That them?' he asked.

Nina shrugged. 'Must be.'

Nodding, he closed the distance, parked the vehicle at a bend in a dry riverbed and got out. The Himba tribe stood back, watching.

Danny walked forwards slowly, knowing the chief would present himself. Nina followed his lead. The chief approached, and in halting Swahili, the three negotiated pictures for money and water. Nina had brought fifteen gallons with her for trade.

For a people that walked miles for a cupful of water, it was an overwhelming gift, and suddenly Nina and Danny were welcomed like old friends. The Himba swept them into the village, where they were fed maize porridge and sour milk. Later, when the night was blue with moonlight, they were led to a mud hut, where they lay together on a mat of woven grass and leaves.

Nina rolled onto her side to face Danny. In the shadowy light, his face looked young, although like her, he had old eyes. It was a hazard of the trade. They'd seen too many terrible things. But it was what had brought them together.

They'd met in wartime Congo. From then on, they'd been together all over the world—in the Sudan, Zimbabwe, Afghanistan, Nepal, Bosnia. They'd both become specialists on Africa. Both had London apartments that collected messages and dust. Often they spent months without seeing each other.

'I'm goin' to be forty next month,' Danny said, quietly.

She loved his Irish accent. The simplest sentence sounded edgy. 'Don't worry, twenty-five-year-olds still swoon when they see you. It's your I-used-to-be-in-a-rock-band look.'

'It was a punk-rock band, love.'

She snuggled closer, kissing him. Danny pulled her close. 'How come we can talk about anythin' but us?'

'Who was talking about us?'

'I said I was almost forty.'

'And I'm supposed to see that as a conversation starter?'

'What if I miss you when you're gone?'

'You know who I am, Danny. I told you at the very beginning.'

'That was more than four years ago. Everythin' in the world changes except you, I guess.'

'Exactly.' She moved the tiniest bit away.

His arms held her. 'I didn't ask for anything,' he whispered.

You did, she thought. You just don't know it yet.

Nina squatted on the high ridge above the makeshift village. It was six in the morning. Below her walked a Himba woman, a heavy pot on her head and a baby in a sling at her bare breast. Nina zoomed in the telephoto lens.

Unaware of Nina, the woman paused at the riverbank and looked out over the empty sand where water should run. Her expression sharpened, turned desperate as she reached down to touch the child in her arms. It was a look of bone-deep fear—knowledge that she had no idea how to feed her child. There was nowhere to go to find water.

Nina caught it on camera and kept shooting until the woman walked on. Nina had taken hundreds of pictures this morning, but she knew that The One was of the woman at the riverbank.

Nina covered the lens and stood up, stretching her aching joints. As she walked back to the village, Danny came up beside her. 'Hey, you. Ready to go?'

She leaned against him, feeling good about her shots. 'I think I got what I needed, yeah.'

'Does this mean we can go and lie by a pool for a week?'

'There's nothing I'd rather do.' She repacked their gear while Danny spoke to the village elder and paid him for the pictures. She set up her satellite phone, positioning it until she found a signal.

As she expected, the magazine offices were closed, so she left a message for her editor and promised to call from the Chobe River Lodge in Zambia. Then she and Danny climbed back into the busted-up old Land Rover, drove through the lunar landscape of Kaokoveld and hopped on a plane headed south. By nightfall, they were at the Chobe River Lodge on their own private deck, watching the sun set over a herd of elephants on the opposite shore.

Nina stretched out on the lounge chair and closed her eyes. The night smelled of murky water and baked mud. For the first time in weeks, her pixie-cut black hair was clean. Pure luxury.

She heard Danny come through their room to the deck. He took an almost imperceptible pause before each step, a tiny favouring of the right leg that had taken a bullet in Angola.

'Here you go.' He put two glasses on the teak table beside her.

She tilted her face up to thank him and noticed several things at once: he hadn't brought the gin and tonic she'd asked for. Instead, he'd put down a straight shot of tequila. He'd forgotten the salt, and worst of all, he wasn't smiling. She sat up. 'What's wrong?'

'Maybe you should take a drink first.' He handed her a yellow envelope. 'Telegram.'

'Did you read it?'

'Course not. But it can't be good news, now, can it?'

Journalists and photojournalists the world over knew about telegrams. It was how your family delivered bad news, even in this satellite and internet age. When she saw it had come from Sylvie, her first thought was, Thank God. But that relief died as she read: YOUR FATHER HAD A HEART ATTACK. MEREDITH SAYS IT LOOKS BAD. SYLVIE.

She looked up at Danny. 'It's my dad . . . I need to go now—'

'Impossible, love,' he said gently. 'The flight from Johannesburg's at six tomorrow morning. I'll get us tickets.'

'Us?'

'Aye. I want to be there for you, Nina. Is that so terrible?'

Relying on people for comfort had never felt natural. She didn't know what to say. So she did what she always did at times like these: she reached down for the buttons on his pants. 'Take me to bed, Daniel Flynn. Get me through this night.'

*I*nterminable was the word that came to mind to describe the wait, but that only made Meredith think *terminal,* which made her think *death,* which brought up all the emotions she was trying to suppress. Her usual keeping busy wasn't working. She'd buried herself in insurance information, researched heart attacks on her laptop, and come up with the best cardiologists in the country. The second she looked away from the screen, her grief came rushing back.

She stared at the multicoloured fish in the waiting-room tank. Sometimes one actually caught her attention and, for a nanosecond, she forgot that her father might be dying.

She felt Jeff come up behind her. 'Mere,' he said quietly, putting his hands on her shoulders. 'Let me hold you.'

She shook her head. How was it he didn't understand? She felt so damn breakable, she could barely move.

Her husband sighed and let her go. 'Did you get hold of your sister?'

'I left messages everywhere I could. You know Nina. She'll be here when she's here.' She looked at the clock. 'What is taking that damn doctor so long? I'm calling the head of the department.'

Jeff said something she didn't hear, because the door to the waiting room opened and Dr Watanabe appeared.

'How is he?' her mother asked in a voice that carried through the room. Only the heaviness of her accent showed she was upset.

Dr Watanabe said, 'Not good. He had a second heart attack when we were taking him to surgery. He's very weak.'

'What can you do?' Meredith asked.

The compassion in the doctor's eyes was terrible. 'Nothing. The damage to his heart is too extensive. Now we just wait . . . and hope he makes it through the night. You can see him one at a time.' He took Mom by the elbow and led her away.

Focus on the details, Meredith thought. Find a way to fix this.

Memories gathered at the periphery of her vision. She saw her dad in the stands at her high school gymnastic meets, cheering with embarrassing vigour, and at her wedding, weeping openly as he walked her down the aisle. Only last week he'd said, 'Let's go get a couple of beers, Meredoodle, just the two of us, like we used to.'

And she'd blown him off, told him they'd do it soon. Had it really been so important to drop off the dry cleaning?

'I guess we should call the girls,' Jeff said. 'Fly them home.'

Meredith hated him for saying it. He'd given up already.

'Mere?' He slipped his arm round her waist. 'I love you.'

She let him hold her as long as she could bear and then eased away. Saying nothing, she followed the path her mother had walked, feeling utterly, dangerously alone.

The door to her father's room was closed, but a window revealed the interior. He lay in a metal-framed bed surrounded by tubes and IV lines and machines. Beside him, her mother sat in a plastic chair. Even now she looked strangely, almost defiantly, serene.

Meredith stood there and wiped her eyes. The doc had said one at a time, but finally she went inside. 'How is he?'

Her mother sighed heavily, got up and walked out of the room.

Meredith touched her father's hand. 'Hey, Daddy,' she whispered. 'It's your Meredoodle. I love you. Talk to me, Daddy.'

The only answer was the winter wind, tapping on the glass while the snow flurried and danced beneath the outside light.

Nina parked her rental car in the dark hospital parking lot and ran inside, praying that she wasn't too late.

In the waiting room on the third floor, she found her sister positioned like a sentinel next to an absurd aquarium full of tropical fish. Nina skidded to a stop. 'Mere?' she said quietly.

Meredith turned to her. Even with the length of the waiting room between them, Nina could see how tired her sister looked. Her chestnut hair was a mess, and her brown eyes looked too big for her colourless face. 'You're here,' she said, walking towards Nina and taking her into her arms.

Nina drew back. 'How is he?'

'He had a second massive heart attack. At first, they were going to try to operate . . . but now they're saying he won't survive it. Dr Watanabe doesn't think he'll make it through the weekend. But they didn't think he'd make it through the first night, either.'

Nina closed her eyes. Thank God she had made it home in time to see him. But how could she lose him? He was her level ground, her North Star, the one person who was always waiting for her to come home. She opened her eyes. 'How's Mom?'

Meredith stepped sideways. And there she was, sitting in a cheap upholstered chair. Even from here, Nina could see how scarily contained her mother was. She hadn't risen to welcome her home, hadn't even looked her way. Rather, she was staring straight ahead and, as usual, she was knitting.

'How is she?' Nina asked again.

Meredith shrugged, and Nina knew what that meant. Mom was alien, indecipherable to them, however much they'd tried.

Nodding at her sister, Nina left her and crossed the room. At her mother's side, she sank to her knees. Suddenly she wanted to be told their love would somehow cure him, even though she knew it was a lie.

'Hey, Mom,' Nina said. 'I got here as quickly as I could.'

'Good.'

She heard a tiny fissure in her mother's voice and dared to touch her thin, pale wrist. 'He's a strong man with a will to live.'

Her mother looked down at her slowly. Nina was shocked by how old and weary she looked, yet how strong. But then, her mother had always been a woman of contradictions. She'd worried acutely about letting her children leave the yard but hardly looked at them in the house; she'd claimed there was no God even as she decorated her holy corner. 'You think that is what matters?'

Nina was taken aback by the ferocity in her mother's voice. 'I think we have to believe he'll get better.'

'He is in room four thirty-four. He has been asking for you.' Her mother got up and started walking. Nina had no choice but to follow. Meredith took her hand as they walked down a brightly lit hallway.

At a closed door, Mom stopped. 'Go in, Nina.'

Nina took a deep breath and went inside, closing the door behind her. The room was quiet except for the mechanical sound of the machines. He looked small, a big man who'd been whittled down to fit in a child's bed.

'Nina.' His voice was so soft she hardly recognised it.

She forced herself to smile. Her father was a man who valued laughter and joy. 'Hey, Daddy.' The little girl word slipped out; she hadn't said it in years.

He knew, and he smiled. A faded, tired version of his smile.

Nina wiped the spittle from his lip. 'I love you, Daddy.'

'I want'—he was breathing hard now—'to go home.'

'You can't, Dad. They're taking good care of you here.'

He reached for her hand. 'Let me die at home.'

This time she couldn't will her tears away. 'Don't . . .'

He stared up at her, still breathing hard. 'Only you will convince Mere.'

'It won't be easy,' she said. 'You know Meredith likes everything in its place. She'll want you here.'

The smile he gave her broke her heart. 'You hate easy.'

'I do,' she said quietly, stung by the sudden thought that without him, no one would know her that well.

He closed his eyes. For a second, Nina thought she'd lost him, but the machines soothed her. He was still breathing.

She sank into the chair beside his bed, knowing why he'd asked this favour. Mom could do it, of course, could force his move home, but Meredith would hate her mother for it.

Dad had spent his life trying to create love where none existed—between his wife and his daughters—and he couldn't give up even now. All he could do was hand his need to her and hope she could accomplish what he wanted. She remembered how often he'd called her his rule-breaker, his spitfire, and how proud he'd been of her courage to go into battle.

Of course she would do as he'd asked. It was perhaps the last important thing he'd ask of her.

That night, after the arrangements had been made to have Dad discharged, Nina drove home in her rental car. Her first view in a long time of Belye Nochi made her breath catch.

The house looked as beautiful and out of place as ever in its snowy valley. On the porch, she stomped the snow off her hiking boots and opened the door. In the kitchen, her mother's precious brass samovar glinted in the light from an overhead fixture.

She told Meredith to go home. As soon as her sister was gone, she grabbed her backpack and camera bags off the kitchen table and headed up the narrow stairway. She went into the bedroom she and Meredith had shared. Although it appeared symmetrical—twin beds, a pair of matching desks and two white dressers—a closer look revealed the two very different girls who'd lived here, and the separate paths their lives would take. Even as girls, they'd had little in common. The last thing Nina really remembered them doing together was the play.

Mom had changed that day and so had Meredith. True to her word, her sister had never listened to another of Mom's fairy tales, but it had been an easy promise to keep, as Mom never told them a story again. Nina was frowning when she happened to glance outside.

There was her mother, sitting on her bench in the winter garden. Tiny white Christmas lights were entwined in the wrought-iron fence, making the garden look like a magical place in the middle of all that night.

Nina went out. 'Mom?' she said, sitting beside her mother. For what seemed like an eternity, neither of them spoke.

'Your father thinks I cannot handle his death,' Mom said.

The calm way she said it brought Nina up short. 'Can you?'

'You would be amazed at what the human heart can endure.'

'That doesn't mean the pain isn't unbearable. In Kosovo, I—'

'Do not tell me about your work. These are discussions you have with your father. War does not interest me.'

Nina knew better than to reach out to her mother. 'Sorry. Just making conversation.'

'Do not.' Mom reached down to touch the red holly berries peeking through the snow, framed by glossy green leaves. Not that her mother could see these colours, of course. Her birth defect precluded her seeing the true beauty in her garden. Her sister had never understood why a woman who saw the world in black and white would care so much about flowers, but Nina knew the power of black-and-white images. Sometimes a thing was its truest self when the colours were stripped away.

CHAPTER THREE

NINA HAD SPENT a lot of time with injured or dying people, standing witness, revealing universal pain through individual suffering. She was good at it, too, able to be both completely in the moment and detached enough to record it. But the day her father came home from the hospital, she couldn't put her grief in a box.

She was standing in her parents' bedroom with her back to the window. In the big bed, with pillows piled round him, her dad looked thin and old and fading.

Nina moved in towards the bed and stood beside Meredith. Mom was on his other side.

'I will be back in a moment,' Mom said.

Dad nodded at her. The look that passed between her parents was so intimate that Nina felt almost like an intruder.

As soon as Mom was gone, Dad turned to look at Meredith. 'I know you're afraid,' he said quietly.

'We don't need to talk about it,' Meredith said.

'Unless you *want* to talk about it,' Nina said, reaching down for his hand. 'You must be afraid of dying, Dad.'

'Oh, for God's sake,' Meredith said, stepping back from the bed.

Nina had lived alongside death for years and knew there were peaceful passings and desperate ones. As hard as it was to contemplate his dying, she wanted to help him. She brushed the white hair away from his forehead.

'Your mom,' he said with effort. 'She'll break without me . . .'

'You know I won't let Mom down,' Meredith said unsteadily.

'She can't do it again . . .' Dad said. 'Help her. Promise me.'

'Can't do what again?' Nina asked.

'Who are you, a detective?' Meredith snapped. 'Back off. He told us to take care of Mom. Like he even had to ask.' It wasn't until she bent to kiss his forehead that Nina saw her watery eyes. 'I'll be back in an hour, Dad. I love you.' And she was gone.

As Nina looked down at his pale, now-sleeping face, the tears she'd been fighting turned him into a grey smear in the huge bed. She wanted to say, *I love you, Dad,* but the words wouldn't let go. Quietly she left his room. In the hallway, she passed her mother, and when their pain-filled gazes met, Nina reached out her hand.

Mom lurched away and went into the bedroom, shutting the door.

Meredith and Jeff met the girls at the train station that night. It was a subdued welcome, full of sad looks and unspoken words.

'How's Papa?' Jillian asked after the car doors were shut.

'Not good. He'll be so glad to see you, though,' Meredith said.

Maddy's eyes filled with tears. 'Can we see him tonight?'

'Of course, honey. He's waiting for us.'

Jeff started the engine. They tried to make conversation, but the words had trouble rising above the pall that hung in the car.

At Belye Nochi, they went inside and made their way upstairs. Meredith led them into the bedroom. 'Dad, look who's here.'

Nina was sitting on the stone hearth, her back to a bright fire. At their entrance, she stood. 'These can't be my nieces,' she said, hugging them tightly, but her usual booming laugh was gone.

'Your papa has been waiting for you two,' Mom said, rising from the rocking chair by the window. She was as warm to her granddaughters as she was cold to her daughters.

They hugged Mom, then turned to Dad, motionless in the bed. 'My granddaughters,' he said quietly. Meredith could see how affected they were by the sight of him.

Jillian was the first to lean down and kiss him. 'Hey, Papa.'

Maddy's eyes were damp. When she opened her mouth to say something, no words came out. Dad reached up a mottled, shaking hand and pressed it to her cheek. 'No crying, Princess.'

Maddy wiped her eyes and nodded.

Dad tried to sit up. Meredith arranged the pillows. Coughing hard, he looked at Mom. 'We're all here. It's time, Anya.'

'No,' Mom said evenly.

'You promised. *Now*," he said with a sternness Meredith had never heard before. Mom sank back into the rocking chair.

'Your mother has agreed to tell us one of her fairy tales. After all these years. Like she used to.' Dad looked at Mom. 'The peasant girl and the prince, I think. That was always my favourite one.'

'No,' Meredith said—or maybe she just thought it.

Her father looked up. 'Yes.' There was a strength in his voice.

Nina sat down at Mom's feet, just as she'd done years ago, before the night the Christmas play changed everything. 'Here, Mad,' she said, patting the floor. 'Come and sit by me.'

Jeff chose the big armchair by the fireplace, and Jillian snuggled in alongside. Only Meredith couldn't seem to make her legs work.

'Sit . . . Meredoodle,' Dad said and, at the nickname, she sat woodenly on the Oriental carpet, as far from her mother as possible.

In the rocking chair, Mom sat very still. '*Her name is Vera, and she is a poor peasant girl. A nobody. Not that she knows this, of course. No one so young can know such a thing. She is fifteen years old, and she lives in the Snow Kingdom, an enchanted land that now is rotting from within. Evil has come to the kingdom; he is a dark, angry knight who wants to destroy it all.*'

Meredith felt a chill. She remembered how it once had been: Mom would come into their room at night and tell them wondrous tales of stone lions and frozen trees and cranes who swallowed starlight. Always in the dark. Her voice would bring them all together for a time, but in the morning, those bonds would be gone.

'*He moves like a virus, this knight; by the time the villagers begin to see the truth, it is too late. The infection is already there; winter snow turns purplish black, puddles in the street pull travellers down into muck, trees stop bearing*' *fruit. Perhaps the fair villagers would have done nothing anyway. They are the kind of people who keep their heads down to avoid danger.*

Vera does not understand this. How can she at her age? In June, when the air smells of flowers, she cannot help but dream of her own bright future. On this night, for some reason, she wakes at midnight and gets out of bed quietly, so as not to waken her sister, and she goes to her window. From here, she can see all the way to the bridge. It is the time of white nights, when at its darkest, the sky is a deep royal purple scattered with stars. The streets are never quiet. At all hours, villagers gather; lovers walk across the bridge, and courtiers leave the cafés very late, drunk on mead and sunlight.

But as she is breathing in the summer night, she hears her parents arguing. Vera tiptoes to the door, pushing it open a crack. Her mother stands wringing her hands. "You cannot keep doing dangerous things, Petyr. Every night we hear of villagers turned to smoke."

"But you cannot ask me to do this."

"I do ask you. Write what the Black Knight tells you to. They are just words." Her mother is crying. "I am afraid for you."

Vera closes the door, confused. She has never before seen her strong mother afraid. But Papa will never let anything bad happen to them.

She means to ask her mother about the argument the next day, but when she wakens, the sun is shining. She rushes outside.

Her beloved kingdom is in bloom, and so is she. How can anything be bad when the sun shines? She is so happy that even the thought of taking her younger sister to the park doesn't bother her.

"Vera, look! Watch me!" twelve-year-old Olga calls out to her, launching into a series of cartwheels.

"Nice." Vera closes her eyes, leaning back into the park bench.

"Two roses do I bring to thee."

Vera opens her eyes and looks up at the most handsome boy she has ever seen. Prince Aleksandr. Every girl recognises his face.

His clothes are perfectly made and decorated in golden beads. Behind him stands a gleaming white carriage, drawn by four white horses. And in his hand, two roses. She responds with the poem's next line, grateful that her father has made her read so much.

"You are young to know poetry," he says, and she can tell that he is impressed. "Who are you?"

She straightens, sitting up. "Veronika. And I am not that young."

"Really? I'll wager your father would not let you walk with me."

"I don't need anyone's permission, Your Highness," she lies.

He laughs, and it is a sound like music. "Well then, Veronika, I will see you tonight. At eleven o'clock. Where shall I find you?"

Eleven o'clock. She is supposed to be in bed then. Perhaps she can put blankets in her bed and climb out of the window. Her glance shoots to her sister, walking towards them. "On the Enchanted Bridge."

"I think you will leave me standing there alone."

Olga comes closer. "No, Prince Aleksandr. I'll see you then."

"Call me Sasha," he says.

Just like that, she falls in love with this young man, who is all wrong for her. Above her station. And dangerous to her family. But this does not matter to Vera, for already love has begun. She and her prince sneak away, get married, and live happily ever after.

'The end,' Mom said, smiling briefly at her granddaughters.

'Anya,' Dad said sharply. 'We agreed—'

'No more.' Mom stood up and walked out of the room.

The fairy tales had always been among Nina's best childhood memories, though she hadn't heard one in decades. But why would her father bring them up now? Surely he knew it would end badly. Meredith and Mom hadn't been able to leave the room fast enough.

She went to stand beside him. They were alone now.

'I love the sound of her voice,' he said.

Nina suddenly understood. 'You wanted us all to be together.'

Dad sighed. 'Know what a man thinks about now? Mistakes.'

She reached for his hand. 'You didn't make many of those.'

'She tried to talk to you until that god-awful play. I shouldn't have let her hide. She's just so . . . broken, and I love her so much.'

'It doesn't matter, Dad. Don't worry.'

'It matters,' he said, his voice weak. 'She needs you . . . and you need her. Promise me. After I'm gone, get to know her.'

'How? I've tried. She won't talk to us. You know that.'

'She'll tell her stories,' he said. 'Make her finish the peasant girl and the prince. You've never heard it all the way to the end. Just try, OK? Promise me.'

Nina touched the side of his face, feeling his tears. 'OK, Dad.'

'Love you,' he whispered, his voice slurred.

'I love you, too.' She kissed his forehead and left him alone.

Drawing in a deep, steadying breath, she went downstairs. In the kitchen, she found her mother standing at the counter. Dozens of beets and yellow onions lay scattered around her cutting board. A giant pot of borscht simmered on the stove.

'Hey,' Nina said, leaning against the doorway.

Her mother turned slowly. Her white hair was coiled in a ballerina bun at the nape of her neck. Against the pallor of her skin, those arctic blue eyes seemed impossibly sharp. And yet there was a brittle look to her Nina didn't remember, and that made her bold.

'I always loved your stories,' she said.

Mom wiped her hands on her apron. 'Fairy tales are for children.'

'Dad loves them. Maybe you could tell the rest of the peasant girl and the prince tomorrow.'

'He is dying. It is a little late for fairy tales, I would say.'

Nina knew then: her promise couldn't be kept. There was simply no way to get to know her mother. There never had been.

The minute Meredith left her bedroom, she heard noise: dogs were barking; the girls were talking loudly; a television was on somewhere. For the first time in months, it felt like home again.

Downstairs, she found Jeff and Jillian in the kitchen, setting the table. The dogs were poised, waiting for breakfast scraps.

'Dad told me to let you sleep,' Jillian said.

'Thanks,' Meredith said. 'Where's your sister?'

'Still in bed.'

Jeff handed Meredith a cup of coffee. 'You OK?' he asked.

'Rough night,' she said. 'Did I keep you awake?'

'No.'

She remembered how entwined they used to be when they slept. Lately they slept so far apart that one's restless night didn't affect the other.

'Mom?' Jillian said, putting down napkins. 'Can we go and see Papa and Baba again this morning?'

Meredith reached for the stack of toast on the counter. 'I'm going to go down now. Why don't you all come after breakfast?'

Jeff nodded. 'We'll take the dogs for a walk and be right down.'

She took her coffee upstairs, where she exchanged her robe and pajamas for a pair of comfortable jeans and a cable-knit turtleneck. Saying a quick goodbye, she hurried out of the house and walked the quarter mile to her parents' home.

All night she'd dreamed about her dad. She needed to sit beside him, let him tell her some stories from his life so she could hold that knowledge close. They knew how he'd joined the army and met Mom while on active duty, but that was pretty much it.

And she wanted to apologise for running out after the fairy tale. She knew it had hurt his feelings. If it mattered, she'd listen to every damn stupid story her mother had to tell.

At the front door, she knocked once and went inside.

'Mom?' She called out, closing the door. She could tell immediately that coffee hadn't been made. 'Nice, Nina,' she muttered.

She put the coffee on and went upstairs. At her parents' bedroom door, she knocked. There was no answer, so she opened it.

Her parents were cuddled together in bed. 'Morning. I've got coffee going. And the samovar.' She threw open the curtains. Sunlight shone through the huge bowed window.

Turning, she looked at her parents again. They lay spooned together, with Dad on his side and Mom tucked up against his back with her arms round him, whispering to him in Russian.

'Mom?' Meredith said, frowning. For all of her mother's Russianness, she never spoke that language in the house.

The look her mother gave chilled Meredith to the bone. The word *No* bubbled from deep inside, but Meredith couldn't say it.

'I am trying to warm him up. He is so cold. So cold.'

Her father lay too still, his eyes closed. He looked peaceful, but a pale blue cast rimmed his lips. It was barely there, but she saw that the man she loved wasn't there any more. He'd never again pull her into a bear hug and whisper, *I love you, Meredoodle.*

Mom made a sobbing sound and rubbed his shoulder and arms. 'I have some bread saved for you. Wake up.'

Meredith had never heard her mother sound so desperate. She'd never heard *anyone* sound like that. It was the sound you made when the floor dropped out from beneath you and you were falling.

Meredith felt the sting of tears but knew she couldn't give in now. She'd be lost. She went to the phone and dialled 911. When she had given the information, she returned. 'He's gone, Mom.'

Her mother looked up at her, wild-eyed. 'He's so cold,' she said, sounding plaintive and afraid. 'They always die cold . . .'

'Mom?' Meredith helped her mother to her feet and into her black flannel robe. 'I'll make you tea. We can have it while they . . . take him. Come on. Let's go downstairs.' She took her mother by the arm, feeling like the stronger of the two for the first time ever.

'He is my home. How will I live without him?'

'We'll all still be here, Mom,' Meredith said, wiping her own tears. It was a hollow reassurance. Her mother was right. He was home, the heart of them. How would they stand life without him?

Nina had been out in the orchard since before dawn, trying to lose herself in photography. For a short time, it had worked. As she headed back to the house, the smell of freshly brewed coffee drew her into the kitchen.

Meredith was at the sink, head bowed, watching the water run.

'Aren't you going to yell at me for not making coffee?'

'No.' Meredith turned slowly. 'He's gone,' she said.

The world tilted off its axis. Pain unlike anything she'd ever known collected in Nina's chest. An absurd memory flashed: she was eight, following her dad through the orchard, when she'd caught her toe and gone flying. 'Nice trip, Neener Beaner,' he'd said, laughing, scooping her onto his big shoulders. 'See you in the fall.'

She walked forwards, her vision blurred by tears, stepping into her big sister's arms. Had she told him how deeply she loved him?

Meredith wiped her eyes. 'They'll be . . . coming for him soon. Mom's up with Dad. I couldn't get her to leave him.'

'I'll go and try. And then . . . what?'

'We start making plans. And phone calls.'

The thought of it, of watching his life turn into the details of death, was almost more than Nina could bear. By the time she was upstairs, she was crying softly.

She knocked on the door of her parents' room and waited. At the silence, she turned the knob and went inside. Surprisingly, the room was empty except for her father, his covers drawn so tightly they looked like a layer of new-fallen snow. He looked pale and old and peaceful.

Nina drew in a deep breath and stared down at him for a long time, memorising every detail. 'Goodbye, Daddy,' she said softly.

Backing away from the bed, she moved to the window.

Mom was out there in the snow, sitting on the bench in her winter garden. She was barefoot and in her nightgown. Her long white hair was unbound and fell in tangles round her pale face.

Nina hurried downstairs and slipped back into her wet boots. She went outside and walked through the thick snow until she was at her mother's side. She draped her coat over Mom's thin shoulders, then took off her boots and put them on her mother's feet.

'Come on,' Nina said. 'Let's go inside.'

Mom stared at her, slowly frowning. Confusion clouded those brilliant blue eyes. She shook her head, and tears glazed her eyes.

'He's gone. Evan is gone,' her mother said. 'I do not want him buried. Not in ground that freezes. We'll scatter his ashes.'

Nina heard the familiar steel in her mother's voice.

'OK, Mom,' she said, standing up. Her feet were freezing. 'I'm going to go in. Meredith will need help. And don't stay out here too long; you'll catch pneumonia.'

'You think I could die from the cold? I am not a lucky woman.'

It made no sense. Nina put a hand on her mother's shoulder, felt her flinch at the contact. As ridiculous as it was, that little flinch hurt Nina's feelings. Even now, Mom wanted only to be alone.

Nina went back to the house and found Meredith in the kitchen. In the look that passed between them was the realisation that this was who they were now. She and Mom and Meredith. From now on, they'd be a triangle, distantly connected, instead of the circle their dad had created. The thought made her want to run for the airport. 'Give me some phone numbers,' she said. 'I'll help with the calls.'

More than 400 people filled the church to say goodbye to Evan Whitson; dozens had come back to Belye Nochi to pay their respects and raise a glass. Judging by the dishes Meredith had washed, a lot of glasses had been raised. As expected, Nina had been a marvellous host; Mom had moved through the crowd, head high; and Meredith had done the heavy lifting. She'd set out the food, napkins, plates and glasses, and she'd washed dishes almost continuously. She was doing what she always did when stressed: hiding behind chores.

She was elbow deep in soapy water when, at about midnight, Jeff and the girls came into the kitchen to find her. He took her in his arms, and the tears she'd held back came pouring out. He stroked her hair, saying the great lie: 'It will be OK.' When nothing was left inside, she drew back. 'I guess I've been holding that in.'

'That's what you do.'

'You say that like it's a bad thing. Should I fall apart?'

'Maybe.'

It made her feel more separate when he said things like that. He seemed to think she was a vase that could be glued back together.

'I've been there,' he said. 'You helped me through my parents' deaths. Let me help you.'

'I'm fine. Really. I'll fall apart later.'

'Meredith—'

'Don't.' She hadn't meant to say it so sharply. 'I mean, don't worry about it. I'm fine. Why don't you take the girls home?'

'Fine,' he said, but there was a guarded look in his eyes.

After everyone had gone, Meredith stood in the clean kitchen, alone, and wished she'd made a different choice. How hard would it have been to say, *Sure, Jeff, take me home . . .?*

She threw the dishrag on the counter. In the living room, she found Nina standing in front of an easel that supported a large picture of Dad. In a pair of khaki pants and a black sweater, with her short black hair a mess, she looked more like a teenager than a famous photographer.

But Meredith saw the grief in her sister's bottle-green eyes. She knew Nina, like her, knew neither how to express it nor even fully feel it, and she hurt for both of them and for the woman upstairs in her empty bed. She went to Nina. 'We have each other,' she said.

'Yeah,' Nina agreed, although their eyes betrayed them both. They knew it wasn't enough.

For the next three days, Nina tried to be a real part of the family, but her every attempt was a failure. Without Dad, they were like random pieces on a board game without a common goal or a rule book. Mom stayed in bed, knitting, while Meredith's competence had never been so apparent. She'd gone back to work the day after the funeral, so she was running the orchard, taking care of her family and still managing to come to Belye Nochi three times a day to micromanage Nina's chores.

Nothing Nina did was right; Meredith did everything again. Vacuuming, dishes, laundry. Nina would have said something, but honestly, she didn't give a damn. It was the grief that was killing her. She thought, He's gone, at the oddest times, and it hurt so badly she'd catch her breath, or stumble or drop a glass. She wasn't doing anyone any good, least of all herself.

Once she'd had that thought, there was no getting rid of it. She tried to talk herself out of it, told herself she couldn't run away, not four days before Christmas. But at three o'clock, she went upstairs to her room and called Sylvie in New York.

'Hey, Sylvie,' she said, when her editor answered.

'Hi, Nina. I've been thinking about you. How's your dad?'

'Gone.' She tried not to react to that word, but it took effort.

'Oh, Nina. I'm sorry.'

Everyone was sorry. 'I need to get back to work.'

'Are you sure? You can never get this time back.'

'Believe me, Sylvie, the last thing I want is this time back.'

'Well, I do need someone in Sierra Leone.'

'A war zone sounds perfect,' Nina said.

'You have serious issues, you know that, right?'

'Yeah,' she said. 'I know.' They talked for a few more minutes, and Nina hung up. Feeling better—and worse—she went downstairs and found Meredith in the kitchen doing the dishes. *Of course*. Nina reached for a towel. 'I was going to do that, you know.'

'These are lunch and dinner dishes from yesterday, Nina.'

'Whoa, slow down. It's dishes, not—'

'People dying of hunger. I get it. You do things that *matter*. Me, I just run the family business and take care of our parents and clean up after my important sister.' Nina felt as if all her faults had just been laid bare. 'I'm sorry.' Meredith wiped her forehead. 'How long are you staying?'

'Not long. The situation in Sierra Leone—'

'Spare me. You're running away.' Meredith finally almost smiled. 'Hell, I'd do the same thing if I could.'

Nina felt as bad about herself as she ever had. She cared about what her selfishness would cost her sister, and about the promise to her father she'd quickly seen was impossible to keep, but God help her, she didn't care enough to stay. 'What about his ashes?'

'She wants to scatter them on his birthday in May.'

'I'll come back for that.'

'Twice in one year?' Meredith said.

Nina looked at her. 'It's some year.'

For a moment, it looked like Meredith might crumble; just let go and cry, and Nina felt her own tears start. Then Meredith nodded curtly and wiped her eyes. 'Be sure and say goodbye to the girls.'

CHAPTER FOUR

In the weeks following her father's death, Meredith held herself together by strength of will alone. Grief had become her silent sidekick. Christmas and New Year's had been disastrous, of course. And Jeff kept saying that if she'd just cry, she'd be OK. She knew crying wouldn't help, because she cried in her sleep.

And so she went on, moving from one thing to the next with a desperate kind of zeal. It wasn't until the girls went back to school that she realised how exhausted she was. And now sometimes she and Jeff went whole days with little more than a nod in passing.

She rinsed out her coffee cup and went downstairs to the home office Jeff used for writing. Knocking quietly, she opened the door.

Jeff sat at his desk. 'How's the book going?' she asked.

'Wow. You haven't asked me that in weeks.'

'Really?' Meredith frowned. In the early days, when he'd been a struggling journalist, she'd read every word he wrote. Even a few years ago, when he'd first tried fiction, she'd been his best critic. That book hadn't sold to a publisher, but she'd been glad when he'd started another. 'I'm sorry. I've been a mess. Can I read what you have so far?'

She saw how easy it was to make him smile and felt a pang of guilt. She mentally added 'Read Jeff's book' to her to-do list.

He leaned back. 'Let's go to dinner tonight. You need a break.'

'Maybe tomorrow. Tonight I need to pay Mom's bills.'

'You're burning the candle at both ends.'

Meredith hated it when he said that. What was she supposed to stop doing? 'It's only been a few weeks. Cut me some slack.'

'Only if you cut yourself some.'

She had no idea what he meant. 'I've got to go. See you tonight.'

Meredith drove down to her parents' house and found her mother at the dining-room table, muttering in Russian. Spread out in front of her was all the jewellery Dad had bought her over the years.

'Hey, Mom. What are you doing?'

'We have these jewels. And the butterfly is somewhere.'

'Are you getting dressed up for something?'

Her mother looked up sharply. Only then did Meredith see the confusion in her eyes. 'We can sell them.'

'We don't need to sell your jewellery, Mom.'

'They'll stop handing out money soon. You'll see.'

Meredith scooped up the costume jewellery. There was nothing of real value here: Dad's gifts were more heartfelt than expensive. 'Don't worry about the bills, Mom. I'll be paying them for you.'

'You?'

Meredith nodded and helped her mother to her feet, surprised at the easy acquiescence. Mom let herself be led up the stairs.

'Is the butterfly safe?'

Meredith nodded. 'Everything is safe, Mom,' she said, helping her mother into bed.

'Thank God,' Mom said with a sigh. She closed her eyes.

Meredith stood there a long time, staring down at her sleeping mother. When she was confident that Mom was sleeping deeply, she went downstairs and called the office.

Daisy answered quickly. 'Meredith Whitson Cooper's office.'

'Hey, Daisy,' Meredith said. 'I'm going to work from Belye Nochi today. My mom's acting a little strange.'

'Grief will do that to a person.'

'Yeah,' Meredith said. 'It will.'

If Meredith had been burning the candle at both ends then, by the end of January, there was nothing left but the flame. Every morning she ran five miles, made her husband and her mother breakfast, and left for work. By eight o'clock, she would be at her desk. At noon, she would return to check on Mom. Then it was back to work until six, grocery shopping on her way home, stopping at Mom's until seven or eight, and home by eight thirty for whatever dinner she and Jeff could throw together. Without fail, she would fall asleep on the sofa by nine and would wake up at three in the morning.

Now it was barely noon; she was already exhausted as she hit the intercom button and said, 'Daisy, I'm going home for lunch. I'll be back in an hour.'

Outside, snow was falling again. She drove slowly to her mom's house, parked and went inside.

'Mom, I'm here.'

There was no answer.

She dug through the refrigerator and found the *pierogi* she'd defrosted the night before. She was popping them in the microwave when she caught a glimpse of a dark shape in the winter garden.

She got her coat and trudged through the snow. 'Mom,' she said. 'You've got to quit this. Come in. I'll make soup and *pierogi*.'

'We have soup? From the belt?'

Meredith shook her head. Whatever. Mom was growing weirder by the day. 'It's lentil. Come on.' She helped her mother to her feet—bare and cold—and led her to the kitchen, where she wrapped her in a blanket and sat her at the table. 'Are you OK?'

'Do not worry about me, Olga,' Mom said. 'Check on our lion.'

Meredith frowned. 'Mom, I think we need to see Dr Burns.'

'What have we to trade?'

Meredith sighed and took the plate of *pierogi* from the microwave. She set the golden pastries in front of her mother. 'They're hot. Be careful. I'm going to call the doctor. Stay here, OK?'

She called Daisy and asked her to make an emergency appointment with Dr Burns. Then she came back to the kitchen. 'You ate all the *pierogi*?' she said, surprised. 'Good.' She helped Mom into socks and boots. 'Put on your coat. I'll warm up the car.'

When she came back, Mom was in the doorway buttoning up her coat incorrectly.

'Here, Mom.' Meredith rebuttoned the coat. She had almost finished when she realised it was warm. She reached into the pockets and found the *pierogi*, wrapped in paper towels. *What the hell?*

'They're for Anya, not you,' Mom said, pulling away.

'I know they're yours,' Meredith said. 'I'll leave them right here, OK?' She put them on the hallway table. 'Come on, Mom.'

She led her mother out to the SUV and drove to town, parking in front of the Cashmere Medical Group's brick office.

Georgia Edwards was at the desk, looking as perky as she had in her cheerleading days at Cashmere High. 'Hey, Mere,' she said.

'Hi, Georgia. Did Daisy get an appointment for my mom?'

'You know Jim. He'd do anything for you Whitsons. Take her down to Exam A.'

'This is ridiculous,' Mom said, suddenly seeming to realise where they were. She lifted her chin, walked briskly to the first exam room, and took the only seat. Meredith followed her inside.

Moments later Dr James Burns walked in. His compassionate eyes made Meredith think of her father; they'd been golf partners for years. He hugged her; in the embrace was shared grief, a silent *I miss him, too.*

'So.' He stepped back. 'Anya, how are you?'

'I am fine, James. Thank you. Meredith is jumpy, you know.'

He pulled a wheeled stool out and sat on it. 'Let's examine you.'

'Fine.'

Jim checked her mother's temperature and looked down her throat. Then he rolled back. 'What day is it, Anya?'

'January thirty-first, 2001. Wednesday. We have a new president. George Bush, the younger. And Olympia is the state capital.'

Jim paused. 'How are you, Anya? Really?'

'My heart beats. I breathe. I go to sleep, and I wake up.'

'Maybe you should see someone,' he said gently. 'A doctor who will help you talk about your loss.'

'Americans believe words change a thing. They do not.'

'OK,' he said, making a few notes on the chart. 'Why don't you go to the waiting room while I speak to Meredith?'

Mom left the room immediately. 'There's something wrong with her,' Meredith said when they were alone. 'She's confused a lot. Today she put her lunch in her pockets. She's worried about a lion, and she called me Olga. Could she have Alzheimer's?'

'Her mind seems fine, Meredith. She's grieving. Give her time. Your parents were married for five decades. Just listen to her if you can. Talk to her. And don't let her be alone too much.'

'Believe me, my mom is alone whether I'm in the room or not.'

'So be alone together.'

'Yeah,' Meredith said. 'Sure. Thanks, Jim, for seeing us.'

On a blistering hot day, more than one month after she'd left Washington State, Nina stood amid a sea of desperate, starving refugees. As far as she could see, there were people huddled in front of sagging tents. Their stoicism was remarkable.

Nina was as filthy and hungry as those around her. She'd lived in this camp for two weeks now. Before that, she'd been in Sierra Leone, ducking and hiding to avoid being shot or raped.

She squatted in the red soil. Sprawled half out of a tent, an old, wizened man lay dead. His emaciated wife rocked him in her arms.

For the first time in Nina's career, the tragedy of it all was nearly unbearable. She carried her own grief with her everywhere now, and when she took pictures, the lens was no protection. As she eased the camera from her eye, she realised she was crying.

She opened her pack, pulled out her satellite phone, positioned it correctly, and called Danny.

At the sound of his voice, she felt something in her chest relax. 'Danny,' she said, yelling to be heard over the static.

'Nina, love. Where are you?'

'Guinea. You?'

'Zambia. The whole DCR thing is exploded.'

'I'm tired,' she said, surprising herself. She couldn't remember ever saying that before, not while she was working.

'I can be at Mnemba Island by Wednesday.'

Blue water. White sand. Ice. Sex. 'I'm in.'

Two days later Nina was stepping onto a sleek white motorboat, speeding across the sea to Mnemba, a small atoll in the Zanzibar archipelago. She made her way down the beach. There were nine private bandas, hidden by dense vegetation. Nina saw the #7 sign.

Danny was in a bamboo chair, his feet propped on a coffee table, sipping a beer and reading. She leaned against the railing. 'That beer isn't quite the best-looking thing in the room, but it's close.'

Danny tossed down his book. Even with his stubble-coated jaw, he looked beautiful. He pulled her into his arms and kissed her until she pushed him away, laughing. 'I'm filthy,' she said.

He kissed her grimy palm. 'It's what I love best about you.'

'I need a shower,' she said.

He took her by the hand, led her to the outside shower, and washed her beneath the hot water. Then he carried her to the bed.

Later, when they both could breathe again, they lay talking, her head cradled in the crook of his arm. There was a pause, and she knew he was going to say what she didn't want to hear.

'I had to hear from Sylvie that your da died.'

'What was I supposed to do? Call and cry?'

He rolled onto his side, pulling her with him. 'I'm from Dublin, remember? I know about losin' people, and about runnin' from it.'

'What do you want from me, Danny? What?'

'Tell me about your da.'

She stared at him. Her feelings of loss were so intense that if she let herself feel all of it, she'd never find a way back.

'I don't know how. He was . . . my sun, I guess.'

'I love you like that,' he said quietly.

Nina wished that made her feel better, but it didn't. She knew about unequal love, how you could be crushed from the inside if one person was more in love than the other. Hadn't she sometimes seen that kind of wreckage in Dad's eyes when he looked at Mom? If Danny ever looked at her like that, it would break her heart.

Still, the thought of losing him made her anxious. 'Can't we just—'

'For now,' he said. But she knew it wouldn't end there.

Still tired and aching from a night spent tossing and turning beneath the covers, Meredith eased out of bed, went to the window, and stared out at the darkness. Dawn hadn't shown its face yet.

She dressed in her running clothes. Downstairs she turned on the coffeepot and whistled for the dogs. In the cold early February dark, she pushed herself hard, doubled back, then veered into Belye Nochi. She slipped out of her running shoes, went into the kitchen where she started the samovar, and then climbed the stairs. She was still breathing heavily when she opened Mom's door.

And found the bed empty. Hell.

Meredith went outside to the winter garden and sat beside her mother, who wore a nightdress and a mohair blanket draped round her shoulders.

As Meredith dared to reach out and cover her mother's cold hand with her own, she noticed the new addition to the garden, a bright new copper column standing next to the old verdigris-aged one. 'When did you order that, Mom?'

'I wish I had some chocolate to give him. He loves chocolate. Don't make Anya go alone.'

'Come on, Mom.' Meredith helped her rise. 'Come on.'

Her mother straightened slowly. Following her into the kitchen, Meredith called Jeff and said she wouldn't be home for breakfast. 'Mom was in the garden again. I had better work here today.'

'Big surprise.'

'Come on, Jeff. Be fair—'

He hung up.

For the rest of the day, she worked from the kitchen table; in addition to paying taxes and reading crop reports and overseeing warehouse costs, she paid Mom's bills and washed her clothes.

Finally, at eight o'clock, when the dinner dishes were done, she went into the living room. Mom sat in Dad's favourite chair, her eyes closed even while her fingers wielded the knitting needles.

'It's time for bed,' Meredith said, striving not to sound tired.

'I can manage my own schedule,' Mom said.

And so it began, the endless grind of getting Mom to bed. At just past nine, Meredith finally pulled the covers up. 'Sleep well,' she said. 'Dream of your garden. The crocuses will be blooming soon.'

'Are they edible?' Mom said, frowning.

That was how it happened lately; one moment her mother was there, and just as suddenly she'd be absent. Each time, Meredith worried the changes *had* to be Alzheimer's.

Meredith soothed her not-mother as she would a frightened child. 'It's OK, Mom. We have plenty of food downstairs.'

Mom sighed, and within moments she was asleep. Downstairs, Meredith put a load in the washer, then finished two care packages for Jillian and Maddy. It was ten o'clock by the time she got home.

She found Jeff in his home office. 'Hey,' she said, coming into the room.

He didn't turn round. 'Hey.'

'How's the book going?'

'Great.'

'I still haven't read it.'

'I know.' He turned to her then.

The look he gave her was full of disappointment. Suddenly she saw the two of them from a distance. 'Are we in trouble, Jeff?'

She could see he was a little relieved by her question. 'Yeah.'

'Oh.' She could see he wanted to talk, but frankly, this was the last thing she needed now. Knowing it was a mistake, she left his office and went up to the bedroom they'd shared for so many years. She stripped down to her underwear and climbed into bed. A couple of sleeping pills should have helped, but they didn't and, later, when he slipped into bed, she knew he knew she was still awake.

She pressed up against his back and whispered, 'Good night.'

It wasn't enough, wasn't anything, and they both knew it. The conversation they needed to have was out there, like a storm cloud, gathering mass in the distance.

CHAPTER FIVE

EVERY DAY, MEREDITH VOWED to talk to Jeff about their troubled marriage, but the truth was, she didn't really want to talk about it. By spring, they both knew they truly were in trouble—the knowledge was in every look, every non-touch, every fake smile, but neither of them brought it up. They worked long hours and kissed each other good night and went their separate ways at dawn.

But driving to her mother's house from work in late March, Meredith found her spirits lifted by the warm front that had swept through the valley. Ice-blue water ran in gullies by the roadways, and sparkling droplets fell from the wakening apple trees.

She turned onto Mom's driveway, parked and walked up to the gate. In the kitchen, she stopped short. Her mother was standing on the counter holding a piece of newspaper and a roll of duct tape.

'Mom! What are you doing? Here. Take my hand.' Meredith rushed over and reached out, helping her mother climb down.

Mom's face was chalky; her hair was a mess; her feet were bare. Behind her, on the stove, something was popping and hissing. 'I need to go to the bank,' she said. 'We haven't much to trade.'

'Mom . . . your hands are bleeding. What have you done?'

Mom glanced towards the dining room.

Meredith walked slowly past the cold samovar. In the dining room, the wallpaper had been torn away in huge strips. In places, dark blotches stained the blank walls. Dried blood? Had her mother worked so feverishly that she'd scraped the skin off her fingertips? Ragged strips of wallpaper had been placed in a bowl in the centre of the table.

Behind her, the pot on the stove boiled over. Meredith turned it off. It was full of water and strips of wallpaper. 'What the hell . . .?'

'We will be hungry,' Mom said in explanation.

This was way past ordinary grief. Gently Meredith took hold of her mother's bloody hands. 'Let's get you washed, OK?'

Upstairs in the bathroom, Meredith cleaned Mom's hands. She could see precise cuts on her fingertips. 'What happened, Mom?'

Her mother kept looking round. 'I heard a gun.'

'You probably heard a truck backfire.'

Mom frowned at that. When Meredith had her mother bandaged, she put her into bed. That was when she noticed the bloodied carpenter's knife on the bedside table. Mom had cut herself on purpose. *Oh God.*

Meredith waited until her mother closed her eyes. Then she went down and looked at the damage round her. The boiling wallpaper, the ruined walls. Fear settled in, and it took every scrap of willpower she had not to scream out loud.

She pulled out her cellphone and called Jeff at work. She didn't know how to handle this alone. 'I need you,' she said. 'Mom has gone way round the bend. Can you come over?'

'I'll be there in ten minutes.'

'Thanks.'

She made a call to Dr Burns next, then sat on the porch, crying.

True to his word, Jeff showed up in ten minutes. He got out of the car, concern written all over his face but, as he came towards her, there was a loud crash.

Meredith ran inside. Her mother was sprawled on the dining-room floor, clutching a strip of wallpaper in one hand and her ankle in the other. A chair lay on its side.

Meredith tested her already swelling ankle. Jeff bent down beside them and then carried her mother to the ottoman. 'Here, Mom,' Meredith said. 'I've got an ice pack.'

'Thank you, Olga,' her mother said.

Jeff led Meredith into the kitchen. 'Wow,' he said.

'Yeah.' She stared at him, not quite knowing what to say, then moved forwards as Dr Burns came into the house, looking harassed.

'Hello, you two,' he said. 'What happened?'

'She was tearing down wallpaper and fell off a chair. Her ankle is swelling up like a balloon,' Meredith said.

Dr Burns smiled tiredly at her. 'Show me.'

But when they went into the living room, her mother was sitting up knitting, as if this were just an ordinary afternoon.

'Anya,' Jim said, going to her. 'What happened here?'

Mom gave him a dazzling smile. Her eyes were completely clear. 'I was redecorating the dining room, and I fell. Silly of me.'

'Redecorating? Why now?'

She shrugged. 'We women. Who knows.'

'May I take a look at your ankle?'

'Certainly. This pain is nothing,' she said.

Gently he examined her ankle and wrapped it in a bandage. 'And what about your hands?' he asked, examining her fingertips. 'It looks like you cut yourself on purpose.'

'Nonsense. I was redecorating. I told you this.'

He smiled gently. 'Come. Jeff and I will help you to your room.'

Meredith watched nervously as they made their way upstairs. When they returned, she looked at the doctor. 'Well?'

'She's sprained her ankle. It will heal if she stays off it.'

'That's not what I mean, and you know it. You saw her fingers. And I found a knife by her bed. I think she did it on purpose. She *must* have some kind of dementia. What do we do?'

Jim nodded slowly. 'There's a place in Wenatchee that could take her for a month or so. We could call it rehabilitation for her ankle. Insurance would cover that. It's not a long-term solution, but time away from Belye Nochi and memories here might help.'

Meredith winced. 'You mean, a nursing home?'

'No one likes a nursing home,' the doctor said. 'But sometimes it's the best answer. And remember, it's only short-term.'

'Will you tell her she's going there because she needs rehab?'

'Of course.'

Meredith knew her father would never have made this choice. But she couldn't deny how much this would help her. *She sits outside . . . tears down wallpaper . . . falls off counters . . . What would be next?*

'God help me,' she said softly. 'OK.'

That night, she dialled Nina's international cellphone number.

'Hello?' said a heavily accented voice. Irish, Meredith thought.

'Hello? I'm calling Nina Whitson. Did I get the wrong number?'

'No. This is her phone. Who am I speakin' to?'

'Meredith Cooper. I'm Nina's sister.'

'Ah, brilliant. I'm Daniel Flynn. I suppose you've heard of me.'

'No.'

'That's disappointin', isn't it? I'm a . . . good friend of your sister's.' His laugh was low and rumbling. Sexy as hell. 'Daniel's me old man, and a mean son of a bitch he was. Call me Danny.'

'How good a friend are you, Danny?'

'It's four years now, give or take.'

'Four *years*? She never mentioned you or brought you home.'

'More's the pity, eh? It was grand talkin' to you, Meredith, but your sis is givin' me the evil eye, so I'd best hand her the phone.'

Meredith said goodbye as Nina answered, laughing. 'Hey, Mere. What's up? How's Mom?'

'Neens, that's why I'm calling. She's not good. She's confused lately. Doc Burns thinks it's ordinary grief, but—'

'Thank God. I wouldn't want her to end up like Aunt Dora, in a pathetic nursing home, eating jello and watching game shows.'

Meredith flinched. 'She fell and sprained her ankle. Luckily I was there to help, but I can't always be there.'

'You're a saint, Mere. The way you're taking care of Mom and running the orchard. Dad would be proud. Look, I really can't talk now. Do you have something important?'

'No, nothing important,' Meredith said. 'I can handle it.'

'Good. I'll be home for Dad's birthday, don't forget.'

'OK,' Meredith said. 'See you then.'

Nina woke to the sound of gunfire. Rounds exploded; the dingy walls of her hotel room shuddered. A shower of plaster rained down on the floor. She got out of bed and crawled to the window.

Tanks were rolling down the rubble-strewn street. Men in uniforms—boys, really—laughed as they fired their machine guns. She turned and leaned against the wall. Lord, she was tired of this.

It was the end of April. Only a month ago she'd been in Sudan with Danny, but it felt like a lifetime.

Her cellphone rang. She crawled across the floor. 'Hello?'

'Nina? Is that you? I can barely hear you.'

'Gunfire. Hey, Sylvie, what's up?'

'We're not using your photos,' Sylvie said. 'There's no way to sugar-coat it. They're not good enough. What's going on?'

Nina couldn't believe what she'd just heard. She pushed the hair out of her eyes. 'I don't know,' she finally said.

'You shouldn't have gone back to work so quickly. I know how much you loved your father. Is there anything I can do to help?'

'Getting the cover always makes me feel better.'

Sylvie's silence said it all. 'A war zone is no place to grieve. Maybe you've lost your edge because there's somewhere you need to be.'

'Yeah. Well . . . thanks,' Nina said, and hung up.

It was hardly surprising her latest photos were crap. She was too tired to concentrate, and when she did finally fall asleep, dreams of her father invariably woke her. His last words nagged at her, the promise he'd elicited. Maybe that was why she couldn't concentrate. She'd failed to keep that promise.

No wonder she'd lost her mojo. It was back in Belye Nochi, in the hands of a woman she'd promised to get to know.

In the first week of May—only a few days earlier than she'd planned—Nina drove into the Wenatchee Valley. The jagged Cascade Mountain range was still covered in snow, but everything else was dressed for spring.

At Belye Nochi, acres of apple trees were in full bloom. The orchard was alive with workers who moved through the branches checking for bugs or rot or whatever it was they looked for. Nina parked and headed for the house.

She didn't bother knocking. As she went into the kitchen, the house smelled musty. Upstairs it was as quiet and empty as below.

Nina refused to feel disappointed. She knew when she'd decided to surprise Mom and Meredith, it might be a little dicey. She went out to the rental car and drove up towards her sister's house.

At the V in the road, a truck came towards her. She pulled over, waiting. It slowed and stopped beside her, and Jeff rolled down his window. 'Hey, Neens. This is a surprise.'

'You know me, Jeff. Where's Mom?'

'Meredith didn't tell you? She's in Parkview.'

'The nursing home? Are you kidding me?'

'Don't rush to conclusions, Nina. Meredith thought—'

Nina gunned the engine, spun the car and drove off. In less than twenty minutes, she pulled into the nursing home car park.

Inside, the lobby was defiantly cheery. At a fake wood desk, a woman wearing a badge saying SUE ELLEN was talking on the phone.

'Excuse me,' Nina said tightly. 'I'm looking for Anya Whitson's room. I'm her daughter.'

'Room one forty-six. To your left.'

Nina walked down the hallway. On either side, the few open doors revealed small rooms, each occupied by two elderly people. She remembered when Aunt Dora had been there. They'd visited her every weekend, and Dad had hated every second. *Death on the layaway plan*, he used to say. How could Meredith have done this? How dare she not tell Nina? By the time she reached room 146, Nina was in a rage.

She knocked sharply, and a voice said, 'Come in.'

Her mother sat in a recliner, knitting. Her white hair was unkempt, and her clothes didn't match, but her blue eyes were bright.

'Why the hell are you here?'

'Language, Nina,' her mother said.

'You should be at home.' Nina moved forwards woodenly, noticing the recreated Holy Corner set up on a dresser.

Just then, Meredith walked in carrying a tote bag bulging with Tupperware containers. 'Nina,' she said, coming up short.

Meredith looked flawless, as usual, in crisp black pants and a pink shirt. Even so, she'd lost too much weight.

Nina turned on her. 'How could you do this?'

'Her ankle—'

'Who gives a damn about her ankle? Dad would hate this.'

'Stop it,' Mom hissed. 'What is wrong with you two?'

'She's an idiot,' Meredith responded. Moving to a table, she set down the big bag. 'I brought you some cabbage *pierogi* and *okroshka*, Mom. And I've chosen some yarn I thought you might like, along with a new pattern. I'll be back again after work.'

Mom nodded but said nothing.

Meredith left without another word. Nina hesitated and then followed. Out in the hall, she saw her hurrying away. 'Meredith!'

Her sister flipped her off and kept going.

Nina went back into the pathetic little room, with its single bed and ugly recliner and fake wood dresser. Only the Russian icons gave a hint about the woman who lived here. 'Come on, Mom. You're getting the hell out of here. I'm taking you home.'

'You?'

'Yeah,' Nina said firmly. 'Me.'

At Belye Nochi, Nina had slept the best, most dreamless sleep she'd had in months, and she awoke ready to take on the world.

She knocked on her mother's bedroom door. 'Mom?'

'Come in.'

Nina opened the door and found her mother in the rocking chair by the window, knitting. 'Hey, Mom. Are you hungry?'

'I was last night and again this morning, but I made sandwiches. Meredith has asked me not to use the stove.'

'I slept for a whole day? Shit. Promise me you won't tell Meredith.'

Mom looked up sharply. 'I do not make promises to children.' At that, she went back to her knitting.

Downstairs, Nina meandered round the kitchen, trying to figure out what to make for lunch. In the freezer, she found dozens of containers of food, each one marked and dated in black ink. Her mother had always cooked for a platoon instead of a family. Nina's eye went straight to the stroganoff and homemade noodles.

Comfort food. She put some water on to boil and popped the sauce in the microwave. She was about to set the table when, out of the window, a blast of sunlight caught the orchard in full bloom.

She ran for her camera bag and went outside, where she immediately took pictures of everything—the trees, the blossoms, the dappled shade, and with every click of the shutter, she thought of her dad and how much he loved this time of year. When she finished, she walked back, passing her mother's so-called winter garden.

On this surprisingly sunny day, it was a riot of white blossoms upheld by lush green leaves. She sat down on the ironwork bench and began taking pictures again: a flawless, pearlescent magnolia blossom, the copper column with its blue-green patina . . .

Nina lowered her camera. There were two columns now. The new one was shiny, with an elegant scroll stamped into it. In the upper half, there was an ornate etching. Leaves, ivy. The letter E.

She turned to the other column. Pushing vines and flowers aside, she now saw Russian letters entwined in the scrollwork; it looked like a word. An A and what appeared to be the P symbol, a circle that might be an O, and something that looked like a spider.

Behind her, the smoke alarm went off, buzzing through the open door. 'Damn.' Nina ran for the house.

Meredith came up with a plan and stuck to it. She'd decided that two afternoons and an evening with Mom would be enough time for Nina to understand the nursing-home decision. So at twelve thirty, she left the office and drove to Parkview. She waved as she sailed past Sue Ellen to Mom's room and opened the door.

Inside, a pair of coverall-clad men were cleaning. All of Mom's personal items were gone. On the bed, instead of the brand-new bedding Meredith had bought, there was a plain blue mattress.

'Where's Mrs Whitson?'

'She moved out,' one of the men said, without looking up.

Meredith blinked. 'Excuse me?'

'Moved out.'

Meredith spun on her heel and walked back to the front desk. 'Sue Ellen,' she said. 'Where is my mother?'

'She left. With your sister, just like that. No notice or nothing.'

'Well, this is a mistake. My mother will be back—'

'There's no room now, Meredith. Mrs McGutcheon is taking her place. We don't expect to have a room again until after July.'

Meredith was too mad to be polite. Saying nothing, she marched out of the building and got in her car. For the first time in her life, she didn't give a damn about the posted speed limit and in twelve minutes she was at Belye Nochi and out of her car.

Inside, the whole house reeked of smoke. In the kitchen, she found dirty plates piled in the sink and an open pizza box on the counter. More than half of the pizza was left in the box.

A misshapen pot sat slumped over the stove. Meredith didn't need to reach for it to know that it had melted to the front burner. She was about to charge up the stairs when she glanced out at the sideyard. Through the wood-paned French doors, she saw them: Mom and Nina were sitting together on the iron bench.

Meredith opened the French door so hard it clattered against the wall. Crossing the yard, she heard her mother's familiar story voice and knew that the bouts of confusion weren't over.

' . . . *she mourns the loss of her father, who is imprisoned in the red tower by the Black Knight, but life goes on. This is a terrible, terrible lesson that every girl must learn. There are still swans to be fed in the ponds of the castle garden, and white summer nights when lords and ladies meet at two in the morning . . .* '

'That's enough of the story,' Meredith said. 'Let's go inside.'

Nina said, 'Don't stop her—'

'I don't want to hear it.' Meredith helped Mom to her feet and led her into the house, where she got her settled upstairs with her knitting.

She found Nina in the kitchen. 'What the *hell* are you thinking?'

'Did you hear the story? It was the peasant girl and the—'

Meredith took her sister by the wrist and pulled her into the dining room, switching on the lights.

It looked exactly as it had on the day Mom fell off the table. Strips of wallpaper were gone; the blank valleys looked like old wounds. Here and there, reddish black smears stained the walls.

Outside, somewhere in the fields, a truck backfired. Meredith turned to Nina, but before she could say anything, she heard footsteps on the stairs.

Mom hurried into the kitchen. 'Did you hear the guns?'

'That was just a truck backfiring, Mom. Everything is fine.'

'My lion is crying.' Mom's eyes were glassy and unfocused.

'There's no lion here, Mom,' Meredith said in a soothing voice. She gently took the huge coat her mother was carrying. The confusion left as quickly as it had come. Mom straightened, looked at her daughters, and walked out of the kitchen. As her footfalls creaked upstairs, Nina turned to Meredith. 'What the hell?'

'You see?' Meredith said. 'She goes . . . crazy sometimes. That's why she needs to be someplace safe.'

'You're wrong,' Nina said. 'That wasn't nuts.'

'Oh, really? And just what was it?'

Nina faced her. 'Fear.'

Nina was not surprised when Meredith started cleaning the kitchen, and with a martyr's zeal. She knew her sister was pissed off. She should care about that, but she couldn't. Instead, she thought about the promise she'd made to her father.

Make her tell you the story of the peasant girl and the prince. All of it.

At the time, it had seemed pointless, impossible. A dying man's last desperate hope to make three women sit down together. But Mom *was* falling apart without him. He'd been right about that. And he'd thought the fairy tale could help her.

Meredith banged a pot down on one of the remaining burners and then swore. 'We can't use the damn stove until we can get rid of this pot you melted.'

'Use the micro,' Nina said distractedly.

'That's your answer? Use the micro. That's all you have to say?'

'Do you remember the story of the peasant girl and the prince? Dad made me promise—'

'Oh, for God's sake. We won't help, making her tell us fables.'

'You want to lock her away. Why? So you can, "lunch with the girls"?'

'How dare you say that to me? *You*.' Meredith moved closer. 'He used to trawl through magazines, looking for his "little girl's" pictures. Did you know that? He checked the messages every day for calls that hardly ever came. Don't you *dare* call me selfish.'

'Enough.' Mom was standing in the doorway, dressed in her night-gown, with her hair uncharacteristically unbound. Her collarbones stuck out prominently beneath her veiny skin. With her pallor, she looked almost translucent. Except for those amazing eyes alight with anger. 'Is this how you honour him, by fighting?'

'We're not fighting,' Meredith said. 'We're worried about you.'

'You think I have gone crazy,' Mom said.

'*I* don't,' Nina said, looking up. 'I noticed the new column in the winter garden, Mom. I saw the letters.'

'What letters?' Meredith demanded.

'It is nothing,' Mom said.

'It's *something*,' Nina said. 'We know nothing about you.'

'The past does not matter.'

'It's what you've always said, and we let you. Or maybe we didn't care,' Nina answered. 'But now I do.'

Mom sighed. 'You will keep asking me, won't you? Meredith will try to stop you because she is afraid, but there is no stopping you.'

'Dad made me promise. He wanted us to hear one of your fairy tales all the way to the end. I can't let him down.'

'I know better than to make promises to the dying. Now you have learned this lesson, too.' Mom paused. 'It would break your father's heart to hear you fighting. You are lucky to have each other. Act like it.' Then she walked back up the stairs.

'Look, Nina,' Meredith said after a long silence. 'I don't give a damn about her fairy tales. I'll take care of her because I promised Dad and it's the right thing to do. But trying to get to know her is a kamikaze mission, and I've crashed once too often. Count me out.'

'I know how hard you tried with her. I'm your sister,' Nina said. 'And I understand why you put her in that terrible place. You thought she was going looney tunes.'

Meredith turned away. 'She *is* looney tunes.'

'I'm going to get her to tell me all of the fairy tale or die trying.'

'Do what you want.' Meredith sighed. 'You always do.'

Meredith tried to lose herself in work, but nothing she did was right. It felt as if a screw in her chest were tightening with every breath she took. The pressure building up behind it was going to blow any minute. After the third time she yelled at an employee, she tossed a packet of papers on Daisy's desk, said tensely, 'File this, please,' and walked away before she could do more damage.

She got in her car and just drove. At first, she had no idea where she was going, but somewhere along the way, she found herself following an old forgotten road. In some ways, it led back to her youth.

She parked in front of the Belye Nochi gift shop. It was a lovely little building set back from the highway and ringed by flowering apple trees. She stared at the white clapboard building. Come summer, there would be flowers everywhere—in planters by the door, in baskets on the porch, twined up the fence line.

The day she had approached Dad with the plan to convert the old roadside stand into a gift shop, she'd been a young mother with a baby on each hip. *Dad, tourists will love it.*

Meredoodle, that's a killer idea . . .

She'd poured her heart and soul into this place, stocking it with things she loved. And it had been a rousing success. When she'd quit the gift shop and moved into the warehouse, it had been to make her father happy. Looking back now, that was when it had begun, this life of hers that seemed to be about everyone else.

She put the car in reverse and drove away, wishing vaguely that she hadn't stopped by. By the time she pulled into her driveway, it was dusk.

Inside the house, she fed the dogs and started dinner, then took a bath. Drying off, she glanced at the king-size bed along the far wall. She remembered suddenly the day she and Jeff had bought it. It had been too expensive, but they'd paid with a credit card, and when it was delivered, they'd come home from work early and fallen onto it, laughing, christening it with their passion.

The second she had the thought, she found a sexy nightgown and went downstairs, where she made a fire and poured herself a glass of wine and waited for Jeff to get home.

At eleven o'clock, she was still waiting. By the time he finally walked in, she'd had three glasses of wine and dinner was ruined.

'Where the hell have you been?' she said.

He frowned. 'What?'

'I made us a romantic dinner. It's ruined now.'

'You're pissed off that I'm home late? You've got to be kidding.'

'Where were you?'

'Researching my book.'

'In the middle of the night?'

'It's hardly the middle of the night. But I've been doing it since January, Mere. You just haven't noticed. Or cared.' He walked away and went into his office, slamming the door behind him.

She followed him. 'I *wanted* you tonight,' she said.

'Well, pardon me. You've ignored me for months. It's been like living with a ghost, but now all of a sudden I'm supposed to change gears and be here for you? It doesn't work that way.'

'Fine. I hope you're comfortable here tonight.'

'It'll be a hell of a lot warmer than *your* bed.'

She walked out, but when she slammed the door, the anger left her and she felt lost. She went upstairs and crawled into their bed. In twenty years of marriage, it was the first time he'd slept on the sofa after a fight, and without him, she couldn't sleep.

At five o'clock, she gave up trying and went down to apologise. He was already gone.

Later that day, Daisy walked into Meredith's office carrying a manila folder. 'I've got the field and orchardist reports.'

'Great,' Meredith said. 'Just leave them on my desk.' Daisy hesitated, and Meredith thought, Oh, no. Here it comes. She'd known Daisy since childhood and hesitant she was not.

'I heard about Nina kidnapping your mom from the nursing home.'

'That's a bit overdramatic. I'll handle it,' Meredith said tiredly.

'Of course you will, honey, but should you?' Daisy put the folder down. 'I can run this place, you know,' she said quietly. 'Your dad trained me. All you have to do is ask for help.'

Meredith nodded. It was true. Daisy *did* know the orchard better than anyone except herself. She'd worked there twenty-nine years. 'Thanks. Can you get Dr Burns on the phone for me, Daisy?'

'Of course.' Daisy headed for the door.

A moment later Daisy put through the call and Jim answered.

'Hey, Jim,' she said. 'It's Meredith.'

'I heard from Parkview today.' He paused. 'Nina?'

'Naturally. She's seen *The Great Escape* one too many times. Can you recommend another nursing home?'

Jim said, 'I've spoken to your mom's doctor at Parkview, and the P.T. who helped her rehab. I also visited her once a week. None of us witnessed any significant confusion.' He drew in a deep breath. 'Bottom line: I can't diagnose what isn't visible to me, so her insurance for long-term care won't be activated.'

Meredith felt as if a huge weight had been placed on her shoulders. 'Now what? She was cutting herself, for God's sake.'

'I know,' he said gently. 'I've made some calls. There's a senior complex in Wenatchee that's nice. It's called Riverton. She would have an apartment with a backyard big enough for gardening. There's an opening in June, but they'll need a deposit quickly.'

Meredith wrote it all down. 'Thanks, Jim. I appreciate your help.' She hung up, picked up her bag and headed out of her office.

At Belye Nochi, Nina was in the kitchen reheating goulash.

Nina smiled at her. 'I'm watching the pot, see? No fire yet.'

'I need to talk to you and Mom. Where is she?'

Nina cocked her head towards the damaged dining room. 'Guess.'

'Damn it, Neens.' Meredith walked through the dining room and went out to Mom, who was sitting on the iron bench. At least she was dressed for the cool weather this time.

'Mom?' Meredith said. 'I need to talk to you. Can we go inside?'

Mom straightened; only then did Meredith realise how soft and rounded she'd looked before.

Together, they walked back into the house. In the living room, Meredith got Mom settled in a chair and then built a fire. By the time she was finished, Nina was with them, sprawled out on the sofa, with her stockinged feet propped on the coffee table.

'What's up, Mere?' she asked.

Meredith kept her gaze on her mother. 'Dr Burns agrees with me that the nursing home isn't the right place for you, Mom. But we think this house is too much to handle. Jim found a nice condominium-like complex in Wenatchee. You'd have a lovely one-bedroom with its own kitchen. If you didn't feel like cooking, there's a dining room.'

'What about my winter garden?' Mom asked.

'There's a backyard with it. You could build a winter garden there. The bench, the fencing, the columns; everything.'

'She doesn't need to move,' Nina said. 'This is her home, and I'm here to help out.'

'Really? How long can we count on you?' Meredith snapped. 'You might have the best intentions in the world, but if something terrible happened in India tomorrow, all we'd see is your ass as you walked out of the door. I can't be with Mom every second.'

'And this would make it easier on you,' Mom said.

Searching her face, all Meredith saw was resignation. 'Yes.'

'Then I will go. I do not care where I live any more,' Mom said.

'I'll pack up everything you need,' Meredith said. 'So you're ready to go next month. You won't have to do a thing.'

Mom stood up. She looked at Meredith, her eyes soft with emotion, then went upstairs. The bedroom door slammed shut.

'She doesn't belong in some glorified nursing home,' Nina said.

Meredith hated her sister for that. 'What are you going to do about it? Are you going to promise to stick around for years? Oh, wait. Your promises don't mean crap.'

Nina slowly stood. 'I'm not the only one who breaks promises in this family. You promised Dad you'd take care of Mom.'

'And that's what I'm doing.'

'Really? What if he were here right now, listening to you talk about moving the winter garden and packing up her things and moving her into town? Would he be *proud* of you, Meredith?'

'He'd understand.' Meredith wished her voice was stronger.

'No, he wouldn't, and you know it.'

'Damn you. You've no idea how hard I tried, how much I wanted . . .' Meredith's voice broke. 'Damn you,' she said again. As she ran for the door, she noticed the goulash burning. The drive home took less than two minutes. The dogs greeted her exuberantly, and she knelt down to pet them. 'Jeff?' she called out.

Getting no answer, she poured herself a glass of wine. In the living room, she turned on the gas fireplace and sat on the marble hearth, letting the real heat from a fake fire heat her back. She told herself Nina was wrong. Dad *would* understand . . .

A thump sounded nearby, and she looked up slowly, expecting to see

Luke or Leia in the room, tail thumping a quiet greeting, begging for a little attention.

Jeff stood in the doorway.

'Oh. You're home.'

'I'm going,' he said quietly.

She didn't know whether to be relieved or disappointed that they wouldn't be able to talk tonight. 'Do you want me to hold dinner?'

He took a deep breath and said, 'I'm leaving.'

'I heard you. I don't—' It sunk in suddenly. 'Leaving? Me? Because of last night? I'm sorry about that. I shouldn't have—'

'We need some time apart, Mere.'

'Don't do this,' she whispered, shaking her head. 'Not now.'

'There's never a good time. I waited because of your father, then because of your mother. I told myself you still loved me, that you were just overwhelmed, but . . . I don't believe it any more. There's a wall round you, Mere, and I'm tired of trying to climb it.'

'It'll be better now. In June—'

'No more waiting,' he said. 'We only have a few weeks before the girls come home. Let's use it.'

She felt herself falling apart, but for months she'd been burying her emotions, and she didn't know what would happen if she stopped. So she said in as even a voice as she could muster, 'OK.'

She saw the way he looked at her then, the resignation. It hurt her almost more than she could stand, letting him go, but she stood up and walked past him, past the suitcase at the front door—the thump she'd heard—and began putting away the breakfast dishes.

Her heart was actually missing beats as she stood at the sink. Never had it occurred to her that Jeff would leave her.

He came up behind her then. 'Do you still love me, Mere?' he asked, turning her by the shoulders until they were facing each other.

She wished he'd asked her that an hour ago, or yesterday, or last week. Any time except now, when even the ground beneath her felt unreliable. She'd thought his love was a bulkhead that could hold back any storm but, like everything else, his love was conditional.

He let go of her and started for the door.

Meredith almost called out, *Of course I love you.* But she couldn't make her mouth open. She just stood there, uncomprehending.

He turned. 'You're like her. You know that, don't you?'

'Don't say that.'

He stared at her a moment, and she knew it was a chance he was giving her, but she couldn't take it. 'Goodbye, Mere,' he said.

CHAPTER SIX

WHEN NINA HAD FINISHED showering and unpacking, she went downstairs. In the kitchen, she found her mother seated at the table, where a crystal decanter waited. 'I thought we'd have a drink. Vodka,' her mother said.

Nina stared at her. In thirty-seven years, she had never been offered a drink by her mother.

'If you'd rather not . . .'

'No. I mean, yes,' Nina said, watching as her mother poured two shot glasses of vodka. She tried to see something in her mother's beautiful face: a frown, a smile. But the blue eyes revealed nothing.

'The kitchen smells of smoke,' Mom said.

'I burned the first dinner. Too bad you never taught me to cook.'

'This is reheating, not cooking.'

'Did your mother teach you to cook?'

'The water is boiling. Put in the noodles.'

Nina went to the stove and poured some of her mother's homemade noodles into the boiling water. Beside them, a saucepan bubbled with stroganoff sauce. She reached for a wooden spoon. 'Hey, I'm cooking,' she said, then took a place at the table and lifted her glass. 'Cheers,' she said.

Mom clinked her glass against Nina's and downed the vodka.

Nina did the same. Minutes passed. 'So what do we do now?'

'Noodles,' was Mom's reply.

Nina rushed back to the stove. 'They're floating,' she said.

'They're done.'

'Another cooking lesson. This is awesome,' Nina said. She dished up, and returned to the table, carrying a bottle of wine.

'Thank you,' Mom said. She closed her eyes in prayer for a moment and then reached for her fork.

'Have you always done that?' Nina said. 'Prayed before dinner?'

'Quit studying me, Nina.' Mom began to eat.

The savoury scent of the stroganoff wafted up. 'Thank goodness you have enough food in the freezer to feed a starving nation,' Nina said, pouring them both some wine. When silence answered her, she said, 'Thank you, Nina, for saying so.'

She tried to concentrate on the food, but the silence got to her. 'Enough,' she said finally. 'If Meredith has her way, I'll be here until you move to Senior World, and I'll be damned if I'll eat every meal in silence. We must have talked at dinner when I was a kid.'

'That was the three of you.'

'How come you never really look at me or Meredith?'

'You are imagining things.' Mom took a sip of wine. 'Eat.'

'OK, but we are going to talk. I'll start. My favourite movie is *Out of Africa*. I love watching giraffes in the Serengeti, and I'm surprised to admit that sometimes I miss snow.'

Mom took another sip of her wine.

'I could ask about the fairy tales instead,' Nina said. 'I could ask why you only told them to us with the lights out, or why Dad—'

'My favourite author is Pushkin. I miss . . . the true *Belye Nochi*, and my favourite movie is *Doctor Zhivago*.'

'So we have something in common after all,' Nina said. 'We like big love stories with unhappy endings.'

Her mother pushed back from the table suddenly, and stood up. 'Thank you for dinner. I am tired now. Good night.'

'I'll ask again, you know,' Nina said. 'For the fairy tale.'

Mom paused, just a step, and then kept going up the stairs. When her bedroom door thudded closed, Nina stared up at the ceiling. 'You're afraid, aren't you?' she mused aloud. 'Of what?

Bundled up in her robe, Meredith sat on her porch, rocking in a wicker chair. The dogs lay beside her feet. Every now and then one of them whined. They knew something was wrong. Jeff was gone.

In the distance, she could see the first copper glimmer of dawn. She'd been out there all night. Tightening her robe round her, she went inside and up the stairs. She put on her running clothes and ran until she couldn't breathe without pain.

At home, she went straight to the shower. When she was dressed, she knew that no one would be able to look at her and know that her husband had left her in the night. She was holding her car keys when she realised it was Saturday.

She felt her knees buckle; she almost sank to the floor. Oh, she could go to work anyway, but she would be alone, in the quiet, with only her own thoughts to distract her.

She went out to the car and drove to Belye Nochi.

There, the living-room light was on. Smoke rose from the chimney. Of course, Nina was up. She was still running on Africa time.

In the kitchen, she saw more dirty dishes piled in the sink and the open decanter of vodka on the counter. It pissed her off suddenly. Sharply. Disproportionately. She attacked the dishes so loudly that pans clanged together as she threw them into the soapy water.

'Whoa!' Nina came into the room wearing a pair of men's boxer shorts and an old Nirvana T-shirt. Her face crinkled in a smile. 'I didn't think pot-tossing was your sport.'

'You think I've nothing better to do than clean up your mess?'

'It's a little early for high drama.'

'That's right. Make a joke.' Meredith clutched the counter edge.

'Meredith, what's wrong?' Nina said.

Meredith almost gave in. She almost said, *Jeff left me.* 'I'm fine.'

'You don't act fine.'

Meredith turned round. 'Honestly, Nina, you don't know me well enough to say that. How was Mom last night? Did she eat?'

'We drank vodka together. And wine. Can you believe it?'

Meredith felt a sharp pang at that; it took her a moment to realise she was jealous. 'Vodka?'

'I know. Shocked the hell out of me, too. And I found out her favourite movie is *Doctor Zhivago.*'

'I don't think alcohol is her best bet these days, do you? I'm going to start packing her things for the move next month. She'll be more comfortable there if she has her stuff around her.'

'She won't be comfortable.' Now Nina looked angry. 'It doesn't matter how organised you are. You're still putting her away.'

'You going to stay, Nina? For ever? I'll cancel the reservation.'

'You know I can't do that.'

'Yeah. Right. You can criticise, but you can't solve. Now I'm going to the garage to get boxes. You're welcome to help.'

'I'm not going to pack her life into boxes, Mere. I want to open her up, not close her away. Don't you get it? Don't you care?'

'No,' Meredith said, pushing past her. She left the house and walked over to the garage. While she waited for the automatic door to open, she had trouble breathing. She doubled over and sucked in air. When she turned on the light, there was Dad's old Cadillac.

They'd gone on a dozen family road trips in the 1956 convertible, which had been his pride and joy. And whenever they stopped for the night and camp was set up, Dad would come for her while he smoked his pipe. *I thought my best girl would like to take a walk.*

She touched the red hood. No one had driven this car in years.

He was the one person she'd have told about what happened last night.

Nina planned to wear her mother down. If Meredith's performance in the kitchen was proving anything, it was that time was of the essence. With every rip of newspaper, another piece of Mom's life was being wrapped up. If Meredith had her way, there would soon be nothing left.

At breakfast, Nina stepped carefully round her ice-cold sister. She made Mom a cup of sweetened tea and a piece of toast and carried them upstairs. Mom lay in bed, her gnarled hands folded primly on the blanket. With the door open, they could both hear Meredith packing. 'You could help your sister.'

'I would if I thought you should move. I don't.' Nina handed Mom the tea and toast. 'You know what I realised making your breakfast?'

Mom sipped the tea. 'I suppose you will tell me.'

'I don't know if you like honey or jam or cinnamon.'

'All are fine.'

'The point is, I don't know.'

'Ah. That is the point.' Sighing, Mom took another sip of tea.

'I want to hear the peasant girl and the prince. All of it. Please.'

Mom set the tea down on the bedside table and got out of bed. Moving past Nina, she went into the bathroom, closing the door.

At lunch, Nina tried again. This time Mom picked up her sandwich and carried it outside. Nina followed her out to the winter garden and sat beside her. 'I mean it, Mom.'

'Yes, Nina, I know. Please leave me.'

Nina sat there another ten minutes, just to make her point.

Inside, Meredith was marking a box with the word 'Tupperware'. 'She'll never tell you,' she said at Nina's entrance.

'Thanks for that.' Nina reached for her camera. 'Keep boxing up her life. Everything neat and labelled. You're a barrel of laughs. Honestly, Mere, how can your kids and Jeff stand it?'

Returning to the house at just past six, Nina saw that the kitchen was empty. Boxes were stacked carefully between the pantry and fridge. She glanced out the window and saw that her sister's car was still there. Meredith must be in another room, knee-deep in newsprint.

Nina opened the freezer and burrowed through the endless rows of containers. Meatball soup, chicken stew with dumplings, lamb and vegetable moussaka, pork chops braised in apple wine, red pepper paprikash, chicken kiev, strudels, savoury breads.

Nina chose one of her favourites: a beef pot roast stuffed with bacon and horseradish. She defrosted it in the microwave, then put it in the oven. With this meal, the aroma would bring Mom to her.

Sure enough, at six forty, Mom came down. 'You made dinner?'

'I reheated it,' Nina said, putting two place settings down on the small oak table in the kitchen. 'There you go, Mom.'

Meredith walked in, noticed the two settings. Her face scrunched in irritation. Or maybe relief. With Meredith it was hard to tell.

'Do you want to eat with us?' Nina asked. 'There's plenty.'

'Sure,' she said. 'Jeff won't be home tonight . . . until late.'

'Good. Here. Sit.' Nina set another place and got the crystal decanter. 'We start with a shot of vodka.'

Meredith sat down. 'What?' she said, looking up.

Mom poured three shots. 'It does no good to argue with her.'

Nina sat down and held up her glass. Mom clinked hers to it. Reluctantly, Meredith did the same. Then they drank.

'OK,' Nina said. 'Meredith, since you're here, you have to join in a new tradition Mom and I have come up with. It's revolutionary, really. It's called dinner conversation.'

'So we're going to talk, are we?' Meredith said. 'About what?'

'I'll go first so you can see how it goes: my favourite song is "Born to be Wild", and my best childhood memory is the trip to Yellowstone, where Dad taught me how to fish.' She looked at her sister. 'And I'm sorry if I make my sister's life harder.'

Mom put down her fork. 'My favourite song is "Somewhere Over the Rainbow", my favourite memory is a day I spent beneath a lime tree in a garden, and I'm sorry that you two are not friends.'

'We're friends,' Nina said.

'This is stupid,' Meredith said.

'No,' Nina said. 'Staring at each other in silence is stupid. Go.'

Meredith gave a sigh. 'Fine. My favourite song is "Candle in the Wind", my favourite memory is when Dad took me skating on Miller's pond, and I'm sorry I said we weren't close, Nina. But we aren't. Maybe I'm sorry for that, too. Now let's eat. I'm starving.'

Nina hadn't even finished eating when Meredith began clearing the table. The second she was up, Mom thanked them for dinner and disappeared, her footsteps quick on the stairs.

Nina couldn't really blame Meredith. As soon as their little conversational jump leads had been used, only Nina had tried to make small talk, and her amusing stories about Africa had been met with a lukewarm response from Meredith and nothing from Mom.

Nina thumped the vodka on the table. 'Let's get drunk.'

Meredith, elbow deep in soapy water, said, 'OK.'

Nina thought she had misheard. 'Did you say—?'

'Don't make a lunar mission out of it.'

'Wow,' Nina said. 'Have we ever got drunk together?'

Meredith dried her hands. 'You've got drunk while I was in the room.'

Nina grinned. 'That doesn't count. Pull up a chair.'

'I'm not drinking vodka, though.'

'Tequila it is.' Nina ran to the living room, grabbed a bottle from the bar, and snagged limes on her way back. She poured two shots, sliced a lime, and pushed the glass towards her sister.

Meredith wrinkled her nose.

'It's not heroin, Mere. Talk a walk on the wild side.'

Meredith reached out, grabbed the shot, and downed it. When her eyes bulged, Nina handed her the lime. 'Here. Bite on this.'

Meredith made a whooshing sound. 'One more.'

Nina drank her own shot and poured them each another, which they drank together. Afterwards, Meredith sat back in her chair, pushing a hand through her perfectly smooth hair. 'I don't feel anything.'

'You will.' Nina paused, then said, 'Hey, how do you manage to keep looking so . . . neat all the time? You've been packing boxes all day but you still look ready for lunch at the club.'

'Only you can make looking nice sound like an insult.'

'It wasn't an insult. Honestly. I just wonder how—Forget it.'

'There's a wall round me.' Meredith poured another shot.

'Yeah. Like a force field. Nothing reaches your hair,' Nina said, laughing, but then Meredith gulped down her third shot, her mouth flitting downwards. 'Is something wrong?'

Meredith blinked slowly. 'You mean, besides the fact that my father died at Christmas, my mom is going crazy, my sister is pretending to help me, and my husband . . . is gone tonight?'

'Yeah, besides that. You know your life rocks. You're one of those wonder women who do everything right.'

'You can do everything right,' Meredith said, staring blankly past her, 'and still end up in the wrong. And alone.'

'I should have called Dad more from Africa,' Nina said. 'I knew how much my calls meant. I thought there was time . . .'

'Sometimes the door just slams shut and you're all by yourself.'

'There is something we can do now to help him,' Nina said.

Meredith looked startled. 'Help who?'

'Dad,' Nina said impatiently. 'Isn't that who we're talking about? He wanted us to get to know her.'

'Not the fairy tales again,' Meredith said. 'You're obsessive.'

'And you aren't? Come on. Come with me. We can *make* her tell us the story. You heard her tonight: she said there was no point arguing with me. That means she's going to give up fighting.'

Meredith stood up. She was a little unsteady on her feet. 'I *knew* better than to try to talk to you. I'll be in the bathroom packing.'

Nina watched her leave the kitchen. Tucking the decanter of vodka under one arm and grabbing Mom's shot glass, she went upstairs. At the bathroom's half-open door, she paused, listening to the clink and rattle that meant Meredith was back at work.

'I'll leave the door open,' she said, 'in case you want to listen.'

No answer came from the bathroom. Nina walked to her mother's room, knocked and walked in. Her mother sat in bed, propped on a mound of pillows. 'I did not invite you in,' she said.

'Nope. But here I am. It's like magic.'

'And you thought I would want vodka?'

Nina moved to the side of the bed. 'I know you will.'

'Why is that?'

'I made a promise to my dying father.'

Her mother flinched as if she'd been struck.

'You loved him. I know you did. And he wanted me to hear your fairy tale about the peasant girl and the prince. All of it. On his deathbed, he asked me. He must have asked you, too.'

Her mother sighed. 'Why do you care so much?'

'Why did he?' Mom didn't answer. Nina stood there, waiting.

Finally Mom said, 'Pour me a drink.' Nina poured her mother a shot and handed it to her. Mom drank the vodka. 'I will do it my way.' She set the empty glass aside. 'If you interrupt me, I will stop. I will tell it in pieces at night. We will not speak of it during the day. Do you understand?'

'Yes.'

'In the dark.'

Nina went and turned off the lamp. She sat on the floor, waiting. A rustling sound as her mother got comfortable in the bed.

'Where should I begin?'

'At Christmas, you ended when Vera was going to sneak out to meet the Prince.'

A sigh. And then Mom's story voice, sweet and mellifluous: '*After she comes home from the park, Vera spends the rest of that day in the kitchen with her mother, but her mind is not on the task at hand. She knows her mama knows this, that she is watching her carefully, but how can a girl concentrate on straining goose fat into jars when her heart is full of love?*

"Veronika, pay attention," her mama says.

Vera sees that she has spilled a big blob of goose fat on the table. She wipes it up with her hand and throws it into the sink.

"And you throw it away? What is wrong with you?"

Her sister giggles. "Maybe she is thinking of boys. Of a boy."

"Of course she is thinking of boys." Wiping moisture from her brow, Mama stirs the lingonberries on the stove. "She is fifteen."

"Almost sixteen."

Her mama turns. In the last days of summer, they preserve food for winter. The tables are full of berries to be turned into jam; there are onions, mushrooms and potatoes to be put in the cellar; cucumbers to be pickled; and beans to be canned in brine. "Almost sixteen," she says. "Two years younger than I was when I met Petyr."

"What did you feel when you first saw him?"

Mama smiles. "I have told this story many times."

"You always say he swept you away. But how?"

Mama reaches out for a wooden chair and sits down.

Vera is shocked. Mama is not a woman who stops working to talk. Vera and Olga have grown up on stories of responsibility and duty. As peasants beholden to the imprisoned king, they must keep their heads down and hands working, for the shadow of the Black Knight falls with the swiftness of a steel blade.

Still, her mother is sitting down now. "He was a tutor then, and so good-looking he took my breath away. When I told your baba, she tsked and said, "Zoya, be careful. You will need your breath."

"Was it love at first sight?" Vera asks.

"I say it was the mead we drank, but it wasn't. It was just . . . Petyr. My Petya. His passion for life swept me away, and before I knew it, we were married. My parents were horrified, for the king was in exile, and your father's ambition scared them. A poor country tutor teaching children, he dreamed of being a poet."

Vera sighs at the romance of it. Now she knows she must sneak out tonight. She even knows Mama will understand if she finds out.

"All right," her mother says. "Let's get back to work."

As the hours pass, Vera finds her mind more and more distracted. While she prepares the beans for pickling, she imagines an entire love story for her and Sasha. It will not matter he is a prince and she a poor tutor's daughter.

"Vera." Her father is in the room, frowning at her. It is not the first time he has spoken.

"Papa," she says. He looks tired and nervous.

"Where is Zoya?" he asks, looking around.

"She and Olga went for more vinegar."

"By themselves?" He nods distractedly and chews on his lip.

"Papa? Is something wrong?"

"No, no. Nothing." Taking her in his arms, he pulls her into an embrace so tight that she gasps and has to wiggle out of it.

In the years to come, Vera will replay that embrace a thousand times in her mind. She will smell the dusty sun-baked leather of her father's jerkin and feel the scratch of his stubbly jaw against her cheek. She'll imagine herself saying, "I love you, Papa."

But the truth is that she has romance and sneaking out on her mind, so she says nothing to her father and goes back to work.

That night, Vera cannot lie still. Sounds float in through the open window: people talking, music from the park. Someone is playing a violin on this warm, light night, probably to woo a lover.

"Are you scared?" Olga asks for at least the fifth time.

Vera rolls over and hugs her sister. "When you are older, you'll see, Olga. There is a feeling in your heart when you meet the boy you'll love. It's like . . . drowning and then coming up for air."

Vera springs out of bed. With a small hand mirror, she can only see herself in pieces—long black hair, ivory skin, pink lips. She is wearing a plain blue gown with a lace collar—the best she has. "Oh, well," she says, and turns to her sister. "How do I look?"

"Perfect."

She knows it is true. She is a pretty girl, some even say beautiful.

Tiptoeing to her window, she blows her sister a kiss and climbs out. She is sure someone below will shout that a girl is sneaking out to meet a boy. But the people on the street are drunk on light and mead. She jumps the last few feet and runs across the cobblestone street.

There he is. Standing by the street lamp at her end of the Fontanka bridge. From here, everything about him is golden—his hair, his jerkin, his skin. "I didn't think you'd come," he says.

She cannot seem to talk. The words are trapped in her chest. She looks at his lips, and it is a mistake. In a flash, she is leaning towards him, and still it is a surprise when he kisses her. She starts to cry, and though her tears turn into tiny stars, there is nothing she can do to stop their falling. Now he will know she is a silly peasant girl who falls in love over nothing and cries at her first kiss.

He wipes the tears from her eyes and says quietly, "I know."

She starts to make an excuse—she is not even sure what it will be, but before she can speak, Sasha pulls her down into a crouch and says, "Be quiet," in a voice so sharp she feels stung by it. "Look."

A black carriage, drawn by six black dragons, is moving down the street. Silence falls. People freeze. It is the Black Knight . . .

The carriage moves like a hunting animal, the dragons breathing fire. When it stops, Vera feels a chill. "That is where I live."

Three hulking green trolls get out and go in Vera's door. "What are they doing?" she whispers. The minutes tick by slowly until the door opens again.

Vera sees it all in some kind of slow motion. The trolls have her father. He is not fighting, not arguing, not even talking.

"Papa!" Vera cries out.

Across the street, her father looks up and sees her. It is as if he alone heard her cry out. He shakes his head as if to say stay there, and then he is shoved into the carriage and he is gone.

Sasha lets her go. Without a backwards glance, she runs across the street. "Mama, where have they taken him?"

For a second, her mother seems not to recognise her own daughter. "You should be in bed, Vera."

"The trolls. Where are they taking Papa?"

When her mother doesn't answer, she hears Sasha's voice behind her. "It's the Black Knight, Vera. They do what they want."

"I do not understand," Vera cries. "You are a prince—"

"My family has no power any more. The Black Knight has imprisoned my father and my uncles. You must know that. It is dangerous to be a royal in the Snow Kingdom these days. No one can help you," he says, wiping tears that do not turn to starlight this time. Rather, they are like cold bits of stone.

"Veronika," Mama says. "We need to get inside. Now." She pulls Vera away from Sasha, who stands watching. "She is fifteen years old," she says, holding Vera close as they climb the steps.

When Vera looks back out to the street, her prince is gone.

From then on, Vera's family is changed. No one smiles any more; no one laughs. Days melt into weeks, and Vera begins to lose hope that her father will return. She turns sixteen without a celebration.

"I hear they are looking for workers at the castle," her mother says one day during supper. "In the library and the bakery."

"Yes," Vera says.

"I know you wanted to go to university," her mother says.

Already that dream is losing substance. It is something her father had dreamed for her, that one day she, too, would be a writer and poet. She has no choices now. Not a peasant girl like her. She understands at last. There will be no school. "I do not want to smell like bread. I will go to the royal library tomorrow."

She is sixteen. How can she possibly understand her mistake? Who could know that people she loved would die because of it?

'What do you mean people will die?' Nina turned on the lamp when Mom fell silent. 'We've never heard that part of the story.'

'Yes, you have. It scared Meredith, so I sometimes skipped it.'
Unmoving, eyes closed, Mom looked like a ghost. 'I am tired. You will
leave me now. Bring me my knitting.'

Nina retrieved the bulging bag from by the rocking chair. In no time,
Mom's hands were moving over the blue-green mohair yarn. Nina
heard the *click-click-click* of the needles as she closed the door.

She pushed the bathroom door open. The room was empty.

Meredith hadn't intended to listen to her mother's fairy tale. She finished
labelling a box and had dragged it into the hallway, and there she heard
the words from her childhood: '*Maybe she is thinking of boys. Of a boy . . .*'
Before she had thought about it, she was standing at the door, listening.

It wasn't until she heard Nina's voice say, 'What do you mean people
will die?' that the spell had broken. Hurrying downstairs, she was in her
car and home in no time, to her empty house and her empty bed.

CHAPTER SEVEN

THE NEXT MORNING, when Meredith came into Mom's kitchen, Nina was
at the table wearing the clothes she'd been in yesterday, with her short
black hair spiked out in all directions. There were books on the table,
and pieces of paper covered with her bold scrawl. 'You look wrecked,'
Meredith said.

'Good morning to you, too.'

'Have you slept at all?'

'Some. I know you don't care, but she mentioned the Fontanka
bridge last night. It was always the Enchanted Bridge before, wasn't it?'

'The fairy tale,' Meredith said. 'I should have known.'

'Listen to this. The Fontanka is a branch of the river Neva, which
flows through the city of Leningrad.'

Meredith poured herself a cup of coffee. 'She's Russian. The story
takes place in Russia. Stop the presses.'

'You should have been there, Mere. Last night was all new.'

No it wasn't. 'Maybe you were just too young to remember.'

'How can you not be interested? We never heard the end of it.'

'I'm tired, Neens. I don't know if you know how that feels, really. You're always so in love with everything you do. But I've spent forty years on this property, and God knows I've tried to get to know Mom. She won't let it happen. She'll lure you in; you'll see sadness in her eyes or a softening in her mouth and you'll believe in it because you want to so much. But she just doesn't love us. And frankly, I've got problems of my own right now.'

'What problems?'

'Nothing. It was just an expression.'

'You're lying.'

'I don't want to fight with you, Neens. Now *please* quit trying to make me care. I can't. Not again. OK?'

The pity in Nina's eyes was almost unbearable. 'OK.'

'Good. Now I'm going to run to the store, and then I'll come back and do some more packing. Make sure she eats a good meal.'

Nina spent the rest of the day alternately taking pictures and surfing the internet in her father's study. Not that she found much, except that Russia's rich fairy tale tradition had dozens of peasant girl and prince stories, and often they ended unhappily.

Finally, as night fell outside, Meredith opened the study door and said, 'Dinner's ready.'

Nina winced. She'd meant to help with dinner. 'Thanks.'

She closed down the computer, then went into the kitchen, where she found Mom seated at the table. There were three place settings.

Nina looked at her sister. 'You're staying for dinner again? Should we call Jeff and invite him?'

Meredith took a casserole out of the oven. 'He's working late.'

'Again?'

'You know news. The stories happen at all hours.'

Nina got the decanter of vodka and three shot glasses and brought them to the table. She sat down next to Mom and poured.

Her hands in oven gloves, Meredith carried the hot casserole dish to the table and set it down on a pair of trivets.

'*Chanakhi*,' Nina said, breathing in the aroma of lamb and vegetable casserole. 'Great choice.'

Meredith pulled up a chair and sat down between them.

Nina handed her a straight shot of vodka. 'It's a new tradition.'

'It smells like pine needles,' Meredith said, wrinkling her nose.

'The taste is quite different,' Mom said.

They chinked the glasses in a wordless toast and drank. Then Nina reached for the serving spoon. 'I'll dish up. Meredith, why don't you start?'

'The three things again?'

'You can do as many as you want. We'll follow your lead.'

Mom said nothing, just shook her head.

'Fine,' Meredith said. 'My favourite time of day is dawn. I love sitting on my porch in summer, and Jeff . . . thinks I run too much.'

While Nina was figuring out her response, Mom surprised her by saying, 'My favourite time of day is night. *Belye Nochi*. I love cooking. And your father thinks I should learn to play the piano.'

For a moment, they all looked at each other.

'He *thought* this. Do not rush me to the doctor's, Meredith.'

Nina filled in the awkward silence. 'My favourite time of day is sunset. Preferably in Botswana. In the dry season. I love answers. And I think there's a reason Mom hardly ever really looks at us.'

'It is meaning you want?' Mom said. 'You will be disappointed. Now eat. I hate this dish when it is cold.'

The rest of the meal proceeded in silence; the only sounds were spoons scraping on china and wine glasses being set down. When dinner was over, Mom walked away. Meredith went to the sink.

'I'm going to hear more of the story,' Nina said. 'You could—'

'I need to go through Dad's study. I need some of his files,' Meredith said. 'I've been putting it off.'

Meredith knelt on the forest-green carpet. A pair of Blackwatch tartan club chairs stood cocked toward the giant mahogany desk. The walls were a rich cobalt blue, and everywhere she looked was a family photograph. She sat back, overcome at what she was to do in there. Only his clothes would be more difficult to go through.

But it had to be done. Mom would need documents in the coming months. Insurance information, tax records, banking information. So Meredith took a deep breath and opened her father's file drawer. For the next hour, she picked through the paper trail of her parents' lives, sorting everything into three piles: Keep, Maybe and Burn.

She was grateful for the concentration it took. Only rarely did her mind wander into the swamp of her broken marriage. As she reached inside another drawer, she heard the thump of the front door and the sound of Nina's voice in the living room.

Of course. Night had fallen and driven Nina back into the house, where she'd undoubtedly exchange one obsession—her camera—for another. The fairy tale.

Meredith grabbed a file and saw the label: *Bepанetpobha*. She was pretty sure that the letters were Russian. Inside, she found a single letter, postmarked twenty years ago, from Anchorage, Alaska, and addressed to Mrs Evan Whitson.

Dear Mrs Whitson,

Thank you for your recent reply to my query. While I am certain that you could provide invaluable insight into my Leningrad study, I understand your decision. If you ever change your mind, I would welcome your participation.

Sincerely,

Vasily Adamovich

Professor of Russian Studies, University of Alaska

Behind her, through the open study door, she heard her mother begin to speak. Meredith hesitated, telling herself that none of this mattered. Then she heard the word 'Vera' and, dropping the strange letter onto the 'Keep' pile, started to listen.

Nina put her camera on the table and walked over to her mother, who sat in Dad's favourite chair, knitting. Even on this warm May evening, a chill hung in the living room, so Nina built a fire.

'Are you ready?' she asked her mother.

Mom looked up and sighed. Her face was drawn. 'The lights.'

Nina turned off the lights. The fire gave the darkness a blazing heart, and she sat on the floor in front of the sofa.

Her mother began slowly. *'In the year following her father's imprisonment in the Red Tower, Vera becomes somebody, and in the Snow Kingdom, in these dark times, that is a dangerous thing to be. She is no longer just an ordinary peasant girl, the daughter of a poor country tutor. She is the eldest daughter of a banned poet. She must be careful. The black carriages are everywhere by the time she is seventeen, as are the whispered stories of people being turned to smoke and lost for ever.*

She just tries to get by. She wakens every morning and dresses in a shapeless dress. Her shoes are ugly, and her socks do not match. Like this, she makes kasha for her sister, who has become a pale shadow of Vera, and for her mother, whose crying can be heard most nights. Vera tries to comfort her, but she cannot be comforted.

So they go on. Vera works long days at the castle library. In rooms scented by dust, leather and stone, she turns in the last of her father's dreams for her—that she will become a writer—and takes joy in the words of others.

Vera is terrified that one day the black carriages will come for her. Or worse—for Olga or Mama. It is only when she is truly alone—in bed at night, with Olga snoring gently beside her—that she allows herself to even remember the girl she'd once imagined herself to be.

It is then, in the quiet darkness, that she thinks of Sasha and how his kiss made her cry. She tries to forget, but even as months pass with no word from him, she cannot forget.

"Vera?" her sister whispers in the dark.

"I'm awake," she answers.

Olga immediately snuggles closer to her. "I'm cold."

Vera holds her. She knows that as older sister she should say something to lift her spirits, but she hasn't enough of herself to share.

Finally Vera gets out of bed and dresses quickly. She goes into the cold kitchen, where a pot of water-thinned kasha sits on the stove. Mama is gone already. She leaves before dawn for her job at the royal food warehouse. Vera reheats the kasha, sweetening it with honey. Sitting on the bed, they eat breakfast in silence.

'Today, huh?' Olga finally says, scraping the bowl for the last speck of food.

'Today,' Vera confirms. It is the same thing she has said to her sister every Friday since Papa was taken away.

Outside, winter is gnashing its teeth. She walks briskly. In the slicing snow, she takes the trolley across town to a place that has become as familiar to her as her own arm.

At the entrance to the Great Hall of Justice, she opens the stone door and goes inside. Woollen-clad women move forward in a queue. Two hours pass, until at last Vera is at the front of the line. She walks up to the marble desk, where a goblin sits in a tall chair. His golden eyes open and close like a serpent's. "Name," he says.

She answers in as even a voice as she can.

"Give me your papers." His voice is a hiss in the quiet.

She slides papers across the cold desk, watching his slim, hairy hand close over them. It takes courage to stand there. What if he has her name on a list? It is dangerous to keep coming here, or so her mother tells her. But coming here is the only hope she has.

He hands the papers back to her. Each time, the answer is the same. "The case is being studied," he says. "Next."

She stumbles away quickly. It is good news. Her father has not been sent to the Barrens . . . or worse. Soon the Black Knight will realise his error. He will learn that her father is no traitor.

Friday after Friday, Vera goes to see the goblin.

And then her mother tells her they must move.

"There is nothing to be done about it, Vera," she says, sitting slumped at the kitchen table. The past year has taken its toll on her, left its mark in wrinkles.

She smokes a cheap cigarette. "My wages at the warehouse have been cut. We cannot pay the bills here."

Vera would like to argue with her mother as she used to, but there is not enough money for firewood at night, and they are cold.

"Where will we go?" Beside her, Vera hears Olga whine.

"My mother offered."

Vera is surprised by this. "We don't even know her."

"My parents did not approve of your father. Now that he is gone . . ."

"He's not gone," Vera says, deciding right then she will never like her grandmother, let alone love her. "When do we move?"

"Tonight. Before the landlord comes to collect the rent."

Vera sighs quietly and goes into her room. There is little enough to pack up. A few clothes, some blankets, a hairbrush.

"A man will bring the furniture tomorrow," Mama says.

In no time, they trudge through the snow to their new home. The building is small, and cheap curtains hang in the windows. Up the stairs they go, to the last apartment on the second floor.

The woman who answers their knock is heavy and sad-looking, wearing a floral housecoat that has seen better days. Her grey hair is covered by a kerchief. She is smoking a cigarette. "Zoya," she says. "And these are my grandchildren. Veronika and Olga. Which is which?"

"I am Vera," she says, standing tall.

The woman nods and shows them inside. "There will be no problem with you, yes? We do not need the trouble you have had."

"There will be no trouble," Mama says quietly.

Vera stops dead. The apartment is minuscule—a single room with a small wood-burning stove and a sink, a table with mismatched chairs, and a bed pushed against the wall. A half-opened door reveals an empty closet. The bathroom must be communal.

How can they all live here, crammed like rats in a shoe box?

"Come," her grandmother says. "I will show you where to put your things."

Later, in this room that smells of boiled cabbage and too many people, Vera climbs into the bed with her mother and her sister.

Beside her, Olga begins to cry. Vera takes hold of her hand.

The year Vera turns seventeen, she is angry all the time. She works from dawn to dark, and when she gets back, she cooks dinner with Mama and her grandmother, then carries firewood for the night. Work, work, work. Only on Fridays is it different.

"You should quit going there," her mother says as they leave the apartment. It is five in the morning and dark as jet in the streets.

Vera squeezes her hand. "See you tonight," she says.

*She walks to the Great Hall of Justice. She enters the long queue. "Name,"
says the goblin when it is her turn.*

*At her answer, he reads her papers. Abruptly, he gets up from his chair.
Down the hall, in a great glassed chamber, she sees him talking to other goblins and then to a man in black robes.*

*Finally, the goblin takes his seat, pushes the papers back. "There is no one
of that name in our kingdom. You are mistaken. Next."*

*"But you do have him, My Lord. I have been coming here for more than a
year. Please check again."*

"He's not here," the goblin sneers. "Gone. Get it? Next."

*Her father is gone. They have killed him, whoever they are. The trolls in
their shiny black carriages and the Black Knight for whom they work.
Questions cannot be asked. They would draw attention to this execution the
Black Knight wants to deny. In the library, Vera wipes the tears from her eyes
and goes about her work.*

*On her walk home, it seems winter is rising from the ground itself. Brittle
black leaves fall from the trees. Beneath a leaden sky, even the mint-green
castle looks forlorn. She walks in her door.*

*The room is crowded with furniture from their old life. They must move
their ottoman when they open the closet door. Her father's mahogany desk is
covered with jars of pickles and onions.*

*She finds her mother at the stove. Olga is peeling potatoes. Her mother
takes one look at her. "It is Friday," she says at last.*

Olga rises from her chair. "Did you learn something?"

Vera can feel the colour draining from her face.

*"Come, Olga," Mama says. "Put on your coat and your valenki boots.
Your grandmother will be home soon. We are going for a walk."*

*When everyone is ready, they go outside, into a blurry white world. The
hush of falling snowflakes mutes everything around them. As they enter the
Grand Park, street lamps are lit through the square. There are no people here
on this cold, early evening.*

*The giant bronze statue of a winged horse rises up from the snow. "These
are dangerous times," Mama says when they are in front of it. "There are
people that cannot be spoken of in the closeness of an apartment. We will
speak of him now, not again, yes?"*

Olga stamps her foot in the snow. "What is going on?"

*"I went to the Great Hall today to ask about Papa," Vera says, feeling tears
sting her eyes. "He is gone."*

"What does that mean?" Olga says. "Do you think he escaped?"

It is Mama who has the strength to shake her head. "No, he has not escaped."

She glances round and moves closer, so that the three of them are touching, huddled together in the shadow of the statue. "They have killed him."

Olga makes a terrible sound, like she is choking, and Vera and Mama hug her tightly. When they draw back, all are crying.

"You knew when they took him," Vera says. "But you let me go every Friday?"

"You had to learn in your way. And I hoped, of course . . ." Their mother pulls them into a fierce hug. "He loved you two more than his own breath," she whispers. "That will never die."

"I miss him," Olga says, starting to cry again.

"Yes," Mama says in a throaty voice. "For ever. That's how long we'll have an empty place at the table. But we will not speak of him again. Not even to each other." She puts her hand into the big pocket of her wool coat and pulls out a cloisonné butterfly.

Vera has never seen anything so beautiful. This is not the kind of piece their family can own—it is something from kings or wizards.

"Petyr's father made this," her mother says. "It was to be for the little princess, but the king thought it shoddy work, so your grandfather learned to make bricks instead of pieces of art. He gave it to your father on our wedding day. And now it is what we have to remember someone who is lost to us. Sometimes, if I close my eyes when I hold it, I can hear our Petya's laugh."

"It's just a butterfly," Vera says. No substitute for his laughter.

"It is all we have," her mother says gently.

Vera wraps herself in grief, and as spring blooms across the kingdom, she begins to feel burdened by melancholy.

"It is not fair that I cannot go to university," she whines to her mother one warm day. They are kneeling in the black earth, weeding their small garden. Both have already worked a full day in the city; this is their summertime routine. A day's labour in the kingdom and then a two-hour cart ride beyond the walled city to the countryside, where they rent a small patch of ground.

"You are too old to be whining about fairness," her mother says.

"I want to study the great writers and artists."

Her mother sits back and looks at Vera. In the golden light that falls at ten o'clock at night, she looks almost pretty again. "You work in the greatest library in the world—three million books," she says. "The royal museum is on your way home, and your sister works there." She makes a tsking sound. "Do not tell me a young woman needs to go to university to learn. If you believe such a thing, you are not . . . his daughter." It is the first time she has mentioned Vera's father, and it has the intended effect.

Vera slides sideways into the warm dirt, looking down at the fragile green rosette of a baby cabbage beside her.

I am Petyr Andreiovich's daughter, *she thinks, and in that reclamation, she remembers the books her father had read to her at night and the dreams he'd let her dream.*

For the remainder of that week, Vera contemplates the discussion in the garden. At work, she wanders round the library, walking amid the stacks with the ghost of her father beside her. Her mind struggles to find the path. She knows now that all she needs is someone to help her understand the books she might read.

And then one day she is at the counter, organising parchment rolls, when a familiar face appears. It is an aged man, walking with a cane across the marble floor, his tattered cleric's robes trailing behind him. At a table near the wall, he sits and opens a book.

Vera approaches him slowly, knowing that her mother would not approve of her plan, but a plan it suddenly is.

"Excuse me," she says softly to the man, who looks up at her.

"Veronika?" he says after a long moment.

"Yes," she says. This man used to come to the house, in the older, better days. She does not think to mention her father, but he is here between them, as surely as the dust. "I am sorry to bother you, but I seek a tutor. I haven't much money."

The cleric removes his glasses. When he speaks, his voice is a whisper. "I cannot help you myself." He sighs. "But I know some students who perhaps are not so afraid as an old man. I will ask."

"Thank you."

"Be careful, young Veronika," he says, putting on his glasses again. "And tell no one of this conversation."

"This secret is safe with me."

The cleric doesn't smile. "No secret is safe."'

CHAPTER EIGHT

IT WAS ALMOST MIDNIGHT when Meredith got home. Exhausted by the day, she still played with the dogs for a while after feeding them. She was in the kitchen making herself a cup of tea when a car drove up.

Jeff. Who else would it be at twelve thirty? She stood gripping the sink, her heartbeat going crazy as the front door opened.

Nina walked into the kitchen, looking vaguely pissed off.

Meredith felt a rush of disappointment. 'It's past midnight. What are you doing here?'

Nina walked over to the counter, grabbed a bottle of wine, found two coffee mugs and filled them both. 'Well, the story is becoming pretty damn detailed for a fairy tale, but since you're afraid of it, I'll say what I came for. We need to talk.'

'Tomorrow is—'

'Tomorrow you'll be all armoured up. Come on.' Leading Meredith to the living room, she got the fire going by pressing a button. *Whoosh* went the gas flames, and on came the heat and light. 'Here,' she said, handing Meredith a cup of wine.

Meredith sat on one end of the sofa. 'What do you want?'

'My sister.'

'I don't know what you mean.'

'You were the one who took me trick-or-treating when Dad was working, remember? You always made my costume. And when I tried out for cheerleader, you helped me and were happy for me when I made it, even though you hadn't. And when Sean Bowers asked me to the prom, you were the one who said not to trust him. We might not have had much in common, but we were *sisters*."

Meredith had forgotten all of that. 'That was a long time ago.'

'I went away and left, and Mom is not an easy person to be left with. And we don't know each other very well. But I'm here now.'

'I see you.'

'Do you? Because frankly, you've been a bitch the last few days. Or maybe not a bitch, just kind of mopey, and one woman who won't talk to me at dinner is my quota.' Nina sat on the sofa and leaned forwards. 'I'm here, and I miss you, Mere. I think—'

'Jeff left me.'

'What?'

Meredith couldn't say it again. She shook her head, felt the sting of tears. 'He's living at the motel by his office.'

'That *jerk*,' Nina said.

Meredith laughed. 'Thanks for not assuming it was my fault.'

'What happened?' Nina asked quietly.

'He asked me if I still love him.'

'And?'

'I didn't answer. And I haven't called him, haven't begged him to come back. No wonder he left me. He said I was like Mom.'

'So now I think he's a prick and a jerk.'

'He loves me, and I've hurt him. That's why he said it.'

'Who gives a damn about his feelings? That's your problem, Mere. You care too much about everyone else. What do *you* want?'

Meredith hadn't asked herself that question in years. She'd gone to the college they could afford, not the one she'd wanted; she'd married younger than planned because she'd been pregnant; she'd come home to Belye Nochi because Dad needed her. When had she ever done what she wanted?

Strangely, she thought about the early days at the orchard, when she'd started the gift shop and stocked it with things she loved.

'You'll figure it out, I promise.' Nina came and hugged her.

'Thanks. I mean it. You helped.'

Nina sat back. 'Remember that the next time I burn the hell out of the stove or leave a mess in the kitchen.'

'I'll try,' Meredith said, clinking glasses. 'To new beginnings.'

'I'll drink to that,' Nina said.

'You'll drink to anything.'

'Indeed I will. It's one of my best traits.'

For the next two days, Mom shut down, turned from quiet into stone-like, even refusing to come down for dinner. Nina would have been upset by it, but the reason was obvious. All of them were feeling the same way. Dad's birthday was approaching.

The day dawned bright and sunny. Nina pushed the covers back and got out of bed. From her window, the apple trees seemed to be dancing, and millions of white blossoms shimmied in the light.

She grabbed her clothes and dressed. She wasn't sure what she'd say to her mother on this tenderest of days; she just knew she didn't want to be alone. She knocked on Mom's door. 'Are you up?'

'Sunset,' Mom said. 'I'll see you and Meredith then.'

Disappointed, Nina went down to the kitchen. After a quick breakfast, she set off to Meredith's house, but all she found there were the huskies. Of course, Meredith had gone to work.

'Damn.' Since the last thing she wanted to do was roam through the quiet house on Dad's birthday, she went back, got her car keys and headed for town. Along the way, she stopped now and then to take photographs, and at noon she ate greasy American food at the diner on Main Street.

By five o'clock she was back at Belye Nochi. She found Meredith in the kitchen, putting something into the oven.

'Hey,' Nina said.

Meredith turned. 'I made dinner. I thought . . . afterwards . . .'

'Sure,' Nina said, walking over to the French doors, looking out. 'How do we do this?'

Meredith came up beside her, putting an arm round her shoulders. 'I guess we just open the urn and let the ashes fall. Maybe you could say something.'

'You're the one who should say something. I let him down.'

'He loved you so much. And he was proud of you.'

Nina felt tears start. Outside, night began to fold across the orchard in ribbons of pink and palest lavender. 'Thanks,' she said.

'It is time,' Mom said behind them.

She stood in the doorway holding a rosewood box inlaid with ivory. She was practically unrecognisable in a purple chiffon evening blouse and canary-yellow linen pants.

'He liked colour,' she said. 'I should have worn more of it . . .' She smoothed the hair from her face and glanced out of the window at the setting sun. Then she drew in a deep breath and walked towards them. 'Here,' she said, holding out the box to Nina.

It was silly. It was just a box full of ashes, not really her dad, and yet, when Nina took it from her mother, grief rolled over her. She couldn't move. She saw Mom and Meredith leave the room and walk outside.

A breeze came through the open doors, brushing her cheek, bringing with it the scent of apples. A cluster of white blossoms landed on the floor at her feet.

Dad?

'Come on, Nina,' Meredith called.

Nina headed for the garden. Meredith and her mother were already there, standing stiffly by the magnolia tree. The last bit of sunlight illuminated the new copper column.

Nina hurried across the grass, noticing a second too late that it was slippery. It all happened in an instant: her toe caught on a rock, and she started to fall, and suddenly the box was flying. It crashed into one of the copper columns and splintered.

Nina hit the ground hard enough to taste blood. She lay there, dazed, hearing Meredith's 'Oh, no' repeat over and over. Then Mom was pulling her to her feet, saying something in Russian. It was the gentlest voice she'd ever heard from her mother.

'I dropped it,' Nina said, and started to cry.

'Do not cry,' Mom said. 'Just think if he were here. He would say, "What the hell did you expect, Anya, waiting until dark?"'

Her mother actually smiled.

Meredith's mouth quirked up. 'We'll call it an ash-tossing.'

Mom was the first to laugh. The sound was so totally foreign that Nina gasped, and then she started to laugh, too.

They stood there, laughing in the winter garden, with the apple trees all round them. And later, when Mom and Meredith had gone inside, Nina stood there alone, staring down at the velvety white magnolia blossoms dressed in grey ash. 'Did you hear us laughing? The three of us together? We laughed for you, Dad . . .'

She would have sworn she felt him beside her then. She knew what he'd have said. *Nice trip, Neener Beaner. See you in the fall.*

'I love you, Dad,' she whispered.

Dinner was chicken kiev with gratin potatoes and a green salad. There was a decanter of vodka in the centre of the table.

'That's my kind of centrepiece,' Nina said, taking a seat while Mom poured three shots. Meredith sat down beside her sister.

'A toast,' their mother said quietly. 'To our Evan.' She clinked her glass against the others and downed the alcohol in one swallow. 'Your father loved it when I drank.'

'It's a good night for alcohol.' Meredith drank her vodka and held her glass out. The second shot burned down her throat. 'I miss hearing his voice when I come into the house,' she said.

Mom immediately poured herself another shot. 'I miss the way he kissed me every morning.'

'I got used to missing him,' Nina said. 'Pour me another.'

'He would not want us speaking about him in this way,' Mom said. 'He would want . . .'

In the silence that followed, they looked at each other. Meredith knew they were thinking the same thing: How do you just go on?

You just do, she thought, and so Meredith said, 'My favourite holiday is Thanksgiving. I love everything about it. And I'll say it now: I hated those damn family road trips we used to take. Remember the time we stayed in teepees? It was one hundred degrees, and Nina sang "I Think I Love You" for four hundred miles.'

Nina laughed. 'I *loved* those camping trips. And Christmas is my favourite holiday, because I can remember the date.'

'I loved your father's adventurous spirit,' Mom said. 'Although those camping trips were hell. Nina, you should never sing in front of people if they cannot leave.'

'Ha!' Meredith said. 'I knew I wasn't crazy.'

Mom sighed. 'He always promised to take me to Alaska. To see again the *Belye Nochi* and the Northern Lights. That is the thing I miss most about Evan. He was always beside me.' She looked up suddenly, as if realising all at once that she'd shown something of herself. She pushed back from the table.

'I always wanted to go to Alaska, too,' Meredith said. She didn't want her mother to leave the table, not now.

'I am going to my room.' Mom stood up and walked out.

That night, Meredith and Nina stayed up late talking about Dad and trading memories. Afterwards, when Meredith lay in her lonely bed, she began what would be a new life habit: talking to her dad in the quiet times. She told him all about Jeff and her inability to say what her husband wanted to hear. She knew what her dad would have asked her. It was the same question Nina had posed.

What do you want?

All the next day, as she tried to work, that question came back to her, until finally she had an answer of sorts.

She didn't know what she wanted, but she knew what she *didn't* want. She was tired of running too fast and hiding behind a busy schedule, tired of pretending problems didn't exist.

After work, she drove to the Wenatchee World building.

'Hey,' she said from the doorway of Jeff's office.

He looked up from the paperwork on his desk. She could tell that he hadn't been sleeping well. His unshaven jaw made him look different— younger, hipper, someone she didn't know.

He got up slowly, ran a hand through his hair. 'Meredith.'

'I should have come sooner.'

'I expected you to.'

She glanced out of the window, at the cars rolling past. 'You were right to leave. We need to figure out where to go from here.'

'Is that what you came to tell me?' She felt his gaze searching for something. 'Because that's not what I'm waiting to hear.'

'I know.' She hated to disappoint him, but she couldn't give him what he wanted. 'I'm sorry, Jeff. But you got me thinking. For once, I don't want to put everyone's happiness above my own. And right now, I don't know what to say to you.'

'Can you say you *don't* love me?'

'No.'

He thought about that, and she felt the distance between them in a way she hadn't before. He nodded and reached down for his reading glasses. She was about to ask about his book when there was a knock at his door. A beautiful young woman in tight jeans poked her head into his office. 'You still up for pizza and beer, Jeff?'

Jeff looked at Meredith, who shrugged. Smiling a little too brightly, she said goodbye in a steady voice, left the office and drove home. There, she fed the dogs and ate a dinner of Raisin Bran. Suddenly she didn't want to be there alone.

Ten minutes later she was at Belye Nochi, calling out for Nina.

She found Mom in the living room, knitting. 'Hey, Mom. I'm going to start packing again. Have you eaten?'

Her mother didn't look up. 'Nina made dinner. Thank you.'

'Where is she?'

'Out.'

Meredith waited for more and got nothing. 'I'll be upstairs.'

Dragging boxes, she went into her parents' closet. The left side was Dad's. Facing Mom's side, she scooped up the sweaters on the shelf and dropped them to the floor. Kneeling, she began folding, so intent that she was surprised when she heard Nina's voice.

'Are you comfortable, Mom?' Nina said.

Meredith moved to the closet door, opening it just a crack.

Mom was in bed with the bedside lamp on beside her. Nina was sitting on the floor in front of the cold hearth.

'Fine,' Mom said. She sighed and turned off the light.

'Belye Nochi,' Mom said, the words suddenly full of passion and mystery. *'It is the season of light in the Snow Kingdom, where fairies glow on bright green leaves and rainbows swirl through the midnight sky. The street lamps come on, but they are decorations only, golden oases along the streets, and on the rare days when rain falls, everything is mirrored in the light. On this day, Vera is cleaning bookcases at the library, and humming a song her father taught her.*

"The library is to be quiet."

Vera drops her rag. The woman facing her is storklike: tall and rail-thin, with a beak of a nose. "I am sorry, ma'am. I thought . . ."

"Do not. You never know who is listening."

The words may be a warning or a rebuke. "I apologise, ma'am."

"Good. A student from the college requests your assistance. Cleric Nevin sent him. Help him, but do not neglect your duties."

"Yes, ma'am." The cleric has a student who will teach her! Vera hurries down the wide marble steps to the main hall of the library.

"Veronika." She hears her name and turns slowly.

He looks exactly as she remembers, with his shock of golden hair that is too long and curly. His wide jaw has been freshly shaven, but it is his green eyes that capture her once again.

"Your Highness," she says, trying to sound casual. "It is good to see you. How long has it been?"

"Don't."

"Don't what?"

"You know what happened on Fontanka bridge."

Her smile slips; she tries to find it. She will not show herself to be naïve and silly. Not again. "That was just a night. Years ago."

"It was no ordinary night, Vera."

"Please. Don't tease me, Your Highness." To her horror, her voice breaks just a little. "And you never came back."

"You were fifteen. I was eighteen. I have been waiting for you."

For the first time in her life, Vera pretends to be ill. She goes to the librarian and complains about pains in her stomach, begging to go home early.

It is a dangerous thing to do, but a girl cannot act out of fear when love is at hand. Still, she is smart enough to go directly home when she is let go. At the apartment, she opens the door slowly and peers inside.

Her grandmother stands in front of the stove, stirring something in a big black cauldron. "You are home early," she says.

"The library was not busy," Vera says, feeling her face redden. "I'm going out to the country to pick cucumbers and cabbage."

"Very well." Her grandmother's baggy dress is ragged at the hem, and her stockings are pocked with snags.

"Tell Mama I will be home late. I will not be home for supper."

"Be careful," her grandmother says. "You are young . . . and his daughter. It does not do well to be noticed."

Vera nods. She carries their rusted old bicycle to the door.

Never has she flown so on her rickety bicycle down the streets of her beloved Snow Kingdom. All along the river, she can feel the beating of her heart. Sasha. He has waited for her.

At the intricate scrollwork entrance of the park, she eases to a stop. The beauty of the castle grounds amazes her. Bordered on three sides by water, the park is a magnificent green haven in the walled city. The air smells of limes. Marble statues line the paths.

She does as they planned: she walks her bike down the path, trying to look calm. But her pulse is racing.

And then he is there, standing beside a lime tree, smiling at her.

He is beside her in an instant. "This way," he says, leading her to a spot deep in the trees where a blanket and basket are laid out.

At first, they sit cross-legged on the warm wool, their shoulders touching. Through the green bower, she can see sunlight dappling the water. Soon, she knows, the paths will be full of lords and ladies and lovers eager to walk outside in the warm light of a June night.

"What have you been doing this past year?" she asks, not daring to look at him. He has been in her heart for so long it is as if she knows him already, but she doesn't. She is afraid to move forwards.

"I am at the cleric's college studying to be a poet."

"But you are a prince, and poetry is forbidden."

"Do not be afraid, Vera. I am careful."

"My father said the same thing to my mother."

"Look at me," Sasha says quietly, and Vera turns to him.

It is a kiss that, once begun, never really ends. Interrupted, yes. Paused. But from that moment onward, Vera sees the whole of her life as only a breath away from kissing him again. On that night, they begin the delicate task of binding their souls together.

Vera tells him everything there is to know about her and listens to his own story—how it was to be born in the northern wilds and left in an orphanage and found later by his royal parents. His tale of loneliness makes her promise to love him for ever.

At this, he turns a little, until he is lying alongside her, their faces close. "I will love you that long, Vera," he says.

They walk hand in hand through the pale purple glow of early morning. The alabaster statues look pink in the light. Out in the city, they are among people again, strangers who feel like friends on this white night. Northern Lights dance in impossible hues.

At the bridge, beneath the street lamp, they look at each other.

"Come tomorrow for dinner," she says. "To meet my family."

"What if they do not like me?"

"They will love you, Sasha. Trust me."

"Give me one more day. Do not tell anyone about us. Please."

She smiles at the thought of another magical night like this. "I'll meet you tomorrow at one."

"I'll be waiting on the bridge over the castle moat."

Vera lets go of him at last and walks across the street. Heaving her bike up to the second floor, she opens the door. The first thing she notices is the smell of smoke, then her mother at the table smoking a cigarette. An overflowing ashtray sits at her elbow.

"Mama!" Vera cries. The bicycle clangs into the wall.

"Hush!" Mama says. Her face is clamped tight with anger. "And where are your vegetables from the garden?"

"I hit a bench with my bike and fell into the street. Everything was lost." The lie spills out. "I had to walk all the way home."

"Seventeen is very young." Mama puts out her cigarette. "You are not so ready for life and love as you believe in these times."

"You were seventeen when you met Papa."

Her mother sighs. It is a sound of defeat, as if she already knows everything that has happened between her daughter and some boy.

"You would do it again, wouldn't you? Love Papa, I mean."

"No," her mother says softly. "I would not love him again. Not if I knew how it would feel to live with a broken heart."

"But—"

"I know you don't understand, Vera. I hope you never do. Now come to bed. Allow me to pretend you are still my innocent girl."

"I am," Vera protests.

Her mother climbs into the narrow bed. "Not for long, though, Veronika. For you want to be in love."

Is this the reason Sasha asked for one more day? Did he know that Mama would resist? Climbing in next to her, Vera finds warmth in her arms.

"Be careful," her mother whispers. "Do not lie to me again."

The next morning, Vera wakes early enough to wash her hair in the kitchen sink and painstakingly brush it dry.

"Where are you going?" Olga says sleepily from the bed.

Vera presses a finger to her lips and makes a shushing sound.

Her mother angles up on one elbow. "There is no need to shush your sister, Veronika. I can smell the rose water in your hair."

Vera says nothing.

Her mother throws back the flimsy covers. She and Olga peel sideways, and stand together in their ragged white nightgowns. "Bring your young man here on Sunday," Mama says. "Your grandmother will be out."

Vera throws her arms round her and hugs her. Then the three of them eat breakfast and walk to work. When Mama turns towards the warehouse and Olga toward the museum, Vera catches a trolley.

When she enters the library, the librarian stands in the magnificent foyer, her toe impatiently tapping the marble.

Vera skids to a stop. "Madam Plotkin. I am sorry to be late."

"Seven minutes, precisely. And you were seen yesterday in the park."

"Oh, no. Madam Plotkin, please—"

"Do you value this employment?"

"Yes, ma'am, very much. And I need it. For my family."

"If I were the child of a criminal of the kingdom, I would be careful. I trust you will not be sick again."

Trapped like a bird banging against a glass window, all day Vera imagines Sasha waiting on the bridge. She is desperate to run out, but her fear is *greater than her love, it seems. Loss of this employment would ruin her family, so she stays.*

Hour after hour she stares at the clock, willing the black hand to move . . . to move . . . and finally her shift is over.

Outside, she runs down the steps, across to the trolley. At her stop, she jumps off and runs for the corner.

The street is empty. Then she sees the black carriages. Two of them, parked in front of the moat bridge. Vera does not move. It takes all her courage to breathe. They know she is a peasant girl sneaking out to meet a royal, and they have come for her. Or maybe they came for him. Even a prince is not safe from the Black Knight's reach.

Tears sting her eyes, and she wipes them away. Her eyes are burning when she looks up and sees a wavery image of a young man standing beneath a dark street lamp. From here, it looks like Sasha, with his unruly hair and strong jawline. Even as she picks up her pace, she tells herself she is being a fool, that he is gone. Still, within a metre or so, she is running. A split second before he begins to move towards her, she knows it is her Sasha, now running towards her.

"Vera," he says, pulling her into his arms, kissing her.

"You waited all day?"

"A day? You think that is all I would wait?" He pulls her close.

Together they cross the street. The Royal Theatre rises up like a green-and-white spun-sugar confection. In the queue along the pavement, people are dressed in furs and jewels and white gloves.

Sasha takes her to a door and up a flight of dark stairs. They slip into a private box. Vera stares across the hall in awe, seeing the gilt décor and crystal chandeliers. In this box—obviously being repaired—even tools and disarray can't hide the plush mohair of the seats. She turns to Sasha. "We have to leave. I do not belong here."

He pulls her into the shadows against the wall. Blue velvet curtains cushion them. "This box won't be used tonight. If someone comes, we'll say we are cleaners. There are our brooms."

The well-dressed patrons stream in. The lights flicker, and a hush falls over the audience. The gold and blue velvet curtains part.

The music begins with a high, pure note, sweeps into a symphony of sound. Galina Ulanova—the great ballerina—leaps across the stage like a ray of light. Vera leans as close as she dares.

For more than an hour, the story of a princess kidnapped by an evil wizard plays out across the stage. When the wizard is brought to his knees by love, Sasha leads Vera to a velvet-draped ottoman tucked in the shadows at the back of the box.

She knows what is going to happen now; she can feel it coming to life between them, uncoiling. He lies down, pulling her down on top of him, and when he slides his hand under her dress, she starts to shake a little. It is as if her body is taking charge of itself.

"Are you sure of this, Verushka?" he whispers.

The endearment makes her smile. "I am sure."

By Sunday, Vera is an entirely different girl. Or perhaps now she is a woman. She and Sasha have met secretly after work every day since the ballet, and Vera has fallen so deeply in love with him that she knows there will never be a way out of it.

"Are you sure about this, Verushka?" he asks her as they climb the steps to her front door.

She takes his hand. She is sure enough for the both of them. "Yes." But when she reaches for the door, he grabs her hand.

"Marry me," he says, and she laughs and kisses him.

"Of course I will."

They climb the narrow stairs. She opens the door with a flourish. The small apartment is shabby but clean. Her mother has been cooking, and the sweet, savoury scent of boar stew fills the room.

"This is my prince, Mama."

Her mother and Olga stand at the table, dressed in pretty floral blouses with plain cotton skirts. Vera sees them through Sasha's eyes: her tired, once beautiful mother; and Olga, ready to burst into womanhood, smiling so brightly her crooked teeth seem ordinary.

Her mother comes round the table. "We have heard much about you, Your Highness. Welcome to our home."

Olga giggles. "We've really heard a lot. She can't shut up."

Sasha smiles. "She talks to me of you also."

Mama shakes Sasha's hand, gazing up at him. When she seems satisfied, she moves to the samovar. "Would you like some tea?"

"Yes, thank you," he says.

"You attend the cleric's college, I hear," Mama says.

"Yes. I'm a good student, too. I will make a good husband."

She flinches a little but pours the tea. "What are you studying?"

"I hope to be a poet some day, like your husband."

Vera sees it all as if in slow motion: her mother hears the terrible words, and the fragile glass cup in her hand falls to the ground.

"A poet?" Mama says. "A prince is dangerous enough . . ."

Vera cannot believe that she forgot to warn Sasha of this. "Don't worry, Mama. You needn't—"

"You say you love her," Mama says bitterly, "and I can see in your eyes that you do, but you will do this to her anyway, this dangerous thing that has been done to our family already."

"I wouldn't endanger Vera for anything," he says solemnly.

"You can't stop us from marrying," Vera says.

Her mother looks at her, and in those eyes she loves is a nearly unbearable disappointment. Vera feels her confidence ebbing.

She places a hand on her stomach. In months to come, she will remember this moment and understand that already his child is growing inside her, but all she knows is she is afraid—'

'Stop.' Meredith pushed the closet door open and stepped out of her hiding place. The bedroom was blue with moonlight, and in it Mom looked exhausted. Meredith walked over to her. 'Are you OK?'

'You were listening,' Mom said, looking down at her own hands. 'Why?'

Meredith shrugged. Honestly, she had no answer for that.

'Well, you are right,' Mom said, leaning back. 'I am tired.'

It was the first time Mom had *ever* said she was right about something. 'Nina and I will take care of you. Don't worry.' She almost reached out to stroke her mother's hair, as she would have done to a child who looked as worn out as Mom did. Almost.

Nina came up to the bedside and stood beside Meredith.

'But who will take care of you two?' Mom asked suddenly.

Meredith started to answer and stopped. It dawned on her that this was both the most caring thing Mom had ever said to them, and that she was right to ask it.

Mom would be gone some day, and only they would be left. Would they take care of each other?

CHAPTER NINE

In the morning, Nina went down to her dad's office, booted up the computer, and ran searches on every word in her mother's story she could think of. She was so caught up in gathering information that when Meredith touched her shoulder, she actually jumped.

'You look like you haven't slept,' Meredith said.

Nina looked up. 'It's the fairy tale. Last night was all new, right? We've never heard that part before.'

'It was new,' Meredith said.

'Did you notice the changes? Vera's mother is smoking cigarettes, and Vera is pregnant before she gets married. When did you ever hear stuff like that in a fairy tale? And listen to this: Galina Ulanova, a great Russian ballerina, danced at the Mariinsky Theatre in Leningrad until 1944. Check it out in this picture.'

Meredith leaned closer. 'That's exactly how Mom described it.'

Nina hit a few keys, and a picture of the Summer Garden came up. 'Also real. In St Petersburg, which used to be Leningrad. Notice the marble statues and the lime trees? And here's the famous Bronze Horseman statue—not a winged horse, but a man on horseback.'

Meredith frowned. 'I found a letter in Dad's files. From a professor in Alaska. He was asking Mom about Leningrad.'

'Really?' Nina scooted closer to the computer, her fingers flying on the keyboard as she pulled up the biography of Galina Ulanova again. 'She was most famous in Leningrad in the 'thirties.' She typed in 'Leningrad 1930'.

On screen, a list of links came up. One of them—'Great Terror'—caught Nina's attention, and she clicked on it. 'Listen to this,' she said when the website appeared. '"The thirties were characterised by the Great Purge of the Communist Party, in which Stalin's secret police arrested peasants, perceived political radicals, ethnic minorities and artists. It was a time of widespread police surveillance, middle-of-the-night arrests, secretive "trials", years of imprisonment and executions."'

'Black vans,' Meredith said, reading the rest. 'The secret police came in black vans to get people.'

'The Black Knight is Stalin. It's a story within a story.' Nina and Meredith looked at each other and, in that look, Nina felt the first true connection of their lives. 'Some of it is real,' she said quietly.

'And have you noticed that she hasn't been confused lately?' Meredith said. Kneeling by the boxes she'd packed, she found the *Верапеtробhа* file and handed over Professor Adamovich's letter.

Nina read it. 'So we know for sure Mom has a connection to Leningrad, and the fairy tale takes place there, and at least some of it is probably real. I'm going to ask the obvious: is she Vera?'

'Vera sees colour,' Meredith said. Acromatopsia, Mom's birth defect was called. 'Maybe Mom is Olga. Keep her talking. I'm going through this house from stem to stern. If there's anything to find, I'll find it.'

'Thanks,' Nina said. 'It feels good to be together on this.'

During dinner that night, Nina concentrated on acting normally. She drank her vodka and ate her meal and made her pretence at conversation, but all the while, she was watching Mom closely, thinking, Who are you? It took an act of will not to voice the question. So when her mother stood up after the meal and said, 'I am too tired for storytelling tonight,' Nina was almost relieved.

She helped her sister with the dishes, then went into Dad's study and ran more searches on the internet, but she found no facts she hadn't known already. The envelope from the professor stuck out from underneath her notes. She picked up the letter and read it again. Her mother had seen or experienced something important enough to have been the subject of a research project. But what?

Nina turned her attention to the dusty green file folder marked '*Верапетровна*'. She stared at the letter lying on top, studying it again. 'What did you want to know from her, Vasily Adamovich?'

That was when she saw it, when she said his name out loud.

Nina sat upright. It was in his signature. When he signed his name, Vasily, the V looked like a B.

Nina's heart was pounding as she read the file label. Was there a space after the *a*? Could it be a first and last name? She broke the word at the second capital letter and was left with '*Вера*'.

'Vepa'? She ran a search for the Russian alphabet. 'Вера' was 'Vera'. Then she translated the rest of the letters. *петровна*. Petrovna.

A little more research and she understood Russian names. First was the given name, then the patronymic—a male or female identification of the father—and then the surname. So this file contained two of three names—'ovna' was the suffix for a daughter. Vera Petrovna meant Vera, Petyr's daughter.

Nina sat back in her chair, feeling the adrenaline rush that always came with nailing a key part of a story. Vera was a real person. Real enough to put her name on a file, and important enough to keep that file for twenty years.

It wasn't a complete answer. But this Vasily Adamovich knew the connection between Mom and Vera, and that connection was important enough to include in a research study.

And with that, Nina came up with a plan.

At five thirty the next morning, Meredith went for her run. By seven o'clock, she was out in the orchard and walking the rows with her foreman, checking on the new fruit's early progress, and by ten she was at her desk, reading crop projections.

But all she could really think about was the fairy tale.

I'm just going to ask the obvious: is she Vera?

She put aside the crop reports and turned to her computer. For the next hour, she ran random searches: Leningrad, Stalin, Vera, Olga, Fontanka bridge, Great Terror. Nothing of real value came up. She found a long list of Vasily Adamovich's published works. He'd written about almost every facet of Russian and Soviet life, from the earliest days of the Bolshevik revolution, through the murder of the Romanovs and the rise of Stalin and the terrors of his regime, to Hitler's attack during World War II. Whatever had happened to the Russians in the twentieth century, he'd studied it. When she added 'Retirement' to the search, she came up with an unexpected link to a newspaper article.

Dr Vasily Adamovich, a former professor of Russian Studies at the University of Alaska in Anchorage, suffered a stroke yesterday at his home in Juneau. Dr Adamovich is well known in academic circles for his prolific publishing schedule. He retired from teaching in 1989 and volunteered frequently at his neighbourhood library. He is recovering at a local hospital.

Meredith picked up the phone and dialled Information, asking for the public library in Juneau, Alaska. The operator gave her several listings.

On the fourth call, she got lucky. 'Hello,' she said. 'I'm trying to find a Dr Vasily Adamovich.'

'Oh, Vasya,' the woman answered. 'No one has called for him in a while, I'm sad to say. Last I heard, he was in a nursing home.'

'Do you know which one?'

'No, I'm sorry, I don't.'

'OK, well, thank you for your help.' Meredith hung up the phone.

Daisy walked into her office. 'There's a problem down in the warehouse. Nothing urgent. If you're busy, I can solve it for you.'

'Yeah, why don't you do that?'

'And then I'll go to Tahiti. On the company credit card.'

'Uh-huh, thanks, Daisy.'

Daisy sat down opposite Meredith. 'That's it,' she said. 'Start talking. I just told you I was going to Tahiti on the company dime. What's going on?'

Meredith paused; Daisy had been around the Whitsons as long as anyone could remember. 'When did you first meet my mom?'

Daisy's eyebrows lifted. 'Well, let's see. I guess I was about ten. It was all the buzz, 'cause your daddy was datin' Sally Herman when he went to war, and when he came home, he was married.'

'So he barely knew her?'

'I don't know about that. My mom said she'd never seen a man so in love. She took care of Anya most of that first year.'

Meredith frowned. 'What do you mean?'

'She was sick. You knew that, right? She was in bed for a year or so.'

'Sick how? What was wrong with her?'

'I don't know. Mom never said much about it, really.'

'OK, thanks, Daisy.' She watched Daisy leave the office and close the door behind her.

Over the next few hours, Meredith managed to get a little work done. But at five o'clock, she gave up and left the office.

Ten minutes later, when she walked into her mother's house, the smell of baking bread greeted her. She found Mom in the kitchen, draped in a baggy white apron, her hands white with flour.

'Hey, Mom.'

'You are here early.'

'I thought I'd do more packing. Where's Nina?'

'She said something about errands and left an hour ago.'

Meredith started to go towards Dad's office, but she paused. The last time she'd packed up Mom's things, she hadn't looked for anything, hadn't gone through pockets and felt at the back of drawers.

Glancing at the kitchen, seeing her mom still kneading dough, she eased towards the stairs.

In the long, wide closet, her mother's black and grey clothing lined one wall. Turtlenecks and long skirts and flowy pants. She went deeper in, to Mom's chest of drawers. Guilt made her grimace as her fingers trailed beneath underwear and socks, felt the smooth wood of drawers.

Nothing hidden. Disappointed, she stood looking at the clothes, all perfectly organised, everything in its place; the only thing that didn't fit was a sapphire-blue coat at the very back of the closet.

Meredith remembered the coat. She'd seen her mother wear it to a performance of *The Nutcracker* when they were little. Dad had kissed Mom and insisted, 'Come on, Anya, just once . . .'

She pulled it out. The cashmere coat was in a classic forties style, with broad shoulders, a fitted waist and wide cuffed sleeves. Meredith put it on; the silk lining was deliciously soft.

But Mom had rarely worn it. Neither, though, had she thrown it away, and it was an odd thing to have saved. Putting her hands in the pockets, Meredith looked at herself in the mirror on the door.

That was when she felt something sewn into the lining behind the pocket. She felt a fraying edge and extracted a tattered photograph.

The black-and-white image was slightly blurry, and the paper was creased and veined, but it was of two children, about three or four years of age, holding hands. At first, she thought it was her and Nina, but then she noticed the old-fashioned heavy coats and boots.

'Meredith!' Nina was thundering up the stairs like an elephant.

Meredith opened the closet door. 'I'm in here, Nina.'

'There you are. I was look—'

Meredith grabbed her arm. 'Is Mom still in the kitchen?'

'Yes, why?'

Meredith held out her hand. 'Look what I found.'

Nina took the photo and stared down at it. 'Vera and Olga?'

Meredith's heart actually skipped a beat. 'You think?'

'I can't tell if they're boys or girls. But this one kinda looks like Mom, don't you think?'

'Honestly? I don't know. And I found out from Daisy that Mom was sick when she married Dad.'

'Now I'm certain about my plan,' Nina said.

'What plan?'

'I'll tell you at dinner. Mom needs to hear this, too. Let's go.'

Together they went downstairs. Mom was seated at the kitchen table. On the counter, there were dozens of loaves of bread and several bags from the local Chinese restaurant.

Nina dished the Chinese food into serving bowls and brought it to the table, positioning it round the vodka and shot glasses.

'You seem . . . buoyant,' Mom said.

'I have a surprise.' Nina lifted her shot glass. 'Cheers!'

'What is it?' Meredith asked.

'First we talk,' Nina said, reaching for the beef with broccoli. 'Let's see. My favourite thing to do is travel. I love passion in all of its guises. And my boyfriend wants me to settle down.'

Meredith was shocked by that last bit. It was so intimate. To her surprise, she decided to match it. 'I love to shop for beautiful things. I used to dream of opening a string of Belye Nochi gift stores, and . . . my husband left me.'

Mom looked up sharply but said nothing.

'I don't know what's going to happen,' Meredith said at last. 'I think maybe love can just . . . dissolve.'

'No, it does not,' her mother said.

'So how do—'

'You hang on,' her mother said. 'Until your hands are bleeding and you do not let go.'

'Is that how you and Dad were happy for so long?' Nina asked.

Mom reached for the chow mein's serving spoons. 'Of course that is what I am speaking of.'

'Your turn,' Nina said to Mom.

Meredith could have kicked her sister. For once they were actually *talking,* and Nina turned it right back to the game.

Mom stared down at her food. 'My favourite thing to do is cook. I love the feel of a fire on a cold night. And . . . I am afraid of many things.' She picked up her fork and began to eat.

Meredith sat back in amazement. It was impossible to imagine her mother afraid of anything, and yet it must be true. She wanted to ask, *What frightens you?* but she didn't have the courage.

'It's time for my surprise,' Nina said. 'We're going to Alaska.'

Meredith frowned. 'We who?'

'You, me and Mom.' Nina produced tickets. 'On a cruise ship.'

Meredith was too stunned to say anything. She knew she should say she had to work, the dogs couldn't be left alone—anything—but the truth was, she *wanted* to go. Daisy could run the business for a short while.

Mom looked up slowly. Her face was pale; her blue eyes seemed to burn through the pallor. 'You are taking me to Alaska? Why?'

'You said it was your dream,' Nina said simply. Meredith could have kissed her. 'And you said it, too, Mere.'

'But . . .' Mom said, shaking her head.

'We need this,' Nina said. 'The three of us. We need to be together, and I want Mom to see Alaska.'

'In exchange for the rest of the story,' Mom said.

'Yes. We want to hear the whole . . . fairy tale, Mom, but this is separate. I saw your face when you said you'd always dreamed of going to Alaska. Let us take you.'

Mom got up and went to stare out at the winter garden, which was now in full vibrant bloom. 'When do we leave?'

The next morning, Nina stood at the fence line, camera in hand, watching workers stream onto the property. Up and down the rows of trees, workers climbed ladders, hand-wrapping the fledging apples to protect them from bugs and the elements.

She was just about to go back into the house when a blue car pulled up in front of the garage. The driver's door opened. All Nina saw was a shock of grey-threaded black hair, and she started to run.

'Danny,' she cried, throwing herself into his arms.

'You're not an easy woman to track down, Nina Whitson.'

Smiling, she took him by the hand. 'Let me show you around the place.'

With an unexpected pride, she showed him around the orchard her father had loved. Now and then she shared memories from her past; mostly she told him about the story her mother was telling.

Finally, she said, 'Why are you here?'

He smiled. 'First things first, love. Where's your bedroom?'

Afterwards, Danny rolled over onto one elbow and looked down at her. He was smiling, but there was something pinched in it. 'You asked why I was here.'

'Give a girl a chance to breathe, won't you?'

'You're breathing,' he said quietly.

'OK,' she forced herself to say. 'Why are you here?'

'I was in Atlanta. From there, this was nothin'.'

'Atlanta?' she said, but she knew what was in Atlanta.

'CNN. They've offered me my own show. In-depth world stories.' He smiled. 'Neens, I've been gallivanting for decades. My bum leg hurts all the time, and I'm tired of keeping up with twenty-year-olds. Mostly, I'm tired of being alone so much.'

'Congratulations,' she said woodenly.

'Marry me,' he said, and his earnestness made her want to cry.

'If I said yes,' she said, 'Would you forget CNN and stay in Africa with me? Or maybe go to the Middle East, or Malaysia?'

'We've done all that, love.'

'And what would I do in Atlanta? Learn to make the perfect peach pie and welcome you home with a glass of Scotch?'

'Come on, Neens. I know who you are.'

'Do you?' Nina felt as if she were falling suddenly. Her eyes stung. How could she say yes . . . How could she say no? She loved this man. But the rest of it? Settling down? The only life she'd ever wanted was the one she had now.

'Come to Atlanta with me for the weekend. We'll talk to people, see what's available for you. Come on, love, give us a chance.'

'I'm going to Alaska with Mom and Meredith.'

'I'll have you back in time. I swear it.'

'But . . . the fairy tale . . . I can't just leave the story. Maybe in two weeks, when we're done . . .'

Danny pulled away from her. 'There will always be another story to follow, won't there, Neens?'

'That's not fair. This is my family history, the promise I made to my dad. You can't ask me to give that up.'

'Is that what I asked?'

'You know what I mean.'

''Cause I thought I proposed marriage and didn't get an answer.'

'Give me more time.'

He leaned down and kissed her, slow and soft. And when he made love to her again, she learned something she hadn't known: sex could mean many things; one of them was goodbye.

CHAPTER TEN

IT WAS ONE OF THOSE RARE crystal-blue days in Seattle where Mt Rainier dominated the city skyline. The waterfront was empty this early in the season. Meredith stared up at the giant cruise ship docked at Pier 66. Dozens of passengers lined up for departure.

'You guys ready?' Nina asked, flinging her backpack over one shoulder.

'I don't know how you travel so light,' Meredith said, lugging her suitcase. As they reached the gangplank, Mom stopped.

Meredith almost ran into her. 'Mom? Are you OK?'

Mom tightened her coat round her and stared up at the ship.

Nina touched Mom's shoulder. 'You crossed the Atlantic by boat, didn't you?' she said gently.

Meredith frowned. Ridiculously, it pissed her off that it was Nina who'd figured that out. Just like it was Nina who'd figured out that Bepa meant Vera and that a trip to Alaska would take them to Vasily Adamovich.

'With your father,' Mom said. 'I don't remember much of it except this. Boarding. Leaving.'

'You were sick,' Meredith said.

Mom looked surprised. 'Yes.'

'Why?' Nina asked. 'What was wrong with you?'

'Not now, Nina,' Mom said. 'Let us go and find our rooms.'

At the top of the gangplank, a uniformed man led them to their side-by-side cabins. 'You have places at the early sitting for dinner. We're serving cocktails on the bow as we pull out of port.'

'Cocktails?' Nina said. 'We're in. Let's go, ladies.'

'I will meet you there,' Mom said. 'I need to get organised.'

'OK,' Nina said. 'Don't wait too long. We need to celebrate.'

Meredith followed Nina to the bow of the ship. Hundreds of people had gathered on deck, and a mariachi band was playing. Uniformed waiters carried umbrella-topped drinks on silver trays.

Meredith leaned against the railing and sipped her drink. 'Are you ever going to tell me about Danny? He is totally hot, by the way, and he flew out to see you. Why didn't he stick around?'

Behind them, the ship's horn honked. People all around them clapped and cheered as the giant ship pulled away from the dock.

'He wants me to move to Atlanta and settle down.'

'You don't sound very happy about that.'

'I live for my career. Why can't we just say we'll keep loving each other and travel until we need wheelchairs?'

Even a month ago Meredith would have given Nina platitudes, but she had learned a thing or two. Every choice changed the road you were on. 'I admire that about you, Neens. You have a passion and you follow it. No one can tell you what's right for you.'

'If you had it to do over again, would you still choose Jeff?'

Meredith's answer came effortlessly. 'I'd marry him again.'

Nina put an arm round her sister. 'Yeah,' she said, 'but you still think you don't know what you want.'

'I hate you,' Meredith said.

Nina squeezed her shoulder. 'No, you don't. You love me.'

Meredith smiled. 'I guess I do.'

The hostess led them to a table by a massive window. Through the glass were miles of empty ocean, the waves tipped in light from a fading sun. When their waiter showed up, Meredith ordered a strawberry daiquiri, Mom ordered vodka and a glass of wine, and Nina said she'd have vodka and a margarita on the rocks.

'To us,' Nina said when the drinks arrived. 'To Meredith, Nina and Anya Whitson. Together for maybe the first time.'

Mom flinched and didn't look at them. Meredith noticed a tiny frown gather at the edges of her mouth when she looked out at the sea. She ate her meal, followed the conversation, added her three new answers, but after dessert, she stood almost immediately.

'I am going back to my room,' she said. 'Will you join me?'

Nina was on her feet in an instant, but Meredith was slower to respond. 'Are you sure, Mom? Maybe you should rest tonight.'

'Thank you,' her mother said. 'But no. Come.'

Meredith and Nina had to rush along behind her through the busy passageways. As expected, Mom's suite was as neat as a pin. The only unexpected thing was the bottle of wine and three glasses on the coffee table. She poured herself a glass, then went to a club chair in the corner, sat down, and put a blanket over her lap.

Meredith sat in the loveseat opposite her.

'Before you turn out the lights, Mom,' Nina said, 'I have something to show you.' She pulled a photograph out of her pocket.

Mom drew in a sharp breath. 'You went through my things?'

'We know the fairy tale takes place in Leningrad and that some of it is real. Who is Vera?' Nina asked. 'Who are these children?'

Mom shook her head. 'Do not ask me.'

'We just want to know you,' Meredith said gently.

Mom stared at the photograph. The room went still. 'You are right. This is no fairy tale. But if you want to hear the rest of it, you will allow me to tell the story in the only way I can.'

Nina sat down by Meredith, holding her hand. 'OK.'

'OK, then.' Mom leaned back in the seat. For once, the lights were on as she started to speak: *Vera fell in love with Sasha on that day in the Summer Garden, and for her, this will never change. Vera is passionately in love with her husband, and when their first child is born, it seems like a miracle. Anastasia, they name her. When Leo is born the next year, Vera cannot imagine being happier, even though it is a bad time in the Soviet Union because of Stalin's evil. People are disappearing and dying. Vera and Olga still cannot safely say their father's name. But in June of 1941, it is impossible to worry, or so it seems to Vera as she tends their garden on the outskirts of the city. She still works in the library while Sasha studies at university. They become good Soviets, or at least quiet ones. Sasha is a year away from finishing his degree, and he hopes to find a teaching position at a university.*

"Mama, look!" Leo calls out to her, holding up a tiny orange carrot. Vera knows she should chastise him, but his smile is so infectious that she is lost. At four, he has his father's golden curls. "Put the carrot back, Leo. It still needs time to grow."

"I told him not to pull it up," says five-year-old Anya, who is as serious as her brother is joyous.

"And you were right." Vera struggles not to smile. Though she is only twenty-two, the children have turned her into an adult; it is only when she and Sasha are alone that they are really still young.

It is late afternoon when they return to Leningrad, and the streets are crowded with people shouting. As Vera reaches the Fontanka bridge, she hears through a speaker: "Citizens, at four o'clock this morning, without declaration of war, German troops attacked our country . . ."

All Vera can think is that she must get home. The children are crying long before she gets back to their new apartment near the Moika embankment. Though she is a mother, she is a daughter, too, and a wife, and it is her mother and husband whom she wants to see now.

In the apartment, no lights are on. Mama and Olga are at the windows, covering them in newsprint and tape. Mama stumbles back, saying, "Thank God," and takes her in her arms.

Vera can see Olga has been crying; her freckled cheeks are tracked in tears, and her strawberry-blonde hair is a mess.

"Vera," Mama says briskly. "You take Olga and go to the store. Buy whatever you can that will last. Anything. I will run to the bank and get all our money." She kneels in front of Leo and Anya. "You will stay here alone and wait for us to return."

The three of them leave the apartment, locking the door behind them. From the other side, there is crying almost immediately.

Vera looks at her mother. "I cannot just leave them locked in—"

"From now on, you will do many unimaginable things," her mother says tiredly. "Now let us go before it is too late."

Outside, the sky is blue and lilacs scent the air. It seems impossible that war hangs over Leningrad on a day like this . . . until they come to the bank, where people crowd at the closed door waving their passbooks and screaming; women are crying.

"We are too late already," Mama says.

"What is happening?" Olga pulls nervously at her hair.

"The banks are closed. Too many people tried to take out their money." Mama leads them to the grocer's. Shelves are practically empty. Already prices are tripling.

Vera has trouble making sense of this. War has just been announced, and yet the supplies and banks are gone already and the people around her looked dazed and desperate.

"We have been here before," Mama says simply.

In the store, they have only enough money for buckwheat flour, dried lentils and lard. Carrying their meagre supplies through the crowded streets, they make it to the apartment at just past six.

Her children are crying, and it breaks Vera's heart. She scoops them up, thinking never again will she follow her mother's advice about this one thing: she will never leave her children alone again.

"Where is Papa?" she asks. Anya shrugs her small shoulders. He should have been home by now.

"I'm sure he's fine," her mother says. "It will be difficult to get through the streets."

Finally, at eight o'clock, he comes in, his hair damp with sweat.

"Verushka," he says, pulling her into his arms. "The trolleys were full. I ran all the way here. Are you OK?"

"Now we are," she says.

That night, while her grandmother snores in the hot darkness, Vera sits up in her bed. In the shadowy darkness, their apartment seems even smaller. With three narrow beds in the living area and the children's cots in the kitchen, there is barely room to walk.

Not far away, Mama and Olga are awake, too, sitting up in their bed. Beside Vera, Sasha is as silent as she's ever seen him.

"I don't know what we're supposed to do," Olga says. "Maybe the Germans will save us. Comrade Stalin—"

"Shhh," Mama says sharply, glancing at her sleeping mother. "Tomorrow we will go to work, and the next day, and the next. Now we must go to sleep. Here, Olga, roll over. I will hold you."

Vera hears them settle down to sleep. She stretches out beside her husband, tries to feel safe in his arms. She leans forwards to kiss him, and when his lips are on hers, there is nothing else, but then he draws back. "You will have to be strong, Verushka."

"We will be strong," she says, holding him in her arms.

"You know I have to go," he says. "I am a university student and poet. And you are the daughter of a criminal of the state."

"You cannot go. I won't let you."

"It is done," he says. "I joined the People's Volunteers. We will kick the Germans' asses in no time and I will be home."

"Promise you'll come back to me," she says.

"I promise," he says easily.

Vera knows some promises are pointless to ask for and useless to receive. "It is a promise I will hold you to, Aleksandr Andreiovich."

In the morning, she wakens early. In the quiet darkness, she finds her one photograph of them, taken on the day of their wedding.

She looks down at their bright and smiling faces. Tears blur the image as she takes it out of the frame and folds it in half and then in half again. She tucks it in the pocket of his coat.

She hears footsteps behind her, feels his hands on her shoulders. "I love you, Verushka," he says, kissing the side of her face.

She is glad he is behind her. She is not sure she has the strength to look him in the eyes when she says, "I love you, too, Sasha."

In no time at all, he is gone.

Vera and Olga are lucky in their jobs in the Hermitage Museum and the Leningrad Public Library. Now both of them crate up masterpieces of art and literature so the history of the Soviet State will never be lost. When work is over, Vera walks to the Summer Garden to remember the day she met Sasha, but it is getting harder to remember. Already the Bronze Horseman is covered in sandbags. Everywhere people are building air-raid shelters.

Today Vera stops by the bank and withdraws her 200 roubles allowed for the month. She stands in line for bread and a tin of cheese. When she finally gets home, at eight o'clock, she finds Anya and Leo playing war in the living room.

"Mama!" Leo cries when he sees her. His face breaks into a gummy grin, and he throws himself into her arms.

"How are my babies? What did you two do in school today?"

"I am too old for baby school," Anya informs her.

Vera pats her daughter's head and goes to the kitchen. She is putting water on to boil when Olga comes into the apartment.

"Have you heard?" she says breathlessly, then lowers her voice. "The children of Leningrad, they're being evacuated."

On the morning of the evacuation, Vera wakens feeling sick. She cannot do it, cannot put her babies on a train bound for somewhere far away. She lies in bed staring up at the water-stained ceiling.

"Vera?" Mama says from the other bed.

Vera turns onto her side.

"You cannot think it," Mama says, and Vera wonders if one day she will know what her children are thinking before they do.

"How can I not?" Vera says. How can she blindly do this thing?

"Comrade Stalin knows where our children can go so they will be safe. And all workers' children must go. That is all there is."

"What if I don't see them again?"

Mama peels back the cover and pads quietly across the small space between them. She pulls Vera into her arms, stroking her black hair as she used to when Vera was young. "We women make choices for others, not for ourselves, and bear what we must for our children. Your job is to hide that your heart is breaking and do what they need you to do."

Vera hears Leo in the kitchen, no doubt talking to the stuffed rabbit that is his best friend. She thinks, It has begun. Her mother whispers words, but she cannot understand them. The roar in her head is too loud. She eases out from bed, dressed in a skirt and a sweater. They are all sleeping in their clothes now. An air raid can come at any time.

Olga whines that she is still sleepy; her grandmother blows her nose; Anya informs everyone that she is hungry. It is all so ordinary. Vera swallows the lump in her throat. Leo, her lion, is laughing now, telling his poor, one-eyed tattered rabbit that they will feed the swans in the Summer Garden today.

"It is war," Anya says, looking impossibly superior.

"Actually," Vera says, "we are going on a walk." She feels physically ill, but she picks up their coats. Last night she stayed up late, sewing money and letters into the lining of her children's coats.

Leo is on his feet in an instant, gleefully clapping his hands, saying, "Walk!" over and over. Even Anya is smiling. In only five days, since the announcement of war, their old life has disappeared.

Breakfast passes in quiet glances and lowered gazes. At the end of the meal, Vera's grandmother rises. When she looks at Vera, her eyes fill with tears and she turns away. "Come, Zoya," she says in a harsh voice. "It does not look good to be late."

Biting her lip, Vera's mother goes to her grandchildren and kneels down, taking them in her arms and holding them.

"Don't cry, Baba," Leo says. "You can walk with us tomorrow."

Across the room, Olga bursts into tears. "I am going now, Mama."

Mama hands Vera 100 roubles. "It is all we have left."

Vera nods and hugs her one last time. "Let's go, children."

Smiling too brightly, Vera leads her children to a part of the city where they have never been. Inside the building they enter, there is pandemonium. Queues snake away from desks chaotic with paperwork, manned by Party members with dour faces.

Vera knows they should go directly into the first queue, but suddenly she takes her children to a corner and kneels down. "Do you remember when Papa went off to join the People's Volunteers, he told us we would all have to be strong?"

"I'm strong," Leo says, showing off a pudgy pink fist.

"Yes," Anya says, suspicious now. She is looking at the coats in Vera's arms and the suitcase she has brought from home.

Vera takes the heavy red woollen coat and puts it on her, buttoning it up. "It is too hot for this, Mama," Anya whines, wiggling.

"You're going on a trip," Vera says evenly. "Just for a week or two, but you might need your coat. And here in this suitcase I have packed a few clothes and some food. Just in case."

"You are not wearing a coat," Anya says, frowning.

"I have to work and stay at home, but you will be home before you know it, and I'll be waiting for you. When you get back—"

"No," Anya says firmly. "I don't want to go without you."

"I don't want to," Leo wails.

"We have no choice. War is coming, and our great comrade Stalin wants children to be safe. You're going to take a short train ride until our Red Army triumphs, then come home to Papa and me."

"You want us to go?" Anya asks, her blue eyes filling with tears.

No, Vera thinks, even as she nods. "I need you to take care of your brother," she says. "OK? Can you be strong for me?"

"Yes, Mama," Anya says.

For the next five hours, they stand in one queue after another. The children are processed and sorted and sent to other lines. By the end of the afternoon, the evacuation centre is overrun with children. Finally the train arrives. At first, no one wants to move, but when the metal wheels scream, they run like a herd, mothers trying to get their babies seats on the train that will save them.

Party members patrol like sharks, forcing mothers and children apart. Leo sobs, clutching Vera. Anya cries silently.

"Stay together. Do not give your food to anyone else. There is money sewn into your pockets, and my name and address."

"Where are we going?" Anya tries to be grown up; it is heartbreaking in one so young. At five, she should be playing with dolls.

"To a summer park near the Luga river. You will be safe there, Anya. And in no time, I will come for you."

"Get on board," a comrade yells out. "The train is leaving."

But Vera cannot do it. She cannot put her children on the train alone. She pretends to be a nonessential worker who has lost her paperwork in the crush, and goes with them. She will see they are safe and then return to the library.

They have been travelling only a few hours when the train slows. Gunfire erupts around them. There is the whine of an airplane engine, and the explosions start. A Party woman makes her way through the car. "Everyone off the train!"

The Germans are here with their tanks and their guns.

Vera grabs her children and runs with the crowd. Bombs drop, and all is smoke and screaming. They cram inside a barn. A bomb hits close. "We need to leave," Vera says. "If a bomb hits us—"

"Citizen," someone says, "The Party wants us here."

"Yes, but I am taking my children out of here."

Vera and her children make their way out of the barn. The countryside is grey with smoke. A building explodes. Vera hefts Leo in her arms, holds on to Anya, and begins the long walk home.

In the years to come, she forgets the hardships of that journey, how her children's feet bled, how their food ran out, how they listened each night for air raids. By the time she stumbles into her mother's arms, she is battered and bloody. But none of this matters.

What matters is her wonderful white city. The Germans are moving toward Leningrad. Hitler has vowed to wipe it off the map.

Vera knows what she must do. Tomorrow, very early, she will go south again to protect all she loves. It is every citizen's job.

"*We have to stop them at Luga,*" *she says to her mother, whose face crumples in understanding.* "*They need workers there.*"

Mama does not ask why or how or why you? All of those answers are clear. It is only the first full week of war, and already Leningrad is becoming a city of women. Every man between fourteen and sixty has gone to fight. Now the girls are going off to war, too. "*I will take care of the children,*" *is all her mother says, but Vera can hear* You come back to us *as clearly as if it had been spoken aloud.*

"*I won't be gone long,*" *Vera promises.* "*All will be fine.*"

Mama only nods. Both of them want to believe.'

'I think that is enough for tonight,' Mom said.

Moving almost cautiously, Meredith crossed the small carpeted space and stood beside her. 'You don't look as tired tonight.'

'Acceptance,' Mom said, staring down at her own hands.

Nina moved in beside her sister. 'What do you mean by that?'

'You were right, Nina. Your father made me promise to tell you this story. I did not want to. And . . . fighting a thing tires you out.'

'Is that why you went so . . . crazy after Dad died?' Nina asked. 'Because you were ignoring his wishes?'

Mom gave a little shrug. 'That is perhaps one of the reasons.'

'OK,' Meredith said. 'We'll come and get you in the morning.'

'I do not want—'

'We do,' Nina said. 'Tomorrow morning the three of us are going to be together. You both know I won't change my mind.'

'She's right,' Meredith said, smiling. 'She's a bitch when she doesn't get her way.'

'How would we know?' Mom said.

'Was that a joke?' Nina said, grinning. 'Come on, sis,' she said, slinging an arm round Meredith. They left for their own room.

Their room was surprisingly spacious. There was a sitting area—a loveseat that made into a bed—a coffee table, a television and two twin beds. A pair of sliding doors led to their private verandah.

'Dibs on the bathroom,' Meredith said, and Nina couldn't help laughing. It was a sentence from their youth. When Meredith came out in flannel pajamas, Nina took her turn. For the first time in years, she and her sister ended up in side-by-side twin beds.

Nina pulled the covers up. 'The picture,' she said after a moment. 'It's Anya and Leo, right?'

'Probably.'

Nina turned to look at her sister. The question that had been with them all night was gathering weight and mass. 'If Mom really is Vera,' she said slowly, 'what happened to her children?'

Nina had been all over the world, but rarely had she seen scenery to rival the magnificence of the Inside Passage. The water was a deep blue, and there were islands everywhere—rough, forested hillocks. Behind it all were rugged snow-draped mountains.

She had come out early this morning and been rewarded with breathtaking shots of dawn breaking across the water. She finally stopped shooting at about seven. By then, her hands were frozen.

'Would you like some hot chocolate, ma'am?'

Nina turned to find a deck steward holding a tray of hot chocolate. Before wrapping her fingers round a warm cup, Nina scooped a blanket from a deck chair and swung it round her shoulders, and stared out at a trio of dolphins jumping alongside the bow.

Meredith came up beside her. 'That's a sign of good luck.'

Nina opened one arm, and let Meredith snuggle beside her, under the blanket. 'It's cold as hell out here, but beautiful.'

'You were restless last night,' Meredith said, reaching for Nina's hot chocolate. 'Why were you tossing and turning?'

'I found him.'

Meredith turned to her. 'What do you mean, you "found him"?'

'Dr Adamovich. He's in a nursing home on Franklin Street in Juneau. I had my editor track him down.'

Meredith bit down on her lip and looked out at the water. 'What are we supposed to do? Can we just show up at his door?'

'I didn't really think it through. I know. I know. Big surprise. I just got so amped when I found him. I know he'll have answers for us.'

'He wrote to *her*. I don't think we can tell her. She's too fragile.'

'That's why I wasn't sleeping. We can't tell her we've been researching her life, and we can't just show up at his nursing home.'

'We will go and see the professor.'

Nina gasped at the sound of her mother's voice and turned round.

'Mom,' Meredith stammered.

'You heard it all?' Nina said, her voice uneven.

'I heard enough,' Mom said. 'It is the professor from Alaska, yes? The one who wrote to me years ago?'

Nina nodded. She pulled the blanket off and wrapped it round her mother's shoulders. Mom held the blanket closed and sat down in a deck chair. Nina and Meredith took chairs on either side.

'I'm sorry,' Nina said. 'I should have told you at the beginning.'

'You thought I would not agree to the trip.'

'Yes. It's just wanting to get to know you. How can I—how can *we*—not want answers? You are part of who we are.'

'It is time, I suppose,' Mom said quietly. 'Your father thought we should talk. It's probably why he kept the letter all these years.'

'What does the professor want to talk about?' Meredith asked.

'Leningrad,' Mom said. 'For years the government hid what happened. We Soviets are always so afraid, and I was afraid to talk about it. But I am eighty-one years old tomorrow. Why be afraid?'

'Tomorrow is your birthday?' they said at once.

Mom almost smiled. 'It was easier to hide everything. Yes, tomorrow is my birthday. I will see this professor with you, but you should know now: you will be sorry you began all of this.'

'Why say that?' Meredith asked. 'How could we be sorry?'

It was a long moment before Mom answered. 'You will.'

Ketchikan was a town that had been built on salmon: catching it, salting it, processing it. The rain gauge attested to the dampness of the climate.

They walked towards Creek Street. Here, the old red-light district had been transformed into a boardwalk of shops and restaurants. They found a cosy little diner and sat down at a knotty pine table by the window. They ordered three halibut and chips and iced tea.

As they ate, they talked about the gold nugget jewellery in the shopwindows, the first nation's tribal art and the bald eagle they'd seen on a totem pole. It was a conversation that could have been had by any family on vacation, but to Nina it felt almost magical. As her mother spoke about things that interested her, she seemed to soften. It was as if every ordinary word loosened something in her.

The waitress cleared their plates, but instead of placing the bill on the table, she set a piece of birthday cake in front of Mom.

'Happy birthday, Mom,' Meredith and Nina said together.

Mom stared down at the lit candle.

'We always wanted to have a birthday party for you,' Meredith said. She reached out and put her hand on Mom's.

'I have made so many mistakes,' Mom said softly.

'Everyone makes mistakes,' Meredith said.

'No. I . . . I didn't mean to be that way . . . I was just trying . . . I couldn't look at you, I was so ashamed.'

'You're looking at us now,' Nina said, although it wasn't strictly true. Mom was still staring at the candle as if it held some secret answer to a long-posed question. 'You want to tell us your story, don't you?'

Mom shook her head.

'You're Vera,' Nina said quietly.

'No,' Mom said, 'that girl is not who I am.'

'But she's who you were,' Nina said.

'You are a dog with a bone, Nina.' Mom sighed. 'Yes. Long ago I was Veronika Petrovna Marchenko. This is my first birthday party with my daughters. There will be time later for the rest of it.'

CHAPTER ELEVEN

AT DINNER, THEY TALKED about ordinary things. They drank wine and toasted Mom's eighty-first birthday. After a delicious meal, they wandered through the giant ship and found their way to a theatre, where a man in a sequined jumpsuit was performing magic. Mom clapped at each new trick, smiling like a kid.

When the show was over, they walked back to their staterooms, strangely silent. Something had changed today, but Meredith didn't know quite what. All she knew was that she had lost the ability to stay separate now. For more than twenty-five years, she'd kept up her side of the wall, and in that distance, she'd found at least a facsimile of strength. Now she had almost none of that left.

At their door, Nina stopped. 'I had a great day. Happy birthday.' She moved forward awkwardly and pulled Mom into an embrace.

Meredith wanted to follow suit, but when she looked in her mother's eyes, she felt too vulnerable. 'I know you must be tired,' she said. 'We should go to bed. Tomorrow we cruise Glacier Bay.'

Mom nodded. 'Thank you for my birthday,' she said so softly they almost couldn't hear, and then she went into her room. Nina unlocked their door. 'Dibs on the bathtub,' she said. Meredith barely noticed. She felt poised on the brink of something. She grabbed a blanket and went to their deck. Here and there on the coastline, lights shone, marking peoples' lives.

'I suppose that is you, Meredith.' She was startled by her mother's voice, coming from the darkness of the veranda to her right.

'Hey, Mom,' she said. They were alike in that way, she and her mom. When they were troubled, both wanted to be outside and alone.

'You are thinking about your marriage,' Mom said.

Meredith sighed. 'I don't suppose you have any advice for me.'

'To lose love is a terrible thing,' Mom said softly. 'But to turn away from it is unbearable. Will you spend the rest of your life replaying it in your head? Wondering if you walked away too easily? Or if you'll ever love anyone that deeply again?'

It was like listening to melted pain. 'You know about loss.'

'We all do.'

'When I first fell in love with Jeff, I couldn't stand to be away from him. And then I . . . could. We got married so young.'

'Young has nothing to do with love.'

'I stopped being happy. I don't even know why or when.'

'I remember when you were always smiling. Back when you opened the gift shop. Maybe you never should have taken over the business.'

Meredith was too surprised to do more than nod. She hadn't thought her mother ever noticed her. 'It meant so much to Dad.'

'It did.'

'I made the mistake of living for him, the orchard and my kids. Now they're so busy with their own lives they hardly ever call.'

'Jillian and Maddy flew away because you gave them wings and taught them to fly.'

'I wish I had wings,' Meredith said quietly.

'This is my fault,' Mom said, standing up.

'Why?' Meredith said, moving closer to the rail that separated the two decks. She felt her mother come towards her until suddenly they were standing face to face. Finally, she could see Mom's eyes.

'I am telling my story to explain.'

'When it's over, will I know what I did that was so wrong?'

Her mother's face seemed to crumple. 'You will know, when it is all done, that you are not the one who did anything wrong. Now come inside. I will tell you about the Luga line tonight.'

Meredith followed Nina into their mother's room and took a seat beside her sister on the loveseat. Mom leaned back into the pillows of her bed.

'*Vera cannot believe that she must leave her children again,*' she said softly. '*But with all the men away, fighting, they must defend against the Germans. And so she kisses her babies goodbye for the second time in a week. They are four and five, too young to be without their mother, but war changes everything, and just as her mother had predicted, Vera is doing what would have been unimaginable even a few months ago.*

In no time at all, she and Olga are crammed together in the back of a transport truck surrounded by dozens of other girls their age. There is not one of them smiling.

When they reach the Luga line, there are girls and women as far as the eye can see, stabbing at the ground with pickaxes and shovels. Their faces are streaked with dirt, and their dresses are ruined. But they are Russians—Soviets—and no one pauses or complains.

As the comrade tells Vera what to do, Olga moves in close, takes her hand. It is their last moment of peace. After that, they take up pickaxes and trudge to the line. Dropping into the trench, they hack at the earth. Day after day, they dig.

At night, they huddle in a barn with the other girls. The whole place smells of dust and mud and sweat and smoke.

On their seventh night, Olga says, "Look at my hands. I'm bleeding." She says it with a kind of confused wonder, as if the blood is not hers. Vera sees the broken blisters on her palm.

"You have to keep your hands wrapped. I told you this."

"They were watching me today. Comrades Slotkov and Pritkin. I know they know about Papa. I could not stop to adjust the wraps."

Vera frowns. She has heard this from her sister before, but now she recognises that something is wrong. Olga does not make eye contact with her.

Outside, the alarm blares. The sound of aircraft builds, and fear in the barn becomes palpable. Girls move and lie flat. Bombs drop. Somewhere, someone is screaming. Olga flinches and methodically rips off blistered skin. Blood bubbles up from her palm.

"Don't do that," Vera says, pulling her sister's hand away.

Vera has been thinking this change in Olga is sleep deprivation and hunger, but now she sees the speck of craziness in her sister's eyes. Olga is unravelling.

"Come here, Olgushka," Vera says, pulling her sister into her arms. They crawl into their bed of hay.

Olga's voice is dreamy-sounding. "Tell me a story, Vera. About princesses and boys who bring you roses."

Vera is weary to the bone, but she strokes her sister's dirty matted hair and uses the only thing she has—her voice—to soothe their spirits. "The Snow Kingdom is a magical walled city, where night never falls and white doves nest on telephone lines . . ." When Olga's eyes grow heavy, she kisses her. "Sleep now."

"Will we see Mama tomorrow?" Olga asks sleepily.

"Not tomorrow, no," Vera says, tightening her hold. "But soon."

The weeks go by. If not for the Germans bombing everything in sight, the birds would be singing here, the pine trees would be green instead of black. As it is, the trench is a huge slash in the earth. Girls crawl around it; soldiers run between here and the front. If this line breaks, Leningrad will fall. This they believe, so they keep digging, no matter that bombs are as present as sunlight.

Vera tries not to think about anything except the serving spoon in her hand. The pickaxe broke last week. All day long, stab, twist, pull. Until her shoulder aches and her neck hurts and her blistered palms burn. Yet all she can worry about is Olga. Her sister digs without complaint, but when the bombs start, Olga just stands staring up at the planes.

Overhead, German planes fill the sky, their engines droning while the alarm rings out over the line. Girls scurry out of the trench. They are screaming, pushing each other. Vera yells for her sister and starts to move. "Come on—!"

"It sounds like Mama's sewing machine." Olga is still standing.

Vera looks back. "Run!" she yells at the moment the bomb hits.

Olga is flung like a ragdoll. She falls in a broken heap. Vera is screaming, crawling to where Olga lies beneath a pile of rubble.

Blood gushes from the side of her mouth and slides through the mud on her cheek. "Vera." She shudders. "I forgot to get down."

Vera holds her sister, trying to keep her alive by loving her so much. "I love you, Olga. Don't leave me. Please . . ."

Olga smiles and coughs. Blood gushes from her nose and mixes with dirt. And she is gone.

In August, Vera is released from work on the line. She is one of thousands of dazed women walking in silent groups for home. When she finally makes it to Leningrad, everywhere she looks are mounds of broken cement—dragon's teeth, they are called—meant to bar the tanks. Huge iron beams criss-cross the city boundaries, and tired soldiers move in marching columns through the streets.

Finally, Vera stands on her own street. Step by step she is at her own front door and in her home again. And there is her mama, at the stove in a faded dress. At Vera's entrance, she turns. Her smile is heartbreaking; worse is the way it fades away.

"Mama!" Leo screams. Anya is beside him in an instant, and they throw themselves into Vera's arms.

They smell so good, so pure . . . Leo's cheeks are as soft and sweet as a ripe plum, and Vera could eat him up. She holds them too long, too tightly, unaware that she has begun to shake and to cry. Slowly releasing them, she stares across the kitchen at her mother. In that look, Vera feels her childhood leave her at last.

"Where's Aunt Olga?" Leo asks, looking past her.

"Olga is gone," Mama says, a tremble in her voice. "She is a hero of the *state, our Olga. That is how we must think of her." She takes Vera in her arms, holding her so hard that neither can breathe. There is only silence between them. In that silence, memories pass back and forth like dye in water, and Vera understands.*

They will not speak of Olga again, not for a long time.

"You need a bath," Mama says after a time. "And those bandages on your hands need changing, so come along."

Those *first days back in Leningrad seem like a dream to Vera. During the day, she works with other library employees, packing up the most valuable books for transport. At the end of her shift, she trudges through the streets and gets into the first queue she finds.*

She doesn't know what they are selling at this market, and she doesn't care. She stands in line for hours. When she reaches the front, only jars of pickles are left. She buys the three she can afford.

In the apartment, she finds her mother and grandmother sitting at the kitchen table, passing a cigarette back and forth.

Saying nothing—they all say little these days—she goes past them to the children's beds. Leaning down, she kisses their tender cheeks. Exhausted and hungry, she goes back into the kitchen. Mama has put out a plate of cold kasha for her.

"Winter is coming," Mama says. "We need food and a burzhuika. I will go to the marketplace tomorrow."

"What will you trade?"

"My wedding ring," Mama says.

The city becomes one long line. Rations are being cut, and often there is no food to be had. Vera wakes at four in the morning to stand in line for bread, and after work, she walks miles to the outskirts of town, bartering with peasants—a litre of vodka for a bag of potatoes, an outgrown pair of valenki for a pound of lard.

It is not safe, and she knows it, but this search for food is all there is. Vera keeps her precious bag of potatoes hidden inside her dress. She is less than a mile from the apartment when the air-raid alarm goes off. Before she can run for a trench, something explodes. One building after another is destroyed. And then . . . silence.

Vera runs for home. Her building is intact. But only half of the building next door remains; the other is a pile of smoking rubble. Her family is in their basement, and when the all-clear sounds, they go back upstairs and put the children in bed.

It is only the beginning. The next day, Vera and her mother find a burzhuika at the market, where Mama's gold ring is not enough; she opens her coat and hands over a large jar of sugar. The stove is a small, ugly cast-iron thing that they drag home.

"That was a lot of sugar," Vera says quietly as Mama walks by.

"Yes. Baba brought it to us. She is working late now at the Badaev warehouses," Mama says, coughing.

"Are you OK, Mama?"

"I am fine. It is just the dust in the air from the bombings."

Before Vera can think of what to say, the air-raid alarm sounds.

"Children!" she calls. "Come quickly." Vera grabs the coats from the wall and bundles her children up. Out to the hallway, down the stairs. The tiny basement is packed with people. In the distance, incendiary bombs fall like rain. When the all-clear finally sounds, the whole city seems to be in flames.

"We are safe," Vera says, smiling as brightly as she can.

"Will you tell us a story, Mama?" Leo says. Vera carries both her children back to the apartment and climbs into bed with them.

"There is a peasant girl," Vera says, trying to sound calm.

"Her name is Vera," Anya says, snuggling close.

"Her name is Vera. And she is a poor peasant girl. A nobody. But she doesn't know that yet . . ."

In the morning, Baba is still not back; she is one of the thousands who are never seen again after the bombings. The Badaev warehouses are burned; all of the city's food stores are gone.

September drips into October and disappears. Every day after work, Vera comes home to her cold apartment and sits down to a meal at six o'clock. Only it is not much of a meal any more. A potato if they are lucky, with some kasha, maybe. The children complain constantly, while Mama coughs quietly in the corner.

Once the snow starts to fall, it never stops. Pipes freeze. Trolleys come to a stop and remain stuck in the accumulating snow. There are no marching troops in the road any more, just poor bundled-up women like Vera, moving through the white landscape in search of anything resembling food.

Vera trudges on. She is so hungry it is difficult to keep moving. She tries not to think about the hours spent in line today and focuses on the sunflower oil and oil cakes she was able to get.

She puts one foot in front of the other and slowly makes her way.

The apartment is warm. She notices instantly that another chair is broken. It lies on its side, two legs missing. Leo is sprawled on the kitchen floor, playing with a pair of metal trucks. She sees the way his cheeks have caved in on themselves, the way his eyes seem too big for his face. He doesn't look like a baby boy at all.

"Did you get food?" he says.

"Did you?" Anya says, rising from her place on the bed.

"Oil cakes," Vera says.

Anya frowns. "They hurt my teeth."

Vera's heart actually hurts when she hears this. But oil cake is what they have. No matter it used to be fed to cattle and has more cellulose than flour. What matters is, you have something to eat.

She goes over to the fallen chair and breaks another leg off. Cracking it in two pieces, she feeds it into the burzhuika and puts water in a pot to boil. She will put yeast in it to fill their bellies. To Anya, she says, "Watch the water. How is Mama?"

Anya stands there. "Quiet," is all she says.

Vera nods. In the other room, her mother is in bed, wrapped up in blankets. Vera sits down at her bedside. "I got some oil cakes today. And a little sunflower oil."

"I am not hungry. Give mine to our babies."

It is what Mama says every night. At first, Vera argued, but then she started to see Anya's cheekbones and heard the way her son cried in his sleep for food. "I'll make you some tea."

"That would be nice," Mama says, letting her eyes drift shut.

Vera knows how hard her mother works to stay awake simply to watch her grandchildren. She hasn't been out of bed in weeks.

"There will be more food next week," Vera says. "I heard they're sending a transport across Lake Ladoga as soon as it freezes. Then we'll all be fine."

Mama pats Vera's hand and sighs quietly.

Every day that winter, Vera wakes thinking one of two things: It will get better today, or It will be over soon. She doesn't know how it is possible to believe this simultaneously, but there it is. Each morning, she reaches for her children, who are in bed with her. When she feels the beating of their hearts, she breathes again.

It takes courage to get out of bed. Even wearing every piece of clothing she owns beneath all their blankets, she isn't warm, and once out of bed, she will be freezing. While they sleep, water freezes in the kitchen. Their eyelashes stick to skin, sometimes so hard that blood is drawn when they open their eyes.

Still, she climbs out over her children, who moan in their sleep. Mama, on her other side, doesn't make a sound. In stockinged feet, Vera grabs the axe and hacks through the last of the bed that was her grandmother's. Then she starts a fire and puts water on to boil.

While she's waiting, she kneels in the kitchen, prises up a floorboard, and counts their stores. A bag of onions, half a bottle of sunflower oil, a nearly empty jar of honey, two jars of pickles, six potatoes and the last of the sugar. She has just measured out a small amount of tea when there is a knock at the door.

At first she hardly recognises the sound, it is so foreign. Since the air raids have stopped, there's very little coming together of people. But she moves to the door and turns the key.

He stands there like a stranger. Vera shakes her head. She has become hungry enough and sick enough to see ghosts.

"Verushka?" he says, frowning.

At the sound of his voice, she feels her legs give out. If this is dying, she wants to give in, and when his arms come round her, she is sure she is dead. No one has held her in so long.

"Verushka," he says again, and she hears the question in his voice, the worry. He doesn't know why she hasn't spoken.

She laughs. "Sasha," she says. "Am I dreaming you?"

"I'm here," he says. When he tries to kiss her, she draws back in shame. Hunger has made her breath terrible. But he won't let her pull away. He kisses her as he used to. When finally she can bear to let him go, she stares up at him.

His hair is shaved down to nothing, his cheekbones are more pronounced, and there is something new in his eyes—a sadness, she thinks—that will be a mark of their generation. "You didn't write."

"I wrote. Every week. There is no one to deliver the letters."

"Are you done? Are you back now?"

"Oh, Vera. No." He closes the door. "It's cold in here."

"And we're lucky. We have a burzhuika."

He opens his ragged coat. Hidden beneath it is half a ham, six sausage links, a jar of honey. Vera goes lightheaded at the sight.

He sets the food down on the table. Taking her hand, he walks to the bed in the archway and stares down at the sleeping children.

Tears come to his eyes, and she understands: they do not look like his babies any more. They look like children who are starving.

Anya rolls over in bed, bringing Leo with her. She opens her eyes. "Papa?" she says. She looks like a little fox, with her pointed chin and sunken cheeks. "Papa?" she says again, elbowing Leo.

"Quit hitting me," Leo whines.

"Are these my little mushrooms?" Sasha says.

Leo sits up. "Papa?"

Sasha scoops his children into his arms as if they weigh nothing. For the first time in months, their laughter fills the apartment. They fight to get his attention, squirming like puppies in his arms.

"I learned to make a fire, Papa—"

"I can cut wood—"

"Ham! You brought us ham!"

Vera sits down beside her mother, who smiles. "He's back," Mama says, struggling to sit up as Vera repositions her pillows. "Go spend the day with him. No lines. Just go." She coughs into a grey handkerchief. They both pretend not to see the bloody spots.

"I'll make you some sweet tea. And you will eat some ham."

Mama nods and closes her eyes again. "He is so proud of you, your papa," she says on a sigh.

Vera feels an unexpected tightness in her throat. She goes into the kitchen, where Leo's laughter warms her more than any burning bed ever could. She fries up ham and sliced onions. A feast.

They all sit on the mattress to eat as there are no chairs any more.

"I say we go to the park," Sasha says.

"It's all boarded up," Anya tells him. "No one plays there."

"We do," Sasha says, smiling as if this is all an ordinary day.

Outside, the snow is falling. A veil of white obscures the city. The sand-bagged Bronze Horseman is only visible in pieces. The frosted trees are strung with icicles. There are no wooden fences or railings left in the city, but no tree has been cut down for firewood.

The children drop onto their backs, making snow angels and giggling. Vera sits by Sasha on an iron bench. She takes his hand.

"They are making an ice road across Ladoga," he says at last, and she knows it is what he has come to tell her.

"I hear trucks keep falling through the ice."

"For now. But it will work. I will get you passes when it's safe."

She does not want to talk about any of this. Only food matters now, and heat. She wishes he would just hold her and kiss her. Maybe they will make love tonight, she thinks. But how could she? She is too weak to sit up sometimes.

"Vera," he says, making her look at him.

She blinks. "What?" She stares into his bright green eyes, and suddenly she is remembering the first time they met.

"You stay alive," he says.

She frowns, trying to listen carefully; then he starts to cry, and she understands. "I will," she says, crying now, too.

"And keep them well. I'll find you a way out. I promise. You just have to hang on a little while longer. Promise me." He shakes her. "Promise me. The three of you will make it to the end."

She licks her cracked, dry lips. "I will," she says, believing in it.

He kisses her. He tastes like sweet summer peaches, and when he draws back, she says, "It's your birthday tomorrow."

"Twenty-five," he says.

She leans against him; his arm comes round her. For a few hours, they are just a young family playing in the park. It is the best day of Vera's life, as impossible as that sounds. The memory of it is gold, and she walks home, holding his hand, feeling herself protect it. It is a light she will need in the months to come.

But when she gets home, she knows instantly something is wrong.

The apartment is dark and freezing. She hears her mother coughing, and she runs to her, yelling at Sasha to build a fire.

Her mother's breathing is noisy and strained. The flesh round her mouth is darkening. "Verushka," she whispers.

Or did she really speak? Vera doesn't know. "Mama," she says.

"I waited for Sasha," Mama says.

Vera wants to beg with her, to plead, to say that he is not back, he is only visiting, and that she needs her mother, but she—

I can't say anything.

All I can do is sit there, staring down at her, loving her so much.

"I love you," Mama says softly. "Never forget that."

"How could I?"

Mama struggles to lean forwards. The effort is terrible to watch, and I take her in my arms. She's like a stick doll now. Her head lolls back.

"I love you, Mama," I say. It is not enough, those three little words that suddenly mean goodbye. But I can't say anything more.

I hold her close, and when I look down, she is gone.

CHAPTER TWELVE

THE SILENCE WAS SO THICK and grey Meredith expected to taste ash. She looked at her mother, still in bed with the covers pulled up to her chin, as if a bit of wool could somehow protect her.

'Are you OK, Mom?' Nina said, getting up.

'How could I be?'

Meredith got up, too. She took her sister's hand, and they walked to the bed. 'Your mother and your sister knew how hard you tried.'

'Do not do that,' Mom said. 'Make excuses for me.'

'It's not an excuse, Mom,' Meredith said as gently as she could. 'They must have known how much you loved them.'

'But *you* didn't,' Mom said, looking at both of them in turn.

Even a week ago Meredith might have lied. Now she said, 'No. I never thought you loved me.'

'All these years,' Nina said, 'we wondered what was wrong with us. We couldn't figure out how a woman who loved her husband could hate her own children.'

Mom flinched at the word *hate* and waved a hand. 'Go now.'

'It wasn't us, was it, Mom?' Nina said. 'You didn't hate your children. You hated yourself.'

At that, Mom crumbled. There was no other word for it. 'I tried not to love you girls,' she said quietly. 'Now go. Leave before you say something you'll wish you hadn't. Please.'

Meredith heard the way Mom's voice caught on *please* and shook. 'OK,' she said. 'We'll go.' She leaned down and kissed her mother's soft, pleated cheek. For the first time ever, she pulled her into an embrace and whispered, 'Good night, Mom.'

Sitka was one of the most charming of all Alaskan towns. With no dock long enough to accommodate large cruise ships, it waited patiently for its visitors to arrive in small launches. Nina took one picture after another. On this day of blue sky and golden sunlight, forested islands rose from the flat sapphire sea like a necklace of jagged jade pieces in front of snowy mountains.

On shore, the three of them stood gazing at the town laid out before them. From here, they could see a spire rising high into the sky, its top a three-tiered Russian cross. They walked up Harbour Drive, and there were bits and pieces of Sitka's Russian past everywhere—street names and store names and restaurant menus.

Mom said almost nothing as they passed one reminder of her past after another. But when they pushed through the doors of St. Michael's Church, she stumbled and would have fallen if both girls hadn't reached out to steady her. There were glittering Russian icons everywhere. Some were paintings on wooden boards; others were jewel-studded masterpieces on silver or gold. White arches separated the rooms, their surfaces decorated in gold scrollwork.

Mom stood there a long time. At first, she looked at everything, touching what she could. Finally she ended up at a small altar draped in heavy white silk adorned with crosses of gold thread. There were candles all around, and a pair of Bibles lay open.

'Do you want us to pray with you?' Nina asked.

'No.' Mom wiped her eyes, although Nina had seen no tears. Then she walked out of the church and up to the cemetery. It was on a small rise, studded with fragile-looking trees and bushes. The grave markers were overgrown with moss. It looked as if no one had been buried there in years, and yet Mom looked at every grave.

Nina took a picture of her in front of a mossy headstone knocked askew by some long-ago storm. The late spring breeze plucked at her bound white hair. She looked . . . ethereal almost, too pale and slim to be real, but the sadness in her blue eyes was as honest as any emotion Nina had ever seen. 'Who are you looking for?'

'No one,' Mom said, then added, 'Ghosts.'

They stood there a moment longer, then Mom straightened her shoulders and said, 'I am hungry. Let us find somewhere to eat.' She put her sunglasses on and coiled a scarf round her throat.

The three of them walked back down town, where they found a small restaurant on the water that promised *Sitka's Best Russian Food*. Inside, there were a dozen or so tables, most full of people. They didn't look like tourists, either. There were broad-shouldered men with beards, women in kerchiefs and dated floral dresses.

A woman greeted them with a bright smile. She was maybe fifty-five or sixty and had given up the diet fight long ago. Silvery curls framed her face. 'Hello there. Welcome to Stacey's.'

Nina glanced at the woman's name tag. 'Are you *the* Stacey?'

She laughed. 'Guilty.' Reaching for three menus, she led them to a table by the window. Outside, a fishing boat motored in to shore.

'What do you recommend, Stacey?' Meredith asked.

'I guess I'd have to say the meatballs. And we make our noodles from scratch. Although the borscht is to die for.'

'How about vodka?' Mom said.

Stacey looked down at her. 'Is that a Russian accent?'

'I have not lived there for a long time,' Mom said.

Stacey beamed. 'Well, you're our special guest. Don't you even look at the menu. I'll bring you something.' Stacey bustled away, paused briefly at a few tables, then disappeared behind a curtain.

Moments later she was back with three shot glasses, a frosted bottle of vodka, and a tray of black caviar with toast points. 'This is my treat,' she said. 'We get too few Russians. *Vashe zdorovye.*'

Mom looked up sharply. Nina wondered how long it had been since she had heard her native language. '*Vashe zdorovye,*' Mom said, reaching for her glass. After Stacey had left, the three of them clinked glasses, drank down their shots and reached immediately for the caviar.

'My daughters are becoming good Russians,' Mom said. There was a softening in her voice as she said it. Nina wished she could see her eyes, but the sunglasses still hid them from view.

For the next twenty minutes or so, they talked about ordinary things, but when Stacey returned with the food, no one could talk about anything else. There were tiny succulent meatballs, wild mushroom soup with a bubbly gruyère crust, and a salmon-stuffed veal roast with caviar sauce. When the apple-and-walnut strudel showed up, Nina cut off a piece. 'Oh my God,' she said.

Mom took a bite. 'It is like my mama used to make.'

'Really?' Meredith said.

'I could never make that dough without thinking of my mother.' Mom shook her head. 'Once, when I served it to your father, he said the strudel was too salty. This was from my tears, so I put the recipe away and tried to forget it.'

'And did you?'

Mom glanced out of the window. 'I forgot nothing.'

'You didn't want to forget,' Meredith said.

'Why do you say this?' Mom asked.

'Your story. You have it memorised word for word; you say it like a rosary. You wanted to remember, and you wanted to tell us.'

'Until the play,' Mom said. 'I am sorry for that, Meredith.'

Meredith sat back in her seat. 'I've waited for that apology all my life, and now that I have it, it doesn't matter. I care about you, Mom. I just want us all to keep talking.'

'Why?' Mom said quietly. 'How can you care? Either of you?'

'We tried not to love you, too,' Nina said.

'I would say I made it easy,' Mom said.

'No,' Meredith said, 'never easy.'

Mom reached out and poured three more vodkas. Lifting her glass, she looked at her daughters. 'What shall we drink to?'

'How about family?' Stacey said, appearing just in time to pour a fourth shot. 'To those who are here, those who are gone, and those who are lost.' She clinked her glass against Mom's. 'That's what we say in our house.'

Nina downed hers. 'Is that an old Russian toast?'

'I've never heard it.' Mom smiled. 'It is very good.'

On the walk back through town, Mom was quick to smile or to point out a trinket in a store window. It was like seeing a butterfly emerge from its chrysalis. And somehow, seeing her mother in this new light made Meredith feel differently about herself. Like her mom, she smiled more easily, laughed more often. Not once on this trip had she worried about the office, or her girls, or missing the ship.

'Look,' Mom said as they came to the end of the street.

Meredith followed her mother's pointing finger. Across the street, she saw a family, laughing together, posing for silly pictures. There was a woman with long brown hair, a handsome blond man, and two tow-headed, giggling little girls.

'That is how you and Jeff used to be,' Mom said quietly.

Meredith felt a new kind of realisation at that. She wasn't young any more. Her days of frolicking with her little girls were long gone. They would always be a family, but if she'd learned anything in the past few weeks, it was that a family wasn't a static thing. There were always changes. You couldn't control its direction. All you could do was hold on for the ride.

As she stood there staring at the strangers, she saw her life in moments. She and Jeff at the prom, dancing to 'Stairway to Heaven' . . . her in labour, screaming at him to stay away with those ice chips . . . taking Jillian to her first day of kindergarten . . . Jeff trying to hold her when Dad was dying, saying, *Who takes care of you, Mere?*

'I've been an idiot,' she said to no one except herself, forgetting for a moment she was standing in the middle of a busy pavement.

'It's about time,' Nina said, smiling. 'I'm tired of being the only screw-up in this family.'

'I love Jeff,' Meredith said, feeling both miserable and elated.

'Of course you do,' Mom said.

Meredith turned to them. 'What if it's too late?'

Mom smiled, and Meredith was struck by the beauty of the face she'd studied for decades. 'I am eighty-one, telling my life story to my daughters. Every year, I thought it was too late to start.'

Nina pulled out her cellphone. 'Call him.'

'Oh, we're having fun. It can wait.'

'No.' Mom laid a hand on Meredith's arm. 'Look at me. I am what fear makes of a woman. Do you want to end up like me?'

Meredith slowly reached out and removed her mother's sunglasses. Staring into the aqua-blue eyes that had always mesmerised her, she smiled. 'You know what, Mom? I'd be proud to have your strength. What you've been through would have killed an ordinary woman. So, yeah, I do want to end up like you.'

Mom swallowed hard.

'But I don't want to be afraid, you're right. So give me that damn cell-phone, Neener Beaner. I've got an overdue call to make.'

'We'll meet you on the boat,' Nina said.

'Where?'

Mom actually laughed. 'The bar with the view, of course.'

Meredith watched her sister and mother walk away, then sat down on the bench and glanced at her watch. She dialled Jeff's number.

It rang so many times she almost gave up.

Then, finally, he answered, sounding out of breath. 'Hello?'

'Jeff?' It was all she could do to hold tears back. 'It's me.'

'Meredith . . .'

She couldn't pinpoint the emotion in his voice. Once, she'd known every nuance. 'I'm in Sitka,' she said, stalling.

'Is it as beautiful as they say?'

'No,' she said. She wasn't going to waste time on the kind of facile conversations that had got her into this mess. 'I mean, yes, but I don't want to talk about that. I want to say I'm sorry, Jeff. You asked me if I loved you, and I hit the brakes. But I was wrong and stupid. I *do* love you. I love you, and I miss you, and I hope I'm not too late, because I want to grow old with the man I was young with.' She drew in a breath. Had she hurt him too much? Waited too long? When the silence went on, she said, 'Say something.'

Jeff sighed. 'I've tried to fall out of love with you, Mere. I couldn't do it, but I thought sure as hell you had.'

'I didn't fall out of love with you, either. I just . . . fell. Can we start over?'

'Hell, no. I don't want to start over. I like the middle.'

Meredith laughed at that. She didn't want to go back and be young again, either, not with all the uncertainties and angst. She just wanted to feel young. 'I'll . . . I'll be naked more. And work less.'

'And I'll make you laugh more. God, I've missed you, Mere.'

Juneau was the epitome of the Alaskan spirit—a state capital built with no roads leading in or out. The only way to get there was by boat or air. Surrounded by towering mountains, the rough-and-tumble city clung tenaciously to its pioneer and native roots.

If they hadn't been on a quest—or it hadn't been raining so hard—Nina felt sure they would have taken an excursion out to see the Mendenhall glacier. But as it was, the three of them were standing at the entrance to the Glacier View Nursing Home.

'Are you afraid, Mom?' Meredith asked.

'I wasn't under the impression he'd agreed to see me,' she said.

'Not precisely,' Nina said. 'So are you afraid?'

'I should have done this years ago. Perhaps if I had . . . No, I am not afraid to tell the story to this man who collects such memories.'

'Perhaps if you had, what?' Meredith asked.

Mom's face was shadowed by the black woollen hood she wore. 'I want you both to know what this trip has meant to me.'

'Why do you sound like you're saying goodbye?' Nina asked.

'Today you will hear the terrible things I did,' Mom said.

'We all do terrible things, Mom,' Meredith said.

'Do we?' Mom made a sound of disgust. 'This is the talk-show babble of your generation. Here is what I want to say before we go in. I love both of you.' Her gaze softened. 'My Ninotchka . . . my Merushka.' She turned and walked into the nursing home.

Nina rushed to keep up with her. At the desk, she smiled at the receptionist. 'We are the Whitson family,' Nina said. 'I wrote to Dr Adamovich and told him we'd be seeing him today.'

The receptionist flipped through a calendar. 'Yes. His son will be here at ten to meet you. Would you like coffee while you wait?'

'Sure,' Nina said.

The waiting room was filled with photographs of Juneau's colourful past. The present was not so different, judging by the image of a bear wandering past a coffee shop. The minutes ticked past. 'I wonder what the *Belye Nochi* is like here,' Mom said.

'According to my research, it's better the further north you go,' Nina said. 'But sometimes you see the Northern Lights from here.'

'The Northern Lights,' Mom said. 'My papa used to take me in the middle of the night, when everyone was asleep. He'd whisper, "Verushka, my little writer," and out we would go, into the streets, to stare up at the sky. It was beautiful. God's light show, he said.'

A man dressed in a flannel shirt and faded jeans walked into the room. With a thick black beard that covered half of his face, it was hard to make out his age. 'Mrs Whitson?' he said.

Mom slowly stood.

The man stretched out his hand. 'I am Maksim. My father, Vasily Adamovich, is the man you have come so far to see.'

'It is many years since your father wrote to me.'

Maksim nodded. 'I'm sorry to say that he had a stroke in the years between. He can barely speak and can't move his left side.'

'So we are wasting your time,' Mom said.

'Not at all. I have taken up a few of his projects, and the siege of Leningrad is one of them. It's such important work, gathering these survivor stories. The Soviets were good at keeping secrets.'

'Indeed,' Mom said.

'So if you'd like to come into my father's room, I'll record your account for his study. He may not appear to react, but I can assure you that he is happy to finally include your story. It will be the fifty-third first-person account he has collected. Later this year I am going to St Petersburg to petition for more records. Your story will make a difference, Mrs Whitson. I assure you.'

Mom simply nodded.

'Follow me, please,' Maksim said. Turning, he led them down the brightly lit corridor to a room at the very end of the hall.

In the centre was a narrow hospital-style bed, with a couple of chairs obviously brought in for this meeting. In the bed lay a shrunken man with a bony face and toothpick arms. His right hand began to tremble, and the right side of his mouth tried to smile.

Maksim leaned down, whispered something in his ear. The man in the bed said something, but Nina couldn't understand a word.

'He says he is so glad to see you, Anya Whitson. He has waited a long time. Vasily Adamovich welcomes you all.'

Mom nodded.

'Please, sit down,' Maksim said, indicating the chairs. On a table by the window was a copper samovar and several plates of *pierogi* and strudel and sliced cheese with crackers.

Vasily said something, his voice crackling like a dried leaf.

Maksim shook his head. 'Sorry, Papa. I can't understand. I'm going to record Anya—May I call you Anya? Is recording OK?'

Mom stared at the gleaming samovar and the silver-wrapped glass teacups. *"Da,"* she said softly, flicking a hand in dismissal.

For a moment, the room was utterly still. Then Mom drew in a long, slow breath and released it. 'I have told this story in a single way for so long, I hardly know how to start now.'

Maksim hit the record button, and the tape started to roll.

'I am not Anya Petrovna Whitson. This is the name I took, the woman I became.' She took another deep breath. *'I am Veronika Petrovna Marchenko Whitson, and Leningrad is my city. In June of 1941, I am coming home from the country, where I'd been gathering vegetables to can for the coming winter . . .'*

Nina closed her eyes, letting the words form pictures in her imagination. She heard things she'd listened to as a fairy tale; only this time there were no princes or goblins. There was only Vera, falling in love, having her babies . . . then digging on the Luga line. Nina had to wipe her tears when Olga died, and again when Vera's mother died. As the portrait of Leningrad under siege became darker, so the light from the window faded. Maksim turned on a lamp, but still they were all in the dark when Mom said, *'I hear my son say, "What's wrong with Baba," and it takes all my strength not to cry. I pull the blanket up to Mama's chest. Should*

I have forced her to eat? This question will haunt me. If I had, I would have been pulling the blanket up on one of my children.

"Mama," Leo says again.

"Baba has gone to be with Olga," I say, and as hard as I try, my voice cracks, and then my children are crying.

It is Sasha who comforts them. I have no comfort left in me. I am afraid if one of them touches me, I will crack apart like an egg.

I sit next to my dead mother for a long time, in our dark, cold room. Then Sasha is beside me suddenly. He folds me into a hug.

"We will be away from here someday," he promises. "We will go to Alaska, just like we always talked about. It won't always be like this."

"Alaska," I say, remembering this dream of his, of ours. "Yes."

But a dream like that—any dream—only makes my pain worse.

I look at him, and though he says something, I see his thoughts in his green eyes, or maybe it is my own thoughts reflected. Either way, we break apart, and Sasha says to our slumped, red-eyed children, "Mama and I must go and take care of Baba."

Leo, sitting on the floor, starts to cry again, but it is a pale imitation of my son's sadness. I have seen him burst into tears when he is healthy. Now he just leaks water from his eyes, too exhausted to do more.

"We'll stay here, Papa," Anya says. "I'll take care of Leo."

"My good children," Sasha says. He keeps them busy while I wash Mama, dress her in her best dress. I kiss her cheek, whisper goodbye.

Then it is time. Sasha and I dress for the cold. Out we go, into the black day. We tie Mama to the sledge, and Sasha drags it through the knee-deep snow. At the cemetery, the bodies are stacked like firewood at the gates, so we find an open space beneath a tree I hope will be the protector for her I was not. I will always know this tree, recognise it. From now on, I will always remember her on the fourteenth of December, wherever I am. It is not much, but it is something.

"It is all we can do," Sasha says as we trudge for home.

All I want to do is lie down. I am so hungry and so tired and so sad. I do not even care if I die. "Yes," I say. Whatever.

But Sasha is urging me forwards, and when we get home and our children climb into bed with us, I thank God my husband is there.

"Don't you give up," he whispers to me in bed that night. "I will find a way to get you out of here."

In the morning, he whispers that he loves me, and he leaves.

In late December, the city slowly freezes to death. It is dark almost all the time. Birds drop from the sky like stones. Twenty degrees below zero becomes normal. The water mains burst.

292 | Kristin Hannah

We do as little as we can, my children and I. Our apartment is black all the time—there is only the briefest spasm of daylight. Our little burzhuika is heat and life, but in the morning, we waken with frost on our cheeks. Leo has developed a cough that worries me.

I get up in the cold and take however long I must to feed wood in the stove. There is a ringing in my ears, and a kind of vertigo often sends me sprawling. Still, I smile when I kiss my babies awake.

Anya groans at my touch, and this is better than Leo, who just lies there. I would give anything to hear him say he is hungry.

I make us each a cup of hot water laced with yeast. I take a piece of thick black bread—the last of this week's rations—and I cut it in thirds. I want to give them it all, but without me, they are lost. We eat as slowly as possible. I put half of mine in my pocket and put on all my clothes.

My children snuggle close in bed. "Don't go, Mama," Leo says.

"I have to." It is the conversation we have every morning. There is very little fight left in them. "Shall I try to find us some chocolate?"

"Chocolate," he says dreamily, slumping back into his pillow.

Anya looks up at me. Unlike her brother, she is not sick; she is just wasting, like me. "You shouldn't tell him there will be chocolate."

"Oh, Anya." I pull her into my arms, hold her as tightly as I can.

"I don't want to die, Mama," she says.

"You won't, moya dusha. We'll make sure of it."

My soul. She is that. They both are. And because of that, I get up and get dressed and go to work. You think that things cannot get worse, but they can. They do.

It is the coldest winter on record in Leningrad. Rations are cut and cut again. Page by page I burn my father's beloved books. I sit in the freezing dark holding my bony children as I tell them the stories. Anna Karenina. War and Peace. Onegin. I tell them how Sasha and I met so often that soon I know the words by heart. It feels further and further away, though. Some days I can't recall the past, but I can see the future: it is in the stretched, tiny faces of my children, in the boils that have begun to blister Leo's pale skin.

Scurvy. Lucky for me, I work in the library. Books tell me that pine needles have vitamin C, so I drag branches home on my sledge.

I can hear my babies breathing in the bed beside me. Leo's every breath is phlegmy. I feel his brow. He is not hot, thank God.

I know what has wakened me. The fire has gone out.

I want to do nothing about it. I could just lie here, hold my children, and go to sleep for ever. There are worse ways to die. Then I feel Anya's tiny legs brush against me, and I remember my promise.

There is a ringing in my ears. Halfway to the stove, I feel myself falling.

When I wake from my faint, I go to the book case. Only the best of the treasures are left: I cannot burn my father's poetry. Instead, I take the axe and crack off a piece of the book case. It burns hot.

I stand by the fire. I can feel how I am swaying. I know suddenly that if I lie down, I will die. Did my mother tell me this? "I won't die in my bed," I say to no one, going to the only furniture left. My father's writing desk. Wrapping myself in a blanket, I sit down.

I pick up his pen and find the ink is frozen solid, but I carry the metal inkwell to the stove. Making a cup of hot water to drink, I light the lamp. I have to do something to keep alive. So I will write.

I am Vera Petrovna, and I am a nobody . . .

I write and write, on paper that I will soon have to burn, with a hand that trembles violently. Still, I write and the night fades.

Somewhere in the late morning, a pale grey light bleeds through the newsprint, and I know I have made it through the worst of it.

I am about to put the pen down, when there is a knock at the door. I open the door to a stranger. A man in a black coat and a military cap.

"Vera Petrovna Marchenko? It is me, Dima Newsky from down the hall." He hands me a bottle of red wine, a bar of chocolate and a sack of potatoes. "My mama is too ill to eat. She won't make it through the day. She asked me to give this to you. For the babies."

"Thank you." I can't remember his mother, my neighbour. Still, I take the food. I might even kill him for it. "Do you want to come—"

"No. I am not here long. It's back to the front tomorrow."

When he is gone, I stare down at the food in awe. I am smiling when I waken Leo and say, "We have chocolate . . ."

In January, I strap poor Leo to the sledge. Anya is too cold to get out of bed. I tell her to stay in bed and wait for us.

It takes three hours to walk to the hospital, and when I get there, people have died in line, waiting to see a doctor. A nurse comes over and looks at Leo. I see pity in her eyes. Leo is somehow both bony and swollen, his arm covered with boils. She gives me a piece of paper. "Here. This will get him aspirin at the dispensary."

When I get home, I cook everything I can find. I strip the wallpaper and boil it. The paste of flour and water thickens into a kind of soup. I boil a leather belt of Sasha's and make a jelly from it. The taste is sickening, but I get Leo to eat a little of it.

In the middle of January, a friend of Sasha's comes to our apartment. I can see he is shocked by what he sees. He gives me a box. As soon as he is gone, we crowd round it. Even Leo is smiling.

Inside are evacuation papers. We are to leave on the twentieth.

Beneath the papers is a coil of fresh sausage and a bag of nuts.

In utter darkness, I pack up the whole of my life, not that there is much left. Honestly, I do not know what I have taken and what I left behind. I remember my writings and my father's, and my last book of poetry by Anna Akhmatova. I take all the food—the sausage, a half bag of onions, four pieces of bread and the nuts.

I have to carry Leo. With his swollen feet and boil-covered arms, he can barely move, and I don't have it in me to waken him when he sleeps. When Anya and I get to the station, we are exhausted. In the train, we cram together, but no one talks. The musty air smells of body odour and death. It is a smell we all recognise.

I give Leo and Anya some wine to drink, but Leo is not happy with that. It is not safe to take out my food. I do the only thing I can think of: I cut my finger and put it in his mouth. Like a newborn baby, he sucks on it. It hurts, but not as much as hearing the congestion in his lungs or feeling the heat in his forehead.

In a quiet voice, I tell them of the fairy-tale love that seems so far away. Somewhere along that trip, I begin to call my husband a prince and Comrade Stalin the Black Knight. The trip lasts for so many hours, my story is the only thing that keeps us all sane.

Finally we reach Lake Ladoga. There is ice as far as I can see.

We are at the start of the ice road the army has been working on for months. Everyone is calling it the road of life. Soon, they say, transports of food will rumble towards Leningrad instead of falling into freezing water. Of course, the Germans bomb it constantly.

I check my children's clothes. Everything is in place. Leo and Anya are wrapped in newsprint and then in all the clothes they own. We wrap scarves round our heads and necks. Outside, it hurts when I take a breath. Beside me, Leo starts to cough.

A full moon rises in the black sky, turning the snow blue. We stand around, all of us, matted together like cattle.

"What do we do, Mama?" Anya says.

"We find a truck. Here, take my hand."

My eyes sting as I start forward. Leo is in my arms, and as thin as he is, he weighs me down. Every step takes concentration. I have to lean into the howling wind. The only real thing in this icy white world is my daughter's hand in mine. Somewhere, far away, I hear an engine roaring. It is a convoy, I hope.

I walk and walk, and there is nothing. Just ice and the distant popping of guns. I think I must hurry, and then Sasha is beside me. I can feel the warmth of his breath. He is whispering about love and the place we will build in Alaska. He tells me it's OK to rest.

"Just for a moment," I say. Closing my eyes, I fall to my knees.

The world is totally quiet. Someone laughs, and it sounds just like Olga. I will go and find her as soon as I have a nap.

"Mama. Mama. Mama." She is screaming in my face.

I open my eyes slowly and see Anya. My daughter has pulled off her scarf and wrapped it round my neck.

"You have to get up, Mama." She is tugging at me.

I look down. Leo is limp in my arms, but I can feel his breathing.

I unwrap the scarf and re-cover Anya's face. "Never take your scarf off again. Do not give it to anyone. Not even me."

"But I love you, Mama."

And there is my strength. Gritting my teeth against the pain that will come, I stagger to my feet and start moving again.

One step at a time, until a lorry materialises in front of me.

A man dressed in baggy white camouflage is standing beside the door, smoking a cigarette. The smell makes me think of my mother.

"A ride across the ice?" I say, hearing how weak my voice is.

The man's face is not drawn or gaunt. He is Somebody, or in the Party, at least, and I feel hope plummet. He looks at Leo. "Dead?"

"Just sleeping. Please," I say, desperate now. All around, trucks are leaving, and I know we will die if we do not find a ride soon. I pull out the cloisonné butterfly made by my grandfather. "Here."

The man just frowns. "What good is a trinket?"

I pull off my glove and give him my wedding ring. "Please . . ."

He takes one last drag of the cigarette, pockets my gold ring. "All right, Baba. Get in. I will take you and the grandchildren."

I am so grateful, I don't realise what he has said until we are all packed in the cab of his truck. Baba. He thinks I am an old woman.

I pull the scarf off. My hair is as white as my skin.

It is daylight when we get across the ice. Not much light, of course, but enough. I can really see where we are now.

Endless snow. Trucks lined up, filled with food for my poor Leningrad. Soldiers dressed in white. Not far from here—300 yards, maybe—is the train station that is our next destination. The bombing starts almost immediately. Our driver stops and gets out.

Honestly, I do not want to get out, though I know there is gasoline in the tank and no camouflage on the truck. We are warm . . . Then I look down at my Leo. He is not breathing. I rip open his coat and pull up the newspaper. His chest is just a brace of bones and blue skin. "Wake up, Leo! Breathe!" I put my mouth on his, breathing for him.

Finally, he shudders. A sweet little breath slips into my mouth.

He starts to cry. I hold him to me, crying, too, and say, "Don't you leave me, Leo. I couldn't bear it."

"His hands are so hot, Mama," Anya says.

I touch Leo's forehead. He is burning up. My hands are shaking as I reposition the newspaper and button up his sweater and coat.

We are going out into the cold again.

Anya leads the way out of the truck. I am so focused on Leo that I hardly notice the bombing and gunfire around me. Somewhere nearby a truck explodes. All around us soldiers are running.

At last I find the dirty white tents of the infirmary, but it is a place for the dying and the dead. People lie in their own freezing filth. I dare not put Leo down. It seems we wander around for hours. Finally, I find an old man wearing white, staring at nothing. "Please," I say, "my son is burning up."

The man's hands tremble as he reaches for Leo. I see the boils on his fingers. He touches Leo's forehead and looks at me.

It is a look I will never forget. Thank God there are no words for it. "Get him to the hospital at Cherepovets." He hands me four white pills. "Two a day, with clean water. When did he eat last?"

I shake my head. How can I say it is impossible to get him to eat?

"Cherepovets," is all he says, and then he turns and goes away.

I take Anya's hand, and we make our way to the train station. Our papers are in order, and we climb into a carriage. There is no seat, so we sit on the cold floor. I hold my Leo on my lap. When it gets dark, I take out my bag of nuts. I give Anya as many as I dare and eat a few myself. I manage to get Leo to take one pill.

It is a long and terrible night. I keep leaning down to see if Leo is breathing. I remember the train stopping once. The big doors open, and someone yells out, "Any dead? Send them out."

I hang on to Leo, screaming, "He's breathing, he's breathing." When the door closes, Anya moves closer. I can hear her crying.

It is no better in Cherepovets. We have one day to spend here, waiting for the train. At first I think this is a blessing, that we will have time to save Leo, but he is getting weaker. I try not to see this truth, but it is lying in my arms. Now there is blood in his cough. He is burning hot and shivering. He will neither eat nor drink.

The hospital is an abomination. Everyone has dysentery and scurvy. Every hour, trucks leave loaded with corpses. I stand in the cold hallway holding my son. When people pass, I whisper, "Help him. Please."

A nurse stops. She takes him gently. "He's dystrophic. Third stage. There is no fourth." At my blank look, she says, "Dying. But if we could get fluids into him . . . maybe. I could take him to the doctor. It would be a difficult few days, maybe, though."

She is so young. I don't know how to believe her or how not to.

"I have evacuation papers to be on a train to Vologda tomorrow."

"They won't let your son on that train. Not one so sick."

"If we stay, it will be impossible to get tickets. We'll die here."

The young nurse says nothing to this. Lies are a waste of time.

"We could start helping Leo now, couldn't we?" I say. "Maybe he will be better by tomorrow."

She cannot hide her pity for me. "Of course. Maybe he will."

And he is. After a night where Anya and I lay curled on the floor by his dirty cot, I get to my knees and he is awake. For the first time in a long time, his blue eyes are clear. "Hi, Mama," he says in a scratchy voice that cuts right through my heart. "Where's Papa?"

I pull Anya up beside me. "We are right here, baby. We are on our way to your papa. He will be waiting for us in Vologda."

I am smiling and crying as I look down at my son. Maybe it is the tears that blur my vision, or more likely it is hope. Common sense is gone with the sound of his voice. I don't see how blue his skin is, how the boils have burst and are seeping yellow. I don't hear the thickness of his cough. I just see Leo. My lion. My baby.

So when the nurse comes by to tell me that I should get on the train, I am confused. "He's getting better," I say.

Silence stretches out between us. She looks at Anya.

For the first time, I see how pale Anya is, how grey her lips are, the angry boils on her throat. Her hair is falling out in clumps.

I look round. "You said they won't let my son on the train."

"Too many evacuees. You and your daughter have papers?"

"You're saying I should leave him here to die? Alone?"

"I'm saying he will die." The nurse looks at Anya again. "You can save her." She touches my arm. "I'm sorry."

I watch her walk away. I don't know how long I stand there, frozen, but when I hear the train's whistle, I look down at the daughter I love more than my own life, and the son of mine who is dying.

"Mama?" Anya says, frowning up at me.

I walk her out of the hospital. At the train, I kneel in front of her. She is so small, wrapped as she is in her bright red coat and wearing valenki that are too big for her feet.

"Mama?"

"I can't leave Leo here." He can't die alone is what I want to say, but how can I say such a thing to my five-year-old? Does she know I am making a

choice no mother should ever have to make? Will she someday hate me for this? "But you are my strong one. You will be OK alone."

She starts to cry. "No, Mama. I want to stay with you."

I reach into my pocket and take out a piece of paper. I write "Anastasia Aleksovna Marchenko" on the paper and pin it to her lapel. "P-Papa will be waiting for you in Vologda. You find him. Tell him I'll be there by Wednesday. You two can meet Leo and me."

It feels like a lie. Tastes like one. But she trusts me.

I don't let her hug me. I can see her reaching, and I push her back into the crowd around us. She hits a woman who stumbles sideways, cursing softly.

I push my daughter at the stranger, who looks at me with glassy eyes. "Take my daughter," I say. "She has papers. Her father will be in Vologda. Aleksandr Andreiovich Marchenko."

"No, Mama." Anya is wailing, reaching for me.

I mean to push her away, but I can't do it. I yank her into my arms and hold her tightly.

The train whistle blows. Someone yells: "Is she going?"

I unwrap Anya's arm. "You be strong. I love you, moya dusha."

How can I call her my soul and then push her away? But I do. I do. At the last minute, I hand her the butterfly. "Here. Hold this for me. I will come back for it. For you."

"No, Mama—"

"I promise," I say, lifting her up into a stranger's arms.

She is still crying, screaming my name when the train doors shut.

I watch the train grow smaller until it disappears. The Germans are bombing again. I hardly care. I walk through the snow towards my son. I tell myself I have done the right thing. I will keep Leo alive by sheer force of will, and Sasha will find Anya in Vologda, and the four of us will meet on Wednesday.

It is such a beautiful dream. I keep it alive one breath at a time.

Back at the hospital, it is cold and dark. The smell is unbearable. In his sagging cot, Leo coughs in his sleep almost constantly, spasms that spew lacy blood designs across the woollen blankets.

When I can stand it no more, I crawl into the cot and pull him into my arms. He burrows against me like the baby he once was, murmuring my name. His breathing is a terrible thing to listen to.

I stroke his hot forehead to let him know I am here. I sing his favourite songs and tell his favourite stories. Now and then he rouses, smiles drunkenly at me, asking for chocolate.

"No chocolate," I say, kissing his grey cheek. I am singing to him, when I realise that he is not breathing any more.

I kiss his cheek, so cold, and his lips, and I think I hear him say, "I love you,

Mama," but of course it is only my imagination. How will I ever forget how this was . . . How he died a little every day? How I let him. Maybe we should never have left Leningrad.

I think I will not be able to bear this pain, but I do. For all of that day and part of the next, I lie holding him. Finally, I ease away.

As much as I want to lie with him for ever, to just slowly starve to death with him, I cannot do it. I made a promise to Sasha.

So, with empty arms and a heart turned to stone, I leave my son by himself, lying dead on a cot. I know all I will ever have of him now is a date on the calendar and the stuffed rabbit in my suitcase.

I will not tell you what I do to get a seat on the train going east. It doesn't matter anyway. I am not really me. I am this wasted white-haired body that cannot rest, although I long just to lie down and close my eyes and give up. The ache of loss is with me always.

Anya. Sasha. These are the words I cling to. From my place on the train, I see the ruined countryside. Bodies in heaps. Scars on the land. Always there is the sound of aircraft and gunfire.

The train moves slowly, stopping in small towns. Starving people fight to get on board. There is talk of heavy fighting in front of us.

And then, miraculously, we arrive at Vologda.

The doors open. Out in the cold, I stand there, and as the others peel away from me, I hear the drone of planes, and I know what it means. The air-raid alarm sounds, and my fellow passengers start to run for cover. I can see people flinging themselves into ditches.

But Sasha is there, not a hundred yards in front of me. He is holding Anya's hand. Her coat is bright red against the snow.

I am crying before I take my first step. My feet are swollen and covered with boils, but I don't notice. I just think of my family and run. I want Sasha's arms round me so badly that I hear the bomb fall too late. Did I think it was my heart, that whistling sound?

Everything explodes at once: the train, the tree beside me, a truck by the road. I see Sasha and Anya for a split second, and then they are in the air, flying sideways with fire behind them.

When I wake up, I am in a hospital tent. I lie there until my memory resurfaces, and then I get up. All around me is a sea of burned, broken bodies. People are crying and moaning.

It is a moment before I realise I can see no colours. Everything is black and white with grey. My hearing is muffled, as if there is cotton in my ears. The red-orange fire is the last colour I will ever see.

"You should not be up," a man says. His tunic is torn in places.

"My husband. My daughter. A little girl in a red coat and a man. They were . . . The train was bombed . . . I have to find them."

"I'm sorry," he says, and my heart is pounding so hard I can't hear anything past ". . . no survivors . . . just you."

I stumble from bed to bed, but all I find are strangers.

Outside, it is snowing hard and freezing cold. The damage done by the blast is covered now in white, though I can see a heap that must be bodies. Then I see it: a small, dark blot on the snow, lying folded up against the nearest tent. I walk toward it. It is my Anya's coat. Or what is left of it. I cannot see the bright red any more, but there is her name, pinned to the lapel. Half of the coat is missing; I can see bloodstains on the lining.

I hold it to my nose, breathe deeply. I can smell her in the fabric.

Inside the pocket, I find the photograph of her and Leo I'd sewn into the lining. See? I'd said to her on the day we hid it. Now your brother will always be with you. And I will meet you on Wednesday.

The last thing I said to her was a lie.

No one will give me a gun. Every man I ask tells me to calm down, that I will feel better tomorrow. I should have asked another mother who had killed a child by moving him, and another by letting her go.

The pain is unendurable. And I deserve to be as unhappy as I am. I move like a ghost through the snowy countryside. There are so many other walking dead on the road that no one tries to stop me. When I hear gunfire or bombing, I turn towards it.

I find what I am looking for on the eighth day. It is the front line. I walk past my countrymen, who call out to me and try to stop me. I walk up to the Germans and stand in front of their guns. "Shoot me," I say, and I close my eyes.

CHAPTER THIRTEEN

'BUT I AM NOT a lucky woman,' Mom said with a sigh.

Silence followed that last, quietly spoken sentence.

Nina wiped the tears from her eyes and stared at her mother in awe. How could all that pain have been in her all along?

Mom stood up quickly. She took a step to the left and stopped, then to the right and stopped. It was as if she'd awakened from a dream to find herself in a strange room from which there was no escape. At last, she went to the window and stared outside.

Nina looked at Meredith, who looked as ruined as Nina felt.

'My God,' Maksim finally said, turning off the tape recorder.

Mom pressed a hand to her chest as if she thought her heart would tumble out of her body. What was she seeing? Nina stared at the woman who had raised her and saw the truth at last. Her mother was a lioness. A warrior. A woman who'd chosen a life of hell for herself because she wanted to give up and didn't know how.

'They take me prisoner instead,' Mom said. 'I try to die. Try . . . Always I am too weak to kill myself.' She looked at them. 'Your father was one of the soldiers who liberated the work camp. We were in Germany by then, years later. When he asked me my name, I was not paying attention; I was thinking that if I'd been stronger, my children would have been with me on this day, and so I whispered, 'Anya'. I could have taken it back later, but I welcomed the pain of hearing her name. I went with your father—married him—because I wanted to be gone, but I never really expected to start over—I was so sick. I hoped to die. But I did not. And how can you not love Evan? There. That is it.' She started for the door.

Nina was on her feet in an instant. Without a word or a look, she and Meredith bookended Mom, each taking hold of one arm.

At their touch, she seemed to stumble. 'You shouldn't—'

'No more telling us what to feel, Mom,' Nina said softly.

'No more pushing us away,' Meredith said, touching Mom's face, caressing her cheek. 'You've lost so much.'

'Not us, though,' Nina said. 'You'll never lose us.'

Mom started to fold like a broken tent, but they got her back to her chair. Then they kneeled in front of her, looking up, just as they'd done so often in their lives. But now the story was over, or mostly told, and from here on, anyway, it would be *their* story.

For all of her life, when Nina had looked at her mother's face, she'd seen hard eyes and a mouth that never smiled. Now she saw the hard lines were fought for, over the softness that lay beneath.

'You should hate me,' Mom said, shaking her head.

Meredith put her hands on Mom's. 'We love you.'

Mom shuddered. Tears filled her eyes and, at the sight of them, Nina felt her own tears rise again.

'I miss them so much,' Mom said, and then she was crying. How long had she held back that simple sentence by force of will, and how must it feel to finally say it? *I miss them*. A few little words. Everything.

Nina and Meredith folded her into their arms, letting her cry.

When Mom finally drew back, her face was ravaged by tears, but she had never looked more beautiful. She put a hand on each of their faces. 'Moya dusha,' she said quietly.

At Vasily's bedside, Maksim rose and cleared his throat, reminding them they weren't alone. 'That is one of the most amazing accounts of the siege I've ever heard,' he said, taking the tape from the machine. 'Over one million people died. You tell their story, too. Thank you.'

Vasily made a croaking, chirping sound in the bed. Maksim leaned close. 'What? I don't understand . . .'

Nina turned to her mom. 'Thank you,' she said quietly. Mom leaned forwards, kissed her cheek.

'My Ninotchka,' she whispered. 'Thank *you*. You were the one who wouldn't let go. This is why you matter to the world. You shine a light on hard times. Your pictures do not let people look away from that which hurts. I am so proud of what you do. You saved us.'

'You did,' Meredith said. 'You got us here.'

While Nina was trying to figure out what to say to that, Maksim said, 'I'm sorry to be rude, but my father is not feeling well.'

Mom went to the bed and stared down at Vasily, his face left lopsided by the stroke. There were tears on his temples and water stained the pillow where they'd fallen. She reached down and touched his face, saying something in Russian.

'Here,' Maksim said, handing Mom a stack of cassette tapes. 'He wants you to deliver these to his former student. Phillip Kiselev has a lot of the original material, and he's just across the water in Sitka. Planes leave every hour.'

'We've been there,' Mom said. 'The boat won't be going back.'

'Actually,' Meredith said, looking at her watch, 'the boat left Juneau forty minutes ago. It will be at sea all day tomorrow.'

'Phillip was his right hand for years in this research. His mother and my father knew each other in Minsk.'

Nina thought how a little thing could mean so much. 'Of course we'll deliver them. We'll have time to catch the boat in Skagway.'

Meredith took the tapes and the piece of paper with the address on it. 'Thank you, Dr Adamovich. And Maksim.'

'No,' Maksim said solemnly. 'Thank *you*. I am honoured to have met you, Veronika Petrovna Marchenko Whitson.'

Mom nodded. She leaned down to whisper something in Vasily's ear. When she drew back, the old man was trying to smile.

'I could be in Los Angeles by now,' Nina said as she followed Meredith out of the seaplane.

'For a world traveller, you complain a lot,' Meredith said.

'I'm just saying, this "Alaskan planes leave every hour" thing is very African. It's really more of an idea than a schedule.'

They walked up the dock into Sitka. There was almost no one about; the cruise ships had moved on. At a small bed-and-breakfast, they found rooms with decks looking out to Mt Edgecombe. While Nina took a shower, Meredith sat on the deck with her feet on the railing. It was ten o'clock, and finally darkness was falling.

'I thought I'd see the *Belye Nochi* from here,' Mom said from her deck next door.

'I guess we're not far enough north,' Meredith said. She heard a door shut quietly and knew she was alone again. She leaned back in her chair. Then the glass door behind her slid open. She thought it was Nina, but it was Mom. 'Hey,' Meredith said. 'I thought you'd gone to bed.'

Mom sat in a chair and coiled her hands nervously. 'I cannot sleep with the tapes in my room. I need to give them away.'

'Tonight? It's ten o'clock, Mom.'

'*Da*. I asked downstairs. This address is three blocks away.'

Meredith turned in her chair. 'You mean this. What's wrong?'

'Honestly? I do not know. But I want to be done with this task.'

'I'll call him.'

'There is no listing. I called Information. We are going to have to just show up. Tomorrow he will be at work and we'll have to wait.'

Somehow holding onto the physical evidence of her life scared her mother. 'OK,' Meredith said. 'I'll get Nina.' She got up, and as she passed her mother, she paused to put a hand on her shoulder. She couldn't walk past her lately without touching her.

She knocked on the bathroom door, got no answer, and went in. Nina was drying her hair.

'Mom wants to drop off the tapes tonight,' Meredith told her.

'Oh. OK,' Nina said.

In less than ten minutes, they were on their way, the three of them, walking up the dark pavement in the direction the innkeeper had shown them. It still wasn't full-on night; the sky was a plum colour, with stars everywhere.

The houses on this street were old-fashioned, with porches and peaked roofs. The smell of roses was heavy in the air.

'This is the house,' Meredith said, looking at the map.

'The lights are on. That's cool,' Nina said.

Mom stood there staring at the house. Its porch railing was the same ornate fretwork as they had at home, and more along the eaves gave the place a fairy-tale appearance. 'It looks like my grandfather's *dacha*. Very Russian, and yet American, too.'

Nina moved, took her arm. 'You sure you want to do this now?'

Mom's answer was to move resolutely forwards and knock.

The door was opened by a short heavy-set man with beetling, black eyebrows and a train-catcher moustache. If he was surprised to find three unknown women on his doorstep at ten thirty, he showed no sign. 'Hello there,' he said.

'Phillip Kiselev?' Mom said, reaching for the bag of tapes.

'There's a name I haven't heard in a while. I'm Gerald Koontz.'

'Oh. I am sorry. We have mistaken information.'

Meredith had the address in her hand. 'Dr Adamovich must—'

'Vasya?' Gerald's moustached lip flipped into a big, toothy smile. He turned, yelled, 'They're friends of Vasya's, honey.'

'Not really,' Mom said. 'I am sorry to have bothered you.'

Just then a woman came bustling towards them. She was dressed in a pilled pink satin robe, and her grey hair was pinned in rollers.

'Stacey?' Nina said in surprise. A second later Meredith recognised their waitress from the Russian restaurant.

'Well, if it isn't my new Russian friends! Come in. Gere, they stopped by the diner the other day. I broke out the caviar.'

'Oh.' Gerald grinned. 'She must have liked you on the spot.'

Nina moved first, pulling Mom along.

'Here, here,' Stacey said. 'Have a seat. I'll make us tea, and you can tell me how you found me.' She seated them in a comfortable living room, complete with an ottoman and a holy corner, where candles were burning. 'You're friends of Vasily's?'

'Not friends,' Mom answered, sitting stiffly.

There was a crash somewhere, and Gerald said, 'Oops. Grandkids,' and ran from the room.

'We're babysitting our son's children this week. I'd forgotten how *busy* they are.' Stacey smiled. 'I'll be right back with tea.' She hurried out of the room.

'Do you think Dr Adamovich was confused? Or did Maksim get the address wrong?' Meredith said as soon as they were alone.

'Kind of coincidental that these people are Russian and that they knew the doctor,' Nina remarked.

Mom stood up so suddenly she hit the coffee table with her shin, but she didn't seem to notice. She walked across the room to the holy corner. From here, Meredith could see the usual decorations: an altar-like table, a couple of icons, a family photograph or two, and three burning votives.

Stacey came back into the room and set her tray down on the coffee table. She poured tea and handed Meredith a cup. 'Here you go.'

'Do you know Dr Adamovich?' Nina asked.

'I do,' Stacey said. 'He and my father were great friends. I helped him with a research study. Typing, that sort of thing.'

'The siege research?' Meredith asked.

'That's right,' Stacey said.

'These are tapes.' Nina indicated the paper sack at her feet. 'Mom just told her story to Dr Adamovich, and he sent us here.'

Stacey paused and looked up. 'What do you mean, her story?'

'She was in Leningrad then. During the war,' Meredith said.

'And he sent you here?' Stacey turned and looked at Mom, who stood so still and straight she seemed to be made of marble.

Stacey went to Mom and stood beside her. The teacup she carried rattled in its saucer. 'Tea?' she asked, looking at Mom's stern profile.

Meredith didn't know why, but she stood up. Beside her, Nina did the same thing. They came up behind Mom.

Meredith saw what had attracted her mother's attention. There were two photographs on the table. One was a black-and-white picture of a young couple. In it, the woman was tall and slim, with black hair and an oversized smile. The man was blond and gorgeous.

'Those are my parents,' Stacey said. 'On their wedding day. My mother was a beautiful woman. Her hair was so soft and black, and her eyes . . . I still remember her eyes. Isn't that funny? They were so blue, with gold . . .'

Mom turned slowly.

Stacey looked into Mom's eyes, and the teacup fell to the floor, breaking to pieces. Her plump hand was shaking as she reached for something on the table, but not once did she look away. She held out a small jewelled butterfly.

Mom dropped to her knees, saying, 'Oh my God . . .'

Meredith wanted to help her, but she and Nina stood back.

It was Stacey who knelt in front of her. 'I am Anastasia Aleksovna Marchenko Koontz, from Leningrad. Mama? Is it you?'

Mom drew in a sharp breath and started to cry. 'My Anya . . .'

Meredith's heart felt as if it were breaking apart and overflowing all at once. Tears streamed down her face. She thought of all that these two had been through, and all the lost years, and the miracle of it was almost more than she could believe. She and Nina put their arms round each other and watched their mother come alive. There was no other word for it. It was as if these tears—of joy, perhaps for the first time in decades—watered her parched soul.

'How?' Mom asked.

'Papa and I woke up on a medical train going east. He was so hurt. Anyway, by the time we got back to Vologda . . . We waited,' Stacey said, wiping her eyes. 'We never stopped looking.'

Mom swallowed hard. Meredith saw her steel herself. 'We?'

Stacey put a hand out. Mom clutched it, and Stacey led her out of a set of French doors. Beyond lay a perfectly tended backyard. Stacey flipped a switch, and a string of lights came on.

That was when Meredith saw the small square garden-within-a-garden tucked in the back. She heard her mother say something in Russian, and then they all walked down a stone path. A white ironwork fence with ornate curlicues and pointed tips framed a patch of ground. Inside was a polished copper bench that faced three granite headstones. There were flowers all round. Overhead, the sky erupted in amazing magical colour. The Northern Lights.

Mom sat—collapsed, really—on the copper bench, and Stacey sat beside her, holding her hand. Meredith and Nina stood behind, each putting a hand on Mom's shoulder.

VERONIKA PETROVNA MARCHENKO

1919–

Remember our lime tree in the Summer Garden

I will meet you there, my love.

LEO ALEKSOVICH MARCHENKO

1938–1942

Our Lion

Gone too soon

ALEKSANDR ANDREIOVICH MARCHENKO

1917–2000

Beloved husband and father

'Last year?' Mom turned to Stacey, whose eyes filled with tears.

'He waited his whole life for you,' she said. 'But his heart just . . . gave out last winter.'

Mom closed her eyes and bowed her head.

Meredith couldn't imagine the pain of that, how it must feel to know that the love of your life had been alive, looking for you all these years, and to miss him by months.

'He always said he'd be waiting for you in the Summer Garden. At the tree.'

Mom slowly opened her eyes. 'Our tree,' she said, staring at his marker for a long time. Then, slowly, she did what she always did, what she could do that so few others could: she straightened her back and lifted her chin. 'Come,' she said in that magical voice. 'We will have tea. There is much to talk about. Anya, I would like to introduce you to your sisters. Meredith used to be the organised one, and Nina is a little crazy, but we're changing, all of us, and you will change us even more.' Mom smiled, and if there was a shadow of sadness in her eyes, it was softened by the joy in her voice.

EPILOGUE

2010

HER NAME IS VERA, *and she is a poor girl. A nobody. No one in America can really understand her, or the place in which she lives. Her beloved Leningrad—Peter's famous Window to the West—is like a dying flower, still beautiful to behold but dying from within.*

Not that Vera knows this yet. She is just a girl, full of dreams.

Often in the summer, she wakes in the middle of the night. At her window, she leans out, seeing all the way to the bridge. In June, when the air smells of limes and new flowers, she can hardly sleep for excitement.

It is Belye Nochi. The time of white summer nights when darkness never falls and the streets are never quiet . . .

I cannot help smiling—after all these years, I have finished my journal at last. Not a fairy tale—my story, as true as I can tell it. My father would be so proud of me. I am a writer at last.

It is my gift to my daughters, although they have given so much more to me, and without them, of course, these words would still be trapped inside, poisoning me from within.

Meredith is home with Jeff; they are preparing for Jillian's wedding. Maddy is at work, managing the gift shops her mother runs. I have never seen Meredith so happy. She and Jeff travel often. They say it is to research his novels, but they simply love to be together.

Nina is upstairs with her Daniel, whom she loves more than she realises. They have followed each other round the world on one amazing adventure after another. Supposedly they are packing now to leave again, but I suspect they are making love. Good for them.

And Anya—she will always be Anya to me—is at church with her family. They come down often and fill this house with laughter. My eldest daughter and I spend hours together in the kitchen, talking in Russian, remembering the ghosts, honouring them at last.

I open the journal one last time and write **For my children** in as bold a hand as I can manage. Then I put it aside. I cannot help closing my eyes. Falling asleep comes easily these days, and the room is so warm on this late December day.

I am a lucky woman. I did not always know that, but I do now. I am loved in my old age, and more importantly perhaps, I love.

I open my eyes, startled by something. For a moment, I am uncertain of my surroundings. Then I see the familiar fireplace, the Christmas tree, and the picture of me that hangs above the mantel.

At first, I didn't like Nina's photograph. I look so terribly sad. But it has grown on me. It was the beginning of this new life, when I finally learned that with love comes forgiveness. It is a famous photograph; people all over the world have seen it and call me a hero. Ridiculous. It is simply the image of a woman who threw much of her life away and was lucky to get some of it back.

In the corner of the room, my holy corner still stands. The candles burn from morning to night. Both of my wedding pictures stand upright, reminding me every day that I have been fortunate. Beside the photograph of Anya and Leo, a dirty grey-pink rabbit sits. His fake fur is matted and he is missing one eye.

I walk into the dining room. From here, I can see my winter garden, where everything is covered with snow. I think of my sweet Evan, who saved me when I needed saving and gave me so much.

I am barefooted and wearing only a flannel nightgown. If I go outside, Meredith and Nina will worry that I am going crazy again, that I am slipping. Only Anya will understand.

Still, I open the door. The cold air hits me so hard that for a beautiful, tragic second, I am back in my beloved city on the Neva.

I walk across the new-fallen snow, feeling it freeze my feet.

I am almost to the garden when he appears. A man, dressed all in black, with golden hair set aglow by the sunlight.

I go to the bench, hold on to its cold black frame.

He moves towards me. When he draws near, I stare into the green eyes of the man I've loved for more than seventy years.

Green. The colour takes my breath away, makes me young again.

He is real. And here. I can feel his warm presence, and when he touches me, I shiver and sit down. I can say nothing except 'Sasha . . .'

'We've waited,' he says, and at the sound of his voice, a shadow peels away from the blackness of his coat and takes its own shape. A smaller version of the man.

'Leo,' I say, unable to say more. My arms ache to reach out for my baby boy, to hold him. He looks so robust, his cheeks pink with life. Then I see that same cheek slack and grey-blue, sheened in frost. I hear him say, 'Mama . . . don't leave me . . .'

Pain makes me gasp out loud, but Sasha is there, taking my hand, saying, 'Come my, love. To the Summer Garden . . .'

The pain is gone.

I look up into my Sasha's green, green eyes and remember the grass in which we sat so long ago. It was there that I fell in love. Leo clings to me as he always did, and I scoop him up, laughing.

'Come,' Sasha says again, kissing me, and I follow.

I know that if I look back, I will see my body, old and withered, slumped on that bench in the snow; that if I wait, I will hear my daughters discover what has happened and begin to cry.

I do not look back. I hold on to Sasha and kiss my Lion's throat.

I have waited so, so long for this, to see them again. To feel like this. And I know my girls will be OK now. They are sisters, a family. And in ten years, we have loved enough for a lifetime.

I think, Goodbye, my girls. I love you. I have always loved you.

And I go.

Kristin Hannah

At the heart of *Winter Garden* is the very special relationship that often exists between mothers and daughters, and Kristin Hannah portrays this bond with particular poignancy and tenderness. It's not surprising, then, to learn that Kristin's own mother had everything to do with her daughter's career path to becoming a highly successful writer.

Kristin did not start out with dreams of writing. Instead, she planned to be a lawyer. But in her third year of law school, her mother was diagnosed with breast cancer, and the prognosis did not look good. For the next several weeks, Kristin spent her days at law school and her evenings by her mother's bedside in a Seattle hospital. 'As any of you know who have been through this sort of thing,' recalls Kristin, 'there are many things you don't want to talk about. We spent a lot of time looking for happy thoughts. It just so happened that what my mom wanted to discuss were her beloved romance novels.'

At one point, Kristin's mother turned to her and said, 'You know, you're going to be a writer.' Shortly after that they tried to write a book together. They did not finish the book, but Kristin learned something important from her mother: Anything is possible, including the dream of becoming a writer.

Sadly, Kristin's mother did not win her fight against cancer. A few years passed, and Kristin was busy with other things, including marriage and a job practising law. Then, during a difficult pregnancy, she was bedridden and had too much time on her hands. At her husband's suggestion, she unearthed the novel she had begun with her mother. With renewed determination, she started to write. The finished product, a historical romance was 'awful,' says Kristin. But the seed had been planted and Kristin continued pounding out stories. Many rejections later, her talent was finally recognised when her novel, *A Handful of Heaven*, was published in 1991. 'I went from a young mother with a cooler-than-average hobby to a professional writer, and I've never looked back,' says Kristin. 'In all the years between then and now, I have never lost my love of, or my enthusiasm for, telling stories. I am truly blessed to be a wife, a mother and a writer.'

In general, it takes Kristin about a year to write each book. She spends three months coming up with ideas, researching the story, and developing characters. Writing a first draft takes the next five months. Often Kristin goes through several starts and stops during this phase. The final process of editing and rewriting involves another four months. It's not unusual for Kristin to do ten drafts of a novel. Fortunately for her readers, her dedication and perfectionism are apparent in each well-crafted and memorable story.

A few of my favourite things—looking at this list gives you an instant snapshot of me!

Favourite movies:
Return of the King (all three *Lord of the Ring* movies, actually); *Gone with the Wind; Matrix; It's a Wonderful Life; The Way We Were; The Godfather; Bladerunner; Eternal Sunshine of the Spotless Mind; West Side Story.*

Favourite classic and current book:
To Kill a Mockingbird by Harper Lee and *The Shadow of the Wind* by Carlos Ruiz Zafon.

Favourite food:
Freshly caught lobster or Dungeness crab, with clarified butter; chateaubriand with Béarnaise sauce; fettuccini alfredo; strawberry milkshake; pina colada; my husband's chicken piccata.

Favourite places:
The beach in Kauai; the slopes of Northern Idaho; the Seattle waterfront; the San Juan Islands; southeastern Alaska; Costa Rica; New York City; San Francisco; London; Edinburgh; Nashville; the Hood Canal in Washington state.

Favourite good luck charm:
My mom's engagement diamond, which I wear on a chain.

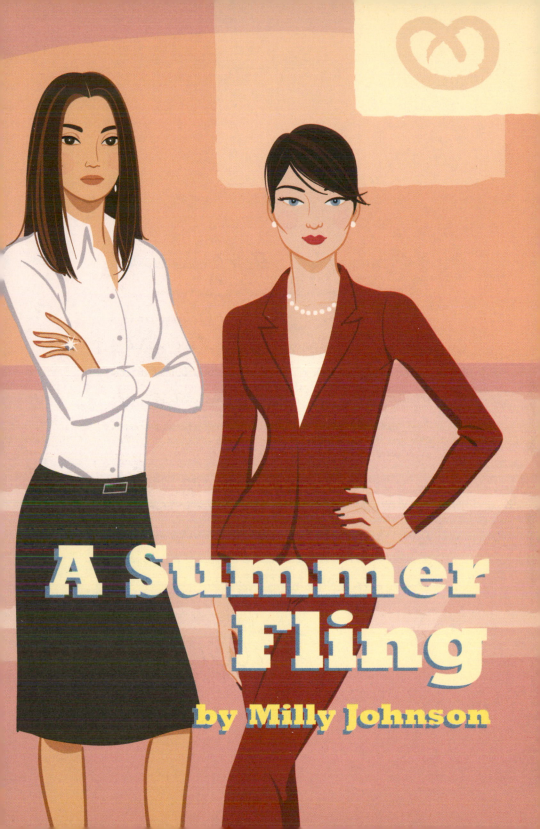

A Summer Fling

by Milly Johnson

'A Summer Fling' is about five women—
Christie, Anna, Raychel, Dawn and
Grace—from very different backgrounds
and with a range of ages, who slowly bond
with each other at work. I really loved writing
about fledgling friendships instead of
long-established ones, as I have done in my
previous novels.

There's a huge cast of people in this book
and it took me a long time to get it right, but
I'm very proud of it and hope that you enjoy the
read . . . and my vampire is going down a
storm with ladies of all ages!

Milly

Chapter 1
April

AFTER ONLY THREE WORDS of Malcolm's speech, Dawn tuned out. She didn't want to listen to his monotonous voice. Nor did she want to think about people retiring from Bakery departments. Her head was too full of confetti and honeymoons and she was counting down the hours until tomorrow morning, when she would finally be choosing her wedding dress.

While Malcolm was droning on about being at the end of an era and raising his thick polystyrene cup full of cheap white wine in Retiring-Brian's direction, she was calculating how long it was to her big day. Every tick of the clock brought her one tiny step closer to being Mrs Calum Crooke.

People were clapping now, so Dawn joined in to make it appear that she was part of the celebrations. Malcolm was smiling, she noticed. Crikey. Probably wind, thought Dawn, watching Malcolm's face return to its normal 'pissed off with the world' cast. Mind you, he *was* very pissed off with the world at the moment. He had presumed, as Deputy Head of Bakery, that he would jump into the top slot when Brian retired. He wasn't best pleased to find out he was being shunted over to Cheese and the new Head of Bakery was going to be an unknown outsider that the MD, Mr McAskill, was bringing in.

That he was going to be 'Cheese Head' and no longer a deputy, didn't do much to take the edge off his disappointment. Bakery was growing and secure, Cheese was sinking. Rumour had it that Mr McAskill was in the process of phasing it out totally. And Cheese was an entirely male department, unlike Bakery, which would now be all female. There would be far less opportunity to look down blouses or sidle up closer to his coworkers than he should do by the photocopying machines. Dawn shuddered as she remembered feeling his hand on her bum on her first day in the department. She had kept herself out of his way as much as possible after that.

Raychel stood alone, swilling the awful wine round in her cup. She was a natural wallflower, but had felt obliged to wave Brian off.

When she heard that he was leaving, she'd presumed that Malcolm would take over as boss, and had started looking at the notice board for any up-and-coming jobs within other departments. She didn't like Malcolm. He was too touchy-feely, and Raychel hated to be touched by anyone—except her husband, Ben. She had been delighted and as surprised as the other three women in the department to hear that Malcolm was being moved to Cheese, and that Grace—the oldest lady in the department—was being made deputy. The big boss, James McAskill, was bringing in a woman from outside as Head of Bakery, which had got the tongues wagging.

Not that Raychel had discussed any of this with her coworkers. They had all been in the same department for ages now but hadn't progressed beyond the 'Morning, nice day' or 'Have a good weekend' stage—give or take a bit of work talk. They were nice-enough women, all different ages, though. And now there was going to be another woman among them. Raychel wondered how she would affect the dynamics of the department, but it didn't matter much. Work was a place to earn a crust, nothing else.

Anna gave Brian a big kiss on the cheek. As bosses went, he was a nice man whose retirement had been long in his sights and he had let Malcolm run the department. Thank goodness that creep was leaving as well. 'Please' and 'Thank you' didn't feature in his vocabulary and he would bark 'Tea!' at any of them when he wanted a drink. Plus she hated the way his eyes flicked to her breasts when he was talking to her.

Anna listened to Brian getting all excited about spending the summer in a caravan on the coast and she envied him that enthusiasm. She had not one single thing to look forward to this weekend or after. She couldn't get interested in the story lines of *Coronation Street*, didn't fancy anything particular to eat, had lost the ability to lose herself in a book and knock out the image of her fiancé bonking the nineteen-year-old hired help in his barber's shop. Life stretched before Anna—longer, greyer and wetter than the entire British coastline in February.

Grace picked up Malcolm's retirement present to look at it—a carriage clock that had a very loud tock. She could almost hear it saying 'slow death, slow death, slow death' to the beat.

'You next, with any luck!' said Brian in her ear.

'Oh yes, maybe.' *God forbid.* The thought of standing where Brian was now, admiring her own clock, being toasted in warm plonk, brought on a cold, clammy sweat at the back of her neck.

'I just can't understand why you'd want to up the ante when you'd got the chance to leave this place and live a life of leisure. Could have been your retirement do as well,' said Brian with a smile.

'You know me, I like a challenge,' said Grace. She had worked with Brian for just over three years now and knew he would *so* enjoy spending his days pottering round busily doing nothing. Apart from his cheery disposition, he reminded her so much of her husband Gordon—too much for comfort—as he prattled on about the joys of retirement.

Grace's thoughts drifted off. Was she not normal in panicking every time the word 'caravan' entered a conversation? The children were adults now but she was still very close to them and didn't want to spend weeks away from them and her grandchildren with only Gordon for company.

She had always said that she would leave him when the children grew up. She wondered how many other women had resolved to do the same and were still there years after the kids had moved out because they simply weren't brave enough to go.

Her eyes caught Malcolm refilling his cup with wine. She could easily believe the rumours he was being moved to Cheese because he wasn't efficient enough to handle the growing Bakery department. Malcolm Spatchcock was neither liked nor respected, although his ego was so big that he was oblivious to that fact.

Grace hoped only that she wouldn't be wishing Malcolm back after meeting her new boss. Still, *Mrs Christie Somers* would have to be really bad to knock Malcolm down in the unpopularity stakes.

The wine and crisps were gone now and people were starting to drift off. Grace's weekend stretched out long and stark in front of her. Babysitting her granddaughter tonight while Gordon went to the Legion and her daughter and son-in-law went out for some posh meal. Shopping, washing and cleaning tomorrow, then on Sunday morning she would make the lunch, clear up, iron and then sit down in front of *Heartbeat* before a hot bath and bed, ready for the week ahead.

She said good night to Brian and her three coworkers. They all seemed nice women, although they didn't mix much. Still, the atmosphere at work was so much lighter than it was at home. Gordon's hair had gone grey in his thirties, but when did he get so grey in his head? Life would have been so much easier for Grace had she done the same.

Calum's loud beer-snoring woke Dawn. She went downstairs to try and sleep on the sofa but what she gained in peace levels, she lost in comfort. The sofa was old and past it; they really could do with another one but every spare penny was being put aside for the wedding. Well, every spare penny of hers, that was; Calum contributed what was left out of his 'social fund'. But she was going to have the fairy-tale wedding: the frock, the flowers and the fancy cake. She knew it was the start to a marriage that her mum and dad would have wanted for her.

Calum was still in bed when she pulled up in front of her future mother-in-law's council house. She beeped the horn, and a minute later Muriel wobbled down the path in leggings, a grubby-looking fleece and flip-flops. Not that Dawn would ever be ashamed to be seen with her. Muriel was Muriel, and Dawn loved her to bits, just as she was.

'Morning, lovely,' said Muriel with an excited little half-toothless grin. The Crookes were a rough family, but they had taken Dawn to their bosom. This was especially important to Dawn since her own parents had died in a car crash sixteen years ago, leaving a gaping hole in her heart. She missed them so much. She wished it was her mum sitting in the car beside her now, helping to pick out her wedding clothes. But Muriel Crooke was the next best thing.

Their first stop was 'Everything but the Bride' on the outskirts of town by the new Tesco. Dawn knew instantly that she wouldn't find her dress in there. It was as if there was only one standard pattern for all the frocks—big wide skirt and puffy sleeves—with slight variations of neckline or ribbon/sequin detail. They weren't harassed by the sales assistant whose ear was stuck on the phone.

'. . . I asked you if that length felt comfortable and you said yes. If you come in here in flats to be measured up and you're wearing heels on the day, how can that be our fault?'

Muriel pulled a face, making Dawn chuckle. They slid out of the shop and Dawn took a big gulp of air.

They drove through Penistone to stop number two: 'Love and Marriage', a far superior site on the Holmfirth Road. They had barely stepped in the shop when an assistant bore down on them, offering help.

'Just looking, thanks,' said Dawn.

'Are you searching for anything in particular?' pressed the assistant, giving Muriel a sneaky look up and down.

'I don't know,' said Dawn, wishing she could just wander round for a bit, undisturbed.

'This is nice, Dawn,' said Muriel, picking out a long, cream dress. 'Can't find the price tag though.'

'Nine thousand,' said snotty assistant woman.

'Pounds?' gasped Muriel. 'You're having a laugh?'

'It's a Vladimir Darq. The reason it's so cheap is that it's secondhand.'

Muriel's jaw dropped.

'He's a famous designer,' said the assistant. 'You *have* heard of him?'

'Can't be that famous if I've never heard of him!' sniffed Muriel.

'I have,' nodded Dawn. 'I didn't realise he was a wedding dress designer though.'

'He doesn't make bridal gowns any more,' said the assistant. 'This dress was from his very last collection—very much sought after.'

'I'm not looking for anything that . . . fancy,' said Dawn. Of course the assistant knew she meant 'expensive' by 'fancy'.

'Our range starts at five thousand for this one,' said the assistant, presenting a plain white satin dress in a thick polythene cover.

'Oh,' said Dawn. She made noises of having to go home and look at some magazines first, in order to leave the shop with some dignity.

'She thinks she's in bloody Paris!' Muriel said as they left.

It was as they were coming back to Barnsley, via the small, pretty village of Maltstone, that Dawn braked hard opposite the church.

'I didn't know there was a bridal shop here,' she said, reversing into a parking spot in front of a bay window full of the prettiest display of bridalwear. Above the door hung a sign in romantic, swirly text, saying simply 'White Wedding'.

The doorbell tinkled daintily as Dawn and Muriel entered.

'It's a Tardis!' said Muriel overloudly. The narrow shop seemed to go on for ever in length. Racks of dresses lined the walls, and showcases of tiaras and shoes ran floor to the cottage-low ceiling. Dawn's mouth opened in a round O of delight. *This is more like it!*

A very slim and smart assistant greeted them with a big smile. On her plain, black fitted dress she wore the name badge 'Freya'.

'Can I help you?' Freya asked Dawn politely.

'I'm getting married and I, er . . . need a dress,' replied Dawn shyly.

'Well, do feel free to look,' said Freya. 'But don't judge the dress until you have tried it on. You'd be surprised how many brides go out looking for one particular style only to find it doesn't suit them at all.'

'Thank you,' said Dawn. 'I don't know where to start.'

'Well, let's start with colour,' said the assistant. She studied Dawn's pale, heavily freckled skin and her shoulder-length copper hair. 'May I recommend ivory rather than white? White isn't always flattering, especially to people with pale skin like yourself. Size 10, at a guess?'

'Spot on,' returned Dawn.

'Are we going to be a summer bride or a winter one?' asked Freya.

'June,' said Dawn.

Freya pulled out a long, tapering gown, shaking out the creases.

'This is silk, ivory as you see, a bow on the back, beaded detail on the front bodice. Very flattering for the smaller-busted woman.'

'Not do me any good then,' snorted Muriel and laughed so hard that her enormous breasts jiggled like two giant blancmanges.

'It's lovely,' said Dawn, 'but it's not leaping out at me.'

'OK,' said Freya, and carefully slid it back onto the rack. 'What about this?' She presented something swimming with ruffles.

'Oooh,' squealed Muriel.

'Too fancy,' said Dawn quietly. 'Sorry, it's not me at all.'

'Oh, don't apologise,' said Freya. 'Finding out what you don't want is the most effective way to lead us to what you do want. So, fewer frills . . .'

She pulled out a very unfussy number in satin. 'This one, perhaps?'

'Neck's too high.' Dawn shook her head. 'That's gorgeous though.' She pointed to a rather full-skirted confection in white. Freya didn't look convinced, but hung it up in the changing room for her all the same. A couple of minutes later, Dawn emerged to show herself off.

'Where's your sheep, Bo Peep?' asked Muriel with a snort.

The dress drowned Dawn and, true enough, the white material made her skin look like the colour of uncooked pastry. Freya nodded in an 'I told you so' way, but kindly. And she was holding up a gown that made Dawn's eyes shine.

'It's from our vintage collection,' explained Freya.

Long and flowing, it had a beautiful scooped neck with peach rose-bud detail, a full skirt, three-quarter sleeves and was made of ivory silk. Dawn's hands reached greedily for the hanger. She closed the dressing-room curtain and when she opened it again and emerged in the dress, both Muriel and Freya gasped with delight.

'Gorgeous,' said Freya. The ivory lent her pale skin some colour, her neck looked extended by inches and the fitted bodice gave the illusion of curves where there were few.

'Oh. My. God. This is the one,' said Dawn. She was almost in tears.

'It is lovely,' said Muriel. 'How much is it?'

'It's fifteen hundred pounds.'

'Fifteen hundred for a secondhand frock!' Muriel laughed, mirthlessly.

Dawn gulped. It was over her budget, but she knew anything else would be second best.

'I don't care—I'll take it,' she heard herself say.

An hour later, Dawn had spent another two hundred and fifty pounds on shoes, a medium-length ivory veil, a tiara and some matching earrings. She hid the purchases on her Visa card and tried not to let worries about the expense spoil the excitement.

'Look at this one,' said Gordon. 'It's an eight berth.'

Grace dutifully left the sink, peered over his shoulder at the caravan catalogue and then returned to scrubbing the Sunday dinner pans, which were infinitely more interesting.

'Plenty of room for Sarah, Hugo and Sable and the baby, when it arrives, and our Laura and Joe.'

And Paul too, Grace added to herself, but there wouldn't have been much point saying it aloud. Paul was as good as dead to his father.

'It's got central heating and a built-in washing machine and dishwasher.' He looked at Grace standing with the tea towel. 'It's got more than we've got here. It would be just ideal for us when you retire.'

'I'm only fifty-five, Gordon.'

'Only?' he snorted. 'You've got to be in the next batch of early retirements. I can't understand why you haven't been asked already!'

Grace shrugged, but didn't say any more.

'I don't know, anyone else at your age would be looking forward to winding down. Can't you imagine, long summers and walks by the sea? According to the brochure, there's even a social club on site and Skegness, Mablethorpe and Ingoldmells are only a short drive away.'

'Gordon, wouldn't you prefer to go on lots of fortnights abroad in the sun? Italy, Spain, France?'

'Oh, I can't be doing with all that heat.'

'We don't have to go in August!'

'Anyway, we couldn't take the grandkiddies abroad. Our Sarah wouldn't agree to that.'

Grace doubted that. Sarah was greedy as far as baby-sitting was concerned. Grace never minded helping her daughter out; Sable was her granddaughter and she loved her dearly, but Sarah presumed that if her mother wasn't at work, she should be on hand 24/7 for her convenience.

'We should go for a weekend and take a look at some of these in the flesh,' suggested Gordon.

'Gordon, we've talked about this before and I don't really want to,' said Grace, standing her ground for once.

'You don't know what you'd like until you try it,' he said, which was ironic seeing as he would have spontaneously combusted had he ever tried anything out of his very small comfort zone. 'It'll be lovely having our own caravan instead of renting someone else's, just you wait and see,' he said. Gordon Beamish always knew best.

Chapter 2

CHRISTIE SOMERS studied herself in the huge hall mirror, smoothed the red suit down over her hips and then whisked round with a flourish.

'Niki, will I do? What do you think? Is this too bright?'

'When do you not dress in primary colours?' her brother said, shaking his head in mock exasperation. 'Don't tell me you're nervous and want to hide yourself inside a black suit?'

'I have no black clothes, so it's just as well that's a ridiculous observation,' said Christie. 'You know I don't do nerves.'

'Yes I do, and I also know that you must be the only woman in the world without black clothes.' Niki grinned at his little sister.

'Possibly,' said Christie. 'But my new department is full of women and I don't want them thinking I'm a power-suited ogre.'

'Just because you always dress beautifully doesn't mean you're an ogre. Even though you are,' said Niki, bending to give her a kiss on the head. Their wide smiles, serious cheekbones and bright-blue eyes made them instantly recognisable as siblings.

'It will be funny going back to work after so long a break,' said Christie, looking in the mirror again.

'James knows what he's doing,' said Niki. 'He wouldn't have offered you this job had he thought you couldn't do it. He's a businessman first, friend second. You'll be fine and it will do you good. I have every confidence in you and, more to the point, James has every confidence in you.'

'OK,' said Christie to her reflection. 'Let's start as we mean to go on.'

Grace arrived first into the department after the weekend. She found that the Maintenance fairies had been at work. A thick new carpet had been laid and a huge executive mahogany desk replaced the standard-issue one that Brian had been working from. There was a whiteboard now on the wall and a rather arty iron coat stand. Mr McAskill wasn't a man renowned for splashing his cash on fripperies so the gossip machine would be well cranked up by this expenditure.

No sooner had Grace switched on her PC than Dawn came in.

'Hiya,' she said breezily. 'Car park's a bit full this morning, isn't it?'

'Yes, it is,' said Grace. They were still at that polite stage, having lightweight interchanges that they'd have with a hairdresser. *Had a nice weekend? Lovely weather we're having!*

'This carpet new? It's like a bouncy castle, isn't it?' Dawn jumped up and down on it, enviously wishing the carpets in Calum's house were as thick and fresh—and free from cigarette burns and spilled beer stains.

'Yes, it is,' said Grace, spotting an unfamiliar clock on the wall as well. 'Quite a lot of things seem to have appeared since Friday.'

'Morning, everyone,' said Raychel, walking in shyly, and just behind her, chestnut-haired Anna arrived with an even quieter greeting, equally mesmerised by all the changes in the department. They all seemed a bit nervy that morning. They had hardly got to know each other and now there would be a mighty impact on even those flimsy dynamics. It felt as if it were the first day in a new class and they were all waiting for the teacher to come in and take control.

Just then a surge of excitement Mexican-waved towards them. The exalted figure of James McAskill appeared at the far end of the office alongside a woman in a bright-red suit, red shoes and coordinating bag. A personal appearance from him was unusual in itself, but the fact that he was smiling while he was talking to this woman was extraordinary. Immediately, the status of the new Bakery boss went up by a few notches. Grace noticed that Malcolm was looking over with great interest from his new department farther down the open-plan office.

'Ladies,' said Mr McAskill, 'may I present Mrs Christie Somers. Christie, may I present the ladies of my Bakery department. This is Grace'—he gestured to them one by one—'Dawn, Anna and Raychel.'

'How do you do,' said Christie in a confident, cigarette-smoky drawl. From her clothes to her voice, there was nothing quiet about this woman.

'I've just been giving Christie a guided tour and, can you believe it, I got lost,' said James McAskill with a beaming smile. Mr McAskill never smiled, despite being the multimillionaire MD and majority shareholder of the chain of mini-supermarkets, White Rose Stores, which his grandfather had started and he had developed to incredible success.

'I'm sure I'll find my way round in no time,' said Christie Somers.

'I'll leave you to get settled in then, my dear,' said Mr McAskill. Had the others known each other better, they would have exchanged furtive glances at that point. *My dear?*

'So I get the posh desk, do I?' said Christie as James McAskill left her to settle herself in with her new team. 'This one?' She indicated the curved desk behind the privacy screen.

'Yes, that's yours,' said Grace with a kindly smile.

'That screen will have to go,' said Christie. 'Can't see what's going on behind that thing!'

Malcolm had insisted on the screen. That way he could play games on the Internet without anyone seeing he was skiving.

'I'll call Maintenance for you, shall I?' asked Grace.

'No, just show me the way to the telephone directory and I'll do it myself,' said Christie.

Lord, she was different from Malcolm, thought Grace.

'So, first things first. Let's all go for a coffee and bond,' said Christie. 'I think I can just about remember my way to the canteen.'

'What, now?' said Dawn.

'Yes.'

'All of us?'

'Yes.'

'What—and leave the phones?' said Grace. Cardinal sin. Malcolm would have had them all beheaded for less.

'I'm sure that voicemail can pick them up for half an hour. Come on. I need to meet you properly and for that we need coffee and biscuits,' said Christie. She marched off in the direction of the stairs, the others trailing behind her like little ducks behind their mam.

Twenty minutes later, the five women were halfway down their coffees in the canteen. James McAskill had told Christie that he thought he had the ideal mix in his department now. But still, Christie thought, he couldn't have found a more varied selection of females if he'd tried. The older one, Grace, was fifty-five and very well named too, with her lovely white-blonde hair that fell in a delicate swoop of silver to her jawline. She had, apparently, been especially keen to take up the deputy position, even turning down the chance of early retirement for it. Then there was Anna, thirty-nine, quiet and unsmiling, hiding behind her twin curtains of long chestnut hair. She twiddled constantly with a small, diamond-studded ring on her wedding finger and her eyes looked dull, as if she hadn't had quality sleep for a long time. Then there was Dawn, thirty-three, a young woman with an outward smile on her freckly face, but too many worries behind those large, toffee-coloured eyes. Last, but not least, the 'baby', Raychel, twenty-eight—a beautiful girl with gentle, grey eyes and gypsy-black curls, who, Christie suspected, hid her light well and truly under a bushel. She doubted she had them wrong; she rarely did. She'd inherited her psychologist father's genes and was constantly analysing people.

'James has great plans for Bakery,' Christie said. 'He wants to launch his Suggestion Scheme from here. We will be in charge of administrating all the ideas that come in from colleagues in the field about Bakery. If it works, he'll be rolling the scheme out to other departments.'

'That's good news,' said Grace. Her job was safe for a while longer.

'What was the last boss like then?' asked Christie.

'Brian? Very nice man,' returned Grace.

'He was all right, was Brian,' added Dawn. 'Think he was getting tired, though, by the end. He left most of the running to Malcolm.' She gave an involuntary shudder when she said his name, which Christie couldn't help but notice.

'Malcolm Spatchcock, that would be?' Christie asked. James had warned her about him. Not that he was one for gossip, but he felt it fair to tell her that Malcolm had not been very pleased to be removed to Cheese, even though it was a promotion. Christie had picked up from that conversation that Malcolm Spatchcock was not one of James's favourite people, although he would never have said as much.

'He's gone to be the Business Unit Manager of Cheese,' said Dawn dryly, adding under her breath, 'Cheese B.U.M. Appropriate.'

Raychel gave a little snort trying to hold a giggle in.

Anna said nothing, just nodded in agreement. In the months they'd been working together, she'd barely spoken. She was a grafter not a talker, the others had each decided.

'It's so lovely to meet you all and share a coffee and break the ice a bit,' said Christie, smiling at each and every one of them. 'I like to run a nice, cheerful ship. We spend a lot of time on board at work so the last thing I want is for it to be a miserable experience.'

Niki was chopping carrots when Christie got home that night.

'Salmon steaks and assorted veg for tea,' said Niki.

'Lovely!' said Christie, kicking off her shoes and wriggling her toes.

'Well?' prompted Niki. 'How was it?'

'Lovely!' said Christie again. 'The women I'm working with are all incredibly nice people and I think I'm going to like it very much.'

'Smashing,' said Niki. 'How was James?'

'James was James,' nodded Christie. 'Sweet as always, although I get the impression everyone's a little scared of him. They're all in awe of him.'

'Well, he's an impressive man,' said Niki.

'I think everyone is wondering what my connection is to him,' smirked Christie.

'Let them,' replied Niki. 'Anyway, are any of your girls attractive enough for me?'

'They're all very attractive.' Christie grinned at him. 'And they're all either married or engaged—no empty ring fingers, alas.'

'Damn!' said Niki with mock frustration.

'Raychel and Dawn are far too young for an old geezer like you, anyway. Now Grace is about five years older than you but stunning. You'd make a very striking couple.' Christie smiled playfully.

Niki dropped the salmon steaks onto the grill. 'If you're changing out of that suit, you've got five minutes to do it. I'm not overcooking salmon for you or anyone.'

None of them mentioned it, but all four women felt the change in atmosphere in the department. It was as if someone had filtered the air and made it lighter and fresher.

Christie was introduced to a lot of people over the next couple of days. She was all too aware that many of the unit managers were curious about her personal connection to James McAskill. But they also knew that he wasn't a fool and would not have brought anyone into the business to head such a coveted department if they weren't highly qualified. It became obvious to anyone who had a conversation with Christie Somers that she knew her retail onions.

Christie was equally impressed by her team. James had done a good job of picking them. They had lovely telephone manners and were very efficient in their work. Dawn looked after Christie's diary and was obviously a natural organiser. The only thing that concerned her was that there was no interaction *between* them. She wondered what was going on in their lives that kept them so tightly bound up in themselves.

Malcolm left it until the end of the week before he swaggered over to Christie's desk and introduced himself. He had seen the way McAskill had led her in, and he wasn't an idiot. He knew Christie Somers was someone important. Someone to have on side.

'Charmed to meet you,' he smiled and flicked his eyes quickly over her full-busted figure. He stuck his hand out confidently. 'Malcolm Spatchcock, as in the game bird.'

'Christie,' she returned. 'As in the serial killer.'

He gave a nervous laugh, taken aback at her humour. It flitted through his mind that she was being sarcastic, but there was a wide, welcoming smile on her face and her handshake was firm and friendly.

'Apologies, it's my attempt at an icebreaker,' she explained.

'Very amusing. Well, anything you want to know about Bakery, feel free to ask. I used to run the department.' Malcolm's voice dropped to a whisper. 'Between you and me, the named Head wasn't interested once he'd got his retirement date. I kept the department afloat.'

'Well, thank you. You've done a good job.'

'Worked in Bakery before?' he asked.

'No, never,' Christie replied without elaboration.

'Where did you come from? Morrison's? Handi-Save?'

'Neither of those,' Christie replied. My goodness he was nosy. She hoped he wasn't the type who would try to undermine her at his earliest convenience. If he was, he was in for a shock. Confrontation excited her. She was good at it.

'We should have lunch. I had some good ideas for the department that I never got the chance to implement. It would be a shame to see them go to waste.'

'Yes, indeed. That would be lovely,' said Christie.

'Good, good. We'll get something arranged soon,' said Malcolm with a wink before wending his way back to Cheese, safe in the knowledge that he had had a very successful first meeting with someone who could be a key figure at White Rose Stores.

Christie mused for a few moments. Malcolm was friendly enough, she supposed. Maybe his brashness was overcompensation for nerves. Then her thoughts were hijacked by the sight of the clock. Once again it was 5 p.m. and no one was making a move towards the coat stand.

'Haven't you seen the time, ladies?' said Christie.

They all nodded.

'And?' Christie perched on the edge of Anna's desk.

'Well, we don't usually finish until five thirty,' said Raychel.

'Why? Are you gluttons for punishment?'

'No, but . . .' began Dawn, before clamming up.

'Go on,' urged Christie.

'Well, Malcolm always made it really clear that we should be putting extra time in.'

'What tosh!' said Christie. 'Anyway, I'm Head of this department now so we'll have no more nonsense. If people can't do their jobs in a thirty-five-hour week, then we need to look at getting extra staff.'

'We're perfectly up-to-date with everything,' volunteered Grace.

'There you are then. Now go—the lot of you. And I'll see you at nine on Monday morning and not before. It's Friday night, for goodness' sake. Don't you have men and social lives to go to?'

They all rose nervously and slowly started to get their coats, unable to shake off the feeling that they were sneaking off.

Christie waved them goodbye with a smile. What a lovely bunch of women. She hoped they all did have a smashing weekend. Life was too short to be miserable—as she knew only too well.

Anna realised that by leaving the office at just after five she could catch the earlier train home. She was probably the only woman in the world who wouldn't have seen that as a treat. It just made the evening stretch even longer in front of her, so she went window-shopping in town to kill some time. She caught sight of her reflection in a glass window. The image it threw back at her was that of the ugliest woman in the world: tired, dull eyes with ghoulish circles, cracked, dry lips and a skin tone that was somewhere between old dishcloth and corpse. It was the face of a woman whom no one in the world valued, not even herself. No wonder her fiancé Tony had run off to the fresh-faced Lynette Bottom.

She was days away from being forty and her life was over.

At the station she stood on the spring-chilly platform, hands stuffed deep into her coat pockets. On the opposite platform, other passengers waited for the Sheffield train going south. A man stood apart from them. He was tall, dressed in a long, generously cut, cape-like black coat and a black hat with a wide brim that threw his face into shade. Anna glanced at him to find him staring over at her. She moved her eyes away, flicking them back to see he was still transfixed by her. *Why would he be staring at me? I'm hardly Gwyneth Paltrow!* she mused. *Come on train,* willed Anna, uncomfortable now. She tried not to look over, but the temptation to see if he was still watching was too much. She found that he was.

The train pulled along the track, blocking his view of her. Anna climbed aboard and slotted into a seat. As the train pulled away, Anna stole a last glance from her position of safety. The man was *still* looking at her. Her last view was of him doffing his hat at her with a smile. What's more, she could have sworn she saw the glint of fangs as he did so.

One year ago exactly, Vladimir Darcescu, or Vladimir Darq, as he was more famously known in the world of couture, had stunned London by making his English base a house in Barnsley. For years his business manager had been buying up land as investments, and one very large, expensive plot was in a village called Higher Hoppleton on the out-skirts of Barnsley, an ex-pit town in very deepest Yorkshire.

Two years ago, Vladimir had decided to go up and see the extent of his business manager's madness but instead was pleasantly surprised.

He stayed at the local pub, the Lord Spencer, for three days. Locals greeted him with a friendly 'How do' when he wandered round the shops or took tea in the café in the very beautiful Hoppleton Hall, an old square jewel in the middle of the lovely nearby park. He liked it very much in this village; in fact, he felt at home. The people reminded him of those in Tiresti, his Romanian birthplace. He liked to listen to their banter and he basked in their friendliness.

He particularly liked the ambience of the Lord Spencer. The landlady was a very attractive older lady with a rather droopy chest and sloping shoulders. Vladimir Darq knew that with the right lingerie she could look years younger, and magnificent. It was then that he had his epiphany.

Within the week, Vladimir Darq had had plans drawn up to erect a house on his land, and within the year the gothic-type hall—Darq House—was completed. And he was to stun the fashion world again by announcing that he was branching out into the lingerie business with price labels accessible to all women. He wanted to be able to make any female feel fantastic *and* comfortable. He knew he could do that by dressing them in the right underwear.

And so it was that Corona Productions got wind of his intended project and persuaded him to star in the flagship TV show, *Jane's Dames,* in which a member of the public was transformed without the need for plastic surgery.

Vladimir, however, insisted he choose the woman. But shooting was scheduled to begin in four weeks and he still hadn't found 'the one', though he had trawled supermarkets and shops for her. Then he wondered if he might find his unpolished jewel heading for home at the end of a hard week's work. Which is why he had ended up on a Barnsley railway station platform that Friday in April.

Grace pushed open the door of the garden centre café. Maltstone was a pretty little village with a lovely café at the side of a country stream. She loved it there because it was the special place where she met her boy. She looked round and caught sight of the strapping young man stand-ing and waving to her and she grinned and walked briskly over to the table he occupied.

'Hello, my darling,' she said, and was enfolded in her son's embrace.

'Hello, Mum. Sorry, it's been too long,' he said, as they sat down.

'You're busy, darling, I know,' said Grace with a smile as warm as a lit winter fireplace. 'You're looking well.'

'So are you. But then you always do. I ordered us tea already,' he said, pouring from a waiting teapot. 'How's Dad?'

'Oh, you know, the same,' said Grace. She didn't say he sent his love; they both knew that would have been a lie. 'Anyway, Happy Birthday.' Grace handed over a carrier bag. 'If you don't like it, I've left the receipt in—'

'Mum, you have great taste and I've never had to change a thing you've given me.' He squeezed her hand and Grace hung onto his fingers for a few sad moments. It shouldn't be like this, skulking round seeing her boy. He should be spending his twenty-eighth birthday embraced in his family home, blowing out silly candles on a cake, even at his age. She had always made a big fuss of them all on their birthdays.

'So, what do you have to tell me?' she said, sniffing back a threatening cloudburst of sudden tears.

'Well . . .' He reached down, fiddled in a briefcase and brought up a file, which he opened. He handed over some photos. 'I've bought it, Mum. That is, myself and my business partner, Charles.'

Grace looked down at the old manor house set in its own grounds, which her talented boy was going to turn into an old people's home.

'It's going to be gorgeous, Mum. Every room en suite—fourteen, the architect reckons—a fifty-foot conservatory facing east for breakfasts, a library, Internet, webcams, a pool, a cinema . . .'

'Slow down,' said Grace, but loving his enthusiasm.

'It will be the most beautiful residential home I can make. The place is a mess at the moment, but you should see how many of the original features are still there. And the garden will be lovely with work. Oh, Mum, we can't wait to get started.'

His face was radiant with excitement. This was a deal Paul had been working towards for years. She had no doubt he would be successful at it. He was a fighter, though some of his energies were taken up with fighting things he shouldn't be and that saddened her so very much.

'I'm going to call it Rose Manor, after Granny,' he beamed.

Grace nodded. 'That's a lovely idea. She would have been so proud of you, Paul. And so would your mother.'

'Really? Do you think they would have been bothered by my sexual proclivity as much as Dad is? I often wonder.'

'They would have loved you for being you and been as proud as Punch of you,' said Grace definitely. She might not have been able to grow children in her body, but she had grown them in her heart and she felt every bit their mother. But, even though she had never known Gordon's first wife, Rita, who had died suddenly and tragically, Grace had always been careful never to usurp her position as true mother. Pictures of Rita still sat in frames in the house and every Mother's Day and on Rita's birthday, Grace had taken the children to her grave to lay flowers. It was only right she should have the deepest respect for the woman who had given her the greatest gift ever. She had the feeling that Rita would have been her friend had their lives overlapped.

'Your Nana Rose would have laughed her head off to be told she was having a mansion named after her,' said Grace.

'Do you think?'

'I know so,' said Grace. She had fallen in love with Rose Beamish on their very first meeting. She oozed life and love and laughter despite the asthma that crippled her. She never once moaned, taking her illness in her stride. Grace had been brokenhearted when she died. Gordon had been of the 'It's a blessing' school of sentiment. He wasn't a man for much emotion. But Grace felt the emptiness in the house for a long time after Rose's passing.

'Look, I can't see you next Saturday, but can you sneak off the weekend after—Easter weekend? Meet you here, same time? I'd like to introduce you to Charles. I've told him about you.'

'Aw, bless you,' said Grace, adding, 'So is Charles a *partner* as well as a partner?'

Paul grinned. 'He's a partner. He is someone's *partner* but more about that one later.'

'I'll be here, same time,' said Grace.

The weekends were the worst for Anna. A desert where her thoughts tormented her and the bed seemed bigger than ever. It had been nearly two months now since she had walked in, needing Tony's arms round her more than ever, and saw the note on the table. *Sorry, need some time to think and we need some time apart. There is no one else though—honest.* Obviously, with Tony having an elastic relationship with the truth, there was indeed someone else. Lynette Bottom, aged nineteen with a peachy bottom and bobbly tits. He had taken her on in his barber's shop as a Girl Friday about six months ago. Now she was official bed-warmer. Anna wondered if he'd put her hourly rate up for that.

Anna hadn't heard from him since he had left, which was good in a way, she tried to tell herself, because he hadn't come back for his stuff or asked for a split of assets. And his share of the mortgage and council tax was still going into the bank. So she let him do what he had to, unharassed, under absolutely no pressure, and hoped one day that the answering machine would be flashing a message that he'd had his fun and wanted to come home.

Chapter 3

'MORNING, GIRLS!' said a cheerful Christie to her troupe of four. It was five to nine on Monday morning and they still looked furtive, as if they were sneaking in late. This job was just what she needed. She was so grateful she had mentioned the fact to James McAskill that she was looking for a full-time job. The ladies intrigued her, each in their own unique way; they all seemed locked in their own little worlds. Grace, for instance. How many women in their fifties refused healthy offers of early retirement—not once, but twice? What was she running from? And young Dawn was positively schizophrenic. Sometimes she had that glow of a girl in love, only for it to be replaced by the world's biggest worries showing on her face—what was all that about? Little Ray was a sweetheart, but so jumpy. Nails constantly in her mouth. Anna intrigued her most of all. Had she ever bloomed? Christie wondered. She had the air of one who never had. That would be so unfair if she had not. Everyone should have days to look back on when they could say, 'I was at my most beautiful then.'

'Morning, everyone,' said Malcolm, swaggering through the office. The ladies returned the greeting politely enough.

'Morning, Christie,' said Malcolm, leaning over her desk. 'I thought we might have lunch together. Let me take you through some of the ideas for the department that I never got to implement.'

'Yes, of course,' said Christie. The man was making an effort to be friendly and it would have been very rude of her to rebuff him. 'Shall we say twelve in the canteen?'

'Or we could go to the Italian round the corner?' he angled.

'The canteen is fine by me,' said Christie in such a way that it brooked no discussion.

'Oh . . . er . . . canteen it is then. Catch you later.' He cocked his finger at her and then strolled back down the office with a satisfied grin.

At twelve, Christie clocked Malcolm settled at a canteen table with a generous serving of shepherd's pie and salad. She picked up a plate of ravioli, sprinkled it with parmesan, and joined him.

'Food's not bad here,' he said.

'Yes, it's very good,' said Christie and speared a cushion of pasta.

'Mr McAskill eats here a lot. But I suppose you know that already.'

Christie veered away from the subject that she suspected Malcolm wanted to angle towards.

'So, you were saying you had some ideas,' she deflected.

'Oh, yes. Well, James McAskill, *as you know*, is really into incentivising. I thought you might like to show him this. I sourced some great promotional gifts before I gave up the department for Cheese,' he said, as if he'd had a choice in the matter. He ferreted in his coat pocket and brought out a clear plastic isosceles triangle. Through the middle was the company logo and across the widest part were the words, 'I spoke and White Rose Stores listened.'

'Very impressive,' said Christie. It was awful and she couldn't think of anyone who would be inspired to spend their time trying to improve the business in the hope of getting one of these things in return.

'It's a paperweight,' said Malcolm. He loaded his mouth with potato.

'Very light for a paperweight,' said Christie. 'Wouldn't it have been better in glass?'

'Health and safety issue,' said Malcolm. 'Plus, glass would be too expensive. You could order in bulk to cut costs even further. It would do nicely for when they roll out the idea to other departments because it's a general statement—not tied to Bakery in any way.'

Christie made a series of facial gestures that Malcolm took to mean that she was speechless with admiration. 'I'll bear it in mind, certainly.'

'I know Mr McAskill would love this idea and I don't mind if you were to tell him where it came from,' said Malcolm, with a wink. Christie knew James would view it from all angles and say, 'What on earth is it?' before slam-dunking it in his bin.

Malcolm bought two coffees after their meal was finished and more of his mediocre ideas had been imparted.

'How are you getting on with those women?' said Malcolm, imbuing the last two words with all the joy of sniffing off-milk.

'I like them very much.'

'Funny bunch if you ask me,' said Malcolm. 'That Grace is a snobby piece, thinks she is above everyone. Anna's sullen. Never seen her smile yet. And I understand Dawn is getting married, isn't she?'

'Is she indeed?' asked Christie.

'Word of warning, that sort always make too many personal calls. Don't know anything about the other one, the young one, Raychel, except I would have thought she was a bit boring to have in such an energy-driven project. I'm surprised Mr McAskill picked that lot, to be honest. I'd have had at least one man in there myself.'

'Well, I have to say, I find them all extremely amiable and hard-working,' Christie said brightly.

'You do realise they've already started taking the mick, coming in at nine and going home as soon as the clock hits five?'

'But that's the working day. Why on earth should anyone do more?'

'Because that's what we do at White Rose Stores, my dear,' he said with a very patronising smile.

That gave Christie the perfect escape clause.

'I'm totally indebted to you for the insight,' she nodded. 'I had better get back and make sure they're behaving, in that case.' And with that she purposefully picked up her tray.

'Quite,' said Malcolm with a smug grin, pleased that she had taken his comments on board. 'I think I'm just going to have a small portion of apple pie before I get back to the Cheese grindstone. It's been lovely talking to you, Christie.'

'And you, Malcolm. Very useful. Very . . . revealing.'

'Ta daaahhh,' said Ben at exactly half past nine on the Tuesday night. 'Finished one room at least, thank goodness.'

'Brilliant,' said Ray, drawing the last brushful of paint across the wall. 'Only two more rooms to go.'

'Ah, we'll have it done by the weekend. It's worth it though, isn't it? A free month's rent for a few evenings of this?' asked Ben.

'I suppose so, but there're a lot of walls to paint.'

'The house looks bigger in this colour.'

'Remind me never to wear magnolia trousers then,' said Raychel.

'Give over, you've hardly got a bottom,' said Ben.

'"Give over?" You're turning into a Yorkshireman!'

'Aaarrghh!' screamed Ben, as if that was a fate worse than death. But in truth he didn't miss his roots in Newcastle. Sometimes it was as if there was no life before he and Raychel moved to Barnsley and rented this small terraced house in the Old Town district. He felt settled here. He had a good job and Ray seemed to enjoy hers. And if she was happy, he was happy.

'That four hundred quid we've saved will go nicely towards the first mortgage payment.'

They both started to grin at each other.

'Our first mortgage. Can you believe it?'

'I can't believe we're actually excited about paying out a big wodge of money every month. How sad are we?'

'Very.'

'You OK anchoring yourself permanently to a life in Barnsley?' said Raychel, the smile suddenly sliding from her face.

'Where you go, I go,' said Ben, resting his arms on her shoulders.

'I like it here. Isn't that odd?'

'Why is it odd?' said Ben, giving her a tiny kiss on her head.

'Because of all places, we end up here. Where my parents came from.'

'You never knew the place. It's not as if you have bad memories here.'

'I suppose not,' Raychel mused.

'There's loads of work around for me, Raychel. I've never felt as settled as I do here.' Ben squeezed his wife. 'Maybe we're growing up at last.' He nudged her playfully but she wasn't smiling. He knew where her thoughts were. The past was always waiting for their minds to slip back to it, like a muddy slope with little grip on the sides.

He slapped her bottom lightly to break her out of her reverie. 'You go and have the first bath. I'll get on with making something to eat.'

'No, let's get a curry delivered,' said Raychel, pasting on a smile.

'I won't argue with that,' said Ben. 'Go on, and I'll have the water after you, so no weeing in it.'

'How will you know?' teased Ray on her way out. He pretended to chase her and she squealed.

Ben's smile dropped when she disappeared up the staircase.

'Please God, make us happy in our new flat,' he whispered. He didn't ask to win the lottery or live for ever, he just hoped God would come through for them and give them some peace at last.

Midweek, during the morning, Christie looked up and saw her ladies all beavering away. In her time, she had headed departments that needed pulling into line for their gossip:work ratio, and this was unnatural. Nor did it make for the best working environment, in her opinion.

'Staff meeting, in the canteen please, ladies, two minutes, so switch your phones to voicemail,' she called out.

Down in the canteen, a fresh batch of buttered scones had just been put out. Christie piled five onto her tray. Proper elevenses!

'Help yourselves, girls,' she said, sitting down.

Anna wasn't hungry. She'd hardly eaten anything since the weekend —her appetite had absconded with Tony—but everyone else had taken a scone. She could nibble at it, she supposed. She really ought to eat.

'Right, I want to know three interesting facts about all of you—it can be anything—but things that are important to you,' announced Christie, after swallowing a big bite of scone. 'I'll go first. I'm a widow, no children, and I live with my brother who is a dentist. Two: I love clothes, especially vintage ones, and double-especially shoes, and have far more than I'll ever wear. Three: I love strawberries and I can't damn well eat them because they bring me out in a rash.'

The ladies laughed gently.

'That's cruel, isn't it?' said Grace. 'It's like loving animals but being allergic to their fur.'

'Your turn, Grace.'

Grace racked her brains. Three *interesting* things. She couldn't think of one.

'They don't have to be extreme,' coaxed Christie. 'Just three things about yourself that we don't know.'

'Well, number one, I've been doing yoga for nearly thirty years. I start off every morning with quarter of an hour and finish off every evening with the same.'

'Wish I were that disciplined,' said Dawn. 'I haven't done any exercise for a long time.'

'You've a lovely figure, anyway, though,' said Grace.

'I'm all legs, which is a pain when I'm buying trousers because they're never long enough!'

'Lucky you. I always need to have mine taken up. Anyway, go on, fact number two, Grace,' urged Christie.

'Right, erm . . . well, I have three children: Laura is twenty-nine, Paul is twenty-eight and Sarah is twenty-five, and two grandchildren: Joe, who is Laura's little boy, he's five years old; and Sarah's little girl, Sable, is four; and there's another brother or sister on the way for her.'

'You married, Grace?' asked Raychel, not hearing any mention of a husband in the family run-down.

'Oh, yes, I've been married to Gordon for twenty-three years. He was a plastic injection moulding engineer but he took early retirement.'

Interesting, thought Christie. Her husband took early retirement yet she was fighting it. And from the ages of her children, they were all born out of wedlock. She'd had Grace pigeonholed as someone traditional!

'And your third fact?'

Grace thought hard, then she grinned.

'I've had a coffee with Phillip Schofield.'

'You haven't!' gasped Raychel. 'I love Phillip Schofield!'

'Where was that?' asked Dawn, open-mouthed.

'Starbucks in Leeds train station about four years ago,' said Grace quite proudly. 'All the tables were taken and he asked if he could sit at mine because I was by myself.'

'Did you get his autograph?' Christie asked.

'He signed my serviette,' replied Grace.

'Your turn, Dawn,' said Christie.

'OK, well, I'm getting married in two months. Last Saturday in June. To Calum.'

A tinkle of congratulatory noises was the result of that revelation.

'Big white wedding?' asked Christie.

'Small to medium. I don't have any family. I'm having the big frock and the church and the cake, but not hundreds of guests. Can't really afford to.'

'What will your married name be?' said Raychel, wiping her mouth with a napkin.

'Crooke. Not the most romantic name. Not like yours—*Love!*' said Dawn with a smile. Not that she minded. Being Mrs Crooke was good enough in her book and made her insides warm at the thought of it. 'Second: I've played the guitar since I was a kid and my most prized possession is the guitar that my parents gave me on my seventeenth birthday. They were both killed in a car accident a few weeks later.'

'Oh my God, that's terrible,' said Grace with heartfelt sympathy.

'I know,' nodded Dawn. 'I miss them so much, especially with the wedding coming up.'

'You must,' agreed Christie. 'And do you still play the guitar?'

'Not as often these days,' said Dawn.

'You must be good, though, if you've been playing it all this time. Didn't you ever join a band or anything?' asked Grace.

'No, I'm no way near good enough to join a band,' said Dawn with a smile. A rather sad little smile, thought Christie.

'And thirdly, oh crikey, can't think of anything. Oh, yes, I can: up until two years ago I was a hairdresser.'

'What made you change career?' asked Christie.

'I was getting bored with hairdressing and went on a computer course and I really, really enjoyed it. So when I found a vacancy for this place in the newspaper, I applied and got it. Didn't think I had a chance.'

The girl doesn't have a lot of self-confidence, deduced Christie. Funny how it was always the pretty, capable ones who didn't.

All eyes turned to Raychel, who had very pink cheeks as a result. Her coworkers smiled encouragingly.

'Three things quickly, Raychel, then you can escape the spotlight,' said Christie, patting her hand.

'I must be the most boring person on the planet,' said Raychel, taking a deep breath. 'OK. I'm married to Ben, who is a builder.'

'Is he a Barnsley lad?' asked Dawn.

'No, he's a Geordie.'

'Oh, I wondered if you'd moved here to be with him. You're from Newcastle as well, presumably, with that accent, aren't you?' Dawn popped the last bit of her scone into her mouth and chewed.

'We used to live in London and he met a bloke down there that was looking for workers up here,' Raychel explained.

'Funny. Most people are moving down south for work and there's you moving the other way!' Dawn commented. 'Been married long?'

'Ten years.'

'Blimey!' said Anna, her first contribution of the morning.

'How many children do you have then?' asked Dawn, who drew the conclusion that anyone who got married so young had to be pregnant. But Raychel surprised her.

'No children and no plans for them. Right, number two.' She tapped with her fingertips on the table as she thought. 'I like to paint pictures. I've always been into art. I'd have liked to have been an artist.'

'Are you any good?' asked Dawn.

'I don't know,' said Raychel. 'I just enjoy doing it. It relaxes me. Bit like your yoga does for you, Grace. And thirdly, I'm moving into a new flat next month and I can't wait. We've got one of the new apartments in Milk Street, where the old dairy used to be. Right at the top.'

'A penthouse then,' winked Christie.

'It's lovely,' said Raychel with a contented sigh. 'I'm going to measure up for curtains at the weekend and I can't wait. How sad is that?'

'I think it's lovely,' said Dawn, who wished she and Calum could move into a new place.

'Anna?' Christie tilted her head at the quiet woman with the sad eyes.

'Happily engaged to, and living with, Tony, who's a barber; I hate cats; and I love Hammer Horror films.'

'I used to love the old Hammer Horrors,' said Grace. 'I had a bit of a thing for Christopher Lee.'

'Once, the nuns at school asked me what I wanted to be when I grew up,' said Anna, sliding back into a memory. 'I told them I wanted to be a vampire. I got a right thrashing for it as well!'

'You have the look of a gothic maid.' Christie weighed Anna up. Full-bosomed, small-waisted and pouty-lipped, the woman would have been transformed with the right neckline and a bit of red lipstick. She had the look of a woman sadly neglected. By herself more than anyone.

'Werewolf or vampire. Which would you go for?' asked Raychel, who had just finished reading *Twilight* and rather fancied the former. The werewolf protagonist reminded her of Ben, all massive and warm.

'No question,' sniffed Anna. 'Vampire every time. Couldn't do with all that werewolf-moulting. It'd block up my Dyson.'

Everyone laughed. Anna had a dry sense of humour, that seemed evident. Christie drained her cup and then noticed that everyone with anything left in their cups followed suit.

'Right, best get back to work then. Thank you for that, ladies. I feel I know you all a little better now.'

Christie led the way out. She was aware that behind her, Grace was twittering to Dawn and Raychel was asking Anna something. She smiled to herself. The thaw had commenced.

Paul rang Grace on her mobile at work that afternoon. 'Mum, you are aware it's the Grand National on Saturday?' he asked.

'My goodness, it's never been a year since the last one? I'll get a newspaper and look at the horses' names.'

'I've looked already. There's one running called The Sun Rose. I'll have to go for it, for my Nana.'

'Oh, well, let's do that then. It's as good an omen as any.'

'Same arrangement as usual?'

'Same arrangement. On the nose.'

'You can pick up your winnings when I see you next week. We'll have lots of cake, the full shebang cream tea. I'll pay.'

He was the most generous soul she knew. 'Oh, Paul, I wish you could meet someone who'd love you for the wonderful person you are!'

I wish you could as well, Mum, said Paul to himself.

Gordon hated gambling and so every year, for as long as she could remember, Grace and Paul had had a secret bet. They didn't study form and distance or anything like that, they just picked a horse with a name that meant something to both of them, whatever the odds. They had won for two years running now, first with Amazing Grace, then last year on the rank outsider, Laura's Boy. Grace put the winnings in the secret bank account she had opened two years ago and which Gordon knew nothing about. She had started squirrelling away some of her money to leave to Paul if anything happened to her. Gordon had cut his son out of his will. It annoyed him no end that she hadn't done the same.

'The Sun Rose?' said Christie, looking over Grace's shoulder at the name she had just written down on her pad. 'Are you betting on horses, Mrs Beamish?'

'Just once a year,' said Grace. 'My boy and I always have a bet on the Grand National.'

'Of course! It's the Grand National on Saturday, isn't it?' said Christie. 'Shall we all have a go?'

'What, together or separate?' asked Dawn.

'Together,' said Christie. 'One up, all up.'

'Anyone got a paper?' asked Anna. 'Let's have a look at some names.' Maybe there would be an appropriate *Tosser of a Fiancé*, or a *Fat-Titted Scrubber* that drew her eye.

'I have,' said Dawn and got out her *Sun* newspaper. She turned to the back pages and looked at the preview of the race.

'Any good names?' asked Raychel.

'Augustus, Elvis Smith, Chocolate Soldier, Mayfly, Hell for Leather, Royal Jelly, Leapfrog, Silver Lady, Milky Bar, The Sun Rose.' Dawn gave a little gasp. 'Wow, I'm reading the *Sun*!' she said. 'That has to be a sign.'

Anna half tutted, half smiled. 'I would have thought with your name being *Dawn* that it would strike more of a chord. Dawn . . . sun rising?'

Dawn gasped, open-mouthed. 'Crikey, I never thought of that!'

'What are the odds on it?' asked Christie.

'Fifty to one,' said Grace. 'That's the horse my son and I have picked.'

'He's a grey. Can't remember the last time a grey won the National. Hmm . . .' Christie read on. The horse didn't have a lot of form so he was either going to be a total loser or a surprise in the unveiling.

'I'm happy if everyone else is,' said Anna, who knew nothing about horses and wasn't really bothered who won, if the truth be told.

'Me too,' said Raychel. 'Fiver each?'

'Count me in,' said Dawn. 'Let's go mad and make it a tenner.' She was throwing so much money away these days, what harm would another few quid do?

Malcolm watched them from the next section. It was quite obvious they were picking horses for the National. He spotted McAskill rounding the corner. *This should be interesting,* he thought and waited. McAskill's whole pet department was either reading the horse-racing bit of the newspaper or faffing about with their purses. He wouldn't like that. As Malcolm watched, James McAskill and Christie started arguing about something, but laughing too. Open-mouthed, Malcolm saw Mr McAskill open up his wallet and hand some paper money over to Christie. The bloody woman was fireproof.

Dawn had the television on for the big race as she studied the brochure of wedding favour examples. Sugared almonds always looked very pretty but they were horrible things to eat. She thought that maybe she should wrap a single chocolate for everyone. It would be far nicer and a damned sight cheaper as she badly needed to cut some costs on this wedding somewhere. She had spent nearly all her savings, and hadn't even thought about flowers or the cake or the honeymoon yet!

The horses were getting into position. Her ears picked up the name of one: June Wedding. She wished she'd known that one was running; that would have had to have been her choice. Too late now, obviously. Suddenly they were off. A horse fell at the first. There were thirty fences in all. By the time the horses had got to the Chair at the fifteenth, Dawn was leaning forward and shouting encouragement. Elvis Smith had the lead from the beginning. He was still in first place as they passed the open ditch, Becher's Brook—for the second time—then at the Canal Turn he lost the lead to Chocolate Soldier. He slid into third place behind Mayfly but then Chocolate Soldier refused Valentine's. Royal Jelly was belting up on the inside, then the enthusiastic commentary started cranking up her adrenalin levels. She hadn't a clue where June Wedding was. The horses approached Melling Road. Elvis Smith was back in front after a mad spurt. Suddenly The Sun Rose tore up the inside, overtaking everything but the lead horse. The commentator was screaming by the twenty-ninth as there seemed to be nothing between Elvis Smith and The Sun Rose.

'Come on, boy,' Dawn screamed at the screen. 'Come on!'

'Elvis Smith's going to do it,' said the commentator. Just as The Sun Rose burst past in the last nanosecond and crossed the line, winning by a short but definite distance.

'Jesus H!' said Dawn. She couldn't remember the last time she had been as thrilled as that. Her heart was galloping as if she'd just finished running the race herself. Dawn hadn't a clue how much money that meant the work's betting syndicate had won but she overrode her initial impulse to tell Calum about it. If he knew she was collecting that sort of money, he'd only put less in the wedding pot. She picked up her brochure and got back to the argument of sugared almonds versus chocolate truffles in silence.

She learned from the newspaper the next morning that June Wedding was the horse that had fallen at the first fence.

Grace was staring out of the window after putting all the Sunday lunch pots and pans away. Sarah and Hugo had gone off for an hour or twelve to look for some new conservatory furniture, leaving Sable kicking a ball about in the garden with her granddad and Joe. He was a lovely boy, Joe, very much like Paul, kindhearted and quiet, happiest with his nose in a book or scribbling in a pad.

Gordon had been smiling nonstop all weekend. He smiled when he went out to the Legion on Friday night and he had smiled and been Mr Jovial all the way through to Sunday lunch. It wasn't a nice smile though. There was something about the way it sat on his lips that disturbed her.

She was trying to work out what Gordon could possibly be up to—because as sure as eggs were eggs, he *was* up to something—when Laura handed Grace a cup of tea and interrupted her thoughts.

'Mum? Hello! Tea!'

'Oh, sorry, love, in a world of my own there.'

'So much for Sarah being an hour. She's already been over two,' said Laura, joining her mother watching through the window as Sable stormed off in a little strop because Joe hadn't passed the ball to her.

'She's pregnant,' said Grace. 'She needs as much help as I can give her.'

'She shouldn't have got pregnant again if she couldn't cope,' continued Laura. 'We all know she's having this baby to cement up the cracks in her marriage.' She looked at Grace. 'You know she's expecting to go straight back to work after the birth and for you to look after the baby, don't you? She and Hugo are banking on you getting early retirement as soon as possible.'

'Well, they're going to be rather disappointed,' said Grace with a heavy sigh. Yes, she knew that if she ever gave up her job, her workload and domestic drudgery would triple. God help her when she was eventually forced to retire.

'I can't see why they don't employ a nanny,' said Laura, then she answered her own question. 'Well, I suppose I can, if I think about it. She's not going to let another woman in the house when she's all pregnancy-fat and risk Hugo's eye wandering again.' She took a long sip of tea. 'Have you seen Paul recently?'

'Yes,' said Grace. 'And I'm seeing him next Saturday as well.'

'Has he said anything to you?' asked Laura mysteriously.

'Anything about what, dear?'

'Oh, nothing in particular,' said Laura. 'Just anything.'

'He's told me all about Rose Manor,' said Grace.

'Have you seen the pics? Lovely, isn't it?'

'Yes, it is, or at least it will be when he's done all the work.' Grace had no doubt of her son's abilities to turn the wreck of a house into something lovely. He was a perfectionist, a hard worker with vision, and she couldn't have wished for a better son. She had been only twenty-one when an infection in her womb had resulted in her needing a full hysterectomy. Then, with cruel irony, she'd had to nurse Laura through the same just after Joe was born. At least her daughter had a little comfort in her memories of one child growing in her body.

They stood and sipped their tea some more, staring out at Gordon in the garden with the children. Both thinking on the same lines.

'It's ridiculous this Paul and Dad thing, don't you think?' said Laura.

'There's nothing I can do,' said Grace. 'I wish I could. I can't even broach the subject—he just walks out of the room.'

Joe suddenly fell to the ground, clutching his head and crying hard, which wasn't like him at all. Laura rushed out.

'What's the matter, love?' called Grace a few steps behind her daughter as Joe cuddled into his mum's shoulder.

'He's all right,' said Gordon and grabbed the boy's arm. 'Come and play, Joe.'

'Gordon, what happened?' asked Grace.

Joe struggled against his granddad's grip.

'It's nothing,' said Gordon in that 'Don't-make-a-fuss' voice of his.

'He's bleeding, Dad. What happened, sweetheart?'

'Sable threw a rock at me,' said Joe.

'Didn't,' said Sable with her tongue stuck out.

'Come and play football and stop being stupid,' said Gordon, pulling Joe away from his mother's embrace.

'Let him go, Dad, he's hurt,' said Laura.

'He's not *that* hurt,' barked Gordon. 'Stop crying, Joe. Kick that ball.'

Instead though, Joe sprang back to his mother's arms.

Gordon snapped nastily, 'For goodness' sake, stop mollycoddling him. He's all right. Joe, come back here and kick this ball.'

'I don't want to play any more,' said Joe.

'KICK THIS BLOODY BALL!' yelled Gordon. Laura felt her boy wince and she tightened her arms round him.

'Leave him alone, Gordon,' said Grace. 'The boy's hurt.'

'You'll make him soft!' spat Gordon, puce-faced. 'He'll turn out like that other one. That what you want? Another nancy boy in the family, as if one isn't enough? That make you both proud, will it?'

Gordon pushed, in none too gentlemanly a fashion, past Grace into the house as Joe sobbed against his mum's breast. Laura looked at her father's disappearing back and Grace saw that she was shaking her head with blatant disgust. Grace realised it was the first time she had seen her husband through her daughter's eyes.

Chapter 4

'WE DID QUITE WELL on Saturday, didn't we?' said Dawn, unbuttoning her coat the following Monday morning.

'We certainly did,' said Christie. 'The Sun Rose finished at fifty-five to one in the end.'

'Bloody Norah,' said Anna. 'We won a lot of money, didn't we?'

'Don't forget to add on the forty pounds James donated as well. All in all, it wasn't bad for an afternoon's work,' added Christie with a wink.

'You're not joking!' It was the only good news Anna had had in ages. She could buy herself a rocking chair and a lifetime's supply of Horlicks.

'Did we win?' asked Raychel, rushing in at just on nine o'clock.

'You didn't hear the result? Where on earth have you been all weekend?' asked Anna with a good-humoured tut.

'We've been doing house stuff,' said Raychel. 'I think Ben and I spent four hours in Ikea alone on Saturday. Then Ben put it all together. Sorry I'm late, Christie. I got caught up in a traffic snarl.'

'I hadn't even noticed,' said Christie. God forbid she would ever be the sort of boss who made a fuss over a few minutes!

He sounded a good sort, did Ben, thought Anna. How come she never got one like that? She had never been lucky in love.

'I'll collect the winnings later,' promised Christie.

'We should have a meal out with some of it to celebrate,' suggested Dawn. She knew if she had it in her pocket, Calum would only 'borrow' it from her, with no intention of ever paying it back. And she could never manage to say no to him.

'That's a good idea,' said Christie. 'Are there any nice restaurants or pubs round here?'

'What about that new Thai place next to the Rising Sun pub up the road?' said Dawn. 'It's only five minutes' walk away. Ooh, Rising Suns again. Must be an omen.'

'Fine by me, if everyone is in agreement? We'll arrange something after the Easter break?'

Everyone either nodded or mumbled and Christie was delighted to accept that as a definite yes.

There was a happy buzz when Christie distributed well-stocked brown packets of horse-race winnings. Each of them put thirty pounds into an envelope for their future celebratory meal. Christie mused about what the others would do with their balances. She would bet that Dawn's would go towards her wedding and Raychel's towards her house, but what of Grace and Anna? They were harder to guess at.

Christie would buy a bottle of champagne with hers, and raise a glass to her late husband, as she always did at this time of year. She reflected a lot around the anniversary of her widowhood. She wished Peter had died when it was autumn or winter and not when the bluebells that he loved so much were starting to flood the forests, when everything in nature was awakening and coming alive; it seemed so unfair. She made sure she enjoyed this time of year for him, for both of them.

Christie liked the smiles that had started passing between the women. It didn't take anything away from their efficiency that they would share a brief natter about 'that shade of blouse really suiting Grace with her colouring' or asking, 'What happened in *Corry* in the last five minutes last night, because the phone rang and I missed it?' Christie was sure that if there had been an office thermometer to check, she would find that it was rising by a degree with every passing day.

That evening, the Dartley train was in when Anna reached the platform. She had missed her usual one after calling into Iceland for some bits and pieces. As she ran for it, she noticed the man in black on the opposite platform again. When his eyes landed on her, he looked as if he couldn't believe his luck that he had seen her again. To Anna's horror, he pointed over at her. He was beckoning. *Yeah, like she was going to go over to him.* Anna's heart rate increased. She jumped on the train, risking a direct look as the train started moving. The man had gone. Then she noticed him descending the last step on her side of the platform. How the heck did he get there so fast?

Well, she supposed blackly, if he was a serial killer, what did it matter? Her life was over anyway. She hoped, when he did eventually catch up with her, that his method would be quick and painless.

Vladimir Darq watched the train pull out of the station seconds before he had a chance to jump on it. *Damn.* He had found the one he was looking for and he couldn't get to her. Every night he had waited at the train station for her to return and now she had and he had missed her. He thought of the shopping she was carrying and it came to him then that maybe she usually caught an earlier train? Third time lucky. He wouldn't miss her again.

The building had that happy last-day-before-a-break feel on Thursday. Dawn was going to be doing some more weddingy things and was all giddy about that; Raychel was joyfully twittering on about preparing for her house move and, though Anna didn't bubble over like the others, Christie hoped she was looking forward to spending a quiet long week-end with her man. Only from Grace's corner did she feel a cool draught. Christie noticed her staring into space on a few occasions.

'Everything OK?' she asked.

Grace snapped her mind back to the here and now.

'Absolutely fine,' she said, convincing neither of them.

The Easter holiday loomed long in front of Grace. Thank goodness there was a lovely Saturday afternoon with Paul to look forward to and Joe's face to enjoy when he saw how many eggs the Easter Bunny had left for him at his grandparents' house. If Gordon's stupid smile didn't scare away the Bunny from visiting, that was.

At five o'clock, Christie bade her ladies a good holiday. The department was to be shut until Tuesday, for Easter. It looked, to Christie, as if Grace especially needed a restful break.

Gordon had volunteered to take Grace to and from work that day. He wanted to take her car in for a service, he said, because he'd heard a rattle. They hadn't spoken much since the Joe incident on Sunday. What was the point? If Gordon didn't want to talk about something, he didn't talk about it.

He was already waiting for her in the car park when she came out of work. The car had been washed and polished and valeted inside, she noticed as she climbed into it. They both mumbled a hello at each other as she clicked herself into the seat belt.

'Did you get the rattle fixed then?' she asked.

'What rattle?' he said absently, then, 'Oh no, there wasn't one. I must have been imagining things.'

Grace knew then that he hadn't taken her car into the garage. He hadn't heard a rattle. He was up to something and her instincts were proved correct when he set off, taking an immediate right turn instead of the left that would have put them on the road for home.

'Gordon, where are we going?' she asked wearily.

'Never you mind,' said Gordon with that incredibly annoying smile.

'Gordon?'

Gordon didn't say anything and flicked on the right indicator as he approached the roundabout, which told Grace they were taking the motorway south.

Anna stood on the railway platform, heart thumping in her chest. The weirdo in black, thankfully, wasn't there. Maybe she should have got any impending attack over and done with. She visualised a touching hospital scene where Tony rushed to her bedside and gently stroked the part of her skull that the stranger had stoved in with an axe. He would pledge undying love and come back to care for her.

The barriers dropped, the train came down the track and Anna relaxed. A cool breath puffed onto the back of her neck. She turned to find the man in black behind her, his eyes locking with hers. She saw fangs, clear as day. She was going to feature in the *Barnsley Chronicle* as the first woman in Barnsley to become undead, she thought, then everything went black. His gloved hands came out and caught her as she fainted.

She came to seconds later, though it felt much longer, with a crowd gathering round her, the strange man cradling her in his arms on the ground and some silly cow saying, 'Someone phone the emergency services! There's a woman having a heart attack!'

She remembered being helped to her feet. She kept saying, 'I'm fine, I'm fine,' but she heard that daft woman shriek, 'You should have left her lying down. I'm St John Ambulance-trained. I know these things.'

But then Anna's brain seemed to fast-forward a little and the next thing she knew she was being led over to the station café for a cup of tea with lots of sugar in it. Fast-forward again some more seconds and Anna was sitting in a quiet corner, and Fang-man was sitting opposite her. She did a double take and shook her head. Did vampires drink Yorkshire Tea—because this one did—and offer Cadbury's shortcakes? She couldn't remember that from her Bram Stoker edition.

'Are you diabetic?' he asked in a deep voice, with an accent reminiscent of black forests and dark castles. He proffered the biscuits.

'No,' said Anna. 'Well, I wasn't this morning anyway.'

'Then you passed out solely because of fear of me,' the man said. 'I am so sorry.' He had pale skin and very black hair, past shoulder length and tied at the back. His beard was the same colour, a thin, expert line that swept over a strong chin and square jaw.

'I'm sure it's not entirely your fault I fainted,' said Anna, omitting to add that she couldn't remember the last decent meal she had eaten and as a consequence she'd been having moments of light-headedness.

'I have been waiting for you,' the man went on. He had very blue eyes, with golden flecks in them. They were fringed with thick, black lashes that a woman would have killed for. His eyebrows were heavy arches and masculine, a small space between them above his nose.

'Why? What do you want me for?' said Anna defensively. 'Why are you loitering round stations?'

'Not loitering, searching,' he answered. 'And not just stations, but libraries, supermarkets, shops. I look for a woman.'

Anna opened her mouth to reply but she hadn't a clue what to say to that. Apart from *Perv*.

The man reached into his voluminous coat and pulled out a very stylish business card that he handed to her.

Vladimir Darq.

That's all it said, plus a mobile number. How arrogant was that? It smacked of someone who should be instantly recognisable. The funny thing was, the name *did* ring a bell, although she couldn't for the life of her remember where she had heard it before. *Crimewatch*?

'What do you want with me then, Mr Darq?' She pronounced it 'Dark'. He didn't correct her so she presumed that was right.

'You,' he began, staring at Anna with such intensity that she felt herself blushing, '. . . you are the woman for whom I have been searching.'

Nutter alert.

'OK, that's me going home now,' said Anna, pushing back her chair.

'Please, hear me out,' he said. 'Five minutes. That's all I ask.'

Anna sat again because she had no choice. The moment she stood, the blood rushed from her head and she felt woozy again.

'My name is Vladimir Darq. I am a designer,' he began.

Yes, of course, thought Anna. *That rings a big bell now*. Gok Wan had dressed some of his women in Darq gowns. If he was the real Vladimir Darq and not some saddo imposter.

'You may know me as a maker of gowns. Only gowns. But no longer!' He waved away his entire collection with one sweep of his hand. 'I have diversified into a new area—lingerie. I don't want to design for A-list divas any more. I want to design for women who want to feel as if they are A-list inside here,' and he thumped his chest where his heart was positioned. 'I have a question: do you watch *Jane's Dames*?'

'I love *Jane's Dames*,' gasped Anna. It was a new programme that competed with Gok Wan's, and was presented by a young, gorgeous, style guru-in-the-making called Jane Cleve-Jones.

'*Jane's Dames* are making a new series. They have approached various designers—I am, of course, one of them—and each of us has a model that we intend to transform. My specialised area will be the lingerie. I need a woman who wants to feel beautiful, earthy—*Darq*, as I call it. I believe that every woman has a Darq side but alas, most women don't even suspect it. Then I see you and I know without a doubt that you are the one. I want you to be my model. I want you to inspire other women to wear my clothes. I want to design for women like you.'

'Old, past-it lumps, you mean?' said Anna, with a mirthless laugh.

'*Nu*, not at all,' said Vladimir Darq, leaning across the table. 'Women in their late thirties, early forties who think they are no longer sexy or maybe they have never felt that way. I see it in the slump of your shoulders that you do not feel desired. I would guess that others have not made you feel very good about yourself. I am right, of course.'

Anna felt teary and gulped. That small movement in her throat was all Vladimir Darq needed to see to know he was correct in his assumptions. Not that he had had any doubt. 'I can transform you,' he whispered, his voice a velvet caress. 'And you will inspire other women to be beautiful.'

'Beautiful?' said Anna with a dry snort of laughter. The word had never been applied to her. No one had ever said, 'Anna Brightside, you are beautiful.' Or lovely, or pretty for that matter. In her twenties, she rarely drew male attention, despite her flawless skin and hair the colour of autumn. Then, in her thirties, she met Tony, with his smooth banter and voracious sexual appetite. Being the object of his lust had lifted her to some state of desirability. Until he dropped her for Miss Pert-Tits, of course. And now here was a bloke dressed up as a vampire telling her that he had magic underwear that would make her beautiful. At thirty-nine? Had he lost his guide dog? Or was he Care in the Community?

'I'm having trouble believing all this,' began Anna, confusion pulling her brows together. 'I mean, this is Barnsley train station. And you say you're Vladimir Darq and want to put me on the telly? I'm beginning to think I'm still passed out and this is a dream.' Even more so because every time his lips parted, she saw a hint of fangs in his teethline.

'What is your name, please?'

'Anna. Anna Brightside.'

'Then please, Anna Brightside, you think it over,' he said. 'Look me up on the Internet and see that I am in good faith.' He leaned in extra close and said in a voice that brooked no debate, 'We start filming on Saturday, May the ninth. You will do this with me.'

'Oh, will I?' said Anna. *Cocky git.*

'Yes, you will, and I will expect your call soon to confirm,' said Vladimir Darq. 'It is *soarta*—fate—that we have met. *Soarta!*' And before Anna could say another word, he had stood, lifted up her hand, kissed the back of it, and clicked his heels together like Kaiser Wilhelm. Then he was gone in a swirl of black coat.

'Bloody hell,' said Anna.

Calum had managed to surpass himself: he had delivered a hat trick. Dawn had come in from work to find that her two-pound coin pot had been raided and the Easter egg she'd had iced with the words 'Foxy Fiancé' was half eaten on the kitchen work surface. Calum had obviously found them both secreted at the bottom of the wardrobe. Thank goodness she'd hidden her Grand National winnings a bit more securely, she thought. Then she had found chocolatey fingerprints all over her veil in the carrier bag. She'd sat on the sofa fuming until he turned up pissed at half past ten. He had laughed in that casual way he had, shrugging his shoulders as though totally baffled that she was making such a fuss, while she cried that he'd spoiled her surprise for him. Then he'd shouted back at her that she was a nag and he'd be better off back with his ex, Mandy Clamp. She'd screamed back that he was a selfish pig and he had slapped her across the face, claiming she was hysterical. Then he had gone to bed, leaving her sobbing in the sitting room.

Grace woke up the next morning to the sound of heavy rain battering against the side of the walls of the tinny caravan in which she had just spent a cramped and uncomfortable night. She turned over to view the clock—ten past six—then she buried her head under the blanket on the narrowest bed she had ever had the misfortune to encounter. She tried to get back to sleep, but the bubbling rage inside her made that impossible.

A picture of Gordon's self-satisfied face as he'd turned off down the motorway the previous evening flared in her head and flooded her whole being with expletive-flavoured feelings. She'd known instantly then that she was being kidnapped and forced somewhere she didn't want to go. She would have put her life savings on it being Blegthorpe (a place name that Gordon had been popping into conversations for months), where she would be tortured with tours of caravan sites. And boy, had she been right! Gordon had packed a case for her. It contained a pair of old black trousers that she wore when she was cleaning, a blue skirt and a fawn top, three bras and one pair of knickers. He'd put in her hairbrush and a couple of towels, no make-up but three pairs of shoes. No nightdress, no tights.

She could hear the low burr of Gordon's annoyingly contented snoring in the next bedroom. She was half tempted to take the car keys and drive home. She hated Gordon for this but decided to throttle back her rising temper and play Gordon's game. One, because she was too tired to resist him and two, because then she could at least say she had tried to like blustery, boring Blegthorpe but, surprisingly enough, had failed dismally.

So, on Saturday, while she should have been sharing tea and scones in the lovely Maltstone Garden Centre café with her son, she was taking refuge from a force-eighteen gale in a basic, no-frills dump, eating a sandwich made from tasteless cheese, cheap white bread, spread with margarine and drinking tea from a mug that had a big chip knocked out of the rim. Gordon was tucking into a greasy fish the size of a small whale.

'Can't beat good old seaside fare,' he said, hooking a fish bone out from between his teeth.

'What time do you have to be at that caravan park?' asked Grace. She took a sip of tea and hoped Paul had got her message and that he didn't think anything was wrong because she hadn't turned up to meet him.

'Half an hour,' said Gordon, checking his watch. 'I've just time for a pudding. Want anything?'

I want to scream, thought Grace, but she answered, 'No thanks.'

After he had eaten a monster-sized portion of treacle sponge and custard, they braved the outside to find the wind had dropped and the sun was playing peek-a-boo behind very grumpy-looking clouds.

'This will be bonny in the summer,' said Gordon, zapping the car open. He whistled an annoying loop of 'I Do Like To Be Beside the Seaside' all the way to Bayview Caravan Site, three miles down the coast.

They called in at the reception office and a lady with a too-small suit straining over a very generous apple-shaped figure welcomed them warmly and led them over to caravan number one after a chirpy bit of sales banter. Inside, Grace had to admit it was impressive. Four rooms, three with double beds and built-in wardrobes, and a bathroom that a cat could have looked forward to a fair swinging in. It was very nice, just not her sort of thing at all. She was sick of camping and caravanning holidays; she wanted holidays where someone else was making her meals for her and there was guaranteed sunshine. She wanted to spend a week or two in a place where she could truly unwind instead of merely transferring domestic chores from one destination to another.

'This is our new model, the "Monte Carlo",' said Small-Suit. 'Twenty thousand pounds, but if you buy it this weekend we have a special offer of eighteen.'

How many weeks in Sorrento would eighteen thousand pounds buy? She watched Gordon's shoulders flinch at the price. He knew how much the caravans were because he'd done his homework. Said aloud though, it sounded scary to a man who had never flashed his cash about freely.

'I don't think we'd need as much space as this,' said Gordon. 'Can you show us something else?'

'Certainly,' said Small-Suit. She had gauged now that this couple weren't going to be the biggest spenders and showed them the 'Cannes'. It had had one lady owner for the past five years. *A colour-blind one at that*, thought Grace, judging by the ghastly mix of orange soft furnishings. It was like being inside a giant rotting mango.

'Twelve thousand, three hundred pounds for a quick sale, this one,' said Small-Suit. 'It's a six berth, one of those being a double. But it does boast a separate dining area.'

The shower room was generously proportioned and Gordon obviously hoped Grace would be impressed by the galley kitchen—her future domain. She could see his brain working behind his glittering eyes, imagining them there in tropical sunshine British summers, Grace happily baking apple pies while entertaining the children and feeding the new baby and loading the washing machine and sweeping the floor with a broom stuck up her bottom, while he read yet more seed catalogues and waved amicably over to the neighbours.

'We'll be saying yes to this one,' said Gordon. 'It's got a lovely feel to it.'

'Gordon!' said Grace crossly. 'Excuse me, could I just have a word?' She pulled Gordon's sleeve, leading him into the corner.

'It's a lot of money, Gordon,' said Grace.

'You'll be getting a lump sum soon, I'm sure of it,' said Gordon.

'You can't rely on that,' said Grace.

'Well, OK then, we can still afford it from the savings. No pockets in shrouds, Grace. It's a good price and we're having it.'

What a time for him suddenly to become extravagant, thought Grace. She wanted to scream at him that there was no way she would spend whole summers in Blegthorpe, but she knew the fight was lost before it started. Gordon didn't lose arguments; instead he wore his opponent down with persistence, and she was too tired to fight back after a night of rubbish sleep. She felt trapped, imprisoned by Gordon's will more than ever since Paul had fallen out with his father.

Grace watched helplessly as he opened his cheque book and wrote out the 10 per cent deposit. He was smiling while his pen moved. 'Chirpy' wasn't a word Grace would ever have associated with her husband. It was weird to see him so elated.

They spent that night in the 'Robin Hood Club', listening to a mediocre singer, before a break for bingo. Gordon picked up a couple of die-hard caravanners at the bar who came over to join them. They enthused over sea air and camping life and invited Gordon and Grace over for morning coffee and to look over their brand new Rolls Royce of Caravans, the 'Monaco'. Grace tried to smile but inside she was screaming. Gordon Beamish, however, had come home.

Maltstone churchyard was a serene place for the dead to sleep, was Raychel's first thought as she and Ben threaded through the grass and stone crosses and angels to a pretty corner, a mass of bright and faded colours, flowers, teddy bears and cards: the children's graveyard.

'What do you think?' said Raychel.

'I think it's perfect,' said Ben. 'It's a lovely spot, pet.'

There was a tree at the edge of the grass border where a wood started. Raychel opened her handbag and took out a small cross and a tiny, fluffy toy rabbit. She parted the grass at the side of the tree. Bluebells were in flower and the air was full of their musty scent.

'Here?'

'Yes,' said Ben.

Raychel kissed the cross and lifted it to Ben's face so he could do the same. 'Happy Easter, my darling Angel,' she said, kneeling to anchor the cross between the sweet blue flowers in the soil. 'Dear God, please look after her for us. Amen.'

'Amen,' said Ben, helping Ray to her feet. He wrapped his arm around her as tears welled in his eyes and he sniffed hard.

Raychel smiled. 'I know she isn't there. I know she's up in heaven but I need somewhere to come that's nearby and pretty like this.'

'You don't have to explain to me, darlin',' said Ben. 'Come on, let's go home. We'll come again. She knows we will.'

As they turned to go, Ben blew a kiss heavenwards and hoped it would be delivered to her. The baby had died before she had been given a name, so they had picked 'Angel' for her. Ben and Raychel, her big brother and sister, were the only ones who would ever remember and grieve for little Angel.

According to the Internet, Vladimir Darq was forty-two years old and originated from Romania. He had enjoyed huge success as a designer of exclusive gothic gowns and wedding dresses for A-list clients before he disappeared for a year, emerging recently in Milan with a breathtaking taster-display of sumptuous lingerie. According to an *Observer* article, his new market was to be '*the forgotten woman*', the one who thought herself ordinary. The price points would match her purse, too. Vladimir Darq had designed a bodyshaper that no woman could afford to be without, he proclaimed confidently.

There were quite a few sites featuring him, even an online fan club and forums trying to find out things about him. He was, it seemed, a real international man of mystery. Or was he indeed a man? There was a weighty amount of speculation on a few gothic sites that he was, in fact, not marketing himself as a vampire, but was the real thing. It accompanied obviously Photoshopped pictures of him with pale golden eyes, bleached white skin and exaggerated fangs. Apparently, he preferred to do all his business in the evening because he hated the sun, which added fuel to the fire. All tabloid newspaper nonsense really.

Unmarried, childless, he was pictured alongside a few beautiful models and with his arm round his 'friend', the photographer Leonid Szabo. Anna might have known Vladimir Darq would be gay. Let's face it, any man who was interested in her couldn't possibly be heterosexual.

Chapter 5

'HELLO, EVERYONE,' said Christie, breezing in. 'Had a nice Easter?'

'Lovely, thank you,' came a ripple of consensus.

Anna hoped she wouldn't have to elaborate. What could she have said? *Fainted in the train station and was asked to dress up in underwear by a gay vampire.* And she had a belting headache from crying herself to sleep. Well 'sleep' was pushing it a bit. She couldn't remember when she'd last managed to have a full night's kip as her dreams were full of Tony. Two large coffees and ibuprofen for breakfast hadn't shifted the pain in her temple.

As Anna went to the loo, she noticed Malcolm watching to see what the boxes were that Maintenance had just brought up to Christie. If he paid as much attention to his own department as to theirs, he might have ended up giving Cheese a chance to survive. It was looking more and more likely that it would be merged with Deli within the year.

Anna went into the deserted toilet and sat on the closed seat, resting her head against the coolness of the partition wall. The pain went much further than her temple. It reached down into her guts, squeezed tightly and kept the pressure on until she felt she could bear it no more. Not content with haunting her dreams, she had opened a secondhand *Barnsley Chronicle* on the train to see that Tony had won an award for his barbering. He was there on the front page 'pictured with his partner, Lynette Bottom'. *Partner.* That one word, applied to Lynette Bottom, hurt—so much. And just to pile on the insult to the injury, they were smiling like love's young dream. Her own life was in bits and she had apparently been whitewashed out of Tony's.

Anna burst into tears; the drops fell fat and warm down her cheeks and she didn't care that they were dragging her mascara with them. She couldn't sleep, couldn't eat, couldn't concentrate; she couldn't find any joy or hope in anything. And, if that wasn't enough, in three days she would be forty—Mayday in every sense of the word. Fat, frumpy, forgotten-and-forty day. *Life ends, not begins, day.*

The boxes contained lots of innovative gifts to reward colleagues who sent in good suggestions to improve the business. Dawn volunteered to pack them all away in the store cupboard and Christie encouraged her to get on with it. The girl was in her element when she was organising. It was only when the task was finished and Christie called a coffee break that they noticed Anna had been missing for a considerable time.

'Where did she go?' asked Christie.

'I thought she'd gone to the toilet,' said Raychel.

'Not for all that time, surely?'

'I'll go and have a look, shall I?' volunteered Dawn.

She entered the loo, which was deathly quiet, but the end cubicle door was locked.

'Anna, you in there?' There was no response.

There was barely more than a slit between the door and the floor to look under, so Dawn went into the adjacent cubicle and climbed on top of the toilet seat to look over into the next. There she saw Anna, sitting on the loo lid, head against the partition wall, tears cascading down her face.

Dawn almost fell off the seat when the main toilet door opened, but thankfully it was only Christie.

'We thought there was a Bermuda triangle in here and you'd disappeared as well. Is she all right? What's going on?'

'She's not really,' Dawn hedged. However nice Christie was, she was still their boss. If Anna was inebriated, she didn't want to drop her in it.

Christie rapped on the door.

'Anna, love, open the door. Are you ill?'

Anna leaned forward, her head dropping into her hands.

'We need to get inside,' said Christie. She whispered through the door, 'Anna? Anna, can you open the door?'

'No, please just leave me,' said Anna.

'I'm coming in,' said Dawn, tucking her skirt up in her knickers, springing from the loo seat and hooking her long leg over the top of the cubicle. 'Oops—bang go my tights!'

Christie heard Dawn land and a second later the door was open. She came in and bent over Anna, who looked like a zombie.

'Anna, Anna love, whatever is it? Have you taken anything?'

'No, no. I am so sorry, Christie,' Anna sobbed.

'Why, love, what's happened?' Christie stroked Anna's hair back from her face and that kind, gentle action smashed the last few bricks holding back the mother lode of Anna's grief. She fell forward into Christie's arms and a confession poured out of her.

'I lied to you all. I'm not happily living with Tony. He left me in February. There was a note saying there was no one else and there was. I'd just come home from hospital after a miscarriage. I needed him so much and he wasn't there.'

'Oh, love,' said Christie, squeezing Anna into her.

'It was my fourth. I can't seem to carry babies longer than six weeks.'

'God,' said Dawn, at a total loss for anything constructive to say but feeling the need to say something at least in a sympathetic tone.

'I'm going to be sick, I'm sorry,' said Anna, quickly pushing Christie away to a safe distance and throwing open the toilet lid.

'Sweetheart,' said Christie with a pitiful sigh.

'I'm a wreck,' said Anna, reaching weakly for the loo roll.

'Men can be such thoughtless bastards,' Dawn said kindly. Her skirt was still tucked up in her drawers.

'Oh God, look at your tights,' said Anna. 'I am so sorry.'

'Anna, it's only a pair of tights,' Dawn replied. 'I'll go and get you a cup of water. Sit down before you fall.'

She left Anna in the capable hands of Christie, who said, 'I'm driving you home, young lady. You're not well. When was the last time you ate something? There was nothing but bile in your stomach to throw up.'

'I'll be fine.' Her legs were as shaky as a newborn foal's.

Dawn came back in with a cup of water and a packet of wet wipes, which she handed over to Christie.

'Grace sent these in,' she said. 'Here, get this down you. I got it from the water cooler, so it's nice and cold.'

Anna gulped at the water while Christie pulled out a couple of the wet tissues and began to wipe Anna's face as if she were a little girl.

'I'm so sorry,' Anna said again.

'Shush,' whispered Christie. 'Are you OK to stand? We're going to get your coat and your bag and I'm taking you home now.'

Anna opened her mouth to protest, but she was too weak. 'Thank you,' she relented.

Anna felt as frail as a kitten as she walked back into the office where

Grace was waiting, holding Anna's coat open and ready for her to slip her arms into. At her side, Raychel was holding her bag. Anna looked at them both, so much kindness shining in their eyes that she wanted to sink to the floor and sob with shame and gratitude in equal measure.

'I'll see you later, ladies,' said Christie, leading Anna down the office. 'Come on, pet, let's get you home and tucked up.'

It was a nice, quiet road end where Anna lived, very close to Dartley train stop. Courtyard Lane was well named as it was a square of narrow, terraced houses round a neat courtyard garden at its centre.

The house gave out so many mixed signals. It was a lovely mix of heavy old furniture and matching reproductions. Quite dark and gothic in its taste: a strong red on the walls, a brave blue showing through from the hallway. But the surfaces were dusty and the carpet could have done with a good vacuum. It looked *tired*. It looked a perfect reflection of Anna at that moment in time.

Christie hunted in the kitchen cupboards for cups after announcing that she was putting the kettle on. She made two coffees and returned to the lounge where Anna was sitting on the sofa looking drowsy.

'I used the de-caff,' said Christie. 'Looks like you need a good sleep.' She opened her handbag and brought out some tablets. 'Here, these'll take the headache away with any luck.'

'I feel a bit better after being sick,' said Anna, but she took the tablets anyway. She felt as if she had been turned inside out.

Christie noticed the photographs displayed round the room: Anna snuggling up to a good-looking guy—Tony presumably.

'Thank you, Christie, for bringing me home. I'm so sorry to put you to all this trouble.'

'If you say that once more I'll thump you,' said Christie. 'You're not well and shouldn't have been at work. Didn't you take any time off when you had your miscarriages?'

'I didn't need to,' replied Anna. 'I lost them so early. Except for the last one. But even then I was in hospital Friday night and out Saturday morning. I didn't want a fuss.'

'And *he* left you that Friday night?' Christie affirmed calmly, which belied the disgust she felt.

'It's been hard for him too, to cope with losing so many,' said Anna. She knew she was making excuses for him but she wanted to believe that he was hurting and weak rather than a total bastard with a pipe cleaner for a backbone.

'Yes, of course, poor him,' said Christie tightly.

'I'm so sorry,' said Anna, bursting into a hard, primal sob. 'I'm forty on Friday. That isn't helping!'

'Good grief,' said Christie. 'You should be flinging open the door to that fortieth year and dragging it over the threshold.'

'I'll be old,' said Anna.

'Like hell you will,' snapped Christie. 'Women at forty should be formidable creatures. What on earth makes women think forty is old? Half of them get reborn at that age because they've not lived until forty comes and kicks them up the backside.'

Anna found herself smiling at Christie's force of argument.

'Do you want something to eat?'

'No, I couldn't face it. I just want to sleep.'

'Then you sleep, love,' said Christie. She pulled a couple of throws from the other side of the sofa and tucked them round Anna. Anna's eyes started to shutter down. She heard the front door close and the key being pushed through the letterbox. Then she slept.

Anna went into work the next day even though she still felt a bit shaky. But she didn't want to spend any longer than she had to in a house full of memories. Plus she wanted to give Dawn some new tights.

'You silly beggar,' said Dawn when Anna handed them over.

'I feel much better today. Thank you for taking me home, Christie. And for listening.'

'Don't mention it.' Christie waved her away, kindly. 'Glad I could help.'

'Look, it's not much. It's just a gesture to say thank you, everyone, for being so kind yesterday . . .' Anna took out of her handbag four boxes of chocolates that she'd bought at the train station newspaper shop.

'You didn't have to do that,' said Grace. 'I only picked up your coat.'

'I only picked up your bag!' said Raychel.

'You did more than that,' said Anna. She remembered the warmth in their eyes—not pity, but support. There was a difference.

'You'll have to get ill in the office more often,' Dawn said through a coffee cream. Then she corrected herself. 'I don't mean really ill, just ill enough to feel bad enough to bring choc—'

'Yes, we know what you mean, Dawn,' put in Christie. There wasn't an ounce of malice in the girl but she had a very clumsy line of expression. 'Anna, we've been talking. Seeing as it's your birthday on Friday, how about we use our horse-race winnings and celebrate with you?'

'Oh!' was all Anna managed, because that invitation came from left field. But the accompanying smile gave Christie the answer she wanted.

'Marvellous,' she said.

'I can't believe Dad did that to you!' said Paul angrily down the phone as he talked to Grace from his office. 'What right does he think he has to force you to go somewhere you don't want to like that? I tell you, Mum, he's getting worse as he gets older. He's a control freak.'

'I'm just glad you got my message,' said Grace, mobile to her ear as she sat on the park bench having her sandwich lunch. 'My phone died on me when I was texting you. I was so looking forward to seeing you and Charles, too.'

'You'll see Charles soon, I promise you that,' Paul growled. 'Mum, I hate to say this but Dad's losing it.'

'Don't be silly, love—'

'I mean it. Laura told me what happened with Joe and the football.'

'Don't, Paul, he isn't that bad,' said Grace, feeling more disloyal by the minute because she wasn't feeling what she was saying.

'The trouble with Dad is that we've all grown up and he can't tell us what to do any more. Why is there always so much anger in him? I've never understood it.'

Grace sighed. She knew why, of course. The anger was born out of frustration. Years and years of sexual frustration, of being impotent and being too stupidly proud to seek help. Not something she could tell her son, of course.

'Paul, love—'

'I'm telling you, Mum. I don't know how you've stood him all these years. You can't have been happy.'

'Of course I have,' said Grace. 'You have made me the happiest woman alive.'

'Just tell me something, then: if he hadn't had three young kids when you met him, would you have ever married him?'

Grace opened her mouth to answer that of course she would, but she knew it wasn't the truth, and so did Paul. Her marriage was as dry as dust, held together only by her children's love. His children's love.

'I'm fine, we rub along in our own way,' said Grace, changing the subject swiftly and attempting cheeriness. 'Now, when am I seeing you? I still have your Easter egg to give you.'

'Mum, I'm a grown man!'

'You're never too old for an Easter egg,' she said. Although Gordon had always been too old for silly things like that.

'I've only got one empty box left after this,' said Raychel, packing up the canvases she had painted. Ben had often told her she should sell them, but Raychel didn't want to do anything to draw attention to herself. She was happy painting them purely for the enjoyment of it. She had always been clever at arts and crafts. She had sewn all their bedding and made the curtains, which they were leaving behind for the next tenant. Everything in their flat was going to be fresh and new and clean.

'There's loads at work,' said Ben. 'I'll ask the boss if I can take some; he'll let me, I know he will.' Ben liked his boss. He was a huge bear of a man who didn't cut corners in his work and paid good wages and on time. They were lucky in having plenty of work on as John Silkstone had a good reputation locally as a craftsman who charged fair prices.

'Smashing,' replied Raychel, and bent to empty the sideboard next. She opened the top drawer and took out the treasure box that she kept there. She slid off the lid and at the top of the pile of letters and cards from Ben sat the little yellow cardigan in a crinkly plastic bag. It had never been worn. She had knitted it herself in preparation for their baby sister's arrival when Raychel was just a girl herself. She could hardly bear to look at it, but neither could she ever throw it away.

Ben watched her trembling fingers reach out to stroke it tenderly through the plastic and he stepped in quickly.

'Come on, let's stop packing for today, pet. Enough for today.'

When Anna got to the train station after work, there was no man in black facing her. Nor was he behind her, about to breathe on her neck. She felt an unreasonable stab of annoyance that he wasn't haunting her that night. She sat on a bench on the platform and pulled out the black-edged card bearing Vladimir Darq's name. *Go on, ring it.* She thought of his promises to locate her 'Darq' side. She thought of Tony and winning him back with her revitalised inner goddess. It was worth a try; anything was worth a try. She pressed down the first two numbers on her phone, lifted it to her ear and heard it burr three times, then a man's voice—*his*—answered with a clipped, 'Hello.'

'Erm, it's me, from the train station, Anna Bri—'

'Yes, I know who you are.'

'I'm ringing to say—'

'My address is Darq House in Higher Hoppleton,' he cut her off. 'What is your address?'

'Erm, two, Courtyard Lane—that's Dartley.'

'Be ready Saturday night at seven p.m., please,' he interrupted with a no-negotiating East European accent. 'A car will be sent for you. You will come here and I will prepare you for filming. Wear your most comfortable, not your best, underwear. I repeat, your *most comfortable*.'

And with that, the line went dead.

Chapter 6
May

WITHOUT EXCEPTION, all five women were really looking forward to their night out together, albeit for different reasons. Dawn knew that every Friday she expected to stay in with Calum and every Friday, without fail, he would promise that he'd come back in after a couple of pints only to turn up long after she had gone to bed. So it would make a refreshing change to go out and enjoy herself. Anna was so dreading being alone on her birthday that even an evening with four relative strangers seemed like a gift. Grace wanted to have a night off from Gordon's incessant talk about their future life in Blegthorpe. And Raychel knew she was far too reliant on Ben for company. Sometimes she felt as if she was choking him with her neediness.

The Rising Sun pub was only up the road from White Rose Stores HQ at the edge of the industrial estate. They called in for a drink to whet their appetites for the meal later in the new Thai restaurant next door, aptly called the Setting Sun.

The Rising Sun had recently had a refurb to make it look like a cowboy saloon. Posters at either side of a small stage announced that 'The Rhinestones' were playing the following week. Dawn was quite sorry they wouldn't be performing that night; she loved any sort of country-and-western music. She only had to hear the first few bars to be back to her childhood with her singing-mad dad and his gee-tar.

They found an empty table. No sooner had they sat down than a waitress with a silver bucket full of ice and a bottle of champagne turned up. Another waitress followed behind with five long glass flutes.

'A little present from James McAskill,' explained Christie to her party of open-mouthed administrators. *What was this woman to James McAskill that she had such sway?* they thought. But they took advantage of his kindness and raised their glasses in Anna's direction and said in unison. 'Happy fortieth birthday, Anna!'

'So how come you haven't any mates or family to go out with tonight, then?' said Dawn. Anna coloured.

'My dear girl, you have such a way with words,' said Christie, shaking her head.

Anna knew that Christie had spoken to the others about the split with Tony because she had told her that she had.

'Well, you know about my errant partner of course,' Anna began to explain. 'Mum and Dad are divorced. Mum got remarried and lives in Ireland; Dad got remarried and lives in Cornwall. I've got a much younger sister, Sally, but she changed her name to Rainbow Storm and went to live on a French commune. I've had a few cards from couples that Tony and I used to go around with, but they're more his mates than mine. And I appear to have drifted apart from all the friends I had before I met Tony. That's why I'm a Billy-No-Mates saddo today.'

Grace nodded. She knew how easy it was to find yourself isolated.

And Ben had been Raychel's only companion. How could she have friends when she could never trust anyone but Ben? Ever. They were united by things that set them apart from everyone in the world.

'Friendships are so important,' said Christie. 'I feel for you being alone. Which is why you are going to have a wonderful meal with us tonight and toast the fact that this day is the first day of the rest of your life.' Christie had been thinking a lot about her ladies and was so glad they were here round this table. Once upon a time she had been wrong in cutting herself off from everyone and floating out into a sea of loneliness. She had been lucky, at least, in being pulled back to shore by wonderful people who cared for her.

'Happy birthday, Anna. This is a little something from us all.' Grace lifted a bag from under the table and put it down in front of Anna, who was genuinely taken aback. She hadn't expected a present.

'I don't know what to say!' she said breathlessly.

'Oh, just get it opened, girl,' said Christie.

Anna reached tentatively into the bag. There were cards, a book, bubble bath, chocolates, a bottle of champagne and all sorts of ribbons and sweeties and a pen with a wobbly '40' on top.

'We thought there might be something in there at least that you liked,' said Raychel. 'We had a stab at what your tastes are.'

'Seeing as we hardly know each other,' added Dawn.

'Thank you all so much,' said Anna. A lot more thought had gone into the girls' presents than the cheques her parents had sent her.

'You've done us a favour,' said Dawn. 'You gave us the excuse to organise this meal.'

'Oh well, my rotten love life is good for something then,' said Anna.

The champagne finished, they gathered up their coats and bags and moved next door to the Setting Sun. An exquisitely made-up Thai waitress met them at the door with her palms pressed together in greeting.

'Dinner for five in the name of Somers,' said Christie. They were led over to a beautifully set table and given the biggest menus Anna had ever seen. It would have been quicker to read *War and Peace*. They ordered their meals and drinks and relaxed.

'Here's hoping our horse-race win changes our fortunes,' said Christie.

'Hear hear,' said Anna. 'In fact . . . no, it doesn't matter.'

'Oh, go on, you can't start something and then stop it,' said Dawn.

'Well . . .' began Anna again. She really ought to tell someone about her visit to Vladimir Darq tomorrow, as a security measure if nothing else. 'Something strange happened to me recently. This bloke followed me in the train station . . .' And she proceeded to tell them the full tale.

'Goodness me!' said Grace. 'He does live in Higher Hoppleton, though. I've read about him in the newspapers.'

'Isn't he the one that looks like Count Dracula?' said Dawn.

'A Transylvanian vampire in Higher Hoppleton,' mused Christie.

'Should I go, do you think?' Anna asked.

'Of course you must go,' said Grace adamantly. 'It's just what you need: an adventure. Perfect timing on his part.'

'But being on TV in my underwear? I'm not sure I could. And they always feel you up on those shows, don't they?'

'No one seems to complain when Gok Wan grabs their hooters,' said Christie. 'But I warn you, if the man gives you anything like a proper fitting service, you're looking at something akin to invasive surgery.'

'Oh God, no. Really?' Anna paled.

'Oh yes, you'll have to strip off and let him look at you.'

'Get away! You're having me on.'

'I am not,' said Christie, amused by the look of horror on Anna's face.

'Oh, just go for it. I mean, what would your alternative plans for the evening be?' said Dawn.

'Fair point,' conceded Anna thinking inwardly, *Bloody hell! Stripping right off in front of millions of people!* It was all a bit surreal.

The Thai food was good and plentiful. They followed it with coffees.

'What a lovely way this has been to round the week off,' said Christie. 'We should do this again.'

'I'd like that,' said Anna. 'I've had a great evening. Thank you all so much.' She meant it too. Their company had given her spirits such a lift. She dreaded to think what her birthday would have been like had she been alone in the house.

'Me too, I've had a smashing time,' said Dawn. It was a nice change from the Crookes' company.

Yes, thought Christie. This evening had done them all good.

'Well, happy birthday, Annie,' said Dawn and raised the last of her coffee in the air. Four other cups nudged against it. 'May this day be the start of better times ahead for you.'

Anna just wished she believed it could be.

Grace went to visit Paul on Saturday morning at his beautiful apartment on the posher outskirts of Sheffield. She rang the intercom and Paul buzzed her in. He greeted her at his door, taking the belated Easter eggs from her with good-hearted humour and his usual loving hug. She was pleasantly surprised to see Joe there with his uncle.

'Hello, sweetheart,' said Grace, giving her grandson a kiss on his head. He looked quite sorry for himself.

'He's got toothache,' Paul whispered. 'Laura's just nipped out for some oil of cloves for him and milk for me. His big Uncle Paul is taking his mind off it by playing a game of cards. Aren't we, Joey?' He gave the boy an affectionate squeeze on his shoulder.

'Paul, where are . . . oh, hello!' A tall, smart, incredibly handsome black man came into the lounge from the dining room.

'Mum, this is Charles, my business partner.'

'Hello,' said Grace with a smile. 'How lovely to meet you at long last.'

'Mrs Beamish, delighted,' said Charles in a beautifully plummy English accent. 'I've heard a lot about you.'

'All good, I hope,' said Grace, with a hint of a blush.

'Every single word,' said Charles.

A buzzer went and Paul's intercom camera showed Laura holding up a four-pint carton of milk.

'She volunteered to fetch it,' said Paul. 'We offered but she wanted to cool off. She's been ringing round for a dentist and getting nowhere.'

When Laura came in, she gave Grace a big hug.

'Calmer now, sweetheart?' said Charles, pulling her to him and giving her a squeeze.

'Oh, I see!' said Grace.

'We've just started courting, Mum. I was dying to tell you but I didn't know if he'd want to see me again after the first date,' said Laura.

'I didn't know if you'd want to see *me* after the first date,' said Charles. 'I was so nervous I spilled my wine all over her skirt.'

Charles and Laura looked at each other sweetly and Grace couldn't help but mirror their smile. *What a lovely man*, she thought. She just hoped it would last. Laura was a bit like poor Anna in the love department. She'd always had a rotten deal when it came to boyfriends, Joe's father being the cherry on the cake. He had left Laura when she was five months' pregnant, writing himself out of the boy's life before he was even born. Laura was well overdue some love and attention.

Laura put the kettle on. Paul had bought cakes and made sandwiches because he had decided they were going to have a high tea on his roof terrace. It was a summer haven up there, an organised chaos of plants and trellis and water features.

'So we're all good for caravanning holidays in Blegthorpe then,' said Paul, popping a small pastry into his mouth and giving Grace a wink.

'Oh, don't even joke,' said Grace wearily.

'You and Dad, alone together 24/7 in a giant can. Lovely.'

'Don't ever retire, Mrs Beamish,' said Charles. 'That's the key.' Laura had obviously been filling him in with some details.

'How's the new boss?' enquired Paul.

'She's a very nice woman,' said Grace. 'We all went out for a meal last night. I've never eaten Thai food before. It was beautiful.'

'Good for you, Mum,' said Paul. 'I presume Dad didn't object?'

'Goodness, Paul. He wouldn't stop me going out anywhere.'

'Apart from here. He wouldn't like it if he knew you visited me.'

'He must know that I see you.'

'Maybe he doesn't. Maybe he thinks you wouldn't dare,' said Paul, which awoke Grace to the idea that her son just might be right, even though she couldn't admit it.

'That's ridiculous.'

'Well, you won't be able to go out with your new friends if you're stuck in Blegthorpe!' Paul wagged his finger at his mum.

'You have to start saying no,' said Laura. 'No one's ever said no to Dad, that's the problem.'

'I did,' said Paul with a proud smirk. 'Hence the reason why I am banished from the family home. He thinks I'll be "cured" when I meet the right woman.'

Grace was surprised Paul could laugh so objectively about that day. She knew how hurt he had been when he told his father he was gay, not hoping for endorsement, just acceptance, and Gordon had refused to listen, then stormed out of the house and said that Paul was to have left by the time he came back. She often wished she had been brave enough to walk out with Paul then.

After her lovely interlude with one half of the family, Grace landed back on terra firma with a resounding bump. She came home to find Gordon carrying a crying Sable, whom he pushed into Grace's arms as soon as she walked in.

'Where the heck have you been?' he demanded.

'I went for a walk round the shops,' she lied. She didn't want to risk his reaction by telling him the truth.

'Sarah's been phoning you. Said it kept going onto voicemail.'

'Oh, did it?' Grace searched her bag to find her phone was switched off. She grimaced to discover there had been twenty-four missed calls: ten from her daughter and fourteen from Gordon. 'I thought I'd left it on.'

'Well, you obviously didn't, did you? What's the point in having a mobile phone if you switch it off when you're out? She's been having pains. She was thinking about going up to hospital!'

'Oh, goodness me.' Grace felt panicked. 'Should we go up there?'

'I had to go over and pick Sable up. Sarah was going for a lie down and she said she'd ring if things got worse.'

Grace immediately rang Laura on her mobile. Laura was remarkably unsympathetic and explained why.

'Mum, I've just passed her in the car. She looked fine to me as she was pulling into the multistorey. She's having as many birth pains as I am!'

Grace really was going to have to learn how to start saying no.

It was amazing the things that crossed your mind when you were standing in a pseudo-Transylvanian castle having two men scrutinise your knockers at point-blank range, thought Anna. She wondered what Tony would think. Would he have her bang to rights on grounds of adultery, even if the men in question were gay?

Leonid Szabo was small, slight, very camp in his gestures, and with his frilly shirt and long waistcoat he looked like Adam Ant in his high-wayman days. In stark contrast, Vladimir Darq was looking very alpha male in slim-cut black trousers and the whitest shirt Anna had ever seen. He wasn't exactly classically handsome, with his pale skin, square jaw and thin, precise line of beard on it, but there was something very 'man' about him. Ironically so, given his sexual proclivity.

She'd arrived at the house in a black Mercedes, which had drawn up outside her home at exactly 7 p.m. The Romanian driver was sullen and uncommunicative, but he didn't speak much English. On the outskirts of the small village of Higher Hoppleton, black electronic gates had gained them entry to a long drive, and they had pulled up in front of the biggest door Anna had ever seen. It had opened with an Addams' Family-style creak and she had half expected to find Lurch behind it. But there was only a much smaller man with a bald head and eyeliner, whom she recognised immediately from the Internet as Leonid Szabo: the 'friend' of Vladimir Darq.

The door had opened out into a huge galleried room. Darq House was a newbuild made to look like it was a relic from the Middle Ages. With a mixture of clever architecture and trompe l'oeil painted walls, it looked eerily like a fifteenth-century vaulted castle.

'You must be Anna, come on in,' Leonid had said in a strong accent. He had helped Anna off with her coat, all the while appraising her. Then the man himself had made an entrance, shaken her hand politely and cut straight to the chase.

'Anna, we need to look at you. Stand up straight and stay still.'

Now both men circled her, looking at her body from all angles. Anna felt surprisingly detached. All she could think was that two homosexual men staring at her chest was bizarrely healthier for her than a night in, alone, watching *Casualty* and sobbing into a box of tissues.

The two men spoke to each other rapidly in their native language. Anna could only guess at what they said to each other. It didn't exactly sound as if they were comparing her to Cindy Crawford.

'She's perfect,' Vladimir commented, as if Anna wasn't there. 'Her underwear is of course awful, and doing nothing for her at all.'

'Can we see, please?' asked Leonid.

'What? You want me to strip off?' said Anna.

'Just to your underwear,' Vladimir said.

Anna took a deep breath and started unbuttoning. She didn't feel as embarrassed as she thought she would. Then again, next week she was going to be standing here with these two and a film crew, including the very gorgeous, slim, cellulite-free Jane Cleve-Jones looking at her. That was a much scarier thought.

'This bra isn't a cheap one, I can see that. But it's rubbish.' Vladimir despaired. 'What bra size are you?'

'Thirty-six C.'

'*Nu!*' he said with a humph. 'You aren't.'

'I am!' said Anna. 'I'll prove it. Have you a tape measure?'

'I don't trust tape measures,' said Vladimir, wearing the expression of a man who had just smelled something foul. 'And stand up straight, please.' He rushed behind her and gripped her shoulders, pulling them back. Her boobs seemed to rise twelve feet when he did that.

'Ah, eez better. Posture is everything,' said Leonid.

'Posture and confidence go hand in hand,' said Vladimir, 'and she obviously has no confidence, so she has no good posture.'

Vladimir stroked the skin down her neck to her shoulders as if she was made out of clay and he was smoothing it. She couldn't remember the last time Tony had been as gently attentive. He could roger for

England, but stroking and softness didn't turn up on the menu. She coughed away the thought of Tony and amused herself by looking round the room while she was being discussed in fluent Romanian.

It really was a cleverly built house. The walls looked as if they were fashioned from ancient stone, and had large iron torches bolted to them. A cavernous unlit fire awaited colder months and a huge black dog that was part Great Dane, part Zoltan Hound of Dracula reposed in a basket at the side of it. He'd given Anna a perfunctory glance when she first came in, but didn't deem her important enough to rise up and investigate her.

Everything was so large: the table, the sofas, the candlesticks. And her tits as well, apparently: as the dispute dipped in and out of English, Vladimir seemed to be arguing with Leonid that she was at least a 40D.

As the conversation between them got even more inflamed, Vladimir Darq flounced off, only to appear minutes later with an armful of corsets and bodyshapers, still with long, uncut threads. He clicked his fingers impatiently at Anna to hold her arms out and step into the bodyshaper that he was stretching for her. Then, when he had pulled it up over her knickers, much to her surprise, he whipped off her bra with the ease of an expert magician. She gasped but he didn't acknowledge her shock because he was too busy hooking her up at the back. Once that was done, he plunged his hands into the front and positioned Anna's breasts precisely into the cups as if he was an artist arranging fruit in a bowl. How he managed to avoid giving her impromptu acupuncture treatment while he was pulling the material and pinning darts in it like a madman was anyone's guess.

'See?' he said to Leonid. 'I could tell from looking at her she was all wrong. This is much better. You can see the difference already that good-fitting underwear can give her,' said Vladimir in an animated voice.

'Can I see?' asked Anna tentatively.

'Nu,' replied Leonid.

'Anna, the filming will take place over the next five Saturdays and chart your progress. You are the perfect choice to demonstrate to other ladies that you don't need to be aged twenty and a size zero to be a siren. Any lingerie I make for you, you can keep. The production companies do not pay a wage, only expenses. Are those terms acceptable to you?'

Anna nodded. Being able to keep just one piece made for her by Vladimir Darq would be payment enough. He began to unpin the bodyshaper so Anna could slip out of it. Her bra made her feel extra saggy and blobby when she put it on again.

'Try to stay much the same weight as you are now, Anna, please,' asked Vladimir. 'Dress exactly the same next week as you have tonight.'

'When will the programme be on the TV?'

'I don't know, but they are hoping to turn it around very quickly. I will send a car for you at quarter to seven next Saturday evening.'

'So late?'

'I don't work in the daylight,' he said, as if that were obvious.

'Oh, no, I suppose not,' said Anna. *Blimey*, she thought. He couldn't really be a vampire, could he?

Dawn went upstairs to rouse Calum at 11 a.m. He'd been drunk again on Saturday night, even though it was supposed to be her night for drinking and his for driving. He'd told her to leave the car and they'd get a taxi. It wasn't just the money, it was the principle. Then they'd bumped into his mates and Calum had wanted to go on to a club with them. Dawn was too tired by that time and annoyed with him, so she'd driven home and he'd ended up getting a taxi back in the small hours anyway.

They went to Muriel's for lunch. All the family were there, squeezed around a big table like the Waltons. Like the sort of family Dawn had always dreamed of belonging to, and now she was about to. She was squashed in between Calum's younger sister, Demi, and his older sister, Denise. Denise, Demi and Dawn—even the alliteration of their names made her feel like one of theirs.

'Got some good news for you,' announced Muriel. 'Bette across the road is going to make the bridesmaids' frocks. That'll save you an arm and a leg.'

'Oh!' said Dawn, trying to muster up a diplomatic refusal. 'Well, actually I've seen some lovely ones in Laura Ashley—'

'Laura Ashley!' scoffed Demi. 'They'll be poncey.'

'No, not at all, they're lovely and—'

'Bette will make anything at a fraction of shop prices. You just tell her what you want and she'll sort it. She's a brilliant sewer.'

'Oh, well, thank you,' gulped Dawn. If Bette was so brilliant, she could make the same ones that she had seen in Laura Ashley.

The veg was limp and boiled to death, the beef was hard on the outside and too pink on the inside. The potatoes were lumpy, the gravy was lumpier; only the Yorkshire puddings stood superb, puffing proudly out of the tin moulds.

'This is a bit shit, Mam,' said Demi.

'Now, now! Just 'cos you were dumped last night, no need to make everyone feel as bad as you do,' said Calum.

'You can shut up,' said Demi.

'Just eat it or leave it!' said Muriel. 'Look at them Yorkshires. Bloody gorgeous they are. Cheers, everyone!' She raised her glass of plonk. 'You should have had me doing the catering at your wedding, Dawn.'

'Well, I'm not coming if you are,' said Demi.

'That reminds me,' said Dawn, turning to Calum. 'We have to go to the Dog and Duck and finalise the menus.'

'Oh, I did that for you on Friday. More or less, anyway. I just need to know if you want sloppy peas or carrots with the beef. Didn't you tell her, Cal?' announced Muriel.

'I forgot,' said Calum.

'Sandra—the landlady—wanted to know quick, so me and our Calum picked while we were up there,' said Muriel.

Dawn gulped down her annoyance. 'What . . . what menu did you pick then?' she asked Calum, but Muriel answered.

'Vegetable soup to start, beef dinner, then treacle sponge or fudge cake. Sandra's given you a right good price an' all. And she's putting a karaoke on and a buffet at night.' She cracked Calum with the spatula that she'd used to lever the Yorkshires out of their tins as she saw Dawn's face drop. 'Don't tell me dopey lad hasn't told you that bit either? He said you'd be OK with it.'

Dawn gulped again. At this rate her gulping muscle was going to beat a previous world record. 'A karaoke?'

'Ooh, I love karaoke,' said Denise.

'The buffet sounded OK,' said Calum, forking up another Yorkshire pudding. 'It'll be cheap an' all.'

'Why didn't you ring me first so I could have had a say in it?' Dawn said between clenched teeth.

'Me mam said it was the best menu,' shrugged Calum, as if that answered the question sufficiently.

'I'll put a bit towards it because I'm inviting some of my friends as well,' said Muriel.

'Aw, thanks, Mam,' said Calum, reaching for more meat.

Dawn fell quiet. She didn't want strangers there, or a karaoke. She wanted a live band and dancing. And she wanted to pick her own menu.

'I don't think I want a karaoke,' she braved quietly.

It was as if the atom bomb had landed in the middle of the gravy. Everyone stopped chewing and rotated their heads in her direction.

'Why not?' said Denise. She was usually smiley but when that smile dropped it altered her whole face to a replica of Demi's.

'What's wrong with a karaoke? Is it not good enough for you?' said Demi with an unpleasant sneer.

'No, it's not that . . .' Gawd, Dawn found herself wishing she hadn't opened her mouth. She had just witnessed the Crooke women swapping raised eyebrows.

Dawn immediately felt herself backing down. 'It's just that, well, I was thinking more of a live band but—'

'Live band?' scoffed Calum. 'Who'd you have in mind? Take That?'

There was a ripple of laughter round the table and it contained unkind tones that chilled Dawn to the core.

'OK, then, a karaoke it is. That'll be fun,' said Dawn, forcing a smile. She felt like she'd just escaped a savaging by a pack.

'We should have a karaoke after this dinner, cheer your miserable face up a bit,' said Denise to her sister.

'I don't need cheering up, he were a knobhead. I'm well shot.'

'He were king of the knobheads,' said Calum. 'It's not like it's the first time he's cheated on you and you've only been going out two minutes.'

'Hark at Mr Faithful!' said Demi. 'Ow! What did you kick me for?'

'What's this?' said Dawn, suddenly picking up on a nasty vibe. There was something zapping between Calum and his sister that she didn't like the look of.

'It's nowt, she's a stirring little cow,' said Calum.

'It's nothing, really,' said Denise, adding to the impression that nothing was, in fact, a very big something. And that something had happened after she drove home last night and Calum went clubbing.

'It's not my fault I'm so attractive,' admitted Calum with a grin.

'What isn't?'

'Ignore them all,' said Denise kindly. 'It's that cow, Mandy Clamp. You know what's she like around our Calum.'

'Wh . . . what do you mean?'

'She's after my body,' said Calum, treating it like a big joke.

'I didn't exactly see you pushing her off,' sniped Demi.

'She only moved in because you weren't around, Dawn,' said Denise.

Tears rose in Dawn's eyes and she was outed before she could push them down again.

'No point in getting upset,' said Demi. 'He won't change. They don't. If they've got away with it once, they'll get away with it again.' With tears in her own eyes, she flounced off, sending her plate zooming across the table to clash into her brother's.

'Nothing happened, Dawn. I swear. Did it, Den?'

'Not that I saw,' said Denise, keeping her eyes down on her dinner. *That was a very careful, diplomatic answer*, thought Dawn.

'Oh ho, I know that look: nag-alert!' said Calum, pointing at Dawn, who tried to protest that she wasn't going to do anything of the sort.

'You need to get a grip, lady.' Muriel's voice came quiet but hard across the dinner table. It hurt, especially because Dawn had deliberately made a conscious effort *not* to say anything. Calum had used her to deflect attention away from himself.

Suddenly she didn't feel a part of this family at all.

Grace was just finishing her Sunday dinner. Joe was there with Laura, Sarah and her husband, Hugo, and Sable, and Gordon was at the head of the table taking the meat carving very seriously. Paul should have been there; lately she had found herself wanting to scream that at Gordon.

'How's the job going, Mother?' said Sarah. 'New boss not too much of a bitch, I hope?'

'It's very enjoyable and the new boss is lovely, thank you, dear,' said Grace. She suspected Sarah had an ulterior motive for enquiring about her job satisfaction.

'You scared Mum silly yesterday, Sarah, saying you had pains,' said Laura, with blue-eyed innocence.

'I did have them,' said Sarah. 'I was very worried, which is why I rang for Dad to pick up Sable. Thank goodness they subsided just before I was going to drive up to hospital.'

'Yes, that was lucky,' said Laura with more than a touch of sarcasm, adding, 'and in plenty of time before the shops shut.'

'Are the people at your job nice, Nana?' said Joe.

'They're all very nice, thank you, Joe,' said Grace.

'Are they all your age?' asked Sarah, reaching for the gravy boat.

'No, Raychel is in her twenties, Dawn in her thirties, Anna was forty just last week and my boss is late forties.'

'So no competition if an early redundancy comes up?' said Sarah.

'Can't be long,' said Gordon. 'I've a good mind to ask them myself what's going on.'

Grace looked at him, horrified. 'You can't do that!'

'What's the worst they can say?'

'You could affect any payout I get,' said Grace, thinking on her feet. 'If they think I'm desperate to go they won't pay as much.' *Whew!*

'A very good point,' said Hugo, shovelling in a huge roast potato.

Gordon seemed satisfied by Hugo's endorsement. That thankfully closed off that avenue of conversation. At least for the afternoon.

'No pud for me, Mum,' said Laura. 'Joe and I are off for a walk.'

'We're taking a dog with us!' said Joe excitedly.

'You haven't eaten all your dinner, so you wouldn't have got any pudding anyway,' said Gordon to Joe.

'He's having a bit of on-and-off toothache. I doubt he'd have wanted a pudding,' replied Laura stiffly, after seeing her boy's face drop.

'Well, take him to the dentist then,' said Gordon with a humph.

'Mine's on holiday and I can't get anyone to look at him before next Friday. I should have lied and said it was an emergency.'

'I'll ask around,' said Grace. 'I'm sure my boss said her brother was a dentist. He might be able to help.'

'You haven't bought a dog, have you?' asked Hugo.

'No, he belongs to my friend, Charles,' said Laura.

'Oh, starting courting, have you?' said Sarah. 'Do we know him?'

'You won't know him,' said Laura.

'And what does he do?' pushed Sarah.

'He's an architect,' said Joe, butting in proudly.

'Oh, really,' said Sarah, impressed by that.

'As a matter of fact, he'll be here any minute to pick us up. Joe, get your shoes on, love.'

'Bring him in,' said Grace.

'No chance!' laughed Laura. 'Maybe a few weeks down the line.'

Joe had barely got his first shoe on when there was a car horn beeping outside.

'Let's have a look at him.' Sarah rushed to the window. 'Damn, you can't see much of him! He's parked the wrong way round.'

'Oh, dear,' pouted Laura. 'You'll have to wait then.'

With a flurry of kisses and byes and waves they went out down the path towards the waiting car. Gordon moved to the window and Grace wondered what he had seen out of it to make his back stiffen and his eyes lock like a Rottweiler before an attack.

Chapter 7

'CHRISTIE, DO YOU MIND me asking?' said Grace as soon as she laid eyes on her boss. 'Did you say that your brother was a dentist?'

'Yes, he's a private dentist,' said Christie. 'What's the problem?'

Grace told her all about Joe.

Christie made a quick phone call and a couple of minutes later she said to Grace, 'He can see your grandson at twelve, is that OK for you?'

'Oh, thank you so much,' said Grace. 'Where's his surgery?'

'Prince Street. Opposite the church.'

'I know it. Thank you,' said Grace. *What a kind woman you are, Christie Somers*, thought Grace, as she rang Laura to ask if it was OK to take Joe out of school.

The plaque on the door read: 'Nikita Koslov and Robin Green', alongside a string of qualifications that looked incredibly impressive. Grace rang the bell and she and Joe entered a spacious and tidy reception room with a central table full of magazines and comics. Joe picked out a *Dr Who* mag while Grace spoke to the receptionist and filled in a form. Then she went to sit next to him.

Soon it was their turn to go up the grand oak staircase, which led to two dentists' rooms. 'Well, hello there,' said a booming voice, as rich and deep as an expensive Christmas cake. The owner of it strode forward with a hand outstretched. 'You must be Joe. Come and take a seat, while your big sister sits on that chair and waits for you.'

'Oh Gawd,' said the dental assistant, raising her eyes heavenwards.

'And you're Grace,' said Niki, seizing Grace's hand firmly.

Grace smiled. This man was instantly recognisable as Christie's brother by his twinkly blue eyes. His hair was silver-white, short and spiked up. He was a completely different body shape to his smaller, rounder sister, though, being long-limbed, slim and straight.

'Now then, young man, relax and go for a nice ride on this chair, totally free of charge. Can you open your mouth for me? Fan-tas-tic! Ah ha—I see the little devil! That's going to need to come out, I'm afraid. But don't worry, Joe, because I am the best dentist in the world and you aren't going to feel a thing.'

He injected Joe's mouth so gently that the boy never made a murmur. While the anaesthetic took effect, Nikita Koslov encouraged Joe to concentrate on the spot-the-difference pictures that were stuck up on his ceiling. The tooth was out in a jiffy and a couple of minutes later, Joe was rinsing out his mouth and picking out a sticker with a lion on it saying, 'I've been super-brave.'

'Thank you *so* much,' said Grace.

'No problemo at all,' said Niki. 'Joe has been brilliant. A star patient. And any friend of Christianya's is a friend of mine, of course.'

'I didn't know that's what Christie was short for,' said Grace, thinking, *What a beautiful name*.

'Russian ancestry,' said Niki. 'Noblemen who escaped the homeland in the Revolution. Who knows, if we'd stayed, I might have been tsar by now. That's the King of Russia to you, Joe.'

'Really?' said Joe, wide-eyed with fascination.

'Absolutely,' said Niki, winking at him. He had a lovely smile, just like Christie's. Genuine and friendly, spreading right up to his eyes.

He held out his hand to Joe and shook it seriously.

'Well, Joe, I hope the next time I see you will be in less painful and happier circumstances.'

Joe returned the handshake with a medically lopsided grin.

'Right, Joe, let's go and pay our bill,' said Grace.

'Absolutely not, wouldn't hear of it!' said Niki.

'No, please. I couldn't let you do this for nothing.'

'I insist and it's my surgery so I win this argument,' said Niki, holding up a shushing finger. 'A favour for a friend of my sister.'

'That's incredibly kind of you,' said Grace.

'Pleasure. Goodbye, Grace,' smiled Niki. His fingers closed round Grace's hand. They were strong and warm. It was the oddest feeling but it was as if something like a soft, benign electrical current passed between them. Grace was aware of an involuntary increase in her heart-rate as Christie's brother showed them out.

From the way Ben answered the door, it was obvious that it was to someone he knew. Raychel could hear a pleasant interchange taking place and then Ben was ushering a man into the sitting room. The visitor was invisible under a stack of thick, empty boxes.

'Here, put them down here,' said Ben.

'Right,' said the man.

'Ray, this is John, my boss.'

'Hello, Mrs Ben,' said John, straightening up, but when his eyes touched on Raychel's face, his mouth dropped open like a dead fish's.

Raychel started to go hot in that familiar way whenever anyone had prolonged eye contact with her.

'Forgive me for staring,' said John. 'You just look so much like . . . Do you mind? Can I ask? Are you from round here? Originally?'

'Newcastle,' said Raychel, frozen in his headlight gaze.

'No family at all down here then?' said John.

'No, we're all from up there,' said Raychel.

'Wow, that's so . . .' John shook his head. He seemed genuinely winded by the sight of Raychel.

'Do you want a cuppa, John?' said Ben.

'No, lad. I'll let you get on. Nice to meet you . . . Raychel,' said John, taking a last lingering look at the young woman and really making an effort not to make her feel any more uncomfortable than she obviously was, but *My God*, it was hard to keep his eyes off her.

Outside, John Silkstone instinctively pressed the home number on his mobile, then clicked off before it connected. The lass had said she had no connections with Barnsley, so was it worth getting the missus upset or excited? But the likeness to his wife Elizabeth was uncanny—there simply *had* to be a connection. She had been searching for years for her older sister, Bev Collier, who had run away from home in the early eighties when she was pregnant. He needed to think very carefully before venturing anywhere near this giant can of worms.

'So, are we going out again tomorrow?' asked Anna. 'Only I've got such a busy schedule I need to pencil it in the diary.'

Dawn laughed. 'You can count me in. You can tell us all the details about your night with the Darq one as well.' It had been a very busy week. They hadn't had any chance to chat.

'Well, that would be nice,' said Christie.

'It will have to be a quick one for me,' said Raychel. 'We're moving into our new flat this weekend and I'm busy, busy, busy. But it would be nice to have a drink in that pub again.'

The following night saw them chattering away and walking round the corner together to the Rising Sun. The small stage in front of the bar wasn't empty this time. It was full of equipment and men in cowboy shirts and hats faffing around with mikes and instruments. Presumably these were The Rhinestones.

'Shall we have a kitty?' suggested Dawn, opening up her purse and holding up a fiver. 'I haven't any change, but it could go towards next week if this is to be a regular occurrence. What do you all think?'

The others seemed to agree and coughed up a fiver each. After Christie had ordered wine at the bar they went to find a table away from the tuning-up band, a little to Dawn's disappointment.

'So come on then,' said Raychel, once they had all taken off their coats and the wine was poured. 'What happened with the designer?'

'Oh, where to begin?' said Anna. 'A Merc picked me up and took me to his house, which is absolutely gorgeous, like a castle off a Hammer Horror set. And then he had a good look at my bra and told me it was appalling.'

'Not one for much elaboration, are you?' said Christie, with a grin.

'The filming starts tomorrow. That's when I'll have stories to tell.'

'It must be so exciting,' said Dawn, grinning. 'I looked Vladimir Darq up on the Internet. He's rather dishy, isn't he?'

'Gay blokes always are,' sniffed Anna.

'What time are you going?' asked Raychel.

'He's sending a car at quarter to seven. He said he doesn't work during the day.' Anna shifted forward in her seat and whispered as if he could overhear her, 'And he's got fangs.'

'Fangs?'

'Like a vampire.'

'He plays on the image of being Romanian then, obviously,' said Christie. 'As one would.'

'What do you mean?' said Dawn.

'Romania—vampires—Dracula,' explained Grace.

'Never been one for all that gothic stuff. That's more my sort of thing,' said Dawn, pointing to the band who had started playing, and were very good. Especially that tall rhythm guitarist at the back. She'd had the brilliant idea of asking them to play at her wedding as soon as she heard his fingers on the strings. At least that would make the evening karaoke more bearable.

'Grandson's tooth doing OK?' Christie asked Grace.

'Thanks to your brother, yes,' replied Grace.

'He's a lovely man is my big brother,' smiled Christie. 'Why he never found the right woman is totally beyond me. He's kind, generous, patient, faithful.'

'Well, there's your answer then,' sighed Anna. 'If he'd been a total bastard, he'd have pulled a nice bird, wrecked her life and been instantly attractive to loads of other women.'

'And are you ready for the move tomorrow?' Christie asked Raychel.

'More or less. I've just got a bit of cleaning left to do for the next person in the house.'

'Yeurch. I shan't be asking to swap you weekends,' said Anna.

'Me neither. I'd rather get felt up by a gay vampire than scrub out ovens,' said Dawn.

They downed their glasses and put their coats on and said their goodbyes. Dawn volunteered to take the glasses back to the bar because she wanted to listen to the band for another five minutes. And as she neared the stage, she fell instantly in love. She noticed that the tall rhythm guitarist was playing a vintage Fender Stratocaster: the same guitar her dad had had. She closed her eyes and listened to the sound and imagined her dad on the stage, his fingers on the strings.

There was applause as the song ended but Dawn was still swaying, locked in a bittersweet daydream. When she toppled, it was the rhythm guitarist whose hands steadied her.

'You OK there, ma'am?' he drawled in a voice straight off a John Wayne western. It seemed the band had stopped for a break.

'Oh, yes, sorry,' said Dawn, feeling a bit of a twerp. 'I was listening to your guitar. My dad used to have a vintage Stratocaster too.'

'*Used to?* He let it go?' questioned the guitarist.

'Not really. He was buried with it. Which is a bit of a conversation stopper, sorry,' sighed Dawn.

'Oh, I'm sorry to hear that. It must have been real special to him.'

'Oh, yes it was.'

'And do you play like your daddy, ma'am?'

'Oh, I'll never be as good as he was,' said Dawn bashfully.

'Which guitar do you have?'

'A Gibson Les Paul. Nineteen fifty-seven.'

He whistled respectfully. 'Wow. You in a band yourself then, ma'am?'

'No, my father was, though,' said Dawn.

'The Beatles?' he teased.

Dawn laughed. 'Of course. He was George.'

'Then may I buy you a drink, Miss Harrison?'

Dawn opened up her mouth to say *No, thank you*. But what came out was, 'Yes, please. Just a Diet Coke, though.'

'So, what's your everyday name then, Miss Harrison?' said the tall, dark guitarist as the barmaid put two Diet Cokes in front of them.

'Dawny. Dawny Sole.' She added the 'Y' on to make her feel like a different person from the Dawn Sole who had a fiancé and was in the midst of imminent-wedding preparations.

'I'm Al Holly. Miss Dawny Sole, it sure is nice to meet you.'

The cowboy held out a large, slim-fingered hand and shook her own. His voice was having the same effect on her that the lead guitar on Chris Isaak's 'Wicked Game' had. It was bouncing round inside her, twanging her own strings and stirring up all sorts of things inside her that it shouldn't have.

'I wondered . . . how long you were going to be around for?' stuttered Dawn. She bit off the part about asking if he'd be available to play for her wedding.

'Well, Kirk—the bass guitarist right there—has come to spend a few weeks with his parents, who moved back over here a couple of years ago, so we're playing a few gigs in the area and we're hoping to head home at the end of June. Why? You thinking of coming and joining us?'

'I wish!' said Dawn. The idea of running away from all those wedding bills with just her guitar and a few pairs of knickers in a bag flashed through her head and felt very attractive.

'You could bring your guitar along and show us all how it's done,' said Al Holly. 'Maybe I don't believe you can play at all and here you are just trying to chat me up.'

'No, no, I'm not, really,' said Dawn, thrown into a sudden small panic. Was she flirting too much?

'Then you'll have to bring your Gibson along and prove it before we leave,' said Al Holly with a grin.

'I might just do that,' said Dawn, grinning back.

Raychel twirled round in her lovely new flat that had views over the whole town. Everything was so clean; the walls were all snow-white with fresh paint and no one had ever cooked in the kitchen oven or put their dirty clothes in the washing machine.

Their new bedroom was so cosy. The second bedroom was going to be a kind of all-sorts room with their computer and Raychel's painting paraphernalia. There was no point in using it for a bedroom; it was unlikely that there would ever be guests. And it would never be a nursery.

Dawn called at Muriel's at ten to sort out Demi and Denise's bridesmaids' dresses with Bette. She had two cups of coffee before Demi woke up. When she did venture downstairs, it wasn't a pretty sight.

'Dawn's been waiting forty minutes for you, you lazy cow,' said Denise.

'I'm up now, aren't I?' barked Demi at her sister. Dawn heard her muttering, 'Anyone would think it was the bloody Royal Wedding!' under her breath as she went upstairs to put on a bit of make-up.

Five minutes later, they were marching across the road. Muriel obviously knew Bette well enough to open the door, go on in and then announce, 'Only us, Bette.'

The largest woman Dawn had ever seen waddled towards them in a poky front room filled with smoke fug. Bette greeted Dawn warmly, after killing her cigarette in the ashtray on a coffee table. Muriel sat on the sofa arm while the others squeezed themselves down on Bette's sofa and the big lady herself occupied an armchair, which creaked in pain.

'I've collected some patterns for you to look at,' said Bette, her voice sounding as if it was coming out of her voice box via a cheese grater. She emptied a carrier bag full of pattern packets onto the coffee table. Most of them looked as if they were out of some 1970s nightmare.

'This is all right,' said Muriel, tapping her nail-bitten finger on a long, swishy number.

'I'm not wearing that!' said Demi. 'I'll look a right chuffing frump.'

'Take that bottom frill off and drop the neck a bit and it's lovely, that,' said Bette, lighting up again.

'I suppose if you drop the neck it would look all right. I don't want to look like a doll,' said Demi, who was rubbing her head and would agree to wearing a black bin-liner just to get out of there and back to bed.

'Well, I'm OK with it,' said Denise. 'If you take that frill off.'

'Well, that was easy,' said Bette, reaching into another carrier at her side. 'Here's your material samples. You wanted peach?'

Dawn was pleasantly surprised to find the lovely shade that matched the tiny roses on her own dress. She intended to make sure it was replicated on the wedding stationery and chocolate favours. Then, fresh fag-a-dangle, Bette measured Denise and Demi's vital statistics. She was wheezing as though she had completed a full body workout by the end.

'Leave it with me,' said Bette, giving Dawn a wink on the way out.

The Mercedes arrived for Anna exactly on time. Leonid once again answered the door and pulled her excitedly into the vaulted room, which was now populated by a small film crew. Mark, the director, introduced himself and a punky cameraman with a white Mohican hairdo called Bruce. Vladimir was standing at the back of the room with a tiny, white-haired, pinch-faced woman of about sixty, and the tall, gamine Jane Cleve-Jones who was even more gorgeous in real life than she was on screen. Seeing that she had arrived, the trio came over and Vladimir nodded a welcome. Jane introduced herself with two alternate air kisses at Anna's cheeks. Everyone seemed very friendly. Even the dog rose out of the basket and came over with a slow walk, tail wagging, and pushed his head into Anna's hand, sniffing her.

'What's his name?' asked Anna.

'Luno,' Vladimir said, and introduced the stern-looking woman with the white hair. 'Anna, this is your make-up lady: may I present Maria Shaposhnikova.'

The tiny woman held her hand out and shook Anna's with the strength of a wrestler.

'Maria is a master. I work with no one else,' said Vladimir.

'Can I get you some refreshment?' Leonid asked, looking at Anna's shaking hands. 'A glass of wine maybe?'

He held up a long crystal decanter full of dark-red liquid.

'Maybe just a little one,' said Anna, receiving the pewter goblet that he handed to her. It was a lovely, fiery wine.

The film crew had a lot to get through, so Anna was shoved in a chair and stripped of make-up by Maria and a lot of swoops of cotton wool.

'Aarrgh, I've got no make-up on—get the crucifixes out, everyone!' laughed Anna, then she clamped her hands over her mouth. Not the most appropriate joke to make in this house.

The camera was quite a frightening piece of equipment, Anna decided, as its big lens-eye trained on her for the first shot. Everything went quiet and Anna did as she was directed, which wasn't difficult because all she had to do was stand there while Jane and Vladimir talked about her.

'Why did you pick Anna to be the face of your "Every Woman has a Darq Side" project, Vladimir?'

'I could see instantly that Anna feels she is much older than she is and as a result her confidence has gone. I am going to show women that whatever their size or age, there is always a goddess in them waiting to show herself.'

'Cut!' said Mark.

There were a lot of short 'action' sequences, Anna noticed. It was all fascinating but not as glamorous as she had imagined.

Anna was feeling quite relaxed until the moment when the director asked if she could strip off now.

'Just to your undies, Anna. We need to ask Vlad why he thinks they are so bad.'

Anna took a deep breath and slipped off her shirt and skirt. She imagined that everyone would burst out laughing, but she soon realised that they were professionals doing a job.

Leonid took some shots of Anna with a very big and heavy-looking camera. They needed some stills, he explained. Then filming commenced again.

'So, Vladimir,' began Jane. 'What is wrong with Anna's underwear?'

'What is right with it?' He laughed without humour. 'The bra is too small and there is no support at all for a bust.'

'It's pretty, though,' put in Jane.

'Pretty bad, you mean. Look how the straps are making a groove in her shoulders,' he carried on, lifting up the said strap and showing the camera the indentation it was making on her skin. 'As for the knickers . . .' He made a sound of despair.

'Cut,' called Mark. 'Excellent.'

Then Anna had to stand in front of the mirror and tell Jane what she saw in her reflection. Where to start?

'My bust is too big, my waist isn't thin enough, my hips are too wide . . .' The list went on and on. By the time she had got to her knees looking like crepe paper the tears were shining in her eyes. They plopped down her cheeks as she 'fessed up that she felt totally worthless and hideous and old. She was so deeply embedded in her self-massacre that she forgot the camera was there.

'Cut!' called Mark. 'I think that's enough for today, boys and girls.'

'Sorry,' said Anna as Jane handed her a tissue.

'You were fab and so natural,' said Jane supportively, rubbing Anna's shoulder. 'Women everywhere will identify with you.'

'Anna, before you go, please try something on for me,' said Vladimir. He held up a stiff, dark-red corset.

Even keeping her eyes forward, Anna could tell that her chest was three feet higher with the garment on than it was without it. Vladimir leaned over her from the back and she could smell his cologne. Something she had never come across before: exotic and spicy but at the same time as fresh as wild Christmas trees.

He expertly laced up the back then stepped away to look at her. Then he marched forward again and straightened her shoulders.

'*La naiba!* As soon as I look at you, you try to curl into a ball! You are wearing a Vladimir Darq exclusive; how can you wilt like a dead flower?' he said crossly.

Thus reprimanded, Anna pulled her stomach in and pushed out her chest. He nodded by way of approval.

'You are married?' he asked.

'No,' said Anna. 'Engaged.'

'I couldn't work out if you were unhappy because you are with a man or unhappy because you are without a man.'

'Both,' said Anna as she placed her hands on her waist, which felt very much smaller. Where had all the flab gone? No doubt it was all crushed up inside the material, but she couldn't feel it if it was.

'What does that mean?'

'My partner left me in February.'

'For another woman?'

'Yes. Don't pull any punches, will you?'

He ignored the barb.

'That explains the sloping shoulders.' He pulled the ribbon tighter at the back and made her yelp.

'Ow! His aren't sloping.'

'No, he is parading like peacock, huh?'

Yep, that just about summed Tony up. A peacock.

'Men can be such monsters,' Vladimir said in a surprisingly gentle way. Which, she thought, was a bit rich coming from a bloke who probably got his nutrients from draining people of their blood. 'OK, that's enough for today.' And he started to unlace her. She hadn't noticed the camera was still rolling and Bruce was smiling behind it. He'd get major Brownie points for this when Mark saw the footage.

The next day, Grace was washing up the Sunday dinner plates when there was a knock at the back door. She opened it to a smiling Charles in a smart, pale-blue shirt and jeans.

'Come in, Charles, Laura won't be long. Would you like a cup of tea?'

'Thank you, but no, I won't,' he said. 'Oh hello, Mr Beamish . . .' Gordon had walked into the kitchen. He stared at Charles's hand, which was outstretched in greeting, then his eyes lifted to Charles's face.

'Who are you?' said Gordon coldly.

'I'm Charles, Charles Onajole. I'm a friend of Laura's, and young Joe's, of course,' came the courteous reply. His hand was still out-stretched but more awkwardly now as Gordon had not come forward to return the greeting. There was an uncomfortable silence in which Charles was eventually forced to let his hand· drop back down. Gordon's jaw tightened and he said in a quiet voice, which was never-theless full of menace, 'I think you'd better get out of my house, lad.'

Charles's eyes flickered as his brain tried to fathom what on earth he had done to earn such a reaction to his greeting. But it was painfully obvious, because there was really no mistaking that look on Gordon's face. Silently, Charles turned and went out of the door. Grace, watching this interchange, was dumbstruck by Gordon's rudeness to a guest.

'Gordon, what on earth—'

Then Laura came down with Joe trotting behind and Grace bit down on what she was about to say.

'Was that Charles?' she asked, then picked up on the vibe in the room. 'What's up?'

'There was a nigger in my house, that's what's up!' snarled Gordon, not seeming to care that Joe was present.

'Joe, go and join Charles in the car,' said Laura quickly, pushing her son out of the door. She was shaking when she turned back and Gordon rounded on her immediately.

'I don't want you in here either, if you're sleeping with *him!*'

Laura looked from Grace to her father, unable to comprehend where this hate had come from.

'Dad, what's the matter with you?'

'All I can say is—thank God you can't have any more kiddies!'

'Gordon!' Grace cried out in disgust.

Laura burst into tears. It was beyond cruel, and Grace leaped to her daughter's side.

'God forgive you for that, Gord—'

But Gordon was in no mood for listening. He made a none-too-gentle grab at his daughter's arm.

'You. Out!' he raged. Grace stepped forward to put herself between father and daughter and ended up being pushed into the table where a cup fell off and covered her skirt in cold tea.

'Mum, are you OK?' said Laura, coming forward to help her mother.

'Laura, love, go,' said Grace, pushing Laura safely out of the house. 'I'm fine.' Although she wasn't fine at all, she was shaking with the worst mix of emotions, but her priority was to get her daughter away from any more vicious, wounding words.

Grace closed the door and turned to face her husband, who was standing frighteningly still and breathing tightly. He looked like a bomb due to explode at any minute.

'Did you know? Did you know he was a blackie?'

'Stop it, Gordon. Stop talking like that!'

Gordon shook his head in disbelief and stared at Grace as if she was insane. 'The world's gone bloody mad.'

He marched out, leaving Grace still in shock, her heart thumping and her limbs quivering. She didn't know this man, hating like something out of the Deep South in the 1920s. Yes, she had witnessed his temper spill on a few occasions over the years, but not to the extent that she was seeing it these days. And now it seemed that two of her children weren't welcome in the house.

Oh, come here, you're useless,' said Elizabeth Silkstone, reaching up to straighten the knot on her husband's tie as they were about to go into church. John Silkstone was a big man and he carried a suit well. He made her knees knock in a suit, still. She was aware that he was staring intently at her while she unloosened his clumsy effort and started again.

'What are you staring at?' she snapped.

'I'm not,' he lied. Had she not opened her mouth then, he would have told her about his burning suspicion that Raychel Love, the wife of his newest worker, young Ben, was closely related to her—was possibly the child of her sister who went missing nearly thirty years ago. It was bursting out of him to say something. But it wouldn't be fair, not today. They would be witnessing their friend Helen's wedding in less than half an hour. What John had to say would have to wait until later. There was a time and a place, and this was neither.

Chapter 8

'OI, ARE YOU PART of this conversation or what?' said Anna, nudging Dawn, whose eyes were drawn to the cowboy guitarist. He had waved at her when they first walked in and she was lost in watching him play.

'Sorry,' said Dawn. 'I just love those guitars.'

'How are your wedding plans going?' asked Raychel.

'Oh, so so,' said Dawn.

'You don't look very thrilled about it,' said Raychel. 'I was so excited when I got married, although we only had a register office do and none of the trimmings.'

'It's not that I'm not excited . . . I just feel . . . like . . . as if . . .'

'Spit it out, lass,' said Christie.

Dawn huffed and came straight out with it, feeling immediately disloyal to her in-laws-to-be as soon as the words had left her.

'I just feel that it's not my wedding any more. I feel that it's been taken over and my choices have been pushed into second place.'

'Who's doing that to you?'

'Well . . . my new mother-in-law is quite a force to be reckoned with. She's paying for some of the stuff and she thinks that gives her the right to choose. They've booked a karaoke and a beef dinner in a dingy pub and I wanted a band and chicken in white wine in a bistro . . .' Dawn snapped her mouth shut before any more came tumbling out.

'And what's your fiancé had to say about it?' asked Christie gently.

'Oh, he's a bit under the thumb. His mother's, not mine.' A tear rolled down Dawn's cheek and she felt Grace's hand upon her own.

'Weddings are very stressful,' she said in that lovely calm voice she had. 'You try and make sure you get what you want, though. Your mother-in-law has had her big day. This is your turn.'

'I half wish we'd just carried on living together and not bothered with all this palaver,' said Dawn, blowing her nose on a tissue. *But you leaped on that drunken proposal Calum made, didn't you, and you ran with it before he could sober up and change his mind?*

'What's your Calum like then?' asked Anna.

'Quiet,' said Dawn, thinking how to describe him. Quiet sounded more acceptable than comatose. 'He's a fork-lift truck driver. Five years younger than me, medium height, slim build, blond hair, likes a pint.'

'He sounds very . . . stable,' said Christie, nodding kindly.

'What made you fall in love with him?' asked Raychel.

'I used to do his mum's hair when I was a hairdresser. She's lovely, really,' Dawn recalled. 'She asked me along to a night out. Her daughters were there and we all had such a laugh. Then she asked me to tea at theirs and there was Calum, all killer smile, floppy hair. He'd just broken up from his girlfriend and his mum suggested we went out. So we did and suddenly I was part of their family.'

'How did he propose? Was it a down-on-one-knee job?' asked Anna.

'Nope. We were all out one night and he . . .' *got absolutely hammered,* 'got a bit tipsy and just came out with it and suddenly the family were all celebrating.' Dawn smiled. 'I was so happy.' It was just a shame that her new fiancé was catatonic under a table five minutes after asking her to marry him. She thought it best to leave that bit out for her workmates. But all of them, without exception, picked up on the fact that the 'other half' in this relationship seemed to be the family, not the man himself.

'The big question is—do you love him?' asked Anna.

''Course I do,' replied Dawn quickly.

'Then that's all that matters,' said Christie. 'You'd be surprised how many people marry someone they don't love because they have other reasons for doing so. And I'm afraid they'll almost always be disappointed if that's the case.'

Grace felt her lip tremble. She volunteered to go and fetch the second round from the bar before those tears pricking at the back of her eyes made a show.

Dawn stayed behind when the others had gone, watching Al on his guitar. He had the same rapturous look on his face that her dad had whenever he got lost in his music. As the song ended he came back to the present world and smiled at her and held up a finger. *One more song, then we break.*

She could have listened to their music all night, even though to most people in the bar they were just a pleasant background hum.

'Hello again, Miss Dawny Sole,' came that smooth caramel voice over her shoulder as she ordered two Diet Cokes at the bar.

'Oh, hello, Mr Holly. And how are you today?'

'I'm just fine, ma'am, just fine. You bought that for me? Thank you.'

'I didn't want you thinking I don't stand my round,' said Dawn. 'I might find myself badmouthed all over America.'

'Shame on you!' said Al. 'I'm Canadian.'

'You all sound the same to me,' Dawn smiled playfully, quite aware that whatever her gracious intentions had been, she had opened international flirting barriers, no passports required.

Al laughed and took a long drink of Coke. Dawn watched his Adam's apple rise and fall in his throat.

'So what brings you here again? You got a recording contract you want me to sign?' Al asked.

'I only wish I had,' said Dawn. 'We come here every Friday after work, just for an hour or so, to end the week on a jolly note.'

'What do you do?'

'I work in an office,' said Dawn. 'Are you a full-time musician?'

'I am now. I was a carpenter but my parents died and so I decided to live out my dream for a few years. I'll retire at thirty-five and buy a small farm and strum my guitar in the evenings on the porch and frighten all the animals.'

Dawn laughed. 'You're like me then, an orphan,' she said. Something else they had in common.

'I guess so.' He leaned down and whispered conspiratorially in her ear, 'But I'm living my dream and I suspect you're not.'

'Oh, and what do you think my dream would be then?' Dawn asked. He'd hit a nerve and it showed in the shake in her voice.

'I think you'd like to be strumming alongside me on that stage.'

'Yeah, right,' said Dawn. 'I'm not good enough by half.'

'I'll be the judge of that. Bring your guitar and come along on Sunday morning to our practice session.'

Dawn found herself agreeing to meet Al Holly on Sunday at the Rising Sun with her guitar in tow.

Anna had had a call from Jane Cleve-Jones to say that there was a change of plan. Vladimir had had to go to Milan and so they were going to film at her house. 'We'll have a good look through your wardrobe,' Jane had said.

The crew had arrived by seven thirty, although there was no Maria because she was with Vladimir in Milan.

Anna's wardrobe was totally garbaged, as she expected. Jane had brought some clothes with her that she thought would suit Anna, including V necks, which Anna never wore.

'Why not? They accentuate your bust perfectly and lengthen your neck!' enthused Jane.

She dressed Anna in red and dark-blue and purple outfits and matching killer heels. But Anna wouldn't admit that the reflection in her wardrobe mirror was pleasing to the eye. Her confidence levels were too damaged to accept any praise.

'Right then, let's wrap that for today,' said Mark. 'Back at Vlad's next week, Anna, for a seven-o'clock-in-the-evening start. Bloody vampires!'

Calum was still asleep in bed when Dawn drove off to the Rising Sun at nine o'clock without her Gibson. She couldn't find it anywhere. Calum had obviously moved it, because she knew she hadn't. She didn't have enough time to look for it now and waking him would only bring her more 'nagging' accusations, plus she didn't want him asking her where she was going. So she picked up her old acoustic guitar instead.

'What am I doing?' she asked herself when she pulled up outside the pub. It suddenly didn't feel as innocent as just going and strumming along with some other like-minded musicians.

They had already started practising when she got there. Al waved and the music stopped.

'Boys, I'd like you all to meet Miss Dawny Sole. Dawny—this is Kirk, Samuel and Mac.'

They all said a friendly hello and Dawn noticed that they'd already got a stool for her. She took her guitar out of its battered old case.

'I've had to bring this one,' she said. 'I seem to have mislaid my Gibson.' She was aware she had missed the opportunity to say that her boyfriend must have moved it. Deliberately missed the opportunity.

It was still a very nice instrument and she sat fine-tuning the strings on it while the band members asked her questions about her dad and his band and Samuel fetched her a coffee. It was obvious that Al had filled them all in on quite a few details. They strummed idly and then Samuel led the music into a tune she recognised because her dad used to play it and her mum used to sing it: 'I'll Take My Chances With You.' And just as all the horses had started to run together in the Grand National, the band and Dawn were suddenly all playing it and Samuel started singing and Dawn opened her mouth and her voice joined his and her heart lifted. It was the most exhilarated she could remember feeling in years.

'You've a lovely voice, Dawny,' said Samuel. 'What else do you know?'

'Loads of things. Anything from Tammy Wynette to Chris Isaak.'

'We once opened for Chris,' said Al.

'NO!' said Dawn, who had rather a thing about Chris Isaak. And for the same reason she had a bit of a thing for Al Holly: because they were from similar moulds, physically as well as musically. 'I wish I could afford him to play at my wedding.' It was out before she could stop it.

Al's head made the smallest jerk, but she saw it. There was nothing else for it but to say what she'd been putting off.

'I'm getting married at the end of June, you see, and I wondered if you'd be around to play at my wedding. Obviously I'd pay you. I'd rather have you than Chris Isaak anyway. It's Saturday the twenty-seventh.'

'Ahh—that's the day we leave for London. That's a real shame. I'm sorry, honey, no can do,' said Samuel.

'Oh, never mind, it was just a thought,' said Dawn. She tried not to sound as disappointed as she felt. There would be no relief from the karaoke now. Then again, did she really want Al Holly to play the background music while she twirled round a dance floor with Calum?

They played some more and when their practice session came to an end, Dawn walked to the door with Al, who was gallantly carrying her guitar for her. They only made it as far as the porch because a heavy downpour was in full pelt. Al pulled her back when she attempted to walk out in it.

'You'll get drenched,' he said.

'I live in England,' laughed Dawn. 'This is what we're used to.'

'So, you're getting married, Dawny Sole,' said Al.

'Yes,' said Dawn.

Al nodded slowly as if all sorts of things were running through his mind. She wished she knew what they were.

'And is your fiancé in a band?' said Al at last, and in such a way that the answer would be of heightened importance.

'No, he's not,' answered Dawn.

The rain stopped so suddenly it was as if a tap in heaven had just been switched off. They fell into step across the car park.

As they reached Dawn's car and she fiddled in her bag for her keys, Al asked, 'Is he into your music?'

'God, no, he's not into music at all.'

Al handed Dawn her guitar and said, 'Then he isn't for you. Any fool would see that. Have a good week, Dawny Sole. Hope to see you again Friday.' And with that, Al Holly turned and strode back inside, leaving Dawn numb, speechless and feeling that she had just received a precisely aimed wake-up slap across the face.

There was a hand-delivered letter in Raychel's mailbox when she went down to collect the Sunday newspapers. It just had her name on the front, in a lovely scrolling font. She waited until she was back in the flat again with Ben before she slit it neatly open with a knife. It was a short letter written on pretty, pale pink paper:

Dear Raychel,

I am Elizabeth, the wife of John Silkstone who Ben works for. I believe I may also be your aunt. My husband, who isn't a man to say these things lightly, is convinced you are the daughter of my missing sister, Beverley. He tells me that the likeness that you have to me is too much to be a coincidence. I will know as soon as I see you if he is right or wrong. I wish you no harm or distress but I have been searching for my sister for many years with no success at all. Please, meet with me just once and then I will bother you no more. Please.

Kindest,

Elizabeth Silkstone

Ben read over her shoulder. He noticed how she gripped the letter as she read it over again.

'I think we made a mistake moving to Barnsley,' Raychel said, with a cross edge in her voice.

'Oh, don't say that, pet,' said Ben. He liked this lovely new flat, and the friendly, buzzing little town and working for John Silkstone.

'Will you tell your boss that I can't help his wife,' she said. 'My mother didn't have a sister.'

'But you know she did.'

'She said she did and then she said she didn't. Who knows which bits were lies and which bits were the truth. It's not as if I can tell your boss's wife anything of comfort, is it?'

Ben pulled her round to face him, his big hands warm on her shoulders. His voice was soft when he began to speak.

'Ray, you know that I would never let anything or anyone hurt you again. John Silkstone is a really good man. If his wife has been looking for her sister for all these years, let her see you once, then, like she says, she can put it to bed.'

'And what if it's true?' said Raychel. 'What if I am the person she's looking for? The answer is no, Ben. *No.*'

The strength in her words belied the tremor in her voice.

When she reached home, Dawn was determined to find her missing guitar. Calum was in the pub. She stabbed in a text, telling him to ring home because it was important.

Her mobile phone rang within the minute.

'What's up?' Calum's impatient voice jumped down the receiver.

'Have you moved my electric guitar by any chance?' asked Dawn.

'I thought you said it was important!'

'It is to me!'

'Why would I move it?'

'Well, I don't know, but I thought I'd check, seeing as it's missing.'

'No, I haven't seen it. I'll be back in a bit. I'm having my usual one pint only, then I'll be in for my dinner.' And before Dawn could ask anything else, the line went dead.

'Yeah, OK,' she said into the air. The 'one pint only' joke was so thin it was positively threadbare. In fact, more and more she was feeling that it was better when he *was* in the pub.

Sure enough, a good hour and a half passed before Calum showed his face. In that time, Dawn had turned out every cupboard in the house, but still she didn't find it.

'Put an insurance claim in,' was Calum's only suggestion.

'What, and say that my guitar got stolen by aliens? Because it can't have just vanished.'

'Well, it has. What do you want it for anyway? You never play it.'

'I'm going to start playing it a lot more.'

'Well, wait till I'm out before you do!' he said, muttering about her playing being akin to a right row.

He went to bed immediately after his Sunday lunch, which he ate alone because Dawn was, once again, checking round just in case she had missed an obvious hiding place.

Dawn could still recall her dad's face when he brought it from behind his back and presented it to her on her seventeenth birthday. *Dee Dee, take good care of it and it will last you a lifetime.*

A crazy idea came to her. Maybe if she went through the motions of replacing it, it would suddenly turn up. That had happened to her before with a bracelet she had once lost. It was worth a try because her guitar couldn't have just vaporised. It must be in a stupidly silly place she hadn't yet thought of.

She went into the kitchen and pulled the laptop out from the drawer to get a street value. She typed in the make and model and the first entry took her to eBay. She couldn't believe how many guitars were listed. There was a Gibson, like her own, at a ridiculous bargain starting price of £304—although twelve bids had driven it up to £1,400. There were five days to go before the auction ended. Wow, she thought, there was going to be an exciting war over that one in the final half an hour. She looked at the item location: Barnsley. *Barnsley?* Her eye flashed over the screen, trying to find the seller. *Cal412.* Calum's birthday was 4 December. Dawn's head started to prickle with anxiety. He wouldn't have done that, would he? Her confusion segued into anger at the real-isation that, yes, he would because this wasn't an exact replica of her guitar, it *was* her guitar. He wouldn't get out of this one by accusing her of nagging.

Dawn tried to compose herself and keep calm, but her whole body had become a racing heartbeat and there was no way she could stop herself running up the stairs and shaking Calum awake. It took a couple of attempts.

'What the fu—'

'My guitar is on eBay and you put it there, didn't you?'

'I knew you'd say that, that's why I didn't tell you.'

'You're selling my guitar! My last-ever birthday present from my parents! What did you expect that I'd say?'

'Shut up, you hysterical cow, and listen. No, I'm not selling it actually, so button it for a minute, will you. I just wondered what it was worth. I was going to pull it off sale at the last minute. But I thought that if it were worth a lot, you might—*might* consider selling it so we could go on a nice honeymoon or something. It's not as if you play it any more so I didn't think there was any harm in just testing the water. It's safe, it's at a mate's house—he took the photo and put it on for me. BUT I WASN'T SELLING IT—OK?'

Dawn's breathing slowed. Was he telling the truth? She could never tell when Calum was lying because he was so good at it. She wanted to believe him so much. She didn't want to think that the man she was marrying would do something as rotten as sell her precious guitar. He even sounded quite selfless until she remembered how often he was at the pub. He could have taken her away to the Bahamas for three months if all his money didn't go over the counter of the Dog and Duck.

'I want that guitar back,' Dawn said, her voice shaking with anger. 'I will never sell it, ever.'

'Fair enough,' said Calum, shrugging his shoulders and settling his head back down on the pillow. 'Can't see why you're making such a fuss; it was only an idea! God, Dawn, get a grip.'

You're very quiet today, Raychel,' said Christie the following morning. 'Everything OK?'

Raychel snapped out of her reverie. 'Sorry, yes, I'm fine.'

'No need to apologise, I'm just enquiring.'

'She'll have got her first mortgage bill,' Anna shouted over. 'That's enough to drive anyone to despair.'

'It's just my time of the month.' Raychel went for an obvious excuse.

'I'll go and get some sugar in my blood. Anyone want anything from the chocolate machine?'

She didn't really want anything but she'd go through the pretence of enjoying something. What she did need was for this day to be over. She was going to Elizabeth Silkstone's house that evening and she was absolutely dreading it.

John Silkstone had taken his son out so that Elizabeth and Raychel could be alone to talk. When the bell rang, Elizabeth opened the door to a whey-faced Raychel with her grey, nervous eyes. The same eyes that she had seen so many times in the mirror before John Silkstone put peace behind them.

'Come in, love, come in.'

It was a beautiful house, the sort of house that Raychel and Ben used to dream of having when they were little. Lots of rooms and light and polish-smelling wood and a big kitchen like the one Elizabeth was now leading her into, telling her to sit down at a massive, thick-topped pine table while she put the kettle on.

There were pencil sketches on the table, being copied from a photo of a small boy.

'Is this your baby?' said Raychel.

'Yes, that's my little two year old, Ellis,' said Elizabeth. 'He's out with his dad,' she added. 'Can I get you a coffee? Tea?'

'Coffee, please. Black.'

'And . . . and have you any plans for children?'

Raychel's eyes flashed towards her. 'If you're truly my aunt, then you'll know that I can't,' she said and with a dry little laugh added, 'Well, I can but I can't.'

'Did you say you take sugar?' said Elizabeth, a shake in her voice.

'My mother told me who my father was,' said Raychel. 'Is it true?'

'I don't know what she told—'

'She told me that my father is my grandfather. She and you and I all have the same dad.'

'She told you that?' said Elizabeth in shock, but she didn't deny it.

'That's why I can't have children,' said Raychel, her voice hard like a protective shell. 'Because I have *dirty blood*, was how she used to put it.'

Elizabeth's face dropped into her hands as she stood waiting for the kettle to boil. She had only been a little girl when her sister, Beverley, ran away, pregnant at fifteen. Elizabeth had been too young to realise that her father had been abusing her sister. Only when his attentions turned to Elizabeth did her juvenile brain tell her that she needed to run to the safety of her Auntie Elsie, who brought her up and kept her safe.

'You aren't dirty,' said Elizabeth. 'None of this could ever have been your fault. I searched for your mother for years and years.'

'You wouldn't have found her,' said Raychel, wrestling with a shake in her voice. 'She didn't want to be found. She changed her name to Marilyn Hunt, then Marilyn Lunn. Then she went to prison when we were thirteen. She's been out for a few years, of course.'

'Prison? What for?' said Elizabeth, wiping at the fat tears plopping down her cheeks. 'What happened to her?'

'God, where to begin!'

Elizabeth slumped into a chair, the kettle forgotten, and Raychel took a deep breath and began.

'My mother said on many occasions that she should have aborted me and she was right. She should never have been allowed to have children. When she wasn't smacking me because she was drunk, or leaving me by myself all night, she was abusing herself—drugs, alcohol, men. My name was Lorraine then and we were always moving, one scruffy place to another. I can't remember much before we ended up in Newcastle except being alone and watching a lot of telly. Isn't that strange? It's as if my early childhood never existed.'

Elizabeth nodded, understanding that sort of loveless childhood. Before her auntie had taken her in.

Raychel went on in an even, emotionless voice.

'Then she moved in with the perfect soul mate for her—a match made in hell—a man called Nathan Lunn. He had a little boy my age— David. He was nervy and quiet, but then he would be because Nathan Lunn used to thrash him stupid. He was a bastard.' Raychel's voice failed her. Elizabeth got her a glass of water.

'Did he hit you too?'

'Oh yes. I got it as much as David did when he was in one of his rages. Though David used to try and take the beatings for me. He'd get in the way and divert Lunn's attention to him—all for me.

'I don't seem to have any time perspective about it all, but David and I became inseparable. We shared a bedroom and we'd talk at night about all the things we were going to do when we were big enough to run away. Then one day the school rang up because they were concerned about some bruises on David's legs and Nathan Lunn, being the sensible type, went mad and nearly killed him for that. He broke one of David's ribs and it punctured a lung in the beating he gave him. I ran to the shop up the road to get the police and Lunn came chasing after me and dragged me back home screaming, but the shopkeeper saw him and, thank God, she rang the police, otherwise he'd have killed us both. The police took me to hospital, an ambulance came for David; he was in intensive care for weeks. Nathan Lunn ran off, but they caught him soon enough. Mum missed all the action; she was comatose upstairs. Heavily pregnant and wrecked on heroin. I don't know how that little girl survived so long inside her. She was stillborn at seven months while Mum was on remand.'

Elizabeth was crying, but now her tears were of rage. She thought of her own son and what she would be galvanised to do if she found out that anyone was hurting him.

'David and I got put into care. Some idiot decided that it would be best for us if we were parted. But we'd always had this pact that if we were ever split, we would meet each other under Big Ben on my sixteenth birthday at midday, just as the clock struck. And when I turned up, he was there waiting for me. He was huge. He'd started beefing himself up so that he could always protect us both. He's obsessed, even now, with staying big and powerful.

'David took the name of that big, dependable clock and I became Raychel, because that was the name of the shopkeeper who rang the police. We changed our surname to Love, just because we liked it. We moved round but we never felt really settled anywhere, until Ben got the job here.'

Elizabeth couldn't think of a single thing to say. She hadn't imagined any of this, not even in her worst nightmares. And Elizabeth Silkstone had terrible nightmares.

'So you see,' said Raychel, smiling strangely and dry-eyed, 'I don't know if you're my aunt or my sister because you're both, aren't you? And Ben is my husband and yet we share a sister.' She laughed and that laugh slid without warning into hard, gulping tears.

'My mother traced me last year and wrote to me,' Raychel began again, wiping her tears away with the heel of her hand. 'She wanted to meet; she said she had things to tell me. I didn't reply. I didn't want to have anything to do with her ever again. I would never have children, even if I could. I'd be too terrified of hurting them.'

So many feelings coursed through Elizabeth, she had no hope of separating them and defining them. But she knew what was most troubling this beautiful young woman standing in front of her because she had lived through the same. She had been terrified that the pattern would be repeated in her, that her rotten genes would out. For a long time she had thought that women coming from 'stock' like her had no business procreating. Then she had got pregnant and inside her a tigress roared that would protect her child at any cost.

'My darling girl,' she said, 'I would kill anyone who tried to hurt my son like you were hurt. Never think that you would make the same choices as your mother. Good God.' The monster that was Raychel's mother was the same sister she had worried about and cried for all those years. She steadied herself with the back of the chair.

'Where was Bev living when you got that letter?'

'She returned to Newcastle when she was released and was calling herself Marilyn Hunt. I kept the letter but never contacted her.'

'Thank goodness you have Ben, and he has you,' said Elizabeth, wanting to cry for Ben, too. She thought of him in the gym, ensuring he was always at the fittest and strongest state his body could achieve. A little boy's fears still present in the big, grown man.

'We're happy now,' said Raychel softly. 'We do lots of nice, daft things together. Things we missed out on. But he still has nightmares and it breaks my heart. I've always felt that we are separate from the rest of the world, as if we don't fit in and shouldn't try.'

'Letting people get close to you can be hard,' said Elizabeth gently. Once she too had felt not worthy enough to be treated kindly. 'But never think that you don't deserve friendship and love because of other people's mistakes. I understand what you're going through.' Elizabeth took the young woman's face in her hands. 'Oh Raychel, I can't tell you how glad I am that you came to see me. But I never imagined any of this.'

'Can I come and see you again?' said Raychel in a quiet, hopeful voice. She surprised herself by asking. She hadn't planned to.

Elizabeth pulled her into a firm embrace. She didn't say anything, neither did she need to.

Chapter 9

FRIDAY AFTERNOON, en route to a meeting, Malcolm just happened to be passing Reception when he saw one of the ladies at the desk having an increasingly heated conversation with a man in a brown coat and a trilby. Kathleen, the receptionist, was shaking her head and whatever she was shaking her head at, the bloke in the hat wasn't having any of it. Malcolm quite fancied Kathleen and he seized on the opportunity to earn some Brownie points.

'Can I help?' Malcolm enquired.

'This "gentleman" wants to speak to the head of HR but, as I've explained, she's on holiday,' said Kathleen in a polite but spiky voice.

'Well, I'm not leaving here until I've spoken to someone with authority,' said the man. Kathleen looked both vexed and exasperated, and her eyes were pleading with Malcolm to help her.

'May I ask what it's regarding?' said Malcolm, with a calming smile.

'And you are?' demanded the man rudely.

'My name is Malcolm Spatchcock. I'm a business unit manager.'

'You're not in Personnel, though, or whatever they call it these days?'

'We're all interlinked,' bluffed Malcolm.

The man mused for a few moments, then obviously decided to trust in the smiling manager in front of him, 'I'm here about my wife. She works in Bakery. Her name is Grace Beamish, and I'm Gordon Beamish.'

'Ah, yes, I know Grace. Until recently I was her manager in Bakery. Why don't you come and sit down over here and tell me what it's about, and then we can see if I can help you.'

'I don't want to sit down, I want someone to tell me why my wife has been passed over for early retirement again and again. If you *were* her boss, you can explain that to me, can't you? Eh?'

Malcolm drew Gordon away from the Reception desk, where Gordon's raised voice was beginning to attract attention.

'I'm slightly confused,' said Malcolm smoothly, rather relishing the fact that he might be about to drop someone in the smelly stuff. 'Mrs Beamish was offered the chance of early retirement on two occasions that I'm aware of, and turned it down.'

Malcolm watched Gordon's jaw tighten. He wouldn't have put the graceful Grace with an old, unsmiling man like this. He thought she would have more taste in husbands.

'She turned it down?' said Gordon, as breathless as if he had been winded. 'She turned it down?'

'Hmm . . . yes. I really can't say any more. I shouldn't divulge a colleague's business. Even to their spouse.'

But there was nothing more to say. Gordon had been told everything he needed to know. He silently turned his back on Malcolm without saying another word and marched out of the building.

Malcolm winked over at Kathleen who blew him a grateful kiss. Now should he say anything to Grace or should he wait for the drama to unfold over the next few days? Malcolm decided on the latter.

The Rhinestones playing in the background of the pub added to the mellowed-out feeling that visited the women after work that night. This was only the fourth time they had been out together yet already it felt an essential part of the week's end.

It was the first time that Dawn had relaxed since Sunday. It had been hard work feigning being cheerful at work, trying hard to push down a nasty cocktail of emotions that felt as if it were poisoning her.

Calum hadn't rushed to bring her guitar home. When it was returned to her on the Tuesday night, she could have wrapped her arms around it and kissed it. In fact, she did.

And now Dawn was here again, staring at Al Holly strumming away and thinking about his parting shot to her last weekend.

'Dawn's getting friendly with the band,' said Grace mischievously. Dawn had let it slip that she had stayed behind for a drink with Al Holly last Friday, although she omitted to add that she had met him on Sunday as well.

'Oh, yes?' said Anna. 'That one at the back that looks like a cross between Elvis and Chris Isaak is a bit of all right.'

She meant Al, looking all mean and moody playing a complicated riff.

'Do tell us more,' said Christie.

'Oh, there's nothing to tell. I just got chatting to one of them about music and we had a drink,' shrugged Dawn.

'Anyone doing anything exciting this weekend, ladies?' asked Christie, raising her glass and issuing a smiley 'Cheers' to them all.

'No doubt I'll be preparing to make more of a fool of myself in front of the whole nation,' sighed Anna.

'And I'm looking at brochures for honeymoon ideas,' said Dawn.

'Where do you fancy going?' asked Raychel.

'Dunno. Where did you go?'

'We couldn't afford the big honeymoon thing,' said Raychel. 'We were only teenagers. We came home from the register office and had fish and chips by candlelight.'

'Aw, how lovely,' sighed Dawn. 'What about you, Grace?'

'I didn't have a honeymoon at all,' said Grace. 'We had the children to look after and Gordon's mother was poorly at the time.'

'Didn't squeeze in a belated one then?' asked Raychel.

Grace shook her head. Their marriage had been more of a business alliance than anything. Gordon gained a housekeeper and companion and she got to borrow some children. Anything as romantic as a honeymoon had no place in a relationship as cold as theirs.

'Where would you have gone, Grace?' asked Dawn.

'I've always wanted to cruise,' said Grace without any hesitation.

Dawn turned to Christie for an alternative destination. Cruising was way out of her budget. Unless it was cruising down the Manchester Ship Canal in a blow-up dinghy. 'Give me an idea, boss.'

'We eloped to Gretna Green, then went to Loch Ness.' Christie smiled. 'It was wonderful. We didn't get out of bed for a week.'

Calum wouldn't have any problem with staying in bed that long. It was just that he wouldn't notice she was in there with him. Ho hum.

'Anyway, what are you doing this weekend, Raychel?' asked Christie.

'Shopping for a tumble drier. How's that for romance?'

'Yeah, but I bet you and Ben stop off for a nice tea somewhere and turn it into a less boring task,' said Dawn. They had all gleaned that Ben and Raychel did such sweet things together, like going for a drive, or to the cinema or visiting the ice-cream parlour out near Penistone; comfortable, coupley things. And when Ben dropped her off and picked her up from work sometimes, they always looked so in love. He tweaked her nose or held her hand and never failed to give her a kiss.

'Grace?'

Grace had barely thought about the extended Bank Holiday weekend to come. There would be no family get-together to lighten her spirits. Just an extra day of Gordon's scintillating company. She wasn't sure she could stand her life with him any longer. She finally felt near the end of the line and needed to do a lot of thinking.

'A belated spring-clean beckons,' she replied with a sigh.

'Well, I shall be doing nothing at all,' said Christie breezily. 'The forecast is sunny and so I intend to sit in the garden, read magazines, drink Pimms and let my big brother cook for me.'

'That the dentist?' asked Anna. 'Good cook, is he?'

'Superb,' said Christie.

'He sounds lovely,' said Anna wistfully. 'He must be gay.'

'Nope,' laughed Christie. 'Straight and wonderful and single.'

'Shame he's not my type then,' said Anna.

'Tell you what you need,' said Christie. 'A bored, married lover on the lookout for a mistress to spoil.'

At that Anna spun.

'What, and do to some poor cow what Tony is doing to me! Why would I want a man that did that to his wife?'

'Whoa,' said Grace, holding up her hands in a peacelike gesture. 'I don't think Christie was being serious, Anna.'

'It was a joke,' said Christie quickly. 'I'm sorry, Anna, it was a clumsy thing to say. I didn't mean—'

'No, no, it's me that should be sorry,' said Anna. 'I'm too sensitive for my own good at the moment. It's the anniversary of our first date today. We used to celebrate it like a proper wedding anniversary, you know, with cards and pressies, even though we aren't married—obviously.' *God, I'm a mess*, she thought.

'Oh, Anna . . .' said Christie and gave her hand a comforting squeeze.

'You weren't to know,' said Anna. 'It's not your fault. I need to take a bit of control of myself.'

Dawn hung behind when the others had gone. She was more than relieved when Al raised his eyes at last, saw her and smiled. She smiled back at him and sat at the bar waiting for him to take his break.

'Hello there,' he said in his drawling, voice. 'You find your guitar?'

'Yes, thank goodness,' said Dawn and went on to tell a lie. 'Silly me, I put it in a safe place and forgot about it.'

'And how was your week?'

'Good,' said Dawn. She felt suddenly guilty. There she was sympathising with Anna about her adulterous fiancé and she was full of floaty feelings for this tall guitar-man in front of her. 'And you?'

'Good, too. Played a lot of places and travelled round,' he replied. 'We won't be practising on Sunday, though, otherwise I would have said come along again. We all really enjoyed your company.'

'Oh, shame,' said Dawn.

'The guys are going sightseeing instead. They want to see something of Yorkshire.'

'And you're not going?' asked Dawn.

'Not with them,' he replied. 'I wondered if you'd like to show me your favourite places, Dawny. How are you fixed for escorting a cowboy round your county? As friends, of course.'

Her insides were a sudden battleground. *No, you can't. Yes, yes, go, you bloody idiot. It's just as friends—his words.*

'Yes, that would be lovely,' she found herself saying, even though she should be picking out honeymoons, sending off invitations. But instead she made arrangements to pick up Al Holly at nine o'clock outside the Rising Sun on Sunday morning, in order to spend the day with him.

When Grace got in from the pub, she picked up a vibe that something wasn't quite as it should be. She made tea, Gordon read the *Barnsley Chronicle* while she washed up and it all seemed, on the surface, a very typical Friday evening, but still she felt an odd undercurrent.

The music for *Coronation Street* ended, which was Gordon's usual cue to go up and get changed for the Legion, but he didn't. He was such a creature of habit that Grace asked, 'Aren't you going out tonight?'

'No, not tonight,' he said quietly.

'Are you feeling all right?'

'Just because I'm not going out, it doesn't mean I'm ill.' He stabbed the remote and switched the television over to *Sky News*. Grace never failed to bristle when he swapped channels without doing her the courtesy of asking. That small action of switching channels set off a massive chain reaction in her brain.

She looked at Gordon, and she knew she had to leave him that weekend. Funny, she had been waiting for a massive event to give her the energy to walk out and, in the end, it was a mere button on the TV remote. She could bear his presence no longer, making choices for her, smashing up her family with his prejudices and anger. It was over. The sudden thought of the freedom to come gave her an injection of euphoria. How should she tell him? She wasn't the type to sneak out like Anna's Tony, leaving a note on the table. She would have to face him head-on. A prospect she wasn't looking forward to at all.

Tuesday, she decided. She would go on Tuesday in the most decent, honest way she could. She would spend the weekend cleaning the house and filling up the food cupboards for him. She would pack a suitcase in readiness and tell him first thing Tuesday morning that their marriage was over. Then she would walk out and go to work and think about the next step from there. She watched *Sky News* but her mind was miles away, mentally making a list of things to do.

When Anna got home, she found a rectangular brown paper parcel waiting for her, propped up against her step. It had obviously been hand-delivered because there were no stamps on it. She opened the door and got the scissors out of the drawer before she'd even got her jacket off. There were about twelve layers of bubble wrap to contend with and finally a square polystyrene case. Puzzled, Anna prised it open to find the white back of a plate with a hanging ring on it. She turned it over to see that the front had a photograph of herself and Tony on it, arms round each other. It was the photo he used to have as the wallpaper on his mobile. And under the photograph on the plate there was a single word printed. *Together.* What the hell did that mean? Was this an anniversary present? She felt a sweet surge of excitement at the thought he might have remembered the date. But if he hadn't, why was Tony sending her photographs on plates when they weren't together? Dear God—was this his way of telling her that he was on his way home?

Anna had thought about the plate for twenty-four hours now, and the only possible conclusion she could come to was that Tony's heart was on its way back to her.

She wished she didn't have to go to Vladimir's but she couldn't let the crew down. She'd leave a note on the door to tell Tony, if he called, that she would be back at 10 p.m. and hope a burglar didn't see it first.

Vladimir Darq seemed rather annoyed by her smile. But not as annoyed as Maria, who was saying 'La dracu' a lot—obviously swearing—as she tried to apply Anna's face make-up.

'Maria says you are smiling too much,' Vladimir said with a huff.

'Right, I'll look miserable then.' Anna assumed an exaggerated pout.

'No, not miserable. Like a statue. Neutral. It is good that you don't seem nervous today, Anna, but what is going on in your head? I presume'—and here he gave a haughty sniff—'that it is something to do with your adulterous man, *Tony*.' He imbued the name with all the qualities of a bowel movement.

'Well, actually, Tony sent me a present that tells me he is getting fed up with his fancy woman,' said Anna, giving a haughty sniff of her own.

'What present?'

'A plate.'

'A plate!' He didn't look as impressed as Anna by the prospect of a plate as a symbol of romance.

'Not any plate. A special plate. With our photograph on it.'

Vladimir's right eyebrow lifted so high Roger Moore would have been envious. It wasn't a gesture lost on Anna.

'Look, I don't know what passes for romance in the gay world—'

'And I do?'

'Well . . . yeah,' said Anna. 'I would have thought so.'

'And why would that be?'

'Well, because I thought you were . . . aren't you?'

'You think I am gay? Because I am a designer—you think I am gay?'

She couldn't tell if that spark in his eyes was anger or amusement.

'I thought . . .'

It was amusement. He threw back his head and laughed.

'*Nebunatico!* You silly girl—oh no, no, no, Anna. I am not gay.'

Anna looked up at this newly reclassified, non-gay, big Romanian bloke and pulled her robe a little tighter round her. God, he'd felt her boobs. How embarrassing!

Vladimir Darq's mouth curved up at one side as he watched her.

'Believe me, Anna, if I had wanted you, you wouldn't be safe. Now, please, stop smiling and let Maria put your make-up on.'

Twenty minutes later, Anna was in conversation with Jane on camera.

'So, here you are wearing a 99p value T-shirt, Anna, on top of a Vladimir Darq bodyshaper—how sexy are you feeling?'

Anna looked into the mirror. Vladimir Darq's bodyshaper had given her the knockers of a nineteen year old and a waist that swooped in and out to a grand pair of hips. For once, instead of curving her back to minimise her chest, she was sticking it up and out. Even wearing the cheapest T-shirt in the world, Anna was looking hotter than she thought possible.

'I can't believe it,' said Anna. 'I didn't think I could have my boobs up here again. I thought they were destined to loll round my waist.'

Jane's attention switched to the designer. 'Vladimir, talk us through what you've done for Anna.'

'It's very simple. I have made a bodyshaper, which I call the "Darqone", that is both comfortable and sexy,' he said confidently.

'How can you do that for every woman and keep the price low?'

Vladimir gave a small laugh as if the answer was obvious. 'I will sell so many that I can keep the price down, of course.'

'Cut,' called Mark. 'We need to see the body thing now, Anna. We'll just get a few shots of it before we call it a day.'

Anna slid the T-shirt over her head.

'Your tits really are fantastic in that top, Anna,' called Bruce from behind the camera.

'Hands on waist, Anna,' instructed Mark. 'And I agree.'

Anna laughed, albeit with a blush.

Vladimir Darq said nothing. He stood by Maria, arms folded, a glower on his face. But he noted that Anna's shoulders were back and how long her neck looked when she wasn't trying to hide herself away.

Vladimir sent Anna home with the Darqone on. He gave her a parcel of more in various gorgeous colours and told her to wear nothing but those all week under her clothes.

The note she had left for Tony was still there on her door when she got back home. He had not called. 'Ah, well,' she sighed, making a beeline for the long mirror in her bedroom. She posed seductively at her reflection, trying to imagine what Tony would think if he saw her now, all pouty-mouthed and attitude. Lynette Bottom would be launched into the nearest wheelie bin and he'd have leaped on her. She felt magnificent.

Calum had been out at his mate's thirtieth birthday do all Saturday night and was just going up the stairs to bed on Sunday morning as Dawn was coming down them.

'Where you off to?' he slurred.

'Meadowhall. Wedding stuff,' she lied.

'Have a nice day.'

She was giddy with excitement and any feelings of guilt she should have had were being squashed with all her might. After all, she was only showing a cowboy around some Yorkshire countryside. A friend. *Yeah, but a 'friend' who makes your heart gallop*, came a counter-argument.

Al was waiting for her, sitting on the wall in the sunshine. He was wearing faded denim jeans and a black T-shirt that made his chest look wide and his waist look small. She found herself smiling as soon as her eyes touched on him.

'Good morning, Dawny Sole,' he said.

'Hi, y'all,' she drawled back and he laughed.

'So, where are you taking me?'

'Wait and see,' she said casually, belying the fact she had pored over the Internet for ages the previous night. There were so many places she could have taken him, but she had made sweet, gentle choices rather than wildly exciting ones. Places she liked, places she would go to to remember him when he had gone back to Canada.

'How about we start with a walk in a nice park?'

'Sounds good to me, honey,' said Al, swinging his body into her passenger car seat. Dawn's foot was very shaky on the clutch.

The ducks and geese at Higher Hoppleton were so well fed they looked at the breadcrumbs scattered by little children with disdain. Dawn had often been the recipient of their disgusted glances, so this time she had lovingly prepared two bags full of Madeira cake.

The ducks waddled forward, quacking a 'That's more like it'.

'Do you feed ducks in Canada?' said Dawn.

'Only to diners,' said Al, grinning again.

'Oh, that's awful,' said Dawn, laughing.

'Sure is a lovely house,' said Al, looking over his shoulder at Hoppleton Hall. 'Can we go in and take a look?'

'Yes, it is on my to-do list,' said Dawn.

'You're my kind of guide, Dawny Sole,' he said, saluting her.

They fed the greedy ducks and then walked round the lovely old Hoppleton Hall, and Dawn's imagination played with the idea that they were a couple on one of many days out. Like Ben and Raychel. Calum never wanted to go anywhere but the pub.

It was just over an hour to the coast. Cleethorpes wasn't the busiest seaside town, but it had sun and sea and sand, some of the things that Dawn wanted to share with Al. She had always wanted to live by the sea or some water. Al, apparently, lived by a lake so big it was like an ocean, he said, making Dawn sigh. Cleethorpes was busy but they dropped on a good parking space just as a family were leaving it.

Dawn headed straight for the nearest novelty shop and bought two Kiss Me Quick hats.

'It's illegal not to wear one of these at the seaside,' she said, and then dragged Al off for his first taste of British fish and chips, doused with salt and vinegar, and they ate them from the paper as they sat on a bench and looked out at the sea and kids with buckets and spades and donkeys with tinkly bells and teenagers showing off to each other with skimpy bikinis and sloppy shorts and volleyballs.

'I love water,' said Al. 'The lake I live alongside is full of fish. Ever been fishing, Dawny?'

'Dad used to take me fishing,' said Dawn, sliding into a memory that was as cosy as a pair of old slippers.

'Your mom ever remarry?' asked Al, licking his fingers.

'Mum and Dad died together. Car crash. Some idiot boy racer.' She shook her head as she thought of the community service sentence that the little teenage twit got for destroying three lives.

'I'm so sorry,' said Al. 'I didn't realise.'

'They're buried next to each other. Dad and his guitar, Mum and her piano.' Dawn's smile was fond and sad. 'I'm joking, of course. Mind you, it was the only thing that wasn't in her coffin. It was like a car boot sale with all the flowers and bits of music and poems and stuff that all their musician friends put in.'

'How old were you?'

'Seventeen.'

'That's young.'

'Too young at any age to lose people like them.' Dawn felt her eyes getting a bit watery.

'Come on, let's hit the beach,' said Al, scrunching up the empty fish and chip papers and launching them perfectly into the nearby bin. He grabbed Dawn's hand and pulled her down the steps to the sand. He held her hand for the length of six steps only but the effect on her was catastrophic. It was sending feelings that she shouldn't be having to every part of her, feelings that she couldn't muster for the man she was marrying. It brought everything she was into question.

Al tugged his boots and socks off and Dawn slipped off her sandals. They walked along the wet sand, the flow of the sea washing over their toes and thrilling them with the chill.

'You get to the seaside often, Dawny?'

406 | Milly Johnson

'Not that much,' she said. 'It's a bit far away from Barnsley.'

'Far away? Naw! Everything is so close in England,' he said. 'You want to try living in Canada.'

'We were going to live in the States,' said Dawn. 'Mum and Dad were getting ready to emigrate. They wanted to live the simple life and play music in bars. They just wanted me to get through school first.'

'And would you have enjoyed that?'

'Yes,' she said, without needing to think.

'Then why aren't you doing it now?'

'Because my dreams died with them.'

'Why?'

'Because . . .'

The words dried up; she couldn't expand on her answer. Strangely enough, she had never asked herself that.

'I know, it's easy for me to say,' Al conceded. He suddenly stopped and turned to her. A sea breeze blew a strand of her hair across her face. He reached out and took it in his fingers and tucked it behind her ear. She wanted to push her face against that hand and feel his long fingers on her cheek. She looked up and found that his eyes were locked on to hers. He reached out again and tapped the side of her head gently.

'All your dreams are sleeping in here still, Dawny. Just sleeping.'

Dawn's heart was booming. She didn't dare move. Was she imagining things or were they leaning closer to each other?

'Sorry!' said a young boy, diving between them for a big inflatable beach ball and spraying them with sand. It stopped whatever was going to happen next. They sprang back from each other and started wandering back to the car park in silence.

'I am now going to drive you round some of our finest countryside,' she said, trying to get back into Dawn-the-Tourist-Guide mode.

'Sounds good to me, girl,' said Al. He slid in a CD and they both sang along to Nicolette Larson and her smoky, soft-rock voice.

'Do you do everything to music?' she asked.

He raised his eyebrows mischievously and she tutted.

'I mean, are you like me? Do you like music in the background when you're eating, do you cook to music, do you sing in the bath?'

'Yep, all of those. And sometimes I do nothing and listen to it too.'

It sounded lovely, just lying back, eyes closed and doing nothing but listening. She could imagine what the answer would have been if she'd suggested to Calum they try that one day. Then she forced Calum out of her thoughts; it wasn't that difficult to do today.

They crossed moors and hopped down country lanes, taking a long and winding road back to Barnsley and the Rising Sun.

'What's he called?' Al suddenly asked her.

'Calum.' She didn't want to talk about him. This was a different world in which Calum Crooke didn't exist.

'What kind of a man is he?'

'He's, er, nice-looking, he's got a great family; they've been really kind to me. He's quiet. He's a family man. He's close to his parents and his sisters. They're all very funny.'

'Sounds like you're more in love with the family than with him.'

'No, I'm not,' said Dawn, with a defensive edge to her voice. 'It's just that they come as a package. That's the sort of family they are.'

'Would your mom and dad have liked him?'

Would they? She had avoided asking herself that question.

'Mum and Dad would have wanted me to be happy. And I am.'

Down one of the lanes, Al suddenly asked Dawn to stop the car.

'Here?' she said. 'What for? There's nothing here.' But she pulled in all the same, by a gate leading to a wood. They walked where the last blur of spring bluebells carpeted the ground.

'Look at that, it's just so pretty,' said Al.

'It is,' said Dawn. 'Don't you have them in Canada?'

'Not British ones. We have hybrids but they aren't the same as these.'

He closed his eyes and breathed in the delicate scent.

'This has been a beautiful day,' he said at last, not looking at her. 'I know we can only be friends, but I'm wishing there was a parallel universe somewhere out there and in it . . . you're free . . .'

Dawn gulped as he slowly turned towards her. Al Holly picked up her hand, laid a small kiss on the back of it and said, 'You may think this is a corny chat-up line, but it isn't. Today has been one of my favourite days ever and I'll always remember it. Thank you.'

Dawn couldn't reply. Her breath caught in her throat. She was glad then that he made 'Let's go' noises and headed back to the car, because she was able to wipe a rogue tear away, unseen.

When she dropped him off at the pub, he gave her a big lopsided grin and told her that he had a surprise in store for her on Friday so she had better come to the Rising Sun and meet him as usual.

That night, Dawn dreamed of dancing at her own wedding. But she wasn't in Calum's arms. She was being spun round the dance floor in a breathtaking waltz by Al Holly in his cowboy gear. The scent of bluebells was heavy in the air. She woke up at the moment when Al Holly's lips were about to descend onto hers.

Grace rolled her neck round on her shoulders and tried to focus on the clock. She'd give anything to stretch her arms back, but that was impossible as both her hands were tied with a belt to the table leg. She tried to think what was happening to her and her last point of recall. She had been ironing. There had been a Bond film on, so it must have been Bank Holiday Monday afternoon. Gordon had made her a hot chocolate and she had sipped at it while she was doing his shirts, even though he'd put too much powder in and made it overpoweringly sweet—too much to finish it. She wanted to leave him with a clean house and all his washing done. She remembered feeling sorry for him while she was putting the shirts on the hangers. She could remember nothing after that.

He'd drugged her, she knew he had. It was laughably unbelievable, and not the sort of stuff that happened to fifty-something suburban couples in real life. But she wasn't laughing and it was happening, because she was tied to a table leg on the floor and Gordon was sleeping on a chair with his head on the table above her. She noticed the phone had been unplugged in the corner and the connection was snipped off, lying next to the cord. She tried to push the table leg up so she could unloop the belt strap, but it was too heavy, plus she noticed, midstruggle, that he had nailed the belt to the wood. *How long have I been like this? What time is it? What day is it?*

The only thing she knew was that she had to stay calm. Gordon had totally flipped. She didn't know what he was capable of in his state of mind. She had drunk only half the chocolate—what if she had drunk it all? He could have killed her.

She didn't know if it was the right tactic but she needed to take some control. She had to get out of that front door and safely.

'Gordon,' she called softly, though her throat was dry. 'Gordon, love.' The 'love' stuck in her craw. She felt anything but affection towards the man sleeping nearby.

'Gordon,' she called again and again, until he snorted and his eyes sprang open and he sat up as if he didn't know where he was or what he'd done. Then his wits caught up with him and Grace saw in his face that he knew exactly what the situation was.

'Gordon, I need the toilet,' said Grace.

'You'll have to do it there,' he said, stretching his back.

'Gordon, I can't do that. Please, let me get up.'

Gordon rubbed at his temples as he sighed wearily. 'I don't know what to do with you, Grace, I really don't.'

'What do you mean . . .' She realised that her voice had begun to rise and she had to force herself to throttle back on the volume.

He looked at her as if she should have known what he was talking about. Then he was up on his feet, railing at her.

'You lied to me, Grace. You lied to *me*.'

Grace cowered as his fists curled up and rose, but they didn't make contact with her on their descent, only the top of the table.

'Well, you've no excuse now. You'll pack in your job, retirement or no retirement, that's final.'

'I can't miss out on a retirement package, love,' said Grace, trembles taking over her voice. 'There's some coming up, I heard.'

'You've turned down two, you lying bitch!' This time the back of Gordon's hand came crashing into the side of Grace's face. And she wet herself on the impact.

'Oh God,' she managed. Grace was afraid now. He knew. How had he found out? She was to discover the answer to that in his next breath.

'I went to your work and had an interesting talk with someone about you,' he said in a horribly knowing way.

'Who?'

'Never you mind who,' said Gordon. 'But he told me you'd had your chance to retire, *twice*, and you turned it down, *twice*.'

Grace knew HR wouldn't give out details like that. *He told me*, Gordon had said. *He*. Surely he didn't mean Malcolm?

Grace groaned. She was frightened and sore, her dignity in shreds.

'Gordon, I'm in pain. Please!'

'And why are you suddenly going to the pub on Fridays? Don't tell me it's with those women you work with. You must think I'm stupid.'

'It *is* with the women I work with!'

Again Gordon's hand came soaring down towards her cheek. Grace cowered, waiting for the sting, but his hand hovered an inch from her, shaking with anger.

'Look what you're making me do!' he screamed at her, then burst into tears. They ran through the fingers that covered his eyes. Then, just as suddenly, they stopped and he spat at her, 'You're ruining everything! You can't leave me, Grace. I won't let you.'

Grace battled against responding to him. She wasn't in a position to inflame the situation any further, but if she had been untied, she knew she would have flown at him with every bit of strength she possessed. Instead, she forced herself to remain as still as she could. She let him think she might have slipped back into unconsciousness.

He wiped his eyes roughly. 'I'll get you a cloth and a towel,' he said, as if she had just asked for them. 'Shan't be a minute, love.'

Chapter 10

'You lost weight?' Raychel asked Anna.

'Nope,' said Anna, smiling because she hadn't but she looked decidedly trimmer thanks to Vladimir's Darqone creations. They really did work. They gave her a lovely shape, even under her crappy clothes. That had a knock-on effect of making her feel, dare she admit it, *sexier*.

Over the next hour, Christie and Dawn would ask her the same question about her weight. Grace didn't, because she hadn't come in, which was strange.

'Has Grace rung in yet?' Christie asked as she came out of her meeting with the buyers at 10 a.m. It wasn't like Grace to be late for work.

'No, she hasn't,' answered Raychel.

'I wouldn't have thought Grace'd be the type not to turn up without saying anything,' said Dawn.

'I totally agree,' said Christie. Grace was *not* that type at all.

Christie retrieved Grace's home number from HR, which she hoped would give them a result, even though they didn't have any record of her mobile number. She rang and, as bad luck would have it, all she got was a dead line. Then she had a brainwave. She rang Niki at the surgery. He must have Grace's grandson's details on file. She could get hold of Grace's daughter that way—it was a start at least.

'What do you want her number for?' he asked.

'Grace hasn't come in. I'm a bit worried about her. I'm thinking of going round to her house if I can't get hold of her.'

'Christie, for goodness' sake—'

'Niki, you of all people know what I'm like.'

'Yes, unfortunately I do,' said Niki with an exasperated sigh. 'Where does she live?'

'Thirty-two Powderham Crescent in Penistone.'

'Look,' Niki said. 'If you're serious about going, I'll meet you there. I don't want you getting into trouble or coming to any harm.'

Christie rang Laura's mobile. It burred so many times she felt sure it would click onto voicemail, but at the last second a voice answered.

'Hello,' said Christie. 'Look, you don't know me, but I work with your mother and we're a little worried that she hasn't arrived yet. Do you have a contact number for her, so I can check we have the right one on file? And her mobile number, please?'

'Yes, yes, of course,' said Laura hurriedly. 'We're just driving back from—' Annoyingly, the phone cut off. Then, seconds later, it rang again in Christie's hand. Laura dictated the home number, which was the same as the one on Grace's HR file, then Laura supplied Grace's mobile number. Just as she finished, the line cut off again and however much Christie rang back, she couldn't get past the voicemail.

She rang Grace's mobile and that too went straight to voicemail. Her lovely voice invited the caller to leave a message, which Christie did. 'Grace, it's Christie. I'm at work. Can you let us know that you're all right? Can you ring me on my direct line?' Then she left the number. Her intuition was strongly telling her that something was very wrong.

'I can't get through. Anyone know where Powderham Crescent is?'

'It's on that huge estate near Penistone,' said Raychel. 'Just before you get into the town after the big roundabout and it's on the left.'

'I think I might just take a drive there,' said Christie.

'Isn't that a bit . . . over the top?' said Anna tentatively.

'I don't know,' said Christie. 'But something isn't right and I won't get any work done for worrying so I might as well go.'

'So long as you don't go barging in like the SAS to find her watching *Morning Coffee*,' said Raychel. But she sensed as much as the others that Grace would never have taken a day off without letting anyone in the department know.

'I'll be back as soon as I can,' said Christie. 'If James asks where I am, tell him. If anyone else asks, tell them it's none of their business.' Then she grabbed her coat and walked down the office towards the stairs.

Christie found number thirty-two, a quiet little house on a corner, surrounded on three sides by a perfect lawn and five-foot conifers. Christie parked in front of it and walked tentatively down the path.

She stretched her hand towards the door knocker, then pulled it back at the last second. She stole across to the front window and peered through. There was no sign of any disturbance. She would have liked to get round to the back but the tall side gate was locked. She returned to the front door and pressed the flap of the letterbox open. There was a faint noise of a radio and voices so soft that Christie wasn't sure if she was imagining them or not.

She heard a car draw up and turned to see that it was Niki, still in his white dentist's tunic.

'You're too protective for your own good,' she levelled at him.

'I know what scrapes you've got yourself into since you were old enough to walk,' said Niki. 'You never did err on the side of caution.' He took a long look at the house. 'Nothing seems untoward. Are you sure she hasn't just broken down in the car and can't get a signal on her mobile to let you know?'

'I hope that's the case,' said Christie. She rapped on the door knocker and rang the bell at the side, too, for good measure. Through the door glass, she saw a flash of light as if a door at the end of a passage had opened slightly and closed again.

'Someone's in, I'm sure of it,' she said and bent to the letterbox, pushed the flap up and shouted through it: 'Grace, are you in there? Grace, are you all right?'

Just then, a brand-new Volvo pulled up at the side of the road and stopped behind Niki's bumper. A young man with a concerned look on his face hurriedly got out.

'Hi. Are you Christie? I'm Paul, Grace's son. My sister's just rung asking me to call over and check on Mum, then her phone cut off and I can't get her back again. What's happening?'

'Hello, Paul, I don't know what's wrong, if anything. Yes, I'm Christie, I work with your mother but she didn't come in today and that worried me. There's someone in the house, I'm sure of it.'

Paul looked through the windows and tried the side gate also. Then, with no other option available, he rapped on the door too.

'Mum, Dad, let me in. It's Paul.'

A man's blurry silhouette appeared behind a rectangle of patterned glass in the door and a voice said, 'Go away. What do *you* want?'

Despite everything, Paul was relieved. It had been crossing his mind that his parents were tied up at the back, victims of armed robbers.

'Dad, is Mum there? Let me in.'

'Go away.'

'Dad, what's going on? Are you all right?'

'Of course we're all right,' said Gordon. 'Why shouldn't we be?'

'Mum should have been in work today,' said Paul.

'She doesn't go to work any more.'

Christie and Paul looked at each other.

'Dad, what's happening? Where's Mum?'

'Go away,' said Gordon, and his silhouette disappeared.

'What now?' said Niki, no longer thinking his sister had overreacted.

'I'll ring the police,' said Paul, even though it felt rather dramatic to do that, to ring the police about your parents. He shook his head at the scenario he was in the middle of as his finger landed on the first 9. He gave it another second for it all to make sense—it didn't—then he keyed in the remaining 99 and lifted the mobile to his ear.

Curtains were twitching across the road. Paul wished the police would hurry up. He had visions of a man with a gun at his mum's head telling his dad to get rid of the people at the door. Was the 'Mum doesn't work any more' line a clue to tell him that they weren't all right really? He tried talking through the letterbox again.

'Dad, let me in. Is Mum OK?'

There was no answer. The three of them stood, not sure of what to do in the ten minutes until a police car rounded the corner.

A corpulent police sergeant and a younger male constable emerged from their car. Paul filled them in on the few details he had to hand. The sergeant checked for himself that the front door was locked and the gate could not be accessed. He called through the letterbox and rang the bell but there was no response. He made the decision on what to do then quickly.

'Best get the number one key ready,' he said, in the manner of a man who had been here many times before. The constable immediately went to the car boot where the large door ram was kept. He put on the protective helmet, goggles and gloves stored alongside it as the sergeant rapped hard on the door and called through the letterbox again.

'Mr Beamish. It's the police. Can you please open this door now, sir?'

There was no response. The sergeant pulled out a steel ASP baton and flicked it down so it extended in readiness. Then he nodded to the constable and stepped aside. The constable crashed the ram next to the keyhole and the whole building seemed to vibrate with the intense noise it made. The door swung instantly open into a house so quiet it could have been deserted. The sergeant quickly checked the lounge for activity, then stepped cautiously forward to the kitchen door at the end of the hallway. He pushed it open, called out both Gordon and Grace's names again and then, holding the ASP firmly in a position that was ready both for defence or attack, he moved forward, the young constable at his heels. Paul and Niki were close behind, despite being urged to stay back.

But the sight that greeted them was the most surreal part of it all. Gordon was sitting at the table drinking a mug of tea and reading a magazine, and underneath that same table was a barely conscious Grace, her arms tied in front of her to one of the thick wooden legs. Niki doubled back down the passage and out of the house. He knew there was a surgery up the road. Grace needed a doctor, quickly.

Gordon looked up at the people who had suddenly poured into his kitchen. His eyes scanned them and stopped at the young constable. He pulled himself up onto his slippered feet.

'What do you want?'

'Come on, sir,' said the sergeant as he saw Gordon's fist begin to shape. He quickly assessed the situation and grabbed the arm of the man he had thought he had come in to rescue and twisted him round while reciting his rights. Only when the cuffs slid on his wrists did Gordon start struggling, as if he had come back to the real world and realised what was happening to him, but he was no match for the big sergeant, who pulled him easily out of the room as he muttered, 'What's going on? What do you think you're doing? Get off me! Grace! Grace!'

Paul and Christie sank to their knees round Grace and while they untied her, the constable spoke down his radio asking for another unit to come and take Gordon down to the station. Grace cried out at the sweet pain of being able to move her arms. Then Niki returned with a doctor from the nearby surgery, who introduced himself to the constable as Dr Mackay and said that Mrs Beamish was one of his patients. Paul and Christie moved away to give him space to tend to Grace. She was in a terrible state. Limp, bruised, her clothes in damp disarray and her muscles crippled from being in one position for so long. Niki left the room, instinctively aware that Grace wouldn't want to be seen like that by anyone she barely knew, least of all a male.

'You need an ambulance,' said Dr Mackay, pressing keys on his mobile.

'I don't need an ambulance,' croaked Grace. 'I just want some water.'

Paul and Christie helped Grace gently to her feet and she immediately fell backwards onto a chair.

'You're going to hospital now,' said the doctor in a soft but no-nonsense Irish brogue, putting his phone back into his pocket. He rubbed at her cold, stiff, aching hands. Grace doubted the blood would ever flow back properly into them.

'Dear God, woman, how long have you been like this?'

'What day is it?' Grace asked. Her whole body throbbed.

'It's Tuesday morning, love,' said Christie, lifting a glass of water to her lips.

'Since yesterday then,' said Grace breathlessly.

'Mum, I'll get you some things for hospital,' said Paul softly. He was wiping his eyes. *His own father.* He couldn't absorb any of it. He just wanted to concentrate on his mum for now. He didn't want to think about his father.

'No, Paul, I don't want to—'

'You're going, Mum. That's an end to it.'

'The ambulance is here,' called Niki from the hallway. He couldn't equate the smiling, elegant lady holding the hand of her jolly little grandson with the poor, pitiable, half-dressed creature he had just seen. How could a man do that to such a lovely woman? His own wife?

The ambulanceman and the doctor started to lead Grace gently outside but her legs were so stiff that she had to surrender to the wheelchair they had brought out for her.

Paul was answering the young constable's questions but wanted to break off to go with his mother.

'Stay, Paul, help the police,' said Grace.

'You can't go by yourself, Mum.'

'Christie, will you come?' It was pure instinct. She wanted a woman with her. A friend. She wanted Christie Somers.

'I'll follow on in my car,' said Christie. 'Niki, will you let the girls at the office know I shan't be back today?'

'Of course I will,' said Niki.

'I'll be there as soon as I can, tell Mum that,' Paul called to Christie. The police would be at the house for a while and he would need to sort out the front door, which was shattered. At least he could do these practical things for her, so she had one task less to worry about. He had to keep his mind busy before it exploded.

In the hospital, Grace allowed her bruised face to be photographed, despite repeating that she didn't want to press charges. But that might not be her decision, said the policeman who came to take a statement.

When Laura arrived, she burst into tears at the sight of her mother's injuries. Like Paul, her emotions were ricocheting between anger and relief, confusion and hatred.

'You can't go back to that house. You must stay with Joe and me.'

'I shan't go back, don't worry,' said Grace. 'But I'm not coming to you. I'm going to stay with Christie for a while.'

Her son and daughter protested gently but, much as Grace loved them, she wanted the generous, uncomplicated company of Christie Somers. She didn't want to be a reminder to her children of what their father had done. They were hurting enough as it was.

So, when Christie had asked her in the hospital if she would like to stay with her and Niki, she had accepted with gratitude.

'Don't tell Sarah yet,' said Grace to her children.

'She'll have to know!' said Paul.

'No, don't, Paul. She's got enough on her plate with her pregnancy. Protect her as much as you can.'

'You just think about yourself, Mum,' said Laura. She loved this woman so much it half killed her to see her lying on a hospital trolley with wounds her own father had caused. She had cried a lot after he had thrown her out of his house, but had still been prepared to forgive him, because he *was* her father after all. Now, after this, she never wanted to see him again.

Understandably, Grace was not at work the next morning. Dawn, Anna and Raychel rushed forward as one to ask about her when Christie came through the door. Intuition, again, had told her that she should disclose to these women what had happened to Grace. Her secret would be safe with them. They were her friends now and, being in the know, would be armed to fend off any gossip being circulated.

'She's fragile,' said Christie. 'I don't think she slept very well last night, but at least she was sleeping peacefully when I left this morning.'

'I can't believe it,' said Dawn. 'What a psycho!'

'Her kids must be in bits,' said Anna. 'I mean, what do you feel when your father does something like that to your mother?'

'The bastard,' said Raychel, which made the others stare at her. They'd never heard her swear before, nor envisaged there could be such a hard edge to her soft voice.

'Well, obviously, let's keep it quiet,' said Christie. 'I know I don't need to say that. Grace isn't someone who would want anyone knowing her business. Officially, Grace is off with a cold.'

The figure of Malcolm crept into her peripheral vision. Christie turned her full stare onto him.

'What's up?' asked Anna.

'I'm sure he had something to do with what happened,' snarled Christie. 'Someone—a man—told Grace's husband that she had twice turned down early retirement. I believe that triggered him.'

'And you think that man was Malcolm?' said Raychel.

'Oh, yes, I'd put money on it,' said Christie.

'If it is him, then that's so evil,' said Dawn, staring at him with eyes narrowed to slits.

'You don't think Grace will go back to her husband, do you?' asked Raychel.

'How could she?' said Anna, her face creased up in disgust. 'How could you go back to someone who treated you like that?' However, her voice toned out at the end as she remembered her own situation. How ironic: this show of strength from a woman who was waiting pathetically in the wings for an adulterous fiancé to return to her.

'The girls all send their love,' said Christie across the dinner table. 'And don't worry, there's been no gossip that I've heard of. I told HR you'd rung in and were off with a cold.'

'There will be gossip,' said Grace, shaking her head at the thought of it. 'The local newspaper will get wind of it.' She thought of all those curtains twitching at the arrival of the police and the ambulance.

'Well, if they do, they do,' said Christie. 'James McAskill said to take off as much time as you like.'

'Does he know?' gasped Grace.

'Not the full story. He trusts my judgment on things.'

'I shall be in work tomorrow,' said Grace. 'The sooner I get back to normal the better. Foundation will cover this bruising if I put it on thickly enough.'

'Whatever you think best,' said Christie. 'And, I'll say this now, if you feel it's too much—you come straight back here.'

Grace nodded. She felt protected and safe at Christie's house and was clinging to that feeling of security. She also knew that if she didn't step out of its big front door soon, she might never do so again.

When Grace walked into work, she was immediately surrounded by her workmates asking, 'What the hell are you doing in?' They sat her down with a coffee and a big plate of biscuits and the office box of tissues, because their concern brought the tears racing up to Grace's eyes.

'How are you feeling, or is that a totally daft thing to say?' said Dawn.

'I feel OK,' said Grace calmly. And strangely enough, she did. She felt remarkably detached from the events of the past few days. She wasn't even panicked by the inclusion of a paragraph in the *Evening Star* about a local woman in Penistone who had been imprisoned by her husband and was then rescued by police. 'An unnamed man has been held in connection with the incident,' it was reported. It did not say that the unnamed man had been sectioned under the Mental Health Act, as the police had informed the family.

'Coming to the pub with us tomorrow?' asked Anna. 'Totally understand if you don't want to, but it wouldn't be the same without you.'

'I'd like to,' replied Grace.

'Great,' said Dawn. To her shame, Friday nights could not come fast enough for her.

To Dawn's horror, the stage was empty when the five of them walked into the Rising Sun the next evening.

'Aren't the band playing tonight?' she asked a passing waitress.

'I think they've finished,' she replied, whizzing past with a basket of condiments for some diners.

Dawn felt hot and faint. She ordered the wine for them all, feeling adrift. Was that why Al Holly wanted to spend the day with her last weekend? Was that his way of saying goodbye without mentioning the actual word? Was that 'the surprise' he said he had for her tonight?

'My mistake,' said the waitress, appearing at her shoulder. 'They've been held up on the motorway, apparently. They'll be here in a bit.'

Dawn's mood lifted instantly. God knows what she'd be like when she saw him. Since Sunday, the days had crawled towards this weekend like a tortoise with arthritic knees.

'What's happened to your husband since?' Anna tentatively asked Grace. 'Don't talk about it, if you don't want to.'

'He's in hospital,' said Grace, with no emotion in her voice. 'He's under psychiatric observation.'

'Will you go back to him?' said Raychel softly.

'No,' said Grace with not a hint of a waver.

Dawn arrived with a tray of glasses and a bottle of merlot and slipped into the stream of conversation.

'Has he been violent towards you before?' she asked.

'No,' Grace said, with a long outward breath. 'He always had a ready temper but I never thought he'd be capable of anything like that.'

'It's scary.' Dawn shivered. 'What leads someone to meltdown like that?'

'I suspect in a lot of cases it's a very long, slow-burning fuse to the dynamite,' Christie sighed. She wondered what sort of marriage Grace had that her husband came into work to enquire about her retirement prospects. Even from that snippet alone, he sounded a very controlling man. That type usually broke rather than bent under pressure.

Grace took a sip of wine. 'Knowing Gordon, he is now probably saying to himself, "What a load of fuss over a simple domestic argument." I wouldn't be surprised if he expected me to have his tea on the table when he gets home and say no more about it.'

Raychel nodded, remembering how quickly Nathan Lunn recovered from his rages and carried on from the point just before he lost it.

Grace knew she wouldn't be far off the mark. Her husband, who would be her *ex*-husband as soon as possible, would fight her all the way, she knew that. He would think she was overreacting. He would not see he had done anything to apologise for. Grace took a deep breath and prepared to share a secret she had told no one yet.

'I was going to leave him.'

'Did he know?' Anna said.

'No, but I think he suspected and hadn't a clue what to do about it.'

Christie nodded. 'Rejection can be a huge trigger for violence.' She watched Grace's brain whirring and she nudged her. 'You're safe now,' she whispered. 'And among friends.'

'Yes,' said Grace. 'And I want to say that I do regard you *all* as my friends.' She took a deep breath to steady her rising emotion.

'Sounds like he did you a favour,' grinned Dawn, then seeing the jaws drop around her, she gasped. 'Oh hell, that came out all wrong!'

Grace rescued her with a tinkly laugh. 'Dawn, you're a tonic.'

'How far ahead have you thought?' enquired Anna softly.

'One day at a time,' interrupted Christie.

'I'm going to have to start planning soon,' said Grace. 'I can't stay with you for ever.'

'For goodness' sake, Grace, the house is enormous. I am sure there are people living with us that I have never seen,' smiled Christie. 'Besides, I think Niki rather likes having someone to show off his cooking skills to. I've got rather blasé, alas. Chicken, mushroom and asparagus spear risotto is on the menu for tonight.'

'Must be nice!' said Dawn with a little laugh. 'Calum made me a chip butty once. Micro chips. That's about as adventurous as he gets.' Then she was distracted as, from the corner of her eye, she saw Samuel arrive on the stage and rush to set up, followed by the others and finally Al.

'What's up with you?' said Anna. 'You look like someone's just switched on a light inside you.'

'Me?' said Dawn, trying to will her heartbeat to slow down.

'It's one of those guitarists, isn't it?' said Raychel with a teasing smile. 'You fancy him.'

'I don't!' she protested. 'I just think they're nice blokes, that's all. I like their music.'

'Sorry we're late, folks,' Samuel's voice blasted down the microphone some minutes later. 'We got held up in your wonderful British traffic, but we're here now and we're starting with this one.' And they slid effortlessly into their first number.

'Have you booked them for your wedding then?' asked Anna.

'No, they're leaving on that day.'

'Oh, that's a shame.'

'Yeah,' said Dawn. She didn't want to think about that. 'I'll go up and get some crisps, shall I? I'm a bit peckish.'

The bar was more packed than usual. Dawn had only just managed to order a couple of bags of cheese and onion by the time the first song was completed.

'This one is a special number,' drawled Samuel. 'It's called "I'll Take My Chances With You" and we have a guest singer to perform it. I'd like you to give a warm Rising Sun welcome to Miss—Dawny—Sole.'

Absently, Dawn began to clap along with everyone else. It took three seconds for her brain to engage, then her head whisked round to the stage to see the band members beckoning to her.

No, no, no, no, no! she thought. This couldn't be happening. Her head was planning an escape route but her legs, totally disconnected from her panicking brain, were betraying her and moving forward.

Al slipped his guitar round her neck and picked up another from behind him.

'Go, girl,' he whispered into her ear. His breath puffed on her neck and fanned flames in her heart.

The intro began. Dawn looked at the sea of faces staring at the local woman. Her only option was to sing and get through it, and then leave the stage and die in a corner. In the background, she could see Christie, Raychel, Anna and Grace standing to watch her.

Dawn opened her mouth and heard the first shaky bars leave her. Then it hit her that she was singing in a band, *a real band.* She thought of watching her mum and dad perform this, then she thought of her mum and dad watching her, now, at this moment, and a strength gathered in her voice. She saw people in the audience smiling, their heads absently nodding. Her voice floated out past them to the walls and she saw Anna sticking up a congratulatory thumb at her. And she was aware that her fingers were moving across the guitar strings in perfect harmony with the rest of the band and it all felt so *right.*

As Al played the final riff and the applause and cheers rose in the air, Dawn found herself grinning as she turned to Al. She fought the surge of euphoria that made her want to fling her arms round him by saying that she was going to kill him. And he winked at her and said, 'You're wasting yourself, honey. Wait for me.' And for a moment she didn't know if he meant when her friends had gone, or for ever.

'You *are* a dark horse,' said Anna with true admiration, as Dawn came back to the table.

'That was wonderful,' said Grace. 'You looked so at home on that stage. How can you hide that talent away so secretly?'

'Oh, give over,' said Dawn, blushing and beaming at the same time.

'You have a true gift.' Christie patted her on the arm. 'You're a total natural. Your voice is perfect for that kind of music.'

'Honestly, you looked as if you were born to it,' added Raychel. 'You really enjoyed doing that, we could tell.'

Dawn decided she would stay for one drink only with Al Holly. She was in danger of getting involved with him and if he tried to take up where he had left off last Sunday, she didn't know if she could resist.

But Al surprised her. He talked about banal things like motorway holdups and transport cafés. He didn't invite her to practise with them on Sunday and Dawn didn't ask to. They parted that night as friends who would soon go their separate ways and had just shared two Cokes together. It was how it should be, said Dawn to herself; it was right that it should be that way. But, as Al returned to the stage and she went out to her car, disappointment weighed her footsteps down and her heart wasn't feeling it was the right thing at all.

Anna found she was smiling all the way home. What a lovely evening that was, better still because Grace came too. And there was Anna thinking *her* relationship was crap! At least Tony didn't have a violent bone in his body.

She crossed the road from the railway station. Her lonely little house was in sight. But there was a film on that night she would enjoy and, bugger it, she'd ring and get a Tandoori Butter Chicken delivered and enjoy it with a glass or two of that riesling presently chilling in her fridge. She got her key out of her handbag and almost stepped on another surprise Tony-present—a single red rose lay on the doorstep.

Sarah rang Grace on the Saturday afternoon to ask how she was, but her opening tone was lukewarm. She always addressed Grace as Mother. It lent a distance between them that Grace had tried, but failed, over the years to close and it felt a particularly chilly word to use at the moment. Out of all her children, Sarah had been given the most: attention, toys, leeway. But she was the coldest of them all, with her father's gift of being able to shove a stopper in his bottle of emotions.

Paul and Laura had told their sister most of what they knew. They hadn't been that surprised at her cool response that 'Dad was obviously ill and Mum must have antagonised him'.

'I've phoned the hospital but they don't know when Dad will be coming home,' Sarah said. 'Have you been to see him?'

'No, Sarah, I haven't,' said Grace. 'Nor will I be going to see him.'

'Haven't you rung?'

'No.'

Sarah gave an incredulous laugh. 'You can't leave him in there!' she said. 'He's sick—he needs help.'

'I can't get involved, Sarah. It's a police matter,' said Grace in an even voice that masked the hurt that Sarah's attitude was causing her. 'I don't know if the police will hold him or release him. I don't know if he'll go to trial or—'

'Trial?' screamed Sarah. 'You can't let him go to *trial!* He's my *father!*'

'It's not for me to decide, Sarah.'

The thought of a trial made Grace's head ache. She could not be disloyal to *their father* whatever she thought about *her husband.*

'You'll have to both pull yourselves together,' said Sarah with a long, impatient exhalation of breath. 'You can't split up at your age.'

'We already have split up!' Anger strengthened Grace's voice.

'Don't be silly,' said Sarah. 'You've been together for over twenty-three years. Twenty-three years! You can't just leave him to rot!'

Grace took a fortifying breath. 'Sarah, I *have* left him,' she said definitively. 'I am divorcing him. It's something I'm afraid you'll have to accept, love. Your mum and dad have split up.'

'Except you're not my mum, are you?' said Sarah spitefully, before she slammed the phone down.

'**W**ell, look-ee here!' whistled Bruce as Anna walked into Vladimir Darq's house at the tardy time of ten past seven.

'What? What's up?' replied Anna quickly.

'You, that's what's up!' said Bruce. 'You look different.'

'You're wearing a V neck that isn't black too, well done!' said Jane, giving her the customary two-cheek kiss. 'I think that shade of blue is definitely your colour. What do you think, Vladimir?'

Anna felt her cheeks flare up at the amount of attention she was receiving from the whole room. Especially when Vladimir strode over and started studying her intensely.

'Yes, it's good on you, Anna.' Then he groaned. 'The shoulders, Anna, they are dropping again. *La dracu!* You drive me crazy!' And he flounced off as if in a very bad mood.

Bruce pulled a face and mouthed, 'What's up with him?' at Jane, who shrugged her shoulders.

'He's been pacing about for ten minutes,' she whispered to Anna.

'It wasn't our fault we were late. We had to take a detour because a lorry had broken down and blocked the road,' Anna explained.

'Maybe it's a full moon,' giggled Bruce.

'You do look different, though,' Jane smiled. 'Really straight-backed and sassy. And thinner. Have you lost weight?'

'Can't, can I?' said Anna. 'He won't let me.'

'We want some footage of you in that bodyshaper and then some higher price-point corsets tonight, Anna darling,' said Mark. 'Leonid's knocking around somewhere, so we can get some stills.'

Anna stripped off and put on her robe. It felt so natural now. It was only like stripping down to a bikini on the beach, really. Give or take a vampire rearranging her knockers at regular intervals.

Maria worked her magic on Anna's face in her surly, silent but efficient manner. Then Vladimir came in to view the finished product.

'You have the smile under control this week,' he observed. 'I take it you haven't heard from *Tony* since the *plate*.'

He was so sniffy Anna wanted to giggle but she reined it in.

'Actually he left me a rose. A red one. On my doorstep.'

Vladimir stood stiffly in front of her, legs astride, arms folded, hair magnificent. 'I must remember that one. The next time I drag a woman's heart through the mud, I will send her a plate and a rose and she will forgive me everything.'

'I didn't say I'd forgiv—'

'Presumably he still lives with the other girl. Still he goes home with her every night and then deceives *her* once a week by leaving presents for you at your door.'

Ouch! He punctured Anna's puffed-up spirit with one expert dart. Anna felt her body slump as if someone had whipped out her spine.

Vladimir pulled Anna fiercely in front of him and when she raised her eyes, they locked with his.

'Why do people do this?' hissed Vladimir, passion throttling up the volume. 'Why do they sell themselves so cheaply and wonder why they feel undervalued? I don't understand!' Softer now. 'Anna, this *Tony* shines a light on you and you flower; he turns it off and you wither. I want you to feel your worth *here*.' He placed the flat of his hand on her breast, above her heart, and yet it was in no way a sexual gesture.

Vladimir took Anna's chin in his hand and lifted it. He saw that his words had sunk in and was satisfied—temporarily at least. Anna made a conscious effort to keep her back straight in front of him and her trembling lip as controlled as possible.

Vladimir called to Mark, 'We are ready.'

Leonid took some shots of Anna posing, then she changed into some absolutely gorgeous corsets in sumptuous velvets and heavy satins. Vladimir wasn't very gentle lacing her into them, but she didn't give him the satisfaction of complaining.

'So, how have you felt this week dumping the old underwear and wearing only the Darqone?' Jane asked, for the camera.

'People have definitely noticed and asked me if I've lost weight,' replied Anna with utter sincerity. 'It's been very comfortable and I have felt more confident that everything seems to be in the place it was when I was much younger.'

'And going to the loo? How easy has that been, Anna?'

'Surprisingly easy,' came the answer. 'The poppers on the gusset are very good. I've had bodies before where they were uncomfortable and not very easy to fasten. And I've thrown them in the washing machine, tumble dried them and they've come up good as new.'

Jane looked impressed at the bonus information. Anna answered her raised eyebrow look. 'Well, I got picked for this programme because I'm just an ordinary woman and how these things wash is important to us. I wouldn't risk the higher-end ones in the tumble drier but, well priced as the Darqone is, it wouldn't be a good buy if it all fell apart after a couple of washes.'

Mark gave her a big thumbs-up and then called for a cut.

'Thank you, Anna,' said Vladimir in a less thorny voice now. 'That was a point worth mentioning.'

'Happy to help,' said Anna.

'That's it then, thank you, everyone,' Mark clapped. 'Same time next week for the big finale.'

The last one. Next week was the last time she would be in Vladimir Darq's house. It blindsided Anna at how saddened she was by that thought. Weekends really wouldn't be the same. She wasn't sure what the next chapter in her story would be. Maybe in two Saturdays she would be sharing a takeaway with Tony on their sofa? She really didn't know how slumped her shoulders would, or wouldn't be, by then.

Chapter 11
June

DAWN WASN'T HER USUAL chirpy self by half and hadn't been all week. Not even on the Thursday morning when she came in with four wedding invitations did she seem like an excited bride-to-be.

'I'd love it if you could come,' she said.

''Course we will,' said Christie. 'Dawn, can I ask—are you all right? You look so low, love.'

'Oh, I'm fine,' said Dawn, pinning on a smile. 'I just have so much to organise it's wearing me down a bit, to be honest.'

'Aren't you getting any help from anyone?'

'Oh, yes, loads,' said Dawn as chirpily as she could manage. That was partly the trouble. Hardly any of Dawn's plans for her wedding had escaped from being Muriel-ised. And she was trying so hard to fight against second thoughts about Calum and the wedding—especially as so much was organised and paid for. Damn Al Holly and his bloody Strat!

'Anyway, enough about me, how are you, Grace?' said Dawn, deflecting attention away from herself. 'Just because I haven't asked this week, it doesn't mean I haven't thought about you.'

'I'm fine, pet,' said Grace with a lovely smile. 'I just have a lot of things to think about, too. The house will have to be sold and I can't imagine that Gordon is going to be very flexible on that front. I'm taking it all in bite-sized pieces.'

'I think that's very wise,' said Raychel. She was involving herself more in their conversations recently, rather than hanging back. Part of her was really freeing itself. And it felt so good. 'Pub tomorrow after work as norm?'

'I think I can safely plan that far ahead, yes,' said Grace.

'You as well, Dawn?' asked Raychel.

Dawn smiled for the first time since last Friday.

'That guitarist can't keep his eyes off you!' said Anna, nudging Dawn.

'He can so!' protested Dawn.

'He looks very sexy with that floppy Elvis hair,' said Christie.

'And the guitar makes him even sexier,' added Anna. 'Imagine him playing you like that.'

'Oh, wow!' said Dawn dreamily, forgetting to play it cool.

'I told you, you fancied him!' came a merry chorus, pointing fingers at Dawn and poking her.

'I don't fancy him,' she laughed, 'but I do think he's nice. How could I not? We like the same music.'

'So you're making beautiful music together,' teased Christie.

'I didn't say that!' said Dawn. 'But he is a really lovely bloke. If I weren't getting married, I might let myself fancy him.' Then, for the benefit of Anna, she added quickly, 'But I am, so I'm not allowed.'

'Ah, don't panic. We're only having you on,' said Anna, hoping that she hadn't frightened Dawn into refuting that she liked the guitarist.

'So what are we all up to this weekend?' asked Christie. 'Anna, how's the filming going?'

'I'm getting into my stride.' Anna winked. 'Though half of me thinks I must be mad. I'm going to have no control about what footage they use. There's a bit of a difference in an experienced film crew seeing my bad underwear and the rest of England—including all the pervs. Like Malcolm, for instance.'

'Bet he tapes it so he can see you on a continuous loop,' grinned Dawn.

'Stop, you'll make me vomit!'

'I've got my bridesmaids' dresses fitting tomorrow,' said Dawn.

'What colour are you going for again?' asked Raychel.

'Peach,' came the answer. 'The same colour, actually, that's on the ribbon on the wedding invites. I've got all the favours to wrap up in the same colour tissue paper.'

'You sound chirpier today than you have all week,' said Anna.

'Maybe it's that guitarist who's cheering you up,' said Raychel.

'Oh, don't you start!' said Dawn. She didn't deny it though, because when Al Holly was nearby she couldn't stop that smile rising up from within her and spreading across her face.

They all stayed for an extra drink so Dawn missed Al's break. She was twitching to get to him but couldn't exactly leave the company so she stayed after the others had gone until the end of that night's gig. She sat at the bar and just watched him. She started to imagine, as Anna had said, that he was playing her like she was a guitar and had to thrash the thoughts down with a mental sledgehammer.

'Ah, Dawny Sole,' said Al, coming straight over to her after resting his guitar on the stand. 'And how are you this evening?'

'I'm good, and you?'

'I'm good too. Drink?'

'Er . . . please. What are you having?'

'I've finished work so I'm having a beer.'

'I'll just have a Diet Coke, thank you. A small one.'

Al paid for the drinks.

'Come and sit outside,' he said, picking up the drinks and leading her to the back of the pub where there was a beer garden. There was a free bench and table in the corner by the boundary hedge and that was where Al Holly headed. They sat opposite each other, their drinks and a candle between them, their hands sitting dangerously close on the surface of the table.

'What a lovely evening,' said Dawn, trying not to look at Al Holly's unblinking eyes. The candlelight was dancing in them. 'Are you going straight home when you leave here? To Canada?'

'Well, we have a few days in London, then we head off for home,' said Al Holly. 'Got a month relaxing by a lake fishing in the sun, then we set off for America on tour. You ever been?'

'Me? Naw,' said Dawn. 'My foreign experience is limited to one Greek island, and France, as a schoolgirl. I don't know why I bother even having a passport.' She had renewed it for her honeymoon. Why?

Al took a long drink of beer and Dawn suddenly wanted to drag her hands through his hair. He was gorgeous, he was beautiful. Too beautiful to bear this.

'Al, I have to go,' said Dawn, suddenly panicked by the surge of her feelings.

'I understand,' he said, staring thoughtfully at his beer.

How can you? thought Dawn. *How can you understand that when I look at you my whole life seems to fall apart in the background?*

She stood up and looped her bag over her shoulder. Al Holly scratched his head and sighed.

'Hear me out, Dawny. I am not in the habit of making a play for other men's girls but I like you a lot. I think we have that kindred spirit thing going on and I really look forward to seeing you for this little time on Fridays. But I'm not trying to complicate things for you and if I have, I'm really sorry. I hope you'll be here next Friday and not stay away.'

'Next Friday, erm . . .' She would have had time to compose herself by then. She should say 'No'. She should tell the others she couldn't go to the pub again after work for a few weeks, then she wouldn't be drawn close to this man like a moth to a flame. It could end only with third-degree burns to her wings. No, tell him no, end it now.

'Yes, I'll be here,' she said.

As Anna rounded the corner to her house, she could see that there was another parcel, peeping out from behind her wheelie bin. She couldn't wait until she got inside to open it. She ripped the paper off to find a heart-shaped box of Ferrero Rocher. She looked round to see if she could see Tony peeping out from a hiding place. Surely he was going to make a move soon? First a photo-plate, then a rose and now this: a third week of presents with no follow-up.

Tony Parker, what the hell are you up to?

Dawn was at Muriel's for 10 a.m. and for once Demi was up and dressed. It appeared she had a brand-new boyfriend on the scene and he had obviously injected a bit of life into her.

Denise didn't seem impressed with him.

'He's another dicksplash,' she confided in Dawn. 'I'm sure he has a girlfriend already. Anyway, what are we doing for your hen night? Where do you fancy? Blackpool? Too far maybe . . . hmm, let me think.'

'Oh, I wasn't going to bother,' said Dawn.

She watched Denise's face form into something quite unpleasant. 'God, you can be a miserable beggar, Dawn!' she said. 'Well, you're having one whether you like it or not. *We* want one if we're going through all this bridesmaid crap for you.' Her reaction shocked Dawn. She had thought Denise was more on her side than that.

Across the road, big Bette sipped delicately from a china cup and beamed as the bridesmaids modelled her creations.

The dresses were orange and Demi's neckline was so low she could have been wearing it and still appeared on the centre pages of *Playboy*.

'I got Bette to lower my neckline a bit as well,' Denise said, adjusting her much smaller bosom inside her dress. 'Hope you don't mind.'

'No, 'course not,' said Dawn, hating herself because what she wanted to say was, 'Yes, I bloody well do mind. And if that is peach, then I'm Cheryl Cole!' Plus the fabric smelled of cigarette smoke. How could it not, being stored in the fug of this house?

'Chuffing hell, I feel like a space hopper,' said Demi, voicing some of what was in Dawn's head. 'Thought it was supposed to be peach!'

'Well, they didn't have that exact shade of peach in the warehouse so I went for the next best thing. Plus this was a lot cheaper,' Bette explained, dunking a digestive into her cup. 'I ran it past Mu first.'

Why didn't you run it past ME—I'm the bride! screamed Dawn inside.

'Itches like hell,' said Denise.

It looked as if it did too. The material was cheap and tacky and made even the slim Denise appear thick-waisted.

'Oh, you pair of moaners!' Muriel chipped in. 'You can change straight after the wedding. Eeh, it's a bonny colour. Nice and bright for summer.'

Dawn took a deep breath and sucked back the comment that Pumpkin Orange was much more suitable for Hallowe'en. And she didn't want the bridesmaids changing straight after the wedding. Rage was bubbling in her and she was scared to unleash it fully, so it seeped out through pinholes.

'I'd bought peach ribbon for the favours and the invitations!'

'No one notices stuff like that!' said Muriel, waving it off as another one of Dawn's pernicketies.

'I do,' said Dawn, getting about as shirty as she could.

'Ooh, you want to save your "I do's" for the big day,' laughed Bette, sending her five chins into vibrations.

'Oi, Mam, talking of "do's", she don't want a hen do,' said Denise, thumbing at Dawn.

'It's just that I don't have anyone to invite,' Dawn tried to explain.

'You've got us and Bette,' said Muriel. 'And I dare say Demi and Denise have some mates that'll want to come and beef up the crowd.'

'Calum's having his stag the Saturday before the wedding,' said Demi.

'Is he?' It was the first Dawn had heard of it.

'Oh, didn't he tell you?' gloated Demi.

Dawn felt suddenly outlawed by them all. Blood in this family was about twelve million times thicker than water. She was wishing more with every passing hour that she'd never started this whole wedding process. She had liked the family much more before their relationship got smothered by cakes and karaokes.

'Well, it would be nice to have a hen do, I suppose,' said Dawn, caving in. *What would be the point in marrying Calum if his family hated her?* However much she didn't want to admit it to herself, belonging to a loving family again had influenced her decision to be Calum's wife. Of course it had.

'Good, you can leave all the arrangements to us then,' said Denise, her face returning to her usual cheeky, cheerful look. 'I promise you, we'll have a night to remember.'

Dawn suspected it would be more a night to forget.

Vladimir was waiting outside Darq House, a tall, unsmiling figure with strange, beautiful eyes scanning the drive for her. Anna gulped as he opened the car door and presented his hand to help her out.

'Our last shoot, Anna,' he said. 'Are you ready?'

'As I'll ever be,' she said, thinking how cool his skin was, despite the lovely warm air of the evening.

'Hiya, babe,' called Bruce. Mark blew her a kiss, Leonid nodded, Jane gave her a hug.

'Full make-up and your grand finale photoshoot time!' smiled Jane, pointing Anna to Maria's chair and gently shoving her forward.

As Maria brushed and dabbed, Anna listened to Leonid and Vladimir conversing in very fast Romanian. God, she would miss these manic evenings. She'd even miss the untalkative Maria, who was now lifting up her hair and twirling it round, dropping it and rearranging it. Anna loved having her hair played with. She found herself drifting off, her eyes closing, and then she felt a sharp jab in her shoulder.

'Don't go to sleep,' barked Vladimir, making her jump to attention.

'I wasn't!' she protested.

For once, there was a screen to allow Anna to strip off completely and put on the highest price-point lingerie set that Vladimir had made. She went behind it, slipping out of her clothes and into the velvety knickers he had made, which caressed her bottom. They actually pushed her stomach in flat while allowing her to breathe and bend. Never mind 'highest price-point'; these things were price*less*. Then she called for him to assist her with the corset, a beautiful red one that made her feel very queenly. The Darqone was an amazing creation and would transform the figures of thousands of women, but his premier collection was *so* worth saving up for. His fingers worked slowly and carefully on the hooks and as she felt his cool breath blow against her neck she shivered.

There were, strangely, no mirrors around that evening so the only reflection she had was the one in her mind. She hoped when she did see the mirror that it wouldn't shatter the illusion she was holding of herself: small-waisted, busty, long-legged, lips a sex-slash of scarlet.

He held up a pair of stockings. Black and sheer and sparkly, she had never seen hosiery as gorgeous. To her horror, he bent to help her put them on.

'No, I'm fine, I can do it!' she rushed, feeling the heat in her cheeks again as her brain presented her with a mini-play of Vladimir smoothing the stockings onto her legs, clipping the deep lace at her thigh. The ferocity of her imagination shocked her.

Vladimir then helped Anna into the dress he had made, red velvet with a fishtail skirt. It was very plain and very gorgeous. He was silent as he zipped her up and smoothed the material over her back. Finally, he held up the highest pair of shoes—blood-red—she had ever seen. She would need oxygen after getting into them. Luckily she didn't have to walk far, just stand there and look like a woman worth shagging for the camera. *Yeah, easy.* Actually, she did feel worth shagging in these clothes.

'Anna, how do you feel?' Vladimir asked her.

'Nice,' she replied in a breathy voice.

'Nice?' he growled. '*Nice?*'

'OK, I feel fantastic,' said Anna, clicking her tongue at his indignation. 'Can I see myself now?'

'*Nu*,' replied Vlad. 'Anna, I want you to remember how you feel.'

'Oh, ho, that sounds suspiciously like I don't look as good as I feel,' sighed Anna with disappointment.

'Let me show you your mirror for today,' he said. He beckoned her out from behind the screen and she did her best to walk gracefully.

The jolly banter going on between the film crew dried up immediately.

Maria and Leonid raised their heads to see her and their eyes widened so much their eyeballs nearly dropped out. Leonid dropped his camera and swore in his native tongue. '*La dracu!*' Which was mirrored in English when Bruce said 'Fucking 'ell!' Maria was shaking her head now in total and utter disbelief—and then she actually smiled.

'Well, well, well,' said Mark. 'Anna, you look . . . look . . . what's the word I'm searching for?'

'I'm not sure there is one,' smiled Jane. 'We might have to make one up. Marvefanwondertastic. Gorgemazing.'

Anna puffed out her cheeks. She was faced with so much evidence that she actually might look rather tasty that it battered through the barrier of her poor self-image and a pleasant warmth spread inside her.

Leonid greedily captured her image with the lens. Then it was necessary for Anna to lose the gown and stand there in some very moody shots in Vladimir's fabulous, luxurious underwear.

Anna pouted and posed like a pro. She lapped up the feeling that she was sexy and curvy and womanly. Everyone broke into rapturous applause when Mark called it a wrap.

'This will be magic, Anna,' said Mark. 'We're going to be turning this around fast as a special to pilot the new series, so be in front of the TV on Thursday the eighteenth.'

'Which month?'

'This month.'

'So soon!' croaked Anna.

Vladimir handed her a goblet of wine. 'Rest and enjoy,' he said.

'Let me get out of this corset; I don't want to spill anything on it,' returned Anna.

'No, sit, please,' insisted Vladimir, so Anna sank into a chair and Vladimir took the one opposite her, his large arms resting on his thighs. There was a light dancing in his eyes and the faintest hint of a smile playing on his soft, generous lips.

'So, do you think it went all right then?' she asked.

Vladimir stared hard at her, his brow creased in the middle. Then, when he realised she wasn't joking, he threw back his head and laughed.

'You joke? It was fantastic. You were fantastic, Anna, a queen. I was right to wait until I had found you. I know this for sure.'

'Blimey,' said Anna, taking a big glug of wine. Her system was thrown into shock by this lifetime's worth of compliments.

Soon the camera crew were all packed up and were almost ready to leave. Back-to-normal-life-land was just around the corner now for Anna. Back to waiting for a boyfriend finally to make his mind up as to who had the superior tits—his fiancée or his teenage concubine.

Anna tipped the last of the wine into her mouth and then slipped into her ordinary clothes behind the screen. Bruce was waiting for her at the other side of it when she emerged. He gave her a kiss on her cheek. And then Mark appeared with the world's biggest bouquet. 'From us all,' he said. 'Some flowers for a woman who has totally blossomed before our eyes.'

Anna burst into tears, for all sorts of different reasons. She was totally overwhelmed by the gift, but also she would miss these Saturdays so much. But all that paled into nothing when she thought of never again feeling Vladimir Darq's hands on her shoulders, his breath on her skin.

'You're going to love the show,' smiled Jane as she climbed into the crew van. 'You've been wonderful. Stay gorgeous.'

They drove away with waves and smiles and blown kisses and Anna wiped at her leaky eyes and waved back until her arm was sore.

Then Leonid and Maria kissed her, three cheeks each, and vigorously shook her hand. She would even miss Maria pulling her this way and that and arguing with Vladimir. *Vladimir.*

The car pulled up to take her home. She didn't want to go. She had to go. It was all over now. Vladimir lifted up a smart black case.

'As promised,' he said. 'An exclusive set of Vladimir Darq lingerie designed for you.'

'Thank you. I shall treasure them,' replied Anna, hoping her voice wouldn't embarrass her by crumbling. She didn't dare look up at his pale-blue eyes flecked with gold and ringed with black. She wasn't sure she would hold it together if she did.

'I will be in touch,' he said, opening the door for her. *'Course you will,* she thought. He bent and put a kiss on her cheek. His lips were soft and cool but the place where they touched her burned all the way home.

Grace and Niki and Christie ate outside. Citronella candles kept the insects away from the king prawn and avocado salad starter, the gruyere and mushroom chicken and the summer pudding and clotted cream. After devouring homemade chocolate mint ice-cream truffles, Niki left his sister and Grace together in the garden with a cognac each. He apologised for being a typical bloke because he wanted to check the sports results on the TV.

'He likes you very much,' said Christie, as soon as her brother was out of earshot. She was a lot further down her glass of those very large cognacs than Grace was.

'I like him too,' said Grace.

'No, I mean he *likes* you.'

'Christie Somers, you sound as if you're at school, matchmaking.'

'He sparkles when you're around. Of course he wouldn't dream of making a move on you while you're a guest in our house, he's far too gallant,' Christie trilled.

'*Tut.* You're imagining things.'

'I'm my father's daughter and I know my psychology, Ms Beamish! I think he's scared a lot of women off by being too good-looking and too nice. Funny creatures, aren't we, women? Even if we find what we want, we're too scared to believe it and we run from it.'

'Yes, aren't we?' said Grace.

'Except I was the exception to the rule and didn't,' said Christie. 'I ran to love with my arms open wide and it was wonderful.'

'Do you think you'll ever marry again?'

Christie shrugged. 'Who knows what the future brings? But Peter Somers is a hell of a hard act to follow. I sometimes curse him for that.'

'Were you very happy?'

Christie smiled. 'He was the most wonderful man: kind, passionate, funny. He was my married boss, older than me. He was living in a sex-less, childless, unhappy marriage and I loved him away from his wife. For a long time I thought I was cursed because I broke up his marriage. But I would have done it all again to have him. And in a way I'm lucky, because some people never find the love of their life but at least I can say I did. For a while. My punishment is that I'll never find anyone like him again and I wouldn't want to take a lesser man to my bed. We all pay for our sins in the end.'

'Could you have children?'

'I presume so, but I don't know for sure. We thought we had all the time in the world. We planned to have them late on when we'd got our travelling bug out of our system, but he died before then. We missed our chance.'

'Oh, Christie.'

'Life makes no guarantees—I accept that, I've had to. There are certain things, like children and longevity, that are privileges, not rights. All we can do is play the hand we are dealt. So let's toast our health and our future happiness and a Malcolm-free existence in the office. My God, I know it's evil but I hope the lazy bastard gets kicked out soon.'

Grace accepted the turn of conversation and poured them both another cognac, which they drank together in comfortable silence. The way only good friends, close friends, can do.

Chapter 12

ON MONDAY MORNING Anna was so preoccupied that Grace had to ask her four times if she wanted a coffee.

'Earth calling Anna, can you read me?' said Grace.

'Sorry, yes, er, what did you say?'

'Do you want a coffee? It's my turn to get them.'

'Yes—yes, please. Sorry.'

Her mobile rang at that moment. It was Vladimir Darq. Her hands were shaking as she answered it.

'Anna, my car will call for you at eight p.m. on Saturday,' he said. 'I have something that I want to give you—it won't take very long.' Then he added pointedly, 'It isn't a plate.' He put the phone down before she could say a single word in answer.

'Can't believe we are at the end of another week!' said Christie, pouring the bottle of chilled zinfandel into five glasses. 'Anyone doing anything exciting this weekend? It seems like only two minutes since I was asking that question last Friday.'

'I'm going for a final dress fitting,' said Dawn.

'Christie and I are off to the theatre,' said Grace.

'And my brother is coming as well,' said Christie. 'He has rather a crush on Grace.'

'Get in there, Gracie,' said Anna, which mirrored exactly what Paul and Laura had said. It was, apparently, obvious to them also that Niki rather liked their mother. Did she like him enough to say 'Yes' if he invited her out to dinner? Paul had asked her. The thought terrified Grace, to be honest. The idea of starting a new, *normal* relationship, with all that it entailed, was scary stuff. Especially with a fifty-five-year-old body, although it was still in fantastic shape, thanks to years of yoga. But then Niki was fifty too. Did men feel the same insecurity about their bodies with new partners?

'What are you going to do now that filming is over? Won't you feel lost?' Raychel asked Anna.

'Well,' Anna leaned forward to impart her information. 'Mr Darq is sending a car for me tomorrow night. Says he's got something for me.'

'What?' asked Dawn, her eyes lit up with excitement.

'Haven't a clue. I won't be there long apparently, so he says.' She had thought of his hand on her heart more times than she cared to count that past week. *Vladimir Darq.* He was taking up more and more of her thought space, which concerned her. There was no point in forming an attachment with someone like him. But she was aware that that was exactly what was happening.

'And I'm going shopping with my aunt,' said Raychel after taking a deep breath.

She cut through most of the story and told them that she had been contacted by an estranged aunt who was, by fantastic coincidence, living in the area.

'What an amazing story,' said Christie. 'I didn't think things happened like that in real life. You must be delighted.'

'It's a long story,' said Raychel. 'I gave you the abridged version.'

'And the happy ending,' said Dawn. 'So that'll do nicely.'

After the others had left, Dawn sat at the bar and watched the band.

'Are you going to sing again?' asked the barman when she gave him a drinks order. 'You were fab.'

'It was a one-off,' said Dawn, secretly glowing.

'Shame,' said the barman. 'You fitted in so well with that band. Maybe you should ask them to take you with them when they go.'

Dawn laughed, but the barman's words were too close for comfort. They brought pictures in her head of her touring on a bus with the boys, setting up the stage with them, jamming together outside with a backdrop of Canadian mountains and warm, orangey sunsets.

Al Holly's arm circled her waist. The contact lasted barely a second but it was enough to send fireworks rocketing up towards her brain and then onwards to the moon.

'You looked lost in thought,' he said. 'Anything interesting?'

'Sort of,' said Dawn. 'How are you? Have you had a good week?'

'Yes, good,' he smiled, his eyes as twinkly as polished rhinestones. 'And how are you, Dawny Sole? I was going to invite you on stage to sing with us again tonight but you were talking with your friends. I didn't see you even look up at me once.'

'Every time I looked up, you were looking down,' replied Dawn. 'Seems we didn't have our eyes coordinated.'

'I looked at you quite a lot,' said Al. 'Not sure how I'm going to spend my Fridays not seeing you out there at the back of the room.'

'Bet you say that to all the girls,' said Dawn, her smile shaky.

'No, Dawny,' said Al, 'I don't. I ain't no womaniser. My music is my woman. But if . . .'

The room melted into a big blur behind Dawn. There was nothing but her and lovely Al Holly and she was desperate for him to finish his sentence. But he didn't.

Dawn could have battered him. But she wasn't free to be flirted with. There was no point in complicating anything. *Yeah, right, like it wasn't already complicated!* A huge part of her didn't want to be right and honourable and decent. It wanted Al Holly to lean into her and kiss her hard on the lips and show her what he tasted like.

'Diet Coke, please. A small one.'

'We . . . er . . . have a private party to play for this evening. I can only stay for five minutes.'

'I—'

'Dawn—' They both started to speak simultaneously. Al's hand twitched upwards. Then dropped back to his side. Then it made a smooth arc to her face. His fingers had barely touched her cheek when a man's voice called across the bar.

'Al. We're ready to go, man. Oh, hi there, Dawny. How are you?'

Al sighed. 'Samuel's timing was never all that good.'

'Maybe his timing is too good,' said Dawn. Samuel had saved them from God knows what, because if she had kissed Al Holly then, she didn't know what bombs it would set off inside her.

'Will you be here next week?'

'Of course I will.'

'Bye.'

'Bye.'

He touched the tip of her nose. Just one little touch with his finger and those bombs detonated inside her, each one setting off another in a different part of her body.

Bugger—she was falling hook, line and sinker for a country boy and she wished that before he left her for ever, she could taste his lips on her own. Just once.

To say that Anna was nervous that Saturday evening as she waited for her car was the equivalent of saying that the 'sun was a bit hot'. What the heck did he have to give her? Whatever it was was secondary to the fact that she was going to see him again. The anticipation was killing her. She had paced a furrow in the hall carpet by the time she heard the car pull smoothly up outside her front door.

Vladimir was waiting for her outside his house, wearing a Nehru-collared long, open jacket that made him look sexily authoritarian. She gulped as he presented his hand to help her out of the car.

'Anna, how nice to see you again,' he said. They went inside Darq House. Luno came stalking over, his tail whirring like a helicopter blade, and pushed his muzzle into Anna's hand.

'Hi, boy, I've missed you,' she whispered to him. Luno stayed for a pat, then returned to his basket, slumping down but keeping his eyes on his master, who was pouring two goblets of wine, one of which he handed over to Anna.

'*Noroc!*' he said, which she took to mean 'Cheers!' and repeated the word back to him before taking a sip.

'Anna, next week it is the *Balul Luna Plina*.'

'The what?'

'A Full Moon Ball. I hold it here in Darq House.'

'A ball?'

'Yes. You will be coming, of course.'

'Me?'

'Yes, Anna. I want you to come as an honoured guest of mine.'

'Oh God, I haven't got a dress posh enough for anything like that. What sort? Long, short?'

He held up one finger to silence her, got up from his seat, disappeared for less than a minute and returned with a long, soft, silver case over his arms. He unzipped and opened it and held up the most beautiful long gown in a shade of blue reminiscent of a late-night sky.

'I told you I had something for you,' he said.

'Well, you were right, it's not a plate!' gasped Anna. 'That can't be for me, can it?'

'Yes, of course,' said Vlad. 'Don't worry, it will fit. You don't need to try it on before. Trust me. Put it on next Saturday only. I will send the underwear to you before then, but I need to work some more on it first.'

'Do I bring a bottle?'

Vladimir gave her a disapproving look. She guessed the answer was no.

'Thank you, Vladimir, it's gorgeous. I've never had a dress like it.'

'Of course, it's a Vladimir Darq. How could you?'

Anna smiled and lifted her eyes to the man with the black hair and the full red lips in front of her, and had to look away again fast. He was too gorgeous. How could she go back to ordinary Saturday nights watching Ant and Dec and eating a ready meal for one? Anna felt suddenly empty inside and gulped at her red wine.

'You know that the show is going to be broadcast on Thursday night at nine p.m., Anna? The lingerie will be in the shops the next day—so the timing is perfect.'

'Yes, I know.' Only five days to find out if she'd made the biggest chump of herself and wrecked Vladimir Darq's career single-handedly. There was nothing she could do now but wait for it, watch it and die of shame afterwards.

Anna put her goblet down. She didn't want to outstay her welcome. 'Well, thank you for this beautiful dress.'

'My car will pick you up at quarter to nine next Saturday evening.' He kissed her hand. She cradled that hand all the way home.

Mr Williamson, Anna's neighbour, delivered a parcel for her five minutes after she had got back from work.

'A gentleman dropped it off earlier,' he said. 'I said I'd give it to you.'

Tony? Anna presumed it was another of his gestures which, frankly, were becoming annoying. But as soon as Mr Williamson produced it from his old-man shopping bag, she knew it couldn't possibly be from anyone else but Vladimir Darq. Wrapped exquisitely in silver tissue paper was the most beautiful boned corset in the same blue as her dress, plus matching knickers and the sheerest blue stockings. The corset was encrusted with tiny blue beads, each one hand-stitched on. Why had he gone to that amount of trouble when no one would see it? More work had gone into that corset than the dress—and a *lot* of work had gone into the dress. Her heart began to thump in a way that it hadn't done for Tony's rose, or his plate or his Ferrero Rochers.

On Thursday at home time, a thought crossed Anna's mind and jetted from her mouth with the speed—and volume—of Concorde.

'Shite, I've no shoes!'

'Are you aware you said that out loud?' said Dawn.

'I've no shoes for Saturday! I'll be at Vladimir Darq's house at a Full Moon Ball and I've got the frock but no shoes!' She filled them in on the dress he had made for her, and the ball he was hosting.

'Wow!' said Dawn. 'Imagine getting that sort of attention from a man.'

'What size are you?' asked Christie.

'Five. Oh, flaming hell! Where am I going to get shoes to match? It's a dark-blue dress! I've only got black high heels!'

'No one will see them, surely, if it's a long dress?' said Raychel.

'Vladimir will notice. I'll notice! You can't imagine how gorgeous that dress is, so I don't want to wear shoes that don't match. I want to feel fab from the feet up and I *don't* want to let him down.'

'I'm a size five, too,' said Christie. 'I'll fix you up. I've got every colour of shoe known to man. In fact . . . why don't we all have a nice girly evening at mine? We can watch the show with you, Anna.'

'Ooh, that sounds lovely,' said Raychel, looking forward to it already.

You've got a gorgeous house, Christie,' said Dawn that evening as she spooned the last of her pasta into her mouth.

'Dad was lucky that the previous owners didn't rip all the original cornices and ceiling roses out. So many old houses lost their original features through the fads of the day.'

'You lived here long then?'

'Most of my life,' said Christie. 'Niki and I grew up here. I moved out when I got married, only to move back in when I was widowed.'

'It's nice you get on so well with your brother,' said Anna. 'My sister's nuts. She thinks hedgehogs are gods and smokes "herbs".'

'Niki gets on with everyone,' said Christie fondly.

'He can't half cook as well!' said Anna, eyeing up his culinary contribution to the evening, which sat in a big bowl waiting to be served. He had made them all a 'Bad Girl's Trifle' for dessert. It was very boozy, very chocolatey and very full of calories.

'Shall we have coffee in a little while? After I've sorted Anna out?' Christie suggested with a twinkly smile. 'She doesn't trust my claims that I can complete her outfit. Come on, ye of little faith,' Christie said, rising from her chair and heading off upstairs.

Anna followed quickly. She was desperate to see what Christie had for her, although she doubted they would find a match.

The others came up behind, after Christie beckoned them, and went into Christie's bedroom, which was like a miniature country house room with its oak panels on the wall and a large, heavy, four-poster with velvet drapes tied at the corners. Christie went over to a door at the side of a huge wardrobe and pulled it open to reveal another cavernous room filled with banks of clothes—modern and vintage—in every colour of the rainbow. There were cabinets full of bags and purses, pashminas and stoles, and racks and racks of shoes.

'Chuffing hell, where's Mr Benn?' said Anna.

Christie laughed. 'I've always loved clothes.'

'Good grief,' said Grace, looking at a shimmering silver evening dress behind glass. 'Do you wear any of them?'

'I used to,' said Christie. 'When Peter was alive. We went to a lot of parties and did a lot of cruising round the world. Something I intend to start doing again when I'm ready.'

When I'm ready? wondered Grace. What a great hole Peter Somers must have left, for her to take so long to recover.

'Good God, I don't believe it!' said Anna, homing in on a pair of long, slim blue shoes from a rack with at least twelve other pairs in dark blue. 'They can't be the same colour, that would just be too spooky.' She pulled out a small square of material that Vladimir had included with the dress, presumably for the purpose of accessorising, and placed it against the shoe.

'It's a match. I don't believe it!'

'It's not quite,' said Christie. 'But you'd need to be lit with a thousand-watt bulb to notice the difference.'

'Try one on,' said Raychel.

Anna threw off her shoe and put the blue stiletto on. It slipped beautifully onto her foot.

Anna gasped. 'Can I borrow them, Christie?'

'Say no, Christie. That would be really funny,' giggled Dawn.

'Of course you can borrow them, silly. There's a bag to match somewhere. Ah, here it is.'

Anna held it reverently, then thumbed open the clasp. 'Christie, are you sure? It's never been used. Look, there's the price label still on. Oh, no, hang on, it's not the price—it says—' Her voice cut off.

Christie reached slowly for the bag and read the handwritten label. *For you, my darling girl.*

'I—' Christie crumpled against the wall and Grace leaped forward.

'Good grief, love, what is it?'

'Nothing, I'm fine.'

'You're not!' said Anna, coming to the other side of her for support. 'Dawn, get that chair!'

Dawn pushed the chair behind Christie only a split second before she fell backwards onto it. She struggled for composure, and then she burst into tears.

They closed around her like flower petals protecting their precious centre. Then Anna ran to Christie's en suite and grabbed some tissues; Raychel raced to get a glass of water; Dawn hunted down a flannel to soak with warm water—she didn't know why. Grace remained with her arms round the woman who had given her comfort in the same way through her recent dark times, as Christie sobbed into her shoulder.

Then, like a summer shower darkens a blue sky and ceases as quickly as it started, Christie recovered. She raised her head to see these four dear women she had become so fond of in such a short time.

'Forgive me,' said Christie. 'He used to give me so many presents.

I never knew he'd bought that for me. I've never seen it before.'

'What a lovely thing to do,' Dawn said softly. 'He sounds a really great bloke.'

'I miss him so much. It's taken me years to move on just a few steps. I will never find another man like him. Even though a lot of people think that James McAskill is warming my bed.'

'Then they're stupid,' said Dawn decisively. 'None of us thinks that.' She knew she spoke for them all.

'James McAskill and I go back forty years. He was the proverbial boy next door,' began Christie, pointing left. 'I never met people as cold as his parents were: so negative, so critical. He used to play with Niki and myself when we were small. He found a lot of love and warmth with my family in this house. He was, is and always will be, one of my dearest friends. The truth is as simple as that. When Peter died, it was James—and Niki, of course—who stopped me following him. But I want you to know that it's only since I started working with you all that I've truly felt part of the real world again.'

Anna gave Christie a hug. 'You're magic, Christie Somers. Pure magic.'

Christie made a huge cafetière of coffee and all five women sat in her lounge, marking off the seconds to the programme starting.

'Nervous?' Dawn asked Anna.

'I should be sitting on a commode, not a sofa,' replied Anna, as a commercial came on saying: *Jane's Dames is sponsored by Treffé chocolates.*' Dawn grabbed Anna's right hand, Grace her left one as she screamed, 'Oh my GOD!'

'*Hi, I'm Jane Cleve-Jones with Jane's Dames and tonight I'm going to sunny Barnsley in South Yorkshire to meet forty-year-old administrator Anna Brightside, who thinks her reflection is her enemy. We've got five weeks to locate her inner mojo and capture it in photographic form to prove to her it exists!*'

A picture of Anna in a frumpy, round-necked jersey jumped out of the screen. That was *so* going in the bin when she got home.

'*Anna isn't just forty—she's a string of other F-words, too, because she's feeling fat, frumpy and forgotten. Can international designer of underwear Vladimir Darq make our Anna feel flighty, fabulous and fantastic instead?*'

'Oh my Lord, I didn't realise I was being filmed then!' Anna would have covered up her eyes but her hands were being too tightly held, for there she was sitting in a robe talking to Jane while Maria was taking all her make-up off. She had thought they were off-camera!

'*When my partner left me, I just fell to bits. I feel so old and blobby and I can't find the energy to do anything about it. Sorry.*' And then Anna burst into tears on screen. She felt her hands being sympathetically squeezed by her coworkers.

Then it switched to a mini-biography of Vladimir and a very moody shot of him in his house, surrounded by his underwear collection. He began to speak: *'Anna is a classic case of a damsel in distress and I am here to rescue her and all women like her. When will women learn they should be at their most confident and beautiful at forty? They hide themselves away in stupid clothes but with the right underwear on, a woman can be amazing!'*

There flashed an image of Anna on screen in the red velvet dress.

'Wow!' came a chorus from either side of her.

'But first, let's see what Anna finds so bad about herself.'

'Aargh!' Anna shrieked as she watched herself strip down to her undies and stand in front of the mirror, going through a list that her boobs were too wide, stomach not flat enough, hips too big, legs not long enough, blah-di-blah . . .

'Are you looking at a different body from the rest of us?' Christie tutted.

Anna studied herself and, surprisingly, even though the camera was supposed to add half a stone, she didn't look quite as bad as she thought she would. Give or take the awful underwear, which, on screen, Vladimir was ripping to bits (not literally—alas, she thought).

'This bra is too tight and not supportive at all.'

'It's comfortable,' Anna retorted.

'How can it be?' replied Vladimir sternly. *'It's gouging grooves into your shoulders. And these knickers! La Naiba! Take these off and throw them away! Good underwear can do more for a figure than extreme surgery.'*

Then there was Anna clad in some of her awful clothes in her bedroom and Vladimir Darq's voice-over.

'Anna is a beautiful, sensuous woman and I wish she could see herself through my eyes.'

Four sets of eyebrows were raised in Anna's direction.

'Women with no self-worth are too concerned with what other people think about them. I want Anna to feel sexy because she is sexy. Look at her beautiful clear skin, her eyes, her hair, her cheekbones, her fantastic breasts—and all she can see is her stomach. She thinks all she is is one big stomach—ach!'

Then the adverts came on. Christie put a brandy in Anna's shaking hands when Grace and Dawn released their grip.

'Thank you, I need this,' she said, taking a gulp.

'I don't know why, you look fab even in awful underwear and no make-up on,' said Dawn. 'Can't wait to see you in that red dress again.'

'That's nothing to the blue one he's made me.' Anna threw the last of the brandy down her throat. 'How the heck I'll have my hands steady enough to do my own make-up on Saturday is anyone's guess.'

'Shhh, it's back on!' Dawn settled back on the big squashy cushions.

'What Anna doesn't know is that we projected a sixty-foot picture of her onto a building in Leeds and asked the locals what they thought about our girl.'

'Look at that bloke walking towards the camera—it looks like Gok Wan,' Raychel pointed.

'And, surprise surprise, a certain gentleman filming up the road here just happens to be passing.'

'Bloody hell, it *is* Gok Wan!' gasped Anna.

'So, Gok, what do you think about our lovely Yorkshire rose?'

'She is fan-tas-tic—look at that womanly figure and that hair! I have to say, Vladimir Darq is one of my favourite ever designers and, if anyone, he's the man to make that gorgeous girl feel like the gorgeous girl she is.'

Then Anna was back in Vladimir's house and he was trying to do up a front-fastening corset. Anna tried to take over and he slapped her hand away.

'You look like an old married couple,' sniggered Dawn.

I wish, thought Anna.

Vladimir was now standing with Anna, who was dressed in the Darqone. The screen was split, showing her both in that, and in her old rubbishy undies. Then she was wearing a simple V-neck T-shirt above the good and bad sets of underwear.

'Quite a difference.'

Vladimir and Jane were now discussing the availability and price points of his designs while Maria was expertly dabbing at Anna's face.

Then Anna was standing, hand on hip, in the most beautiful red corset and stockings. The picture segued into one of her in the red gown looking like a 1950s starlet with an amazing hourglass figure. Leonid was snapping madly at her and Anna Brightside was beaming from the inside out.

'Oh, wow, Anna!' Raychel clasped her hands together as if in prayer. 'You look amazing.'

Anna didn't say anything. Vladimir had not let her see herself. She hadn't had a clue she looked like that. It wasn't her, it couldn't be her. That woman was sex on legs. That woman *was someone to sew hundreds of tiny beads onto a blue corset for.*

'Darq Side Lingerie will be available in the High Street from the nineteenth of June. Finally, Vladimir, do you have anything to say to Anna and the self-proclaimed "forgotten women" out there?'

Vladimir Darq smiled at the camera, the tiniest hint of fangs showing. *'There are no forgotten women out there because Vladimir Darq has remembered you. And, Anna, I hope you are sitting with friends and a glass of wine and saying to yourself, "Darq was right, I am sexy after all."'*

Cue the music.

Anna let out a big breath. It felt like the first time she had breathed since the programme began.

'That was so brilliant, lady!' Christie gave her a big hug.

'Dare I venture out tomorrow?' asked Anna.

'With your head held high, *girlfriend*,' grinned Christie.

Chapter 13

THE NEXT MORNING Anna walked onto the train station platform and felt as if she had been rubbed over by a fluorescent highlighter. Did that fellow commuter with the black coat really take a long second look at her? She felt her cheeks flaring with colour.

'Excuse me,' asked Black Coat. 'Were you on *Jane's Dames* last night?'

She could have said it a bit more quietly, thought Anna. A few people turned to give a prolonged glance or twelve.

'Er . . . yep, that was me,' smiled Anna bashfully.

Black Coat's mouth stretched into a wide smile. 'I thought you were marvellous. I'm going out at lunch time to buy one of those Darq bodyshapers. You really sold it to me.'

'Thank you. Thank you so much,' said a stunned Anna. She felt a couple of people staring but Anna Brightside fought the old urge to curve into herself. She imagined Vladimir Darq behind her, pushing her shoulders out. She stuck out her chest, lifted her chin and smiled.

'So, are you looking forward to your hen night then?' asked Raychel later, in the Rising Sun. It was perfectly obvious that Dawn wasn't, judging by the look of horror on her face after being reminded of what was happening the following night.

So no one quite believed her when she said, 'Yes, I've come round to the idea now. It will be fun.'

'Where are you going for it again?'

'Blegthorpe-on-Sea. Have you ever been?'

No one had except Grace. She shook her head along with everyone else though. It would have been very hard to try and convince Dawn she was going to have a marvellous night in that godforsaken hole.

'I see Mr Guitarist is staring over a lot, as usual,' Christie noted, pouring out the wine.

Dawn felt herself colouring. 'We're just friends.'

'Yeah, and I'm Basil Brush,' said Anna. 'Are you going to snog him before he goes home?'

'Anna!' said Dawn, with virginal affront. 'I didn't think you'd be saying anything like that!'

Neither did Anna, but she was in less of a position to get on her soapbox these days, with her head split between a possibly returning boyfriend and a possibly vampiric underwear designer who was giving her erotic dreams.

'Dawn, the sexual tension between you two couldn't be cut with a chain saw,' said Christie. 'We've all seen it building for weeks. You staring at him, him staring at you. What's going on with you both?'

'Nothing. Honest. I couldn't,' Dawn shrugged. 'It wouldn't be right however much—' She cut off. She sounded so sad that no one jumped in to tease her about the unfinished sentence.

'Ben's a lovely kisser,' put in Raychel at last.

'I haven't been kissed in a long time,' said Grace with a gentle laugh.

'Maybe it's about time you were then?' said Christie, her eyes mischievously widening. Grace narrowed her eyes at her friend and shook her head in exasperation.

Anna exhaled loudly. 'It's supposed to be very nice and romantic, but I've never really thought it was all that wonderful a thing to do—snog. Tony isn't a snogger.' He might have used a snog as an introduction to open proceedings but after that he wasn't interested.

'Well, I'm a big believer in a kiss being able to tell you more than anything,' said Christie. 'You'—she turned to Anna—'have obviously been kissing the wrong men. And you'—she pointed at Dawn—'need to listen to what your heart is telling you.'

After the others had gone, Dawn waited at the bar, watching the band. Al Holly raised his head and smiled at her. She thought of his lips pressing down onto hers and, wrong as it was, she didn't fight the fantasy. What was that Christie said about listening to her heart? She couldn't help but listen to it, because it was shouting at her.

He made his usual beeline over to her when they had finished.

'Howdy,' he said.

'Hello there, pardner,' said Dawn. *He will be gone next week. You will be*

Calum's 'pardner', the respectable Mrs Crooke, and there will be another band on this stage. The thought hit her hard.

'Dawny,' he said, suddenly urgent, 'can you come with me for a moment? There's something I need to show you.'

''Course,' said Dawn, following him as he marched purposefully through the standing drinkers, out of the door, down the beer garden, past the benches and on to where the lighting stopped and the grass began to slope down to the wood behind the pub.

Dawn looked up. She knew the moon was one day off being full because Anna was going to the Full Moon Ball tomorrow, but it looked as near full as damn it. It was huge, like a perfect hole in the sky, a portal to another world where things were brilliantly lit and uncomplicated.

'Dawny.' Al looked up, seemingly having some internal battle with himself. 'I didn't bring you out here to look at the moon. I brought you out here to kiss you underneath it. Just once.'

Flaming heck! 'Oh, did you?'

'Yes I did, ma'am,' said Al Holly, and though every nerve in Dawn Sole's body was telling her to back up, she stood unmoving and let Al Holly slide his arms round her, tilt her head back and slowly press his sweet lips against her own. And it was every bit as good as the fantasy.

When he stopped for breath, she came up for air with every intention of pushing him away, but instead she filled her lungs up with oxygen and let him do it again. His body was so warm and strong against her, his arms tight about her, but gentle, as if he were holding something precious and delicate. She drank in the smell of him: spicy aftershave and a hint of peppermint. And when the kiss came to a soft end, the words that came from his mouth made her gulp more than a salmon that had just jumped from a river onto a dry concrete block.

'Dawny Sole, you and I both know that you shouldn't be marrying anyone but me.'

'Don't say that.'

'But I am saying it.' Al's tender hands came up to her face and forced her to look at him. 'I wanted to kiss you once to see if you felt the same, and you do. I know you do.'

Dawn's knees were in danger of folding beneath her.

'Al, I think you're wonderful, truly I do,' she began, having to throttle back hard on the words that could have so easily pumped out from her vocal cords: *I love you too, I've tried so hard not to, but I do* . . . 'But let's not get carried away. This is like a holiday romance for you. You'll have forgotten me as soon as you get to the airport—'

'The hell I will!'

'We barely know each other.'

'Then come with me and let me find out all about you.'

'I can't give up everything I have,' said Dawn.

'What do you have? You're marrying a man you don't love, who doesn't like your music, who doesn't put a smile on your face, and all because you want to belong to a family. I know you an awful lot better than you think I do, Dawny Sole. You're filling up my heart, girl. I've never felt like this about anyone. It's knocked me off my feet and I've tried to ignore it but I can't and I don't want to.'

'Don't say any more, please.'

'One final thing, then I'll go,' he said. 'You think about what I've said. And let me tell you that you are one special woman. You are beautiful and you're funny and you have the voice of one smokin' angel. And I've been fighting against this but I can't do it any more without telling you what my heart is crying out for me to say. I want you, Dawny Sole, more than I've ever wanted anyone in my life.'

Dawn tore her eyes away from him. If only she was free, things would be so different. But she wasn't. This was so wrong. *But why does his body feel so right against me?*

Al stepped back. His hands left her shoulders.

'You have seven and a half days until I leave for London. You have seven and a half days to pack your suitcase, grab your guitar and come with me to live a life you know you want. Hell, it won't be a life of luxury, but you'll be singing and you'll be happy and you'll be loved more than you ever would be if you stayed.'

'Al—'

'Seven and a half days,' he cut in. 'I've said all I should say. It's not what I do, Dawny. I'm a decent man but I'm in love with you and if you don't come, then that will be my punishment for moving in on another man's woman.'

Then he leaned in and kissed her full on the mouth under the big moon, and afterwards big Al Holly walked away, leaving Dawn trembling like a leaf in a tornado.

At 5 p.m. on Saturday evening, Anna carefully laid the corset out on her bed. It was stunning. She had hardly been able to stop looking at it since she received it. It was all the intricacies that intrigued her: the hundreds of glittery dark beads, individually applied. Why? *She is worth it,* said that voice inside her head: a deep, East European voice with an impatient edge. She shivered with desire for him. But after tonight, who knew if she would ever see him again?

Her doorbell rang. It only ever went at this time of night because the gormless local pizza delivery service mixed up her house with next door.

But she was wrong. She opened the door to find the pièce de résistance present from Tony. Tony himself. Beaming, with his arms wide open and bearing a red rose in his mouth.

'Babe!' he said through clenched teeth. He whisked the rose into his hand and then under Anna's nose. She stood in stunned silence.

Over the past months, she had imagined many times what she would do at this point, and that was to throw herself gratefully into Tony's arms and cover his lying, cheating face with kisses of forgiveness while dragging him over her threshold. But now the moment was here, she didn't do anything of that sort at all, and no one was more surprised than she.

'Tony.'

'Yep, that's me, babe. Oh, I have missed you so much.'

His arms came about her and she almost staggered backwards with the force of his embrace. His familiar aftershave enveloped her, but it certainly wasn't travelling up her olfactory passages and making her knees knock now. He was cooing in her hair like an amorous pigeon. Then he pulled back from her and looked at her as if she had returned from a long absence.

'I've come back, babe. I've been an idiot. Let's go inside.'

He tried to push her backwards through the door.

'Whoa, Tony,' she said, extricating herself. If Tony got inside the house, she wouldn't get him out again. And she had her evening to think about. This was Vladimir's big night. She couldn't let him down.

Tony's eyebrows knotted in confusion. It was obvious he thought that five seconds after ringing her bell they'd be in bed, where he would continue to try and ring her bell. And, a few weeks ago, maybe they would have been. But now she was a woman worth sewing small beads on corsets for. Tony would need to appreciate that.

'I'm sorry but I'm going out tonight.'

'You're joking,' he said, lip curling with churlish disappointment. 'Cancel it. Life's just not been the same without you, babe.'

Her wounded ego had a smug moment. *He wants me more than Lynette Bottom.* But it was quickly overridden by the stronger desire to see Vladimir Darq again.

'No, I can't,' she said.

'But I've missed you so much, babe. Did you get my presents?'

'Yes, I got them,' said Anna. 'I was beginning to wonder what you were playing at after so long!'

Tony smiled that cheeky grin of his. 'I figured that if I didn't find them smashed up where I put them that you might still want me.'

That made sense. He was hedging his bets.

Anna rubbed her forehead. 'Tony, I can't think about this right now.'

'I'll come back later, shall I? That is, if you want me to . . . ' he said in such a way that intimated he was backing off already.

'Yes,' said Anna, her voice coming from a last vestige of the old-deserted-lonely Anna place within; but she didn't know if she truly wanted him to, or if it was just some automatic response.

'OK, I will then,' he replied, the grin flooding his face again.

She would sort all this out later, but now she needed to get ready. She wanted to be perfect for Vladimir.

'I don't know what time I'll be back,' she said.

'I'll be here at midnight. If you aren't here by then, I'll wait.'

Anna closed the door and thought, *You've won, girl! Tony is coming home.* So why wasn't every part of her body singing about it?

Half an hour later, she was staring at herself in the mirror and uttering expletives. Her hand was trembling so much that when she applied her eyeliner she might have been preparing to go to a fancy-dress party as a panda with a Goth fixation. She sighed, and grabbed the cotton wool and eye make-up remover in order to start again. Why did Tony have to come stirring up her life—today of all bloody days?

The doorbell sounded just as she was about to have another go at the eyeliner and she opened the door to four grinning and wonderfully familiar friends bearing cases and bags.

'We thought you might need some help getting ready,' said Christie. 'And looking at the state of your eyes, I think we were right.'

Dawn was all dolled up herself. She could stay only about an hour because she was setting off on her hen night, and helping Anna get ready was infinitely better than sitting at home waiting to be whisked off to Blegthorpe.

Dawn, firmly back in her hairdressing mode, curled and pinned Anna's hair into the most beautiful tower, leaving loose tendrils round her face.

'I was all fingers and thumbs to start with, then Tony turned up and made my nerves even worse!' said Anna. She had filled them in on the details of her recent visitor.

'Have you decided what you're going to do?' asked Raychel.

'I'm trying not even to think about it,' said Anna. 'I need to concentrate on Vladimir's ball first. Then when I come home I'll give Tony some head space.'

'You're very wise,' said Grace. 'This is an important evening for you and you deserve a wonderful time.'

While Grace popped the kettle on, Christie set to work on Anna's face. Raychel took over when it came to her eyes.

'Wow!' she approved proudly.

'Let me have a look,' pleaded Anna.

'Wait,' said Raychel. 'Lips first.'

'I've got five minutes left,' said Dawn when Raychel had sealed Anna's scarlet lipstick. 'Please put the frock on and let me see.'

'Have you tried it on already?' asked Christie.

'He said I hadn't to. He said it would fit.' Anna dropped her voice as if Vladimir was in earshot. 'I know it sounds daft, but I thought he'd be able to tell if I did.'

'Right, well, fingers crossed, everyone,' said Christie. Grace brought the dress in. It really was the most beautiful shade of blue.

'Your hooks and eyes are all skewwhiff,' said Christie, as Anna slipped off her robe to reveal the corset Vlad had made for her. 'How the heck did you think you'd manage on your own?'

'I know, I'm useless,' said Anna.

'No, you're not. You're just nervous,' said Dawn. 'I would be as well, everyone looking me up and down all night, no doubt. I bet there will be loads of professional models sticking their noses up at you.'

'Dawn, please shut up,' said Raychel.

'There, you're sorted!' said Christie. 'My goodness, how long did it take him to stitch all those beads on?'

'It's *so* Cinderella, isn't it?' said Raychel, clasping her hands excitedly.

'I don't know,' huffed Anna. 'If it is, it's a bit of a twisted version. Christie and Vladimir are both fairy godmothers and there's no Prince Charming. Well, there is but he's run off with the teenage Ugly Sister.'

They all laughed because it was impossible not to, the way Anna had said it. Then she stepped into the dress, which Grace and Christie lifted upwards. It skimmed over her hips and rested perfectly on her bust as she threaded her arms into the sleeves.

'Bloody hell,' said Dawn, her eyes as wide as the full moon hanging outside the window. 'I take it back. Those models won't be sticking their noses up at you, they'll be too busy turning lime-green with envy.'

A taxi beeped outside and Dawn's delighted smile dropped. She stood to go. 'That's got to be mine. I ordered one to take me down to the bus station. Can I leave my gear here?'

'Yes, of course you can. Go and have a great time,' said Anna.

'You'll have a better one,' she replied. 'You look gorgeous, Anna. Like a totally different woman from the one you were before your birthday. You're like a little bud in a vase that's suddenly become the biggest bloom of the bunch.'

Dawn gave Anna a small peck on the cheek. It was a sad little kiss, Anna thought.

'Now we'll let you see yourself in the mirror!' said Grace.

But Anna surprised them all. 'No, I don't want to see myself.'

'But you look gorgeous, Anna,' said Grace.

'You *feel* gorgeous, don't you?' said Christie with a knowing smile. 'And you're savouring that feeling, aren't you?'

'Yes, Christie,' nodded Anna. 'I couldn't possibly look as good as I feel at this moment.' It was so wonderful to be understood. By friends.

'Here are your shoes,' said Raychel, guiding Anna's toes into them. 'You are stunning, Anna. Dawn's right. You've blossomed before our eyes.'

For once, Anna didn't bat back the compliment; she accepted it wholeheartedly and said thank you. She didn't feel like Anna, the ordinary Barnsley sparrow. She felt like a golden, gorgeous phoenix, rising from the ashes of her former rubbish self-worth.

'Chuffing hell, I'm scared!'

'Don't be saying that tonight in illustrious company,' said Christie, packing her make-up away. Their job was done and now it was time to leave Anna to be picked up by her pumpkin coach.

'Remember, you were chosen to show off your inner siren,' said Grace. 'So let her out, girl. Oh, and, obviously, we want to know every last detail on Monday.'

'Goodnight, darling Anna,' said Christie. 'Have a ball.'

The car arrived, and when Anna stepped out into the night she saw the usually impassive chauffeur take a second and a third glance as he opened the door to let her in. It empowered her to think she might have cracked Mr Impenetrable and she grinned to herself.

Her new-found confidence bobbed temporarily as they turned into the drive at Darq House. As the Merc came up to the designated dropping-off point, a small part of Anna almost wanted to tell the chauffeur to keep driving and take her home. It was suddenly all very serious. Then she saw Vladimir wearing the most exquisite black suit and a moon-white shirt, with an extravagantly tied white cravat at the neck. His hair was loose, a magnificent midnight mane that made him look more vampiric and untamed and romantic than ever before. He came forward to open the door for her and he presented his hand for her to take. She pictured it on her breast, above her heart.

'Anna,' he said, 'good evening. You look . . . beautiful.'

Do I? she was about to say, until a stern voice stopped the words coming out of her throat. *Ah ha—yes, you do. Don't insult the man by inferring that his creation makes you look any less than fantastic.* 'I feel wonderful,' she said. 'It all fits like a glove.'

'Of course,' he said with haughty surprise.

He led her inside as if he were a crown prince and she were his chosen bride. She was aware of being watched and stared at and talked about, and she tried to stop blushing in case it melted her foundation. Then, as she entered, she realised why she was drawing so much attention, for, as well as being escorted in by the man himself, there—hanging from the gallery—was a *huge* poster of herself in a grainy film noir-type shot. It was black and white, the corset picked out in red, and underneath the words: *Every Woman has a Darq Side.* It was amazing.

'What do you think?' said Vladimir.

'I . . . er . . . I'm stunned,' said Anna quietly.

'That's because it is stunning,' he said. He turned to her. '*You* are stunning, Anna.'

Leonid wafted over with two glasses of champagne and pecked Anna on both cheeks.

Someone grabbed Vladimir's attention and he clicked his heels to be excused, in that military way of his.

'Anna Brightside,' began Leonid, with a kind softness to his voice she hadn't heard before, 'you make me so proud. You are a real woman. A lady. Vladimir will owe the success of the Darqone to you.'

'I hope it is successful for him,' smiled Anna. 'But the success will be down to his design alone. It's miraculous.'

'Yes, his order books are very full. I think he is not worrying. But you underplay your part.'

A wisp of a woman in the tallest heels Anna had ever seen in her life gushed at Leonid and did a left, right and left again cheek kiss. Anna recognised her immediately from magazines.

'Leonid, how marvellous to see you,' said Sticky-Thin Woman, smiling with a set of teeth that would have made a crocodile sick with envy.

'This is Oona Quince,' introduced Leonid.

'Yes, I know,' said Anna. 'Wow!'

The Supermodel nodded as if it was normal to hear such flattering exclamations attributed to her. Which it probably was. Anna felt obliged to say how beautiful she looked, which again seemed expected.

'Excuse me, please,' said Leonid, waving at someone and then disappearing. Anna watched him head towards a man wearing a silver tuxedo and greeting people very flamboyantly. When she turned around to Oona, it was to see a much colder-faced woman than the one who had been draped round Leonid not two moments ago.

'So you're Vlad's little pet project,' said Oona spikily, taking a swill from her champagne glass. Obviously not her first of the evening.

'I beg your pardon?' said Anna, smiling politely still.

'You're Vlad's temporary fixation. His *plat du jour*.'

'Am I?' Anna answered, trying not to rise to the bait. If Oona carried on bitching, she'd give her one good push and send her careering off her shoes.

'Enjoy it while you can,' Oona said, her eyes glittering with malice. 'He'll suck you dry and then discard you.'

And with that, Oona turned on her killer heels, switched on her barracuda smile and went off crying 'Dahling' at someone across the room.

Anna closed her agape mouth and started to giggle. Wow, she really must be getting up some noses! Fancy, Oona Quince bitching about her! How good was that? Anna took another sip of her champagne. She owed it to Vladimir to stay sober and dignified. Plus she could observe so much more that way. This was surely *the* place for people watching.

The room next to the great open reception hall was booming out disco music. A live band was playing at eleven million decibels. Leonid was heavily involved in conversation with Silver Jacket Man and Vladimir was chatting merrily to some people. She saw him glance over at her and wave. He made some tiny gesture that she knew meant, 'Are you OK?' and she nodded heartily back. She grabbed a canapé for something to do with her hands and ate and looked around. There were lots of tall, stunning women, who looked as if they had just stepped off glossy mag covers. There were also a lot of drop-dead gorgeous hunks too, with classical aquiline noses and Kirk Douglas chins. But none of them had the effect on Anna's knees that Vladimir Darq did when she caught sight of him in the crowd.

Oona had snatched another champagne flute and was hanging round Vladimir now, trying not to sway. She appeared to be trying to monopolise his attention and he rather expertly wasn't allowing that to happen. Which explained a few things, Anna thought with a wry smile.

By the time Dawn alighted from the minibus at Blegthorpe in her 'Last chance to shag me—I'm the Bride' T-shirt, she was the only one of the thirteen sober.

Demi's best mate, Sherideen, was the worst hit so far and had already vomited on her 'Little Hen Seeks Big Cock' T-shirt. Luckily, there were

454 | Milly Johnson

some spares on the bus that Demi had brought just in case anyone was
sick on themselves—how well she knew her crowd.

They weren't the only hen or stag party there. The town was heaving
with groups of women bearing L-plates and veils. Dawn tried to look
jolly only because she didn't want Denise or Demi scoffing at her for
being miserable, but she could think of better ways of enjoying herself
than carrying a giant inflatable knob round with her in a place she
didn't like, with people she didn't know.

Bette and Muriel were wearing big summer frocks that showed off
their bingo wings to best effect. Bette couldn't stand up for very long,
given her bulk, so she and Muriel found a cosy corner to sit in with
their pints of lager and lime. Luckily, most of the party were too far
gone even to remember Dawn's existence, something at least for which
she was grateful. Dawn watched her 'hens' dancing on tables and flirting with 'cocks'. She pressed her fingernail hard into the inflatable willy
and heard the air sigh out of it. She was so glad that she had told the
girls in the office not to come. She would have been so embarrassed.

Two of the women were virtually unconscious by 2.30 a.m. and
Denise asked Dawn if she would mind ringing for the bus driver to pick
them up now instead of at 5 a.m. Dawn didn't mind at all; in fact she
was ecstatic, but she made a lot of 'Aw!' sounds for effect. She clam-
bered on the bus with them all and did a convincing job of saying what
a fantastic night she'd had and feigned being well tipsy. Even Bette and
Muriel were too drunk to notice that Dawn was stone-cold sober
and playacting her little heart out.

She thought of Al Holly and his proposal. But how could she just up
and leave her whole life to chase a dream? People like her didn't up and
cross the Atlantic with just a guitar and a few pairs of clean knickers
with a man they barely knew. They did nine-to-five jobs and married
men who never put their dirty washing in the laundry bin and had a
perfunctory bonk on Saturday nights and dreamed of lives they weren't
ever brave enough to chase.

Dawn wished she had got drunk after all.

Anna also was stone-cold sober. A few times she had seen Vladimir
about to come over to her, only to be snatched back by someone. He
was a victim of his own success, tonight more than ever. At least she
had the big dog, Luno, for company. He had wandered over when
she flashed a miniature Yorkshire pudding canapé at him. Surprisingly,
he had stayed hanging round her when he had eaten it, settling at her
side with his big head on his shaggy paws.

'You're the girl on the poster, aren't you?' boomed a raucous voice in her ear. She turned round to see a presenter from the *Morning Coffee* breakfast show. *What the hell was his name?*

'Tony Barrett,' he offered, right on cue, holding out a big meaty hand. Of course: *Tony.* How could she forget? 'I had to come over. I think you look absolutely fantastic.'

'Oh, thank you,' said Anna, relieved to be talking to someone.

'And you're even nicer in the flesh! I don't think Vlad could have picked anyone more perfect,' said Tony, leaning in a bit too close and looking down her top. It seemed he had the same charm offensive as the other Tony. He'd probably ask her for a shag with his next breath.

'Well, that's very kind of you to say so,' said Anna, pulling back to give herself some space.

'I'd like to have you on the show. Are you up for that?'

'Sounds great!' smiled Anna, as he fell forward onto her and knocked the remainder of her drink down her dress. Luckily there wasn't much in her glass and it was stain-free champagne, but it gave Tony the excuse to wipe his hand down her front apologetically. It felt like the grope it was. Anna stepped away from his hand politely.

'Anna, come, I need you,' said a welcome voice at her side. Leonid. 'Tony, go away.'

Tony shrugged his shoulders and moved off, knocking into the lady with the canapé tray and sending a couple of mini-quiches Luno's way.

'He's a horrible man,' said Leonid. 'He tries to get anything into bed. Vladimir sent me to say he's so sorry you are on your own so much. You are such a great success.'

'No, he's the success,' said Anna. 'I'm just the shop-floor dummy.'

'He will be with you shortly,' said Leonid, tutting at her self-denigration and giving her a gentle slap on the bottom. 'Don't move.'

He replaced the empty glass in her hand with a full one, and moved off.

She looked across at Vladimir in his gorgeous suit and starched white shirt again, and something definitely happened to her heart that wasn't supposed to happen. He was so charming and at ease with his crowd. But this was his world, after all, and not hers. He was glitz and glamour and chauffeur-driven Mercs. She was a Barnsley woman whose idea of exciting fashion before she met Vladimir Darq had been a sale on in Dorothy Perkins.

Her work here was done. She belonged in Ordinary World and she needed to get back to it sooner rather than later, because complications were already setting in. She was in mortal danger of falling in love and could only get hurt. Yes, he had awoken her inner siren. The trouble was, that siren wanted him. He had lifted her so high she wasn't sure if normal life was possible any more.

It was time to go home and face Tony. She would listen to what he had to say and then decide what she wanted. What *she* wanted.

She took a last look at the beautiful room decorated with giant moons and stars against black velvet drapes and buzzing with music, chatter and stunning people. She raised her glass in Vladimir Darq's direction and took a long sip of champagne.

Good luck, Vladimir. I wish you everything that makes you happy.

Anna patted Luno's big head, then slid out through the front door where the complimentary taxis were waiting. She thought no one had noticed she was gone.

The taxi driver didn't take much of a detour but, as they rounded the corner for Courtyard Lane, Anna saw Vladimir Darq standing by her front door in the moonlight.

'How . . . how did you get here so fast?' was her first breathless question to him when she had got out of the taxi, followed by the second: 'Why are you holding a blue stiletto?'

He held the shoe out to her.

'You dropped this, running away from my ball, Cinderella.'

Anna lifted her dress up so Vladimir could see her feet, both with a shoe on them.

'No, I didn't,' she said.

'Oh, goodness,' he said, rubbing his forehead. 'I found it by the cars. I presumed . . . Someone is going to be rather angry with me then.'

'Hopping mad,' said Anna with a smile.

'Why did you go, Anna?' He pronounced her name as always, more Ah-na, than Anna. Like a sigh.

'Oh, Vladimir, why do you think?' said Anna, with a loaded sigh of her own. 'Look at me. Look at where I live!' She pointed backwards at the small house. 'It's a terrace in the middle of Barnsley. I work in an office. I don't jet off to Milan. I don't have friends who are pop stars. You've made me feel wonderful. Now I have to be wonderful in my own world.'

'You could go to Milan and mix with pop stars.'

'Yeah, course I cou—Mw!'

She had no chance to finish her sentence because Vladimir Darq cleared the distance between them in a nanosecond, seized her roughly in his arms and stifled her words with his lips.

Good God, her brain said on behalf of her mouth, which was otherwise engaged. His arm was round her waist, his other pulling her hair back and stretching out her throat to him. They looked like a Mills and Boon cover. One entitled: *Yours to Devour.*

Chuff, he's going to kill me! she thought. Quickly followed by, *And I don't care!* His lips smudged along her jugular, setting off dormant fireworks on her nerve endings.

She could see his black hair, taste him on her lips, smell the wonderful alpha-male cologne he wore, hear him breathe, feel his strong body pressing against hers . . . She wished only that she had a load more senses with which to experience him because five didn't seem enough. His voice vibrated against her neck saying, 'Anna, you drive me crazy. I want you so much. You do belong to my world. You belong to me.'

This couldn't be happening. She'd had too much champagne and was hallucinating. Could you hallucinate on two glasses though?

Then he straightened her up and looked deep into her eyes.

'I have guests. I have to go back. Tomorrow, at eleven in the morning, I will come for you. I will show you the true world of Vladimir Darq.' He lifted her hand and kissed the back of it, then once again he planted a long, sensuous kiss on her lips. He drew apart from her slowly, torturously, leaving Anna bathing in the aftershock, afraid to open her eyes and see him go.

When she opened them, he was no longer there. What did he mean by 'his true world'? she mused. Was he going to show off the his-and-hers coffins in the basement? The bottles of maidens' blood in his cellars?

She stood there sighing like something out of a Hollywood musical, thinking she would never sleep tonight, not in a million years, when she heard the low rumble of an approaching car. *Tony.* She'd forgotten about him. She'd actually forgotten about him. Half an hour ago, she'd been ready to listen to his excuses, but after that kiss there was no way on this planet that was going to happen.

'Anna! Wow! I didn't recognise you for a minute there. You look amazing. Is it really you? Wow!'

He jumped out of the car and she immediately noticed the suitcases on the back seat.

'I'm early, babe,' he said. 'And so are you. Couldn't wait, huh? Me neither. That dress is fantastic on you. I can't wait to see it on the bedroom floor. Come here, I have missed you so much.' He came forward, arms open wide to enclose her, but she held up an arresting palm.

'Tony.' She couldn't think of anything else to say then but, 'No.'

He froze, arms still open. 'No? What do you mean—*no*?'

'I don't want you back.'

'Oh, come on,' he said, still hanging on to that smile. 'You know you do. That's why you told me to come back at midnight.'

'I didn't tell you. You volunteered,' Anna corrected him.

'Ah—I see. You're playing hard to get!'

'No, I'm not. You'll have to go back to Lynette.'

'I can't,' he said. 'I mean, I don't want to. I want you, not her.'

'Tony, I don't want you.'

'You do. That's why you kept my gifts. Let's go in and talk about it.'

'No,' said Anna, holding up that palm again. 'I don't want you to come inside. I don't want you, Tony. It's over.'

He was still smiling as if he didn't believe her. That was until the sound of a second car's screeching tyres cut through the night air and a pink Fiat Punto ground to a halt about a gnat's leg's length away from Tony's bumper. His smile dropped like a brick then.

'I knew you'd be here, you two-timing twat,' said a very angry, scarlet-faced Lynette Bottom, leaping out onto the pavement. Then Lynette looked at the glamorous woman in blue velvet and her face creased up with confusion and embarrassment. Then she did a double take and realised it *was* Tony's ex-girlfriend after all. Blimey! She pulled her cardigan round her, feeling very dull and scruffy by comparison.

'Well, you can have him,' said Lynette through hot, angry tears. 'He's bloody useless at anything that doesn't involve a pair of scissors and a comb. Like—in bed!'

'Oi!' said Tony.

'Did he tell you I thought I was pregnant last month?'

Anna's breath caught in her throat. 'No, he didn't.'

'You're not pregnant,' said Tony.

'No, but I thought I was and I told you I might be,' said Lynette, twisting round to him. 'And where were you while I was at the doctor's? Sniffing back round here, weren't you, you . . . you . . . arsehole.' She stabbed a finger at Anna. 'Well, you're welcome to him. The bastard left me a note saying, "I need a break" and "There's no one else" and then he crept out, thinking I wouldn't notice. But I saw him loading his suit-cases into the car because his leaving technique is as shite as his foreplay. And I knew he'd slither back here! Have him, he's yours!'

'Thank you for your generous offer, Lynette, but sadly, I must decline,' said Anna, with more control than she could have thought possible. 'Good night to you both. Tony, I'll be in touch about splitting the assets.' From the scream she heard after unlocking the door and shutting it behind her, she thought Lynette might have started splitting Tony's assets already.

Chapter 14

ELIZABETH HELD in her hand the letter that her sister had written to her giving her directions to the hostel where she was staying. She hadn't told Raychel that she had written to Bev, or that she had replied, or that Bev was expecting her daughter to visit her. Elizabeth was trying to remain calm but it was so very difficult. Thank goodness John was driving. He was, clichéd as it was, her rock. He always had been. She was so glad her niece had a rock in Ben, too.

She closed her eyes. She wasn't sure what she would feel when she saw Bev. The monster who had both beaten her own child and stood aside while her boyfriend did the same was also the little girl she had heard crying in her bedroom when they were kids because their dad was an abuser. She didn't know which Bev she would see when Bev opened her door.

The satnav announced that when they turned this corner they would have reached their destination.

'I'll come in with you,' said John.

'No, wait here,' said Elizabeth. 'It's not exactly the sort of area you'd want to leave a nice car anyway.'

'It's not exactly the sort of building I want my wife walking into by herself,' said John adamantly. 'I'll at least see you to Bev's door.'

Elizabeth didn't protest. John would want to see she was safely in. And her nerve was failing by the second.

The entrance area was all cheap wood panelling and a stab at cheering up the walls with some tacky pictures hanging up in plastic frames. There was a serving hatch in the wall, presumably 'Reception'. Through it, Elizabeth could see a woman sitting with her back to the hole, listening to an iPod and watching a portable TV at the same time.

'Hello,' John called through it, getting her attention by hammering on the hatch frame. 'We've come to see Marilyn Hunt.'

'Top floor, room eight,' said the woman, giving him her briefest attention before turning back to the TV again.

'Obviously a very secure hostel,' said John in a whisper.

They walked up a very bare, narrow, twirly staircase three floors up till they got to the top. Elizabeth's heart was racing. She geed herself up, lifted her knuckles and rapped hard. There was the sound of some activity behind the door, then it opened and there stood the sister she hadn't seen since she was a child, the sister she had cried buckets' worth of tears for, searched for, prayed for. She would not have recognised the bloated bleach-blonde who looked so much older than her years. Only in her grey eyes was a hint of the Bev she once knew.

The two women stood staring at each other, unable to move.

'Elizabeth?'

'Yes, it's me.'

'Where's Lorraine?'

'Let's go inside,' replied Elizabeth. 'John, you can go now.' He nodded at her and went slowly back down the stairs.

Bev moved aside to let Elizabeth into her room.

'It's a dump, I know, but it's only a temporary place,' Bev said, gesturing towards the room with some embarrassment.

'It doesn't matter. I didn't come to see where you live.'

'Is she here? Will she be coming up in a bit?'

'She isn't, no.'

It was a functional, basic space but it was immaculately clean. There was a double bed standing along the left wall, and a table, chair and old sofa tarted up with a red throw under a sloping Velux window. To the right, an old walnut wardrobe, bashed pine drawers, and a run of three kitchen cupboards, two drawers and a small, shiny stainless-steel sink.

Bev went over to switch the kettle on.

'Can I get you a drink?'

'Not for me, thanks,' said Elizabeth.

'It's been a long time, hasn't it?' said Bev awkwardly. She was shivering as if she was cold and pulled her cardigan tighter and defensively round her. 'How did Lorraine find you? Is she well?'

'She's well,' was all Elizabeth could manage to respond. She had planned for days what she was going to say to Bev, but the script had been torn up and Elizabeth could no longer predict how she would react in front of 'Marilyn'.

'I don't know what to say to you,' Bev said quietly.

'Me neither,' said Elizabeth, in a much colder voice.

'I need to talk to my daughter, though,' said Bev. 'I need to see her.'

'Talk to me instead. She doesn't want to see you, Bev.'

'She wrote and—'

'I wrote that letter. I wasn't sure you'd agree to see me.'

'Oh.'

'She told me everything and I can't say that I blame her for not wanting to come.'

'I'd hoped she would see me, just one time. I know she wouldn't want to see me any more than once. I don't blame her for that. I wanted to say I'm sorry. For everything I've done to her.'

'You could say that by letter and spare her the face-to-face ordeal.'

'I was doing it for her. I thought she might want . . .' Bev stumbled. She took a big breath. 'I thought she might want to pay me back.'

'What—you wanted her to come here and slap you?'

Bev shrugged. 'Or scream at me. Whatever she needed to do.'

'She's not a vengeful person. She's a wonderful, kindhearted girl.'

'I made so many mistakes with her.'

Marriage and motherhood had softened Elizabeth but at that moment she felt once again like the feral teenager she used to be. 'Mistakes? That's putting it finely, isn't it? How could you? How could you let all those things happen? To your own child?'

'Do you know what happened to *me* as a child? You haven't a clue what I went through.'

'Yes, I do,' said Elizabeth. 'I know what you went through because Dad started on me when you'd gone!'

Bev's mouth dropped open. 'I'm sorry about that,' she said at last. 'I didn't know.'

Elizabeth laughed without the slightest bit of humour. 'Well, you wouldn't, would you? Because you left me to it. Didn't it cross your mind he would try and do to me what he'd done to you? You could have told someone about him when you left, just in case, but you didn't.'

Elizabeth thought back to the pale-faced, moody sister whom she used to tease, not knowing that their father was abusing her. For years, she had punished herself for not realising, for being too young to help.

'I can't turn the clock back but I wish more than anything I could. I used to take a lot of drink and drugs,' said Bev, not meeting her sister's eyes, 'and I'm not trying to use that as an excuse.'

'It isn't an excuse,' Elizabeth butted in.

'No, it isn't. Everything was my fault. I'm clean now. I got myself sorted when I came out of prison. It's taken me a few years, mind. I'm leaving here next week. I've got a little council flat.'

'That's good,' said Elizabeth quietly.

'I can't ever make up for what . . . what I let happen to her. And the other one. The drugs killed her. I couldn't stop taking them. I've had to face the fact that I killed my own child, did Lorraine tell you?'

'Yes,' said Elizabeth.

Bev sank onto the sofa and twiddled nervously with her necklace. 'I've been so scared of meeting Lorraine again. I . . . I felt I had to, though. But I didn't know how to say it.'

'I'll tell her that you're sorry,' said Elizabeth. She wanted to hate this pathetic woman but she couldn't quite manage to.

'It's not just that. There's more.'

'What?' asked Elizabeth, as Bev's face dropped into her hands and she sighed 'Oh God,' over and over.

'Do you remember the Siddalls at school? Charlene Siddall was in my class. She had a twin brother, Michael.'

'I remember them,' replied Elizabeth. She knew of the Siddalls: a rough, large family. The name still cropped up in the *Barnsley Chronicle*, usually connected with drugs and fights and shoplifting.

'I had sex with Michael Siddall,' Bev went on.

'What's this got to do with Ra . . . Lorraine?'

Bev took in a long fortifying breath, but the cruel secret she had kept for over twenty-eight years came out with a whisper.

'He could be Lorraine's dad. I don't know for sure, but he may be.'

'What?'

'When she was a baby, she had the look of him. Tell her I'm sorry.'

Bev began to cry softly into her hands as Elizabeth tried to process that information: that Raychel might not be a child of an illicit union, that she might be able to have children of her own after all.

'Why didn't you tell her that before?' Elizabeth couldn't get to grips with this at all.

'I was a different person then. I was hurt and I wanted to hurt back.'

Then Elizabeth knew. Bev had wanted to hate and punish her daughter for what she herself had gone through. It was so twisted.

Elizabeth covered the distance between them in two strides and, lifting Bev by the edges of her cardigan, she crashed her back into the wall.

'You told a little bairn that her father was her granddad when you didn't know for sure? What kind of an animal are you?'

Bev shrieked but she didn't try to defend herself. 'I know, I know, I'm sorry I did that. I'm sorry I left you, too. I'm sorry I ran off and didn't tell anyone for you.' She was flinching, waiting for the slap that didn't come. But Elizabeth released her grip. There was nothing to be had from more violence. She had seen enough of that.

'I'll tell her what you've said,' said Elizabeth, calming herself. She wanted to go home now and work out how she was going to put this all to Raychel. There was just one more thing she had to do: the reason why Elizabeth had come to face her sister. She reached inside her bag and pulled out a cheque, which she forced into Bev's hand.

'When Dad died, I sold his house. I put the money in an account for you in case I found you. I never touched a penny of it.'

Bev looked at her cheque blankly. Then, slowly, her hand extended towards Elizabeth. 'I don't want it.'

'You have read that cheque correctly, haven't you? There's over forty thousand pounds in that account and it's all yours.'

'I can read. But I don't want it. Take it back.'

'You're turning it down?' asked Elizabeth disbelievingly. 'No one turns that sort of money down.'

'You obviously did. You would have used it otherwise,' said Bev.

Elizabeth moved towards the door. She had done what she came for. But the sound of tearing paper halted her step.

'It isn't mine,' said Bev, still holding the cheque, which was now in eight pieces. 'I don't want that sort of money. I live simply and without any complications. It's taken me a long time to get to this stage.'

Elizabeth still didn't look convinced.

'Please, Elizabeth,' implored Bev. 'Give it to Lorraine. Just don't tell her it came from *him*. Tell her something else, something nice,' Bev went on. 'Don't tell her I gave it to her. That would tie us together and we don't belong together. She needs to be free of me. Please. That's why I wanted to see her today. One last time.'

Elizabeth saw then that Bev meant every word.

'I'll do as you ask.' Elizabeth opened the door to go.

'Elizabeth.' Bev's voice came out small and cracked. It was the long-ago voice Elizabeth remembered of her sister. It dragged her back to the past and tears stabbed behind Elizabeth's eyes.

'Just tell me, she is happy, isn't she?'

'Yes,' nodded Elizabeth. 'She's happy.'

'I'm glad. Goodbye, Elizabeth.'

'Goodbye, B—Marilyn. Good luck.'

'You too.'

Vladimir Darq was a man who considered himself blessed. He had been born to kind and loving parents, and Vladimir Senior had wanted more than a lifetime in the mines for the son who had an amazing artistic talent and who loved to stitch with his seamstress mother. Alas, his parents had not lived to see their son catapulted to the A-list of the fashion world.

Vladimir was the dark darling of designers. The paparazzi adored him, reporters courted him, models tried to bed him and the young Vladimir had woken up many a morning with a beautiful woman beside him. To the outside world, Vladimir Darq had everything. Almost. For in his heart he was still a simple boy from Romania, craving the love and family warmth sadly lacking from his dynamic career.

Seeing Anna at the train station that night had lit something within him. He couldn't explain why the sight of the sad woman with the long chestnut hair had the effect on him that it did. He saw her potential as *the* model for his intended project. But it was more than that for him. Something primal within recognised a connected soul. A fellow being who needed love and to love. Her vulnerability called out to him and his heart answered.

Week by week, he watched Anna bloom, and the smell of her creamy skin almost drove him mad with lust. It took every reserve of strength to keep his lips away from it.

And at the Full Moon Ball, he had wanted the crowds to disperse early and for there to be only he and Anna left. He had planned to lead her out onto his balcony and dance with her in the moonlight. He wanted it to be romantic and lovely for her. He wanted to tell her as they waltzed under the stars that he had fallen in love with her. He wanted her to tell him she felt the same.

He had raced to her house when he discovered she had left. He could no more have stopped that kiss happening than he could have held back a flood. But was it just a kiss for her?

He was actually shaking with nerves as he got in the car to pick her up the next morning.

The wedding rehearsal went ahead after the morning's Sunday church service. There was a slight holdup while both bridesmaids were sick in the graveyard. The groom had only one eyebrow. The other had been shaved off when he was tied naked to a lamppost in Wakefield town centre. He was exceedingly quiet and well behaved during the rehearsal.

As he looked at his future bride by his side, Calum Crooke realised what a good lass he had in Dawn. He had woken up that morning next to Mandy Clamp—his final fling, as arranged by his mates. But Mandy Clamp was a total slapper and not worth risking losing Dawn for. He looked at Dawn, smart in a summer frock, her long red hair tied behind her and her face all nicely made up, and compared her to his sisters, zombie-white and swaying in jeans and knock-off designer tops. His mother, in her omnipresent flip-flops, was pushing them into position and swearing at them in a whisper that really was anything but, and he thought that it was no wonder he went for Clampesque women, because it was all he'd ever known, until Dawn came into his life. She'd worked so hard and he'd been less than helpful. And standing in church then, he felt true shame that he was the sort of man who'd thought it was big and clever to deceive her. When they were married, he was going to make sure he tried very hard to keep it in his trousers.

Vladimir looked grim-faced as he pulled up outside her house and Anna half expected he was going to tell her that he was a bit drunk last night and hadn't meant to kiss her. She stiffened her spine in readiness for a confrontation, but then Vladimir got out of the car, crushed her violently in his arms and planted such a kiss on her lips that she thought if his fangs sank in her throat she would happily bleed to death there in front of the neighbours.

'It's daylight,' she said, with the little bit of breath that he spared her. 'Won't you turn to dust?'

'God save us from story writers,' said Vladimir. 'Get in the car.'

She gladly did as she was told and was driven to Darq House, which an army of cleaners had miraculously restored to its magnificent gothic glory. He showed Anna round his home, his world. He introduced her to the extravagantly sized kitchen fridge, which thankfully had a Marks & Spencer's minced beef pie and a jar of Hellmann's mayonnaise in it, as well as Cristal champagne and Italian white truffles. He took her into the cavernous sitting room with a massive TV, DVDs and CDs lining the shelves on the wall, and the biggest, squashiest sofa ever. He showed her the bathrooms, his office, a storage cupboard full of dog food and rooms stacked high with material and sewing machines. There were no coffins, no bottles of virgins' blood, no Black Mass altars.

Then Vladimir Darq took Anna Brightside upstairs to his gothic bed-room, where he threw her down on his four-poster, pinned her there in the shape of a crucifix and did all manner of unholy things to her.

'**B**loody hell, have you had plastic surgery?' said Dawn to Anna as she swaggered in like Mae West the next day. 'You look about twenty years younger than you did on Saturday when we left you—and you only looked about nineteen then!'

Everyone turned to the phenomenon that was Anna, with her fresh face and sparkling eyes. Even her hair seemed more alive, falling in chestnut curls round her face and bobbing when she moved, as if she were straight out of an old Harmony Hairspray advert.

'I don't know what you mean,' said Anna with a smug grin.

'Emergency meeting, I think,' said Christie, switching her phone to voicemail and leading the way down to the canteen.

'**D**id you see Spatchcock's face as we walked past his desk?' said Raychel.

'I don't care what that twerp thinks of me or any of us,' said Christie.

'I hate him,' said Dawn. 'I never liked him before, but after what he tried to do to Grace, I doubly hate him.'

Anna was last to the table with her cappuccino. The others were waiting for her to begin and so she teasingly said in a very slow voice, 'Once upon a time . . .'

'You are so dead if you don't hurry up,' said Dawn.

'Well, I was standing by myself for most of the evening, to be honest, sharing canapés with the dog—'

'Tell us about that bit later,' said Christie, rolling her hand as if to fast-forward to the juicy bits.

'—So I came home early but Vladimir followed me and kissed me good night and then he collected me from my house yesterday morning and I spent most of the day with him.'

'Doing what?'

'We watched a film, he cooked me dinner—'

'And? You witch!' said Dawn.

'We listened to music, then—'

'Anna!'

'—Then Vlad impaled me—'

'Hallelujah!' said Grace and they all gave Anna a round of applause.

'Did Tony come back?' asked Dawn.

'Oh, yes.'

'I hope you told him what to do.'

'More or less,' said Anna.

'And how did your hen night go?' said Christie, turning to Dawn. She worried about Dawn.

'Awful,' said Dawn. 'But we had the wedding rehearsal yesterday and Calum was . . . like a new bloke. It was so odd. He didn't go out to the pub or drag me to his mother's for lunch. He wanted it to be just me and him.' *He was like he was at the beginning*, she added to herself.

'He'll be getting into wedding mode,' said Grace.

'So the countdown begins?' said Anna.

'Yes, it does,' said Dawn. The countdown clock to her wedding was ticking loudly now, but the one that was tocking for Al Holly boarding a bus with his suitcases was so much louder.

To celebrate the bride-to-be's hen night that Friday night, they went to the Thai restaurant as they had for Anna's birthday. And they raised a glass of champagne to Dawn, each wishing with all their hearts that she knew what she was doing. For once, Dawn was trying awfully hard to bubble about her wedding, saying how lovely her dress was and that her bridesmaids had promised to stay sober, at least through the ceremony. She looked unnaturally cheerful.

'Did you manage to get a honeymoon sorted out then?' said Grace, pouring the last of the champagne into Dawn's glass.

'No,' said Dawn. 'Calum's going to take some time off next month and we'll see about getting a weekend away in Butlins or something.'

'Have you said goodbye to your cowboy?' said Anna.

That did it.

Dawn's head fell into her hands and she broke into agonised sobs.

'Oh, Dawny,' said Anna.

That made it worse. *He* called her Dawny. And he was going tomorrow. For good. Out of her life.

Christie's hand gripped hers. 'You know, if you're at that church door tomorrow and you don't want to go through with the wedding, we'll all be there to support you. You don't have to be afraid.'

'I'm sorry,' said Dawn. She lied about the reason for her tears and fooled no one. 'It's just with Mum and Dad not being there. They so wanted me to have the big white wedding.'

'Darling, I'm sure your mum and dad would just want you to be happy, with or without a meringue frock,' said Grace. She above all knew how hard a loveless marriage could be.

'I will be happy,' Dawn said. 'I promise.'

Al Holly was having a drink at the bar when Dawn went in later. His back was broad and long and she wanted to press her cheek against it and feel its warmth through his black shirt.

He sensed her presence, turned round and gave her a smile. Not the usual lazy smile that lit up his whole face but a reserved, gentle one.

'Dawny Sole, you came,' he said. 'I thought maybe—'

'I came. To say goodbye,' she said, the words sticking to her throat on their exit as if they were barbed and hooked. 'I wouldn't have not come.'

'The bus leaves here at three p.m. tomorrow. You got'—he looked at his watch—'eighteen hours to change your mind and come with us. Girl, I would love you so much—'

'Don't say it, Al.'

His lips dropped to her ear.

'I love you, Dawny Sole. And you love me, too, because I kissed you and I felt your heart against mine and I *know*. Come home with me.'

'I can't.'

He kissed her cheek. A slow, soft kiss that ignited every cell, every nerve, every atom in her body. She would always remember that kiss as the saddest and most beautiful one she ever had.

'Goodbye, dear, lovely, sweet Al Holly. Be happy and safe always,' she said and turned, not looking back once, for then he would have seen the tears streaming down her face.

Chapter 15

'COME HERE, YOU SCRUFF. You've fastened up your buttons all wrong,' said Ben, pulling Raychel none too gently in front of him and redoing the top two buttons of her new shirt.

'Good job I have you,' Raychel laughed. While she was at the wedding, he was helping John put up a playhouse in the garden for young Ellis. She suspected John could have easily done it by himself, but he obviously wanted the young man's company. It was wonderful being part of such a lovely family. And having friends like the women she worked with. And she'd had a huge surprise when Elizabeth handed her a cheque for forty-two thousand pounds, apparently her share in some old forgotten family matured bonds that had been recently discovered. She had protested, but Elizabeth had insisted the money was hers by rights and forced her to take it. There was a lot of sunlight in her life now and just the one cloud left to clear—the identity of her true father. But today that thought was pushed into second place. Today was Dawn's Day.

'Flaming heck, it's like a holding pen for *The Jeremy Kyle Show* in here,' said Anna as they sat alone on the bride's side of the church.

The four women were all watching in amazement as the groom's side of the pews began to fill up with big women in gaudy dresses and scrawny teenagers, a few in smart trousers, most in jeans and trainers and even a few in hooded tops.

'Shh, Anna,' said Christie. 'The sound carries in these places.'

'Did you remember the money, Christie?' asked Raychel. They'd had a collection for Dawn instead of buying her a present.

'It's here in my handbag,' said Christie, patting her bright-yellow bag. She was dressed from head to foot in lemon and looked like walking sunshine. Which, coincidentally, was how the others saw her: a warm, wonderful force. Their centre.

Grace let her eye rove round the church. It was a beautiful building. She would be sitting here again within the year, watching Charles and Laura walk down the same aisle. They, and Paul, had come over on Thursday to break the wonderful news. Christie had opened a bottle of champagne and the women had sat on the patio watching Charles and Paul and Niki playing football with Joe. Like Christie, warmth seemed to ooze out of Niki's soul. It had been one of the smiliest evenings she could remember. It wasn't even sullied by the sad news that Sarah had decided to cut herself off from them, siding with her father. But then she didn't need them any more for baby-sitting duties, it seemed, as Hugo had invested in an au pair from the Eastern bloc. Very young, cheap to employ and pretty no doubt. Paul said that he could see trouble brewing already. Grace hoped Sarah would come round and had written her a letter. Maybe the new baby would help to heal the rift when it arrived. And Gordon would be out of hospital within the week, too, apparently, Paul carefully informed her. Grace had found she wasn't as nervous about that as she thought she might have been. But then she felt truly safe now, especially in the presence of solid, kind Nikita Koslov and his wonderful sister.

'Good grief!' said Anna as what could only be the groom's mother marched to the front of the church in huge pink trousers, an ill-matching pink jacket and a black hat that looked like a castoff from a funeral. She resembled an extra on *Shameless*.

The groom was easy to spot with his one eyebrow. He had a smart penguin suit on with a peach cravat. He looked designer-untidy and good-looking but not at all like they had imagined as a match for Dawn.

'I want to hijack Dawn at the door and run off with her,' said Anna.

'We may all be wrong, of course, and she'll be blissfully happy with him,' said Grace.

'Yeah, and the moon is made of Red Leicester,' said Anna.

Raychel wasn't sure if she should have been praying for Dawn to come to her senses and run off with that Canadian guitarist, but she did, anyway, in the silence.

Then the organ music started full pelt and with hearts full of all sorts of mixed emotions, the four friends stood and turned to see a veiled Dawn, a beautiful, tall Dawn in an exquisite gown and carrying a teardrop bouquet of peach flowers, walk slowly down the aisle. Tears came to their eyes. They tried not to look at the two bridesmaids in satsuma orange behind her, one with her cleavage pushed so up and out that it almost got to the altar before the bride.

They saw Dawn smile at them through the veil. It was the smile of a woman saying, 'Thanks for coming,' not a smile that said, 'This is the happiest day of my life.'

As she got to the altar, Dawn smiled at Calum but inside she was screaming. There was nothing for it now but to go ahead and get married because if she hadn't been brave enough or big enough to halt proceedings before, she wasn't going to be able to do it at this stage. If only someone else would do it for her. *Pleeease!*

'If anyone here prethent knowth why the two thould not be joined in holy matrimony, thpeak now or for ever hold your peath,' lisped the vicar.

There were a few coughs from the groom's side.

Had Dawn's four friends looked down, they would have seen that all of them had their fingers crossed. Each one was wishing or praying or calling to cosmic forces that if this wedding was going to be happy, let it go ahead. And if not, *please God,* let something stop it in its tracks.

In that prolonged silence, Dawn waited for Al Holly to throw open the door, stride down the aisle, pick her up and run out. But he didn't. The vicar began to speak again. Calum and Dawn knelt at the altar. Someone had written 'SH' on Calum's left sole and 'IT!' on his right, which set a lot of shoulders shaking. But Dawn wasn't laughing. She had switched to automatic pilot, reciting vows that no longer meant anything to her.

The bride and groom exchanged the rings they had picked from the Argos catalogue and the church erupted as Calum and Dawn were declared man and wife. Her four friends exchanged glances. That was that then. Dawn was married. For better or worse. It was done. As the bride and groom went to sign the register with the tangerine twosome trotting behind, the music began for the hymn, 'Guide Me, Oh Thou Great Redeemer.'

Grace's lovely voice cut through the out-of-tune cacophony as clear as a nightingale's. It was her favourite hymn. Anna's throat was full of tears and she had to mime her singing. It didn't help that Dawn emerged emulsion-white from the vestry door as the hymn ended on a dodgy descant from some cocky Crookes. She couldn't have been wearing a more fake smile if she'd tried.

The Crookes piled out of the church for the photographs, a huge percentage of them lighting up fags as soon as they got into the grounds.

Christie drove in convoy with the others to the reception. The pub car park was full and she had to pull in on the road, but at least it would be easier to get out.

'I think there must be more people here than there were at Princess Di's wedding!' Grace commented.

'Yes, and I wonder how many of them Dawn actually knows,' replied Christie, accepting a small sherry from a waitress but passing on the 'canapés': a selection of Rubik's cube-sized pork scratchings, foot-long sausage rolls, potted beef sandwiches and sizzling-hot roast potatoes that took the fingerprints off anyone who happened to pick one up.

The diners were squashed at the tables. Anna's eyes found Dawn and saw that her meal was untouched. She looked like a Degas dancer on a Lowry background: totally and utterly out of place.

After the meal, when tar-strength coffee was served, Calum said that he wasn't one for speeches so he was just going to toast the bride, and that was it. The best man more than made up for it with embarrassingly near-the-knuckle stories of Calum's past love life that were meant to reassure the bride that Calum would never stray, but ended up doing quite the opposite, much to the amusement of the, by now, loud and swaying Crooke family and entourage.

People started to move into the main bar, Dawn included. She needed some air.

'Where are you off to?' said Muriel to the bride. 'I've got some aunties and uncles that I want you to meet.'

'I'm off to the toilet,' said Dawn. 'I'll be back soon.'

On the wall, outside the toilet, there was a full-length mirror. Dawn passed it, then doubled back and stared at herself. What looked back at her was the most miserable bride in the world, a truly unhappy woman. She looked again in the mirror and her eyes sprang open. She was going barmy. Her reflection was dressed in white and the colour wasn't draining her at all because she looked tanned and healthy. She had a simpler dress on, ballerina length, cowboy boots, a Stetson, and a waistcoat studded with rhinestones. Behind her was Al Holly, also in white. The smiles were bursting out of their faces because the couple in that mirror were in love. No woman should wear a wedding dress for a man she wasn't in love with and she knew she would never feel the way about Calum Crooke that she had grown to feel about Al Holly.

'Oh God, can I? Dare I?' she asked the bride in the mirror. The bride nodded. Dawn slipped out of the fire exit at the side of the toilet door and into the bright sunshine of the day.

At the other side of the car park, Dawn saw Anna, Grace and Raychel clustered round Christie, who was having a cigarette.

'Hello, love,' said Grace as the beautiful bride strode out towards them. 'Are you having a lovely day?'

'No,' said Dawn, desperately clutching at Grace's hands. 'Oh, girls, I've made the most dreadful mistake. Can you help me?'

'Are you serious?' said Christie.

'I've been pathetic, I know I have. I've married Calum because I was too scared to back out but I don't love him. I love Al Holly and he's asked me to go to Canada with him and I said no but I want to more than anything. Help me!'

Christie dropped her cigarette on the ground and killed it with her yellow heel. 'Right,' she said. 'We'd best get cracking then, hadn't we?'

They sprang into action like a well-oiled military elite force.

'Get in the car,' said Christie, fishing out her keys from her yellow handbag. 'Quick.'

They moved as one into Christie's BMW, Grace in the front, the other three squashed up in the back with Dawn's frock, which was so big it almost constituted another person. They did a totally synchronised belt-up and Christie slammed the automatic gear lever into drive.

'Where am I going? Direct me!' she said, looking in her rear-view mirror at the pub. Their exit hadn't been spotted, despite the squeal of her wheels as she took the corner like James Bond.

'Is that the time?' said Dawn, pointing to the clock on the dashboard.

'To the minute.'

'Oh Jesus. I'm going home first. Turn left here and follow. I'm picking up a suitcase, then I'm catching a bus.'

'Would this be a tour bus full of cowboys?' asked Raychel.

'Yes, it would.'

'Marvellous!' said Anna. 'What time does it leave?'

'I've got half an hour. Oh God, am I doing the right thing?'

'God knows!' said Grace. 'But you're young enough to take a chance, love. And anyone looking at your face over the past few weeks could tell you were doing the wrong thing.'

'I should have stopped this wedding months ago!' said Dawn, dropping her head into her hands.

'That's as may be,' said Grace. 'But you've stopped it now. We'd all be a lot wiser if we could visit our past selves.' As she knew only too well.

As if by magic, every traffic light either stayed or turned to green at their approach. Christie broke the speed limit but reckoned the risk of a fine would be worth it.

'Right, stop at the last house on your right!' commanded Dawn.

Christie screeched up to Dawn's front door. Raychel pulled Dawn out of the car because her frock was making it impossible for her to get out unaided. She was shaking too much to get the key in the lock so Grace snatched it from her and did the honours.

Led by Dawn, they flew up the stairs. Grace pulled two suitcases down from the top of the wardrobe. Anna emptied underwear drawers into them and threw clothes on top. Raychel was gathering shoes. Dawn's dress, by now, felt poisonous on her but there was no time to change.

'Where's your mobile and charger? Passport? Bank books? Make-up? Jewellery?' Grace said, thinking back to the important things she had needed to take from her own house.

Dawn opened a drawer and gathered up everything in it.

'It's all here!' she said.

She grabbed her two guitars from the side of her bed and said, 'That's it. I've got everything I need. Let's go.'

She didn't even give the house a backward glance as they set off like a rocket in the direction of the Rising Sun.

'So you're really going mad and doing it then?' said Raychel.

'Do you think I am mad?' said Dawn.

'I think this is the most sane you've been since I met you,' said Anna. 'Follow your heart, kiddo. Be brave.'

'Oh, and before we forget, here's your wedding present.' Christie fished in her pocket and dropped an envelope of cash into Dawn's lap. Then more fell on top of it as the girls emptied their purses onto her.

'No, I couldn't possibly—'

'Yes, you can, you'll need it,' said Grace.

'But it's a wedding present and I'm not really married.'

'It's for the next wedding.'

Dawn smiled a big wide arc that took up most of her face. Her whole heart seemed to swell up at the thought of getting married in cowboy boots. She knew she would. She'd seen it. She felt her mum and dad relaxing in heaven. They just wanted her to be happy and she jolly well was going to be. For all of them.

'Am I legally married now?'

'Yes,' said Christie. 'But I think you'll find it's voidable. Let a solicitor sort all that out for you. You just concentrate on being love's crazy-cowboy young dream.'

'I'll never be able to thank you all for this. I can't believe I'm doing it.'

'Better late than never,' put in Grace.

'We all want signed CDs when you record those albums,' said Raychel.

'I absolutely love you all to bits,' said Dawn. 'You've been like mothers and sisters to me. I'll miss you like hell.'

'We will miss you too,' said Anna. 'Oh God, now I'm filling up.'

'Hang onto your hats,' said Christie, stealing a look at the clock. It was showing 3 p.m. exactly and there was the tour bus in front, about to nudge out of the car park into the road.

Christie stamped her foot down on the accelerator, honking her horn like a madwoman, then she braced herself, hit the brake and her posh car skidded to a perfect stop alongside the bus.

'Oh, hell, I'm stuck!' shrieked Dawn. The car door handle was lost somewhere in the folds of her dress and her very big handbag.

Raychel had to jump out and open Dawn's door from the outside. Anna pushed Dawn and her giant frock out of the car.

Al Holly came bounding down the bus steps and froze as his feet hit the ground. His face bore all the signs of a man who thought he was hallucinating and if he moved the vision would disappear. Dawny Sole had thought she would fly into his arms but the opposite was true. She moved slowly towards him, her eyes locked on his. *How could I ever have thought I could live without him?* she asked herself.

'You're here,' he said in a croaky whisper. 'Is this a second goodbye?'

'No,' smiled Dawn. 'This is a great big fat hello.'

'Oh, Dawny.' His eyes glistened with emotion as his hand reached out to take hers, shyly, like a little boy and a little girl in the playground. 'I will make you so happy.'

'You'd better,' said Anna, lugging one of Dawn's suitcases.

'Hear hear,' laughed Raychel, struggling with the other case.

Samuel hopped out of the bus and jokingly muttered about women really being the weaker sex as he lifted the cases effortlessly on board.

'Take good care of her,' said Christie to Al.

'Yes, ma'am, I promise I will,' said Al Holly, wearing the soppiest grin a mouth could form into. He put his arm round Dawn and squeezed her into his side. They fitted perfectly together and between them they were giving out vibes that could have fried a passing egg.

Then Dawn leaped forward and hugged each one of her friends in turn. Big squashy hugs full of happy strength. She saved the biggest one for Christie.

'You've been wonderful,' she said. 'I'll never forget all you've done.'

'Be happy, my darling girl,' said Christie. 'Go and be loved and enjoy every minute of it.'

'Take care, I'll miss you so much,' Dawn beamed, blowing them all a big kiss. 'I love you all. I'll be in touch, I promise.'

'You better had be,' said Anna. 'You barmy cow.'

Al Holly took Dawn's hand and pulled her gently onto the bus. They saw Dawn's grinning face framed in one of the windows as the bus engine started up. The four women stood and watched it drive away and grow smaller as it travelled down the road. Their arms were sore from waving by the time it had disappeared.

'What now? Shall we go back to the Dog and Duck and get some cake?' said Anna with innocently raised eyebrows.

'Well, I don't know about you three, but I think a glass of champagne might be in order.'

'I've got no money,' said Anna. 'I gave it all to Dawn.'

Christie smoothly produced a Visa card from her bag.

'Who needs cash these days?' she said.

Epilogue

27 June—the following year

ANNA STOOD in the walled garden behind Darq House in a sumptuous black gown and closed her eyes. She pulled the fragrance from the red flowers that she carried into her lungs and sighed with contentment.

'You all right, love?' said Christie, dressed also in black, a much shorter ensemble with fancy ruffs at the sleeves and neck. Her own inimitable style. Even in black she looked colourful.

'Ohhh, yes,' said Anna.

'Such a beautiful day, too,' said Christie, tipping her head upwards. The sun was gently lowering, its edges melting into the blue of the sky.

Grace wended her way towards them, carrying a bottle of Dom Pérignon. Behind her, Raychel followed with four glasses. Both of them were in stylish black suits.

'Do you remember this date last year, we were drinking champagne then, too?' said Christie as Grace poured her a glass.

'When Dawny became Mrs Crooke.'

'And now she's Mrs Holly and singing her little heart out.'

They kept in regular touch and, thanks to the wonders of webcam, they could see that smile still bursting out at them from the screen.

'Beautiful ceremony,' said Grace, sipping the sparkly champagne.

'Absolutely!' said Raychel. 'And you look gorgeous, Anna.'

'Thank you,' smiled Anna. She felt gorgeous too. She was *only* in her forties and she was going to look back on this decade some day with the sure and certain knowledge that she had sucked it dry.

'There were some fantastic dresses in the congregation,' said Anna.

'Oh, hark at her! She's gone all fashiony already. She's only been Mrs Darq for two hours and she's turned into Zandra Rhodes.'

'Great idea having a black wedding,' said Raychel.

'Aye well, that's what happens when you marry one of the undead.'

To the rest of the world, Vladimir Darq was an enigma, a mystery and a businessman par excellence, thanks to his amazingly successful lingerie range. The Darqone creation was judged to be a wardrobe basic for over one-fifth of the female population in Britain, and it had taken America by storm since its Christmas launch.

Anna alone owned the man who liked to watch Harry Potter films with homemade popcorn and waltz with her in the garden. Still, there were plenty of 'darq' things about him to keep Anna intrigued. His skills in the bedroom were out of *this* world, that was for sure.

Anna patted the bump at the front of her dress, where her baby was snug and warm and growing.

'Christie, come round for dinner next week while Grace and Niki are away. I'm obviously not going anywhere in this state. Don't be lonely.'

'I will do that,' said Christie. She winked at Grace. Grace was going to be cruising round the Mediterranean for a fortnight with her brother. Nikita Koslov was ready to make up for a lot of lost time. Grace was both nervous and giddy about the impending trip. Shopping for fancy underwear for the first time at fifty-six had been a revelation. Especially when you took your son and his new partner along to help you choose it. But Grace had learned from young Dawn that when a chance at happiness came along, you grab on to it with both hands.

The money from her divorce was finally through and a lavish spending spree for cruise clothes did her good. Gordon had been, as expected, hideously uncooperative in their divorce in the beginning. Unexpectedly, it had been Sarah who had convinced him to let go and be reasonable. His first act as a divorcé was to move permanently into his Blegthorpe caravan.

'What date have they given you for the baby?' asked Raychel.

'October the thirty-first,' sighed Anna. 'As if it could be anything else. What about you?'

'Feb the fourteenth. As if it could be anything else!' Raychel grinned back. She felt positively euphoric today because this had been the first day she hadn't been sick. She hadn't realised morning sickness lasted all day, but she didn't really care because she was having the baby she never thought she and Ben would dare to conceive. Thanks to Elizabeth's persuasion, Michael Siddall's twin sister had been willing to provide some DNA to test, once they had assurances they wouldn't be sued by the CSA, and yes, there was a match. That meant that Raychel was not a child of incest as she had believed all her life. Michael wasn't exactly perfect dad material, being in prison for armed robbery, but Raychel had no intention of building relationships with strangers. She had all the family she wanted in Elizabeth, John, Ellis, Ben and the women now surrounding her.

'I'm going to have to have a big reorganisation in my department,' tutted Christie. 'Everyone will think I'm a boss from hell because my staff are leaving me in droves!'

'Give over, there's a queue of applicants to work with you,' smiled Raychel. 'And I hope you don't replace me because I'll be coming back after my maternity leave.'

Anna topped up her glass. 'I think I'm allowed this. The baby won't object, will he?' She smoothed her hand over the front of the wedding gown that her husband had designed for her. Underneath it, she was wearing a loose but incredibly sexy pregnancy corset.

'A toast,' said Christie. 'To Anna and her new husband and all the lovely babies to come.'

'And to us,' added Anna. 'To women, because we're bloody marvellous.'

'To friends,' said Raychel.

'Both here and absent ones busy playing guitars,' added Grace.

They all raised their glasses to each other. Then to the west. To Canada. To the sun.

Milly Johnson

A Summer Fling is a gritty tale of female friendship. Is this important to you and why did you want to explore friendships across the age divide?

I only wish I had as much luck picking fellas as I have with picking friends! My friends have given me a lot of joy and support and laughs, and life for me without them would be a very cold place. In my second ever job, when I was in my early twenties, I worked with three women—one in her fifties, one in her sixties and one in her seventies and I thought I would be bored out of my tree by these 'old fogeys'. How wrong I was. I had such fun with 'The Golden Girls' as I've always called them. We went out for meals, they gave me advice and I realised how much friendship just dashes the age barrier. I always planned to write something to celebrate those wonderful women.

Do you love beautiful lingerie or are you an M&S girl?

I love beautiful underwear and would be first in line for a Vladimir Darq corset. A good fitting bra really does change how you present yourself to the world— your stance and posture alter and that improves your confidence levels no end. I own some beautiful corsets—but I've also got the M&S drawers!

Would you like a Gok Wan makeover?

I did apply to his *Gok's Fashion Fix* programme but I wasn't chosen and the kids were delighted because they were terrified all their schoolfriends would see me in my underwear! I would *love* Gok to make me over because I've never had anything like that. I'm OK in the limelight with my author face on, but exposed as *me*, would be frightening. I've lost a lot of weight recently and realised I have been hiding myself away for a long time in black baggy clothing. Now I'm slimmer, I haven't a clue what looks good on me.

Are you, like Dawn in the novel, a country-and-western fan?

I was brought up on country-and western-music because my dad was a big fan and I love it. I just wish I had the smoky voice to sing it.

Who was your favourite character in this novel?

Vampiric Vladimir. I just loved developing him and making him fit into the real world without too much suspension of belief.

What would you say have been the highlights of your own decades so far?

My twenties were my big learning curve. I just wish I'd appreciated my youth more when I had it instead of taking it as read that I'd always have a stomach that stayed flat! It was filled with dead-end jobs and rubbish boyfriends, I had no money but great mates and life was not too serious and full of dancing in nightclubs. My thirties were the most emotional years—and the grittiest. I was in an awful marriage, but had my two beautiful children and they galvanised me to fight for what I wanted. My forties have been my favourite. I actually grew to like and accept myself a lot more. I stopped dreaming about a writing career and got down to making it happen and it's been wonderful. I just want to squeeze as much as I can out of life whatever age I am now and enjoy my children before they grow up and fly the nest!

You appeared on the television show *Come Dine With Me*, but it has not been shown yet. Did you enjoy it?

Yes, but alas I can't talk about it until it's been aired, hopefully in the autumn. I will say that I absolutely loved it and what I learned most from that week was nothing to do with cooking—I learned that I should stop moaning about life and just get on with it. It was a really intensive week but I wouldn't have missed it for the world.

And was it this experience that led you to take the BBC Radio Presenter course?

Yes. When they asked me to join the Beeb, I thought they were mad. I couldn't see how I would transfer to the other side of the desk, but I'm enjoying learning a new craft—it's great fun and really cranks up the adrenaline levels. I'm a great believer in *Que Sera, Sera*, so I'll let it lead me where it will.

What's the best piece of advice you've ever been given?

'What you can't control, don't worry about.' That took away all my anxieties about things like sitting on aeroplanes to applying for *Come Dine With Me* and *Gok's Fashion Fix*.